PRIDE AND PREJUDICE

JANE AUSTEN

PRIDE AND PREJUDICE

An Annotated Edition

EDITED BY

PATRICIA MEYER SPACKS

The Belknap Press of Harvard University Press

Cambridge, Massachusetts

London, England

2010

Frontispiece: Watercolor of Jane Austen by her sister, Cassandra, painted about 1802. An 1862 letter from Anna Austen (Lefroy) refers to "a sketch which Aunt Cassandra made of her on one of their expeditions—sitting down out of doors on a hot day, with her bonnet strings untied." It is one of only two authenticated portraits of Austen (the other also by Cassandra). Its subject has a remarkably expressive back.

LIBRARY OF CONGRESS CATALOGING-IN-PUBLICATION DATA

Austen, Jane, 1775–1817.

Pride and prejudice : an annotated edition / Jane Austen ;

edited by Patricia Meyer Spacks.

p.   cm.

The text of this edition is essentially that of the first edition (1813).

Includes bibliographical references.

ISBN 978-0-674-04916-1 (alk. paper)

1. Austen, Jane, 1775–1817. Pride and prejudice.   2. Gentry—England—

Fiction.   3. Social classes—England—Fiction.   4. Young women— Fiction.

5. Mate selection—Fiction.   6. Courtship—Fiction.   7. Sisters—Fiction.

8. England—Social life and customs—19th century—Fiction.   9. Domestic

fiction.   I. Spacks, Patricia Ann Meyer.   II. Title.

PR4034.P7   2010

823'.7—dc22   2010013236

For Jude

The world of *Pride and Prejudice*.

Contents

Note on the Text

The text of this edition of *Pride and Prejudice* is essentially that of the first edition (1813). I have corrected one printer's error, identified in the notes, and regularized the spelling of *Phillips,* which appears in the original text sometimes with one *l,* sometimes with two. With the exception of a few tiny changes in punctuation for the sake of clarity, the spelling and punctuation are those of the first printing.

For citations of works available in several modern editions, including Austen's novels, I have used volume and chapter numbers rather than page numbers. Fuller citations locate works less frequently reprinted.

PRIDE AND PREJUDICE

Introduction

Generations of teenage girls—indeed, generations of men and women of every age—have happily read *Pride and Prejudice* without benefit of notes. They may not know the difference between a curricle and a gig or have more than a vague notion just what the nineteenth-century English militia did, but such bits of ignorance hardly impede enjoyment of this novel about wishes fulfilled. Nor need readers know anything about the novel's writer in order to enjoy her work, although details of her life emphasize the magnitude of her accomplishment: she made much out of little.

Here, then, a few details; later, some comments about notes.

In the first posthumous account of Jane Austen, a short essay prefixed to the volume containing *Northanger Abbey* and *Persuasion* (1818), her brother Henry depicted her as pious and saintly: "Though the frailties, foibles, and follies of others could not escape her immediate detection, yet even on their vices did she never trust herself to comment with unkindness. . . . Faultless herself, as nearly as human nature can be, she always sought, in the faults of others, something to excuse, to forgive or forget. . . . She never uttered either a hasty, a silly, or a severe expression." Little happened in her life, Henry Austen explains: "A life of usefulness, literature, and religion, was not by any means a life of event." As a consequence, he has little to say about the novelist. His sister was good, she did her duty, she had talent: enough!

Some subsequent biographers have concluded, on the basis of selective reading of her letters, that, far from saintly, Austen was malicious and nasty. Others paint a writer of complicated personality and character. No one has managed to discover or manufacture for her a life of much event (despite considerable effort to unearth possible love affairs). Her brothers, biographers agree, led exciting lives, but Austen herself, confined to the domestic sphere, neither did nor apparently experienced a great deal.

Kathryn Sutherland, in a chapter called "Personal Obscurity and the Biographer's Baggage," concisely and lucidly summarizes the development of numerous biographical myths about Austen.[1] About certain facts, however, there is no dispute. Born in 1775, the novelist, with five brothers and one sister, grew up in a lively household, in which reading aloud, acting plays, and writing light verse were communal activities. Brothers James and Henry both wrote essays of varying degrees of seriousness, and James also experimented with serious verse. Jane began writing early; in her teens she produced a burlesque *History of England* (illustrated by her sister) and several pieces of fiction. She wrote the first version of *Pride and Prejudice,* called *First Impressions,* at the age of twenty.

The manifest disruptions of Austen's life were such domestic occurrences as the unexpected death of her father and the various moves of the family from one place to another. A record survives of one proposal of marriage, which she accepted, then declined a day later. More ambiguous is the story of her brief youthful attachment to the Irishman Tom Lefroy, with whom she flirted conspicuously in late 1795. Nothing came of the flirtation; Tom Lefroy married an Irish woman. Jane Austen assumed the role of maiden aunt, making frequent visits to her married brothers and helping with their children. Her most significant known relationship was to her sister, Cassandra, with whom she corresponded when they were apart and to whom she was devoted. Most of her extant letters are to Cassandra, who probably destroyed many of those that did not survive.

In short, her brother was correct in suggesting that her brief life (she died at the age of forty-two) contained little external event and little obvious excitement. It produced, however, six memorable novels, as well as the novella *Lady Susan* and fragments of two other full-length fictions. *First Impressions,* the early version of *Pride and Prejudice,* issued from about nine months' work, begun in October 1796, and was the first of Austen's major novels to be drafted. She almost certainly read it aloud to her family: the habit of reading her

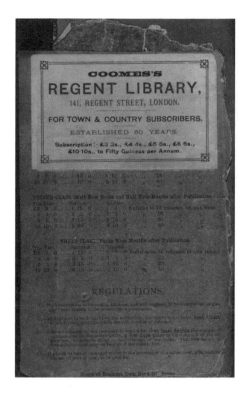

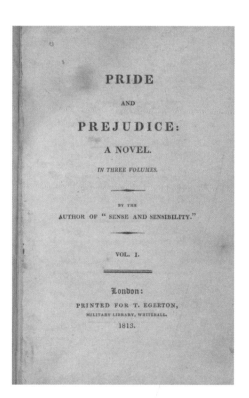

The cover of the Houghton Library copy of the 1813 first edition of *Pride and Prejudice,* in the wrapper of a circulating library. The wrapper show the prices of a subscription (which "will continue to be charged as long as any books remain in the subscriber's possession"), ranging from three guineas to fifty guineas a year.

The title page of the first edition of *Pride and Prejudice,* showing the identification of its writer as "Author of 'Sense and Sensibility.'"

Amy Lowell's bookplate in the Houghton Library first edition of *Pride and Prejudice.* Lowell was an avid collector of books and manuscripts.

creations to this admiring but discriminating audience had been established long before. In November 1797, her father wrote to the London publisher Thomas Cadell, offering the manuscript for publication—an offer declined without sight of the work.

Pride and Prejudice actually appeared in print in January 1813, two years after *Sense and Sensibility,* which had also been drafted long before its publication, although later than *First Impressions.* In the interval between the original version and publication, Austen revised her work. That interval was remarkably long: sixteen years, years that largely coincided with a period of physical instability in Austen's life. Her parents moved with Jane and Cassandra to Bath in early 1801. After that, until 1809, the family had no fixed residence, visiting in the homes of various relatives. Austen appears to have felt depressed by the relocation to Bath, and she would hardly have had ready opportunities for writing in her succession of temporary homes. The 1809 move to Chawton may have provided a renewed sense of permanence and made writing far easier. The fact is that few records survive of the years between *First Impressions* and *Pride and Prejudice,* and we cannot know for sure exactly why so much time elapsed between the different versions of the fiction. Nor is it possible to know the nature of Austen's revisions, since no manuscript now exists; we have only the hint in one of her letters that she cut severely. Thomas Egerton, publisher of *Sense and Sensibility,* published this novel as well, to immediate good reviews. By October, he issued a second edition. Anne Isabella Millbanke (later Lady Byron) wrote that *Pride and Prejudice* was in London "at present the fashionable novel," and other private letters likewise testify to the book's popularity.[2] Claire Tomalin reports that "Henry Austen was told by a literary gentleman that it was much too clever to be the work of a woman. . . . The great world read, laughed and bought."[3]

The great world has continued to read, laugh, and buy. A study of Austen's European reception cites evidence of readership from Denmark, Finland, Serbia, Croatia, and Romania, among other places.[4] The novelist's reputation has steadily risen, especially during the twentieth century, when a proliferation of cinematic adaptations attracted new readers. *Pride and Prejudice* has remained a favorite, reread by many—among others, by Sir Walter Scott, Austen's contemporary and literary rival. "Also read again and for the third time at least Miss Austen's very finely written novel of *Pride and Prejudice*," Scott writes. "That young lady had a talent for describing the involvements and feelings and characters of ordinary life which is to me the most wonderful I ever met with."[5]

The talent Scott identified would become an important basis for assessing Austen's accomplishment. At the beginning, the novelist's realism and her willingness to dwell in the ordinary provided cause for praise. Austen was even compared to Shakespeare, as she would be also in later periods. Yet the concentration on ordinary life also provided grounds for negative assessment: especially by comparison with Scott, Austen lacked romance and passion.[6] She was, as the 1870 *Memoir* by her nephew James Edward Austen-Leigh reiterated, a good woman: passion could hardly be expected. By the late nineteenth century, many admired Austen's evocations of ordinary life, but they did not attribute "genius" to her. She was seen as a hard worker, praiseworthy because, unlike Scott, she was thought not to write for the sake of money. Reviewers typically compared her with other women writers and found her superior to such eighteenth-century predecessors as Frances Burney. But she confined herself to "art," not engaging with significant substance—and "the confinement to art is . . . seen as a feminine quality; greater scope, intellect, moral and social significance as masculine attributes."[7]

Multiplying editions testify to Austen's twentieth-century resurgence: six new editions of *Pride and Prejudice* came out in each of three years (1991, 1994, 1995). Acclaimed film adaptations help to explain but do not entirely account for the novel's popularity. Most years between 1983 and 2003 saw the publication of two or three editions. *Pride and Prejudice,* like Austen's other novels, has come to be considered a classic: safe for teaching in schools, yet full of rich material for feminists, as well as for those sentimental about the English past.

It has also emerged clearly as a repository for and stimulus of fantasy, and thus possibly less safe than it seems. In the film versions—there have been at least eight since 1940—Darcy, romanticized, tends to turn into a Heathcliff figure, passionate, beautiful, and over-whelmingly physical. Colin Firth goes swimming and young women swoon. After the television version of *Pride and Prejudice* in which he starred had achieved enormous popularity, Firth explained his acting strategy. He would think to himself, "This is where he wants sex with her right now," and not do anything at all. "In other words, what he did precisely was to think instead of act. The trick is to assume the look of desire instead of acting upon it."[8] Thus the actor encourages the fantasies of the audience. Maureen Dowd, during a presidential election campaign, could hold forth at length in the *New York Times* on Obama as a Darcy-figure, assuming that her readers would readily understand that she wished to suggest glamour and sexiness.

Continuations and adaptations of and extrapolations from *Pride and Prejudice* provide further persuasive evidence for the novel as a spur to fantasy. Brandy Foster cites "a novel exploring a love affair between Jane Austen and Mr. Darcy that transcends time, a mystery series that stars Jane Austen as a shrewd detective, a Christian Romance series that superimposes twenty-first-century characters onto Austen's plots, an innovative interpretation of *Pride and Prejudice* set in a Jewish retirement community, and a novel whose plot centers on characters reading Austen's novels."[9] Not all of these works focus specifically on *Pride and Prejudice*, but all attest to the novelist's power to engage her readers in imaginative activity. The Winter 2007 issue of *JASNA News*, the newsletter of the Jane Austen Society of North America, reports not only the advent of *Jane Austen for Dummies* but also the publication of *A Letter from Lady Catherine*, about Anne de Bourgh's adventures; the third of a series of mysteries in which the newlywed Darcys play sleuth; and *Pemberley Manor*, about the problems of postmarital communication between Elizabeth and Darcy. A work entitled *Pride and Prejudice and Zombies* (first sentence: "It is a truth universally acknowledged that a zombie in possession of brains must be in want of more brains") remained on the *New York Times Book Review* best-seller list for several months in 2009.

As such instances suggest, the appropriation and elaboration of Austen's fictions continue undiminished in the twenty-first century. Not only is Jane Austen considered common cultural property; not only are her novels read and reread in high school, in college, in book clubs, in the private existences of thousands. She continues to provide, in many ways, stimulus for fantasy.

Fantasies don't demand notes. Why obstruct a novel so accessible as *Pride and Prejudice,* a novel of which readers have taken imaginative possession, with annotation that ties it down? If someone feels free to add zombies to a novel, the book's plot must seem to offer infinite opportunities for expansion. Writers apparently think it easy to elaborate Austen. After all, her novels are light on plot and on obvious kinds of detail. We know about Elizabeth Bennet's dark, intelligent eyes, but little else about how she looks. Jane is beautiful, but the nature of her beauty remains unspecified. The furniture at Netherfield? What the Bennet sisters wear for different occasions? What their house looks like? All absent from the text. Someone who wants to produce a sequel to *Pride and Prejudice* can fill in missing details, imagine a romance for Mary Bennet or postmarital difficulties for Elizabeth, and construct a fiction that aspires to answer Austen enthusiasts' perpetual need for more.[10]

Yet few enthusiasts have found sequels or variations satisfactory in comparison with Austen's fiction. What seems simple in the reading turns out less simple in the writing. *Pride and Prejudice* provides, in fact, a lot of detail—just not the kind that we may expect. And that brings us back to notes, which thrive on detail, and which help readers realize how much richness details provide.

Annotation is interpretation: appropriate for a work in which interpretation constitutes the central activity and central problem. Annotation helps to locate Austen in history, in literature, in language. I could have written such things about the idea of annotating *Pride and Prejudice* before I ever attempted to do just that. I write them now with a new sense of revelation.

Producing these notes taught me more than I thought I had left to learn about *Pride and Prejudice.* I have read the novel probably forty or fifty times. I have taught it, over the course of many years, to undergraduates at every stage of their college educations, to graduate students, and to faculty seminars. Several times I have held forth about it in print. With real shame now, I confess that at the beginning of this project I thought I could annotate the book out of my head.

I was wrong.

The process of writing notes taught me not only how much I didn't know but also the importance of what I learned. I discovered extraordinary definitions of *nice,* learned the history of backgammon, and encountered eighteenth-century views on physiognomy. More important, I became aware of dark suggestions in *Pride and Prejudice,* suggestions that various delightful films have ignored. Writing notes revealed that more than fantasy operates in Austen's construction of plot and showed how complicated an apparently straightforward novel can be. Most important, the process uncovered—or, as Austen herself would say, *unfolded*—the need to understand a historical moment in order to understand the fiction written in it.

The details of *Pride and Prejudice* reveal their richness when one grasps their context. I am thinking now not of the kind of detail most apparent in Austen—about what central characters think and about what everyone says—but of inconspicuous textual moments that seem virtually devoid of importance. When Elizabeth and Jane return from Netherfield, for instance, they must listen to Lydia and Kitty reporting "news" they had missed: "[S]everal of the officers had dined lately with their uncle, a private had been flogged, and it had actually been hinted that Colonel Forster was going to be married" (I, 12). Colonel Forster's marriage will turn out to be of some importance in the plot, since he and his wife will be Lydia's hosts in Brighton. The officers who have dined with Mr. Phillips matter not at all; they only emphasize the inconsequence of the girls' talk. But what about that private?

The maltreated private is the only enlisted man mentioned in the novel. Brutality toward enlisted men was common in the late-eighteenth-century militia, and floggings occurred frequently. These facts now emerge in the notes, which also remind the reader of the obvious but important point that Lydia and Kitty, heartless in their self-centered frivolity, consider a private's flogging no more significant than the guests at their uncle's dinner party or any other item of gossip.

That is only the beginning. Notes exist in the context of other notes, just as details of Lydia's conversation inhabit a narrative of many conversations. And other notes illuminate not only the matter of that private but, as a consequence, the complicated operations of the novel as a whole. Asking myself questions, I discovered—and notes now reveal—for instance, that the militia demanded set quotas of men from every county, and the men who filled these quotas came overwhelmingly from the poorest social classes. A great gap separated officers, with the status of gentlemen, from their soldiers. The contemporary reputation of militiamen emphasized their dangers to women because of their seductive ways and uniforms. England was at war during the period of *Pride and Prejudice*—a fact of which Austen, with four brothers serving in the armed forces, would have been vividly aware. Lacking a war, the militia would not have existed: this body of men, by law, was called up only in times of national danger. The danger from France, during the Napoleonic Wars, was thought imminent. Brighton, to which the men stationed in Meryton move in the course of the novel, seemed a particularly likely target for invasion from France, because of its location and the nature of its harbor.

In light of such historical information, the reference to the private's flogging becomes increasingly meaningful. The text of *Pride and Prejudice* never explicitly mentions war, although covert allusions occur fairly often. Lydia and Kitty, given their natures, of course never think of the possibility that Brighton might be a target of invasion, but neither do their mother, their father, or their more reflective sisters. As the notes accumulate a body of relevant facts, readers may begin to wonder why the Bennets respond enthusiastically to the romance of the military but never concern themselves with military functioning. They may come to think that the single clause about the private works like the startling line in *The Rape of the Lock*, "And Wretches hang that Jury-men may Dine," to point out the myopia of the well-to-do. Perhaps this novel concerned with two or three families in a country village not only celebrates the local but calls subtle attention to its limitations. Love, marriage, money, and trivial but absorbing gossip supply sufficient preoccupations for most of the novel's characters. Mr. Bennet varies the theme by his constant search for absurdity; Mr. Collins varies it by total self-preoccupation. No one ever refers directly to national issues, yet indirect allusions to them abound. Austen's first readers could hardly have failed to notice and to ponder this fact; current readers made aware of it have an opportunity to ponder as well.

The flogged private may serve as a reminder of what happens beyond the limits of Longbourn or Netherfield or Rosings or Pemberley—what in fact happens within Meryton, known to but not thought about by its inhabitants. The wider world impinges yet does not matter, its disturbances ignored. Austen has raised the issue; she leaves it to her readers to determine what it means. Notes can illuminate the question without deciding it.

This single ramifying example may suggest how notes can thicken understanding of the text, but it also reminds us that notes exist primarily to provide information. Information—the kind one finds in notes—may seem to have little bearing on what interests readers most in Austen: matters of imagined individual thought and feeling. We need not understand the private's novelistic function to understand how self-centered and trivial Lydia and Kitty are as members of the Bennet family.

Yet some of the information that notes provide in fact illuminates the personal. For one thing, notes often call attention to Austen's vocabulary, revealing its unexpected obscurities; and vocabulary, as an aspect of linguistic choice, can convey character. As Juliet McMaster puts the point, "Given . . . the fullness and specificity of Austen's created world, what a character says, with the way she says it, is as salient an aspect of identity as her genetic inheritance, her body, her class, certainly her actions."[11] The starting point for understanding the relation between recorded speech and identity is comprehension of the words employed.

In most respects, the vocabulary of *Pride and Prejudice* sounds familiar to twenty-first-century readers. Occasional words refer to actualities no longer part of our experience: *boulanger* (a French dance), *hack chaise* (a hired coach), *white soup* (an elaborate soup made with veal stock and ground almonds). There are anglicisms like *joint* for *roast*. For the most part, though, Austen's limpid prose appears utterly comprehensible.

That comprehensibility, however, proves partly illusory. Many words that still look familiar had different meanings in Austen's time. The short first chapter of *Pride and Prejudice* contains at least seven examples: *let* (meaning leased), *chaise* (carriage), *give over* (give up), *establishment* (settlement in life), *parts* (intelligence), *develope* (uncover, disclose), *mean* (undistinguished). Context helps, of course: it's pretty clear that a chaise and four is not an extended seat on which to recline. The casual reader, however, might well be baffled, without even knowing that she's baffled. Yet more confusing are words like *excessively,* which means something like *very,* with no implication of excess; or *quite,* meaning *altogether, entirely*—an intensifier rather than, as at present, a moderator. Readers need not only to remedy immediate confusion but also to build up a new vocabulary. Moreover, the partly unfamiliar lexicon reminds us that Austen, who seems so familiar, in fact inhabited a culture different from our own. (I shall return later to the matter of speech and identity.)

As we become accustomed to a linguistic register both familiar and alien, we may experience more deeply the paradox common to all Austen novels: their substance seems both familiar, the kinds of conflict and resolution that many or most human beings experience, and "other," the product of social and personal assumptions unlike our own. In *Pride and Prejudice,* the predictable realms of profound difference involve economics and social class. Most readers beyond their early teens could say in advance of reading Austen that eighteenth-century women had fewer economic opportunities than their twenty-first-century counterparts; most would know also that England had a king and an aristocracy and a fairly rigid class system. *Pride and Prejudice,* assuming these facts, dramatizes their implications.

Charlotte Lucas most vividly calls attention to issues of economics and class. Daughter of a man who has been knighted for his service as mayor, a man serene in his conviction of personal importance, Charlotte nonetheless holds precarious class status. The relation between class and wealth is complicated; notes illuminate the complications. Her family has little money and several children (their number remains unspecified in Austen's text). She is twenty-seven years old, impoverished, and plain. She faces the acute problem of what to do: how she can be financially supported. Marriage is the obvious solution, the "best" solution for any woman without economic resources, but no wooers have materialized.

Given this situation, Charlotte has developed a pragmatic and unromantic, indeed cynical, view of marriage. It's better not to know too much about the man you're marrying; you're sure to find things to dislike after the wedding. Marriages made without knowledge are as likely to turn out well as those long meditated. It's reasonable to marry for the sake of an "establishment"—a settled arrangement in life. Romance doesn't matter.

These views contrast with Elizabeth's less fully articulated opinions. Elizabeth, like her sister Jane, believes first of all in love. She thinks it wrong to marry for money; she thinks it important to like and respect the man you marry. As far as the novel tells us, she never worries about what will happen to her if she fails to find the right man, despite her mother's frequent and accurate reminders that there will be no money to support her after her father dies. Her financial position resembles Charlotte's, and she has four sisters who must also marry, but these facts do not inflect her point of view. She differs from Charlotte in being only twenty years old, attractive, spirited, and witty: she has more resources for the marriage market, but she does not think of matters in these terms.

When Charlotte marries the man whom Elizabeth has repudiated on grounds of his stupidity, egotism, and dullness, she becomes the target of Elizabeth's severe and repeated denunciation. The two eldest Bennet girls discuss the marriage more than once, with Elizabeth unswerving in her condemnation, which she sees as a matter of moral principle. She feels no apparent sympathy with Charlotte's dilemma. After she visits her friend at her new home, she sees that Charlotte has managed to make the best of her situation and has found sources of contentment, despite her full awareness of her husband's defects. This realization does not alter Elizabeth's judgment.

Pride and Prejudice trains the reader to identify with Elizabeth. Her charm and wit operate on us as on Darcy; her ways of seeing the world therefore seem plausible. But Charlotte's position merits serious attention, inasmuch as it insists that the novel's imagined world bears significant resemblances to the world in which Austen actually lived, and that the world makes demands. Although wishes get magically fulfilled within the novel, still privates are flogged and young women compromise for the sake of survival. Elizabeth arrives at a fairy tale marriage, but *Pride and Prejudice* insists on alternative possibilities as well. It does not compel readers to judge Elizabeth as wrong in her condemnation of Charlotte, but it urges them to judge. Elizabeth has more than sentiment on her side: she embodies a principled view of what marriage should entail. Economic realities bolster Charlotte's position. The uncomfortable juxtapositions of the two concepts of marriage, and of poverty and principle, demand attention.

Yet the novel's charm, as well as Elizabeth's, may tempt us to slide over the uncomfortable actualities delicately sketched in the background. Notes, reflecting my own process of learning and pondering, elucidate historical realities that support the fictional structure—realities that would have been assumed by Austen's original readers. Again, as in the case of the private, the notes do not make or force final judgments—but they enlarge the grounds for judgment.

The making of judgments constitutes a central activity of characters within *Pride and Prejudice,* who constantly assess one another. Lazy or casual judgments by the community, typically based on superficial evidence, influence everyone. When he first enters the Meryton assembly, Darcy is judged handsome and thrillingly attractive, with his annual income of £10,000. By the end of a single paragraph, he is no longer attractive: his manners are arrogant and he can be dismissed as "proud." Elizabeth, influenced by Darcy's insulting her, accepts the communal verdict, and thus gets the novel's plot under way. Shifting communal interpretations of Wickham and of Lydia corroborate opinion's volatility, but its power remains. Such characters as Mrs. Phillips and Mrs. Bennet rarely get beyond their community's views. Elizabeth does, and the novel challenges its readers to do likewise.

Here, too, notes can help, not only by calling attention to various cruxes of judgment, but by citing critical opinion. Quotations from critical sources suggest the vast range of approaches to and views of *Pride and Prejudice,* and the existence of conflicting opinions about important matters in the novel. They situate the text in an ongoing and lively conversation.

Yet another kind of note sketches Austen's immediate literary context: her own fiction and works by other authors. The novelist consistently returns—sometimes in comic, sometimes in serious mode—to a single set of issues: the problem of poverty in women, the matter of persuasion (to what degree should one properly allow herself to be persuaded by a friend?), the appropriate (and the inappropriate) treatment of social inferiors, and so on. Her interest in such concerns begins early: the juvenilia, fiction written from her early teens onward, treat some of them in burlesque fashion. To be reminded of allusions in both her earlier and her later fiction that presage or echo *Pride and Prejudice,* like accreting vocabulary or knowledge of social and political facts, invites a complex response to the words on the page.

As Austen explicitly declared, her family read novels with enthusiasm—read them aloud and to themselves, talked of them with one another, on occasion wrote letters about them. Even by the time of her first work on the book that became *Pride and Prejudice,* the novelist had developed wide knowledge of her predecessors and contemporaries in the art of fiction. She felt special interest in women's achievements, and references to Maria Edgeworth and especially Frances Burney recur in her text. Samuel Richardson is always in the background: *Sir Charles Grandison* was allegedly Austen's favorite novel. To become aware of literary allusions in *Pride and Prejudice* reveals the novelist's sophistication as well as, once again, the density of her text.

Constructing a frame around the novel, notes establish multiple perspectives that reveal diverse meanings. Thus they return attention to the novelistic text, revealing many possible foci for attention. Although one can happily read *Pride and Prejudice* in the absence of notes, their presence introduces us to a richer, more provocative book.

Pride and Prejudice proceeds by means of conversation. Groups or pairs of characters talk to one another, or individuals in effect talk to themselves. The novel frequently describes Elizabeth as "saying" something that she would be unlikely to say aloud, as when, in the company of Maria Lucas, she witnesses the allegedly remarkable spectacle of Miss de Bourgh stopping at the parsonage gate. Elizabeth is said to say, "I like her appearance. . . . She looks sickly and cross.—Yes, she will do for him very well. She will make him a very proper wife" (II, 5). "Him" refers to Darcy, who, according to Wickham, plans to marry his cousin, Miss de Bourgh. But Elizabeth would not make this little speech to Maria, who knows nothing of Darcy's marital plans and who has no apparent sense of irony: Maria would not understand "I like her appearance" in conjunction with "sickly and cross." Elizabeth must be talking to herself, either silently or aloud. (Accounts of her thought processes frequently sound like internal conversation.) Would she really *cry,* "How despicably have I acted!" and the rest of the long sequence of self-recrimination (II, 13)? She is alone in her room at the time. Does she actually *exclaim,* "To Jane herself, there could be no possibility of objection" (II, 10) and go on out loud for several sentences more, again in solitude? By the middle of the paragraph that starts thus, she is *thinking* about her mother, the transition from exclaiming to thinking imperceptible. Indeed, exclaiming and crying out appear to be metaphors for thought—or, to put it otherwise, thought in *Pride and Prejudice* often sounds like speech.

The interest of the conversations between persons derives partly from clashes of linguistic style. No one who has read *Pride and Prejudice* could mistake an utterance by Lydia for one by Elizabeth, or even one of Mary's speeches for one of Mr. Collins's, although the young clergyman and the young female autodidact appear to rely on the same sort of reading to shape their sentiments. No two figures in *Pride and Prejudice* sound alike. In rhythm, tone, vocabulary, and syntax, they differentiate themselves from one another, each providing the reader a unique source of delight.

The individual flavor of speech is particularly marked in the comic characters, whose ways of talking tell us who they are. Mrs. Bennet, the novel's first speaker, soon reveals her disorganized mind (through her disorganized sentences), her lack of attention to her own meanings, her self-dramatizations, and her unfailing energy in pursuit of her single goal, her daughters' marriage. What she thinks, she says, without much regard for sense. One appreciates her most, perhaps, in conjunction with Mr. Collins. Speaking of the entail, she observes, "It is a grievous affair to my poor girls, you must confess. Not that I mean to find fault with *you,* for such things I know are all chance in this world. There is no knowing how estates will go when once they come to be entailed" (I, 14). As she often does, she employs emotional language (*grievous, poor*) and a rhetoric of blame, this time in the negative: she will not find fault. She conveys her profound puzzlement over the entail, often explained to her, never understood, and her sense of the world as an incomprehensible place.

Mr. Collins, in response, appears to react to what she has said but as usual speaks of himself. The first-person singular pronoun appears four times in the two and a half sentences he utters in response. He insistently engages in his customary self-congratulation: he is sensitive to the misfortunes of others, he explains; he is careful not to appear forward; he can offer assurances; he will not say too much until they are better acquainted. All this emerges, also as usual, in oratorical mode. Whatever his subject, this clergyman perpetually sermonizes.

Mrs. Bennet, who shares with her daughter Lydia a useful ability not to listen, doesn't care what Mr. Collins says—unless he wishes to speak with her about marrying one of her daughters. She talks sometimes just to fill the air. Sometimes—most often with her husband—she talks in hope of provoking a response. Sometimes her hopes spill out, sometimes her fears. Almost always her speech leaves the impression of a woman with little control of her circumstances or her utterance, desperately trying to assert control.

Mr. Collins, in contrast, exactly that combination of servility and self-importance that Mr. Bennet deduced from his introductory letter, sounds like a man who has written out everything in advance. His oratorical air, his Latinate vocabulary, his ponderous sentence structure, and his sheer plethora of words force others to listen, however worthless the substance of his utterance. The most egregious instance of his technique occurs at the Netherfield ball, when he feels obliged to make a speech about the responsibilities of a clergyman. The Bingley sisters silently ridicule him, but people listen, and Mrs. Bennet, at least, is impressed.

Mrs. Bennet and Mr. Collins amuse us (they would annoy us in real life). They exist under the novelist's control, at a comfortable distance from actuality. Manipulated for our pleasure, detoxified by their verbal context, subordinate to the writer's wit, they determinedly pursue their own interests, but they do no real damage. Austen even rewards them both: Mr. Collins gets exactly what he wants, a compliant woman, and Mrs. Bennet ends up with three of her five daughters married. This novelist invariably seems amused as well as appalled by the complex operations of self-love. She demonstrates those operations through her verbal exactitude.

Mr. Bennet, too, is self-absorbed, with a more subtle form of self-love. His speech is more engaging than his wife's; readers are likely to smile at his jokes. His wit, his elegant phrasing, his teasing—all make him appealing, especially because of his high regard for Elizabeth, and especially by contrast with Mrs. Bennet. It is important to the novel's effect, though, that we understand, as even Elizabeth is compelled to understand, his moral insufficiencies: the irresponsibility that wit and elegance conceal.

Lady Catherine de Bourgh—another self-lover—also exhibits a distinctive linguistic profile. Elizabeth characterizes her as precisely as her father has labeled Mr. Collins, as a being of "dignified impertinence" (II, 6). The comic mixture of dignity and impertinence emerges in Lady Catherine's alternate questions and pronouncements: pronouncements about tomorrow's weather, the vast extent of her talents (and her daughter's), the proper size for roasts and the proper way of packing; questions about every aspect of Elizabeth's family and upbringing. Her asserted confidence that Darcy's melancholy air when he departs comes from his regret at leaving her insists on her status as center of everyone's universe, but it and her other proclamations of assurance possibly disguise self-doubt. A faint shadow of pathos clings to even this dreadful woman.

Her final confrontation with Elizabeth reveals Lady Catherine's rhetoric of authority as words without substance to support them. But Elizabeth has understood this fact long before, declining to answer a question about her age and holding forth on the rights of young women in the face of Lady Catherine's astonishment. Sir William Lucas and his younger daughter, as well as Mr. Collins, take the lady at her own valuation, assuming that the language of power corresponds to the actuality. Elizabeth remains unintimidated.

She is unintimidated still when Lady Catherine comes to her home for the express purpose of forbidding any possible match between her and Darcy. "Do not deceive yourself into a belief that I will ever recede," she proclaims. "I shall not go away, till you have given me the assurance I require" (III, 14). But in fact she *does* recede; she goes away with no assurances; she is eventually compelled to accept a marriage she deplores—a marriage that demonstrates the evanescence of her authority.

In retrospect, therefore, the reader must reinterpret Lady Catherine's way of speaking. Both her dignity and her impertinence, it turns out, only disguise her impotence. She may be able to argue the poor into cheerfulness and amity, but she cannot make her daughter accomplished or make her nephew marry that daughter or keep him from marrying whom he likes. Her linguistic resources preserve the façade of power. She convinces Mr. Collins, who depends on her for his prosperity, of her godlike potency. Those not dependent, however, if the very idea of wealth and rank does not cow them (as it cows Sir William Lucas and his daughter Maria), find her language unfrightening and ineffectual.

In other words, we are invited to see through Lady Catherine's language, as Elizabeth sees through it, to comprehend language as defense. Similarly, the linguistic patterns of Mrs. Bennet and Mr. Collins exist to be seen through. Mrs. Bennet's chaotic speech accurately conveys the disorder of her mind, but her talk of her nerves and her professions of never speaking to her daughter again express helpless irritation rather than the illness or the determination they proclaim. Mr. Collins's orotund phrases insist on his desire to behave with perfect correctness and to offend no one. We quickly learn to understand them as signs of self-regard and self-absorption.

The other minor characters whose speech is represented function in much the same way. The Bingley sisters, with their run-on sentences and with lavish exclamation points and question marks suggesting their insistent emphasis, talk to assert their superiority. Lydia, whose favorite word is *fun,* makes heavy use of adjectives and colloquialisms and sounds as mindless as her mother, but she is her mother's daughter in another sense as well. Her frivolity conceals determination to achieve the only success she can imagine: the first marriage among the Bennet sisters. The novel renders Wickham's speech more often in summary than in quotation, but when we encounter his words on the page, they typically include terms of sentiment. He presents himself as a man of feeling—"Till I can forget his father, I can never defy or expose *him*" (I, 16)—yet emerges finally as hardhearted, corrupt, and cynical.

The individual patterns of speech that differentiate and define the characters, in other words, also obscure important truths about them. Elizabeth discerns those truths in some instances, and the reader joins her in discernment. Perhaps we see through Wickham before she does. In any case, the novel demands that we interpret each of its personages. It provides all necessary clues, and sometimes it makes interpretation easy: Collins is not much of a puzzle, nor is Mrs. Bennet, and it doesn't take long to suspect that Lady Catherine is less powerful than she claims. Wickham, though, like Mr. Bennet, is harder to figure out. For some time both men seem altogether charming; only gradually do we realize their flaws.

Interpretation—the reading of human beings and of letters—obviously constitutes a central activity of *Pride and Prejudice.* The plot turns on what Elizabeth makes of Darcy, and he of her. These two figures, examples of the kind of "intricate character" that Elizabeth thinks it most entertaining to ponder, use language in more complicated ways than, say, Mrs. Bennet, but for them, too, language provides a screen. The substance more than the style of their utterance provides vital clues to their nature.

In the central episode of reading and rereading Darcy's letter, Elizabeth exercises her rational faculties, trying to make objective sense of a text. Most of the novel's interpretations, though, rest on less solid ground. Elizabeth, especially, lives surrounded by people who make and share judgments of one another. Characters arrive at their verdicts on the basis, most often, of physical appearance and "manners," and of their emotional responses to both. The Bingley sisters, outraged by Elizabeth's muddy petticoat and contemptuous of her as a result, offer a conspicuous instance. Wickham in particular benefits from this kind of judgment: Elizabeth and Jane alike assume his "amiability" on the basis of his appearance and his "happy manners." Darcy, by the same principle, suffers: his manners are proud and his appearance arrogant.

Because as readers we participate so much in Elizabeth's point of view, we run the danger of participating also in her frequent misinterpretations. The novel both demands our alertness and makes alertness difficult. Clearly the brightest of the Bennet sisters, praised by her father for wit and intelligence that resemble his own, Elizabeth thinks faster and more effectively than most of those around her. Yet she as much as Jane believes that a man of such amiable appearance as Wickham must be in the most serious sense of the word ("kind, lovable") amiable in character, and more firmly than Jane she believes that a man stiff and socially maladroit as Darcy must be less than amiable in nature.

An astute reader may realize early that judgments made on appearances must be undependable and that Elizabeth has too much confidence in her own opinion. Those less suspicious will know on rereading—and many readers of *Pride and Prejudice* are rereaders—that the Bennet sisters misjudge both Wickham and Darcy. In either case, readers face the problem of deciding the proper basis of judgment. The novel does not make it easy to decide. The obvious alternatives to appearances, however, are words and acts. Elizabeth increasingly focuses on both, but most especially words, as she tries to decipher Darcy.

Early in *Pride and Prejudice,* Bingley accuses Darcy of seeking words of four syllables for his letters—therefore, in Bingley's view, not writing "with ease" (I, 10). As a talker, too, Darcy often conveys more dignity than ease. On the subject of Bingley's propensity to act on impulse: "When you told Mrs. Bennet this morning that if you ever resolved on quitting Netherfield you should be gone in five minutes, you meant it to be a sort of panegyric, of compliment to yourself—and yet what is there so very laudable in a precipitance which must leave very necessary business undone, and can be of no real advantage to yourself or any one else?" (I, 10). The two four-syllable words in this sentence do not alone account for its ponderousness, which comes, rather, from Darcy's propensity for long sentences, abstract terms, and generalization. In contrast, Elizabeth's short sentences, personalized utterance, and predominantly short words sound lively and engaging: "'You have only proved by this,' cried Elizabeth, 'that Mr. Bingley did not do justice to his own disposition. You have shewn him off now much more than he did himself'" (I, 10).

We might conclude from these examples that Elizabeth is alert, Darcy more considered. Perhaps we decide, rather, that Elizabeth tends toward ad hominem argument, whereas Darcy discourses with more attention to general principles. Or is it that Darcy is something of a prig, in contrast to Elizabeth in her spontaneity? Elizabeth never comments explicitly on Darcy's mode of speech, but his way of talking presumably contributes to her conviction of his pervasive pride. Pride leads him to separate himself in his own imagining from other men: he is different, he thinks, and superior. So is his speech—superior at least in its apparent carefulness and in its premeditated quality. Partly influenced by Elizabeth's point of view, the reader may well share her conviction that we hear a proud man talking when we hear Darcy holding forth.

As Elizabeth says, though, intricate characters are best worth studying. Neither she nor Darcy always talks the same way, nor do their speech patterns lend themselves to definitive interpretation. As the novel moves toward its resolution, the two of them sound increasingly like each other. Gary Kelly, discussing Austen's use of idiolect ("the peculiar style of individuals"), points out that the most important characters speak a language closer to standard English, their speech resembling "the discourse of the narrator."[12] By the conclusion of *Pride and Prejudice,* Darcy and Elizabeth indeed resemble the narrator as well as each other. Earlier, though, Darcy's speech has sometimes verged on pomposity and Elizabeth has on occasion sounded cheeky. Their achievement of a shared linguistic register marks their movement toward mutuality.

It also marks their virtual abandonment of linguistic disguise. Despite the flexibility and range of their language, Darcy and Elizabeth, like Lady Catherine and Mr. Collins, conceal their real meanings—sometimes even from themselves—in what they say. What Darcy hears as flirtatious exchange actually expresses Elizabeth's real antagonism; what Elizabeth hears as evidence of pride sometimes constitutes an effort toward closeness. Of course what is conveyed depends on the hearer as well as the speaker. The scene in which Collins refuses to believe that Elizabeth means exactly what she says (as, in rejecting his proposal, she certainly does) lends the point comic emphasis. When Darcy, moving toward his second proposal, comes to dinner at the Bennets', he hardly speaks at all. Elizabeth hears coldness, lack of interest; Darcy, as he later explains, is silent because he feels too much. Language apparently does not provide a dependable means of communication. Actions count, too: Elizabeth's realization of what Darcy has done for her family suggests to her that he may love her and causes her to reassess whether she loves him. Even facial expressions may count. Those appearances that characters are all too ready to rely on in isolation become more useful evidence when combined with other kinds of information.

Yet language matters. Unlike the other characters, Darcy and Elizabeth use language in varying ways, depending on context. Darcy announcing that there's not a woman in the room with whom it would not be a punishment to dance sounds nothing like Darcy, much later in the novel, confessing that he has trouble figuring out what to say to people he's meeting for the first time, or Darcy expressing his sympathy for Elizabeth's grief over her sister's elopement, or Darcy explaining himself on paper after his rebuffed proposal. Each of these communications adopts a different linguistic register. Elizabeth's speech when she operates in playful or flirtatious modes hardly resembles her holding forth to Jane about Darcy's alleged mistreatment of Wickham or about the meretriciousness of Charlotte's marriage. The conclusions about character that one might reach on the basis of any single utterance are likely to contradict those produced by subsequent speeches.

Which is exactly the point. Elizabeth's tendency to reach absolute conclusions (Charlotte's marriage is so reprehensible that they can never be friends again; Darcy is proud and wicked; Wickham is the model of male attractiveness) ignores complexity, of evidence and of human nature, and keeps her from arriving at accurate interpretations. Darcy performs better than she in this respect. Although he begins by announcing that none of the Meryton women is worth looking at, he quickly goes on to make distinctions. His interest in Elizabeth soon develops in spite of his initial rejection. To be sure, his first proposal evinces considerable backsliding in this respect: he appears to have returned to repudiating her relatives on the basis of class, whether or not he has actually met them. By the time of the second proposal, however, he can go so far as to attest his "respect" for Elizabeth's family.

Darcy explains his change as a result of the shock he received when Elizabeth claimed that he had not behaved like a gentleman. For Elizabeth, the corresponding shock is Darcy's letter of explanation, cold and haughty though it in some respects is. As she explicitly says, one of the letter's revelations is that events that she thought admitted no explanation or excuse turn out to allow interpretations she has never imagined. Darcy compels her to open her mind, to acknowledge new possibilities. She has precisely the same effect on him.

The novel urges its readers, too, to open their minds: to realize the gap between plausibility and exactitude in making human judgments, to grasp the urgency of such judgments as well as the difficulty of making them, to acknowledge that wishes can come true, while understanding that many lives are lived in disappointment. Employing the structure of romance, it contains within that structure a world in which money matters hugely, in which men and women alike can deceive and manipulate one another, in which war inhabits the margins of attention. Elizabeth marries Prince Charming, but in the background Charlotte remains condemned to Mr. Collins. Economic exigency and human opacity survive as facts of life, even within a happy fiction. Pemberley provides many satisfactions, but the happiness of its residents and visitors cannot obviate the uncomfortable actualities that *Pride and Prejudice* has revealed.

Notes

1 Kathryn Sutherland, *Jane Austen's Textual Lives: From Aeschylus to Bollywood* (Oxford: Oxford University Press, 2005), 55–117.

2 Quoted in Annika Bautz, *The Reception of Jane Austen and Walter Scott: A Comparative Longitudinal Study* (London: Continuum, 2007), 58.

3 Claire Tomalin, *Jane Austen: A Life* (New York: Knopf, 1998), 219.

4 *The Reception of Jane Austen in Europe,* ed. Anthony Mandal and Brian Southam (London: Continuum, 2007).

5 Journal entry, 14 March 1826, quoted in Bautz, *The Reception of Jane Austen and Walter Scott,* 1.

6 See Bautz, *The Reception of Jane Austen and Walter Scott,* 104. I have relied heavily on this careful study of Austen's changing reputation in comparison with Scott's.

7 Bautz, *The Reception of Jane Austen and Walter Scott,* 107.

8 Virginia L. Blum, "The Return to Repression: Filming the Nineteenth Century," *Jane Austen and Co.: Remaking the Past in Contemporary Culture,* ed. Suzanne R. Pucci and James Thompson (Albany: State University of New York Press, 1983), 163.

9 Brandy Foster, "Pimp My Austen: The Commodification and Customization of Jane Austen," *Persuasions On-Line,* http://www.jasna.org/persuasions/on-line/vol29no1/foster.html.

10 Compare Colleen McCullough, *The Independence of Miss Mary Bennet* (Ryde, N.S.W.: HarperCollins, 2008), one of the recent "continuations" of *Pride and Prejudice.*

11 Juliet McMaster, "Mrs. Elton and Other Verbal Aggressors," *The Talk in Jane Austen,* ed. Bruce Stovel and Lynn Weinlos Gregg (Edmonton: University of Alberta Press, 2002), 78.

12 Gary Kelly, "Jane Austen's Imagined Communities," *The Talk in Jane Austen,* 131.

VOLUME I

I

It is a truth universally acknowledged, that a single man in possession of a good fortune, must be in want of a wife.[1]

However little known the feelings or views of such a man may be on his first entering a neighbourhood, this truth is so well fixed in the minds of the surrounding families, that he is considered as the rightful property[2] of some one or other of their daughters.

"My dear Mr. Bennet," said his lady[3] to him one day, "have you heard that Netherfield Park is let[4] at last?"

Mr. Bennet replied that he had not.

"But it is," returned she; "for Mrs. Long has just been here, and she told me all about it."

Mr. Bennet made no answer.

"Do you not want to know who has taken it?" cried his wife impatiently.

"*You* want to tell me, and I have no objection to hearing it."[5]

This was invitation enough.

"Why, my dear, you must know, Mrs. Long says that Netherfield is taken by a young man of large fortune from the north of England; that he came down on Monday in a chaise and four[6] to see the place, and was so much delighted with it that he agreed with Mr. Morris[7] immediately; that he is to take possession before Michaelmas,[8] and some of his servants are to be in the house by the end of next week."

"What is his name?"

"Bingley."

"Is he married or single?"

---

1 This famous first sentence has provided the material for much critical debate. It supplies a topic for an entire "disputatious" issue of a journal—knowledge of which I owe to Edward Neill ("'Found Wanting?' Second Impressions of a Famous First Sentence," *Persuasions*, no. 25 [2003], 76). Neill himself points out that the sentence turns on the ambiguity of *want:* "either a single man lacks a wife by definition, or might be supposed to 'want' in the sense of desiring one." The novel as a whole, he observes, explores the wanting of men less than that of women, who typically either desire or need a man (79). William Galperin puts the same point in broader terms, arguing that the words "represent an imposition where the coercive weight of public opinion ('*must* be in want of a wife') is virtually synonymous with the wish-fulfilling fantasies of women, whose affirmation of 'truth' is a by-product of their vulnerability and subordination. For the probabilistic scenario to thrive, there must be not only wealthy single men and unmarried women available for emplotment in a narrative of eventual and necessary union. There also must exist something on the order of 'universal' inequality since only in such a climate is there sufficient pressure on both single men and women to produce a phenomenon so widespread that it wears the mantle of truth" (*The Historical Austen* [Philadelphia: University of Pennsylvania Press, 2003], 125).

2 This metaphor begins a long sequence of references to marriage as a matter of material possession, in which husbands and money oddly merge. The "universe" sug-

gested by the general acknowledgment alluded to in the previous sentence has dwindled to "a neighbourhood," the two nouns synonymous from the point of view of many characters in Austen's narrative. Mrs. Bennet is particularly preoccupied with husbands as female property, but others in the fiction more quietly share her views. The metaphor has ironic force with reference to a period in which women could hold no financial property in their own names, except by special legal arrangement. They could, however, seek "property" in the guise of a husband.

3 Wife.

4 Rented.

5 Mr. Bennet is precisely right: his wife pretends to be asking questions, but she is actually eager to impart information. Bruce Stovel asks why she doesn't simply tell the news, and answers: "Her pseudo-questions are a transparent guise intended to induce Mr. Bennet to ask a genuine question. . . . His question, if only he would ask it, would request information that he does not possess, and so would imply that in this matter he is dependent, needy, inferior" ("Asking Versus Telling," *The Talk in Jane Austen,* ed. Bruce Stovel and Lynn Weinlos Gregg [Edmonton: University of Alberta Press, 2002], 24).

6 A carriage seating four people, drawn by four horses: in other words, a fairly luxurious piece of equipment, indicative of Bingley's wealth. This is only the first among many forms of conveyance that will be specified in *Pride and Prejudice,* the gradations among them suggesting degrees of prosperity and of style. In *Memoirs of Mr Clifford,* an unfinished tale probably written when Austen was between the ages of twelve and fifteen, she describes her protagonist as "a very rich young Man [who] kept a great many Carriages of which I do not recollect half. I can only remember that he had a Coach, a Chariot, a Chaise, a Landeau, a Landeaulet, a Phaeton, a Gig, a Whisky, an Italian Chair, a Buggy, a Curricle & a wheelbarrow." Her pleasure in the elaborate terminology of transportation and her interest in the physical details of getting from place to place apparently persisted. In later works such as

"Oh! single, my dear, to be sure![9] A single man of large fortune; four or five thousand a year.[10] What a fine thing for our girls!"

"How so? How can it affect them?"

"My dear Mr. Bennet," replied his wife, "how can you be so tiresome! You must know[11] that I am thinking of his marrying one of them."

"Is that his design[12] in settling here?"

"Design! Nonsense, how can you talk so! But it is very likely that he *may* fall in love with one of them, and therefore you must visit him as soon as he comes."[13]

"I see no occasion for that. You and the girls may go, or you may send them by themselves, which perhaps will be still better, for as you are as handsome as any of them, Mr. Bingley might like you the best of the party."

"My dear, you flatter me. I certainly *have* had my share of beauty, but I do not pretend to be anything extraordinary now. When a woman has five grown up daughters, she ought to give over[14] thinking of her own beauty."

"In such cases, a woman has not often much beauty to think of."

"But, my dear, you must indeed go and see Mr. Bingley when he comes into the neighbourhood."

"It is more than I engage for,[15] I assure you."

"But consider your daughters. Only think what an establishment[16] it would be for one of them. Sir William and Lady Lucas[17] are determined to go, merely on that account, for in general you know they visit no new comers.[18] Indeed you must go, for it will be impossible for *us* to visit him, if you do not."[19]

"You are over scrupulous surely. I dare say Mr. Bingley will be very glad to see you; and I will send a few lines by you to assure him of my hearty consent to his marrying which ever he chuses of the girls; though I must throw in a good word for my little Lizzy."

"I desire you will do no such thing. Lizzy is not a bit better than the others; and I am sure she is not half so handsome as Jane, nor half so good humoured as Lydia. But you are always giving *her* the preference."

Pride and Prejudice, however, she also employed modes of transportation as emblems of social status. Thus a curricle, much more elegant than a gig, declares its possessor a prosperous man of fashion, in contrast to the stately barouche, which signifies only wealth. Bingley's chaise and four likewise indicates his possession of money, while telling little about his style.

7 Presumably the steward of the estate, who would handle such matters of business as rental arrangements, about which Bingley and he have come to an agreement.

8 The Feast of St. Michael, 29 September, one of four English quarter days, when rent might be paid if it were to be by quarterly installments. The novel offers several clues about the passage of time in its narrative, alluding, for example, to Christmas, and to the gradual greening of trees during Elizabeth's spring visit to her friend Charlotte. Its action occupies roughly a year, corresponding in this respect to Austen's other novels.

There is no way, however, to ascertain a specific year for the happenings of *Pride and Prejudice.* Since the novel was originally written in the late eighteenth century and revised some time before its publication in 1813, it might be set either at the time of its first composition or later. The clues it offers are ambiguous.

9 Mrs. Bennet's qualifier, "to be sure," suggests—accurately—that she would have no special interest in Bingley were he not single, so his marital state should be self-evident.

10 Four or five thousand pounds a year would have been a very large income. It is virtually impossible to calculate equivalents, but a yearly income of £5,000 would be equivalent to something between $340,000 and $500,000 in 2010 dollars. In 1800, an English laborer or farmer made £15–£20 a year. At the gentry level—the level of the Bennet family—roughly £300 per person per year was required for respectable living. Throughout her novels, Austen characteristically specifies precise incomes and detailed inheritance provisions. Her emphasis is particularly vivid in *Sense and Sensibility,* in which money makes plot.

11 Mrs. Bennet means that *must* literally: it is inconceivable to her that anyone should fail to share her automatic equation between a single man and marriage to one of her daughters.

12 Plan.

13 The etiquette of visiting figures importantly in *Pride and Prejudice.* Until an introductory visit has been paid, no social connection between families can exist. Established members of the community call upon newcomers to inaugurate social relations. Only men can call upon men, so Mrs. Bennet does not have the option of initiating the relationship herself.

In 1814, Austen exchanged numerous letters with her niece, Anna Austen, who was engaged in writing a novel. Austen commented extensively on individual sections of the narrative as Anna sent them to her. Many of her strictures about the text concern the rules of visiting, which she feels strongly characters should not violate. Thus in a September letter she points out that "a woman in her situation would hardly go there, before she had been visited by other Families." She evidently shared the manuscript with others in her family, who held similar views: later in the same letter, she reports that her mother "is more disturbed at Mrs F.'s not returning the Egertons visit sooner, than anything else. They ought to have called at the Parsonage before Sunday" (To Anna Austen, 9–18 September 1814).

14 Stop.

15 Promise.

16 Settlement in life. Marriage would provide a young woman with an established position and—given a man of appropriate assets—a dependable income.

17 As we later learn, Sir William has been knighted during his mayoralty; his wife therefore has the title of Lady Lucas.

18 Because they consider themselves too important to do so.

19 Because they are women.

20 Compare Mrs. John Knightley, in *Emma*, who has "many fears and many nerves" (I, 11). In the course of the eighteenth century, prevailing physiological theory placed increasing emphasis on the nerves as of central importance to the human body—and indeed the soul. George Cheyne, with his treatise *The English Malady* (1733), popularized the understanding of what he called "nervous distempers"; he claimed to suffer from them himself. His suffering, he explained, derived from the fineness of his nerves: a form of weakness but also of highly developed emotional responsiveness.

Such fineness of nerves came increasingly to be associated with women, traditionally creatures of emotion rather than of reason, who could now claim the talent and "genius" that Cheyne linked with refined nerves, along with the disabilities connected to such refinement. Hysteria, earlier attributed to a wandering womb, came to be seen as a disorder of the nerves. The vague symptoms that Mrs. Bennet intermittently claims throughout *Pride and Prejudice* would have been readily seen by her contemporaries as evidence of delicate nerves. Jane Austen's mother also allegedly possessed such nerves. The novelist writes to Cassandra, "They want us to drink tea with them tonight, but I do not know whether my Mother will have nerves for it" (8 April–11 April 1805).

In a learned, witty, and wide-ranging essay, Margaret Anne Doody points out that "Mrs Bennet's nerves are both unethical (attention-seeking, vain) and ethical. Without the 'nerves,' professedly possessed by Mrs Bennet but shared among a number of characters—including Elizabeth and Darcy—there would be no perceptiveness, no physical response to the world, no awakening to the moment" ("'A Good Memory Is Unpardonable': Self, Love, and the Irrational Irritation of Memory," *Eighteenth-Century Fiction* 14: 1 [2001], 84).

21 Doody also observes that "Mr Bennet meets Mrs Bennet's claim with politely worded sarcasm. He himself disdains the physical and the immediate—Mr Bennet is a parody of escape into the realm of pure thought, of sublime abstraction. Mr Bennet spends his time in his library, shutting the door on unpleasant realities and indulging (for too much of his existence) in wishful thinking" (84).

"They have none of them much to recommend them," replied he; "they are all silly and ignorant like other girls; but Lizzy has something more of quickness than her sisters."

"Mr. Bennet, how can you abuse your own children in such a way? You take delight in vexing me. You have no compassion on my poor nerves."[20]

"You mistake me, my dear. I have a high respect for your nerves. They are my old friends. I have heard you mention them with consideration these twenty years at least."

"Ah! you do not know what I suffer."

"But I hope you will get over it, and live to see many young men of four thousand a year come into the neighbourhood."

"It will be no use to us, if twenty such should come since you will not visit them."

"Depend upon it, my dear, that when there are twenty, I will visit them all."[21]

Mr. Bennet was so odd a mixture of quick parts,[22] sarcastic humour, reserve, and caprice, that the experience of three and twenty years had been insufficient to make his wife understand his character. *Her* mind was less difficult to develope.[23] She was a woman of mean[24] understanding, little information, and uncertain temper. When she was discontented she fancied herself nervous. The business of her life was to get her daughters married;[25] its solace[26] was visiting and news.[27]

Poster of the 1940 movie *Pride and Prejudice*. This advertisement of the Greer Garson–Lawrence Olivier Warner Brothers film attempts to appeal to a presumed preoccupation of twentieth-century young women. The promotional copy on the poster reads: "When pretty girls t-e-a-s-e-d men into marriage!"

22 Intelligence.

23 Unveil or disclose.

24 Poor, undistinguished.

25 Given the notion of husbands as property, it seems relatively unsurprising that Mrs. Bennet should conceive her "business" as that of getting her daughters married. Again, the metaphor carries ironic overtones, given that no other kind of business activity could be engaged in by a woman of the gentry class. That the novelist herself was sharply aware of the limitations on allowable female activity emerges in an early letter to her sister. Austen, age twenty, has been exploring various expedients for getting to London. She wants to go by stagecoach, but her brother won't permit this. Finally, she has managed to work out a feasible arrangement, with a brother as protective companion. She writes, "My Father will be so good as to fetch home his prodigal Daughter from Town, I hope, unless he wishes me to walk the Hospitals [as a medical student], Enter at the Temple [to study law], or mount Guard at S[t] James [as a soldier]" (To Cassandra, 18 September 1796). It is a fairly complicated joke. Suffering from the male insistence on protecting women against the possibility of sexual danger, she suggests that men's real concern is to keep women from pursuing independent careers.

26 The hint that Mrs. Bennet needs "solace" for her life may come as something of a surprise, since the woman has already been revealed as silly and tedious. In fact, the "business" of finding husbands for five daughters of small fortune is an arduous one. This is the first of several suggestions that Austen fully realizes the painfulness of economic pressure for women, and the first of several indications that she can sympathize even with her most unattractive characters.

27 Reuben Arthur Brower focuses on this paragraph in an examination of Austen's wit: "Many pages of *Pride and Prejudice* can be read as sheer poetry of wit, as Pope without couplets. The antitheses are almost as frequent and almost as varied; the play of ambiguities is certainly as complex; the orchestration of tones is as precise and subtle. As in the best of Pope, the displays of ironic wit are not without imaginative connection; what looks most diverse is really most similar, and ironies are linked by vibrant reference to basic certainties. There are passages too in which the rhythmical pattern of the sentence approaches the formal balance of the heroic couplet"—and as an example he offers the final paragraph of Chapter I (*The Fields of Light: An Experiment in Critical Reading* [New York: Oxford University Press, 1951], 164).

For a survey of critical attitudes toward Mrs. Bennet's role in the novel and an investigation of how she is represented in film versions of *Pride and Prejudice,* see June Sturrock, "Mrs. Bennet's Legacy: Austen's Mothers in Film and Fiction," *Persuasions On-Line* 29: 1 (Winter 2008), http://www.jasna.org/persuasions/on-line/vol29no1/sturrock.html.

2

MR. BENNET WAS AMONG THE EARLIEST of those who waited on[1] Mr. Bingley. He had always intended to visit him, though to the last always assuring his wife that he should not go; and till the evening after the visit was paid, she had no knowledge of it. It was then disclosed in the following manner. Observing his second daughter employed in trimming a hat,[2] he suddenly addressed her with,

"I hope Mr. Bingley will like it, Lizzy."

"We are not in a way to know *what* Mr. Bingley likes," said her mother resentfully, "since we are not to visit."

"But you forget, mama," said Elizabeth, "that we shall meet him at the assemblies,[3] and that Mrs. Long has promised to introduce him."

"I do not believe Mrs. Long will do any such thing. She has two nieces of her own.[4] She is a selfish, hypocritical woman, and I have no opinion[5] of her."

"No more have I," said Mr. Bennet; "and I am glad to find that you do not depend on her serving you."[6]

Mrs. Bennet deigned not to make any reply; but unable to contain herself,[7] began scolding one of her daughters.

"Don't keep coughing so, Kitty, for heaven's sake! Have a little compassion on my nerves. You tear them to pieces."

"Kitty has no discretion in her coughs," said her father; "she times them ill."

"I do not cough for my own amusement," replied Kitty fretfully.

"When is your next ball to be, Lizzy?"[8]

1 Visited, called on.

2 Clothing was extremely expensive in this period, so it was common for women to refurbish various items of apparel. Neil McKendrick points out that even hats and dresses preserved in museums show repeated signs of alteration. Fashions changed rapidly, another reason for efforts at home refashioning ("The Commercialization of Fashion," in *The Birth of a Consumer Society: The Commercialization of Eighteenth-Century England,* ed. Neil McKendrick, John Brewer, and J. H. Plumb [London: Europa, 1982], 43).

Retrimming hats in ways that corresponded to changing fashion or that altered color schemes or styles could make an old accessory seem new. Austen, at the age of twenty-two, writes to her sister, "next week [I] shall begin my operations on my hat, on which you know my principal hopes of happiness depend" (To Cassandra, 27 October 1798). A few months later, she specifies: "Flowers are very much worn, & Fruit is still more the thing.—Eliz: has a bunch of Strawberries, & I have seen Grapes, Cherries, Plumbs & Apricots—There are likewise Almonds & raisins, french plumbs & Tamarinds at the Grocers, but I have never seen any of them in hats" (To Cassandra, 2 June 1799). Nine days later: "We have been to the cheap Shop, & very cheap we found it, but there are only flowers made there, no fruit—& as I could get 4 or 5 very pretty sprigs of the former for the same money which would procure only one Orleans plumb . . . I cannot decide on the fruit till I hear from you again.—Besides, I cannot help thinking that it is more natural to have flowers grow out of the head than fruit.—What do you think on that subject?" (To Cassandra, 11 June 1799).

Trimming hats, however, was widely seen as frivolous activity. Mary Wollstonecraft, in *A Vindication of the Rights of Woman* (1792), is especially ferocious: "The conversation of French women, who are not so rigidly nailed to their chairs to twist lappets, and knot ribands, is frequently superficial; but, I contend, that it is not half so insipid as that of those English women whose time is spent in making caps, bonnets, and the whole mischief of trimmings, not to mention shopping, bargain-hunting, &c. &c.: and it is the decent, prudent women, who are most degraded by these practices; for their motive is simply vanity" (chap. IV).

To introduce Elizabeth in the act of trimming a hat is the novelist's little joke. Elsewhere, Elizabeth shows little interest in self-adornment or in domestic activity.

3 Social gatherings, generally public (that is, open to anyone who bought a ticket), which provided opportunities for dancing and other entertainment. Private balls became more common as the century continued, but in this period the public assembly provided one relatively rare opportunity for young men and young women to spend time together. Assemblies took place in public assembly rooms. Since anyone who bought a ticket could come, they typically involved the mingling of social classes.

4 Given her nieces, Mrs. Long will be husband-hunting, too, and therefore unlikely to introduce potential rivals to the highly eligible Bingley.

5 No good opinion.

6 Doing you a favor.

7 Mrs. Bennet will often prove unable to contain her feelings. Preoccupied as she is with the subject of marriage, she repeatedly reveals the intensity of her emotional involvement with the matter.

8 In the first edition, this line, spoken by Mr. Bennet, appears as part of Kitty's speech, an obvious mistake: presumably a printer's error.

Day bonnets, fashion plate from Rudolph Ackermann, *Repository of Arts,* 1817. This engraving shows one kind of headwear Elizabeth might have been trimming.

9 Two weeks from tomorrow.

10 Irritating.

11 Caution, attention to circumstances.

12 Take their chances.

13 Duty.

14 Because Mr. Bennet has called upon Bingley, he is now in a position to introduce the young man to others. Moreover, once Mr. Bennet has performed the ritual of introduction for the women in his household, they, too, will be able to introduce others. Without telling his family in advance, Mr. Bennet has gone through the necessary "forms of introduction" by paying the visit that makes further social relations possible.

15 Mr. Bennet's teasing customarily declares his superiority to its targets. The account of him in the previous chapter has him in effect insisting on his contempt for established social forms. Now he reverses course, representing himself as upholding convention and his wife as insufficiently respectful of conventional decorum. In both instances, he emphasizes his difference from and implicit superiority to the women in his family.

16 Mary selects passages of interest to her and writes them down, presumably making collections of such selections. Often called *ana*, collections in which extracts of the wit and wisdom of others mingle with observations by the collector were popular throughout the eighteenth century and into the nineteenth. *Thraliana*, by Hester Thrale Piozzi, is one published example of the genre. Piozzi combined extracts with diary entries from 1776 to 1809, thus producing a record both of her life and of her literary taste. Most assemblages of passages, however, remained private documents. Mary presumably extracts passages purely for her own enlightenment. Her conversation, which relies heavily on popular wisdom in clichéd forms, suggests the kind of quotation that might be appealing to her.

17 Austen's first use of *sensible* here has the modern meaning: giving evidence of having good sense. The

"To-morrow fortnight."[9]

"Aye, so it is," cried her mother, "and Mrs. Long does not come back till the day before; so it will be impossible for her to introduce him, for she will not know him herself."

"Then, my dear, you may have the advantage of your friend, and introduce Mr. Bingley to *her*."

"Impossible, Mr. Bennet, impossible, when I am not acquainted with him myself; how can you be so teazing?"[10]

"I honour your circumspection.[11] A fortnight's acquaintance is certainly very little. One cannot know what a man really is by the end of a fortnight. But if *we* do not venture, somebody else will; and after all, Mrs. Long and her neices must stand their chance;[12] and therefore, as she will think it an act of kindness, if you decline the office,[13] I will take it on myself."

The girls stared at their father. Mrs. Bennet said only, "Nonsense, nonsense!"

"What can be the meaning of that emphatic exclamation?" cried he. "Do you consider the forms of introduction,[14] and the stress that is laid on them, as nonsense?[15] I cannot quite agree with you *there*. What say you, Mary? for you are a young lady of deep reflection I know, and read great books, and make extracts."[16] Mary wished to say something very sensible,[17] but knew not how.

"While Mary is adjusting her ideas," he continued, "let us return to Mr. Bingley."

"I am sick of Mr. Bingley," cried his wife.

"I am sorry to hear *that*; but why did not you tell me so before? If I had known as much this morning I certainly would not have called on him. It is very unlucky; but as I have actually paid the visit, we cannot escape the acquaintance now."

The astonishment of the ladies was just what he wished; that of Mrs. Bennet perhaps surpassing the rest; though when the first tumult of joy was over, she began to declare that it was what she had expected all the while.

"How good it was in you, my dear Mr. Bennet! But I knew I should persuade you at last. I was sure you loved your girls too well to neglect such an acquaintance. Well, how pleased I am! and it is such a good joke, too, that you should have gone this morning, and never said a word about it till now."

"Now, Kitty, you may cough as much as you chuse," said Mr. Bennet; and, as he spoke, he left the room, fatigued with the raptures of his wife.[18]

"What an excellent father you have, girls," said she, when the door was shut. "I do not know how you will ever make him amends for his kindness; or me either, for that matter. At our time of life, it is not so pleasant I can tell you, to be making new acquaintance every day; but for your sakes, we would do anything. Lydia, my love, though you *are* the youngest, I dare say Mr. Bingley will dance with you at the next ball."

"Oh!" said Lydia stoutly,[19] "I am not afraid; for though I *am* the youngest, I'm the tallest."

The rest of the evening was spent in conjecturing how soon he would return Mr. Bennet's visit, and determining when they should ask him to dinner.

word and its cognates will appear many times in *Pride and Prejudice,* often meaning "conscious of," with different shades of implication. The history of the word *sense* and its cognates was long ago set forth in detail by C. S. Lewis (*Studies in Words* [Cambridge: Cambridge University Press, 1960]), who explains that *sensible* could mean "something apprehensible by the senses" or, alternately, "capable of being emotionally experienced" (pp. 156–157). From meaning "able to feel," *sensible* proceeds to the meaning of "actually feeling" (p. 158). It also, however, for reasons Lewis elaborately explains, could mean "having ordinary intelligence, the opposite of silly or foolish" (p. 161). By the end of the eighteenth century, the word "is overburdened with meanings. It can mean (1) perceptible to the senses, (2) sentient, not unconscious, (3) having such *sensibility* as Marianne Dashwood's [in *Sense and Sensibility*], or (4) having (good or common) *sense,* being no fool" (p. 163). Austen would have been *sensible* of all these meanings.

As for Mary, there is some pathos in her yearning to say something sensible when given the opportunity, as she would see it, to shine. Given her father's tendency toward mockery, and considering the tone of his invitation to her, he presumably asks for her wisdom in order to make fun of her. Austen's capacity at least momentarily to solicit sympathy for foolish Mary, as earlier for foolish Mrs. Bennet, suggests the breadth of her comprehension.

18 Reuben Arthur Brower suggests that Mr. and Mrs. Bennet in effect speak different languages (*The Fields of Light: An Experiment in Critical Reading* [New York: Oxford University Press, 1951], 166).

19 Firmly, resolutely.

3

1 Mr. Bennet's pleasure in mildly tormenting the women in his family controls much of his activity.

2 Information.

3 With this brilliant use of the passive voice, suggesting that hopes "were entertained" with no clarity about who entertains them, Austen conveys the possibility that Lady Lucas, her daughters, the Bennet girls, and their mother all cherish the same hopes—which, in the nature of things, can only be fulfilled for one (or two: a girl and her mother) at best.

4 In other words, she will have completed "the business of her life."

5 To return a visit promptly was a conventional courtesy, part of the established ritual. The short length of Bingley's stay emphasizes its conventional nature.

6 Blue was a highly fashionable color for men in this period. When Lydia marries, later in the novel, she will wonder in advance whether her husband-to-be will wear his blue coat at the altar.

NOT ALL THAT MRS. BENNET, however, with the assistance of her five daughters, could ask on the subject was sufficient to draw from her husband any satisfactory description of Mr. Bingley.[1] They attacked him in various ways; with barefaced questions, ingenious suppositions, and distant surmises; but he eluded the skill of them all; and they were at last obliged to accept the second-hand intelligence[2] of their neighbour Lady Lucas. Her report was highly favourable. Sir William had been delighted with him. He was quite young, wonderfully handsome, extremely agreeable, and to crown the whole, he meant to be at the next assembly with a large party. Nothing could be more delightful! To be fond of dancing was a certain step towards falling in love; and very lively hopes of Mr. Bingley's heart were entertained.[3]

"If I can but see one of my daughters happily settled at Netherfield," said Mrs. Bennet to her husband, "and all the others equally well married, I shall have nothing to wish for."[4]

In a few days Mr. Bingley returned Mr. Bennet's visit, and sat about ten minutes with him in his library.[5] He had entertained hopes of being admitted to a sight of the young ladies, of whose beauty he had heard much; but he saw only the father. The ladies were somewhat more fortunate, for they had the advantage of ascertaining from an upper window, that he wore a blue coat[6] and rode a black horse.

An invitation to dinner was soon afterwards dispatched; and already had Mrs. Bennet planned the courses that were to do credit to her housekeeping, when an answer arrived which deferred it all. Mr. Bingley was obliged to be in town[7] the following day, and consequently unable to accept the honour of their invitation, &c.[8] Mrs. Bennet was quite disconcerted. She could not imagine what business he could have in town so soon after his arrival in Hertfordshire;[9] and she began to fear that he might be always flying about from one place to another, and never settled at Netherfield as he ought to be. Lady Lucas quieted her fears a little by starting the idea of his being gone to London only to get a large party for the ball; and a report soon followed that Mr. Bingley was to bring twelve ladies and seven gentlemen with him to the assembly. The girls grieved over such a number of ladies; but were comforted the day before the ball by hearing, that instead of twelve, he had brought only six with him from London, his five sisters and a cousin. And when the party entered the assembly room, it consisted of only five altogether; Mr. Bingley, his two sisters, the husband of the eldest, and another young man.[10]

Mr. Bingley was good looking and gentlemanlike; he had a pleasant countenance, and easy, unaffected manners.[11] His sisters were fine[12] women, with an air of decided fashion. His brother-in-law, Mr. Hurst, merely looked the gentleman;[13] but his friend Mr. Darcy soon drew the attention of the room by his fine, tall person,[14] handsome features, noble mien; and the report which was in general circulation within five minutes after his entrance, of his having ten thousand a year.[15] The gentlemen pronounced him to be a fine figure of a man, the ladies declared he was much handsomer than Mr. Bingley, and he was looked at with great admiration for about half the evening, till his manners gave a disgust[16] which turned the tide of his popularity; for he was discovered to be proud, to be above his company,[17] and above being pleased; and not all his large estate in Derbyshire[18] could then save him from having a most forbidding, disagreeable countenance,[19] and being unworthy to be compared with his friend.

Mr. Bingley had soon made himself acquainted with all the principal people in the room; he was lively and unreserved, danced every dance, was angry that the ball closed so early, and talked of giving one himself at Netherfield. Such amiable[20] qualities must speak for themselves. What a contrast between him and his friend! Mr. Darcy

7 London.

8 The "&c." designates the formal language that would conventionally make part of the apology.

9 The Bennets' county, in east central England, north of London; in Austen's time a predominantly agricultural region.

10 This is the first specific instance of the reporting and believing of false information in the community. The discrepancy between report and fact suggests that the local "universe" relies heavily on rumor, with false news often more titillating than true.

11 Bingley is the first of several characters to be described in terms of their "manners," meaning not only politeness but general bearing. (Darcy, toward the end of this paragraph, will be said to have manners that "gave a disgust" to others.) Manners, it will turn out, are not sufficient to determine merit, although many within the local community assume otherwise. Yet manners *seem* dependable indications of character because, as conduct books reiterated, they reflect a person's attitudes toward others.

Conduct books multiplied through the eighteenth century, addressed mainly to women, but on occasion to men instead, or to both sexes. Some of them provided detailed instructions about manners, including recommendations about appropriate conversational subjects and about how one should serve oneself at dinner. Yet, paradoxically, an overwhelming consensus conveyed by these books had it that good manners simply expressed the possessor's appropriate feelings toward others. As the emanation of social feeling, manners could not logically be taught. One might follow all the rules yet not be thought to have "pleasing" manners.

When Jane summarizes her feelings toward Bingley, after the dance, early in Chapter 4, she praises him by observing that she "never saw such happy manners!—so much ease, with such perfect good breeding!" Some such combination of ease and good breeding appears to be the ideal. Toward the end of *Sense and Sensibility*, Mrs. Dashwood discusses Marianne's present and her past lover, assessing them in terms of their manners: "the Colonel's manners are not only more pleasing to me than Willoughby's ever were, but they are of a kind I well know to be more solidly attaching to Marianne. Their gentleness, their genuine attention to other people, and their manly unstudied simplicity is much more accordant with her real disposition, than the liveliness—often artificial, and often ill-timed of the other" (III, 9). This suggests a similar point in different terms.

Edmund Burke maintains that manners are more vital than law in people's experience: "The law touches us but here and there, and now and then. Manners are what vex and soothe us, corrupt or purify, exalt or debase, barbarize or refine us, by a constant, steady, uniform, insensible operation, like that of the air we breathe in. They give their whole form and colour to our lives" (*Letters on a Regicide Peace,* 1795, quoted in Malcolm Day, *Voices from the World of Jane Austen* [Devon: David & Charles, 2006], 192).

12 Elegant, with the implication that they are expensively dressed; their "air of decided fashion" confirms their stylishness.

13 In other words, he fulfills the minimum requirement of acceptability at a dance: he has a gentlemanly appearance, probably acquired simply by wearing appropriate clothes.

14 Physical nature.

15 An enormous fortune, twice as large as Bingley's, which would make him one of the wealthiest men in the country. Its twenty-first-century equivalent might be as much as $1,000,000 a year.

16 Distaste.

17 To consider himself more socially important than those around him.

18 A county in the north Midlands characterized by fine scenery—especially in the northern Peaks district—and famous for its great houses. It is the site of Chatsworth, the magnificent home of the dukes of Devonshire, which some have thought the model for Darcy's estate, Pemberly. Even in the eighteenth century, the region attracted tourists.

danced only once with Mrs. Hurst and once with Miss Bingley, declined being introduced to any other lady,[21] and spent the rest of the evening in walking about the room, speaking occasionally to one of his own party. His character was decided.[22] He was the proudest, most disagreeable man in the world, and every body hoped that he would never come there again. Amongst the most violent against him was Mrs. Bennet, whose dislike of his general behaviour was sharpened into particular resentment, by his having slighted one of her daughters.

Elizabeth Bennet had been obliged, by the scarcity of gentlemen, to sit down for two dances; and during part of that time, Mr. Darcy had been standing near enough for her to overhear a conversation between him and Mr. Bingley, who came from the dance for a few minutes, to press his friend to join it.

"Come, Darcy," said he, "I must have you dance. I hate to see you standing about by yourself in this stupid[23] manner. You had much better dance."

"I certainly shall not. You know how I detest it, unless I am particularly acquainted with my partner. At such an assembly as this it would be insupportable. Your sisters are engaged, and there is not another woman in the room, whom it would not be a punishment to me to stand up with."[24]

"I would not be so fastidious as you are," cried Mr. Bingley, "for a kingdom! Upon my honour, I never met with so many pleasant girls in my life, as I have this evening; and there are several of them you see uncommonly pretty."

"*You* are dancing with the only handsome girl in the room," said Mr. Darcy, looking at the eldest Miss Bennet.

"Oh! she is the most beautiful creature[25] I ever beheld! But there is one of her sisters sitting down just behind you, who is very pretty, and I dare say, very agreeable. Do let me ask my partner to introduce you."

"Which do you mean?" and turning round he looked for a moment at Elizabeth, till catching her eye,[26] he withdrew his own and coldly said, "She is tolerable; but not handsome enough to tempt *me;* and I am in no humour at present to give consequence[27] to young ladies

Full dress, fashion plate from Rudolph Ackermann, *Repository of Arts,* 1814. The Bennet sisters and other women at the assembly might have worn dresses like the one depicted in this engraving.

Full dress, *Le Beau Monde,* 1806. A gentleman's attire for the assembly.

19 This "forbidding, disagreeable countenance" belongs to the man who at the beginning of the paragraph had "handsome features." His wealth made him handsome; his reserve makes him disagreeable. Once more we see the volatility of communal opinion and the degree to which interpretation depends upon emotion. We may note also the intimate connection between judgment and appearance.

20 An adjective that appears frequently in *Pride and Prejudice.* It is in the early nineteenth century a strong term of approval, implying friendliness and likeability —or even lovability. In *Emma,* Knightley's comments on Frank Churchill suggest that the English word implies also sensitive responsiveness toward others: "No, Emma, your amiable young man can be amiable only in French, not in English. He may be very 'aimable,' have very good manners, and be very agreeable; but he can have no English delicacy towards the feelings of other people: nothing really amiable about him" (I, 18).

21 To dance with a woman, a man had to be formally introduced to her. By avoiding introductions, Darcy avoids dancing with anyone he does not already know.

22 The community has come to conclusions about his nature on the basis of his behavior.

23 Tiresome.

24 Darcy's explanation of his reluctance to dance suggests a combination of awkwardness and arrogance. His unwillingness to dance unless he is particularly acquainted with his partner hints that he has difficulty making polite conversation; his arrogance emerges in his contempt for every available woman.

25 Created being, with no derogatory implication.

26 Elizabeth is close enough to overhear what Darcy says; Darcy might plausibly realize this fact. He catches her eye before he enunciates his rejection, as if he wants her to pay attention. Is this a kind of flirtation? Throughout the first and second volumes of *Pride and Prejudice,* the relation between Elizabeth and Darcy develops by means of antagonism.

27 Social importance: Darcy assumes that Elizabeth would acquire status by dancing with him.

28 In Frances Burney's *Evelina* (1778), a novel that often seems to be in Austen's mind, the young heroine, at her first assembly, hears from a friend about a conversation between the nobleman she has just danced with and two other men. Lord Orville, her dancing partner, characterizes her as "a poor weak girl!" Unlike Elizabeth, Evelina cannot laugh at the insult. *Belinda* (1801), by Maria Edgeworth, contains an important scene in which the protagonist overhears a group of men discussing her in negative terms. She modifies her behavior as a result. Elizabeth differs sharply from most conventional novelistic heroines.

29 In her delight in the ridiculous, Elizabeth resembles her father. This first exemplary episode reveals also the degree to which she uses comedy as defense, protecting against the hurt of Darcy's insult by turning it into a joke.

30 All things considered; for the most part.

31 Singled out.

32 The family with the highest social position. By ingenious analysis of textual detail, Kenneth Smith has concluded that Meryton corresponds to the town of Harpenden in Hertfortshire and that Longbourn is derived from Redbourn, a village two miles southwest of Harpenden. ("The Probable Location of 'Longbourn' in Jane Austen's *Pride and Prejudice*," *Persuasions*, no. 27 [2005], 234–241.)

33 Outcome.

34 Expectations about.

35 Extremely. At this time the adverb served to intensify rather than to qualify the term it modified.

36 A man who asked a lady to dance would be expected to remain her partner for two dances. If he invited her a second time, they would share two more dances.

37 Obviously, Mrs. Bennet has no way of knowing what Bingley felt about Miss Lucas. She fills in her narrative on the basis of her wishes.

who are slighted by other men. You had better return to your partner and enjoy her smiles, for you are wasting your time with me."

Mr. Bingley followed his advice. Mr. Darcy walked off; and Elizabeth remained with no very cordial feelings toward him.[28] She told the story however with great spirit among her friends; for she had a lively, playful disposition, which delighted in any thing ridiculous.[29]

The evening altogether[30] passed off pleasantly to the whole family. Mrs. Bennet had seen her eldest daughter much admired by the Netherfield party. Mr. Bingley had danced with her twice, and she had been distinguished[31] by his sisters. Jane was as much gratified by this, as her mother could be, though in a quieter way. Elizabeth felt Jane's pleasure. Mary had heard herself mentioned to Miss Bingley as the most accomplished girl in the neighbourhood; and Catherine and Lydia had been fortunate enough to be never without partners, which was all that they had yet learnt to care for at a ball. They returned therefore in good spirits to Longbourn, the village where they lived, and of which they were the principal inhabitants.[32] They found Mr. Bennet still up. With a book he was regardless of time; and on the present occasion he had a good deal of curiosity as to the event[33] of an evening which had raised such splendid expectations. He had rather hoped that all his wife's views on[34] the stranger would be disappointed; but he soon found that he had a very different story to hear.

"Oh! my dear Mr. Bennet," as she entered the room, "we have had a most delightful evening, a most excellent ball. I wish you had been there. Jane was so admired, nothing could be like it. Everybody said how well she looked; and Mr. Bingley thought her quite[35] beautiful, and danced with her twice![36] Only think of *that* my dear; he actually danced with her twice; and she was the only creature in the room that he asked a second time. First of all, he asked Miss Lucas. I was so vexed to see him stand up with her; but, however, he did not admire her at all:[37] indeed, nobody can, you know; and he seemed quite struck with Jane as she was going down the dance.[38] So he inquired who she was, and got introduced, and asked her for the two next. Then, the two third he danced with Miss King, and the two fourth with Maria Lucas, and the two fifth with Jane again, and the two sixth with Lizzy, and the Boulanger—"[39]

"If he had had any compassion for *me*," cried her husband impatiently, "he would not have danced half so much! For God's sake, say no more of his partners. Oh! that he had sprained his ancle in the first dance!"

"Oh! my dear," continued Mrs. Bennet, "I am quite delighted with him.[40] He is so excessively[41] handsome! and his sisters are charming women. I never in my life saw anything more elegant than their dresses. I dare say the lace upon Mrs. Hurst's gown—"

Here she was interrupted again. Mr. Bennet protested against any description of finery. She was therefore obliged to seek another branch of the subject, and related, with much bitterness of spirit and some exaggeration, the shocking rudeness of Mr. Darcy.

"But I can assure you," she added, "that Lizzy does not lose much by not suiting *his* fancy; for he is a most disagreeable, horrid man, not at all worth pleasing. So high[42] and so conceited that there was no enduring him! He walked here, and he walked there, fancying himself so very great![43] Not handsome enough to dance with! I wish you had been there, my dear, to have given him one of your set downs. I quite detest the man."[44]

38 Guests at the balls in *Pride and Prejudice* engaged in country dancing, for which couples stood opposite each other in long lines, or sets. When the music began, each couple in turn would work their way down the set by performing a series of steps with each couple they passed. Couples not for the moment engaged in dancing were expected to converse with each other. Since each dance lasted roughly half an hour, there was considerable time for conversation. Those not dancing could also have the pleasure of assessing the performances of the others passing down the set. Thus Bingley has the opportunity to see Jane, to whom he subsequently asks to be introduced.

39 A country dance of French origin. Its name "originates in the mildly improper French popular song *La boulangère a des écus,* which suggests that the baker's wife acquired her money by means less creditable than the sale of bread" (*Jane Austen's Letters,* collected and edited by Deirdre Le Faye, 3rd ed. [Oxford: Oxford University Press, 1995], 356n4).

40 If Mr. Bennet torments his wife, she can also torment him—and she shows considerable defensive capacity to ignore him.

41 Extremely; like "quite," a colloquial intensifier.

42 Haughty.

43 "While [Mrs. Bennet] is not in general a reliable witness," Deborah Kaplan observes, "she captures nicely Mr. Darcy's tendency at the ball to flaunt his power to choose by exhibiting himself detached and free" (*Jane Austen Among Women* [Baltimore: The Johns Hopkins University Press, 1992], 187). Kaplan's book treats *Pride and Prejudice* extensively, illuminating its relation to modern American feminist criticism and to Austen's own female culture.

44 The vigor of Mrs. Bennet's speech reflects the energy of her personality—energy that has only one focus in the novel. Austen makes her an increasingly unsympathetic character yet provides details that allow the reader to understand how she got that way: not only because of her "mean understanding" and "uncertain temper" but also because of her limited outlets.

Edward Francisco Burney, "Frances d'Arblay,"
c. 1784–1785. Frances Burney, an eighteenth-
century novelist, represented here under her married name of d'Arblay, was an important influence
on Austen. *Pride and Prejudice* contains reminis-
cences of her first novel, *Evelina* (1778), and her
second, *Cecilia* (1782).

Portrait of Maria Edgeworth, from
E. A. Duyckinck, *Portrait Gallery
of Eminent Women,* 1813. Maria
Edgeworth, born eight years before
Austen but surviving twenty-two
years after, was a popular novelist
of the period. Austen admired her
and sometimes dramatized situations that her fellow novelist also
employed—as when Elizabeth overhears Darcy's insult at the assembly.

4

WHEN JANE AND ELIZABETH WERE ALONE, the former, who had been cautious in her praise of Mr. Bingley before, expressed to her sister how very much she admired him.

"He is just what a young man ought to be," said she, "sensible, good humoured, lively; and I never saw such happy manners![1] — so much ease, with such perfect good breeding!"

"He is also handsome," replied Elizabeth, "which a young man ought likewise to be, if he possibly can.[2] His character is thereby complete."

"I was very much flattered by his asking me to dance a second time. I did not expect such a compliment."

"Did not you? *I* did for you. But that is one great difference between us. Compliments always take *you* by surprise, and *me* never. What could be more natural than his asking you again? He could not help seeing that you were about five times as pretty as every other woman in the room. No thanks to his gallantry for that. Well, he certainly is very agreeable, and I give you leave to like him. You have liked many a stupider person."

"Dear Lizzy!"

"Oh! you are a great deal too apt you know, to like people in general. You never see a fault in any body. All the world are good and agreeable in your eyes. I never heard you speak ill of a human being in my life."

"I would not wish to be hasty in censuring anyone; but I always speak what I think."

1 Manners are habits indicating good breeding, but the word is used here with overtones of an earlier sense: a person's habitual behavior, including moral character. *Happy* manners are fortunate ones—from the point of view both of the possessor of such manners and of anyone coming into contact with such a person.

2 In calling attention to Bingley's handsomeness, Elizabeth in effect teases her sister for not acknowledging that physical attractiveness accounts for part of the young man's appeal. Edward Neill claims, startlingly, that "Jane Austen's novels are almost indecently erotic" (*The Politics of Jane Austen* [New York: St. Martin's Press, 1999], 61). The reiterated emphasis on appearance, in men and women alike, reminds readers of the physical component of romantic relationships.

Elizabeth's wit, verve, and occasional willingness to defy convention differentiate her from the other characters in Austen's novel, but the saucy girl was already a well-established fictional and dramatic character. Perhaps her most memorable stage incarnation is Millamant in William Congreve's play *The Way of the World* (1700), a glamorous figure who stipulates to her lover all the rights she demands before she will allow herself to "dwindle into a wife."

In fiction, the saucy girl typically plays a secondary role. Samuel Richardson's *Clarissa* (1748) contains Anna Howe, the heroine's closest female friend, who teases her mother, her suitor (whom she means to accept), and Clarissa herself. Charlotte, in *Sir Charles Grandi-*

son (1753–1754), Richardson's second novel, also teases her suitor (even after he becomes her husband) and her parents. The text makes it clear, however, that she needs to reform.

Later writers used such characters to suggest a serious critical perspective on more conventional sentimental figures within a text. A salient example is Frances Burney's *Cecilia, or Memoirs of an Heiress* (1782), a phrase in which probably provides the title of *Pride and Prejudice* (although the *OED* cites examples of the phrase from 1610 onward). In this long novel, Lady Honoria Pemberton supplies frequent comic commentary on the pretensions of the Delvile family and actually, at the book's end, raises questions about Cecilia's hard-won marriage. Frances Brooke's *History of Lady Julia Mandeville* (1763) represents a young widow, Lady Anne Wilmot, who, like Anna Howe, enjoys teasing the lover whom she will accept, and who comments astutely on other characters. Thus she and others, including the hero, Harry Mandeville, visit a *nouveau riche* family, the daughter of which, she claims, is "the bride I intend for Harry Mandeville." She describes the young woman first through her education: "Her mother being above the little vulgar cares of a family, or so unimportant a task as the education of an only child; she was early entrusted to a French chambermaid, who, having left her own country on account of a Faux Pas which had visible consequences, was appointed to instill the principles of virtue and politeness into the flexible mind of this illustrious heiress of the house of Westbrook, under the title of governess. . . . [P]eople must live, and there is 80,000*l.* attached to this animal, and, if the girl likes him, I don't see what he can do better" (4th ed., 2 vol., London, 1765; I, 44–45). Written in epistolary form, the novel therefore provides us with Lady Anne's written words rather than with, as in *Pride and Prejudice,* reports of her thoughts and utterances. Like Elizabeth Bennet, however, Lady Anne evinces a sharp eye and a sometimes sharp tongue.

Finally, there is Robert Bage's *Hermsprong, or Man As He Is Not* (1796), a book that Austen is known to have admired. Its heroine mainly behaves in conventional and sentimental fashion, but her best friend,

"I know you do; and it is *that* which makes the wonder. With *your* good sense, to be so honestly blind to the follies and nonsense of others! Affectation of candour[3] is common enough;—one meets it every where. But to be candid without ostentation or design—to take the good of every body's character and make it still better, and say nothing of the bad—belongs to you alone. And so you like this man's sisters too, do you? Their manners are not equal to his."

"Certainly not; at first. But they are very pleasing women when you converse with them. Miss Bingley is to live with her brother and keep his house;[4] and I am much mistaken if we shall not find a very charming neighbour in her."

Elizabeth listened in silence, but was not convinced; their behaviour at the assembly had not been calculated to please in general; and with more quickness of observation and less pliancy of temper than her sister, and with a judgment too unassailed by any attention to herself, she was very little disposed to approve them. They were in fact very fine[5] ladies; not deficient in good humour when they were pleased, nor in the power of being agreeable where they chose it; but proud and conceited. They were rather handsome, had been educated in one of the first private seminaries in town,[6] had a fortune of twenty thousand pounds,[7] were in the habit of spending more than they ought, and of associating with people of rank;[8] and were therefore in every respect[9] entitled to think well of themselves, and meanly[10] of others. They were of a respectable family in the north of England; a circumstance more deeply impressed on their memories than that their brother's fortune and their own had been acquired by trade.[11]

Mr. Bingley inherited property to the amount of nearly a hundred thousand pounds from his father, who had intended to purchase an estate,[12] but did not live to do it.—Mr. Bingley intended it likewise, and sometimes made choice of his county; but as he was now provided with a good house and the liberty of a manor,[13] it was doubtful to many of those who best knew the easiness of his temper,[14] whether he might not spend the remainder of his days at Netherfield, and leave the next generation to purchase.[15]

Maria Fluart, mocks her and her father for conventional pretensions and, unlike her predecessors in the line of saucy women, refuses to marry.

Elizabeth Bennet is less programmatic than Maria and less aggressive than Lady Honoria; her teasing is largely confined to Jane, in an affectionate mode, and, with more irritation, Darcy. But the pleasure she shares with her father, that of laughing at the ridiculous, separates her from the other women in *Pride and Prejudice.*

3 Openness, kindliness, generosity.

4 Manage the household. Since Bingley does not have a wife, it is appropriate that an unmarried female member of his family should assume this supervisory role.

5 Fashionable.

6 Austen does not think highly of the education provided by such seminaries. In *Emma,* we learn that "Mrs. Goddard was the mistress of a School—not of a seminary, or an establishment, or any thing which professed, in long sentences of refined nonsense, to combine liberal acquirements with elegant morality upon new principles and new systems—and where young ladies for enormous pay might be screwed out of health and into vanity" (I, 3). In *Sense and Sensibility,* a "landscape in colored silks" worked by one of the characters hangs over a mantelpiece, "in proof of her having spent seven years at a great school in town to some effect" (II, 4).

7 They might expect an annual income of £1,000 apiece from a principal of £20,000—modest, compared with Bingley's income, but a fairly substantial sum.

8 High rank.

9 "In every respect" from their own point of view: most readers could readily specify respects in which they might not seem superior. The qualities specified mainly derive from economic well-being, with the addition of the attractive appearance desirable in a lady. The Bingley sisters pride themselves on characteristics that, as the novel will abundantly show, make them marriageable by conventional standards.

10 Ungenerously.

11 Although by this time large fortunes were being made in trade, and members of the nobility intermarried with the newly rich, it was still true that inherited wealth, like Darcy's, based on the possession of land, implied higher social standing than earned wealth.

12 House and land that could be passed on to his descendants, improving their social status.

13 The right to hunt on the estate he has rented. Such a right was available only to the wealthy. It was highly valued by those who enjoyed hunting. *Sense and Sensibility* observes that "a sportsman, though he esteems only those of his sex who are sportsmen likewise, is not often desirous of encouraging their taste by admitting them to a residence within his own manor": hence Sir John Middleton is pleased to settle an all-female family in a cottage on his estate (I, 7).

14 Bingley is easy-going and easily influenced.

15 The complexities of the British class system inhabit the consciousness of all Austen's characters. Those complexities are numerous and subtle. In 1814 Patrick Colquhoun, a prolific writer on many subjects, constructed a table of the various classes. What he called "The Highest Orders" included the royal family, "lords spiritual and temporal," and members of the peerage above the rank of baronet. The second class contained baronets, knights, country gentlemen, and "others with a large income." According to Colquhoun, Great Britain held 234,305 members of this group, to which Darcy would have belonged. Below them were the third class, including clergy, doctors, merchants and manufacturers on a large scale, and bankers. In the fourth class, of which the Bennet family would be members, were persons of moderate income, members of the lesser clergy, doctors, lawyers, and teachers (the author offers no explanation of why doctors appear in both the third and the fourth class). Colquhoun claimed that Great Britain had 1,168,250 of them (*A Treatise on the Wealth, Power, and Resources of the British Empire, in Every Quarter of the World,* 2nd ed., London, 1815, pp. 106–107).

It is often alleged that wealth does not determine social class, but Colquhoun's table suggests that it at least carries considerable weight. His second class lists "others with a large income" right along with knights and baronets; the third, including manufacturers on a large but not a small scale, also indicates that money has a bearing on status. Colquhoun provides no source for his statistics and does not reveal the authority for his classifications. The existence of his system by no means proves that its principles were universally accepted. It suggests, rather, that the division of classes remained contested—a fact that would only have intensified such anxiety as that of the Bingley sisters.

Land remained of primary significance, in Colquhoun's as in other codifications of the system. Darcy has higher status than Bingley not only because his annual income is double that of his friend but because he owns an estate, and one that has been passed down through the family. The Bingley sisters' concern that their brother purchase an estate derives from their desire for heightened status.

Miss Bingley and Mrs. Hurst have relatively little money of their own. They mingle with the wealthy partly in the hope of improving their social standing by association. Marriage between social classes was not the norm, but it was not uncommon either. As early as 1740, Samuel Richardson's *Pamela* had suggested that a servant girl of intelligence, with a number of "accomplishments," could and in a sense should marry an upper-class man. By the end of the century, relatively impoverished aristocratic families might marry their daughters to rich members of the merchant class, and *nouveaux riches* traders and their children could hope to marry into the upper classes. Miss Bingley, it soon will become apparent, hopes to marry Darcy and thus to secure her position in Colquhoun's second class.

The Bennet family have a moderate income but not enough to secure the futures of their daughters. Mrs. Bennet's "business" is not only to marry off her daughters but to ensure that they marry men of prosperity and social standing. Elizabeth will claim, much later in the novel, that she belongs to the same class as Darcy, since she is the daughter of a gentleman. Her mother, however, belongs to a more dubious social level, and

His sisters were very anxious for his having an estate of his own;[16] but though he was now established only as a tenant, Miss Bingley was by no means unwilling to preside at his table, nor was Mrs. Hurst, who had married a man of more fashion than fortune, less disposed to consider his house as her home when it suited her. Mr. Bingley had not been of age two years,[17] when he was tempted by an accidental[18] recommendation to look at Netherfield House. He did look at it and into it for half an hour, was pleased with the situation[19] and the principal rooms, satisfied with what the owner said in its praise, and took it immediately.

Between him and Darcy there was a very steady friendship, in spite of a great opposition of character.—Bingley was endeared to Darcy by the easiness, openness, ductility of his temper, though no disposition could offer a greater contrast to his own, and though with his own he never appeared dissatisfied. On the strength of Darcy's regard Bingley had the firmest reliance, and of his judgment the highest opinion. In understanding Darcy was the superior. Bingley was by no means deficient, but Darcy was clever. He was at the same time haughty,[20] reserved, and fastidious, and his manners, though well bred, were not inviting. In that respect his friend had greatly the advantage. Bingley was sure of being liked wherever he appeared, Darcy was continually giving offense.

The manner in which they spoke of the Meryton assembly was sufficiently characteristic. Bingley had never met with pleasanter people or prettier girls in his life; every body had been most kind and attentive to him, there had been no formality, no stiffness, he had soon felt acquainted with all the room; and as to Miss Bennet,[21] he could not conceive an angel more beautiful. Darcy, on the contrary, had seen a collection of people in whom there was little beauty and no fashion, for none of whom he had felt the smallest interest, and from none received either attention or pleasure.[22] Miss Bennet he acknowledged to be pretty, but she smiled too much.

Mrs. Hurst and her sister allowed it to be so—but still they admired her and liked her, and pronounced her to be a sweet girl, and one whom they should not object to know more of. Miss Bennet was therefore established as a sweet girl, and their brother felt authorized by such commendation to think of her as he chose.

few would have agreed that Elizabeth and Darcy belonged on the same plane; Colquhoun, it will be remembered, puts them two classes apart.

Although the Bennet daughters have little apparent interest in class or wealth (Lydia and Kitty care only about uniforms; Mary focuses on her books; Jane and Elizabeth concern themselves with character rather than status), many characters in Austen's world aspire to rise or fear to fall. Moreover, it is notable that Austen provides rich husbands for her important female characters, whether or not she delineates them as acknowledging a desire for wealth.

16 Owning an estate would improve Bingley's social status and thus, by extension, his sisters'.

17 In other words, he is less than twenty-three years old.

18 Chance.

19 Location.

20 Darcy has already been several times accused of pride. To be haughty is to be proud, arrogant, and supercilious, although haughtiness may also be a form of physical appearance, designating someone "imposing in aspect" or "stately" (OED). The adjective therefore reiterates the accusation of Darcy's pride. It appears only three times in *Pride and Prejudice*, always in relation to Darcy.

21 The eldest unmarried daughter in a family is always designated "Miss," with her family name. Younger daughters are "Miss" with Christian and family names: for example, "Miss Elizabeth Bennet." Of course, if a younger daughter is the only family member, or the eldest present at a social gathering, she will be addressed as "Miss" with her family name.

22 Darcy may be right in discerning little beauty and no fashion among the guests at the assembly, but far more important is his acknowledgment of feeling no interest in them. Such lack of interest may well account for their reciprocal lack of attention to and pleasure in him.

Edward Francis Burney, "An Elegant Establishment for Young Ladies," c. 1805.
This satiric watercolor of a fashionable seminary, the work of Edward Francis
Burney (1760–1848), a favorite cousin of the novelist Frances Burney, suggests the
concentration on deportment and ladylike "accomplishments" that helps to account
for Austen's negative opinion of "elegant" institutions for female education.

5

WITHIN A SHORT WALK OF LONGBOURN lived a family with whom the Bennets were particularly intimate. Sir William Lucas had been formerly in trade in Meryton, where he had made a tolerable fortune and risen to the honour of knighthood by an address to the King, during his mayoralty.[1] The distinction had perhaps been felt too strongly. It had given him a disgust to[2] his business and to his residence in a small market town; and quitting them both, he had removed with his family to a house about a mile from Meryton, denominated[3] from that period Lucas Lodge,[4] where he could think with pleasure of his own importance, and unshackled by business, occupy himself solely in being civil[5] to all the world. For though elated by his rank, it did not render him supercilious; on the contrary, he was all attention to every body. By nature inoffensive, friendly and obliging, his presentation at St. James's[6] had made him courteous.[7]

Lady Lucas was a very good kind of woman,[8] not too clever to be a valuable neighbour to Mrs. Bennet.—They had several children. The eldest of them, a sensible, intelligent young woman, about twenty-seven, was Elizabeth's intimate friend.

That the Miss Lucases and the Miss Bennets should meet to talk over a ball was absolutely necessary; and the morning[9] after the assembly brought the former to Longbourn to hear and to communicate.

1 Knighthoods were awarded for "meritorious service." Sir William's service would have consisted in offering a formal address—perhaps a speech of gratitude—to the king during his time as mayor.

2 Distaste for.

3 Called.

4 For Sir William, a man (as we will learn) of limited financial resources, to give his house a name—an act usually reserved to men of rank and wealth—is another sign of his social pretensions, which amount to delusions of grandeur.

5 This word appears several times in *Pride and Prejudice*, with various shades of meaning. Derived from a root meaning "citizen," it long denoted the behavior appropriate for a member of the community, "civilized" behavior. By Austen's time, however, it often meant decently polite, or not actually rude. Thus it is possible to allude, as later in *Pride and Prejudice*, to "a civil sneer." Sir William's civility, and the kind most often alluded to in the novel, is a matter of form rather than feeling.

6 The court where he was knighted—and "made . . . courteous." His sense of his rank makes him feel obligated to treat others gracefully, by the principle of *noblesse oblige*.

7 With a pun on "court," since it was his presentation at court that made him courteous.

8 A phrase implying both condescension and irony, suggesting that Lady Lucas belongs to a general category and cannot be characterized in any special way.

9 "Morning," the conventional time for making visits, extended from about 11 A.M., immediately after breakfast, to 3 P.M., approximately the time when one might begin dressing for dinner in the country. For young women, paying morning visits was a regular form of recreation, as well as a social duty.

10 Mrs. Bennet's profession that "she hardly knows what" Mr. Robinson said is a stratagem for gaining the pleasure of hearing about his remarks once more.

11 Not a grammatical mistake, but at the time an acceptable form of the past tense.

12 A hired conveyance, thus an indication that Mrs. Long is not sufficiently wealthy to own her own carriage. To keep a horse and carriage required an annual income of about £1,100, roughly equivalent to $110,000 now. Horses were expensive to feed, carriages expensive to buy—and they required upkeep. Mrs. Bennet's imagination is always concrete: she thinks about status in physical terms.

13 Admirable.

14 Charlotte is willing to forgive a man of family and fortune any degree of arrogance. Like the Bingley sisters, she thinks that such appurtenances comprise "every thing in his favour."

15 Elizabeth implicitly claims her own pride as a form of self-respect, inaugurating the novel's complicated discussions of the quality as sometimes virtue, sometimes vice.

16 As usual, Mary's observations offer hackneyed judgments and sentiments, familiar from current conduct books. Her equation of pride with a sense of "self-complacency," however, calls attention to an important aspect of several characters' pride in *Pride and Prejudice*. The discussion of pride in the novel has already begun, with the repeated allusions to Darcy's pride and the passing one to Elizabeth's. The Bingley sisters have

"*You* began the evening well, Charlotte," said Mrs. Bennet with civil self-command to Miss Lucas. "*You* were Mr. Bingley's first choice."

"Yes;—but he seemed to like his second better."

"Oh!—you mean Jane, I suppose—because he danced with her twice. To be sure that *did* seem as if he admired her—indeed I rather believe he *did*—I heard something about it—but I hardly know what—something about Mr. Robinson."[10]

"Perhaps you mean what I overheard between him and Mr. Robinson; did not I mention it to you? Mr. Robinson's asking him how he liked our Meryton assemblies, and whether he did not think there were a great many pretty women in the room, and *which* he thought the prettiest? and his answering immediately to the last question—Oh! the eldest Miss Bennet beyond a doubt; there cannot be two opinions on that point."

"Upon my word!—Well, that is very decided indeed—that does seem as if—but however, it may all come to nothing you know."

"*My* overhearings were more to the purpose than *yours*, Eliza," said Charlotte. "Mr. Darcy is not so well worth listening to as his friend, is he?—Poor Eliza!—to be only just *tolerable*."

"I beg you would not put it into Lizzy's head to be vexed by his ill-treatment; for he is such a disagreeable man that it would be quite a misfortune to be liked by him. Mrs. Long told me last night that he sat close to her for half an hour without once opening his lips."

"Are you quite sure, Ma'am?—is not there a little mistake?" said Jane.—"I certainly saw Mr. Darcy speaking to her."

"Aye—because she asked him at last how he liked Netherfield, and he could not help answering her;—but she said he seemed very angry at being spoke to."

"Miss Bingley told me," said Jane, "that he never speaks much unless among his intimate acquaintances. With *them* he is remarkably agreeable."

"I do not believe a word of it, my dear. If he had been so very agreeable, he would have talked to Mrs. Long. But I can guess how it was; every body says that he is ate up[11] with pride, and I dare say he had heard somehow that Mrs. Long does not keep a carriage, and had come to the ball in a hack chaise."[12]

"I do not mind his not talking to Mrs. Long," said Miss Lucas, "but I wish he had danced with Eliza."

"Another time, Lizzy," said her mother, "I would not dance with *him,* if I were you."

"I believe, Ma'am, I may safely promise you *never* to dance with him."

"His pride," said Miss Lucas, "does not offend *me* so much as pride often does, because there is an excuse for it. One cannot wonder that so very fine[13] a young man, with family, fortune, everything in his favour, should think highly of himself. If I may so express it, he has a *right* to be proud."[14]

"That is very true," replied Elizabeth, "and I could easily forgive *his* pride, if he had not mortified *mine.*"[15]

"Pride," observed Mary, who piqued herself upon the solidity of her reflections, "is a very common failing I believe. By all that I have ever read, I am convinced that it is very common indeed, that human nature is particularly prone to it, and that there are very few of us who do not cherish a feeling of self-complacency on the score of some quality or other, real or imaginary. Vanity and pride are different things, though the words are often used synonimously. A person may be proud without being vain. Pride relates more to our opinion of ourselves, vanity to what we would have others think of us."[16]

"If I were as rich as Mr. Darcy," cried a young Lucas[17] who came with his sisters, "I should not care how proud I was. I would keep a pack of foxhounds,[18] and drink a bottle of wine every day."

"Then you would drink a great deal more than you ought," said Mrs. Bennet; "and if I were to see you at it I should take away your bottle directly."

The boy protested that she should not; she continued to declare that she would, and the argument ended only with the visit.

been described through Elizabeth's eyes, in Chapter 4, as "proud and conceited"—in other words, proud and vain, since *conceited* is a synonym for *vain.* Although Mary's distinction accords with conduct books, and although it applies to some instances in *Pride and Prejudice,* it does not shed sufficient light on the use of the terms in Austen's novel. *Vanity* is a relatively simple concept: it designates self-conceit and desire for admiration, precisely the characteristics of the Bingley sisters. Pride is more complex, as Charlotte's remark about Darcy's justifiable pride may suggest. It can mean—and often does, especially in comments about Darcy—inordinate self-esteem, with a sense of superiority to others. In this respect, it is the first of the Seven Deadly Sins. Darcy is also accused of pride in the sense of "arrogant, haughty, or overbearing behavior." In a more benign meaning, the one that Charlotte draws on, *pride* may designate consciousness of what is due to oneself or to one's position. The novel explores these meanings especially in Darcy, Elizabeth, and Lady Catherine de Bourgh.

17 Austen is singularly vague about the Lucas offspring. She enumerates them only as "several children" and assigns none except Charlotte a name.

18 Fox hunting had become fashionable in the late eighteenth century. The "young Lucas" associates both hunting and hard drinking with the life of the wealthy gentry.

6

1 Visited.

2 The etiquette of reciprocal visiting belongs to an elaborate system of manners. To follow this system's rituals properly is, like possession of one's own carriage, a mark of social status. Social calls took place only during certain hours, during what is called "morning": between roughly 11 A.M. and 3 P.M. The promptness with which a call was returned could be taken to measure the caller's degree of enthusiasm for an acquaintance, as could the length of a formal visit. (In *Emma,* the protagonist arranges for her protégée, Harriet, to spend fifteen minutes in a visit to the family of a man who has proposed to her. Emma considers the man ineligible; the short visit is intended to signal that Harriet is no longer interested in developing close relations with his sisters.) Refreshments might or might not be offered during a visit; ladies might or might not engage in needlework while conversing.

Austen's letters on occasion hint at her impatience with the rituals of visiting. She writes, for instance, to her sister Cassandra about a call from "Lady Eliz. Hatton & Anna-maria": "Yes, they called,—but I do not think I can say anything more about them. They came & they sat & they went" (6 November 1813).

3 What Elizabeth sees often differs from what others perceive. Because of her attractiveness as a character, and because we are often privy to her thoughts, readers tend to assume the correctness of this protagonist's point of view. This is sometimes—not always—a dangerous assumption.

THE LADIES OF LONGBOURN SOON WAITED ON[1] those of Netherfield. The visit was returned in due form.[2] Miss Bennet's pleasing manners grew on the good will of Mrs. Hurst and Miss Bingley; and though the mother was found to be intolerable and the younger sisters not worth speaking to, a wish of being better acquainted with *them,* was expressed towards the two eldest. By Jane this attention was received with the greatest pleasure; but Elizabeth still saw superciliousness[3] in their treatment of every body, hardly excepting even her sister, and could not like them; though their kindness to Jane, such as it was, had a value as arising in all probability from the influence of their brother's admiration. It was generally evident whenever they met, that he *did* admire her; and to *her* it was equally evident that Jane was yielding to the preference which she had begun to entertain for him from the first, and was in a way to be very much in love; but she considered with pleasure that it was not likely to be discovered by the world in general,[4] since Jane united with great strength of feeling, a composure of temper and a uniform cheerfulness of manner, which would guard her from the suspicions of the impertinent. She mentioned this to her friend Miss Lucas.

"It may perhaps be pleasant," replied Charlotte, "to be able to impose on the public in such a case; but it is sometimes a disadvantage to be so very guarded. If a woman conceals her affection with the same skill from the object of it, she may lose the opportunity of fixing[5] him; and it will then be but poor consolation to believe the world equally in the dark. There is so much of gratitude or vanity in almost every attachment, that it is not safe to leave any to itself.[6] We can all *begin* freely—a slight preference is natural enough; but there are very few of us who have heart enough to be really in love without encouragement. In nine cases out of ten a women had better shew *more* affection than she feels. Bingley likes your sister undoubtedly; but he may never do more than like her, if she does not help him on."

"But she does help him on, as much as her nature will allow. If *I* can perceive her regard for him, he must be a simpleton indeed not to discover it too."

"Remember, Eliza, that he does not know Jane's disposition as you do."

"But if a woman is partial to a man, and does not endeavour to conceal it, he must find it out."

"Perhaps he must, if he sees enough of her. But though Bingley and Jane meet tolerably often, it is never for many hours together; and as they always see each other in large mixed parties, it is impossible that every moment should be employed in conversing together. Jane should therefore make the most of every half hour in which she can command his attention. When she is secure[7] of him, there will be leisure for falling in love as much as she chuses."[8]

This silhouette, by an unknown artist, represents Austen's sister, Cassandra.

4 Conduct books typically insisted on the importance of women's concealing their love at least until a man had committed himself to desiring marriage. Many such books made yet more extreme recommendations. Thus Dr. John Gregory's *Father's Legacy to His Daughters* (1784), a work of enduring popularity into the nineteenth century, implies that a "woman of delicacy" will conceal her love even from herself: "It is even long before a woman of delicacy dares avow to her own heart that she loves; and when all the subterfuges of ingenuity to conceal it from herself fail, she feels a violence done both to her pride and to her modesty. This, I should imagine, must always be the case where she is not sure of a return to her attachment" (*The Young Lady's Pocket Library, or Parental Monitor* [Bristol: Thoemmes Press, 1995], 27). Moreover, a good woman should never, even after marriage, reveal to her husband the magnitude of her love: "If you love [a man], let me advise you never to discover to him the full extent of your love, no not although you marry him" (35). Austen does not espouse such views, but she is clearly aware of them. Indeed, she was aware of them early: *Frederic & Elfrida,* one of the first written of her juvenilia, begins with the information that the titular characters "loved with mutual sincerity but were both determined not to transgress the rules of Propriety by owning their attachment, either to the object beloved, or to any one else."

5 Making his attachment permanent.

6 Dr. Gregory again: "What is commonly called love among you is rather gratitude, and a partiality to the man who prefers you to the rest of your sex; and such a man you often marry, with little of either personal esteem or affection. Indeed, without an unusual share of natural sensibility, and very peculiar good fortune, a woman in this country has very little probability of marrying for love" (32).

7 Sure. Charlotte's choice of *secure* in this context, however, may also suggest her tacit equation between marriage and financial security.

8 Charlotte is represented as considerably more intelligent than Mrs. Bennet, but her attitude toward mar-

riage resembles that of Elizabeth's mother. Just as Mrs. Bennet focuses on how a girl can "get" a man (she uses the verb in this connection frequently), Charlotte assumes that every young woman's goal must be to effect a marriage. She claims to consider "falling in love" a frivolous luxury.

9 Married to a husband of social status and/or wealth.

10 Vingt-un (or Twenty-one) and Commerce are both card games. In Vingt-un, now called blackjack, every player receives one card dealt face down and bets that this card plus additional cards dealt face up will beat the dealer's hand without exceeding twenty-one. In Commerce, cards are traded to get the best hand of three cards. Both games can be played with almost any number of participants. Austen reports from Lyme to Cassandra: "My mother had her pool of commerce each night" (14 September 1804).

11 A characteristic that leads to something—in this case, to marriage.

12 Charlotte sees the search for a husband as an arduous competitive pursuit, with "success" difficult to attain.

13 Founded on true grounds, free from error, valid.

14 Charlotte's witty cynicism allows Elizabeth to believe that she doesn't really mean what she says. Lacking the obsessiveness of Mrs. Bennet, she appears to have the status of a humorous observer. Thus Elizabeth can laugh at her commentary without having to take it seriously.

15 Admitted that she was pretty.

"Your plan is a good one," replied Elizabeth, "where nothing is in question but the desire of being well married;[9] and if I were determined to get a rich husband, or any husband, I dare say I should adopt it. But these are not Jane's feelings; she is not acting by design. As yet, she cannot even be certain of the degree of her own regard, nor of its reasonableness. She has known him only a fortnight. She danced four dances with him at Meryton; she saw him one morning at his own house, and has since dined in company with him four times. This is not quite enough to make her understand his character."

"Not as you represent it. Had she merely *dined* with him, she might only have discovered whether he had a good appetite; but you must remember that four evenings have been also spent together—and four evenings may do a great deal."

"Yes; these four evenings have enabled them to ascertain that they both like Vingt-un better than Commerce;[10] but with respect to any other leading characteristic,[11] I do not imagine that much has been unfolded."

"Well," said Charlotte, "I wish Jane success[12] with all my heart; and if she were married to him to-morrow, I should think she had as good a chance of happiness, as if she were to be studying his character for a twelvemonth. Happiness in marriage is entirely a matter of chance. If the dispositions of the parties are ever so well known to each other, or ever so similar before-hand, it does not advance their felicity in the least. They always continue to grow sufficiently unlike afterwards to have their share of vexation; and it is better to know as little as possible of the defects of the person with whom you are to pass your life."

"You make me laugh, Charlotte; but it is not sound.[13] You know it is not sound, and that you would never act in this way yourself."[14]

Occupied in observing Mr. Bingley's attentions to her sister, Elizabeth was far from suspecting that she was herself becoming an object of some interest in the eyes of his friend. Mr. Darcy had at first scarcely allowed her to be pretty;[15] he had looked at her without admiration at the ball; and when they next met, he looked at her only to criticise. But no sooner had he made it clear to himself and his friends that she had hardly a good feature in her face, than he began to find it was rendered uncommonly intelligent by the beautiful expression of her dark eyes.[16] To this discovery succeeded some others equally mortifying. Though he had detected with a critical eye more than one failure of perfect symmetry in her form, he was forced to acknowledge her figure to be light and pleasing; and in spite of his asserting that her manners were not those of the fashionable world, he was caught by their easy playfulness.[17] Of this she was perfectly unaware;—to her he was only the man who made himself agreeable no where, and who had not thought her handsome enough to dance with.

He began to wish to know more of her, and as a step towards conversing with her himself, attended to her conversation with others.[18] His doing so drew her notice. It was at Sir William Lucas's, where a large party were assembled.

"What does Mr. Darcy mean," said she to Charlotte, "by listening to my conversation with Colonel Forster?"

"That is a question which Mr. Darcy only can answer."

"But if he does it any more I shall certainly let him know that I see what he is about. He has a very satirical eye, and if I do not begin by being impertinent myself, I shall soon grow afraid of him."

On his approaching them soon afterwards, though without seeming to have any intention of speaking, Miss Lucas defied her friend to mention such a subject to him, which immediately provoking Elizabeth to do it, she turned to him and said,

"Did you not think, Mr. Darcy, that I expressed myself uncommonly well just now, when I was teazing Colonel Forster to give us a ball at Meryton?"[19]

"With great energy;—but it is a subject which always makes a lady energetic."

"You are severe on us."

"It will be *her* turn soon to be teazed," said Miss Lucas. "I am going to open the instrument,[20] Eliza, and you know what follows."

"You are a very strange creature by way of a friend!—always wanting me to play and sing before any body and every body!—If my vanity had taken a musical turn, you would have been invaluable, but as

16 In *Persuasion,* too, the progress of a man's love is signaled by his changing assessment of a woman's appearance.

17 Of all the characters defined in relation to their manners, Elizabeth is the only one to have "playful" manners. Austen, writing that a friend seems to admire the character of Elizabeth in *Pride and Prejudice,* recently published, adds, "I must confess that I think her as delightful a creature as ever appeared in print, and how I shall be able to tolerate those who do not like *her* at least I do not know" (To Cassandra, 29 January 1813). It is striking, however, that Darcy is first of all attracted by her physical nature—her eyes and her figure. This is clearly an erotic attraction.

18 The fact that Darcy has to listen to Elizabeth's conversation with others in order to proceed toward talking with her himself again suggests his social awkwardness. Someone like Bingley, for instance, would simply converse with a woman who interested him, without feeling the need for intermediate steps.

19 This is the first conversation between Elizabeth and Darcy. They have previously overheard each other, though: Elizabeth accidentally heard Darcy denigrating her appearance and declining to dance; Darcy has just, by design, overheard Elizabeth talking with Colonel Forster. Both thus already have evidence on which to base their interpretations.

20 Piano.

21 Save your breath. The proverb is indeed a familiar one.

22 First-rate.

23 Natural aptitude.

24 Steady effort. It is striking that Mary, who has discoursed on the distinction between vanity and pride, herself suffers from vanity.

25 Darcy's indignation probably comes less from desire for conversation—for which he does not seem eager at social gatherings—than from distaste for the form of dancing going on. In contrast to the country dances that had long been traditional, in which everyone at a gathering might take part, the "two or three officers" and the Lucas and Bennet girls are participating in Scotch and Irish reels, a relatively new fad. Such dances demand lively activity and make conversation impossible, unlike the country dances that involve rather lengthy periods of inaction for each couple, in which conversation is demanded. Darcy appears to be a traditionalist.

26 Both gentlemen and ladies often took lessons from dancing masters as part of their education. To dance well was considered a mark of gentility.

it is, I would really rather not sit down before those who must be in the habit of hearing the very best performers." On Miss Lucas's persevering, however, she added, "Very well; if it must be so, it must." And gravely glancing at Mr. Darcy, "There is a fine old saying, which every body here is of course familiar with—'Keep your breath to cool your porridge'[21]—and I shall keep mine to swell my song."

Her performance was pleasing, though by no means capital.[22] After a song or two, and before she could reply to the entreaties of several that she would sing again, she was eagerly succeeded at the instrument by her sister Mary, who having, in consequence of being the only plain one in the family, worked hard for knowledge and accomplishments, was always impatient for display.

Mary had neither genius[23] nor taste; and though vanity had given her application,[24] it had given her likewise a pedantic air and conceited manner, which would have injured a higher degree of excellence than she had reached. Elizabeth, easy and unaffected, had been listened to with much more pleasure, though not playing half so well; and Mary, at the end of a long concerto, was glad to purchase praise and gratitude by Scotch and Irish airs, at the request of her younger sisters, who with some of the Lucases and two or three officers joined eagerly in dancing at one end of the room.

Mr. Darcy stood near them in silent indignation at such a mode of passing the evening, to the exclusion of all conversation,[25] and was too much engrossed by his own thoughts to perceive that Sir William Lucas was his neighbour, till Sir William thus began.

"What a charming amusement for young people this is, Mr. Darcy!—There is nothing like dancing after all.—I consider it as one of the first refinements of polished societies."[26]

"Certainly, Sir;—and it has the advantage also of being in vogue amongst the less polished societies of the world.—Every savage can dance."

Sir William only smiled. "Your friend performs delightfully;" he continued after a pause, on seeing Bingley join the group;—"and I doubt not that you are an adept in the science yourself, Mr. Darcy."

"You saw me dance at Meryton, I believe, Sir."

"Yes, indeed, and received no inconsiderable pleasure from the sight. Do you often dance at St. James's?"[27]

"Never, Sir."

"Do you not think it would be a proper compliment to the place?"

"It is a compliment which I never pay to any place if I can avoid it."

"You have a house in town, I conclude?"

Mr. Darcy bowed.

"I had once had some thought of fixing in town myself—for I am fond of superior society; but I did not feel quite certain that the air of London would agree with Lady Lucas."

He paused in hopes of an answer; but his companion was not disposed to make any; and Elizabeth at that instant moving towards them, he was struck with the notion of doing a very gallant thing, and called out to her,

"My dear Miss Eliza, why are you not dancing?—Mr. Darcy, you must allow me to present this young lady to you as a very desirable partner.—You cannot refuse to dance, I am sure, when so much beauty is before you." And taking her hand, he would have given it to Mr. Darcy, who, though extremely surprised, was not unwilling to receive it, when she instantly drew back, and said with some discomposure to Sir William,

"Indeed, Sir, I have not the least intention of dancing.[28]—I entreat you not to suppose that I moved this way in order to beg for a partner."

Mr. Darcy with grave propriety requested to be allowed the honour of her hand; but in vain. Elizabeth was determined; nor did Sir William at all shake her purpose by his attempt at persuasion.

"You excel so much in the dance, Miss Eliza, that it is cruel to deny me the happiness of seeing you; and though this gentleman dislikes the amusement in general, he can have no objection, I am sure, to oblige us for one half-hour."

"Mr. Darcy is all politeness," said Elizabeth, smiling.

"He is indeed—but considering the inducement, my dear Miss Eliza, we cannot wonder at his complaisance;[29] for who would object to such a partner?"

27 St. James's Palace, the royal residence. Sir William is asking whether Darcy frequents the court.

28 It would be impolite for a lady to refuse to dance with a particular man; she would customarily declare, as Elizabeth does, that she has no intention of dancing with anyone. Evelina, in Burney's novel, gets into social difficulties because she refuses one man and subsequently accepts the invitation of another.

29 Desire of pleasing.

30 Satisfaction, but with no implication of self-satisfaction.

31 On your marriage.

Elizabeth looked archly, and turned away. Her resistance had not injured her with the gentleman, and he was thinking of her with some complacency,[30] when thus accosted by Miss Bingley,

"I can guess the subject of your reverie."

"I should imagine not."

"You are considering how insupportable it would be to pass many evenings in this manner—in such society; and indeed I am quite of your opinion. I was never more annoyed! The insipidity, and yet the noise; the nothingness and yet the self-importance of all these people!—What would I give to hear your strictures on them!"

"You conjecture is totally wrong, I assure you. My mind was more agreeably engaged. I have been meditating on the very great pleasure which a pair of fine eyes in the face of a pretty woman can bestow."

Miss Bingley immediately fixed her eyes on his face, and desired he would tell her what lady had the credit of inspiring such reflections. Mr. Darcy replied with great intrepidity,

"Miss Elizabeth Bennet."

"Miss Elizabeth Bennet!" repeated Miss Bingley. "I am all astonishment. How long has she been such a favourite?—and pray when am I to wish you joy?"[31]

"That is exactly the question which I expected you to ask. A lady's imagination is very rapid; it jumps from admiration to love, from love to matrimony in a moment. I knew you would be wishing me joy."

"Nay, if you are so serious about it, I shall consider the matter as absolutely settled. You will be having a charming mother-in-law, indeed, and of course she will be always at Pemberley with you."

He listened to her with perfect indifference, while she chose to entertain herself in this manner, and as his composure convinced her that all was safe, her wit flowed long.

7

MR. BENNET'S PROPERTY CONSISTED almost entirely in an estate of two thousand a year, which, unfortunately for his daughters, was entailed in default of heirs male,[1] on a distant relation; and their mother's fortune, though ample for her situation in life, could but ill supply the deficiency of his. Her father had been an attorney in Meryton, and had left her four thousand pounds.[2]

She had a sister married to a Mr. Phillips, who had been a clerk to their father, and succeeded him in the business,[3] and a brother settled in London in a respectable line of trade.

The village of Longbourn was only one mile from Meryton; a most convenient distance for the young ladies, who were usually tempted thither three or four times a week, to pay their duty[4] to their aunt and to a milliner's shop[5] just over the way. The two youngest of the family, Catherine and Lydia, were particularly frequent in these attentions; their minds were more vacant than their sisters', and when nothing better offered, a walk to Meryton was necessary to amuse their morning hours and furnish conversation for the evening; and however bare of news the country[6] in general might be, they always contrived to learn some from their aunt. At present, indeed, they were well supplied both with news and happiness by the recent arrival of a militia[7] regiment in the neighbourhood; it was to remain the whole winter, and Meryton was the head quarters.

Their visits to Mrs. Phillips were now productive of the most interesting intelligence.[8] Every day added something to their knowledge of the officers' names and connections.[9] Their lodgings were

1 The entail, commonly used in this period, was a legal device for controlling the disposition of an estate. In most cases, including that of the Bennet family, it provided that, lacking a male heir in the immediate family, wealth and property should go to the nearest male relative. In other words, neither Mrs. Bennet nor her daughters can inherit Mr. Bennet's estate.

In an important essay that lays out the legal ramifications of the entail and the entail's functions in *Pride and Prejudice,* Sandra Macpherson maintains that "[i]t is difficult to fully comprehend the way the novel thinks about relationship (dynastic and affective) without understanding with some precision the legal logic of entailment" ("Rent to Own; or, What's Entailed in *Pride and Prejudice,*" *Representations* 82 [2003], 2).

2 Mr. Bennet comes from a family of moderate wealth and land; his wife, daughter of a legal agent, would have lower social standing; her siblings also occupy positions of relatively low status. Her fortune of £4,000 would provide an income of at most £200 a year, an inadequate amount for her and her daughters to live on.

3 A country attorney, such as Mrs. Bennet's father and her brother-in-law, had fairly secure social standing in his limited society but would be looked down on by city dwellers. London lawyers in general had higher status.

4 Their respects.

5 Selling clothing, fabrics, and accessories; such shops, however, increasingly specialized in hats.

6 District.

7 The militia was a body for civil defense, called together at times of national crisis. Every county in England and Wales was required to provide its quota of men. In practice, a disproportionate number of these men belonged to the illiterate poor, although their officers were gentlemen. Unlike soldiers in the regular army, militia members could not be sent to serve abroad, but might be stationed anywhere in England.

Pride and Prejudice was both drafted and revised during the Napoleonic Wars of the early nineteenth century, when England feared invasion from France, and its action takes place in the same period. The Napoleonic Wars consisted of a series of conflicts involving various coalitions of European countries. They appeared to continue the wars resulting from the French Revolution, and even their starting point is not certain. Many historians have settled on 1803, when a declaration of war between England and France concluded a brief period of peace. The end point, however, is clear: Napoleon's 1815 defeat at the Battle of Waterloo, followed by the Second Treaty of Paris.

Results of the wars were far-reaching. Among other things, they solidified the status of the British Empire as the leading world power, and they caused the restoration of the French monarchy.

Gillian Russell describes this conflict as the "first truly 'world' war, fought in many theatres on both land and sea" and points out that "the struggle against France had profound effects on many levels of British society—political, cultural, and economic" ("The Army, the Navy, and the Napoleonic Wars," in *A Companion to Jane Austen,* ed. Claudia L. Johnson and Clara Tuite [Chichester: Wiley-Blackwell, 2009], 261). In *Pride and Prejudice,* Austen treats extensively only the erotic effects of military men on women. Given that the threat of invasion does not appear strong at the time of the novel's action (the book never directly mentions war), militia regiments would take up residence in a town for the winter.

The presence of such a regiment was often thought to have a deleterious effect on the morals of local young women, and it was sometimes alleged that young men joined the militia for the sake of the erotic possibilities it might open. As Tim Fulford puts the point, "The militia's reputation . . . [was] more about the risks it posed to English ladies' virtue than the threat it made to Frenchmen's lives" ("Sighing for a Soldier: Jane Austen and Military Pride and Prejudice," *Nineteenth-Century Literature* 57: 2 [2002], 156. Fulford's essay provides a valuable survey of the militia's place in society, as well as in Austen's novel.) Thus Frances Burney, whose work Austen greatly admired, wrote in her second novel, *Cecilia, or Memoirs of an Heiress* (1782), of a Mr. Aresby, "a captain in the militia; a young man who having frequently heard the words red-coat and gallantry put together, imagined the conjunction not merely customary, but honourable, and therefore, without even pretending to think of the service of his country, he considered a cockade as a badge of politeness, and wore it but to mark his devotion to the ladies, whom he held himself equipped to conquer, and bound to adore" (I, 2). In *Britons: Forging the Nation, 1707–1837,* Linda Colley quotes a weaver who frequently noted in his diary "how the local working girls hung on the arms of soldiers, and how avidly they watched every recruiting parade they could get to see" ([New Haven: Yale University Press, 1992], 257). And Mary Wollstonecraft comments that "nothing can be so prejudicial to the morals of the inhabitants of country towns as the occasional residence of a set of idle superficial young men, whose only occupation is gallantry, and whose polished manners render vice more dangerous, by concealing its deformity under gay ornamental drapery. An air of fashion, which is but a badge of slavery, and proves that the soul has not a strong individual character, awes simple country people into an imitation of the vices, when they cannot catch the slippery graces, of politeness" (Chapter I, "The Rights and Involved Duties of Mankind Considered").

At the very least, many regiments had a reputation for conviviality. In *Emma,* Mr. Weston's nature is suggested by his service in the militia: the narrator tells us that he "had satisfied an active cheerful mind and social temper by entering into the militia of his county, then embodied" (I, 2).

This engraving of a uniform worn by the Oxfordshire Militia may suggest why young women found militia officers so attractive.

8 Information.

9 Family connections.

10 The uniform of a minor officer.

11 Gather, deduce.

12 Lydia's capacity to ignore any utterance she does not wish to hear serves her well throughout the novel's action.

not long a secret, and at length they began to know the officers themselves. Mr. Phillips visited them all, and this opened to his nieces a source of felicity unknown before. They could talk of nothing but officers; and Mr. Bingley's large fortune, the mention of which gave animation to their mother, was worthless in their eyes when opposed to the regimentals of an ensign.[10]

After listening one morning to their effusions on this subject, Mr. Bennet coolly observed,

"From all that I can collect[11] by your manner of talking, you must be two of the silliest girls in the country. I have suspected it some time, but I am now convinced."

Catherine was disconcerted, and made no answer; but Lydia, with perfect indifference,[12] continued to express her admiration of Captain Carter, and her hope of seeing him in the course of the day, as he was going the next morning to London.

"I am astonished, my dear," said Mrs. Bennet, "that you should be so ready to think your own children silly. If I wished to think

13 Aware.

14 The characteristic color of British army uniforms.

15 Such a person would probably be part of the regular army, where—unlike the militia—salaries remained stable, war or no war. He might have a private income from his family, as well as his military salary.

16 A circulating library, where books were lent to patrons who paid for a subscription. Such libraries often served as gathering places, so the officers' frequenting of Clarke's does not necessarily indicate their interest

211 THE CHARMS of a RED COAT.
_____ London.Publish'd 1.st Nov.r 1787. by Rob.t Sayer. 53 Fleet Street _____

Anonymous, "The Charms of a Red Coat," 1787. British army officers at this time wore red coats; consequently, they were often called Redcoats, as they were in the American War for Independence. Red coats continued to be worn, at least on occasion, until the beginning of World War I.

slightingly of any body's children, it should not be of my own however."

"If my children are silly, I must hope to be always sensible[13] of it."

"Yes—but as it happens, they are all of them very clever."

"This is the only point, I flatter myself, on which we do not agree. I had hoped that our sentiments coincided in every particular, but I must so far differ from you as to think our two youngest daughters uncommonly foolish."

"My dear Mr. Bennet, you must not expect such girls to have the sense of their father and mother.—When they get to our age, I dare say they will not think about officers any more than we do. I remember the time when I liked a red-coat[14] myself very well—and indeed so I do still at my heart; and if a smart young colonel, with five or six thousand a year,[15] should want one of my girls, I shall not say nay to him; and I thought Colonel Forster looked very becoming the other night at Sir William's in his regimentals."

"Mama," cried Lydia, "my aunt says that Colonel Forster and Captain Carter do not go so often to Miss Watson's as they did when they first came; she sees them now very often standing in Clarke's library."[16]

Mrs. Bennet was prevented replying by the entrance of the footman[17] with a note for Miss Bennet; it came from Netherfield, and the servant waited for an answer. Mrs. Bennet's eyes sparkled with pleasure, and she was eagerly calling out, while her daughter read,

"Well, Jane, who is it from? what is it about? what does he[18] say? well, Jane, make haste and tell us; make haste, my love."

"It is from Miss Bingley," said Jane, and then read it aloud.

"My dear Friend,

"If you are not so compassionate as to dine to-day with Louisa and me, we shall be in danger of hating each other for the rest of our lives, for a whole day's tête-à-tête between two women can never end without a quarrel. Come as soon as you can on the receipt of this. My brother and the gentlemen are to dine with the officers. Yours ever,

"Caroline Bingley"

"With the officers!" cried Lydia. "I wonder my aunt did not tell us of *that*."

"Dining out," said Mrs. Bennet, "that is very unlucky."[19]

"Can I have the carriage?" said Jane.

"No, my dear, you had better go on horseback, because it seems likely to rain; and then you must stay all night."

"That would be a good scheme," said Elizabeth, "if you were sure that they would not offer to send her home."

"Oh! but the gentlemen will have Mr. Bingley's chaise to go to Meryton; and the Hursts have no horses to theirs."

"I had much rather go in the coach."[20]

"But, my dear, your father cannot spare the horses, I am sure. They are wanted in the farm, Mr. Bennet, are not they?"

"They are wanted in the farm much oftener than I can get them."

"But if you have got them to day," said Elizabeth, "my mother's purpose will be answered."

She did at last extort from her father an acknowledgment that the horses were engaged, Jane was therefore obliged to go on horseback, and her mother attended her to the door with many cheerful prognostics of a bad day. Her hopes were answered; Jane had not been gone long before it rained hard. Her sisters were uneasy for her, but her mother was delighted. The rain continued the whole evening without intermission; Jane certainly could not come back.

"This was a lucky idea of mine, indeed!" said Mrs. Bennet more than once, as if the credit of making it rain were all her own. Till the next morning, however, she was not aware of all the felicity of her contrivance. Breakfast was scarcely over when a servant from Netherfield brought the following note for Elizabeth:

"My dearest Lizzy,

"I find myself very unwell this morning, which, I suppose, is to be imputed to my getting wet through yesterday. My kind friends will not hear of my returning home till I am better. They insist also on my seeing Mr. Jones—therefore do

in books. This is a sample of the kind of "news" the sisters acquire from their aunt and offer as the topic for evening conversation.

17 The Bennets have an adequate, although not lavish, income—enough to provide them with a footman, a butler, two housemaids, a housekeeper, and a cook, as well as unspecified outdoor servants. Even poor families in this era customarily had servants. Peter Laslett has pointed out that between 1574 and 1821, servants were "a feature of almost one-quarter of the households of a category as low as . . . tradesmen and craftsmen, in the centre of the social scale, and . . . some la bourers . . . had servants" ("Mean Household Size in England since the Sixteenth Century," in *Household and Family in Past Time: Comparative Studies in the Size and Structure of the Domestic Group over the Last Three Centuries,* ed. Peter Laslett, with the assistance of Richard Wall [Cambridge: Cambridge University Press, 1972], 153). *Everyone* in the gentry class, no matter how poor, had servants. In *Sense and Sensibility,* the impoverished Dashwood women move from one house to another, bringing two servants along. In *Mansfield Park,* the Prices, living in extreme poverty in Portsmouth, well below the gentry, have at least two housemaids, and Mrs. Price complains about their lack of efficiency. According to J. A. Downie, who offers an illuminating discussion of the financial situations of Austen's characters, £2,000 a year, Mr. Bennet's income, is the average income of a baronet ("Who Says She's a Bourgeois Writer? Reconsidering the Social and Political Contexts of Jane Austen's Novels," *Eighteenth-Century Studies* 40: 1 [2006], 69–84).

18 Given Mrs. Bennet's obsession with the possibilities of marriage, she assumes that the letter writer is male.

19 Unfortunate.

20 A coach is a large enclosed carriage, big enough for four to six people, thus appropriate for a family. Its possession is a sign of prosperity, but the fact that the Bennets do not have enough horses to supply both the coach and the farm indicates the limits of their wealth.

21 "Putrid sore throat" was at the time a label for serious infectious diseases, so Jane may in fact be seriously ill.

22 Mud.

23 On one occasion Austen refers to herself as a "desperate walker," observing ruefully that "it is too dirty
even for such desperate walkers as Martha and I to get
out of doors" (To Cassandra, 30 November 1800).

24 Charlotte Brontë, in an 1848 letter to G. H. Lewes,
expressed her opinion of *Pride and Prejudice* in these
terms: "Why do you like Miss Austen so very much? I
am puzzled on that point. . . . I had not seen *Pride and
Prejudice* till I read that sentence of yours, and then I
got the book. And what did I find? An accurate da-
guerreotyped portrait of a commonplace face; a carefully fenced, highly cultivated garden, with neat bor-
ders and delicate flowers; but no glance of a bright,
vivid physiognomy, no open country, no fresh air, no
blue hill, no bonny beck. I should hardly like to live
with her ladies and gentlemen, in their elegant but
confined houses" (quoted in Tony Tanner, *Jane Austen*
[Cambridge: Harvard University Press, 1986], 103). It
is true that much of what happens in an Austen novel
happens indoors. Elizabeth, however, is often associated with the outdoors—not always springing over
puddles, but frequently escaping the literal and metaphorical confinement of her society. ·

25 "Georgian breakfasts were dainty meals of varieties
of bread, cake and hot drinks, served (if the house were
grand enough to possess one) in the breakfast-parlour
rather than the dining-room, and eaten off the new
fine china" (Maggie Lane, *Jane Austen and Food* [Lon-
don: The Hambledon Press, 1995], 28). Late breakfast
hours were more fashionable than early ones. Thus it is
that Jane's note arrives at the relatively unfashionable
Bennet household just at the end of breakfast; there is
time for the Bennets to discuss it and for Elizabeth to
walk (and run) the three miles to Netherfield, yet the
Netherfield residents are still at breakfast.

not be alarmed if you should hear of his having been to me—
and excepting a sore-throat[21] and head-ache there is not
much the matter with me.

> "Yours, &c."

"Well, my dear," said Mr. Bennet, when Elizabeth had read the
note aloud, "if your daughter should have a dangerous fit of illness, if
she should die, it would be a comfort to know that it was all in pursuit of Mr. Bingley, and under your orders."

"Oh! I am not at all afraid of her dying. People do not die of little
trifling colds. She will be taken good care of. As long as she stays
there, it is all very well. I would go and see her if I could have the carriage."

Elizabeth, feeling really anxious, was determined to go to her,
though the carriage was not to be had; and as she was no horse-
woman, walking was her only alternative. She declared her resolution.

"How can you be so silly," cried her mother, "as to think of such a
thing, in all this dirt![22] You will not be fit to be seen when you get
there."

"I shall be very fit to see Jane—which is all I want."

"Is this a hint to me, Lizzy," said her father, "to send for the
horses?"

"No, indeed. I do not wish to avoid the walk.[23] The distance is
nothing, when one has a motive; only three miles. I shall be back by
dinner."

"I admire the activity of your benevolence," observed Mary, "but
every impulse of feeling should be guided by reason; and, in my opinion, exertion should always be in proportion to what is required."

"We will go as far as Meryton with you," said Catherine and Lydia.
—Elizabeth accepted their company, and the three young ladies set
off together.

"If we make haste," said Lydia, as they walked along, "perhaps we
may see something of Captain Carter before he goes."

In Meryton they parted; the two youngest repaired to the lodgings of one of the officers' wives, and Elizabeth continued her walk alone, crossing field after field at a quick pace, jumping over stiles and springing over puddles with impatient activity,[24] and finding herself at last within view of the house, with weary ancles, dirty stockings, and a face glowing with the warmth of exercise.

She was shown into the breakfast-parlour,[25] where all but Jane were assembled, and where her appearance created a great deal of surprise.—That she should have walked three miles so early in the day, in such dirty weather, and by herself, was almost incredible to Mrs. Hurst and Miss Bingley; and Elizabeth was convinced that they held her in contempt for it. She was received, however, very politely by them; and in their brother's manners there was something better than politeness; there was good humour and kindness. Mr. Darcy said very little, and Mr. Hurst nothing at all. The former was divided between admiration of the brilliancy which exercise had given to her complexion,[26] and doubt as to the occasion's justifying her coming so far alone.[27] The latter was thinking only of his breakfast.

Her inquiries after her sister were not very favourably answered. Miss Bennet had slept ill, and though up, was very feverish and not well enough to leave her room. Elizabeth was glad to be taken to her immediately; and Jane, who had only been withheld by the fear of giving alarm or inconvenience, from expressing in her note how much she longed for such a visit, was delighted at her entrance. She was not equal, however, to much conversation, and when Miss Bingley left them together, could attempt little beside expressions of gratitude for the extraordinary kindness she was treated with. Elizabeth silently attended her.

When breakfast was over, they were joined by the sisters; and Elizabeth began to like them herself, when she saw how much affection and solicitude they shewed for Jane. The apothecary came, and having examined his patient, said, as might be supposed,[28] that she had caught a violent cold, and that they must endeavour to get the better of it; advised her to return to bed, and promised her some draughts.[29] The advice was followed readily, for the feverish symp-

26 "Darcy's famous appreciation of [Elizabeth's] brilliant complexion takes on greater significance when linked to medical discourse that associated exercise with a sharper and stronger intelligence, and also with a woman's ability to conceive" (Jillian Heydt-Stevenson, *Austen's Unbecoming Conjunctions: Subversive Laughter, Embodied History* [New York: Palgrave Macmillan, 2005], 71). In other words, Elizabeth's unconventional behavior may make her a more appealing object for courtship. Heydt-Stevenson also points out that Mr. and Mrs. Bennet's willingness to have two of their marriageable daughters staying at Netherfield with no "adult supervision of their chastity"—the Bingley sisters, Bingley himself, Darcy, and presumably Mr. Hurst are all young people—is "remarkable" (73). In the novel's first volume, the question of chastity is never at issue.

27 Darcy's divided response reveals an internal conflict that the novel will articulate in many ways: between immediate emotional reaction and judgment based largely on a sense of convention and of what is owed to his social position.

28 Felicia Bonaparte points out, in the course of a wide-ranging study of the epistemological grounds of reading in *Pride and Prejudice,* that the verb *suppose* appears ninety times in the text ("Conjecturing Possibilities: Reading and Misreading Texts in Jane Austen's *Pride and Prejudice,*" *Studies in the Novel* 37: 2 [2005], 141–161).

29 Doses of liquid medicine. Apothecaries, the lowest medical rank, often examined and prescribed for patients. Surgeons and physicians ranked above them and were more highly trained.

30 A suggestion of how impoverished the lives of upper-class women might be. With servants performing the work of the household, with limited social possibilities, and with, apparently, no intellectual resources, the Bingley sisters indeed have little to do aside from attending to the men of the house.

toms increased, and her head ached acutely. Elizabeth did not quit her room for a moment; nor were the other ladies often absent; the gentlemen being out, they had in fact nothing to do elsewhere.[30]

When the clock struck three, Elizabeth felt that she must go; and very unwillingly said so. Miss Bingley offered her the carriage, and she only wanted a little pressing to accept it, when Jane testified such concern in parting with her, that Miss Bingley was obliged to convert the offer of the chaise into an invitation to remain at Netherfield for the present. Elizabeth most thankfully consented, and a servant was dispatched to Longbourn to acquaint the family with her stay and bring back a supply of clothes.

8

AT FIVE O'CLOCK THE TWO LADIES retired to dress, and at half past six[1] Elizabeth was summoned to dinner. To the civil enquiries which then poured in, and amongst which she had the pleasure of distinguishing the much superior solicitude of Mr. Bingley's, she could not make a very favourable answer. Jane was by no means better. The sisters, on hearing this, repeated three or four times how much they were grieved, how shocking[2] it was to have a bad cold, and how excessively they disliked being ill themselves; and then thought no more of the matter: and their indifference towards Jane when not immediately before them, restored Elizabeth to the enjoyment[3] of all her former dislike.

Their brother, indeed, was the only one of the party whom she could regard with any complacency.[4] His anxiety for Jane was evident, and his attentions to herself most pleasing, and they prevented her feeling herself so much an intruder as she believed she was considered by the others. She had very little notice from any but him. Miss Bingley was engrossed by Mr. Darcy, her sister scarcely less so; and as for Mr. Hurst, by whom Elizabeth sat, he was an indolent man, who lived only to eat, drink, and play at cards, who when he found her to prefer a plain dish to a ragout,[5] had nothing to say to her.

When dinner was over, she returned directly to Jane, and Miss Bingley began abusing her as soon as she was out of the room. Her manners were pronounced to be very bad indeed, a mixture of pride and impertinence;[6] she had no conversation, no stile, no taste, no beauty. Mrs. Hurst thought the same, and added,

1 A rather late, thus fashionable, hour for dinner at this time. Such a dinner hour would be more normal in London, where the streets provided some artificial light for going home, than in the country. The Bingley sisters offer numerous clues of their desire to be seen as fashionable.

2 Dreadful, very bad. *Shocking* was a hyperbolic term of little specific meaning in society slang; it served mainly as an intensifier. The Bingley sisters typically employ a conversational rhetoric heavily dependent on emphatic adjectives and adverbs.

3 A significant noun. Unlike Jane, who likes everyone, Elizabeth is capable not only of disliking but of enjoying her dislike.

4 Contentment.

5 A stew, highly seasoned and made in the French style, another indication of fashionable pretension.

6 It is striking that Netherfield opinion of Elizabeth includes an accusation of pride, as does Meryton opinion of Darcy. The "impertinence" Miss Bingley mentions is probably the same quality earlier designated as "playful" manners.

7 Disheveled.

8 Perhaps an underskirt, not an undergarment, fashionable in the 1780s but certainly not by the time the novel was published in 1813. By this time, the detail of a muddy underskirt would have suggested that Elizabeth was old-fashioned and dowdy. Efrat Margalit makes the dirty petticoat, which she understands as underwear conforming to current fashion, the subject of an essay. Margalit argues that the Bingley sisters, by pointing out that Elizabeth's petticoat is six inches deep in mud, "insinuate that it contrasts with the accepted norms of modesty." Having observed that Elizabeth "looks almost wild," the sisters go on to hint at her sexual audacity, a point emphasized, Margalit maintains, by their talk about her dirty "ancles." In fact, she continues, their commentary reflects more on them than on Elizabeth: "Eager to debase Elizabeth and, by association, to degrade Jane, the sisters unwittingly expose their own coarseness" (http://www.jasna.org/persuasions/on-line/vol23no1/margalit.html).

   Whether or not one imagines Elizabeth as dressed in the "vertical style" of the 1790s (the detail of her "letting down" her gown to hide her petticoat suggests the earlier underskirt fashion), Margalit's larger point remains important. Undergarment or not, a dirty petticoat hints at a lack of fastidiousness and faint sexual aspersion. The malice of the Bingley sisters toward Elizabeth indicates their moral inadequacy.

9 Duty.

10 When it comes to his sister, Darcy feels none of the ambivalence that afflicts him in relation to Elizabeth. He feels free to consider only propriety, without conflicting emotion.

11 Mud.

12 Decorous young ladies were virtually always accompanied in public.

13 Independence, which might imply disregard for one's ties to others, could be seen as a bad quality. In *Mansfield Park*, Sir Thomas rebukes Fanny by accusing her of it: "I had thought you peculiarly free from willfulness of temper, self-conceit, and every tendency to

"She has nothing, in short, to recommend her, but being an excellent walker. I shall never forget her appearance this morning. She really looked almost wild."

"She did, indeed, Louisa. I could hardly keep my countenance. Very nonsensical to come at all! Why must *she* be scampering about the country, because her sister had a cold? Her hair so untidy, so blowsy!"[7]

"Yes, and her petticoat; I hope you saw her petticoat,[8] six inches deep in mud, I am absolutely certain; and the gown which had been let down to hide it, not doing its office."[9]

"Your picture may be very exact, Louisa," said Bingley; "but this was all lost upon me. I thought Miss Elizabeth Bennet looked remarkably well, when she came into the room this morning. Her dirty petticoat quite escaped my notice."

"*You* observed it, Mr. Darcy, I am sure," said Miss Bingley; "and I am inclined to think that you would not wish to see *your sister* make such an exhibition."

"Certainly not."[10]

"To walk three miles, or four miles, or five miles, or whatever it is, above her ancles in dirt,[11] and alone, quite alone![12] what could she mean by it? It seems to me to shew an abominable sort of conceited independence,[13] a most country town indifference to decorum."

"It shews an affection for her sister that is very pleasing," said Bingley.

"I am afraid, Mr. Darcy," observed Miss Bingley in a half whisper, "that this adventure has rather affected your admiration of her fine eyes."

"Not at all," he replied; "they were brightened by the exercise."—A short pause followed this speech, and Mrs. Hurst began again.

"I have an excessive regard for Miss Jane Bennet, she is really a very sweet girl, and I wish with all my heart she were well settled.[14] But with such a father and mother, and such low connections, I am afraid there is no chance of it."

"I think I have heard you say that their uncle is an attorney in Meryton."

"Yes; and they have another, who lives somewhere near Cheap-side."[15]

"That is capital,"[16] added her sister, and they both laughed heart-ily.[17]

"If they had uncles enough to fill *all* Cheapside," cried Bingley, "it would not make them one jot less agreeable."

"But it must very materially lessen their chance of marrying men of any consideration in the world," replied Darcy.

To this speech Bingley made no answer; but his sisters gave it their hearty assent, and indulged their mirth for some time at the expense of their dear friend's vulgar[18] relations.

With a renewal of tenderness, however, they repaired to her room on leaving the dining-parlour, and sat with her till summoned to coffee. She was still very poorly, and Elizabeth would not quit her at all, till late in the evening, when she had the comfort of seeing her sleep, and when it appeared to her rather right than pleasant that she should go down stairs herself. On entering the drawing-room she found the whole party at loo,[19] and was immediately invited to join them; but suspecting them to be playing high[20] she declined it, and making her sister the excuse, said she would amuse herself for the short time she could stay below, with a book. Mr. Hurst looked at her with astonishment.

"Do you prefer reading to cards?" said he; "that is rather singular."

"Miss Eliza Bennet," said Miss Bingley, "despises cards. She is a great reader, and has no pleasure in anything else."

"I deserve neither such praise nor such censure," cried Elizabeth; "I am *not* a great reader,[21] and I have pleasure in many things."

"In nursing your sister I am sure you have pleasure," said Bingley; "and I hope it will be soon increased by seeing her quite well."

Elizabeth thanked him from her heart, and then walked towards the table where a few books were lying. He immediately offered to fetch her others—all that his library afforded.

"And I wish my collection were larger for your benefit and my own credit; but I am an idle fellow, and though I have not many, I have more than I ever look into."

that independence of spirit, which prevails so much in modern days, even in young women, and which in young women is offensive and disgusting beyond all common offence" (III, 1).

In her 1801 novel *Belinda,* Austen's contemporary Maria Edgeworth ("I have made up my mind to like no Novels really, but Miss Edgeworth's, Yours & my own," Austen writes to Anna Austen [28 September 1814]) commented approvingly that "our heroine was not one of those daring spirits, who are ambitious of acting for themselves" (Chapter 11). Anxiety about female independence was much in the air during Austen's period.

14 In marriage.

15 A section of London in the commercial district. By suggesting that this uncle is in trade, Mrs. Hurst is emphasizing Elizabeth's "low connections."

16 First-rate.

17 The sisters appear to forget the fact that their own wealth and their brother's are derived from trade; they attempt to adopt the attitudes of the landed gentry.

18 From a low social class.

19 A card game in which three or five cards are dealt to all players, who compete to win tricks on the basis of their high cards. This was at the time a particularly fashionable game. Elizabeth's reluctance to play, however, speaks well for her. One conduct book writer warns her daughters, about card playing in general, "it will be proper for you to know how to play at the games most in use, because it is an argument of great folly to engage in any thing without doing it well; but this is a diversion which I hope you will have no fondness for, as it is in itself, to say no worse, a very insignificant amusement" (Sarah Pennington, *An Unfortunate Mother's Advice to her Absent Daughters, in a Letter to Miss Pennington, The Young Lady's Pocket Library, or Parental Monitor* [Bristol: Thoemmes Press, 1995], 93).

20 For high stakes. Austen writes to her sister from Bath about an evening entertainment at which there were two pools at Commerce, "but I would not play more than one, for the Stake was three shillings, & I cannot afford to lose that, twice in an even^g" (To Cas-

sandra, 7–9 October 1808). Increasingly through the eighteenth century, gambling became a fashionable diversion for men and women alike. Moralists, novelists, and dramatists, however, used gambling as a sign of corruption. Thus Maria Edgeworth's Belinda rejects a young man whom she is on the verge of marrying—her wedding gown already brought home—when she discovers that he has spent much of his time gambling. She considers such activity to indicate an addiction that will never disappear.

21 The learned lady remained a negative stereotype. Perhaps Elizabeth wishes to disclaim emphatically any intellectual pretensions.

22 Libraries in great houses commonly included acquisitions from many generations of the family. Bingley's failure to add significantly to his father's library could be taken as neglect of family tradition, although Bingley, of course, lacks his own estate to house a library. Books were often sold in simple, plain bindings, with the assumption that they would subsequently be bound in leather for a family collection.

Deidre Shauna Lynch notes that "the early nineteenth century witnessed the apogee of the library within the English country house. . . . The new architectural prominence of the library in the home registered how it had become de rigeur among the propertied classes to number books among one's personal effects. It also suggested, as did the contemporary marketing of elegant reprints of 'standard novels,' how rereading had emerged as a fashionable rite of ownership. Being good and being English—really experiencing pleasure—now meant protracting one's reading and becoming *at home* with one's books" (*The Economy of Character: Novels, Market Culture, and the Business of Inner Meaning* [Chicago: University of Chicago Press, 1998], 144).

23 Piano, a term that would soon come into currency. *Piano-forte,* the original word, comes from Italian words for soft and loud and calls attention to the instrument's versatility and range. In the eighteenth century, the piano-forte came to replace the harpsichord, which had flourished for the previous two centuries. As a

LIBRARY READING CHAIRS.

Designs for a library reading chair, from Rudolph Ackermann, *Repository of Arts,* 1810. A reading chair for a person who takes reading seriously.

Elizabeth assured him that she could suit herself perfectly with those in the room.

"I am astonished," said Miss Bingley, "that my father should have left so small a collection of books. What a delightful library you have at Pemberley, Mr. Darcy!"

"It ought to be good," he replied, "it has been the work of many generations."[22]

"And then you have added so much to it yourself, you are always buying books."

"I cannot comprehend the neglect of a family library in such days as these."

"Neglect! I am sure you neglect nothing that can add to the beauties of that noble place. Charles, when you build *your* house, I wish it may be half as delightful as Pemberley."

"I wish it may."

"But I would really advise you to make your purchase in that neighbourhood, and take Pemberley for a kind of model. There is not a finer county in England than Derbyshire."

"With all my heart; I will buy Pemberley itself if Darcy will sell it."

"I am talking of possibilities, Charles."

"Upon my word, Caroline, I should think it more possible to get Pemberley by purchase than by imitation."

Elizabeth was so much caught with what passed, as to leave her very little attention for her book; and soon laying it wholly aside, she drew near the card-table, and stationed herself between Mr. Bingley and his eldest sister, to observe the game.

"Is Miss Darcy much grown since the spring?" said Miss Bingley; "will she be as tall as I am?"

"I think she will. She is now about Miss Elizabeth Bennet's height, or rather taller."

"How I long to see her again! I never met with anybody who delighted me so much. Such a countenance, such manners!—and so extremely accomplished for her age! Her performance on the piano forte[23] is exquisite."

"It is amazing to me," said Bingley, "how young ladies can have patience to be so very accomplished, as they all are."

"All young ladies accomplished! My dear Charles, what do you mean?"

"Yes, all of them, I think. They all paint tables, cover skreens and net purses.[24] I scarcely know any one who cannot do all this, and I am sure I never heard a young lady spoken of for the first time, without being informed that she was very accomplished."

"Your list of the common extent of accomplishments," said Darcy, "has too much truth. The word is applied to many a woman who deserves it no otherwise than by netting a purse, or covering a skreen. But I am very far from agreeing with you in your estimation of ladies in general. I cannot boast of knowing more than half a dozen, in the whole range of my acquaintance, that are really accomplished."

"Nor I, I am sure," said Miss Bingley.

"Then," observed Elizabeth, "you must comprehend a great deal in your idea of an accomplished woman."

"Yes; I do comprehend a great deal in it."

"Oh! certainly," cried his faithful assistant, "no one can be really esteemed accomplished, who does not greatly surpass what is usually met with. A woman must have a thorough knowledge of music, sing-

stringed instrument, the harpsichord was unable to move from soft to loud and back again.

24 Painting decorations on furniture, embroidering covers for screens, and doing net work with special needles were all characteristic activities of well-bred women, commonly called accomplishments. In her early work *Lady Susan* (c. 1793–1794), Austen comments, in Lady Susan's voice, on the female acquisition of accomplishments, including more substantial ones than those mentioned here: "it is throwing time away; to be Mistress of French, Italian, German, Music, Singing, Drawing &c. will gain a Woman some applause, but will not add one Lover to her list."

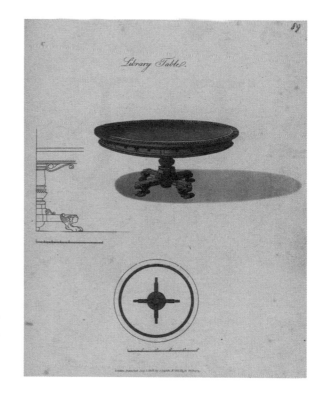

Library table; unknown artist, plate 89 from George Smith, *A Collection of Designs for Household Furniture and Interior Decoration in the Most Approved and Elegant Taste* (London: 1808). Family libraries consisted not only of collections of books but of rooms to house them. Such a table as this would be typical furniture.

25 Darcy's view is not unique. Hester Chapone's *Letters on the Improvement of the Mind* (to which Darcy's phrasing here may allude), first published in 1773, went through numerous editions in the early nineteenth century. "With regard to accomplishments," Chapone writes, "the chief of these is a competent share of reading, well chosen and properly regulated" (*Letters* [London, 1822], 136). The closest she comes to painting tables and such is her remark, "As to music and drawing, I would only wish you to follow as Genius leads" (137). She emphasizes that even the talented young woman will not approach the achievement of a professional artist, and that she should be content with pleasing her family alone. "It is of great consequence," she concludes, "to have the power of filling up agreeably those intervals of time which too often hang heavily on the hands of a woman, if her lot be cast in a retired situation" (137). In *Catharine* (1792), Austen's narrator takes a critical attitude toward a character who cultivates accomplishments rather than serious reading: "those Years which ought to have been spent in the attainment of useful knowledge and Mental Improvement, had been all bestowed in learning Drawing, Italian and Music, more especially the latter, and she now united to these Accomplishments, an Understanding unimproved by reading and a Mind totally devoid either of Taste or Judgement."

The late years of the eighteenth century and the early years of the nineteenth were a period in which female knowledge was increasingly valued—despite the negative "learned lady" stereotype. In 1795 Maria Edgeworth suggested, "A woman may now possess a considerable stock of information without being gazed upon as a miracle of learning; and there is not much danger of her being vain of accomplishments which cease to be astonishing." She adds, "You must have observed that public opinion is at present more favourable to the cultivation of the understanding of the female sex than it was some years ago; more attention is paid to the education of women, more knowledge and literature are expected from them in society" (*Letters for Literary Ladies,* Second Letter).

At the same time, merely decorative accomplishments sometimes became the target of active disap-

ing, drawing, dancing, and the modern languages, to deserve the word; and besides all this, she must possess a certain something in her air and manner of walking, the tone of her voice, her address and expressions, or the word will be but half-deserved."

"All this she must possess," added Darcy, "and to all this she must yet add something more substantial, in the improvement of her mind by extensive reading."25

"I am no longer surprised at your knowing *only* six accomplished women. I rather wonder now at your knowing *any*."

"Are you so severe upon your own sex, as to doubt the possibility of all this?"

Print from *Progress of Female Virtue,* engraved by Antoine Cardon (1772–1813), from original drawings by Maria Cecilia Louisa Cosway (1759–1838) (London: Pub. April 10, 1800, at R. Ackermann's, *Repository of Arts*). Painting was a common "accomplishment" of young women. This engraving associates it with innocence; the caption reads, "While Nature's beauties her free lines pourtray / She knows not that she's fairer than they." Maria Cosway, born and educated in Italy, married an artist and became an ambitious and renowned painter herself.

"*I* never saw such a woman. *I* never saw such capacity, and taste, and application, and elegance, as you describe, united."

Mrs. Hurst and Miss Bingley both cried out against the injustice of her implied doubt, and were both protesting that they knew many women who answered this description, when Mr. Hurst called them to order, with bitter complaints of their inattention to what was going forward. As all conversation was thereby at an end, Elizabeth soon afterwards left the room.

"Eliza Bennet," said Miss Bingley, when the door was closed on her, "is one of those young ladies who seek to recommend themselves to the other sex, by undervaluing their own; and with many men, I dare say, it succeeds. But, in my opinion, it is a paltry device, a very mean art."

"Undoubtedly," replied Darcy, to whom this remark was chiefly addressed, "there is a meanness in *all* the arts which ladies sometimes condescend to employ for captivation. Whatever bears affinity to cunning is despicable."[26]

Miss Bingley was not so entirely satisfied with this reply as to continue the subject.

Elizabeth joined them again only to say that her sister was worse, and that she could not leave her. Bingley urged Mr. Jones being sent for immediately; while his sisters, convinced that no country advice could be of any service, recommended an express to town for one of the most eminent physicians.[27] This, she would not hear of; but she was not so unwilling to comply with their brother's proposal; and it was settled that Mr. Jones should be sent for early in the morning, if Miss Bennet were not decidedly better. Bingley was quite uncomfortable; his sisters declared that they were miserable. They solaced their wretchedness, however, by duets after supper, while he could find no better relief to his feelings than by giving his housekeeper directions that every attention might be paid to the sick lady and her sister.

proval, because they were associated with female efforts to charm men with superficial attractions. Thus, in *Belinda,* Edgeworth has a group of young men discussing Belinda as the niece of a woman who specializes in getting husbands for girls. Last winter, one says, "You heard of nothing, wherever you went, but of Belinda Portman, and Belinda Portman's accomplishments. Belinda Portman, and her accomplishments, I'll swear, were as well advertised, as Packwood's razor strops" (Chapter 2). The suggestion that the struggle to get a man duplicates commercial tactics amplifies the metaphor of business that Austen associates with Mrs. Bennet.

26 Austen had already explored the character of a lady who specialized in the arts of captivation in *Lady Susan,* a study of an adventuress who fully demonstrates the despicableness of cunning—but also its power.

27 The country provided only apothecaries; physicians, with more training, were widely assumed to be more competent. An express was a special messenger.

9

1 Main part.

2 Their personal maids, who, like their mistresses, appear to have pretensions, presenting themselves as "elegant ladies" rather than as members of the servant class.

3 Improvement.

4 Breakfast would normally take place around ten o'clock and would be a fairly elaborate meal, lasting about an hour. Although servants got up very early, it would take them several hours to get fires burning, to bring water inside, to heat water for tea, and so forth. Ladies and gentlemen often used the pre-breakfast hours for such activities as letter writing.

ELIZABETH PASSED THE CHIEF[1] of the night in her sister's room, and in the morning had the pleasure of being able to send a tolerable answer to the enquiries which she very early received from Mr. Bingley by a housemaid, and some time afterwards from the two elegant ladies who waited on his sisters.[2] In spite of this amendment,[3] however, she requested to have a note sent to Longbourn, desiring her mother to visit Jane, and form her own judgment of her situation. The note was immediately dispatched, and its contents as quickly complied with. Mrs. Bennet, accompanied by her two youngest girls, reached Netherfield soon after the family breakfast.[4]

Had she found Jane in any apparent danger, Mrs. Bennet would have been very miserable; but being satisfied on seeing her that her illness was not alarming, she had no wish of her recovering immediately, as her restoration to health would probably remove her from Netherfield. She would not listen, therefore, to her daughter's proposal of being carried home; neither did the apothecary, who arrived about the same time, think it at all advisable. After sitting a little while with Jane, on Miss Bingley's appearance and invitation, the mother and three daughters all attended her into the breakfast parlour. Bingley met them with hopes that Mrs. Bennet had not found Miss Bennet worse than she expected.

"Indeed I have, Sir," was her answer. "She is a great deal too ill to be moved. Mr. Jones says we must not think of moving her. We must trespass a little longer on your kindness."

"Removed!" cried Bingley. "It must not be thought of. My sister, I am sure, will not hear of her removal."

"You may depend upon it, Madam," said Miss Bingley, with cold civility,[5] "that Miss Bennet shall receive every possible attention while she remains with us."

Mrs. Bennet was profuse in her acknowledgments.

"I am sure," she added, "if it was not for such good friends I do not know what would become of her, for she is very ill indeed, and suffers a vast deal, though with the greatest patience in the world, which is always the way with her, for she has, without exception, the sweetest temper I have ever met with. I often tell my other girls they are nothing to *her.* You have a sweet room here, Mr. Bingley, and a charming prospect[6] over the gravel walk. I do not know a place in the country that is equal to Netherfield. You will not think of quitting it in a hurry I hope, though you have but a short lease."

"Whatever I do is done in a hurry," replied he; "and therefore if I should resolve to quit Netherfield, I should probably be off in five minutes. At present, however, I consider myself as quite fixed here."

"That is exactly what I should have supposed of you," said Elizabeth.

"You begin to comprehend me, do you?" cried he, turning towards her.

"Oh! yes—I understand you perfectly."

"I wish I might take this for a compliment; but to be so easily seen through I am afraid is pitiful."

"That is as it happens. It does not necessarily follow that a deep, intricate character is more or less estimable than such a one as yours."[7]

"Lizzy," cried her mother, "remember where you are, and do not run on in the wild manner that you are suffered[8] to do at home."

"I did not know before," continued Bingley immediately, "that you were a studier of character. It must be an amusing[9] study."

"Yes, but intricate characters are the *most* amusing. They have at least that advantage."

5 Civility, as opposed to manners, entails adherence to the proper social forms without expectation that it implies anything more. When Marianne Dashwood sees the errors of her ways toward the end of *Sense and Sensibility,* she lists among her good resolutions an intention to "practice the civilities, the lesser duties of life, with gentleness, and forbearance" (III, 10). As her resolution suggests, civility, like every other human mode, can be practiced in many different ways. It remains, however, one of "the lesser duties."

6 View.

7 *Pride and Prejudice* systematically contrasts the "deep, intricate character[s]" of Darcy and Elizabeth with the simpler and more straightforward ones of Bingley and Jane. Elizabeth will say a few lines later that intricate characters are the most amusing, and the novel bears her out. Peter Knox-Shaw, who argues that ideas of the picturesque play a powerful role in the novel, points out that "intricate" is a word favored by William Gilpin, an eighteenth-century clergyman (1724–1804) who wrote extensively, beginning in 1768, on the picturesque, a concept that became important for late eighteenth- and nineteenth-century aesthetic theory. Knox-Shaw observes that Gilpin values the intricate in the kinds of scene that meet his criteria of the picturesque (*Jane Austen and the Enlightenment* [Cambridge: Cambridge University Press, 2004], 83).

8 Permitted.

9 Interesting, diverting.

Mrs Bennet and her two youngest girls

Hugh Thomson, Illustrations for *Pride and Prejudice,* 1894. Mrs. Bennet with Lydia and Mary. Hugh Thomson (1860–1920), born in Ireland but long a London resident, illustrated many popular novels.

Promenade dress, fashion plate from Rudolph Ackermann, *Repository of Arts,* published between 1809 and 1829. This engraving of a promenade dress may suggest how Elizabeth would be dressed for her walks. The *OED* cites an 1809 issue of *The Examiner* describing such a dress as "a round high frock of fine French cambric."

"The country," said Darcy, "can in general supply but a few subjects for such a study. In a country neighbourhood you move in a very confined and unvarying society."

"But people themselves alter so much,[10] that there is something new to be observed in them for ever."

"Yes, indeed," cried Mrs. Bennet, offended by his manner of mentioning a country neighbourhood. "I assure you there is quite as much of *that* going on in the country as in town."

Every body was surprised; and Darcy, after looking at her for a moment, turned silently away. Mrs. Bennet, who fancied she had gained a complete victory over him, continued her triumph.

"I cannot see that London has any great advantage over the country for my part, except the shops and public places. The country is a vast deal pleasanter, is it not, Mr. Bingley?"

"When I am in the country," he replied, "I never wish to leave it; and when I am in town it is pretty much the same. They have each their advantages, and I can be equally happy in either."

"Aye—that is because you have the right disposition. But that gentleman," looking at Darcy, "seemed to think the country was nothing at all."

"Indeed, Mama, you are mistaken," said Elizabeth, blushing for her mother. "You quite mistook Mr. Darcy. He only meant that there was not such a variety of people to be met with in the country as in the town, which you must acknowledge to be true."

"Certainly, my dear, nobody said there were; but as to not meeting with many people in this neighbourhood, I believe there are few neighbourhoods larger. I know we dine with four and twenty families."[11]

Nothing but concern for Elizabeth could enable Bingley to keep his countenance. His sister was less delicate, and directed her eyes towards Mr. Darcy with a very expressive smile. Elizabeth, for the sake of saying something that might turn her mother's thoughts, now asked her if Charlotte Lucas had been at Longbourn since *her* coming away.

"Yes, she called yesterday with her father. What an agreeable man Sir William is, Mr. Bingley—is not he? so much the man of fashion!

10 Eighteenth-century fiction had, by and large, depicted people as incapable of changing in essentials. They might acquire new characteristics, as Tom Jones acquires prudence, but their fundamental natures would not alter. Austen appears to believe in the possibility of more radical change.

11 In other words, their social circle includes twenty-four families.

12 A condescending phrase, implying that nothing particular can be said about them.

13 Propose to her.

14 Alluding to Orsino's speech at the very beginning of Shakespeare's *Twelfth Night:* "If music be the food of love, play on."

15 Robust.

so genteel and so easy!—He has always something to say to every body.—*That* is my idea of good breeding; and those persons who fancy themselves very important and never open their mouths, quite mistake the matter."

"Did Charlotte dine with you?"

"No, she would go home. I fancy she was wanted about the mince-pies. For my part, Mr. Bingley, *I* always keep servants that can do their own work; *my* daughters are brought up differently. But every body is to judge for themselves, and the Lucases are very good sort of girls,[12] I assure you. It is a pity they are not handsome! Not that *I* think Charlotte so *very* plain—but then she is our particular friend."

"She seems a very pleasant young woman," said Bingley.

"Oh! dear, yes;—but you must own she is very plain. Lady Lucas herself has often said so, and envied me Jane's beauty. I do not like to boast of my own child, but to be sure, Jane—one does not often see any body better looking. It is what every body says. I do not trust my own partiality. When she was only fifteen, there was a man at my brother Gardiner's in town, so much in love with her that my sister-in-law was sure he would make her an offer[13] before we came away. But however he did not. Perhaps he thought her too young. However, he wrote some verses on her, and very pretty they were."

"And so ended his affection," said Elizabeth impatiently. "There has been many a one, I fancy, overcome in the same way. I wonder who first discovered the efficacy of poetry in driving away love!"

"I have been used to consider poetry as the *food* of love,"[14] said Darcy.

"Of a fine, stout,[15] healthy love it may. Everything nourishes what is strong already. But if it be only a slight, thin sort of inclination, I am convinced that one good sonnet will starve it entirely away."

Darcy only smiled; and the general pause which ensued made Elizabeth tremble lest her mother should be exposing herself again. She longed to speak, but could think of nothing to say; and after a short silence Mrs. Bennet began repeating her thanks to Mr. Bingley for his kindness to Jane, with an apology for troubling him also with Lizzy. Mr. Bingley was unaffectedly civil in his answer, and forced his younger sister to be civil also, and say what the occasion required.

She performed her part indeed without much graciousness, but Mrs.
Bennet was satisfied, and soon afterwards ordered her carriage.
Upon this signal, the youngest of her daughters put herself forward.
The two girls had been whispering to each other during the whole
visit, and the result of it was, that the youngest should tax Mr. Bingley with having promised on his first coming into the country to give
a ball at Netherfield.

Lydia was a stout,[16] well-grown girl of fifteen, with a fine complexion and good-humoured countenance; a favourite with her mother,
whose affection had brought her into public[17] at an early age. She had
high animal spirits,[18] and a sort of natural self-consequence,[19] which
the attention of the officers, to whom her uncle's good dinners and
her own easy[20] manners recommended her, had increased into assurance.[21] She was very equal therefore to address Mr. Bingley on the
subject of the ball, and abruptly reminded him of his promise; adding, that it would be the most shameful thing in the world if he did
not keep it. His answer to this sudden attack was delightful to their
mother's ear.

"I am perfectly ready, I assure you, to keep my engagement; and
when your sister is recovered, you shall if you please name the very
day of the ball. But you would not wish to be dancing while she
is ill."

Lydia declared herself satisfied. "Oh! yes—it would be much better to wait till Jane was well, and by that time most likely Captain
Carter would be at Meryton again. And when you have given *your*
ball," she added, "I shall insist on their giving one also. I shall tell
Colonel Forster it will be quite a shame if he does not."

Mrs. Bennet and her daughter then departed, and Elizabeth returned instantly to Jane, leaving her own and her relations' behaviour
to the remarks of the two ladies and Mr. Darcy; the latter of whom,
however, could not be prevailed on to join in their censure of *her*, in
spite of all Miss Bingley's witticisms on *fine eyes*.

16 Healthy.

17 Into society.

18 Great natural good humor.

19 Self-importance.

20 Easy-going, easy to get along with.

21 Self-assurance.

10

THE DAY PASSED MUCH AS the day before had done. Mrs. Hurst and Miss Bingley had spent some hours of the morning with the invalid, who continued, though slowly, to mend; and in the evening Elizabeth joined their party in the drawing-room.[1] The loo table, however, did not appear. Mr. Darcy was writing, and Miss Bingley, seated near him, was watching the progress of his letter, and repeatedly calling off[2] his attention by messages to his sister. Mr. Hurst and Mr. Bingley were at piquet,[3] and Mrs. Hurst was observing their game.

Elizabeth took up some needlework, and was sufficiently amused in attending to what passed between Darcy and his companion. The perpetual commendations of the lady either on his hand-writing, or on the evenness of his lines, or on the length of his letter,[4] with the perfect unconcern with which her praises were received, formed a curious dialogue, and was exactly in unison with her opinion of each.

"How delighted Miss Darcy will be to receive such a letter!"

He made no answer.

"You write uncommonly fast."

"You are mistaken. I write rather slowly."

"How many letters you must have occasion to write in the course of a year! Letters of business, too! How odious I should think them!"

"It is fortunate, then, that they fall to my lot instead of yours."

"Pray tell your sister that I long to see her."

"I have already told her so once, by your desire."

---

1 A room for receiving guests, to which the ladies withdraw after dinner.

2 Away.

3 A card game for two, played with a reduced deck.

4 Letter writing was still considered an art. Not only were collections of letters by well-known figures frequently published; so were books of model letters, from which aspiring correspondents could learn what sort of sentiment supplied an appropriate response to a given situation. (The eighteenth-century novelist Samuel Richardson inaugurated his literary career by publishing such a volume.) Calligraphy as well as content contributed to a letter's perceived excellence. Austen herself, during her long correspondence with her sister, Cassandra, frequently apologized for her "sprawling" handwriting and straggling lines. In an 1813 letter, she writes, "I took up your Letter again to refresh me, being somewhat tired; & was struck with the prettiness of the hand; it is really a very pretty hand now & then—so small & so neat!—I wish I could get as much into a sheet of paper" (To Cassandra, 3 November 1813).

1O

"I am afraid you do not like your pen. Let me mend it for you.[5] I mend pens remarkably well."

"Thank you—but I always mend my own."

"How can you contrive to write so even?"

He was silent.

"Tell your sister I am delighted to hear of her improvement on the harp,[6] and pray let her know that I am quite in raptures with her beautiful little design for a table, and I think it infinitely superior to Miss Grantley's."[7]

"Will you give me leave to defer your raptures till I write again?—At present I have not room to do them justice."[8]

"Oh! it is of no consequence. I shall see her in January. But do you always write such charming long letters to her, Mr. Darcy?"

"They are generally long; but whether always charming, it is not for me to determine."

"It is a rule with me, that a person who can write a long letter, with ease, cannot write ill."

"That will not do for a compliment to Darcy, Caroline," cried her brother—"because he does *not* write with ease. He studies too much for words of four syllables.[9]—Do not you, Darcy?"

"My stile of writing is very different from yours."

"Oh!" cried Miss Bingley, "Charles writes in the most careless way imaginable. He leaves out half his words, and blots[10] the rest."

"My ideas flow so rapidly that I have not time to express them—by which means my letters sometimes convey no ideas at all to my correspondents."

"Your humility, Mr. Bingley," said Elizabeth, "must disarm reproof."

"Nothing is more deceitful," said Darcy, "than the appearance of humility. It is often only carelessness of opinion, and sometimes an indirect boast."

"And which of the two do you call *my* little recent piece of modesty?"

"The indirect boast;—for you are really proud of your defects in writing, because you consider them as proceeding from a rapidity of thought and carelessness of execution, which if not estimable, you

5 Quill pens, the kind Darcy would have used, dulled rapidly with use and had to be "mended" by sharpening the tip with a penknife.

6 A fashionable instrument at the time—played also by Jane Crawford in *Mansfield Park.* In *Persuasion,* the Musgrove family transports a harp by carriage from one house to another in an effort to console Mrs. Musgrove, who is "out of spirits." The harp, it turns out, "seems to amuse her more than the piano-forte" (I, 6).

7 Darcy's sister, clearly, has many "accomplishments."

8 Like Mr. Bennet, Darcy appears to have perfected a rhetoric of ironic politeness.

9 The spontaneity and intimacy of familiar letters were often asserted during the eighteenth century, but it remained a matter of debate whether such letters were really ever "easy" and natural. Dr. Johnson articulated a particularly emphatic view to the contrary: "It has been so long said as to be commonly believed that the true characters of men may be found in their letters, and that he who writes to his friend lays his heart open before him. But the truth is that such were the simple friendships of the *Golden Age,* and are now the friendships only of children. Very few can boast of hearts which they dare lay open to themselves, and of which, by whatever accident exposed, they do not shun a distinct and continued view, and certainly what we hide from ourselves we do not shew to our friends" (*Life of Pope*).

10 Blurs with drops of ink that would have dripped from his pen as he wrote in haste.

11 The word *interesting* had acquired its modern meaning but was still frequently used in an older sense, meaning significant, worth attention.

12 The contrast between Miss Bingley's badinage with Darcy and Elizabeth's calls attention to Elizabeth's intelligence and wit and to the fact that what she says is not dictated by a desire to attract.

James Barry, "Samuel Johnson," 1778–1780. Johnson, the great literary arbiter of the eighteenth century, held forth on the subject of letter-writing as well as virtually every other literary genre.

think at least highly interesting.[11] The power of doing anything with quickness is always prized much by the possessor, and often without any attention to the imperfection of the performance. When you told Mrs. Bennet this morning that if you ever resolved on quitting Netherfield you should be gone in five minutes, you meant it to be a sort of panegyric, of compliment to yourself—and yet what is there so very laudable in a precipitance which must leave very necessary business undone, and can be of no real advantage to yourself or any one else?"

"Nay," cried Bingley, "this is too much, to remember at night all the foolish things that were said in the morning. And yet, upon my honour, I believe what I said of myself to be true, and I believe it at this moment. At least, therefore, I did not assume the character of needless precipitance merely to shew off before the ladies."

"I dare say you believed it; but I am by no means convinced that you would be gone with such celerity. Your conduct would be quite as dependent on chance as that of any man I know; and if, as you were mounting your horse, a friend were to say, 'Bingley, you had better stay till next week,' you would probably do it, you would probably not go—and, at another word, might stay a month."

"You have only proved by this," cried Elizabeth, "that Mr. Bingley did not do justice to his own disposition. You have shewn him off now much more than he did himself."

"I am exceedingly gratified," said Bingley, "by your converting what my friend says into a compliment on the sweetness of my temper. But I am afraid you are giving it a turn which that gentleman did by no means intend; for he would certainly think the better of me, if under such a circumstance I were to give a flat denial, and ride off as fast as I could."

"Would Mr. Darcy then consider the rashness of your original intentions as atoned for by your obstinacy in adhering to it?"[12]

"Upon my word, I cannot exactly explain the matter, Darcy must speak for himself."

"You expect me to account for opinions which you chuse to call mine, but which I have never acknowledged. Allowing the case, however, to stand according to your representation, you must remember,

Miss Bennet, that the friend who is supposed to desire his return to the house, and the delay of his plan, has merely desired it, asked it without offering one argument in favour of its propriety."

"To yield readily—easily—to the *persuasion*[13] of a friend is no merit with you."

"To yield without conviction is no compliment to the understanding of either."

"You appear to me, Mr. Darcy, to allow nothing for the influence of friendship and affection. A regard for the requester would often make one readily yield to a request, without waiting for arguments to reason one into it. I am not particularly speaking of such a case as you have supposed about Mr. Bingley. We may as well wait, perhaps, till the circumstance occurs before we discuss the discretion of his behaviour thereupon. But in general and ordinary cases between friend and friend, where one of them is desired by the other to change a resolution of no very great moment,[14] should you think ill of that person for complying with the desire, without waiting to be argued into it?"

"Will it not be advisable, before we proceed on this subject, to arrange with rather more precision the degree of importance which is to appertain to this request, as well as the degree of intimacy subsisting between the parties?"

"By all means," cried Bingley; "let us hear all the particulars, not forgetting their comparative height and size; for that will have more weight in the argument, Miss Bennet, than you may be aware of. I assure you that if Darcy were not such a great tall fellow, in comparison with myself, I should not pay him half so much deference. I declare I do not know a more awful[15] object than Darcy, on particular occasions, and in particular places; at his own house especially, and of a Sunday evening when he has nothing to do."

Mr. Darcy smiled; but Elizabeth thought she could perceive that he was rather offended; and therefore checked her laugh.[16] Miss Bingley warmly resented the indignity he had received, in an expostulation with her brother for talking such nonsense.

"I see your design, Bingley," said his friend.—"You dislike an argument, and want to silence this."

13 The subject of persuasion, how far one should be persuaded by a friend, and under what circumstances, returns emphatically in Austen's later novel *Persuasion*.

14 Importance.

15 Awe-inspiring.

16 An act of refraining that shows true courtesy. Chapone explains, "To be perfectly polite, one must have great presence of mind, with a delicate and quick sense of propriety; or, in other words, one should be able to form an instantaneous judgment of what is fittest to be said or done, on every occasion as it offers" (*Letters on the Improvement of the Mind* [London, 1822], 128). At the "last stage of perfection in politeness," she goes on to observe, "[w]e should be perfectly easy, and make others so if we can" (129).

It is especially significant that Elizabeth checks her laugh. Like her father, she enjoys laughing at the ridiculous, but this tiny episode indicates that she consciously tries to avoid hurting others.

17 Arguments may seem like disputes to Bingley, but this, like other arguments between Darcy and Elizabeth, seems rather more like flirtation: a little dance of self-display that demonstrates, to readers as well as to the participants, their wit and intellectual nimbleness.

18 Socially important.

19 The reel, a lively and popular dance, could be thought of low social status. Elizabeth may be remembering Darcy's scorn of the dancing at Sir William Lucas's gathering, when Mary played Scotch and Irish airs so that her younger sisters and "some of the Lucases" could dance with officers at the end of the room. It was this spectacle that caused Darcy to remark, "Every savage can dance."

20 A common eighteenth-century locution, not at the time ungrammatical.

"Perhaps I do. Arguments are too much like disputes.[17] If you and Miss Bennet will defer yours till I am out of the room, I shall be very thankful; and then you may say whatever you like of me."

"What you ask," said Elizabeth, "is no sacrifice on my side; and Mr. Darcy had much better finish his letter."

Mr. Darcy took her advice, and did finish his letter.

When that business was over, he applied to Miss Bingley and Elizabeth for the indulgence of some music. Miss Bingley moved with some alacrity to the piano-forte; and after a polite request that Elizabeth would lead the way, which the other as politely and more earnestly negatived, she seated herself.

Mrs. Hurst sang with her sister, and while they were thus employed Elizabeth could not help observing as she turned over some music-books that lay on the instrument, how frequently Mr. Darcy's eyes were fixed on her. She hardly knew how to suppose that she could be an object of admiration to so great[18] a man; and yet that he should look at her because he disliked her, was still more strange. She could only imagine, however at last, that she drew his notice because there was a something about her more wrong and reprehensible, according to his ideas of right, than in any other person present. The supposition did not pain her. She liked him too little to care for his approbation.

After playing some Italian songs, Miss Bingley varied the charm by a lively Scotch air; and soon afterwards Mr. Darcy, drawing near Elizabeth, said to her—

"Do not you feel a great inclination, Miss Bennet, to seize such an opportunity of dancing a reel?"

She smiled, but made no answer. He repeated the question, with some surprise at her silence.

"Oh!" said she, "I heard you before, but I could not immediately determine what to say in reply. You wanted me, I know, to say 'Yes,' that you might have the pleasure of despising my taste;[19] but I always delight in overthrowing those kind[20] of schemes, and cheating a person of their premeditated contempt. I have therefore made up my mind to tell you, that I do not want to dance a reel at all—and now despise me if you dare."

"Indeed I do not dare."

Elizabeth, having rather expected to affront him, was amazed at his gallantry;[21] but there was a mixture of sweetness and archness in her manner which made it difficult for her to affront anybody; and Darcy had never been so bewitched[22] by any woman as he was by her. He really believed, that were it not for the inferiority of her connections,[23] he should be in some danger.

Miss Bingley saw, or suspected enough to be jealous; and her great anxiety for the recovery of her dear friend Jane, received some assistance from her desire of getting rid of Elizabeth.

She often tried to provoke Darcy into disliking her guest, by talking of their supposed marriage, and planning his happiness in such an alliance.

"I hope," said she, as they were walking together in the shrubbery the next day, "you will give your mother-in-law a few hints, when this desirable event takes place, as to the advantage of holding her tongue; and if you can compass it, do cure the younger girls of running after officers.—And, if I may mention so delicate a subject, endeavour to check that little something, bordering on conceit and impertinence, which your lady possesses."

"Have you anything else to propose for my domestic felicity?"

"Oh! yes.—Do let the portraits of your uncle and aunt Phillips be placed in the gallery at Pemberley. Put them next to your great uncle the judge. They are in the same profession, you know; only in different lines. As for your Elizabeth's picture, you must not attempt to have it taken, for what painter could do justice to those beautiful eyes?"

"It would not be easy, indeed, to catch their expression, but their colour and shape, and the eye-lashes, so remarkably fine, might be copied."

At that moment they were met from another walk, by Mrs. Hurst and Elizabeth herself.

"I did not know that you intended to walk," said Miss Bingley, in some confusion, lest they had been overheard.

"You used us abominably ill," answered Mrs. Hurst, "in running away without telling us that you were coming out."

21 Courtliness; especially courtesy to a lady.

22 Although figuratively the word means "fascinated," its literal meaning is "under . . . magical influence" (OED). The great gap between Elizabeth's feelings toward Darcy (she remains preoccupied with his original insult) and his toward her is emphasized by this strong way of conveying his emotion.

23 Family ties.

Plates 27 and 28 from William Gilpin, *Observations, Relative Chiefly to Picturesque Beauty, Made in the Year 1772, on Several Parts of England; Particularly the Mountains, and Lakes of Cumberland, and Westmoreland* (London: Printed for R. Blamire, 1786). *(Top)* This engraving illustrates Gilpin's point about the difficulty of grouping four cattle in picturesque fashion. "The only way, in which they will group well, is to unite *three* . . . and to *remove the fourth.*" *(Bottom)* Similarly, Gilpin explains that to make two cows picturesque, the artist must unite them: "If they stand apart, whatever their attitudes, or situation may be, there will be a deficiency."

Then taking the disengaged arm of Mr. Darcy, she left Elizabeth to walk by herself. The path just admitted three. Mr. Darcy felt their rudeness, and immediately said,—

"This walk is not wide enough for our party. We had better go into the avenue."

But Elizabeth who had not the least inclination to remain with them, laughingly answered,

"No, no; stay where you are.—You are charmingly group'd, and appear to uncommon advantage. The picturesque would be spoilt by admitting a fourth.[24] Good bye."

She then ran gaily off, rejoicing as she rambled about, in the hope of being at home again in a day or two. Jane was already so much recovered as to intend leaving her room for a couple of hours that evening.

24 The picturesque had become a popular aesthetic category, largely as a result of William Gilpin's *Observations, on Several Parts of England . . . relative chiefly to Picturesque Beauty* (1808). Gilpin held forth at some length on aesthetic effects created by cows, which, he claimed, were far more picturesque than horses. "Cattle are so large," he writes, "that when they ornament a foreground, a few are sufficient. Two cows will hardly combine. Three make a good group—either united—or when one is a little removed from the other two. If you increase the group beyond three; one, or more, in proportion, must necessarily be a *little detached*" (*Observations, on Several Parts of England, Particularly the Mountains and Lakes of Cumberland and Westmoreland, Relative Chiefly to Picturesque Beauty*, 3rd ed., 2 vols. [London, 1808], II, 254). To compare the residents of Nethercote to cattle, as Elizabeth implicitly does, is hardly flattering; but of course she includes herself in the same category—and she is quite happy to be *"a little detached."*

11

1 Withdrew. Customarily, ladies removed themselves after dinner to the drawing room, leaving the men to drink, smoke, and talk politics and smut.

2 The Bingley sisters apparently suffer mental impoverishment comparable to that of Lydia and Kitty Bennet. Unlike the Bennet girls, however, they have been thoroughly instructed in the social behavior of the class to which they aspire: they model themselves on their notion of fine ladies, elevating superficiality to an art.

3 Of attention.

4 Needlework. To indulge in graceful needlework, decorative rather than useful, was a frequent occupation of women in company. In a letter Austen seems taken aback by a woman who, during a social call, "sat darning a pair of stockings the whole of my visit" (To Cassandra, 14 September 1804), an activity too utilitarian to be proper. Like the artistic accomplishments discussed by Chapone, needlework served the purpose of passing time. Dr. Gregory observes: "The intention of your being taught needle-work, knitting, and such like, is not on account of the intrinsic value of all you can do with your hands, which is trifling, but to enable you to judge more perfectly of that kind of work, and to direct the execution of it in others. Another principal end is to enable you to fill up, in a tolerably agreeable way, some of the many solitary hours you must necessarily pass at home" (John Gregory, *A Father's Legacy to His Daughters, The Young Lady's Pocket Library, or Parental Monitor* [Bristol: Thoemmes Press, 1995], 21).

WHEN THE LADIES REMOVED[1] after dinner, Elizabeth ran up to her sister, and seeing her well guarded from cold, attended her into the drawing-room; where she was welcomed by her two friends with many professions of pleasure; and Elizabeth had never seen them so agreeable as they were during the hour which passed before the gentlemen appeared. Their powers of conversation were considerable. They could describe an entertainment with accuracy, relate an anecdote with humour, and laugh at their acquaintance with spirit.[2]

But when the gentlemen entered, Jane was no longer the first object.[3] Miss Bingley's eyes were instantly turned toward Darcy, and she had something to say to him before he had advanced many steps. He addressed himself to Miss Bennet, with a polite congratulation; Mr. Hurst also made her a slight bow, and said he was "very glad;" but diffuseness and warmth remained for Bingley's salutation. He was full of joy and attention. The first half hour was spent in piling up the fire, lest she should suffer from the change of room; and she removed at his desire to the other side of the fire-place, that she might be farther from the door. He then sat down by her, and talked scarcely to any one else. Elizabeth, at work[4] in the opposite corner, saw it all with great delight.

When tea[5] was over, Mr. Hurst reminded his sister-in-law of the card-table—but in vain. She had obtained private intelligence that Mr. Darcy did not wish for cards; and Mr. Hurst soon found even his open petition rejected. She assured him that no one intended to play, and the silence of the whole party on the subject seemed to justify her. Mr. Hurst had therefore nothing to do, but to stretch himself on one of the sophas[6] and go to sleep. Darcy took up a book; Miss Bingley did the same; and Mrs. Hurst, principally occupied in playing with her bracelets and rings, joined now and then in her brother's conversation with Miss Bennet.

Miss Bingley's attention was quite as much engaged in watching Mr. Darcy's progress through *his* book, as in reading her own; and she was perpetually either making some inquiry, or looking at his page. She could not win him, however, to any conversation; he merely answered her question, and read on. At length, quite exhausted by the attempt to be amused with her own book, which she had only chosen because it was the second volume of his, she gave a great yawn and said, "How pleasant it is to spend an evening in this way! I declare after all there is no enjoyment like reading! How much sooner one tires of any thing than of a book!—When I have a house of my own, I shall be miserable if I have not an excellent library."

No one made any reply. She then yawned again, threw aside her book, and cast her eyes round the room in quest for some amusement; when hearing her brother mentioning a ball to Miss Bennet, she turned suddenly towards him and said:

"By the bye, Charles, are you really serious in meditating a dance at Netherfield?—I would advise you, before you determine on it, to consult the wishes of the present party; I am much mistaken if there are not some among us to whom a ball would be rather a punishment than a pleasure."

"If you mean Darcy," cried her brother, "he may go to bed, if he chuses, before it begins—but as for the ball, it is quite a settled thing; and as soon as Nicholls[7] has made white soup[8] enough, I shall send round my cards."[9]

"I should like balls infinitely better," she replied, "if they were carried on in a different manner; but there is something insufferably tedious in the usual process of such a meeting. It would surely be much more rational[10] if conversation instead of dancing made the order of the day."

"Much more rational, my dear Caroline, I dare say, but it would not be near so much like a ball."

5 Generally served an hour or so after dinner.

6 Rude behavior, emphasizing the self-indulgence that has already been seen to characterize Mr. Hurst. The word *sopha* had come into English in 1717, derived from an Arabic term designating a raised section of floor, furnished with rugs and cushions, used for councils and for especially esteemed guests. The sofa was thus associated with ease and splendor. William Cowper in 1785 published *The Task,* with *or The Sofa* as subtitle, stimulated by a friend's suggestion that he write a poem about the sofa to alleviate his depression. He associated this item of furniture with the dangerous possibilities of "luxury": according to the genealogy he presented, "first necessity invented stools, / Convenience next suggested elbow-chairs, / And luxury the accomplished Sofa last" (I, 83–85).

7 The housekeeper.

8 An elaborate soup based on veal stock, cream, and almonds. Maggie Lane declares it "the best soup of all" (*Jane Austen and Food* [London: The Hambledon Press, 1995], 55).

The Jane Austen Centre website reproduces a recipe for white soup published in John Farley's *London Art of Cooking* (1783): "Put a knuckle of veal into six quarts of water, with a large fowl, and a pound of lean bacon, half a pound of rice, two anchovies, a few pepper corns, a bundle of sweet herbs, two or three onions, and three or four heads of celery cut in slices. Stew them all together, till the soup be as strong as you would have it, and then strain it through a hair sieve into a clean earthen pot. Having let it stand all night, the next day take off the scum, and pour it clean off into a tossing-pan. Put in half a pound of Jordan almonds beat fine, boil it a little, and run it through a lawn [fine cloth] sieve. Then put in a pint of cream, and the yolk of an egg, and send it up hot."

9 Invitations.

10 The nature of the rational and the irrationality of some of its proclaimed adherents are recurrent themes in *Pride and Prejudice.*

11 A hint of sympathy even for Miss Bingley.

Miss Bingley made no answer; and soon afterwards got up and walked about the room. Her figure was elegant, and she walked well; —but Darcy, at whom it was all aimed, was still inflexibly studious. In the desperation of her feelings,[11] she resolved on one effort more; and, turning to Elizabeth, said,

"Miss Eliza Bennet, let me persuade you to follow my example, and take a turn about the room.—I assure you it is very refreshing after sitting so long in one attitude."

Elizabeth was surprised, but agreed to it immediately. Miss Bingley succeeded no less in the real object of her civility; Mr. Darcy looked up. He was as much awake to the novelty of attention in that quarter as Elizabeth herself could be, and unconsciously closed his book. He was directly invited to join their party, but he declined it, observing, that he could imagine but two motives for their chusing to walk up and down the room together, with either of which motives his joining them would interfere. "What could he mean? She was dying to know what could be his meaning?"—and asked Elizabeth whether she could at all understand him?

"Not at all," was her answer; "but depend upon it, he means to be severe on us, and our surest way of disappointing him, will be to ask nothing about it."

Miss Bingley, however, was incapable of disappointing Mr. Darcy in any thing, and persevered therefore in requiring an explanation of his two motives.

"I have not the smallest objection to explaining them," said he, as soon as she allowed him to speak. "You either chuse this method of passing the evening because you are in each other's confidence and have secret affairs to discuss, or because you are conscious that your figures appear to the greatest advantage in walking;—if the first, I should be completely in your way;—and if the second, I can admire you much better as I sit by the fire."

"Oh! shocking!" cried Miss Bingley. "I never heard any thing so abominable. How shall we punish him for such a speech?"

"Nothing so easy, if you have but the inclination," said Elizabeth. "We can all plague and punish one another. Teaze him—laugh at him. —Intimate as you are, you must know how it is to be done."

Portrait of Edward Austen Knight, Jane's brother, at the time of his world tour. Edward was adopted by the wealthy Knight family and changed his last name to theirs. The Chawton Cottage, where Jane, late in her life, lived with her mother, belonged to one of his estates.

"But upon my honour, I do *not*. I do assure you that my intimacy has not yet taught me *that*. Teaze calmness of temper and presence of mind! No, no—I feel he may defy us there. And as to laughter, we will not expose ourselves, if you please, by attempting to laugh without a subject. Mr. Darcy may hug himself."

"Mr. Darcy is not to be laughed at!" cried Elizabeth. "That is an uncommon advantage, and uncommon I hope it will continue, for it would be a great loss to *me* to have many such acquaintance. I dearly love a laugh."

"Miss Bingley," said he, "has given me credit for more than can be. The wisest and the best of men, nay, the wisest and best of their actions, may be rendered ridiculous by a person whose first object in life is a joke."

"Certainly," replied Elizabeth—"there are such people, but I hope I am not one of *them*. I hope I never ridicule what is wise or good.[12] Follies and nonsense, whims and inconsistencies, *do* divert me, I own, and I laugh at them whenever I can.—But these, I suppose, are precisely what you are without."

"Perhaps that is not possible for any one. But it has been the study of my life to avoid those weaknesses which often expose a strong understanding to ridicule."

"Such as vanity and pride."

"Yes, vanity is a weakness indeed. But pride—where there is a real superiority of mind, pride will be always under good regulation."

Elizabeth turned away to hide a smile.[13]

"Your examination of Mr. Darcy is over, I presume," said Miss Bingley;—"and pray what is the result?"

"I am perfectly convinced by it that Mr. Darcy has no defect. He owns it himself without disguise."[14]

"No"—said Darcy, "I have made no such pretension. I have faults enough, but they are not, I hope, of understanding. My temper I dare not vouch for.—It is I believe too little yielding—certainly too little for the convenience of the world. I cannot forget the follies and vices of other so soon as I ought, nor their offenses against myself. My feelings are not puffed about with every attempt to move them. My

12 In dearly loving a laugh, Elizabeth resembles her father. She takes pains, however, to differentiate herself from him by insisting on careful discrimination about the targets of her laughter: she will not laugh, as Lydia does, just for the sake of laughing, and she has no wish to laugh at everyone, as Mr. Bennet apparently does.

13 Perhaps because Darcy's implicit claim of "real superiority of mind" betrays the vanity he is disclaiming.

14 Jan Fergus remarks about these two sentences, "The doubleness of irony has seldom been more perfectly exercised. While staying completely within the bounds of polite discourse, Elizabeth has managed to say—without saying it—that Darcy is full of defects and that he has been doing his unsuccessful best to hide them" ("The Power of Women's Language and Laughter," *The Talk in Jane Austen,* ed. Bruce Stovel and Lynn Weinlos Gregg [Edmonton: University of Alberta Press, 2002], 106).

15 John Wiltshire characterizes Darcy as he appears in this speech: "He is here both self-important, and struggling towards self-understanding; he is both defensive and striving for an unpractised openness. As with many human confessions it is the way this one is received that determines its intent and meaning" (*Recreating Jane Austen* [Cambridge: Cambridge University Press, 2001], 109).

16 Elizabeth's hostile response perhaps influences the reader to understand Darcy's statement as she does. Wiltshire's commentary on the passage continues, "In this instance what Elizabeth hears in Darcy's speech fits in with her 'premeditated' or previous notions about him, and the reader, whose dominant allegiance is to her, tends to 'hear' Darcy's speech as she does" (109).

17 Elizabeth indeed has an extreme response to Darcy's self-description, and Darcy shows considerable forbearance in his reaction to her.

temper would perhaps be called resentful. — My good opinion once lost is lost for ever."[15]

"*That* is a failing indeed!" — cried Elizabeth. "Implacable resentment *is* a shade in a character. But you have chosen your fault well. — I really cannot *laugh* at it. You are safe from me."[16]

"There is, I believe, in every disposition a tendency to some particular evil, a natural defect, which not even the best education can overcome."

"And *your* defect is a propensity to hate every body."

"And yours," he replied with a smile, "is wilfully to misunderstand them."[17]

"Do let us have a little music," — cried Miss Bingley, tired of a conversation in which she had no share. — "Louisa, you will not mind my waking Mr. Hurst."

Her sister made not the smallest objection, and the piano forte was opened; and Darcy, after a few moments' recollection, was not sorry for it. He began to feel the danger of paying Elizabeth too much attention.

12

IN CONSEQUENCE OF AN agreement between the sisters, Elizabeth wrote the next morning to their mother, to beg that the carriage might be sent for them in the course of the day. But Mrs. Bennet, who had calculated[1] on her daughters remaining at Netherfield till the following Tuesday, which would exactly finish Jane's week, could not bring herself to receive them with pleasure before. Her answer, therefore, was not propitious, at least not to Elizabeth's wishes, for she was impatient to get home. Mrs. Bennet sent them word that they could not possibly have the carriage before Tuesday; and in her postscript it was added, that if Mr. Bingley and his sister pressed them to stay longer, she could spare them very well.—Against staying longer, however, Elizabeth was positively resolved—nor did she much expect it would be asked; and fearful, on the contrary, as being considered as intruding themselves needlessly long, she urged Jane to borrow Mr. Bingley's carriage immediately, and at length it was settled that their original design of leaving Netherfield that morning should be mentioned, and the request made.

The communication excited many professions of concern; and enough was said of wishing them to stay at least till the following day to work on Jane; and till the morrow their going was deferred. Miss Bingley was then sorry that she had proposed the delay, for her jealousy and dislike of one sister much exceeded her affection for the other.

The master of the house heard with real sorrow that they were to go so soon, and repeatedly tried to persuade Miss Bennet that it

[1] Mrs. Bennet, who often seems mindless to the point of real stupidity, frequently reveals unexpected wiliness in her calculations about her daughters' marital prospects. Her "business" of marrying off her daughters demands and arouses all her capacities.

2 Annoying.

3 This instance of Darcy's "wisdom" is not particularly impressive.

4 He assumes that such a hope would encourage her vanity.

5 Aware.

6 Situations in which a man suddenly withdraws attention from a woman in whom he has seemed to be interested appear quite often in eighteenth-century fiction. Ordinarily, such withdrawal produces an intense reaction from the woman in question. Frances Burney's *Cecilia* contains a typical episode. Young Delvile has been warmly responsive to Cecilia, who has begun to be romantically interested in him. Delvile's father is one of Cecilia's guardians. When she comes for a visit to the Delvile castle, the young man changes his attitude: "[H]e breakfasted by himself every morning, rode or walked out alone till driven home by the heat of the day, and spent the rest of his time till dinner in his own study. When he then appeared, his conversation was always general, and his attention not more engaged by Cecilia than by his mother. Left by them with his father, sometimes he appeared again at teatime, but more commonly he rode or strolled out to some neighbouring family, and it was always uncertain whether he was again seen before dinner the next day." Reacting to "a coldness so extraordinary," Cecilia constructs various hypotheses to explain it, but resolves to overcome her own partiality and to follow a similar course; she declines "all discourse but what good breeding occasionally made necessary" (VI, 1).

Elizabeth, in contrast, gives no sign of noticing that Darcy is ignoring her. Her unconcern is unusual and refreshing: the fact that she evinces no interest in the most eligible man in her society—rich, well-born, tall, good-looking, and "in want of a wife"—differentiates her from almost all previous novelistic heroines.

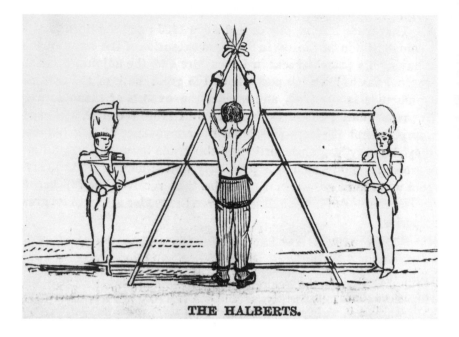

THE HALBERTS.

"Military Flogging," *Illustrated London News*, 1846. Military punishment in the mid-nineteenth century remained much the same as it had been earlier. Typically the soldier was bound with his hands above his head, in front of the troop, and lashed across the bare back. The halberts referred to in the caption were lances that might be used to make a frame for binding.

would not be safe for her—that she was not enough recovered; but Jane was firm where she felt herself to be right.

To Mr. Darcy it was welcome intelligence—Elizabeth had been at Netherfield long enough. She attracted him more than he liked—and Miss Bingley was uncivil to *her,* and more teasing[2] than usual to himself. He wisely[3] resolved to be particularly careful that no sign of admiration should *now* escape him, nothing that could elevate her with the hope of influencing his felicity;[4] sensible[5] that if such an idea had been suggested, his behaviour during the last day must have material weight in confirming or crushing it. Steady to his purpose, he scarcely spoke ten words to her through the whole of Saturday, and though they were at one time left by themselves for half an hour, he adhered most conscientiously to his book, and would not even look at her.[6]

On Sunday, after morning service, the separation, so agreeable to almost all,[7] took place. Miss Bingley's civility to Elizabeth increased at last very rapidly, as well as her affection for Jane; and when they parted, after assuring the latter of the pleasure it would always give her to see her either at Longbourn or Netherfield, and embracing her most tenderly, she even shook hands with the former.—Elizabeth took leave of the whole party in the liveliest spirits.

They were not welcomed home very cordially by their mother. Mrs. Bennet wondered at their coming, and thought them very wrong to give so much trouble,[8] and was sure Jane would have caught cold again.—But their father, though very laconic in his expressions of pleasure, was really glad to see them; he had felt their importance in the family circle. The evening conversation, when they were all assembled, had lost much of its animation, and almost all its sense, by the absence of Jane and Elizabeth.

They found Mary, as usual, deep in the study of thorough bass[9] and human nature;[10] and had some new extracts to admire, and some new observations of thread-bare[11] morality to listen to. Catherine and Lydia had information for them of a different sort. Much had been done, and much had been said in the regiment since the preceding Wednesday; several of the officers had dined lately with their uncle, a private had been flogged,[12] and it had actually been hinted that Colonel Forster was going to be married.

7 That is, to everyone except Bingley.

8 By borrowing Bingley's coach instead of waiting for their own, which their mother has promised for the next Tuesday.

9 The study of musical harmonies.

10 Mary studies human nature entirely through books, instead of paying attention to living human beings. Compare Austen herself, who writes of going to art museums with a friend, "I had some amusement at each, tho' my preference for Men & Women, always inclines me to attend more to the company than the sight" (To Cassandra, 18–20 April 1811).

11 Worn out. Mary has a propensity to prefer the most clichéd moral utterances.

12 Brutal corporal punishment was common in the army at the beginning of the nineteenth century. The large social gap between officers and enlisted men made it relatively easy to inflict such punishment. Sentences of up to one thousand lashes for such serious crimes as mutiny occurred, and the flogging of privates was a frequent event. This is the novel's only allusion to a man below the rank of officer. In making a flogging into an item of gossip on a level with information about who dined with their uncle, Lydia and Kitty exemplify their frivolity and their conversational casualness: they rarely think about what they say, and they clearly don't feel any uneasiness about the idea of flogging. Moreover, like the novel's other characters, they give no evidence of realizing that the militia's presence implies a situation of national danger.

13

1 Because it's Monday, and no fishing would have taken place on Sunday. Maggie Lane takes Mrs. Bennet's concern for the unavailable fish, when she expects Mr. Bingley for dinner, as a sign of bad judgment: "Mrs. Bennet is so ill-judging that she imagines Mr. Bingley's love for Jane will be affected by the presence or absence of fish on the table" (Maggie Lane, *Jane Austen and Food* [London: The Hambledon Press, 1995], 109). In fact, the anxious mother does not care so much about Mr. Bingley's love as about his coming to the point of proposing. She perhaps hopes that evidence of the good table she sets will make Bingley forget that the Bennet family is less wealthy and less fashionable than his own.

2 The housekeeper. Upper servants were generally referred to by their last names.

3 Mr. Bennet's idea of "early attention" is answering a letter more than two weeks after receiving it. He has known of Mr. Collins's impending arrival for a month, but he notifies his family of it only on the very day that the guest is expected.

4 Mr. Collins, as the nearest male relative, would inherit through the entail.

"I HOPE, MY DEAR," said Mr. Bennet to his wife, as they were at breakfast the next morning, "that you have ordered a good dinner to-day, because I have reason to expect an addition to our family party."

"Who do you mean, my dear? I know of nobody that is coming, I am sure, unless Charlotte Lucas should happen to call in, and I hope *my* dinners are good enough for her. I do not believe she often sees such at home."

"The person of whom I speak is a gentleman, and a stranger."

Mrs. Bennet's eyes sparkled.—"A gentleman and a stranger! It is Mr. Bingley I am sure! Why Jane—you never dropt a word of this; you sly thing! Well, I am sure I shall be extremely glad to see Mr. Bingley.—But—good lord! how unlucky! there is not a bit of fish to be got to-day.[1] Lydia, my love, ring the bell. I must speak to Hill,[2] this moment."

"It is *not* Mr. Bingley," said her husband; "it is a person whom I never saw in the whole course of my life."

This roused a general astonishment; and he had the pleasure of being eagerly questioned by his wife and five daughters at once.

After amusing himself some time with their curiosity, he thus explained.

"About a month ago I received this letter, and about a fortnight ago I answered it, for I thought it a case of some delicacy, and requiring early attention.[3] It is from my cousin, Mr. Collins, who, when I am dead, may turn you all out of this house as soon as he pleases."[4]

"Oh! my dear," cried his wife, "I cannot bear to hear that mentioned. Pray do not talk of that odious man. I do think it is the hardest thing in the world, that your estate should be entailed away from your own children; and I am sure if I had been you, I should have tried long ago to do something or other about it."[5]

Jane and Elizabeth attempted to explain to her the nature of an entail.[6] They had often attempted it before, but it was a subject on which Mrs. Bennet was beyond the reach of reason; and she continued to rail bitterly against the cruelty of settling an estate away from a family of five daughters, in favour of a man whom nobody cared anything about.[7]

"It certainly is a most iniquitous affair," said Mr. Bennet, "and nothing can clear Mr. Collins from the guilt of inheriting Longbourn. But if you will listen to his letter, you may perhaps be a little softened by his manner of expressing himself."

"No, that I am sure I shall not; and I think it is very impertinent of him to write to you at all, and very hypocritical. I hate such false friends.[8] Why could he not keep on quarreling with you, as his father did before him?"

"Why, indeed, he does seem to have had some filial scruples on that head, as you will hear."

> "Hunsford, near Westerham, Kent,
> 15th October.

Dear Sir,

"The disagreement subsisting between yourself and my late honoured father, always gave me much uneasiness, and since I have had the misfortune to lose him, I have frequently wished to heal the breach; but for some time I was kept back by my own doubts, fearing lest it might seem disrespectful to his memory for me to be on good terms with any one with whom it had always pleased him to be at variance.—'There, Mrs. Bennet.'—My mind however is now made up on the subject, for having received ordination[9] at Easter, I have been so fortunate as to be distinguished by the patronage of the Right Honourable Lady Catherine de Bourgh, widow of

5 It is indeed a hard thing that female children should be deprived of inheritance in favor of distant male relatives. Mrs. Bennet alone in her family articulates this truth. Her articulation, however, has little force, since it appears to issue from her invincible ignorance about the nature and legal authority of an entail.

6 The entail was a binding legal arrangement; Mr. Bennet, who has not devised it, has no power to alter it.

7 Since *she* cares nothing about him, she assumes that "nobody" cares.

8 Mrs. Bennet has imagined a character and an attitude for this man she has never met. She believes him to be a "false friend," and hypocritical, because she conceives him as preoccupied with a desire for his inheritance, and thus for Mr. Bennet's death. He would therefore only be pretending to wish friendship with the Bennets.

9 Mr. Collins has been ordained as a clergyman.

10   Lady Catherine was the widow of a knight or a baronet, probably a knight. If her title had come from him, she would have been Lady de Bourgh; her status as Lady Catherine, therefore, indicates that she is the daughter of a duke, a marquess, or an earl, the highest ranks of nobility. (Lady Lucas, in contrast, is only a "Lady" by virtue of her husband's title.) Later evidence makes clear that her father was an earl. She has, therefore, married beneath her rank, but she is of high descent—a fact in which Mr. Collins obviously takes great pride.

11   Raised, promoted.

12   Many wealthy landowners held the right to appoint someone to a particular clerical position. Lady Catherine has used this right on behalf of Mr. Collins, whom she has named as rector of a parish, thus providing him with a socially respectable position and an income. A rector, who held the position for life, also acquired the use of a house and of a plot of land (the "glebe"), which he might farm himself or rent. And he had the privilege of collecting tithes.

13   It is worth noting that Mr. Collins places the responsibility of respect toward her ladyship ahead of his duties in the church.

14   An emblem of peace—trite, as Mr. Collins's allusions tend to be.

15   Mr. Collins's use of this adjective epitomizes the artifice of his rhetoric. He has no way of knowing how "amiable" the Bennet daughters are.

16   A week. Mr. Collins proposes visiting for almost two weeks, from Monday to the Saturday of the next week. Since travel was both expensive and slow, long visits were common. Indeed, a two-week stay would have seemed rather short.

17   Perform the day's religious service.

18   Mr. Collins's prose style resembles Mary's moral maxims in seeming all second-hand. His phrases—"bounty and beneficence," "blessing of peace," "beg leave to apologize"—sound as though they've been copied from a manual for clergymen, and his extrava-

Sir Lewis de Bourgh,[10] whose bounty and beneficence has preferred[11] me to the valuable rectory of this parish,[12] where it shall be my earnest endeavour to demean myself with grateful respect towards her Ladyship,[13] and be ever ready to perform those rites and ceremonies which are instituted by the Church of England. As a clergyman, moreover, I feel it my duty to promote and establish the blessing of peace in all families within in the reach of my influence; and on these grounds I flatter myself that my present overtures of goodwill are highly commendable, and that the circumstance of my being next in the entail of Longbourn estate, will be kindly overlooked on your side, and not lead you to reject the offered olive branch.[14] I cannot be otherwise than concerned at being the means of injuring your amiable[15] daughters, and beg leave to apologise for it, as well as to assure you of my readiness to make them every possible amends,—but of this hereafter. If you should have no objection to receive me into your house, I propose myself the satisfaction of waiting on you and your family, Monday, November 18th, by four o'clock, and shall probably trespass on your hospitality till the Saturday se'nnight[16] following, which I can do without any inconvenience, as Lady Catherine is far from objecting to my occasional absence on a Sunday, provided that some other clergyman is engaged to do the duty of the day.[17] I remain, dear sir, with respectful compliments to your lady and daughters, your well-wisher and friend,[18]

William Collins"

"At four o'clock, therefore, we may expect this peace-making gentleman," said Mr. Bennet, as he folded up the letter. "He seems to be a most conscientious and polite young man, upon my word; and I doubt not will prove a valuable acquaintance, especially if Lady Catherine should be so indulgent as to let him come to us again."

"There is some sense in what he says about the girls however; and if he is disposed to make them any amends, I shall not be the person to discourage him."

"Though it is difficult," said Jane, "to guess in what way he can mean to make us the atonement he thinks our due, the wish is certainly to his credit."

Elizabeth was chiefly struck by his extraordinary deference for Lady Catherine, and his kind intention of christening, marrying, and burying his parishioners whenever it were required.

"He must be an oddity, I think," said she. "I cannot make him out.—There is something very pompous in his stile.—And what can he mean by apologizing for being next in the entail?—We cannot suppose he would help it, if he could.—Can he be a sensible[19] man, sir?"

"No, my dear; I think not. I have great hopes of finding him quite the reverse.[20] There is a mixture of servility and self-importance in his letter, which promises well. I am impatient to see him."

"In point of composition," said Mary, "his letter does not seem defective. The idea of the olive branch perhaps is not wholly new, yet I think it is well expressed."[21]

To Catherine and Lydia, neither the letter nor its writer were in any degree interesting. It was next to impossible that their cousin should come in a scarlet coat, and it was now some weeks since they had received pleasure from the society of a man in any other colour. As for their mother, Mr. Collins's letter had done away much of her ill-will, and she was preparing to see him with a degree of composure, which astonished her husband and daughters.[22]

Mr. Collins was punctual to his time, and was received with great politeness by the whole family. Mr. Bennet indeed said little; but the ladies were ready enough to talk, and Mr. Collins seemed neither in need of encouragement, nor inclined to be silent himself. He was a tall, heavy-looking[23] young man of five-and-twenty. His air was grave and stately, and his manners were very formal. He had not been long seated before he complimented Mrs. Bennet on having so fine a family of daughters; said he had heard much of their beauty, but that, in this instance, fame had fallen short of the truth; and added, that he did not doubt her seeing them all in due time well disposed of in marriage. This gallantry was not much to the taste of some of his hear-

gantly deferential tone intensifies the impression that the letter emerges from an artificially constructed being.

19 Elizabeth may mean either a man of sensibility or (more likely) a man of sense.

20 Mr. Bennet takes great pleasure in laughing at others, so he anticipates special entertainment if Mr. Collins is not a sensible man.

21 Mary responds positively to a piece of writing that resembles in style and partly in substance her own utterances.

22 Evidently her husband and daughters fail to realize that from Mrs. Bennet's point of view, any unmarried man constitutes an opportunity.

23 Of grave or severe appearance.

24 Gallantry—courtliness toward the female sex—is not necessarily perceived as a tribute. As Mary Wollstonecraft pointed out, male homage to women is "arbitrary insolent respect," and "the men who pride themselves upon paying [such homage], with the most scrupulous exactness, are most inclined to tyrannize over, and despise, the very weakness they cherish" (*A Vindication of the Rights of Woman,* ch. IV, "Observations on the State of Degradation to which Woman Is Reduced by Various Causes"). The Bennet sisters presumably hear the artificiality of Mr. Collins's compliments —and some of them, at least, perhaps resent the assumption that being well married is their goal in life.

25 Conscious.

26 The likelihood of Mr. Collins's appearing forward and precipitate seems faint indeed.

27 Mr. Collins seems to consider girls and furniture alike as objects to be approved or disapproved. He rather resembles Mrs. Bennet in his objectification of her daughters.

ers;[24] but Mrs. Bennet, who quarreled with no compliments, answered most readily,

"You are very kind, sir, I am sure; and I wish with all my heart it may prove so; for else they will be destitute enough. Things are settled so oddly."

"You allude perhaps to the entail of this estate."

"Ah! sir, I do indeed. It is a grievous affair to my poor girls, you must confess. Not that I mean to find fault with *you,* for such things I know are all chance in this world. There is no knowing how estates will go when once they come to be entailed."

"I am very sensible,[25] madam, of the hardship to my fair cousins,— and could say much on the subject, but that I am cautious of appearing forward and precipitate.[26] But I can assure the young ladies that I come prepared to admire them. At present I will not say more; but, perhaps, when we are better acquainted—"

He was interrupted by a summons to dinner; and the girls smiled on each other. They were not the only objects of Mr. Collins's admiration. The hall, the dining-room, and all its furniture, were examined and praised;[27] and his commendation of everything would have touched Mrs. Bennet's heart, but for the mortifying supposition of his viewing it all as his own future property. The dinner too in its turn was highly admired; and he begged to know to which of his fair cousins the excellence of its cookery was owing. But here he was set right by Mrs. Bennet, who assured him with some asperity that they were very well able to keep a good cook, and that her daughters had nothing to do in the kitchen. He begged pardon for having displeased her. In a softened tone she declared herself not at all offended; but he continued to apologise for about a quarter of an hour.

14

DURING DINNER, MR. BENNET scarcely spoke at all; but when the servants were withdrawn, he thought it time to have some conversation with his guest, and therefore started a subject in which he expected him to shine, by observing that he seemed very fortunate in his patroness. Lady Catherine de Bourgh's attention to his wishes, and consideration for his comfort, appeared very remarkable. Mr. Bennet could not have chosen better. Mr. Collins was eloquent in her praise. The subject elevated[1] him to more than usual solemnity of manner, and with a most important aspect[2] he protested that he had never in his life witnessed such behaviour in a person of rank—such affability and condescension, as he had himself experienced from Lady Catherine. She had been graciously pleased to approve of both the discourses, which he had already had the honour of preaching before her. She had also asked him twice to dine at Rosings,[3] and had sent for him only the Saturday before, to make up her pool of quadrille[4] in the evening. Lady Catherine was reckoned proud[5] by many people he knew, but *he* had never seen anything but affability in her. She had always spoken to him as she would to any other gentleman;[6] she made not the smallest objection to his joining in the society of the neighbourhood, nor to his leaving the parish occasionally for a week or two, to visit his relations. She had even condescended to advise him to marry as soon as he could, provided he chose with discretion; and had once paid him a visit in his humble parsonage, where she had perfectly approved all the alterations he had been making,

1 An important verb. Mr. Collins is elevated—exalted, raised to a higher sphere—by the very thought of his patroness; association with her confirms for him his most grandiose sense of self.

2 Pompous, pretentious facial expression.

3 Her estate.

4 A card game for four players, played with a deck of forty cards.

5 Like Darcy and Elizabeth. The novel's reiterated emphasis on how "many people" judge others as proud underlines the issues of opinion and interpretation that come up repeatedly in *Pride and Prejudice*.

6 This bit of praise suggests that Mr. Collins does not feel at all certain of his own status as a gentleman.

7 The description of Mr. Collins that Mr. Bennet formulated on the basis of his letter—"a mixture of servility and self-importance" (I, 13)—seems remarkably accurate.

8 Mrs. Bennet's views of "great ladies in general" must be based on what she has heard rather than what she knows directly. Community opinion, which produces "universal" acknowledgment of such "truths" as the one articulated in the novel's first sentence, shapes many of her ideas.

9 "Many girls" is here a euphemism for "my girls": Mrs. Bennet is at least as self-referential as Mr. Collins.

10 Lady Catherine is a brilliant rationalizer.

11 Mr. Collins is emphatic about the "condescension" of Lady Catherine and her daughter. He has declared "affability and condescension" to be the evidence of Lady Catherine's "remarkable" behavior to him and has expressed his delight that "she even condescended to advise him to marry." His stress on aristocratic condescension both emphasizes his social insecurity and paradoxically suggests his view that the aristocrats actually consider him an equal, as his reiterated reference to his "humble abode" hints that he thinks it anything but humble. "Condescension," however, does not have quite the meaning we attach to it. In the language of the *OED,* it designates "affability to one's inferiors, with courteous disregard of difference of rank or position" *(OED).* As Austen (and Mr. Collins) use the word, it implies not an open attitude of superiority but only a manifestation of graciousness. Edward Neill, though, argues that such condescension as Lady Catherine's, "which is, supposedly, to set people at their ease . . . is actually a carefully orchestrated form of social 'terrorism'" (*The Politics of Jane Austen* [New York: St. Martin's Press, 1999], 51). It reiterates the gap between aristocrats and their social inferiors.

12 A light, sporty carriage, usually with four large wheels, customarily drawn by two horses.

13 At court. Being formally presented to the monarch in a court ceremony constituted official admittance to

and had even vouchsafed to suggest some herself—some shelves in the closets up stairs.[7]

"That is all very proper and civil, I am sure," said Mrs. Bennet, "and I dare say she is a very agreeable woman. It is a pity that great ladies in general are not more like her.[8] Does she live near you, sir?"

"The garden in which stands my humble abode, is separated only by a lane from Rosings Park, her ladyship's residence."

"I think you said she was a widow, sir? has she any family?"

"She has only one daughter, the heiress of Rosings, and of very extensive property."

"Ah!" cried Mrs. Bennet, shaking her head, "then she is better off than many girls.[9] And what sort of young lady is she? is she handsome?"

"She is a most charming young lady indeed. Lady Catherine herself says that in point of true beauty, Miss de Bourgh is far superior to the handsomest of her sex; because there is that in her features which marks the young woman of distinguished birth.[10] She is unfortunately of a sickly constitution, which has prevented her making that progress in many accomplishments, which she could not have otherwise failed of; as I am informed by the lady who superintended her education, and who still resides with them. But she is perfectly amiable, and often condescends[11] to drive by my humble abode in her little phaeton[12] and ponies."

"Has she been presented?[13] I do not remember her name among the ladies at court."

"Her indifferent state of health unhappily prevents her being in town; and by that means, as I told Lady Catherine myself one day, has deprived the British court of its brightest ornament. Her ladyship seemed pleased with the idea, and you may imagine that I am happy on every occasion to offer those little delicate compliments which are always acceptable to ladies. I have more than once observed to Lady Catherine, that her charming daughter seemed born to be a duchess, and that the most elevated rank, instead of giving her consequence,[14] would be adorned by her.—These are the kind of little things which please her ladyship, and it is a sort of attention which I conceive myself peculiarly bound to pay."

"You judge very properly," said Mr. Bennet, "and it is happy for you that you possess the talent of flattering with delicacy.[15] May I ask whether these pleasing attentions proceed from the impulse of the moment, or are the result of previous study?"

"They arise chiefly from what is passing at the time, and though I sometimes amuse myself with suggesting and arranging such little elegant compliments as may be adapted to ordinary occasions, I always wish to give them as unstudied an air as possible."

Mr. Bennet's expectations were fully answered. His cousin was as absurd as he had hoped, and he listened to him with the keenest enjoyment, maintaining at the same time the most resolute composure of countenance, and except in an occasional glance at Elizabeth, requiring no partner in his pleasure.

society. Young women wore elaborate court dress for the event; only the wealthy were in a position to participate. It's interesting that Mrs. Bennet keeps track of who is presented, since people at her social level would rarely if ever be involved. But fascination with the doings of the elite appears to be a widespread characteristic that survives much social change.

14 Social importance.

15 Delicacy, "a refined sense of what is becoming, modest, or proper . . . delicate regard for the feelings of others" *(OED)*, was a quality much valued in Austen's time, particularly for women. As Dr. Gregory puts the point —before holding forth on the attractiveness of blushing— "One of the chief beauties in a female character, is that modest reserve, that retiring delicacy, which avoids the public eye, and is disconcerted even at the gaze of admiration" (John Gregory, *A Father's Legacy to His Daughters, The Young Lady's Pocket Library, or Parental Monitor* [Bristol: Thoemmes Press, 1995], 11). Well-bred women were thought to have a "natural" sense of delicacy; the woman who did not display such a sense, or who was believed to have lost her delicacy, would be severely criticized. Gentlemen, too, were expected to manifest delicacy.

Anonymous, "The Circulating Library," 1804. Circulating libraries were widely associated not only with fiction but with risqué fiction. The caption of this 1804 print imagines the words of the young woman at the desk as she rejects books with titles suggesting moral instruction in favor of several that concern love, including *Assignation* and *Frederick or the Libertine*.

16 The "everything" that identifies the book would have consisted mainly of a paper label on the front cover, indicating the library's policies and rates. Circulating libraries, responding to the tastes of their paid subscribers, often specialized in novels, a genre widely denigrated on moral grounds well into the nineteenth century. Moralists thought that reading novels would inflame the imaginations of young women in particular. Thus Sarah Pennington: "Of *Novels and Romances,* very few are worth the trouble of reading: some of them perhaps do contain a few good morals, but they are not worth the finding where so much rubbish is intermixed. . . . The most I have met with of these writings, to say no worse, it is little better than the loss of time to peruse. But some of them have more pernicious consequences. By drawing characters that never exist in life, by representing persons and things in a false and extravagant light, and by a series of improbable causes bringing on impossible events, they are apt to give a romantic turn to the mind, which is often productive of great errors in judgment, and of fatal mistakes in conduct" (Sarah Pennington, *An Unfortunate Mother's Advice to Her Absent Daughters, in a Letter to Miss Pennington, The Young Lady's Pocket Library, or Parental Monitor* [Bristol: Thoemmes Press, 1995], 87–88).

Mary Wollstonecraft, who shared the worry about inflamed imaginations, felt even more concerned about the intellectual laxness that she attributed to fiction. "The best method, I believe," she writes, "that can be adopted to correct a fondness for novels is to ridicule them: not indiscriminately, for then it would have little effect; but, if a judicious person, with some turn for humour, would read several to a young girl, and point out both by tone, and apt comparisons with pathetic incidents and heroic characters in history, how foolishly and ridiculously they caricatured human nature, just opinions might be substituted instead of romantic sentiments" (*A Vindication of the Rights of Woman,* chap. XIII, "Some Instances of the Folly which the Ignorance of Women Generates; with Concluding Reflections on the Moral Improvement that a Revolution in Female Manners Might Naturally Be Expected to Produce"). Wollstonecraft, however, wrote two novels herself.

By tea-time, however, the dose had been enough, and Mr. Bennet was glad to take his guest into the drawing-room again, and when tea was over, glad to invite him to read aloud to the ladies. Mr. Collins readily assented, and a book was produced; but on beholding it, (for every thing announced it to be from a circulating library,)[16] he started back, and begging pardon, protested that he never read novels.[17]—Kitty stared at him, and Lydia exclaimed.—Other books were produced, and after some deliberation he chose Fordyce's Sermons.[18] Lydia gaped[19] as he opened the volume, and before he had, with very monotonous solemnity, read three pages, she interrupted him with,

"Do you know, mama, that my uncle Phillips talks of turning away Richard,[20] and if he does, Colonel Forster will hire him. My aunt told me so herself on Saturday. I shall walk to Meryton to-morrow to hear more about it, and to ask when Mr. Denny comes back from town."

Lydia was bid by her two eldest sisters to hold her tongue; but Mr. Collins, much offended, laid aside his book, and said:

"I have often observed how little young ladies are interested by books of a serious stamp, though written solely for their benefit. It amazes me, I confess;—for certainly, there can be nothing so advantageous to them as instruction. But I will no longer importune my young cousin."

Then turning to Mr. Bennet, he offered himself as his antagonist at backgammon.[21] Mr. Bennet accepted the challenge, observing that he acted very wisely in leaving the girls to their own trifling amusements. Mrs. Bennet and her daughters apologised most civilly for Lydia's interruption, and promised that it should not occur again, if he would resume his book; but Mr. Collins, after assuring them that he bore his young cousin no ill will, and should never resent her behaviour as any affront, seated himself at another table with Mr. Bennet, and prepared for backgammon.

Austen suggests a very different view through her famous comment, in the narrator's voice, in *Northanger Abbey*. "There seems almost a general wish of decrying the capacity and undervaluing the labour of the novelist," she writes, "and of slighting the performances which have only genius, wit, and taste to recommend them." She imagines a young woman asked what she is reading: "'Oh! it is only a novel!' replies the young lady; while she lays down her book with affected indifference, or momentary shame.—'It is only Cecilia, or Camilla, or Belinda;' or, in short, only some work in which the greatest powers of the mind are displayed, in which the most thorough knowledge of human nature, the happiest delineation of its varieties, the liveliest effusions of wit and humour are conveyed to the world in the best chosen language" (I, 5). Austen does not italicize the titles of the novels to which she alludes (*Cecilia* and *Camilla,* works by Frances Burney; *Belinda* by Maria Edgeworth).

17 Austen writes in a letter about a Mrs. Martin who wishes her to subscribe to a new circulating library. "As an inducement to subscribe Mrs Martin tells us that her Collection is not to consist only of Novels, but of every kind of Literature &c &c—She might have spared this pretension to *our* family, who are great Novel-readers & not ashamed of being so" (To Cassandra, 18–19 December 1798). In contrast, James Fordyce (see note 14), writing about the books a young woman might read, observes that "there seem to me to be very few, in the style of Novel, that you can read with safety, and yet fewer that you can read with advantage.—What shall we say of certain books, which we are assured (for we have not read them) are in their nature so shameful, in their tendency so pestiferous, and contain such rank treason against the royalty of Virtue, such horrible violation of all decorum, that she who can bear to peruse them must in her soul be a prostitute, let her reputation in life be what it will?" (*Sermons to Young Women,* 3rd American ed. from 12th London ed. [Philadelphia, 1809], 75). Mr. Collins may share Fordyce's view, which is more emphatic even than Pennington's or Wollstonecraft's.

18 James Fordyce's *Sermons to Young Women* (1766) was a conservative conduct book that preached the value of female passivity. The unlikelihood of Lydia's being able to listen to it may be suggested by Fordyce's emphatic recommendation that women cultivate "an unaffected bashfulness" (57). Mary Wollstonecraft singles out Fordyce for forceful criticism in *Vindication of the Rights of Woman* (1792). She says she would not allow the *Sermons* in the library of any pupil of hers, and she offers several examples of ways in which he denigrates women under the guise of praising them. A striking instance of the clergyman's attitude is a passage suggesting that if husbands become indifferent, wives are to blame. "Had you behaved to them with more *respectful observance,* and a more *equal tenderness; studying their humours, overlooking their mistakes, submitting to their opinions* in matters indifferent, passing by little instances of unevenness, caprice, or passion, giving *soft* answers to hasty words, complaining as seldom as possible, and making it your daily care to relieve their anxieties and prevent their wishes, to enliven the hour of dullness, and call up the ideas of felicity: had you pursued this conduct, I doubt not but you would have maintained and even increased their esteem, so far as to have secured every degree of influence that could conduce to their virtue, or your mutual satisfaction, and your house might at this day have been the abode of domestic bliss." Wollstonecraft comments, "Such a woman ought to be an angel—or she is an ass—for I discern not a trace of the human character, neither reason nor passion in this domestic drudge, whose being is absorbed in that of a tyrant" (chap. V).

19 Yawned.

20 Discharging a servant.

21 A board game for two, in which pieces are moved according to rolls of dice. Allegedly the world's oldest game, backgammon is said to have originated with the Royal Game of Ur in ancient Mesopotamia. Its rules were codified by Edmond Hoyle in 1745, and it was particularly popular with English clergymen in the eighteenth century.

"Protested
that he never read novels"

Hugh Thomson, Illustrations for *Pride and Prejudice,* 1894. Mr. Collins reacts
to the sight of a novel.

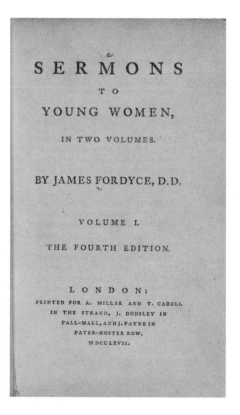

SERMONS
TO
YOUNG WOMEN,
IN TWO VOLUMES.

BY JAMES FORDYCE, D.D.

VOLUME I.

THE FOURTH EDITION.

LONDON:
PRINTED FOR A. MILLAR AND T. CADELL
IN THE STRAND, J. DODSLEY IN
PALL-MALL, AND J. PAYNE IN
PATER-NOSTER ROW.
MDCCLXVII.

Title page of James Fordyce, *Sermons to
Young Women,* 1767. This didactic work is
Mr. Collins's idea of a good book for read-
ing aloud to women.

15

MR. COLLINS WAS NOT A SENSIBLE MAN, and the deficiency of nature had been but little assisted by education or society; the greatest part of his life having been spent under the guidance of an illiterate[1] and miserly father;[2] and though he belonged to one of the universities,[3] he had merely kept the necessary terms, without forming at it any useful acquaintance.[4] The subjection in which his father had brought him up, had given him originally great humility of manner; but it was now a good deal counteracted by the self-conceit of a weak head, living in retirement, and the consequential[5] feelings of early and unexpected prosperity.[6] A fortunate chance had recommended him to Lady Catherine de Bourgh when the living[7] of Hunsford was vacant; and the respect which he felt for her high rank, and his veneration for her as his patroness, mingling with a very good opinion of himself, of his authority as a clergyman, and his rights as a rector, made him altogether a mixture of pride and obsequiousness, self-importance and humility.[8]

Having now a good house[9] and very sufficient income, he intended to marry;[10] and in seeking a reconciliation with the Longbourn family he had a wife in view, as he meant to chuse one of the daughters, if he found them as handsome and amiable as they were represented by common report. This was his plan of amends—of atonement[11]—for inheriting their father's estate; and he thought it an excellent one, full of eligibility[12] and suitableness, and excessively generous and disinterested on his own part.

1 Ignorant (not literally unable to read).

2 This is the closest the novel comes to conveying a little sympathy for Mr. Collins, who is consistently the object of mockery. His miserly, illiterate, autocratic father is partly responsible for his foolishness—although the narrator is careful to point out also "the deficiency of nature" in him.

3 He attended Oxford or Cambridge, universities that at this time had residence requirements (which Mr. Collins has fulfilled by keeping "the necessary terms") but demanded little else of their students.

4 Acquaintances who might be useful for establishing him in a career, but also acquaintances who might be intellectually and morally useful.

5 Self-important.

6 This bit of biography helps to account for Mr. Collins's apparent mixture of social insecurity with a sense of superiority. Being brought up in subjection to an "illiterate" father would presumably sap his confidence, but his "early . . . prosperity" and the patronage of a noblewoman help him to think very well of himself.

7 Clerical position, which would provide its possessor with sufficient income on which to live.

8 This is precisely the mixture indicated by his insistence on Lady Catherine's condescension and on the humbleness of his abode. Ivor Morris, in a curious little book focused on Mr. Collins as a character, describes

him as "secure in the two assumptions that are the bedrock of his being: the certainty of his excellence, and the necessity of his welfare" (*Mr Collins Considered: Approaches to Jane Austen* [London: Routledge and Kegan Paul, 1987], 2).

9 The narrator's summary makes it clear that Mr. Collins's abode is not humble.

10 His notion of marriage, in other words, is based on economic rather than erotic considerations.

11 The use of a biblical term suggests what will become increasingly apparent: that Mr. Collins, constantly claiming the privileges of a clergyman, has little grasp of Christian principles.

12 Desirability.

13 Folios are volumes of the largest size, made up of sheets of paper folded only once.

14 Accustomed.

His plan did not vary on seeing them.—Miss Bennet's lovely face confirmed his views, and established all his strictest notions of what was due to seniority; and for the first evening *she* was his settled choice. The next morning, however, made an alteration; for in a quarter of an hour's tête-à-tête with Mrs. Bennet before breakfast, a conversation beginning with his parsonage-house, and leading naturally to the avowal of his hopes, that a mistress for it might be found at Longbourn, produced from her, amid very complaisant smiles and general encouragement, a caution against the very Jane he had fixed on.—"As to her *younger* daughters she could not take upon her to say—she could not positively answer—but she did not *know* of any prepossession;—her *eldest* daughter, she must just mention—she felt it incumbent on her to hint, was likely to be very soon engaged."

Mr. Collins had only to change from Jane to Elizabeth—and it was soon done—done while Mrs. Bennet was stirring the fire. Elizabeth, equally next to Jane in birth and beauty, succeeded her of course.

Mrs. Bennet treasured up the hint, and trusted that she might soon have two daughters married; and the man whom she could not bear to speak of the day before, was now high in her good graces.

Lydia's intention of walking to Meryton was not forgotten; every sister except Mary agreed to go with her; and Mr. Collins was to attend them, at the request of Mr. Bennet, who was most anxious to get rid of him, and have his library to himself; for thither Mr. Collins had followed him after breakfast; and there he would continue, nominally engaged with one of the largest folios[13] in the collection, but really talking to Mr. Bennet, with little cessation, of his house and garden at Hunsford. Such doings discomposed Mr. Bennet exceedingly. In his library he had been always sure of leisure and tranquillity; and though prepared, as he told Elizabeth, to meet with folly and conceit in every other room of the house, he was used[14] to be free from them there; his civility, therefore, was most prompt in inviting Mr. Collins to join his daughters in their walk; and Mr. Collins, being in fact much better fitted for a walker than a reader, was extremely well pleased to close his large book, and go.

In pompous nothings on his side, and civil assents on that of his cousins, their time passed till they entered Meryton. The attention of the younger ones was then no longer to be gained by *him*. Their eyes were immediately wandering up in the street in quest of the officers, and nothing less than a very smart bonnet indeed, or a really new muslin[15] in a shop window, could recal them.

But the attention of every lady was soon caught by a young man, whom they had never seen before, of most gentlemanlike appearance, walking with an officer on the other side of the way. The officer was the very Mr. Denny, concerning whose return from London Lydia came to inquire, and he bowed as they passed. All were struck with the stranger's air,[16] all wondered who he could be, and Kitty and Lydia, determined if possible to find out, led the way across the street, under pretence of wanting something in an opposite shop, and fortunately had just gained the pavement when the two gentlemen turning back had reached the same spot. Mr. Denny addressed them directly, and entreated permission to introduce his friend, Mr. Wickham, who had returned with him the day before from town, and he was happy to say had accepted a commission in their corps. This was exactly as it should be; for the young man wanted[17] only regimentals to make him completely charming. His appearance was greatly in his favour; he had all the best part of beauty, a fine countenance, a good figure, and very pleasing address.[18] The introduction was followed up on his side by a happy[19] readiness of conversation—a readiness at the same time perfectly correct and unassuming; and the whole party were still standing and talking together very agreeably, when the sound of horses drew their notice, and Darcy and Bingley were seen riding down the street. On distinguishing the ladies of the group, the two gentlemen came directly towards them, and began the usual civilities. Bingley was the principal spokesman, and Miss Bennet the principal object. He was then, he said, on his way to Longbourn on purpose to inquire after her.[20] Mr. Darcy corroborated it with a bow, and was beginning to determine not to fix his eyes on Elizabeth, when they were suddenly arrested by the sight of the stranger, and Elizabeth happening to see the countenance of both as they looked at each other, was all astonishment at the effect of the meeting. Both changed colour, one looked white, the other red. Mr. Wickham, after a few moments,[21] touched his hat—a saluta-

15 Muslin, a lightweight cotton fabric, was fashionable in Austen's time. Introduced to Europe from the Middle East in the late seventeenth century, it had become particularly popular in France by the end of the eighteenth century. It was used for making dresses, so new prints would be eagerly sought. In her letters, Austen several times refers to buying, or wanting to buy, muslin in order to have a dress made of it. Thus, writing to Cassandra on 18 April 1811, she reports having gone to a linendraper's shop to buy checked muslin, and being "tempted by a pretty coloured muslin," of which she buys ten yards for Cassandra "on the chance of your liking it." If it does not suit her sister, she continues, "I sh^d not in the least mind keeping the whole. . . . [T]he pattern is a small red spot." In an early piece of juvenilia, *Frederic and Elfrida,* the eponymous characters, with a friend, visiting "the amiable Rebecca," address her in unison: "Your sentiments so nobly expressed on the different excellencies of Indian & English Muslins, & the judicious preference you give the former, have excited in me . . . admiration." *Frederic and Elfrida* is dedicated to Martha Lloyd, "As a small testimony of the gratitude I feel for your late generosity to me in finishing my muslin Cloak." Later, in *Northanger Abbey,* Austen has Henry Tilney win the approval of Mrs. Allen, the heroine's chaperone, by declaring himself to "understand muslin" and discussing the value and washability of various instances of it. Mrs. Allen concludes, on this basis, that the young man must "be a great comfort to" his sister (I, 3).

16 Grace, stylishness.

17 Needed.

18 Manner of speaking.

19 Fortunate.

20 After her health.

21 Ordinarily a gentleman would touch his hat immediately to acknowledge an acquaintance.

22 His apparent failure to notice would have been dictated by courtesy—and perhaps by prudence as well: desire to avoid an open quarrel between the other men.

23 Doses of medicine (for Jane).

24 This trivial narrative suggests the kinds of path that "news" travels in the community.

25 The name of the regiment, which would serve under the name of the county from which its members were taken. By law, every county had to supply a specified number of men for the militia. The reference to "the ——shire," as opposed to the name of an actual county, employs a convention left over from the eighteenth century, when fiction often utilized a pretense of factuality and substituted blanks for the names of people and places to suggest a purpose of preventing readers from identifying actual persons or localities.

26 Mrs. Phillips's sensibility is no more highly developed than Lydia's or Kitty's.

tion which Mr. Darcy just deigned to return. What could be the meaning of it?—It was impossible to imagine; it was impossible not to long to know.

In another minute, Mr. Bingley, but without seeming to have noticed what passed,[22] took leave and rode on with his friend.

Mr. Denny and Mr. Wickham walked with the young ladies to the door of Mr. Phillip's house, and then made their bows, in spite of Miss Lydia's pressing entreaties that they should come in, and even in spite of Mrs. Phillips's throwing up the parlour window, and loudly seconding the invitation.

Mrs. Phillips was always glad to see her nieces; and the two eldest, from their recent absence, were particularly welcome, and she was eagerly expressing her surprise at their sudden return home, which, as their own carriage had not fetched them, she should have known nothing about, if she had not happened to see Mr. Jones's shop boy in the street, who had told her that they were not to send any more draughts[23] to Netherfield because the Miss Bennets were come away,[24] when her civility was claimed towards Mr. Collins by Jane's introduction of him. She received him with her very best politeness, which he returned with as much more, apologising for his intrusion, without any previous acquaintance with her, which he could not help flattering himself however might be justified by his relationship to the young ladies who introduced him to her notice. Mrs. Phillips was quite awed by such an excess of good breeding; but her contemplation of one stranger was soon put an end to by exclamations and inquiries about the other; of whom, however, she could only tell her nieces what they already knew, that Mr. Denny had brought him from London, and that he was to have a lieutenant's commission in the ——shire.[25] She had been watching him the last hour, she said, as he walked up and down the street,[26] and had Mr. Wickham appeared, Kitty and Lydia would certainly have continued the occupation, but unluckily no one passed the windows now except a few of the officers, who in comparison with the stranger, were become "stupid, disagreeable fellows." Some of them were to dine with the Phillipses the next day, and their aunt promised to make her husband call on Mr. Wickham, and give him an invitation also, if the family from

Longbourn would come in the evening. This was agreed to, and Mrs. Phillips protested[27] that they would have a nice[28] comfortable noisy game of lottery tickets,[29] and a little bit of hot supper[30] afterwards. The prospect of such delights was very cheering, and they parted in mutual good spirits. Mr. Collins repeated his apologies in quitting the room, and was assured with unwearying civility that they were perfectly needless.

As they walked home, Elizabeth related to Jane what she had seen pass between the two gentlemen; but though Jane would have defended either or both, had they appeared to be wrong, she could no more explain such behaviour than her sister.

Mr. Collins on his return highly gratified Mrs. Bennet by admiring Mrs. Philips's manners and politeness. He protested that, except Lady Catherine and her daughter, he had never seen a more elegant woman; for she had not only received him with the utmost civility, but had even pointedly included him in her invitation for the next evening, although utterly unknown to her before. Something, he supposed, might be attributed to his connection with them,[31] but yet he had never met with so much attention in the whole course of his life.

27 Asserted.

28 Throughout *Pride and Prejudice,* Austen uses "nice" in its current sense, meaning pleasant or agreeable. In *Northanger Abbey,* however, written close to the time of the first version of *Pride and Prejudice,* she has Henry Tilney inveigh against this usage. Catherine speaks of a book as "nice," causing Henry to comment, "and this is a very nice day, and we are taking a very nice walk, and you are two very nice young ladies. Oh! it is a very nice word indeed!—it does for every thing. Originally perhaps it was applied only to express neatness, propriety, delicacy, or refinement;—people were nice in their dress, in their sentiments, or their choice. But now every commendation on every subject is comprised in that one word" (I, 14).

The now familiar meaning of "nice" as agreeable was relatively new in Austen's time, having developed only during the eighteenth century. The word had had an extraordinary range of meanings; the *OED* remarks that "the precise sense development in English is unclear." Derived from Romance-language terms meaning "foolish, silly, ignorant," "nice" originally meant exactly that. Its other meanings before Austen include these: wanton or lascivious, showy, effeminate, fastidious, refined, shy, pampered, trivial, risky, and dainty.

29 A card game for an unspecified number of players, in which a player won if he or she held a certain card, the "lottery ticket."

30 The offer of a hot supper, like that of a noisy game of lottery tickets, betrays Mrs. Phillips's vulgarity. In polite society by this time, only cold suppers, if any, were served, except at balls.

31 In supposing that "something" is to be attributed to his relationship to the Bennets, Collins suggests that he thinks his own attractiveness is the primary cause of Mrs. Phillips's hospitality.

16

1 Such scruples may come from Mr. Collins's excessive politeness. His remark recorded at the end of the previous chapter, though, about the great attention he has received, strongly suggests that extreme egocentricity underlies such politeness. How, he may wonder, can the Bennets possibly get along without him for an evening?

2 Lady Catherine's establishment is evidently so splendid that she has different breakfast parlors for summer and winter, the difference depending on the advantageousness of a particular exposure for warm or cold temperatures. By implication, she even has more than one summer parlor. Her splendor appears to serve Mr. Collins as an imaginative extension of his own. He is exceedingly interested in all physical appurtenances of prosperity.

3 A carved decoration surrounding the fireplace, which, made of wood or marble and heavily ornamented, might be extremely elaborate. Nonetheless, £800 is an extraordinarily large sum to spend for such decoration. The detail emphasizes Lady Catherine's great wealth and Mr. Collins's awe at it.

4 We begin to realize the limitations of Mr. Collins's conversational material, which includes only the glories of Lady Catherine (with emphasis on the appurtenances of her wealth) and of himself.

5 The gentlemen have presumably been lingering over their after-dinner wine. The Bennet girls and their

As NO OBJECTION WAS MADE TO the young people's engagement with their aunt, and all Mr. Collins's scruples of leaving Mr. and Mrs. Bennet for a single evening during his visit[1] were most steadily resisted, the coach conveyed him and his five cousins at a suitable hour to Meryton; and the girls had the pleasure of hearing, as they entered the drawing-room, that Mr. Wickham had accepted their uncle's invitation, and was then in the house.

When this information was given, and they had all taken their seats, Mr. Collins was at leisure to look around him and admire, and he was so much struck with the size and furniture of the apartment, that he declared he might almost have supposed himself in the small summer breakfast parlour[2] at Rosings; a comparison that did not at first convey much gratification; but when Mrs. Phillips understood from him what Rosings was, and who was its proprietor, when she had listened to the description of only one of Lady Catherine's drawing-rooms, and found that the chimney-piece[3] alone had cost eight hundred pounds, she felt all the force of the compliment, and would hardly have resented a comparison with the housekeeper's room.

In describing to her all the grandeur of Lady Catherine and her mansion, with occasional digressions in praise of his own humble abode, and the improvements it was receiving,[4] he was happily employed until the gentlemen joined them;[5] and he found in Mrs. Phillips a very attentive listener, whose opinion of his consequence[6] increased with what she heard, and who was resolving to retail[7] it all

Sir Thomas Banks, chimneypiece in Daylesford House, Gloucestershire, built 1789–1793. This elaborate chimneypiece suggests the kind of expensive ornamentation that Mr. Collins so greatly admired in Lady Catherine's establishment. Jane Austen visited Daylesford in 1806.

cousin have been invited for the evening, not for dinner.

6 Importance.

7 Repeat in detail.

8 Evidently they could not stand to hear again about Lady Catherine's splendor and Mr. Collins's importance.

9 A piano, which the Phillipses are evidently too uncultivated to own.

10 Such imitations, on wood or ceramic, would have been made by pasting pictures on the surface, modeled after the decorations on actual china, and varnishing over them.

11 Exuding. Port wine is a sweet, fortified wine (originally from Portugal), customarily drunk after dinner.

among her neighbours as soon as she could. To the girls, who could not listen to their cousin,[8] and who had nothing to do but to wish for an instrument,[9] and examine their own indifferent imitations of china[10] on the mantelpiece, the interval of waiting appeared very long. It was over at last however. The gentlemen did approach; and when Mr. Wickham walked into the room, Elizabeth felt that she had neither been seeing him before, nor thinking of him since, with the smallest degree of unreasonable admiration. The officers of the ——shire were in general a very creditable, gentlemanlike set, and the best of them were of the present party; but Mr. Wickham was as far beyond them all in person, countenance, air, and walk, as *they* were superior to the broad-faced, stuffy uncle Phillips, breathing[11] port wine, who followed them into the room.

Mr. Wickham was the happy man towards whom almost every female eye was turned, and Elizabeth was the happy woman by whom

12 This is Mr. Collins's diction: as usual, a cliché.

13 What is called in America an English muffin.

14 A precursor of bridge, more fashionable—and more demanding—than games like lottery tickets. At whist, four people play in partnerships of two.

15 She could not hope to be told about the relationship because personal conversation would not be appropriate on first acquaintance. Certainly she cannot properly ask a personal question. Wickham's intimate self-revelations are improper—a fact that Elizabeth does not realize at the time he offers them.

he finally seated himself; and the agreeable manner in which he immediately fell into conversation, though it was only on its being a wet night, and on the probability of a rainy season, made her feel that the commonest, dullest, most threadbare topic might be rendered interesting by the skill of the speaker.

With such rivals for the notice of the fair,[12] as Mr. Wickham and the officers, Mr. Collins seemed likely to sink into insignificance; to the young ladies he certainly was nothing; but he had still at intervals a kind listener in Mrs. Phillips, and was, by her watchfulness, most abundantly supplied with coffee and muffin.[13]

When the card tables were placed, he had the opportunity of obliging her in return, by sitting down to whist.[14]

"I know little of the game at present," said he, "but I shall be glad to improve myself, for in my situation in life—" Mrs. Phillips was very thankful for his compliance, but could not wait for his reason.

Mr. Wickham did not play at whist, and with ready delight was he received at the other table between Elizabeth and Lydia. At first there seemed danger of Lydia's engrossing him entirely for she was a most determined talker; but being likewise extremely fond of lottery tickets, she soon grew too much interested in the game, too eager in making bets and exclaiming after prizes, to have attention for any one in particular. Allowing for the common demands of the game, Mr. Wickham was therefore at leisure to talk to Elizabeth, and she was very willing to hear him, though what she chiefly wished to hear she could not hope to be told, the history of his acquaintance with Mr. Darcy.[15] She dared not even mention that gentleman. Her curiosity however was unexpectedly relieved. Mr. Wickham began the subject himself. He inquired how far Netherfield was from Meryton; and, after receiving her answer, asked in a hesitating manner how long Mr. Darcy had been staying there.

"About a month," said Elizabeth; and then, unwilling to let the subject drop, added, "he is a man of very large property in Derbyshire, I understand."

"Yes," replied Mr. Wickham;—"his estate there is a noble one. A clear ten thousand per annum. You could not have met with a person more capable of giving you certain information on that head than myself—for I have been connected with his family in a particular manner from my infancy."

Elizabeth could not but look surprised.

"You may well be surprised, Miss Bennet, at such an assertion, after seeing, as you probably might, the very cold manner of our meeting yesterday.—Are you much acquainted with Mr. Darcy?"

"As much as I ever wish to be," cried Elizabeth warmly,—"I have spent four days in the same house with him, and I think him very disagreeable."[16]

"I have no right to give *my* opinion," said Wickham, "as to his being agreeable or otherwise. I am not qualified to form one. I have known him too long and too well to be a fair judge. It is impossible for *me* to be impartial. But I believe your opinion of him would in general astonish—and perhaps you would not express it quite so strongly any where else.—Here you are in your own family."

"Upon my word, I say no more *here* than I might say in any house in the neighbourhood, except Netherfield. He is not at all liked in Hertfordshire.[17] Every body is disgusted with his pride. You will not find him more favourably spoken of by any one."

"I cannot pretend to be sorry," said Wickham, after a short interruption, "that he or that any man should not be estimated beyond their deserts; but with *him* I believe it does not often happen. The world is blinded by his fortune and consequence, or frightened by his high and imposing manners, and sees him only as he chuses to be seen."

"I should take him, even on *my* slight acquaintance, to be an ill-tempered man." Wickham only shook his head.

"I wonder," said he, at the next opportunity of speaking, "whether he is likely to be in this country[18] much longer."

"I do not at all know; but I *heard* nothing of his going away when I was at Netherfield. I hope your plans in favour of the — —shire will not be affected by his being in the neighbourhood."

"Oh! no—it is not for *me* to be driven away by Mr. Darcy. If *he* wishes to avoid seeing *me,* he must go. We are not on friendly terms, and it always gives me pain to meet him, but I have no reason for avoiding *him* but what I might proclaim to all the world; a sense of

16 An indiscreet utterance: a proclamation of her feelings that has not been asked for, no doubt motivated partly by her memory of the apparent antagonism between the two men.

17 An unsupported categorical statement that resembles her mother's verbal extravagance.

18 Region.

19 Courtliness to the female sex. Wickham is hinting that Elizabeth herself exemplifies the "good society" he seeks. The *OED* includes among its definitions of *gallantry* "amorous intercourse or intrigue" and cites a line from Lord Byron's *Don Juan* (1819): "What men call gallantry, and gods adultery." Wickham's "gallantry" is not necessarily innocent.

20 Appropriate, proper to be chosen.

21 Ordination at this time required no special training. Wickham does not mean that he was educated particularly for the church; only that he was expected to become a clergyman.

22 The living would become available, and be presentable, at the death of the current incumbent.

23 Many wealthy landowners had the right to distribute several ecclesiastical positions.

very great ill usage, and most painful regrets at his being what he is. His father, Miss Bennet, the late Mr. Darcy, was one of the best men that ever breathed, and the truest friend I ever had; and I can never be in company with this Mr. Darcy without being grieved to the soul by a thousand tender recollections. His behaviour to myself has been scandalous; but I verily believe I could forgive him any thing and every thing, rather than his disappointing the hopes and disgracing the memory of his father."

Elizabeth found the interest of the subject increase, and listened with all her heart; but the delicacy of it prevented further inquiry.

Mr. Wickham began to speak on more general topics, Meryton, the neighbourhood, the society, appearing highly pleased with all that he had yet seen, and speaking of the latter especially, with gentle but very intelligible gallantry.[19]

"It was the prospect of constant society, and good society," he added, "which was my chief inducement to enter the ——shire. I knew it to be a most respectable, agreeable corps, and my friend Denny tempted me further by his account of their present quarters, and the very great attentions and excellent acquaintance Meryton had procured them. Society, I own, is necessary to me. I have been a disappointed man, and my spirits will not bear solitude. I *must* have employment and society. A military life is not what I was intended for, but circumstances have now made it eligible.[20] The church *ought* to have been my profession—I was brought up for the church,[21] and I should at this time have been in possession of a most valuable living, had it pleased the gentleman we were speaking of just now."

"Indeed!"

"Yes—the late Mr. Darcy bequeathed me the next presentation[22] of the best living in his gift.[23] He was my godfather, and excessively attached to me. I cannot do justice to his kindness. He meant to provide for me amply, and thought he had done it; but when the living fell, it was given elsewhere."

"Good heavens!" cried Elizabeth; "but how could *that* be? How could his will be disregarded? Why did you not seek legal redress?"

"There was just such an informality in the terms of the bequest as to give me no hope from law. A man of honour could not have doubted the intention, but Mr. Darcy chose to doubt it—or to treat it as a merely conditional recommendation, and to assert that I had forfeited all claim to it by extravagance, imprudence, in short any thing or nothing. Certain it is, that the living became vacant two years ago, exactly as I was of an age to hold it, and that it was given to another man; and no less certain is it, that I cannot accuse myself of having really done any thing to deserve to lose it. I have a warm, un-guarded temper, and I may perhaps have sometimes spoken my opin-ion *of* him, and *to* him, too freely. I can recal nothing worse. But the fact is, that we are very different sort of men, and that he hates me."

"This is quite shocking!—He deserves to be publicly disgraced."

"Some time or other he *will* be—but it shall not be by *me*. Till I can forget his father, I can never defy or expose *him*."

Elizabeth honoured him for such feelings, and thought him hand-somer than ever as he expressed them.[24]

"But what," said she, after a pause, "can have been his motive?—what can have induced him to behave so cruelly?"

"A thorough, determined dislike of me—a dislike which I cannot but attribute in some measure to jealousy. Had the late Mr. Darcy liked me less, his son might have borne with me better; but his father's uncommon attachment to me, irritated him I believe very early in life. He had not a temper to bear the sort of competition in which we stood—the sort of preference which was often given me."

"I had not thought Mr. Darcy so bad as this—though I have never liked him, I had not thought so very ill of him—I had supposed him to be despising his fellow-creatures in general, but did not suspect him of descending to such malicious revenge, such injustice, such in-humanity as this!"

After a few minutes' reflection, however, she continued, "I *do* re-member his boasting one day, at Netherfield, of the implacability of his resentments, of his having an unforgiving temper.[25] His disposi-tion must be dreadful."

"I will not trust myself on the subject," replied Wickham; "*I* can hardly be just to him."

Elizabeth was again deep in thought, and after a time exclaimed, "To treat in such a manner, the godson, the friend, the favourite of

24 Elizabeth's response to Wickham's physical appear-ance, which changes according to her reaction to his words, emphasizes the degree to which her judgments of people (like those of others in her community) often rest on a basis of appearance.

25 This is a distortion of what Darcy actually said (he was not boasting) that emphasizes once more the de-gree to which Elizabeth's pre-judgment of Darcy shapes her capacity even to hear him. She is unable to assess him accurately.

26 In other words, countenance signifies character.

27 He served as steward of the estate.

28 Astonishing.

29 This important speech emphasizes for the first time in the novel the possibility that pride might be a positive characteristic. Elizabeth's earlier remark that she could forgive Darcy's pride if he hadn't hurt hers hints at an equation between pride and self-respect, but Wickham's speech adds a detailed account of how pride can function to good ends.

30 The qualities of generosity, charity, and concern for his tenants that the senior Mr. Darcy had displayed.

his father!"—She could have added, "A young man, too, like *you,* whose very countenance may vouch for your being amiable"[26]—but she contented herself with "And one, too, who had probably been his companion from childhood, connected together, as I think you said, in the closest manner!"

"We were born in the same parish, within the same park, the greatest part of our youth was passed together; inmates of the same house, sharing the same amusements, objects of the same parental care. *My* father began life in the profession which your uncle, Mr. Phillips, appears to do so much credit to—but he gave up every thing to be of use to the late Mr. Darcy and devoted all his time to the care of the Pemberley property.[27] He was most highly esteemed by Mr. Darcy, a most intimate, confidential friend. Mr. Darcy often acknowledged himself to be under the greatest obligations to my father's active superintendence, and when immediately before my father's death, Mr. Darcy gave him a voluntary promise of providing for me, I am convinced that he felt it to be as much a debt of gratitude to *him,* as of affection to myself."

"How strange!" cried Elizabeth. "How abominable!—I wonder that the very pride of this Mr. Darcy has not made him just to you!—If from no better motive, that he should not have been too proud to be dishonest,—for dishonesty I must call it."

"It *is* wonderful,"[28] replied Wickham,—"for almost all his actions may be traced to pride;—and pride has often been his best friend. It has connected him nearer with virtue than any other feeling. But we are none of us consistent; and in his behaviour to me, there were stronger impulses even than pride."

"Can such abominable pride as his, have ever done him good?"

"Yes. It has often led him to be liberal and generous,—to give his money freely, to display hospitality, to assist his tenants, and relieve the poor.[29] Family pride, and *filial* pride, for he is very proud of what his father was, have done this. Not to appear to disgrace his family, to degenerate from the popular qualities,[30] or lose the influence of the Pemberley House, is a powerful motive. He has also *brotherly* pride, which with *some* brotherly affection, makes him a very kind and careful guardian of his sister; and you will hear him generally cried up[31] as the most attentive and best of brothers."

"What sort of girl is Miss Darcy?"

He shook his head.—"I wish I could call her amiable.[32] It gives me pain to speak ill of a Darcy. But she is too much like her brother,—very, very proud.—As a child, she was affectionate and pleasing, and extremely fond of me; and I have devoted hours and hours to her amusement. But she is nothing to me now. She is a handsome girl, about fifteen or sixteen, and I understand highly accomplished. Since her father's death, her home has been London, where a lady lives with her, and superintends her education."

After many pauses and many trials of other subjects, Elizabeth could not help reverting once more to the first, and saying,

"I am astonished at his intimacy with Mr. Bingley! How can Mr. Bingley, who seems good humour itself, and is, I really believe, truly amiable, be in friendship with such a man? How can they suit each other?—Do you know Mr. Bingley?"

"Not at all."

"He is a sweet tempered, amiable, charming man. He cannot know what Mr. Darcy is."

"Probably not;—but Mr. Darcy can please where he chuses. He does not want[33] abilities. He can be a conversible[34] companion if he thinks it worth his while. Among those who are at all his equals in consequence, he is a very different man from what he is to the less prosperous. His pride never deserts him; but with the rich he is liberal-minded, just, sincere, rational, honourable, and perhaps agreeable,—allowing something for fortune and figure."[35]

The whist party soon afterwards breaking up, the players gathered round the other table and Mr. Collins took his station between his cousin Elizabeth and Mrs. Phillips.—The usual inquiries as to his success was made by the latter. It had not been very great; he had lost every point; but when Mrs. Phillips began to express her concern thereupon, he assured her with much earnest gravity that it was not of the least importance, that he considered the money as a mere trifle, and begged she would not make herself uneasy.

31 Celebrated. To cry up means to extol; figuratively, to praise in a loud voice, from the early associations of crying with loudness.

32 Likeable.

33 Lack.

34 Good in conversation.

35 Darcy's wealth and good looks, Wickham suggests, help to make him "agreeable"; he is perhaps conscious that his own good looks contribute to making him seem "amiable" to Elizabeth and others.

36 Object of concern.

37 Darcy's mother, in other words, was the daughter of an earl. She evidently married a commoner; hence Darcy, despite his wealth, has no title, though he descends from a member of the nobility.

38 By marrying.

"I know very well, madam," said he, "that when persons sit down to a card table, they must take their chance of these things,—and happily I am not in such circumstances as to make five shillings any object.[36] There are undoubtedly many who could not say the same, but thanks to Lady Catherine de Bourgh, I am removed far beyond the necessity of regarding little matters."

Mr. Wickham's attention was caught; and after observing Mr. Collins for a few moments, he asked Elizabeth in a low voice whether her relation was very intimately acquainted with the family of de Bourgh.

"Lady Catherine de Bourgh," she replied, "has very lately given him a living. I hardly know how Mr. Collins was first introduced to her notice, but he certainly has not known her long."

"You know of course that Lady Catherine de Bourgh and Lady Anne Darcy[37] were sisters; consequently that she is aunt to the present Mr. Darcy."

"No, indeed, I did not.—I knew nothing at all of Lady Catherine's connections. I never heard of her existence till the day before yesterday."

"Her daughter, Miss de Bourgh, will have a very large fortune, and it is believed that she and her cousin will unite the two estates."[38]

This information made Elizabeth smile, as she thought of poor Miss Bingley. Vain indeed must be all her attentions, vain and useless her affection for his sister and her praise of himself, if he were already self-destined for another.

"Mr. Collins," said she, "speaks highly both of Lady Catherine and her daughter; but from some particulars that he has related of her ladyship, I suspect his gratitude misleads him, and that in spite of her being his patroness, she is an arrogant, conceited woman."

"I believe her to be both in a great degree," replied Wickham; "I have not seen her for many years, but I very well remember that I never liked her, and that her manners were dictatorial and insolent. She has the reputation of being remarkably sensible and clever; but I rather believe she derives part of her abilities from her rank and fortune, part from her authoritative manner, and the rest from the pride of her nephew, who chuses that every one connected with him should have an understanding of the first class."

Elizabeth allowed that he had given a very rational[39] account of it, and they continued talking together with mutual satisfaction till supper[40] put an end to cards; and gave the rest of the ladies their share of Mr. Wickham's attentions. There could be no conversation in the noise of Mrs. Phillips's supper party, but his manners recommended him to every body. Whatever he said, was said well; and whatever he did, done gracefully. Elizabeth went away with her head full of him. She could think of nothing but of Mr. Wickham, and of what he had told her, all the way home; but there was not time for her even to mention his name as they went, for neither Lydia nor Mr. Collins were once silent. Lydia talked incessantly of lottery tickets, of the fish[41] she had lost and the fish she had won; and Mr. Collins in describing the civility of Mr. and Mrs. Philips, protesting that he did not in the least regard his losses at whist, enumerating all the dishes at supper, and repeatedly fearing that he crouded his cousins, had more to say than he could well manage before the carriage stopped at Longbourn House.

39 By labeling Wickham's account "rational," Elizabeth intends to praise it. Her terminology, however, is hardly accurate for such a prejudicial narrative.

40 Supper was usually a relatively light meal, served several hours after dinner—perhaps nine or ten P.M.

41 Tokens for the game, often made in the shape of fish.

17

1 "Amiable appearance" seems a curious guarantee of veracity, emphasizing the superficial grounds upon which judgments are often made. The crucial term here, from Jane's point of view, is "amiable": she assumes that the quality of likability testifies to goodness.

2 Self-interested.

3 As Elizabeth has earlier confessed, she dearly loves a laugh. Jane has a highly developed capacity to resist her sister's laughter.

4 Reputation. The word *character* had in Austen's time two distinct senses in relation to human beings; *Pride and Prejudice* employs both. With an original concrete meaning—a distinctive mark impressed or engraved on a substance—the word was extended, according to the *OED,* to denote "a graphic symbol standing for a sound, syllable, or notion" or "individual handwriting." Its two moral meanings also suggest an actual phenomenon and something that stands for it. *Character* might mean "the sum of the moral and mental qualities which distinguish an individual or a race" or, as here, "the estimate formed of a person's qualities; reputation."

5 Jane thinks first of Bingley's involvement in the situation: she wants most of all to acquit him of any error.

6 Interest in physiognomy, a pseudo-science that purports to read character from facial expression, was widespread in the eighteenth and nineteenth centu-

ELIZABETH RELATED TO JANE THE NEXT DAY, what had passed between Mr. Wickham and herself. Jane listened with astonishment and concern;—she knew not how to believe that Mr. Darcy could be so unworthy of Mr. Bingley's regard; and yet, it was not in her nature to question the veracity of a young man of such amiable appearance[1] as Wickham.—The possibility of his having really endured such unkindness, was enough to interest all her tender feelings; and nothing therefore remained to be done, but to think well of them both, to defend the conduct of each, and throw into the account of accident or mistake, whatever could not be otherwise explained.

"They have both," said she, "been deceived, I dare say, in some way or other, of which we can form no idea. Interested[2] people have perhaps misrepresented each to the other. It is, in short, impossible for us to conjecture the causes or circumstances which may have alienated them, without actual blame on either side."

"Very true, indeed;—and now, my dear Jane, what have you got to say on behalf of the interested people who have probably been concerned in the business?—Do clear *them* too, or we shall be obliged to think ill of somebody."

"Laugh as much as you chuse, but you will not laugh me out of my opinion.[3] My dearest Lizzy, do but consider in what a disgraceful light it places Mr. Darcy, to be treating his father's favourite in such a manner,—one whom his father had promised to provide for.—It is impossible. No man of common humanity, no man who had any value for his character,[4] could be capable of it. Can his most intimate friends be so excessively deceived in him?[5] oh! no."

"I can much more easily believe Mr. Bingley's being imposed on, than that Mr. Wickham should invent such a history of himself as he gave me last night; names, facts, every thing mentioned without ceremony. — If it be not so, let Mr. Darcy contradict it. Besides, there was truth in his looks."[6]

"It is difficult indeed — it is distressing. — One does not know what to think."

"I beg your pardon; — one knows exactly what to think."[7]

But Jane could think with certainty on only one point — that Mr. Bingley, if he *had* been imposed on, would have much to suffer when the affair became public.

The two young ladies were summoned from the shrubbery[8] where this conversation passed, by the arrival of some of the very persons of whom they had been speaking; Mr. Bingley and his sisters came to give their personal invitation for the long expected ball at Netherfield, which was fixed for the following Tuesday. The two ladies were delighted to see their dear friend again, called it an age since they had met, and repeatedly asked what she had been doing with herself since their separation.[9] To the rest of the family they paid little attention; avoiding Mrs. Bennet as much as possible, saying not much to Elizabeth, and nothing at all to the others. They were soon gone again, rising from their seats with an activity which took their brother by surprise, and hurrying off as if eager to escape from Mrs. Bennet's civilities.

The prospect of the Netherfield ball was extremely agreeable to every female of the family. Mrs. Bennet chose to consider it as given in compliment to her eldest daughter, and was particularly flattered by receiving the invitation from Mr. Bingley himself, instead of a ceremonious card. Jane pictured to herself a happy evening in the society of her two friends, and the attentions of their brother; and Elizabeth thought with pleasure of dancing a great deal with Mr. Wickham, and of seeing a confirmation of every thing[10] in Mr. Darcy's looks and behaviour.[11] The happiness anticipated by Catherine

ries. Henry Fielding mocks it in *Joseph Andrews* (1742) through the character of Parson Adams, who hears from the host of an inn of the many betrayals that a neighboring squire has been guilty of. Indeed, the squire has tricked Adams himself, who nonetheless says that "he hath in his Countenance sufficient Symptoms of . . . that Sweetness of Disposition which furnishes out a good Christian." When the host points out that one can't tell anything from a man's face, Adams insists that he has learned from books, the most dependable guide, "that Nature generally imprints such a Portraiture of the Mind in the Countenance, that a skilful Physiognomist will rarely be deceived" (II, 17).

Johann Kaspar Lavater, a Swiss clergyman, wrote an extensive treatise on the subject, *Physiognomische Fragmente* (1775–1778). Translated into English in 1793, it exercised considerable influence. Austen, however, is skeptical. A propensity to judge people on the basis of their looks turns up again in *Emma*, where Emma's initial enthusiasm for Harriet Smith is based mainly on the girl's "soft blue eyes" and her "look of great sweetness" (I, 3). Both Elizabeth and Jane have consistently cited Wickham's looks as evidence of his amiability and authenticity.

7 Elizabeth's belief that she knows "exactly what to think" indicates a clear moral danger: she is all too certain of the validity of her opinions.

8 A plot planted with shrubs.

9 In other words, they deliver themselves of conventional social patter, which Austen also mocked in *Northanger Abbey*.

10 That is, a confirmation of Darcy's wickedness, as described by Wickham.

11 If Wickham's looks can guarantee the truth of his narrative, Darcy's looks may be expected to reinforce conviction.

12 It was widely considered improper for members of the clergy to engage in dancing. Mr. Collins, however, feels sure that neither the high church official to whom he is ultimately responsible nor his patroness would disapprove.

13 Good character.

and Lydia depended less on any single event, or any particular person, for though they each, like Elizabeth, meant to dance half the evening with Mr. Wickham, he was by no means the only partner who could satisfy them, and a ball was at any rate, a ball. And even Mary could assure her family that she had no disinclination for it.

"While I can have my mornings to myself," said she, "it is enough. —I think it no sacrifice to join occasionally in evening engagements. Society has claims on us all; and I profess myself one of those who consider intervals of recreation and amusement as desirable for every body."

Elizabeth's spirits were so high on this occasion, that though she did not often speak unnecessarily to Mr. Collins, she could not help asking him whether he intended to accept Mr. Bingley's invitation, and if he did, whether he would think it proper to join in the evening's amusement; and she was rather surprised to find that he entertained no scruple whatever on that head, and was very far from dreading a rebuke either from the Archbishop, or Lady Catherine de Bourgh, by venturing to dance.[12]

"I am by no means of opinion, I assure you," said he, "that a ball of this kind, given by a young man of character,[13] to respectable people, can have any evil tendency; and I am so far from objecting to dancing myself, that I shall hope to be honoured with the hands of all my fair cousins in the course of the evening, and I take this opportunity of soliciting yours, Miss Elizabeth, for the two first dances especially,— a preference which I trust my cousin Jane will attribute to the right cause, and not to any disrespect for her."

Elizabeth felt herself completely taken in. She had fully proposed being engaged by Mr. Wickham for those very dances:—and to have Mr. Collins instead!—her liveliness had been never worse timed. There was no help for it, however. Mr. Wickham's happiness and her own were per force delayed a little longer, and Mr. Collins's proposal accepted with as good a grace as she could. She was not the better pleased with his gallantry from the idea it suggested of something more.—It now first struck her, that *she* was selected from among her sisters as worthy of being mistress of Hunsford Parsonage, and of assisting to form a quadrille table at Rosings, in the absence of more eligible visitors. The idea soon reached to conviction, as she observed his increasing civilities toward herself, and heard his frequent attempt at a compliment on her wit and vivacity; and though more astonished than gratified herself, by this effect of her charms, it was not long before her mother gave her to understand that the probability of their marriage was exceedingly agreeable to *her.* Elizabeth however did not chuse to take the hint, being well aware that a serious dispute must be the consequence of any reply. Mr. Collins might never make the offer, and till he did, it was useless to quarrel about him.

If there had not been a Netherfield ball to prepare for and talk of, the younger Miss Bennets would have been in a pitiable state at this time, for from the day of the invitation, to the day of the ball, there was such a succession of rain as prevented their walking to Meryton once. No aunt, no officers, no news could be sought after;—the very shoe-roses[14] for Netherfield were got by proxy. Even Elizabeth might have found some trial of her patience in weather, which totally suspended the improvement of her acquaintance with Mr. Wickham; and nothing less than a dance on Tuesday, could have made such a Friday, Saturday, Sunday and Monday, endurable to Kitty and Lydia.

14 A shoe-rose is a piece of shoelace or ribbon tied into a rosette and worn on the front of the shoe. Shoe-roses had become fashionable late in the eighteenth century.

18

1 Such as remembering that people sometimes become ill and are thus unable to attend a social event, or that Wickham might have a conflicting obligation—and remembering his strained relations with Darcy, which despite his proclaimed fearlessness might keep him away from the ball or might prevent Bingley from inviting him.

2 Her use of military metaphors makes joking reference to his profession.

3 News.

4 Conventional inquiries about the family's health and well-being.

Till Elizabeth entered the drawing-room at Netherfield, and looked in vain for Mr. Wickham among the cluster of red coats there assembled, a doubt of his being present had never occurred to her. The certainty of meeting him had not been checked by any of those recollections that might not unreasonably have alarmed her.[1] She had dressed with more than usual care, and prepared in the highest spirits for the conquest of all that remained unsubdued of his heart, trusting that it was not more than might be won[2] in the course of the evening. But in an instant arose the dreadful suspicion of his being purposely omitted for Mr. Darcy's pleasure in the Bingleys' invitation to the officers; and though this was not exactly the case, the absolute fact of his absence was pronounced by his friend Denny, to whom Lydia eagerly applied, and who told them that Wickham had been obliged to go to town on business the day before, and was not yet returned; adding, with a significant smile,

"I do not imagine his business would have called him away just now, if he had not wanted to avoid a certain gentleman here."

This part of his intelligence,[3] though unheard by Lydia, was caught by Elizabeth, and as it assured her that Darcy was not less answerable for Wickham's absence than if her first surmise had been just, every feeling of displeasure against the former was so sharpened by immediate disappointment, that she could hardly reply with tolerable civility to the polite inquiries[4] which he directly afterwards approached to make.—Attention, forbearance, patience with Darcy, was injury to Wickham. She was resolved against any sort of conversation with him, and turned away with a degree of ill humour, which she could not wholly surmount even in speaking to Mr. Bingley, whose blind partiality[5] provoked her.

But Elizabeth was not formed for ill-humour; and though every prospect[6] of her own was destroyed for the evening, it could not dwell long on her spirits; and having told all her griefs to Charlotte Lucas, whom she had not seen for a week, she was soon able to make a voluntary transition to the oddities of her cousin, and to point him out to her particular notice. The first two dances, however, brought a return of distress; they were dances of mortification. Mr. Collins, awkward and solemn, apologising instead of attending,[7] and often moving wrong without being aware of it, gave her all the shame and misery which a disagreeable partner for a couple of dances can give. The moment of her release from him was exstacy.

She danced next with an officer, and had the refreshment of talking of Wickham, and of hearing that he was universally liked. When those dances were over, she returned to Charlotte Lucas, and was in conversation with her, when she found herself suddenly addressed by Mr. Darcy, who took her so much by surprise in his application for her hand,[8] that, without knowing what she did, she accepted him.[9] He walked away again immediately, and she was left to fret over her own want of presence of mind; Charlotte tried to console her.

"I dare say you will find him very agreeable."

"Heaven forbid!—*That* would be the greatest misfortune of all!—To find a man agreeable whom one is determined to hate!—Do not wish me such an evil."

When the dancing recommenced, however, and Darcy approached to claim her hand, Charlotte could not help cautioning her in a whisper not to be a simpleton and allow her fancy for Wickham to make her appear unpleasant in the eyes of a man of ten times his consequence.[10] Elizabeth made no answer, and took her place in the set,[11] amazed at the dignity to which she was arrived in being allowed to stand opposite to Mr. Darcy, and reading in her neighbours' looks their equal amazement in beholding it.[12] They stood for some time without speaking a word; and she began to imagine that their silence was to last through the two dances, and at first was resolved not to

5 To Darcy.

6 Expectation.

7 Paying attention.

8 For the dance.

9 Thus violating the promise she had made to her mother: "I believe, Ma'am, I may safely promise you *never* to dance with him" (I, 5).

10 Charlotte is absolutely consistent in her eye for the matrimonial chance—the best chance being, from her point of view as from Mrs. Bennet's, at a man of "consequence" and wealth. Her caution to Elizabeth indicates how completely she subordinates feeling to economic advantage: no matter how Elizabeth feels about Darcy, she should, from Charlotte's point of view, encourage him.

11 The array of couples required to perform a country dance.

12 The neighbors may or may not have any reaction at all to Elizabeth's dancing with Darcy. What matters is her reading of their looks. Reading of looks generates much of the plot in *Pride and Prejudice*.

R. Sharples, "The Cloakroom, Clifton Assembly Rooms," 1817–1818. This painting of the Clifton Assembly Rooms in Bristol conveys the festive atmosphere of a ball. Ladies and gentlemen gather in the cloakroom before dancing. The painting is the first major work of Austen's contemporary Rolinda Sharples (1793–1838), who had decided at the age of thirteen that she would be a professional painter.

break it; till suddenly fancying that it would be the greater punishment to her partner to oblige him to talk, she made some slight observation on the dance.[13] He replied, and was again silent. After a pause of some minutes she addressed him a second time with

"It is *your* turn to say something now, Mr. Darcy.—*I* talked about the dance, and *you* ought to make some sort of remark on the size of the room, or the number of couples."[14]

He smiled, and assured her that whatever she wished him to say should be said.

"Very well.—That reply will do for the present.—Perhaps by and by I may observe that private balls are much pleasanter than public ones.[15]—But *now* we may be silent."

"Do you talk by rule, then, while you are dancing?"

"Sometimes. One must speak a little, you know. It would look odd to be entirely silent for half an hour together; and yet for the advantage of *some,* conversation ought to be so arranged as that they may have the trouble of saying as little as possible."

"Are you consulting your own feelings in the present case, or do you imagine that you are gratifying mine?"

"Both," replied Elizabeth archly; "for I have always seen a great similarity in the turn of our minds.—We are each of an unsocial, taciturn disposition, unwilling to speak, unless we expect to say something that will amaze the whole room, and be handed down to posterity with all the eclat[16] of a proverb."[17]

"This is no very striking resemblance[18] of your own character, I am sure," said he. "How near it may be to *mine,* I cannot pretend to say.—*You* think it a faithful portrait undoubtedly."

"I must not decide on my own performance."[19]

He made no answer, and they were again silent till they had gone down the dance, when he asked her if she and her sisters did not very often walk to Meryton. She answered in the affirmative, and, unable to resist the temptation, added, "When you met us there the other day, we had just been forming a new acquaintance."

The effect was immediate. A deeper shade of hauteur[20] overspread his features, but he said not a word, and Elizabeth, though blam-

13 In *Northanger Abbey,* Henry Tilney suggests to Catherine that a country dance is "an emblem of marriage." When Catherine disagrees, on the ground that marriage lasts a lot longer, Henry elaborates the analogy. In both instances, he explains, "it is an engagement between man and woman, formed for the advantage of each; and . . . when once entered into, they belong exclusively to each other, till the moment of its dissolution . . . it is their duty, each to endeavour to give the other no cause for wishing that he or she had bestowed themselves elsewhere" (I, 10). Darcy has asked for Elizabeth's hand as a temporary, not a permanent, partner. Henry Tilney's perspective, however, might suggest that the exchanges between the couple as they dance adumbrate the sparring of a tense marriage.

14 Austen had once before played with the possibilities of talking by formula at a social gathering. In *Northanger Abbey,* not published until 1818, but mostly written before 1800, Henry Tilney instructs the young and naïve Catherine in the proper things to say at the tea table. Catherine isn't quite sure whether she's allowed to laugh. Darcy, at any rate, smiles. Tilney's motivation, however, is quite different from Elizabeth's: he wishes to entertain Catherine and himself; she wishes to "punish" Darcy.

15 Such as the assembly at Meryton where Elizabeth first saw Darcy.

16 Brilliance, dazzling effect.

17 Although Elizabeth's self-description as "of an unsocial, taciturn disposition" is by no means accurate, there is in fact considerable truth to her perception that both she and Darcy often speak with the hope of impressing others—she, by her wit; Darcy, by his wisdom. This conversation between the two of them, like many of their exchanges, is a form of sparring. Elizabeth has taken control from the outset by prescribing the terms of their dialogue, and on the whole she maintains dominance.

18 Likeness, representation.

19 *Performance* means the accomplishment of something undertaken. Elizabeth's using the word in this

context, though, also suggests another familiar meaning: "the action of performing a play, piece of music . . . etc." *(OED)*. She has been inventing a script, for Darcy as well as for herself, and then performing her share of it.

20 Haughtiness.

21 Wickham will "suffer all his life" from being deprived of the church position that would have provided him with permanent financial support

22 Extreme.

23 The highest level of society.

ing herself for her own weakness, could not go on. At length Darcy spoke, and in a constrained manner said,

"Mr. Wickham is blessed with such happy manners as may ensure his *making* friends—whether he may be equally capable of *retaining* them, is less certain."

"He has been so unlucky as to lose *your* friendship," replied Elizabeth with emphasis, "and in a manner which he is likely to suffer from all his life."[21]

Darcy made no answer, and seemed desirous of changing the subject. At that moment, Sir William Lucas appeared close to them, meaning to pass through the set to the other side of the room; but on perceiving Mr. Darcy he stopt with a bow of superior[22] courtesy to compliment him on his dancing and his partner.

"I have been most highly gratified indeed, my dear Sir. Such very superior dancing is not often seen. It is evident that you belong to the first circles.[23] Allow me to say, however, that your fair partner does not disgrace you, and that I must hope to have this pleasure often repeated, especially when a certain desirable event, my dear Eliza, (glancing at her sister and Bingley,) shall take place. What congratulations will then flow in! I appeal to Mr. Darcy:—but let me not interrupt you, Sir. You will not thank me for detaining you from the bewitching converse of that young lady, whose bright eyes are also upbraiding me."

The latter part of this address was scarcely heard by Darcy; but Sir William's allusion to his friend seemed to strike him forcibly, and his eyes were directed with a very serious expression towards Bingley and Jane, who were dancing together. Recovering himself, however, shortly, he turned to his partner, and said,

"Sir William's interruption has made me forget what we were talking of."

"I do not think we were speaking at all. Sir William could not have interrupted two people in the room who had less to say for themselves.—We have tried two or three subjects already without success, and what we are to talk of next I cannot imagine."

"What think you of books?" said he, smiling.

"Books—Oh! no.—I am sure we never read the same, or not with the same feelings."

"I am sorry you think so; but if that be the case, there can at least be no want[24] of subject.—We may compare our different opinions."

"No—I cannot talk of books in a ball-room; my head is always full of something else."

24 Lack.

Such very superior dancing is not often seen.

Hugh Thomson, Illustrations for *Pride and Prejudice,* 1894. Sir William Lucas compliments Darcy on his dancing.

25 That is, Wickham.

25 That is, Wickham.

26 "Civil disdain" epitomizes Miss Bingley: her use of the forms of politeness hardly obscures the substance of contempt for those whom she perceives as social inferiors.

"The *present* always occupies you in such scenes—does it?" said he, with a look of doubt.

"Yes, always," she replied, without knowing what she said, for her thoughts had wandered far from the subject, as soon afterwards appeared by her suddenly exclaiming, "I remember hearing you once say, Mr. Darcy, that you hardly ever forgave, that your resentment once created was unappeasable. You are very cautious, I suppose, as to its *being created*."

"I am," said he, with a firm voice.

"And never allow yourself to be blinded by prejudice?"

"I hope not."

"It is particularly incumbent on those who never change their opinion, to be secure of judging properly at first."

"May I ask to what these questions tend?"

"Merely to the illustration of *your* character," said she, endeavouring to shake off her gravity. "I am trying to make it out."

"And what is your success?"

She shook her head. "I do not get on at all. I hear such different accounts of you as puzzle me exceedingly."

"I can readily believe," answered he gravely, "that report may vary greatly with respect to me; and I could wish, Miss Bennet, that you were not to sketch my character at the present moment, as there is reason to fear that the performance would reflect no credit on either."

"But if I do not take your likeness now, I may never have another opportunity."

"I would by no means suspend any pleasure of yours," he coldly replied. She said no more, and they went down the other dance and parted in silence; on each side dissatisfied, though not to an equal degree, for in Darcy's breast there was a tolerable powerful feeling towards her, which soon procured her pardon, and directed all his anger against another.[25]

They had not long separated, when Miss Bingley came towards her, and with an expression of civil disdain[26] accosted her,

"So, Miss Eliza, I hear you are quite delighted with George Wickham!—Your sister has been talking to me about him, and asking

me a thousand questions; and I find that the young man forgot to tell
you, among his other communication, that he was the son of old
Wickham, the late Mr. Darcy's steward. Let me recommend you,
however, as a friend, not to give implicit confidence to all his assertions; for as to Mr. Darcy's using him ill, it is perfectly false; for, on
the contrary, he has always been remarkably kind to him, though
George Wickham has treated Mr. Darcy in a most infamous manner.
I do not know the particulars, but I know very well that Mr. Darcy is
not in the least to blame, that he cannot bear to hear George Wickham mentioned, and that though my brother thought that he could
not well avoid including him in his invitation to the officers, he was
excessively glad to find that he had taken himself out of the way. His
coming into the country[27] at all is a most insolent thing indeed, and I
wonder how he could presume to do it. I pity you, Miss Eliza, for this
discovery of your favourite's guilt; but really considering his descent,
one could not expect much better."

"His guilt and his descent appear by your account to be the same,"
said Elizabeth angrily; "for I have heard you accuse him of nothing
worse than of being the son of Mr. Darcy's steward, and of *that,* I can
assure you, he informed me himself."

"I beg your pardon," replied Miss Bingley, turning away with a
sneer. "Excuse my interference.—It was kindly meant."

"Insolent girl!" said Elizabeth to herself.—"You are much mistaken if you expect to influence me by such a paltry attack as this. I
see nothing in it but your own wilful ignorance and the malice of Mr.
Darcy." She then sought her eldest sister, who had undertaken to
make inquiries on the same subject of Bingley. Jane met her with a
smile of such sweet complacency, a glow of such happy expression, as
sufficiently marked how well she was satisfied with the occurrences
of the evening.—Elizabeth instantly read her feelings, and at that
moment solicitude for Wickham, resentment against his enemies,
and every thing else gave way before the hope of Jane's being in the
fairest way[28] for happiness.

"I want to know," said she, with a countenance no less smiling than
her sister's, "what you have learnt about Mr. Wickham. But perhaps

27 Neighborhood.

28 Having the best possible chance.

you have been too pleasantly engaged to think of any third person; in which case you may be sure of my pardon."

"No," replied Jane, "I have not forgotten him; but I have nothing satisfactory to tell you. Mr. Bingley does not know the whole of his history, and is quite ignorant of the circumstances which have principally offended Mr. Darcy; but he will vouch for the good conduct, the probity and honour of his friend, and is perfectly convinced that Mr. Wickham has deserved much less attention from Mr. Darcy than he has received; and I am sorry to say that by his account as well as his sister's, Mr. Wickham is by no means a respectable young man. I am afraid he has been very imprudent, and has deserved to lose Mr. Darcy's regard."

"Mr. Bingley does not know Mr. Wickham himself?"

"No; he never saw him till the other morning at Meryton."

"This account then is what he has received from Mr. Darcy. I am perfectly satisfied. But what does he say of the living?"

"He does not exactly recollect the circumstances, though he has heard them from Mr. Darcy more than once, but he believes that it was left to him *conditionally* only."

"I have not a doubt of Mr. Bingley's sincerity," said Elizabeth warmly; "but you must excuse my not being convinced by assurances only. Mr. Bingley's defence of his friend was a very able one I dare say; but since he is unacquainted with several parts of the story, and has learnt the rest from that friend himself, I shall venture still to think of both gentlemen as I did before."

She then changed the discourse to one more gratifying to each, and on which there could be no difference of sentiment. Elizabeth listened with delight to the happy, though modest hopes which Jane entertained of Mr. Bingley's regard, and said all in her power to heighten her confidence in it. On their being joined by Mr. Bingley himself, Elizabeth withdrew to Miss Lucas; to whose inquiry after the pleasantness of her last partner she had scarcely replied, before Mr. Collins came up to them and told her with great exultation that he had just been so fortunate as to make a most important discovery.

"I have found out," said he, "by a singular accident, that there is now in the room a near relation of my patroness. I happened to overhear the gentleman himself mentioning to the young lady who does the honours of this house[29] the names of his cousin Miss de Bourgh, and of her mother Lady Catherine. How wonderfully these sort of things occur! Who would have thought of my meeting with—perhaps—a nephew of Lady Catherine de Bourgh in this assembly!—I am most thankful that the discovery is made in time for me to pay my respects to him, which I am now going to do, and trust he will excuse my not having done it before. My total ignorance of the connection must plead my apology."

"You are not going to introduce yourself to Mr. Darcy?"

"Indeed I am. I shall intreat his pardon for not having done it earlier. I believe him to be Lady Catherine's *nephew*. It will be in my power to assure him that her ladyship was quite well yesterday se'nnight."[30]

Elizabeth tried hard to dissuade him from such a scheme; assuring him that Mr. Darcy would consider his addressing him without introduction as an impertinent freedom,[31] rather than a compliment to his aunt; that it was not in the least necessary there should be any notice on either side; and that if it were, it must belong to Mr. Darcy, the superior in consequence, to begin the acquaintance.—Mr. Collins listened to her with the determined air of following his own inclination, and, when she ceased speaking, replied thus,

"My dear Miss Elizabeth, I have the highest opinion in the world of your excellent judgment in all matters within the scope of your understanding, but permit me to say that there must be a wide difference between the established forms of ceremony amongst the laity, and those which regulate the clergy; for give me leave to observe that I consider the clerical office as equal in point of dignity with the highest rank in the kingdom—provided that a proper humility of behaviour is at the same time maintained.[32] You must therefore allow me to follow the dictates of my conscience on this occasion, which leads me to perform what I look on as a point of duty. Pardon me for neglecting to profit by your advice, which on every other subject shall be my constant guide, though in the case before us I consider myself more fitted by education and habitual study to decide on what is right than a young lady like yourself." And with a low bow he left

29 Miss Bingley.

30 A week ago yesterday.

31 Since Darcy is the man of higher rank, it would properly be his prerogative to choose whether to be acquainted with Mr. Collins. Mr. Collins is committing a social sin in introducing himself.

32 "Servility and self-importance" once more.

33 Civility, even "distant civility," satisfies Mr. Collins, who is incapable of perceiving the contempt that formal politeness may conceal.

34 Imagination.

her to attack Mr. Darcy, whose reception of his advances she eagerly watched, and whose astonishment at being so addressed was very evident. Her cousin prefaced his speech with a solemn bow, and though she could not hear a word of it, she felt as if hearing it all, and saw in the motion of his lips the words "apology," "Hunsford," and "Lady Catherine de Bourgh."—It vexed her to see him expose himself to such a man. Mr. Darcy was eyeing him with unrestrained wonder, and when at last Mr. Collins allowed him time to speak, replied with an air of distant civility. Mr. Collins, however, was not discouraged from speaking again, and Mr. Darcy's contempt seemed abundantly increasing with the length of his second speech, and at the end of it he only made him a slight bow, and moved another way. Mr. Collins then returned to Elizabeth.

"I have no reason, I assure you," said he, "to be dissatisfied with my reception. Mr. Darcy seemed much pleased with the attention. He answered me with the utmost civility,[33] and even paid me the compliment of saying that he was so well convinced of Lady Catherine's discernment as to be certain she could never bestow a favour unworthily. It was really a very handsome thought. Upon the whole, I am much pleased with him."

As Elizabeth had no longer any interest of her own to pursue, she turned her attention almost entirely on her sister and Mr. Bingley; and the train of agreeable reflections which her observations gave birth to, made her perhaps almost as happy as Jane. She saw her in idea[34] settled in that very house, in all the felicity which a marriage of true affection could bestow; and she felt capable under such circumstances, of endeavouring even to like Bingley's two sisters. Her mother's thoughts she plainly saw were bent the same way, and she determined not to venture near her, lest she might hear too much. When they sat down to supper, therefore, she considered it a most unlucky perverseness which placed them within one of each other; and deeply was she vexed to find that her mother was talking to that one person (Lady Lucas) freely, openly, and of nothing else but her expectation that Jane would be soon married to Mr. Bingley.—It was an animating subject, and Mrs. Bennet seemed incapable of fatigue while enumerating the advantages of the match. His being such a charming young man, and so rich, and living but three miles from them, were the first points of self-gratulation; and then it was such a comfort to think how fond the two sisters were of Jane, and to be certain that they must desire the connection as much as she could do. It was, moreover, such a promising thing for her younger daughters, as Jane's marrying so greatly must throw them in the way of other rich men; and lastly, it was so pleasant at her time of life to be able to consign her single daughters to the care of their sister,[35] that she might not be obliged to go into company more than she liked. It was necessary to make this circumstance a matter of pleasure, because on such occasions it is the etiquette; but no one was less likely than Mrs. Bennet to find comfort in staying home at any period of her life. She concluded with many good wishes that Lady Lucas might soon be equally fortunate, though evidently and triumphantly believing there was no chance of it.

In vain did Elizabeth endeavour to check the rapidity of her mother's words, or persuade her to describe her felicity in a less audible whisper; for to her inexpressible vexation, she could perceive that the chief of it was overheard by Mr. Darcy, who sat opposite to them. Her mother only scolded her for being nonsensical.

"What is Mr. Darcy to me, pray, that I should be afraid of him? I am sure we owe him no such particular civility as to be obliged to say nothing *he* may not like to hear."

"For heaven's sake, madam, speak lower.—What advantage can it be for you to offend Mr. Darcy?—You will never recommend yourself to his friend by so doing."

Nothing that she could say, however, had any influence. Her mother would talk of her views in the same intelligible tone. Elizabeth blushed and blushed again with shame and vexation. She could not help frequently glancing her eye at Mr. Darcy, though every glance convinced her of what she dreaded; for though he was not always looking at her mother, she was convinced that his attention was invariably fixed by her. The expression of his face changed gradually from indignant contempt to a composed and steady gravity.

At length however Mrs. Bennet had no more to say; and Lady Lucas, who had been long yawning at the repetition of delights which

35 Once Jane was married, she might act as a chaperone to her sisters, who, as unmarried women, could not attend social occasions without proper accompaniment.

36 Supper at a ball is a considerably more formal meal than a routine supper, which could consist of little more than tea and cakes—at least in London. It might include soup (the "white soup" that Bingley was planning to have made) and a variety of cold meats, as well as an assortment of sweets.

37 Performing, exhibiting her talents.

38 Another moment of sympathy for foolish Mary, who desperately desires the approval of others.

she saw no likelihood of sharing, was left to the comforts of cold ham and chicken.[36] Elizabeth now began to revive. But not long was the interval of tranquillity; for when supper was over, singing was talked of, and she had the mortification of seeing Mary, after very little entreaty, preparing to oblige the company. By many significant looks and silent entreaties, did she endeavour to prevent such a proof of complaisance,—but in vain; Mary would not understand them; such an opportunity of exhibiting[37] was delightful to her, and she began her song. Elizabeth's eyes were fixed on her with most painful sensations; and she watched her progress through the several stanzas with an impatience which was very ill rewarded at their close; for Mary, on receiving amongst the thanks of the table, the hint of a hope that she might be prevailed on to favour them again, after the pause of half a minute began another. Mary's powers were by no means fitted for such a display; her voice was weak, and her manner affected.—Elizabeth was in agonies. She looked at Jane, to see how she bore it; but Jane was very composedly talking to Bingley. She looked at his two sisters, and saw them making signs of derision at each other, and at Darcy, who continued however impenetrably grave. She looked at her father to entreat his interference, lest Mary should be singing all night. He took the hint, and when Mary had finished her second song, said aloud,

"That will do extremely well, child. You have delighted us long enough. Let the other young ladies have time to exhibit."

Mary, though pretending not to hear, was somewhat disconcerted; and Elizabeth, sorry for her, and sorry for her father's speech,[38] was afraid her anxiety had done no good.—Others of the party were now applied to.

"If I," said Mr. Collins, "were so fortunate as to be able to sing, I should have great pleasure, I am sure, in obliging the company with an air; for I consider music as a very innocent diversion, and perfectly compatible with the profession of a clergyman.—I do not mean however to assert that we can be justified in devoting too much of our time to music, for there are certainly other things to be attended to. The rector of a parish has much to do.—In the first place, he must make such an agreement for tythes as may be beneficial to himself

This bound sheet music belonged to Austen's own collection. Fond of music, Jane began her day with an hour of practice at the pianoforte.

John Harden, "The Concert, 25th September 1805." Musical entertainment was a common feature of social events in Austen's time. John Harden (1772–1847) was a painter best known for his landscapes.

39 All members of a parish were obligated to pay their clergyman the value of 10 percent of their annual agricultural productivity. The precise value of their production was often a matter of debate, so a clergyman might claim that they owed larger sums than they alleged. Such disputes frequently ended up in law courts.

40 Others have and value "happy" or "easy" or "elegant" manners; only Mr. Collins would think "attentive and conciliatory" the ideal adjectives for modifying *manners.* Despite his elaborate proclamations of politeness and deference, Mr. Collins has an eye for the main chance, as "conciliatory" suggests.

41 Austen herself, at the age of twenty-four, reports "sitting down two Dances in preference to having Lord Bolton's eldest son for my Partner, who danced too ill to be endured" (To Cassandra, 8–9 January 1799). A woman who has refused one man is not permitted to dance with another. In Frances Burney's *Evelina,* a book Austen admired, the youthful heroine makes the mistake of dancing with a more attractive man after refusing a fop; she thus wins the fop's lasting enmity and suffers great embarrassment. Her chaperone, Mrs. Mirvan, blames herself for not having instructed the country girl, but adds that "she had taken it for granted that I must know such common customs" (I, 11).

and not offensive to his patron.[39] He must write his own sermons; and the time that remains will not be too much for his parish duties, and the care and improvement of his dwelling, which he cannot be excused from making as comfortable as possible. And I do not think it of light importance that he should have attentive and conciliatory manners[40] towards every body, especially towards those to whom he owes his preferment. I cannot acquit him of that duty; nor could I think well of the man who should omit an occasion of testifying his respect towards any body connected with the family." And with a bow to Mr. Darcy, he concluded his speech, which had been spoken so loud as to be heard by half the room.—Many stared.—Many smiled; but no one looked more amused than Mr. Bennet himself, while his wife seriously commended Mr. Collins for having spoken so sensibly, and observed in a half-whisper to Lady Lucas, that he was a remarkably clever, good kind of young man.

To Elizabeth it appeared, that had her family made an agreement to expose themselves as much as they could during the evening, it would have been impossible for them to play their parts with more spirit, or finer success; and happy did she think it for Bingley and her sister that some of the exhibition had escaped his notice, and that his feelings were not of a sort to be much distressed by the folly which he must have witnessed. That his two sisters and Mr. Darcy, however, should have such an opportunity of ridiculing her relations was bad enough, and she could not determine whether the silent contempt of the gentleman, or the insolent smiles of the ladies, were more intolerable.

The rest of the evening brought her little amusement. She was teazed by Mr. Collins, who continued most perseveringly by her side, and though he could not prevail on her to dance with him again, put it out of her power to dance with others.[41] In vain did she entreat him to stand up with somebody else, and offer to introduce him to any young lady in the room. He assured her that as to dancing, he was perfectly indifferent to it; that his chief object was by delicate attentions to recommend himself to her, and that he should therefore make a point of remaining close to her the whole evening. There was no arguing upon such a project. She owed her greatest relief to her friend Miss Lucas, who often joined them, and goodnaturedly engaged Mr. Collins's conversation to herself.

She was at least free from the offense of Mr. Darcy's further notice; though often standing within a very short distance of her, quite disengaged, he never came near enough to speak. She felt it to be the probable consequence of her allusions to Mr. Wickham, and rejoiced in it.

The Longbourn party were the last of all the company to depart; and by a manoeuvre of Mrs. Bennet had to wait for their carriage a quarter of an hour after every body else was gone, which gave them time to see how heartily they were wished away by some of the family. Mrs. Hurst and her sister scarcely opened their mouths except to complain of fatigue, and were evidently impatient to have the house to themselves. They repulsed every attempt of Mrs. Bennet at conversation, and by so doing, threw a languor over the whole party, which was very little relieved by the long speeches of Mr. Collins, who was complimenting Mr. Bingley and his sisters on the elegance of their entertainment, and the hospitality and politeness which had marked their behaviour to their guests. Darcy said nothing at all. Mr. Bennet, in equal silence, was enjoying the scene. Mr. Bingley and Jane were standing together, a little detached from the rest, and talked only to each other. Elizabeth preserved as steady a silence as either Mrs. Hurst or Miss Bingley; and even Lydia was too much fatigued to utter more than the occasional exclamation of "Lord, how tired I am!" accompanied by a violent yawn.

When at length they arose to take leave, Mrs. Bennet was most pressingly civil in her hope of seeing the whole family soon at Longbourn; and addressed herself particularly to Mr. Bingley, to assure him how happy he would make them, by eating a family dinner with them at any time, without the ceremony of a formal invitation. Bingley was all grateful pleasure, and he readily engaged for taking the earliest opportunity of waiting on her, after his return from London, whither he was obliged to go the next day for a short time.

Mrs. Bennet was perfectly satisfied, and quitted the house under the delightful persuasion that, allowing for the necessary preparations of settlements,[42] new carriages, and wedding clothes, she

42 Legal agreements concerning the financial arrangements of a marriage. Without a settlement that explicitly provided for a wife's financial well-being, she would have no right to any money at all. Wealth that she brought with her into the marriage would immediately belong to her husband. Settlements, however, assigned money for a woman's support in widowhood and, in some cases, for her use during the marriage.

should undoubtedly see her daughter settled at Netherfield in the course of three or four months. Of having another daughter married to Mr. Collins, she thought with equal certainty, and with considerable, though not equal, pleasure. Elizabeth was the least dear to her of all her children; and though the man and the match were quite good enough for *her,* the worth of each was eclipsed by Mr. Bingley and Netherfield.

Anonymous, "View of a Drawing Room," 1780. This image of tea being taken in a gentleman's drawing room conveys the formality of late eighteenth-century social decorum.

19

THE NEXT DAY OPENED A NEW SCENE[1] at Longbourn. Mr. Collins made his declaration[2] in form.[3] Having resolved to do it without loss of time, as his leave of absence extended only to the following Saturday, and having no feelings of diffidence[4] to make it distressing to himself even at the moment, he set about it in a very orderly manner, with all the observances which he supposed a regular part of the business.[5] On finding Mrs. Bennet, Elizabeth, and one of the younger girls together, soon after breakfast, he addressed the mother in these words,

"May I hope, Madam, for your interest[6] with your fair daughter Elizabeth, when I solicit for the honour of a private audience with her in the course of this morning?"

Before Elizabeth had time for anything but a blush of surprise, Mrs. Bennet instantly answered,

"Oh dear!—Yes—certainly.—I am sure Lizzy will be very happy—I am sure she can have no objection.—Come, Kitty, I want you upstairs." And gathering her work together, she was hastening away, when Elizabeth called out,

"Dear Ma'am, do not go.—I beg you will not go.—Mr. Collins must excuse me.—He can have nothing to say to me that anybody need not hear. I am going away myself."

"No, no, nonsense, Lizzy.—I desire you to stay where you are."—And upon Elizabeth's seeming really, with vexed and embarrassed looks, about to escape, she added: "Lizzy, I *insist* upon your staying and hearing Mr. Collins."

1 The formulation once more suggests a stage play—not inappropriate for the mechanical performance of romantic interest that Mr. Collins is about to offer. Like Mary again, he often conveys an air of having memorized his lines.

2 A well-chosen word for Mr. Collins's form of proposal, which consists largely of assertion.

3 Formally. The episode of Mr. Collins's proposal is one of the few scenes in Austen's work that provoke significant biographical speculation. In 1797, when Jane was working on *First Impressions,* later to become *Pride and Prejudice,* her friend Anne Lefroy invited a young man, the Reverend Samuel Blackall, for a visit. Apparently she thought him a likely match for Jane, but he seems to have been a clumsy and wooden suitor who never actually proposed, although he made his romantic intentions clear by writing to Mrs. Lefroy, "[I]t would give me particular pleasure to have an opportunity of improving my acquaintance with [the Austen] family—with a hope of creating to myself a nearer interest" (quoted in letter to Cassandra, 17–18 November 1798). In 1813, Austen writes to her sister about Blackall's marriage, saying that she would like to know what sort of woman he married: "He was a peice [sic] of Perfection, noisy Perfection himself which I always recollect with regard. . . . I would wish [his wife] to be of a silent turn & rather ignorant, but naturally intelligent and wishing to learn;—fond of cold veal pies, green tea in the afternoon, & a green window blind at night" (To Cassandra, 3–6 July 1813). It is conceivable that Austen

imagined Collins's proposal on the basis of her experience with Blackall. See Claire Tomalin, *Jane Austen, A Life* (New York: Knopf, 1998), 129–130.

4   Mr. Collins's lack of diffidence is significant. Despite his constant explicit and implicit claims of humility, he is in fact supremely confident of his own worth.

5   For Mr. Collins as for Mrs. Bennet, marriage is (at least at the moment) the business of his life.

6   Personal influence.

7   Conscious.

8   Probably, like her mother, she is at her needlework.

9   Because, like her father, she realizes how ridiculous Mr. Collins is.

10   Because he is apparently a reader of moralists, Mr. Collins assumes that every woman will have "natural delicacy." His awareness of Elizabeth as an individual person is confined to her "wit and vivacity"; he sees her primarily as an embodiment of Woman and therefore can believe that he knows her nature and her meanings.

11   Expensively. If a woman were accustomed to lavish spending, she would be unlikely to economize.

Elizabeth would not oppose such an injunction—and a moment's consideration making her also sensible[7] that it would be wisest to get it over as soon and as quietly as possible, she sat down again and tried to conceal by incessant employment[8] the feelings which were divided between distress and diversion.[9] Mrs. Bennet and Kitty walked off, and as soon as they were gone, Mr. Collins began.

"Believe me, my dear Miss Elizabeth, that your modesty, so far from doing you any disservice, rather adds to your other perfections. You would have been less amiable in my eyes had there *not* been this little unwillingness; but allow me to assure you that I have your respected mother's permission for this address. You can hardly doubt the purport of my discourse, however your natural delicacy[10] may lead you to dissemble; my attentions have been too marked to be mistaken. Almost as soon as I entered the house, I singled you out as the companion of my future life. But before I am run away with by my feelings on this subject, perhaps it would be advisable for me to state my reasons for marrying—and moreover for coming into Hertfordshire with the design of selecting a wife, as I certainly did."

The idea of Mr. Collins, with all his solemn composure, being run away with by his feelings, made Elizabeth so near laughing that she could not use the short pause he allowed in any attempt to stop him further, and he continued:

"My reasons for marrying are, first, that I think it a right thing for every clergyman in easy circumstances (like myself) to set the example of matrimony in his parish. Secondly, that I am convinced that it will add very greatly to my happiness; and thirdly—which perhaps I ought to have mentioned earlier, that it is the particular advice and recommendation of the very noble lady whom I have the honour of calling patroness. Twice has she condescended to give me her opinion (unasked too!) on this subject; and it was but the very Saturday night before I left Hunsford—between our pools at quadrille, while Mrs. Jenkinson was arranging Miss de Bourgh's foot-stool, that she said, 'Mr. Collins, you must marry. A clergyman like you must marry. —Chuse properly, chuse a gentlewoman for *my* sake; and for your *own,* let her be an active, useful sort of person, not brought up high,[11] but able to make a small income go a good way. This is my advice.

Find such a woman as soon as you can, bring her to Hunsford, and I will visit her."[12] Allow me, by the way, to observe, my fair cousin, that I do not reckon the notice and kindness of Lady Catherine de Bourgh as among the least of the advantages in my power to offer. You will find her manners beyond anything I can describe;[13] and your wit and vivacity I think[14] must be acceptable to her, especially when tempered with the silence and respect which her rank will inevitably excite.[15] Thus much for my general intention in favour of matrimony; it remains to be told why my views were directed to Longbourn instead of my own neighbourhood, where I can assure you there are many amiable young women. But the fact is, that being, as I am, to inherit this estate after the death of your honoured father, (who, however, may live many years longer,) I could not satisfy myself without resolving to chuse a wife from among his daughters, that the loss to them might be as little as possible, when the melancholy event takes place—which, however, as I have already said, may not be for several years.[16] This has been my motive, my fair cousin, and I flatter myself it will not sink me in your esteem. And now nothing remains for me but to assure you in the most animated language of the violence of my affection.[17] To fortune I am perfectly indifferent, and shall make no demand of that nature on your father, since I am well aware that it could not be complied with; and that one thousand pounds in the 4 per cents, which will not be yours till after your mother's decease,[18] is all that you may ever be entitled to. On that head, therefore, I shall be uniformly silent; and you may assure yourself that no ungenerous reproach shall ever pass my lips when we are married."[19]

It was absolutely necessary to interrupt him now.

"You are too hasty, Sir," she cried. "You forget that I have made no answer. Let me do it without further loss of time. Accept my thanks for the compliment you are paying me. I am very sensible of the honour of your proposals, but it is impossible for me to do otherwise than to decline them."

"I am not now to learn,"[20] replied Mr. Collins, with a formal wave of the hand, "that it is usual with young ladies to reject the addresses[21] of the man whom they secretly mean to accept, when he first applies for their favour; and that sometimes the refusal is repeated a second

12 Given Lady Catherine's high rank, her visiting a woman of lower social position would be considered an honor.

13 In other words, no adjectives come to mind. When we actually encounter Lady Catherine and her manners, this remark by Mr. Collins takes on considerable comic force.

14 But he isn't sure.

15 This is a telling comment: Elizabeth's "wit and vivacity" have presumably attracted Mr. Collins, who has earlier been at pains to compliment her on precisely these characteristics. He wants, however, to be sure that she keeps them in check and is properly subdued in the presence of social greatness.

16 Note how "many years" has turned into "several years." Mr. Collins is eager for his inheritance.

17 Mr. Collins never fulfills his implied promise: he never expresses the "violence of [his] Affection," nor does his language ever achieve animation.

18 Elizabeth will inherit £1,000 from her mother; the money has been safely invested in government bonds, which earn only 4 percent a year, or £40. Mr. Collins promises not to reproach her for bringing so little wealth to the marriage.

19 A striking aspect of this proposal is that virtually everything Mr. Collins has to say is about himself. The drama of the scene, from his point of view, derives entirely from his own process of decision. Although he refers to Elizabeth toward the end of his "declaration," he never *asks* her to marry him.

20 I do not have to learn now. In his metaphorical stage performance, Mr. Collins has cast Elizabeth in the role of conventional young lady, who can only be grateful for his overtures. It is beyond his capacity to imagine a woman wishing to reject him.

21 Marriage proposals.

22 Position in life—perhaps with overtones of another
meaning: post of employment.

23 Speaking of "qualifications" also suggests that Collins is thinking of employing her—as indeed he is.

or even a third time. I am therefore by no means discouraged by what you have just said, and shall hope to lead you to the altar ere long."

"Upon my word, Sir," cried Elizabeth, "your hope is a rather extraordinary one after my declaration. I do assure you that I am not one of those young ladies (if such young ladies there are) who are so daring as to risk their happiness on the chance of being asked a second time. I am perfectly serious in my refusal.—You could not make *me* happy, and I am convinced that I am the last woman in the world who could make *you* so.—Nay, were your friend Lady Catherine to know me, I am persuaded she would find me in every respect ill qualified for the situation."[22]

"Were it certain that Lady Catherine would think so," said Mr. Collins very gravely—"but I cannot imagine that her ladyship would at all disapprove of you. And you may be certain when I have the honour of seeing her again, I shall speak in the highest terms of your modesty, economy, and other amiable qualifications."[23]

"Indeed, Mr. Collins, all praise of me will be unnecessary. You must give me leave to judge for myself, and pay me the compliment of believing what I say. I wish you very happy and very rich, and by refusing your hand, do all in my power to prevent your being otherwise. In making me the offer, you must have satisfied the delicacy of your feelings with regard to my family, and may take possession of Longbourn estate whenever it falls, without any self-reproach. This matter may be considered, therefore, as finally settled." And rising as she thus spoke, she would have quitted the room, had not Mr. Collins thus addressed her,

"When I do myself the honour of speaking to you next on this subject, I shall hope to receive a more favourable answer than you have now given me; though I am far from accusing you of cruelty at present, because I know it to be the established custom of your sex to reject a man on the first application, and perhaps you have even now said as much to encourage my suit as would be consistent with the true delicacy of the female character."

"Really, Mr. Collins," cried Elizabeth with some warmth, "you puzzle me exceedingly. If what I have hitherto said can appear to you in the form of encouragement, I know not how to express my refusal in such a way as to convince you of its being one."[24]

"You must give me leave to flatter myself, my dear cousin, that your refusal of my addresses is merely words of course.[25] My reasons for believing it are briefly these:—It does not appear to me that my hand is unworthy your acceptance, or that the establishment I can offer would be any other than highly desirable. My situation in life, my connections with the family of de Bourgh, and my relationship to your own, are circumstances highly in my favour; and you should take it into further consideration that in spite of your manifold attractions, it is by no means certain that another offer of marriage may ever be made you. Your portion[26] is unhappily so small that it will in all likelihood undo the effects of your loveliness and amiable qualifications. As I must therefore conclude that you are not serious in your rejection of me,[27] I shall chuse to attribute it to your wish of increasing my love by suspense, according to the usual practice of elegant females."

"I do assure you, Sir, that I have no pretension whatever to that kind of elegance which consists in tormenting a respectable man. I would rather be paid the compliment of being believed sincere. I thank you again and again for the honour you have done me in your proposals, but to accept them is absolutely impossible. My feelings in every respect forbid it. Can I speak plainer? Do not consider me now as an elegant female intending to plague you, but as a rational creature,[28] speaking the truth from her heart."

"You are uniformly charming!" cried he, with an air of awkward gallantry; "and I am persuaded that when sanctioned by the express authority of both your excellent parents, my proposals will not fail of being acceptable."

To such perseverance in wilful self-deception Elizabeth would make no reply, and immediately and in silence withdrew; determined, if he persisted in considering her repeated refusals as flattering encouragement, to apply to her father, whose negative might be uttered in such a manner as to be decisive, and whose behaviour at least could not be mistaken for the affectation and coquetry of an elegant female.

24 Elizabeth faces a comic but also rather desperate dilemma: Mr. Collins will pay no attention to anything she says because he feels confident that he knows what she means, regardless of her words. He could hardly demonstrate more fully his essential contempt for women.

25 Customary.

26 Marriage portion, dowry.

27 Like Mrs. Bennet and Charlotte, Mr. Collins considers marriage primarily a business transaction. A woman supplies her personal attractions in exchange for a man's wealth and social status. Collins is, however, nasty in his hints that Elizabeth does not possess sufficient charms to compensate, in the view of less magnanimous suitors than he, for her meager financial resources. As he has abundantly demonstrated, money (Lady Catherine's wealth and his own actual and potential income) is much on his mind. Ivor Morris sums up his view of Mr. Collins as follows: "Mr Collins is the living expression and microcosm of all those things against which [Austen's] soul is in revolt, but with which she must in her personal life come to terms: her world's brittle elegance and dominating materialism, its pomposities and pretensions, its unfeelingness and inhumanities, its stupidities and its mindlessness" (*Mr Collins Considered: Approaches to Jane Austen* [London: Routledge and Kegan Paul, 1987], 160). I find it hard to connect this clergyman with elegance, brittle or otherwise, but the other characteristics Morris specifies indeed mark Mr. Collins and also appear elsewhere as targets of Austen's satire.

28 A persistent stereotype had it that men were rational beings, women creatures of feeling. In asking to be considered rational, Elizabeth is asking Mr. Collins to abandon one of his clichés.

20

1 Mr. Collins has in his imagination converted Elizabeth into a model woman in the James Fordyce mode.

2 From Mrs. Bennet's point of view, financial self-interest should control a woman's response to a matrimonial proposal.

MR. COLLINS WAS NOT LEFT LONG TO THE silent contemplation of his successful love; for Mrs. Bennet, having dawdled about in the vestibule to watch for the end of the conference, no sooner saw Elizabeth open the door and with quick step pass her towards the staircase, than she entered the breakfast-room, and congratulated both him and herself in warm terms on the happy prospect of their nearer connection. Mr. Collins received and returned these felicitations with equal pleasure, and then proceeded to relate the particulars of their interview, with the result of which he trusted he had every reason to be satisfied, since the refusal which his cousin had stedfastly given him would naturally flow from her bashful modesty[1] and the genuine delicacy of her character.

This information, however, startled Mrs. Bennet;—she would have been glad to be equally satisfied that her daughter had meant to encourage him by protesting against his proposals, but she dared not believe it, and could not help saying so.

"But depend upon it, Mr. Collins," she added, "that Lizzy shall be brought to reason. I will speak to her about it myself directly. She is a very headstrong, foolish girl, and does not know her own interest;[2] but I will *make* her know it."

"Pardon me for interrupting you, Madam," cried Mr. Collins; "but if she is really headstrong and foolish, I know not whether she would altogether be a very desirable wife to a man in my situation, who naturally looks for happiness in the marriage state. If therefore she actually persists in rejecting my suit, perhaps it were better not to force her into accepting me, because if liable to such defects of temper, she could not contribute much to my felicity."

"Sir, you quite misunderstand me," said Mrs. Bennet, alarmed. "Lizzy is only headstrong in such matters as these. In every thing else she is as good natured a girl as ever lived. I will go directly to Mr. Bennet, and we shall very soon settle it with her, I am sure."

She would not give him time to reply, but hurrying instantly to her husband, called out as she entered the library,

"Oh! Mr. Bennet, you are wanted immediately; we are all in an uproar. You must come and make Lizzy marry Mr. Collins, for she vows she will not have him, and if you do not make haste he will change his mind and not have *her*."

Mr. Bennet raised his eyes from his book as she entered, and fixed them on her face with a calm unconcern which was not in the least altered by her communication.

"I have not the pleasure of understanding you,"[3] said he, when she had finished her speech. "Of what are you talking?"

"Of Mr. Collins and Lizzy. Lizzy declares she will not have Mr. Collins, and Mr. Collins begins to say that he will not have Lizzy."

"And what am I to do on the occasion?—It seems an hopeless business."

"Speak to Lizzy about it yourself. Tell her that you insist upon her marrying him."[4]

"Let her be called down. She shall hear my opinion."

Mrs. Bennet rang the bell,[5] and Miss Elizabeth was summoned to the library.

"Come here, child," cried her father as she appeared. "I have sent for you on an affair of importance. I understand that Mr. Collins has made you an offer of marriage. Is it true?" Elizabeth replied that it was. "Very well—and this offer of marriage you have refused?"

"I have, Sir."

"Very well. We now come to the point. Your mother insists upon your accepting it. Is it not so, Mrs. Bennet?"

"Yes, or I will never see her again."

"An unhappy alternative is before you, Elizabeth. From this day you must be a stranger to one of your parents.—Your mother will

3 Mr. Bennet's customary elaborate courtesy in addressing his wife is a subtle form of insult—although she does not understand it thus.

4 According to Lawrence Stone, by 1660 "it had been conceded, in the interests of 'holy matrimony,' that children of both sexes should be given the right of veto over a future spouse proposed to them by their parents" (*The Family, Sex and Marriage in England, 1500–1800* [New York: Harper & Row, 1977], 272). In the highest reaches of the aristocracy, different rules applied: great lands and power might be at stake. Samuel Richardson's *Clarissa,* written in the middle of the eighteenth century, develops its narrative from the rejection by the heroine's parents of the young woman's right of refusal. Clarissa declares over and over that she will not marry without her father's consent, but she wishes to retain the right to reject a suitor chosen by her father. Her parents insist that she marry a loathsome man with vast property.

The Bennet girls face no such situation. By the end of the eighteenth century, according to Stone and others, "The choice of a spouse was increasingly left in the hands of the children themselves and was based mainly on temperamental compatibility with the aim of lasting companionship" (*The Family, Sex and Marriage in England,* 392). As Lady Pennington puts the point, "Fortune and Family it is the sole province of your father to direct in: he certainly has always an undoubted right to a negative voice, though not to a compulsive one. As a child is very justifiable in the refusal of her hand, even to the absolute command of a father, where her heart cannot go with it, so is she extremely culpable in giving it contrary to his approbation" (Sarah Pennington, *An Unfortunate Mother's Advice to her Absent Daughters, in a Letter to Miss Pennington, The Young Lady's Pocket Library, or Parental Monitor* [Bristol: Thoemmes Press, 1995], 96). Mrs. Bennet, however, dominated by economic concerns and pursuing the "business" of getting her daughters married, relies on the older view that fathers can dictate their daughters' choices.

5 Mrs. Bennet rings for a servant to get Elizabeth.

6 Mr. Bennet has made no such promise. His wife hears what she wants to hear.

7 On her side.

8 Like so many other characters in the novel, Mr. Collins has his pride.

9 Emma, in Austen's later novel, also receives an unwanted proposal, although her suitor is less ridiculous than Mr. Collins. Her judgment of the proposal resembles the narrator's assessment of Mr. Collins's: "There had been no real affection either in his language or manners. Sighs and fine words had been given in abundance; but she could hardly devise any set of expressions, or fancy any tone of voice, less allied with real love. She need not trouble herself to pity him" (I, 16).

10 Either because the fact of the mother's reproach vindicates him for making the proposal or because he feels satisfaction that Elizabeth is being made to suffer for refusing him.

11 A minor running joke in *Pride and Prejudice* is the variety of situations that Lydia will characterize as "fun."

never see you again if you do *not* marry Mr. Collins, and I will never see you again if you *do*."

Elizabeth could not but smile at such a conclusion of such a beginning, but Mrs. Bennet, who had persuaded herself that her husband regarded the affair as she wished, was excessively disappointed.

"What do you mean, Mr. Bennet, by talking in this way? You promised me to *insist* upon her marrying him."[6]

"My dear," replied her husband, "I have two small favours to request. First, that you will allow me the free use of my understanding on the present occasion; and secondly, of my room. I shall be glad to have the library to myself as soon as may be."

Not yet, however, in spite of her disappointment in her husband, did Mrs. Bennet give up the point. She talked to Elizabeth again and again; coaxed and threatened her by turns. She endeavoured to secure Jane in her interest;[7] but Jane, with all possible mildness, declined interfering—and Elizabeth sometimes with real earnestness and sometimes with playful gaiety replied to her attacks. Though her manner varied, however, her determination never did.

Mr. Collins, meanwhile, was meditating in solitude on what had passed. He thought too well of himself to comprehend on what motive his cousin could refuse him; and though his pride was hurt,[8] he suffered in no other way. His regard for her was quite imaginary;[9] and the possibility of her deserving her mother's reproach prevented his feeling any regret.[10]

While the family were in this confusion, Charlotte Lucas came to spend the day with them. She was met in the vestibule by Lydia, who, flying to her, cried in a half whisper, "I am glad you are come, for there is such fun here![11]—What do you think has happened this morning?—Mr. Collins has made an offer to Lizzy, and she will not have him."

Charlotte hardly had time to answer, before they were joined by Kitty, who came to tell the same news, and no sooner had they entered the breakfast-room, where Mrs. Bennet was alone, than she likewise began on the subject, calling on Miss Lucas for her compassion, and entreating her to persuade her friend Lizzy to comply with the wishes of all her family. "Pray do, my dear Miss Lucas," she added in a melancholy tone, "for nobody is on my side, nobody takes part with me,[12] I am cruelly used, nobody feels for my poor nerves."

Charlotte's reply was spared by the entrance of Jane and Elizabeth.

"Aye, there she comes," continued Mrs. Bennet, "looking as unconcerned as may be, and caring no more for us than if we were at York, provided she can have her own way.—But I tell you what, Miss Lizzy, if you take it into your head to go on refusing every offer of marriage in this way, you will never get a husband at all—and I am sure I do not know who is to maintain you when your father is dead.—I shall not be able to keep you[13]—and so I warn you.—I have done with you from this very day.—I told you in the library, you know, that I should never speak to you again, and you will find me as good as my word. I have no pleasure in talking to undutiful children. —Not that I have much pleasure, indeed, in talking to any body. People who suffer as I do from nervous complaints can have no great inclination for talking. Nobody can tell what I suffer!—But it is always so. Those who do not complain are never pitied."

Her daughters listened in silence to this effusion,[14] sensible that any attempt to reason with her or sooth her would only increase the irritation. She talked on, therefore, without interruption from any of them till they were joined by Mr. Collins, who entered the room with an air more stately than usual, and on perceiving whom, she said to the girls,

"Now, I do insist upon it, that you, all of you, hold your tongues, and let Mr. Collins and me have a little conversation together."

Elizabeth passed quietly out of the room, Jane and Kitty followed, but Lydia stood her ground, determined to hear all she could; and Charlotte, detained first by the civility of Mr. Collins, whose inquiries after herself and all her family were very minute, and then by a little curiosity, satisfied herself with walking to the window and pretending not to hear. In a doleful voice Mrs. Bennet thus began the projected conversation.—"Oh! Mr. Collins!"—

"My dear Madam," replied he, "let us be for ever silent on this point. Far be it from me," he presently continued, in a voice that marked his displeasure, "to resent the behaviour of your daughter.

12 But she has just declared that "the wishes of the entire family" would have Elizabeth marry Collins.

13 Since Mrs. Bennet as a widow will have a likely income of only about £200—the interest on £5,000 invested at 4 percent—it is literally true that she could not support her daughters at anything like the level to which they are accustomed.

14 Outpouring of emotion.

15 Particular.

16 Advancement.

17 Since his conduct has been almost entirely dictated by the doctrine of conduct books, Mr. Collins assesses his own performance by their model.

Resignation to inevitable evils is the duty of us all; the peculiar[15] duty of a young man who has been so fortunate as I have been in early preferment;[16] and I trust I am resigned. Perhaps not the less so from feeling a doubt of my positive happiness had my fair cousin honoured me with her hand; for I have often observed that resignation is never so perfect as when the blessing denied begins to lose somewhat of its value in our estimation. You will not, I hope, consider me as shewing any disrespect to your family, my dear Madam, by thus withdrawing my pretensions to your daughter's favour, without having paid yourself and Mr. Bennet the compliment of requesting you to interpose your authority in my behalf. My conduct may I fear be objectionable in having accepted my dismission from your daughter's lips instead of your own.[17] But we are all liable to error. I have certainly meant well through the whole affair. My object has been to secure an amiable companion for myself, with due consideration for the advantage of all your family, and if my *manner* has been at all reprehensible, I here beg leave to apologise."

21

THE DISCUSSION OF MR. COLLINS'S OFFER was now nearly at an end, and Elizabeth had only to suffer from the uncomfortable feelings necessarily attending it, and occasionally from some peevish allusion of her mother. As for the gentleman himself, *his* feelings were chiefly expressed, not by embarrassment or dejection, or by trying to avoid her, but by stiffness of manner and resentful silence. He scarcely ever spoke to her, and the assiduous attentions which he had been so sensible of himself, were transferred for the rest of the day to Miss Lucas, whose civility in listening to him, was a seasonable[1] relief to them all, and especially to her friend.

The morrow produced no abatement of Mrs. Bennet's ill humour or ill health. Mr. Collins was also in the same state of angry pride. Elizabeth had hoped that his resentment might shorten his visit, but his plan did not appear in the least affected by it. He was always to have gone on Saturday, and to Saturday he still meant to stay.

After breakfast, the girls walked to Meryton to inquire if Mr. Wickham were returned, and to lament over his absence from the Netherfield ball. He joined them on their entering the town, and attended them to their aunt's, where his regret and vexation, and the concern of every body, was well talked over. —To Elizabeth, however, he voluntarily acknowledged that the necessity of his absence *had* been self-imposed.

"I found," said he, "as the time drew near, that I had better not meet Mr. Darcy;—that to be in the same room, the same party with

1 Opportune.

2 Paper that has been smoothed between glaze boards and hot metal plates; a fancy sort of writing paper.

3 A fashionable street in the West End of London.

4 A favorite activity of young women was engaging in extensive correspondences with female friends. In *Mansfield Park,* the narrator refers to "every body at all addicted to letter writing, without having much to say, which will include a large proportion of the female world at least" (III, 13). Henry Tilney, in *Northanger Abbey,* observes, "Every body allows that the talent of writing agreeable letters is peculiarly female"—although his subsequent elaboration has it that the usual style of correspondence among women is characterized by a "general deficiency of subject, a total inattention to stops [i.e., punctuation], and a very frequent ignorance of grammar" (I, 3). Miss Bingley, who has been deeply interested in Darcy's letter writing, writes letters herself strongly marked by their artifice and conventionality.

him for so many hours together, might be more than I could bear, and that scenes might arise unpleasant to more than myself."

She highly approved his forbearance, and they had leisure for a full discussion of it, and for all the commendation which they civilly bestowed on each other, as Wickham and another officer walked back with them to Longbourn, and during the walk, he particularly attended to her. His accompanying them was a double advantage; she felt all the compliment it offered to herself, and it was most acceptable as an occasion of introducing him to her father and mother.

Soon after their return, a letter was delivered to Miss Bennet; it came from Netherfield, and was opened immediately. The envelope contained a sheet of elegant, little, hot pressed paper,[2] well covered with a lady's fair, flowing hand; and Elizabeth saw her sister's countenance change as she read it, and saw her dwelling intently on some particular passages. Jane recollected herself soon, and putting the letter away, tried to join with her usual cheerfulness in the general conversation; but Elizabeth felt an anxiety on the subject which drew off her attention even from Wickham; and no sooner had he and his companion taken leave, than a glance from Jane invited her to follow her upstairs. When they had gained their own room, Jane taking out the letter, said,

"This is from Caroline Bingley; what it contains has surprised me a good deal. The whole party have left Netherfield by this time, and are on their way to town; and without any intention of coming back again. You shall hear what she says."

She then read the first sentence aloud, which comprised the information of their having just resolved to follow their brother to town directly, and of their meaning to dine that day in Grosvenor street,[3] where Mr. Hurst had a house. The next was in these words. "I do not pretend to regret anything I shall leave in Hertfordshire, except your society, my dearest friend; but we will hope at some future period, to enjoy many returns of that delightful intercourse we have known, and in the mean while may lessen the pain of separation by a very frequent and most unreserved correspondence. I depend on you for that."[4] To these high flown expressions, Elizabeth listened with all the insensibility of distrust; and though the suddenness of their removal surprised her, she saw nothing in it really to lament; it was not to be supposed that their absence from Netherfield would prevent Mr. Bingley's being there; and as to the loss of their society, she was persuaded that Jane must soon cease to regard it, in the enjoyment of his.

"It is unlucky," said she, after a short pause, "that you should not be able to see your friends before they leave the country. But may we not hope that the period of future happiness to which Miss Bingley looks forward, may arrive earlier than she is aware, and that the delightful intercourse you have known as friends, will be renewed with yet greater satisfaction as sisters?—Mr. Bingley will not be detained in London by them."

"Caroline decidedly says that none of the party will return into Hertfordshire this winter. I will read it to you—

"When my brother left us yesterday, he imagined that the business which took him to London, might be concluded in three or four days, but as we are certain it cannot be so, and at the same time convinced that when Charles gets to town, he will be in no hurry to leave it again,[5] we have determined on following him thither, that he may not be obliged to spend his vacant hours in a comfortless hotel. Many of my acquaintance are already there for the winter; I wish I could hear that you, my dearest friend, had any intention of making one of the croud, but of that I despair. I sincerely hope your Christmas in Hertfordshire may abound in the gaieties which that season generally brings, and that your beaux will be so numerous as to prevent your feeling the loss of the three, of whom we shall deprive you."[6]

"It is evident by this," added Jane, "that he comes back no more this winter."

"It is only evident that Miss Bingley does not mean he *should*."

"Why will you think so? It must be his own doing.—He is his own master. But you do not know *all*. I *will* read you the passage which particularly hurts me. I will have no reserves from *you*." "Mr. Darcy is impatient to see his sister, and to confess the truth, *we* are scarcely less eager to meet her again. I really do not think Georgiana Darcy has her equal for beauty, elegance, and accomplishments; and the affection she inspires in Louisa and myself is heightened into some-

5 As Bingley has said earlier, when he's in the country he prefers the country; when he's in town, he prefers town. He has also made clear that he is easily persuadable.

6 A beau is an "attendant or suitor of a lady" (OED). Miss Bingley obviously has the more general sense of "attendant" in mind, since she evidently counts married Mr. Hurst as one of the three beaux, along with Darcy and Bingley.

thing still more interesting,[7] from the hope we dare entertain of her being hereafter our sister. I do not know whether I ever before mentioned to you my feelings on this subject, but I will not leave the country without confiding them, and I trust you will not esteem them unreasonable. My brother admires her greatly already, he will have frequent opportunity now of seeing her on the most intimate footing; her relations all wish the connection as much as his own, and a sister's partiality is not misleading me, I think, when I call Charles most capable of engaging any woman's heart. With all these circumstances to favour an attachment and nothing to prevent it, am I wrong, my dearest Jane, in indulging the hope of an event which will secure the happiness of so many?"

"What think you of *this* sentence, my dear Lizzy?"—said Jane as she finished it. "Is it not clear enough?—Does it not expressly declare that Caroline neither expects nor wishes me to be her sister; that she is perfectly convinced of her brother's indifference, and that if she suspects the nature of my feelings for him, she means (most kindly!) to put me on my guard? Can there be any other opinion on the subject?"

"Yes, there can; for mine is totally different.—Will you hear it?"

"Most willingly."

"You shall have it in few words. Miss Bingley sees that her brother is in love with you, and wants him to marry Miss Darcy. She follows him to town in the hope of keeping him there, and tries to persuade you that he does not care about you."

Jane shook her head.

"Indeed, Jane, you ought to believe me.—No one who has ever seen you together, can doubt his affection. Miss Bingley I am sure cannot. She is not such a simpleton. Could she have seen half as much love in Mr. Darcy for herself, she would have ordered her wedding clothes. But the case is this. We are not rich enough, or grand enough for them; and she is the more anxious to get Miss Darcy for her brother, from the notion that when there has been *one* intermarriage, she may have less trouble in achieving a second; in which there is certainly some ingenuity, and I dare say it would succeed, if Miss de Bourgh were out of the way. But, my dearest Jane, you cannot seriously imagine that because Miss Bingley tells you her brother greatly admires Miss Darcy, he is in the smallest degree less sensible of *your* merit than when he took leave of you on Tuesday, or that it will be in her power to persuade him that, instead of being in love with you, he is very much in love with her friend."

"If we thought alike of Miss Bingley," replied Jane, "your representation of all this, might make me quite easy. But I know the foundation is unjust. Caroline is incapable of wilfully deceiving any one; and all that I can hope in this case is, that she is deceived herself."

"That is right.—You could not have started a more happy idea, since you will not take comfort in mine. Believe her to be deceived by all means. You have now done your duty by her, and must fret no longer."

"But, my dear sister, can I be happy, even supposing the best, in accepting a man whose sisters and friends are all wishing him to marry elsewhere?"

"You must decide for yourself," said Elizabeth, "and if upon mature deliberation, you find that the misery of disobliging his two sisters is more than equivalent to the happiness of being his wife, I advise you by all means to refuse him."

"How can you talk so?"—said Jane faintly smiling,—"you must know that though I should be exceedingly grieved at their disapprobation, I could not hesitate."

"I did not think you would;—and that being the case, I cannot consider your situation with much compassion."

"But if he returns no more this winter, my choice will never be required. A thousand things may arise in six months!"

The idea of his returning no more Elizabeth treated with the utmost contempt. It appeared to her merely the suggestion of Caroline's interested[8] wishes, and she could not for a moment suppose that those wishes, however openly or artfully spoken, could influence a young man so totally independent of every one.

She represented to her sister as forcibly as possible what she felt on the subject, and had soon the pleasure of seeing its happy effect. Jane's temper was not desponding, and she was gradually led to hope, though the diffidence of affection sometimes overcame the hope,

8 Self-interested.

9 Two full courses would be a lavish meal, since a single course at this time involved a large variety of dishes, all displayed simultaneously on the table for diners to choose among. A first course would typically include soup, a roast of meat, a dish of chicken and/or one of fish, and a substantial vegetable offering. There would also be numerous side dishes of vegetables, and perhaps a sweet such as a tart. One course would certainly be enough for a "family dinner." If a second course were served, the table would be cleared and a new assortment of four main dishes, possibly including cold roasts, and at least four side dishes, would be placed. Diners helped themselves to whatever was close to them or asked for items of their choice to be passed.

A typical "moderate dinner" reported by a Franco-American visitor in 1810–1811, and cited in the introduction to *The Jane Austen Cookbook* (by Maggie Black and Deirdre Le Faye [London: British Museum Press, 1995]), consisted of oyster sauce, fish, spinach, fowls, soup, bacon, vegetables, and roasted or boiled beef as a first course. The second course would provide creams (involving flavoring such as lemon juice and peel, nuts, sweetening, cream, and the equivalent of gelatin), "ragout," celery, pastry, macaroni, cauliflowers, and game. Dessert would offer cakes along with assorted fruits and nuts.

Although roasts (referred to as "joints") might be served in relatively simple form, vegetable dishes were often elaborate, made into pies and puddings and fricassees. A "ragoo of celery," for instance, contained mace, cloves, pepper, and other herbs, onions, cream, wine, and hard-boiled egg yolks. "Herb pudding" involved oatmeal, breadcrumbs, flour, lard, spinach, parsley, leek, onion, and sage. Fish was frequently served with complex sauces, and meat dishes, too, might involve many ingredients and complicated procedures.

that Bingley would return to Netherfield and answer every wish of her heart.

They agreed that Mrs. Bennet should only hear of the departure of the family, without being alarmed on the score of the gentleman's conduct; but even this partial communication gave her a great deal of concern, and she bewailed it as exceedingly unlucky that the ladies should happen to go away, just as they were all getting so intimate together. After lamenting it however at some length, she had the consolation that Mr. Bingley would be soon down again and soon dining at Longbourn, and the conclusion of all was the comfortable declaration that, though he had been invited only to a family dinner, she would take care to have two full courses.[9]

22

The Bennets were engaged to dine with the Lucases, and again during the chief[1] of the day, was Miss Lucas so kind as to listen to Mr. Collins. Elizabeth took an opportunity of thanking her. "It keeps him in good humour," said she, "and I am more obliged to you than I can express." Charlotte assured her friend of her satisfaction in being useful, and that it amply repaid her for the little sacrifice of her time. This was very amiable, but Charlotte's kindness extended farther than Elizabeth had any conception of;—its object was nothing less, than to secure[2] her from any return of Mr. Collins's addresses,[3] by engaging them towards herself. Such was Miss Lucas's scheme; and appearances were so favourable that when they parted at night, she would have felt almost sure of success if he had not been to leave Hertfordshire so very soon. But here, she did injustice to the fire and independence of his character, for it led him to escape out of Longbourn House the next morning with admirable slyness, and hasten to Lucas Lodge to throw himself at her feet.[4] He was anxious to avoid the notice of his cousins, from a conviction that if they saw him depart, they could not fail to conjecture his design,[5] and he was not willing to have the attempt known till its success could be known likewise; for though feeling almost secure, and with reason, for Charlotte had been tolerably encouraging, he was comparatively diffident since the adventure of Wednesday. His reception however was of the most flattering kind. Miss Lucas perceived him from an upper window as he walked towards the house, and instantly set out to meet

1 Main part.

2 Make her safe.

3 Proposals.

4 Mr. Collins's ease in moving from one woman to another (Jane to Elizabeth to Charlotte) as the object of his devotion derives from his failure to grasp the fact that women have consciousness of their own. He imagines them, at best, in the role of grateful recipient; his slight doubt about Charlotte appears to be precautionary. Essentially Mr. Collins, like Mrs. Bennet, understands women as a form of property, ready to be exchanged. He is not likely to throw himself at anyone's feet—but he's capable of speaking as though he intends just that.

5 Another indication of his high self regard: he assumes that others are as focused on him as he himself is.

6 Because of the conventions of female propriety.

7 Settled and financially secure living arrangement. It is important, in assessing Charlotte's decision to marry Collins, to understand that she fully realizes his stupidity and that neither he nor his courtship has any charms for her.

8 Promising.

9 Entering society. Girls were customarily expected to wait for their older sisters' marriage before coming out themselves.

10 "A single woman, with a very narrow income, must be a ridiculous, disagreeable, old maid! the proper sport of boys and girls," Emma explains to Harriet Smith in Austen's 1815 novel (I, 10). She elaborates by explaining how money makes all the difference: she anticipates for herself, given her comfortable financial foundation, a happy single state. Charlotte is quite right in thinking that marriage must be the "pleasantest preservative from want" for a young woman of small fortune. As Austen writes to her niece Fanny Knight, "Single Women have a dreadful propensity for being poor" (13 March 1817). Virtually the only alternatives to marriage for a woman who wished to retain any vestige of gentility were serving as a governess or becoming a companion (doing tasks and errands for a well-to-do woman and providing her with an object for patronizing) in a wealthy family. The situation of a governess may be suggested by the narrator's account of Jane Fairfax's expectations, in *Emma,* of her life as a governess: "With the fortitude of a devoted noviciate, she had resolved at one-and-twenty to complete the sacrifice, and retire from all the pleasures of life, of rational intercourse, equal society, peace and hope, to penance and mortification for ever" (II, 2). Later in the novel, Jane refers to employment offices for governesses as existing "for the sale—not quite of human flesh—but of human intellect." When her interlocutor thinks she's alluding to the slave trade, Jane explains, "governess-trade, I assure you, was all that I had in view; widely different certainly as to the guilt of those who carry it on; but as to the greater misery of the victims, I do not know where it lies" (II, 17). Frances Bur-

him accidentally in the lane. But little had she dared to hope that so much love and eloquence awaited her there.

In as short a time as Mr. Collins's long speeches would allow, every thing was settled between them to the satisfaction of both; and as they entered the house, he earnestly entreated her to name the day that was to make him the happiest of men; and though such a solicitation must be waived for the present,[6] the lady felt no inclination to trifle with his happiness. The stupidity with which he was favoured by nature, must guard his courtship from any charm that could make a woman wish for its continuance; and Miss Lucas, who accepted him solely from the pure and disinterested desire of an establishment,[7] cared not how soon that establishment were gained.

Sir William and Lady Lucas were speedily applied to for their consent; and it was bestowed with a most joyful alacrity. Mr. Collins's present circumstances made it a most eligible match for their daughter, to whom they could give little fortune; and his prospects of future wealth were exceedingly fair.[8] Lady Lucas began directly to calculate with more interest than the matter had ever excited before, how many years longer Mr. Bennet was likely to live; and Sir William gave it as his decided opinion, that whenever Mr. Collins should be in possession of the Longbourn estate, it would be highly expedient that both he and his wife should make their appearance at St. James's. The whole family in short were properly overjoyed on the occasion. The younger girls formed hopes of *coming out*[9] a year or two sooner than they might otherwise have done; and the boys were relieved from their apprehension of Charlotte's dying an old maid. Charlotte herself was tolerably composed. She had gained her point, and had time to consider of it. Her reflections were in general satisfactory. Mr. Collins to be sure was neither sensible nor agreeable; his society was irksome, and his attachment to her must be imaginary. But still he would be her husband.—Without thinking highly either of men or of matrimony, marriage had always been her object; it was the only provision for well-educated young women of small fortune,[10] and however uncertain of giving happiness, must be their pleasantest preservative from want. This preservative she had now obtained; and at the age of twenty-seven, without having ever been handsome, she felt all the good luck of it. The least agreeable circumstance in the business was the surprise it must occasion to Elizabeth Bennet, whose friendship she valued beyond that of any other person. Elizabeth would wonder, and probably would blame her; and though her resolution was not to be shaken, her feelings must be hurt by such disapprobation. She resolved to give her the information herself, and therefore charged Mr. Collins when he returned to Longbourn to dinner, to drop no hint of what had passed before any of the family. A promise of secrecy was of course very dutifully given, but it could not be kept without difficulty; for the curiosity excited by his long absence, burst forth in such very direct questions on his return, as required some ingenuity to evade, and he was at the same time exercising great self-denial, for he was longing to publish[11] his prosperous love.

As he was to begin his journey too early on the morrow to see any of the family, the ceremony of leave-taking was performed when the ladies moved for the night; and Mrs. Bennet with great politeness and cordiality said how happy they should be to see him at Longbourn again, whenever his engagements might allow him to visit them.

"My dear Madam," he replied, "this invitation is particularly gratifying, because it is what I have been hoping to receive; and you may be very certain that I shall avail myself of it as soon as possible."

They were all astonished; and Mr. Bennet, who could by no means wish for so speedy a return, immediately said,

"But is there not danger of Lady Catherine's disapprobation here, my good sir?—You had better neglect your relations, than run the risk of offending your patroness."

"My dear sir," replied Mr. Collins, "I am particularly obliged to you for this friendly caution, and you may depend upon my not taking so material a step without her ladyship's concurrence."

"You cannot be too much upon your guard. Risk anything rather than her displeasure; and if you find it likely to be raised by your coming to us again, which I should think exceedingly probable, stay quietly at home, and be satisfied that *we* shall take no offence."

ney's final novel, *The Wanderer* (1802), had as subtitle *Female Difficulties*. It narrated the extreme difficulties of a young woman without known family or social status endeavoring to support herself in England at the time of the French Revolution. Her efforts at paid employment include working in a milliner's shop and functioning as a companion—but in fact only marriage solves her problems.

In the light of such evidence, Charlotte's decision to lure and accept Mr. Collins becomes more comprehensible. In the middle of the eighteenth century, Thomas, second Lord Lyttelton, wrote that "after all that sentimental talkers and sentimental writers may produce upon the subject, marriage must be considered as a species of traffic, and as much a matter of commerce as any commodity that fills the warehouse of a merchant." Lawrence Stone, who quotes this observation, says that few would have shared Lyttelton's "cynical view" (*The Family, Sex and Marriage in England 1500–1800* [New York: Harper & Row, 1977], 273) at that time. Charlotte, however, imagined as living at the end of the century, indicates both by her comments on others and by her own procedures that she has much the same perception. She is altogether clear-sighted in her choice, aware of Collins's social and moral unattractiveness. She makes, however, precisely the kind of bargain that Collins has expected Elizabeth to make: her charms for his security.

11 Publicize.

12 Indeed, his reflections often sound much like hers. Both model their opinions on the doctrine of conventional conduct books and frequently parrot moral clichés.

13 Like Mr. Collins, Mary sometimes seems to have a high opinion of herself. She also, however, shows signs of insecurity.

"Believe me, my dear sir, my gratitude is warmly excited by such affectionate attention; and depend upon it, you will speedily receive from me a letter of thanks for this, as well as for every other mark of your regard during my stay in Hertfordshire. As for my fair cousins, though my absence may not be long enough to render it necessary, I shall now take the liberty of wishing them health and happiness, not excepting my cousin Elizabeth."

With proper civilities the ladies then withdrew; all of them equally surprised to find that he meditated a quick return. Mrs. Bennet wished to understand by it that he thought of paying his addresses to one of her younger girls, and Mary might have been prevailed on to accept him. She rated his abilities much higher than any of the others; there was a solidity in his reflections which often struck her,[12] and though by no means so clever as herself,[13] she thought that if encouraged to read and improve himself by such an example as her's, he might become a very agreeable companion. But on the following morning, every hope of this kind was done away. Miss Lucas called soon after breakfast, and in a private conference with Elizabeth related the event of the day before.

The possibility of Mr. Collins's fancying herself in love with her friend had once occurred to Elizabeth within the last day or two; but that Charlotte could encourage him, seemed almost as far from possibility as that she could encourage him herself, and her astonishment was consequently so great as to overcome at first the bounds of decorum, and she could not help crying out,

"Engaged to Mr. Collins! my dear Charlotte,—impossible!"

The steady countenance which Miss Lucas had commanded in telling her story, gave way to a momentary confusion here on receiving so direct a reproach; though, as it was no more than she expected, she soon regained her composure, and calmly replied,

"Why should you be surprised, my dear Eliza?—Do you think it incredible that Mr. Collins should be able to procure any woman's good opinion, because he was not so happy as to succeed with you?"

But Elizabeth had now recollected herself, and making a strong effort for it, was able to assure her with tolerable firmness that the prospect of their relationship was highly grateful[14] to her, and that she wished her all imaginable happiness.

"I see what you are feeling," replied Charlotte,—"you must be surprised, very much surprised,—so lately[15] as Mr. Collins was wishing to marry you. But when you have had time to think it over, I hope you will be satisfied with what I have done. I am not romantic,[16] you know. I never was. I ask only a comfortable home; and considering Mr. Collins's character,[17] connections, and situation in life, I am convinced that my chance of happiness with him is as fair, as most people can boast on entering the marriage state."

Elizabeth quietly answered "Undoubtedly;"—and after an awkward pause, they returned to the rest of the family. Charlotte did not stay much longer, and Elizabeth was then left to reflect on what she had heard. It was a long time before she became at all reconciled to the idea of so unsuitable a match. The strangeness of Mr. Collins's making two offers of marriage within three days, was nothing in comparison of his being now accepted. She had always felt that Charlotte's opinion of matrimony was not exactly like her own, but she could not have supposed it possible that when called into action, she would have sacrificed every better feeling to worldly advantage.[18] Charlotte the wife of Mr. Collins, was a most humiliating picture!— And to the pang of a friend disgracing herself[19] and sunk in her esteem, was added the distressing conviction that it was impossible for that friend to be tolerably happy in the lot she had chosen.

14 Gratifying. Charlotte will become a second cousin by marriage.

15 Recently.

16 "Having a tendency towards romance; readily influenced by imagination" (OED).

17 Meaning either essential nature or, more likely, reputation. It is difficult to understand, however, what Charlotte could possibly know of Mr. Collins's reputation, and she has hardly had time to grasp his essential nature.

18 Now and later, Elizabeth shows a striking lack of sympathy for Charlotte's dilemma. Charlotte, it must be remembered, is twenty-seven years old, on the verge of being an "old maid," a condition generally thought to begin at the age of twenty-eight. Elizabeth's inability to grasp the pressures of her friend's situation suggests the possibility that Austen's heroine may be short-sighted in hastening to "conviction." On first reading, though, one would be unlikely to grasp this fact. In formulating this and other judgments, Elizabeth typically articulates her view with such eloquence and force that it carries conviction even when based on dubious evidence or unexamined assumption.

19 In Elizabeth's eyes, she has violated moral principle in accepting a man whom she neither loves nor respects. This extreme idealistic view marks Elizabeth's sharp difference from those, like her mother, who believe that a woman's chief responsibility is to marry for financial advantage.

23

1 When his daughter marries Mr. Bennet's cousin, she will establish a family relationship with the Bennets, which Sir William imagines as extending to himself, his wife, and his other children. "House," in Sir William's sense, designates "[a] family including ancestors and descendants . . . esp. one . . . of exalted rank, or high renown" *(OED)*. His use of the term supplies one more instance of his social pretensions.

2 Lie.

Elizabeth was sitting with her mother and sisters, reflecting on what she had heard, and doubting whether she were authorised to mention it, when Sir William Lucas himself appeared, sent by his daughter to announce her engagement to the family. With many compliments to them, and much self-gratulation on the prospect of a connection between the houses,[1] he unfolded the matter,— to an audience not merely wondering, but incredulous; for Mrs. Bennet, with more perseverance than politeness, protested he must be entirely mistaken, and Lydia, always unguarded and often uncivil, boisterously exclaimed,

"Good Lord! Sir William, how can you tell such a story?[2]—Do not you know that Mr. Collins wants to marry Lizzy?"

Nothing less than the complaisance of a courtier could have borne without anger such treatment; but Sir William's good breeding carried him through it all; and though he begged leave to be positive as to the truth of his information, he listened to all their impertinence with the most forbearing courtesy.

Elizabeth, feeling it incumbent on her to relieve him from so unpleasant a situation, now put herself forward to confirm his account, by mentioning her prior knowledge of it from Charlotte herself; and endeavoured to put a stop to the exclamations of her mother and sisters by the earnestness of her congratulations to Sir William, in which she was readily joined by Jane, and by making a variety of remarks on the happiness that might be expected from the match, the excellent character of Mr. Collins, and the convenient distance of Hunsford from London.

Mrs. Bennet was in fact too much overpowered to say a great deal while Sir William remained; but no sooner had he left them than her feelings found a rapid vent. In the first place, she persisted in disbelieving the whole of the matter; secondly, she was very sure that Mr. Collins had been taken in; thirdly, she trusted that they would never be happy together; and fourthly, that the match might be broken off. Two inferences, however, were plainly deduced from the whole; one, that Elizabeth was the real cause of all the mischief; and the other, that she herself had been barbarously used by them all; and on these two points she principally dwelt during the rest of the day. Nothing could console and nothing appease her. Nor did that day wear out her resentment. A week elapsed before she could see Elizabeth without scolding her, a month passed away before she could speak to Sir William or Lady Lucas without being rude, and many months were gone before she could at all forgive their daughter.

Mr. Bennet's emotions were much more tranquil on the occasion, and such as he did experience he pronounced to be of a most agreeable sort; for it gratified him, he said, to discover that Charlotte Lucas, whom he had been used to think tolerably sensible, was as foolish as his wife, and more foolish than his daughter![3]

Jane confessed herself a little surprised at the match; but she said less of her astonishment than of her earnest desire for their happiness; nor could Elizabeth persuade her to consider it as improbable.[4] Kitty and Lydia were far from envying Miss Lucas, for Mr. Collins was only a clergyman; and it affected them in no other way than as a piece of news to spread at Meryton.

Lady Lucas could not be insensible of triumph on being able to retort on[5] Mrs. Bennet the comfort of having a daughter well married; and she called at Longbourn rather oftener than usual to say how happy she was, though Mrs. Bennet's sour looks and ill-natured remarks might have been enough to drive happiness away.

Between Elizabeth and Charlotte there was a restraint which kept them mutually silent on the subject; and Elizabeth felt persuaded

3 Her folly, of course, consists in having chosen a marriage of convenience. Mr. Bennet himself, however, having married for other reasons, has lived to find his choice less than satisfactory.

4 Elizabeth has some psychological stake in her insistence on the likelihood of the marriage's unhappiness. She disapproves so strongly of Charlotte's behavior that she in effect wants it punished: her friend's marital unhappiness would implicitly declare that Elizabeth had been right in her opposed view of marriage.

5 Throw back at.

6 The importance of "rectitude and delicacy" to Elizabeth suggests her strong commitment to principle.

7 Mr. Collins much prefers rapturous expressions to rapture.

8 Agree to.

9 Two weeks from Monday.

10 Apparently Collins's entertainment value for Mr. Bennet has worn out.

that no real confidence could ever subsist between them again. Her disappointment in Charlotte made her turn with fonder regard to her sister, of whose rectitude and delicacy[6] she was sure her opinion could never be shaken, and for whose happiness she grew daily more anxious, as Bingley had now been gone a week and nothing was heard of his return.

Jane had sent Caroline an early answer to her letter, and was counting the days till she might reasonably hope to hear again. The promised letter of thanks from Mr. Collins arrived on Tuesday, addressed to their father, and written with all the solemnity of gratitude which a twelvemonth's abode in the family might have prompted. After discharging his conscience on that head, he proceeded to inform them, with many rapturous expressions,[7] of his happiness in having obtained the affection of their amiable neighbour, Miss Lucas, and then explained that it was merely with the view of enjoying her society that he had been so ready to close with[8] their kind wish of seeing him again at Longbourn, whither he hoped to be able to return on Monday fortnight;[9] for Lady Catherine, he added, so heartily approved his marriage, that she wished it to take place as soon as possible, which he trusted would be an unanswerable argument with his amiable Charlotte to name an early day for making him the happiest of men.

Mr. Collins's return into Hertfordshire was no longer a matter of pleasure to Mrs. Bennet. On the contrary, she was as much disposed to complain of it as her husband.[10]—It was very strange that he should come to Longbourn instead of to Lucas Lodge; it was also very inconvenient and exceedingly troublesome.—She hated having visitors in the house while her health was so indifferent, and lovers were of all people the most disagreeable. Such were the gentle murmurs of Mrs. Bennet, and they gave way only to the greater distress of Mr. Bingley's continued absence.

Neither Jane nor Elizabeth were comfortable on this subject. Day after day passed away without bringing any other tidings of him than the report which shortly prevailed in Meryton of his coming no more to Netherfield the whole winter; a report which highly incensed Mrs.

Bennet, and which she never failed to contradict as a most scandalous falsehood.

Even Elizabeth began to fear—not that Bingley was indifferent—
but that his sisters would be successful in keeping him away. Unwilling as she was to admit an idea so destructive of Jane's happiness, and
so dishonourable to the stability of her lover, she could not prevent
its frequently recurring. The united efforts of his two unfeeling sisters and of his overpowering friend, assisted by the attractions of
Miss Darcy and the amusements of London, might be too much, she
feared, for the strength of his attachment.

As for Jane, *her* anxiety under this suspence was, of course, more
painful than Elizabeth's; but whatever she felt she was desirous of
concealing, and between herself and Elizabeth, therefore, the subject was never alluded to. But as no such delicacy restrained her
mother, an hour seldom passed in which she did not talk of Bingley,
express her impatience for his arrival, or even require Jane to confess
that if he did not come back, she should think herself very ill used. It
needed all Jane's steady mildness to bear these attacks with tolerable
tranquillity.

Mr. Collins returned most punctually on Monday fortnight, but
his reception at Longbourn was not quite so gracious as it had been
on his first introduction. He was too happy, however, to need much
attention; and luckily for the others, the business of love-making[11]
relieved them from a great deal of his company. The chief of every
day was spent by him at Lucas Lodge, and he sometimes returned to
Longbourn only in time to make an apology for his absence before
the family went to bed.

Mrs. Bennet was really in a most pitiable state. The very mention
of anything concerning the match threw her into an agony of ill humour, and wherever she went she was sure of hearing it talked of. The
sight of Miss Lucas was odious to her. As her successor in that house,
she regarded her with jealous abhorrence. Whenever Charlotte came
to see them she concluded her to be anticipating the hour of possession; and whenever she spoke in a low voice to Mr. Collins, was convinced that they were talking of the Longbourn estate, and resolving

11 Like Mrs. Bennet's business of getting her daughters married, Mr. Collins's temporary business of love-
making may seem demanding. After all, he must have,
according to his sense of things, many forms to go
through.

to turn herself and her daughters out of the house, as soon as Mr. Bennet were dead. She complained bitterly of all this to her husband.

"Indeed, Mr. Bennet," said she, "it is very hard to think that Charlotte Lucas should ever be mistress of this house, that *I* should be forced to make way for *her,* and live to see her take her place in it!"

"My dear, do not give way to such gloomy thoughts. Let us hope for better things. Let us flatter ourselves that *I* may be the survivor."

This was not very consoling to Mrs. Bennet, and therefore, instead of making any answer, she went on as before,

"I cannot bear to think that they should have all this estate. If it was not for the entail I should not mind it."

"What should not you mind?"

"I should not mind any thing at all."

"Let us be thankful that you are preserved from a state of such insensibility."

"I never can be thankful, Mr. Bennet, for anything about the entail. How anyone could have the conscience to entail away an estate from one's own daughters, I cannot understand; and all for the sake of Mr. Collins too!—Why should he have it more than anybody else?"

"I leave it to yourself to determine," said Mr. Bennet.

Volume II

I

Miss Bingley's letter arrived, and put an end to doubt. The very first sentence conveyed the assurance of their being all settled in London for the winter, and concluded with her brother's regret at not having had time to pay his respects to his friends in Hertfordshire before he left the country.

Hope was over, entirely over; and when Jane could attend to the rest of the letter, she found little, except the professed affection of the writer, that could give her any comfort. Miss Darcy's praise occupied the chief of it. Her many attractions were again dwelt on, and Caroline boasted joyfully of their increasing intimacy, and ventured to predict the accomplishment of the wishes which had been unfolded in her former letter. She wrote also with great pleasure of her brother's being an inmate of Mr. Darcy's house, and mentioned with raptures,[1] some plans of the latter with regard to new furniture.

Elizabeth, to whom Jane very soon communicated the chief of all this, heard it in silent indignation. Her heart was divided between concern for her sister, and resentment against all others. To Caroline's assertion of her brother's being partial to Miss Darcy she paid no credit. That he was really fond of Jane, she doubted no more than she had ever done; and much as she had always been disposed to like him, she could not think without anger, hardly without contempt, on that easiness of temper,[2] that want of proper resolution, which now made him the slave of his designing[3] friends, and led him to sacrifice his own happiness[4] to the caprice of their inclinations. Had his

[1] Ecstatic delight.

[2] Temperament. Bingley's "easy manners" have previously been a subject for approval; they probably derive from the easy temperament that Elizabeth here decries.

[3] Scheming, plotting.

[4] Of course Elizabeth's assumption that his happiness must depend on Jane derives largely from her "prejudice" in favor of her sister.

5 Aware.

6 Substantially.

7 Expression of annoyance.

8 He has not made promises of marriage and then failed to fulfill them—a procedure that would have seriously violated fundamental standards of decorum as well as of decency.

9 "Angelic" Jane resembles the heroines of many sentimental eighteenth-century novels and plays and the descendants of those heroines in nineteenth-century fiction, but she also differs from them in important ways. One may think, for instance, of Mary Brunton's popular novel *Self-Control* (published in 1810, just three years before *Pride and Prejudice*). Laura, the protagonist of *Self-Control,* a work obviously influenced by both *Pamela* and *Clarissa,* is unfailingly good, but good, as the title suggests, by virtue of severe self-discipline. Like Jane, she sees people in the best light and does not reproach them with their failings, although she repudiates vice wherever she finds it.

Jane, in contrast, seems fundamentally good by nature rather than by effort. She makes efforts, to be sure: as she says to Elizabeth, she works to get the better of herself when her disappointment over Bingley's disappearance threatens her cheerfulness. Her habit of thinking the best of everyone, however, involves no effort at all. It comes from her nature.

An important group of eighteenth-century thinkers, David Hume and Adam Smith chief among them, had argued that feeling rather than thought provided the ground for morality. Smith articulated in detail his doctrine of "sympathy," claiming for human beings an innate capacity for imaginative identification with one another that could generate moral conduct. Jane exemplifies the theory: she sympathizes with everyone and behaves generously to all. As Elizabeth says, "sweetness and disinterestedness" characterize her.

But Jane is not Austen's heroine. Elizabeth, unlike her sister, does not always take a generous view, does not always act sweetly, and conspicuously cares about her own "performances." Austen's originality manifests itself in her imagining of such a character as of pri-

own happiness, however, been the only sacrifice, he might have been allowed to sport with it in what ever manner he thought best; but her sister's was involved in it, as she thought he must be sensible[5] himself. It was a subject, in short, on which reflection would be long indulged, and must be unavailing. She could think of nothing else; and yet whether Bingley's regard had really died away, or were suppressed by his friends' interference; whether he had been aware of Jane's attachment, or whether it had escaped his observation; whichever were the case, though her opinion of him must be materially[6] affected by the difference, her sister's situation remained the same, her peace equally wounded.

A day or two passed before Jane had courage to speak of her feelings to Elizabeth; but at last on Mrs. Bennet's leaving them together, after a longer irritation[7] than usual about Netherfield and its master, she could not help saying,

"Oh! that my dear mother had more command over herself; she can have no idea of the pain she gives me by her continual reflections on him. But I will not repine. It cannot last long. He will be forgot, and we shall all be as we were before."

Elizabeth looked at her sister with incredulous solicitude, but said nothing.

"You doubt me," cried Jane slightly colouring; "indeed, you have no reason. He may live in my memory as the most amiable man of my acquaintance, but that is all. I have nothing either to hope or fear, and nothing to reproach him with.[8] Thank God! I have not *that* pain. A little time therefore.—I shall certainly try to get the better."

With a stronger voice she soon added, "I have this comfort immediately, that it has not been more than an error of fancy on my side, and that it has done no harm to anyone but myself."

"My dear Jane!" exclaimed Elizabeth, "you are too good. Your sweetness and disinterestedness are really angelic;[9] I do not know what to say to you. I feel as if I had never done you justice, or loved you as you deserve."

Miss Bennet eagerly disclaimed all extraordinary merit, and threw back the praise on her sister's warm affection.

"Nay," said Elizabeth, "this is not fair. *You* wish to think all the world respectable, and are hurt if I speak ill of anybody. *I* only want to think *you* perfect, and you set yourself against it. Do not be afraid of my running into any excess, of my encroaching on your privilege of universal good will. You need not. There are few people whom I really love, and still fewer of whom I think well.[10] The more I see of the world, the more am I dissatisfied with it; and every day confirms my belief of the inconsistency of all human characters, and of the little dependence that can be placed on the appearance of either merit or sense. I have met with two instances lately; one I will not mention; the other is Charlotte's marriage. It is unaccountable! in every view it is unaccountable!"

"My dear Lizzy, do not give way to such feelings as these. They will ruin your happiness. You do not make allowance enough for difference of situation and temper. Consider Mr. Collins's respectability, and Charlotte's prudent, steady character. Remember that she is one of a large family; that as to fortune, it is a most eligible[11] match; and be ready to believe, for every body's sake, that she may feel something like regard and esteem for our cousin."

"To oblige you, I would try to believe almost anything, but no one else could be benefited by such a belief as this; for were I persuaded that Charlotte had any regard for him, I should only think worse of her understanding, than I now do of her heart. My dear Jane, Mr. Collins is a conceited, pompous, narrow-minded, silly man; you know he is, as well as I do; and you must feel, as well as I do, that the woman who marries him, cannot have a proper way of thinking.[12] You shall not defend her, though it is Charlotte Lucas. You shall not, for the sake of one individual, change the meaning of principle and integrity, nor endeavour to persuade yourself or me, that selfishness is prudence, and insensibility of danger, security for happiness."[13]

"I must think your language too strong in speaking of both,"[14] replied Jane, "and I hope you will be convinced of it, by seeing them happy together. But enough of this. You alluded to something else. You mentioned *two* instances. I cannot misunderstand you, but I intreat you, dear Lizzy, not to pain me by thinking *that person* to blame,

mary importance in her plot. The witty girl who had appeared frequently in eighteenth-century fiction invariably figured as secondary to the heroine—and often as dubiously attractive to men. Thus Maria Fluart, in *Hermsprong,* remains unmarried, and Charlotte, in *Sir Charles Grandison,* has to reform after her marriage. Austen is not only original but daring: she dares to introduce into her fiction the angelically good sister, and yet to insist tacitly on Elizabeth's moral as well as intellectual preeminence.

Unable to act automatically for good on the basis of her feelings, Elizabeth seeks steadily to develop moral discrimination. She makes many mistakes along the way, influenced too often by immediate reactions and by others' views. But she looks at the evidence she is offered; she corrects herself when she can; she insists on the value of principle. She exemplifies moral process rather than moral triumph. Her way is more arduous than Jane's, and more rational. Also, perhaps, more interesting.

10 She sounds strikingly like her father here.

11 Appropriate.

12 Elizabeth *feels* that Charlotte doesn't *think* in the right way. Charlotte's sin appears to be her failure to marry for love, her willingness to marry someone she couldn't possibly love. It's curious that Elizabeth believes lack of love to constitute an error of thought. Of course she would formulate the error as one of thinking because she believes that right thinking about marriage includes acknowledgment of necessary emotional commitment. As is often apparent, Elizabeth operates characteristically on the basis of principle—although she may be misguided in the principles she applies.

13 Elizabeth is more astute and more realistic than Jane, partly because she is not blinded by a desire to think well of everyone. But she isn't realistic about Charlotte. Perhaps Austen wishes to suggest that Charlotte's situation, despite the differences between her and Elizabeth in age and attractiveness, is uncomfortably close to Elizabeth's potential one. As Mr. Collins has said, she may never have another proposal of marriage; she could find herself single, aging, and

poverty-stricken. Her assertion of absolute principle defends her against this realization.

14 Jane is quite right, especially about Elizabeth's attitude toward Charlotte. In calling Mr. Collins conceited, pompous, narrow-minded, and silly, Elizabeth articulates a view that Austen has led the reader to share; but in terming Charlotte's marriage one of selfishness rather than of prudence, she exaggerates considerably. Indeed, Charlotte might be termed *un*selfish for relieving her family of the burden of her support, and she is certainly prudent in her marital choice, given a fairly narrow definition of prudence. Elizabeth's incapacity to empathize with a woman of limited prospects, possessed of limited choices, marks a real inadequacy. She is younger, prettier, and luckier than Charlotte. If Jane feels inwardly compelled to think well of everyone, her sister is equally compelled to articulate absolute views and to feel absolute confidence in her own opinion. It is true that Charlotte's marriage entails a violation of Elizabeth's principles—but not of her own: she has always said that it's best to marry without knowing too much of a man, and she has always considered a man's financial position of primary importance.

15 This plural pronoun refers to women in general: Jane has enlarged her considerations to take in her sex as a whole.

16 She is perhaps describing the "error of fancy" of which she has earlier accused herself.

17 The phrasing suggests that pride, as well as money and "connections," can be a source of importance. This idea provides a new perspective on Darcy's pride.

18 Something objectionable, that is, in the object of the man's affections.

19 Jane is saying that she's less unhappy in supposing that Bingley does not feel affection for her than she would be if she believed he did, because in the latter case she would have to think he was far too subject to outside influences in determining his own actions.

and saying your opinion of him is sunk. We[15] must not be so ready to fancy ourselves intentionally injured. We must not expect a lively young man to be always so guarded and circumspect. It is very often nothing but our own vanity that deceives us. Women fancy admiration means more than it does."[16]

"And men take care that they should."

"If it is designedly done, they cannot be justified; but I have no idea of there being so much design in the world as some persons imagine."

"I am far from attributing any part of Mr. Bingley's conduct to design," said Elizabeth; "but without scheming to do wrong, or to make others unhappy, there may be error, and there may be misery. Thoughtlessness, want of attention to other people's feelings, and want of resolution, will do the business."

"And do you impute it to either of those?"

"Yes; to the last. But if I go on, I shall displease you by saying what I think of persons you esteem. Stop me whilst you can."

"You persist, then, in supposing his sisters influence him?"

"Yes, in conjunction with his friend."

"I cannot believe it. Why should they try to influence him? They can only wish his happiness, and if he is attached to me, no other woman can secure it."

"Your first position is false. They may wish many things besides his happiness; they may wish his increase of wealth and consequence; they may wish him to marry a girl who has all the importance of money, great connections, and pride."[17]

"Beyond a doubt, they *do* wish him to chuse Miss Darcy," replied Jane; "but this may be from better feelings than you are supposing. They have known her much longer than they have known me; no wonder if they love her better. But, whatever may be their own wishes, it is very unlikely they should have opposed their brother's. What sister would think herself at liberty to do it, unless there were something very objectionable?[18] If they believed him attached to me, they would not try to part us; if he were so, they could not succeed. By supposing such an affection,[19] you make every body acting unnaturally and wrong, and me most unhappy. Do not distress me by the idea. I am not ashamed of having been mistaken—or, at least, it is slight, it is nothing in comparison of what I should feel in thinking ill of him or his sisters. Let me take it in the best light, in the light in which it may be understood."

Elizabeth could not oppose such a wish; and from this time Mr. Bingley's name was scarcely ever mentioned between them.

Mrs. Bennet still continued to wonder and repine at his returning no more, and though a day seldom passed in which Elizabeth did not account for it clearly, there seemed little chance of her ever considering it with less perplexity. Her daughter endeavoured to convince her of what she did not believe herself, that his attentions to Jane had been merely the effect of a common and transient liking, which ceased when he saw her no more; but though the probability of the statement was admitted at the time, she had the same story to repeat every day. Mrs. Bennet's best comfort was, that Mr. Bingley must be down again in the summer.[20]

Mr. Bennet treated the matter differently. "So, Lizzy," said he one day, "your sister is crossed in love I find. I congratulate her. Next to being married, a girl likes to be crossed a little in love now and then. It is something to think of, and gives her a sort of distinction among her companions. When is your turn to come? You will hardly bear to be long outdone by Jane. Now is your time. Here are officers enough in Meryton to disappoint all the young ladies in the country. Let Wickham be *your* man. He is a pleasant fellow, and would jilt you creditably."

"Thank you, Sir, but a less agreeable man would satisfy me. We must not all expect Jane's good fortune."

"True," said Mr. Bennet, "but it is a comfort to think that, whatever of that kind may befal you, you have an affectionate mother who will always make the most of it."

Mr. Wickham's society was of material service in dispelling the gloom, which the late perverse occurrences had thrown on many of the Longbourn family. They saw him often, and to his other recommendations was now added that of general unreserve.[21] The whole of what Elizabeth had already heard, his claims on Mr. Darcy, and all that he had suffered from him, was now openly acknowledged and

20 Because wealthy people commonly left London in the summer.

21 Frankness. The use of the term *unreserve*, however, emphasizes Wickham's lack of the reticence about personal matters that is appropriate for a gentleman, although the Bennet sisters do not see it this way.

22 Discussed.

23 Generosity.

publicly canvassed;[22] and every body was pleased to think how much they had always disliked Mr. Darcy before they had known any thing of the matter.

Miss Bennet was the only creature who could suppose there might be any extenuating circumstances in the case, unknown to the society of Hertfordshire; her mild and steady candour[23] always pleaded for allowances, and urged the possibility of mistakes — but by every-body else Mr. Darcy was condemned as the worst of men.

Adam Callander, "The Great House and Park at Chawton," c. 1780. Edward Austen Knight, Jane Austen's brother, owned this rather grand late sixteenth-century house, which has now become a center for the study of women's writing.

2

After a week spent in professions[1] of love and schemes of felicity, Mr. Collins was called from his amiable Charlotte[2] by the arrival of Saturday. The pain of separation, however, might be alleviated on his side, by preparations for the reception of his bride; as he had reason to hope, that shortly after his next return into Hertfordshire, the day would be fixed that was to make him the happiest of men. He took leave of his relations at Longbourn with as much solemnity as before; wished his fair cousins health and happiness again, and promised their father another letter of thanks.

On the following Monday, Mrs. Bennet had the pleasure of receiving her brother and his wife, who came as usual to spend the Christmas at Longbourn. Mr. Gardiner was a sensible, gentlemanlike man, greatly superior to his sister as well by nature as education. The Netherfield ladies would have had difficulty in believing that a man who lived by trade, and within view of his own warehouses, could have been so well bred and agreeable.[3] Mrs. Gardiner, who was several years younger than Mrs. Bennet and Mrs. Philips, was an amiable, intelligent, elegant[4] woman, and a great favourite with all her Longbourn nieces. Between the two eldest and herself especially, there subsisted a particular regard. They had frequently been staying with her in town.

The first part of Mrs. Gardiner's business on her arrival, was to distribute her presents and describe the newest fashions.[5] When this was done, she had a less active part to play. It became her turn to listen. Mrs. Bennet had many grievances to relate, and much to com-

1 Declarations. By Austen's time, the word sometimes suggested insincerity or falsity: professions do not necessarily declare the truth.

2 Many of Mr. Collins's nouns tend to come, in his speech, with specific adjectives attached: thus his humble abode and his amiable Charlotte and his fair cousins, as well as his styling himself the happiest of men.

3 Although their own father had made his fortune by trade.

4 Correct and delicate in taste, refined in manners and habits—a word of high praise in Austen's vocabulary. It is particularly important in this instance, since it makes it clear that Mrs. Gardiner has the bearing and manners of a gentlewoman.

5 Which would come to London (from Paris) earlier than to the provinces.

6 The verb Mrs. Bennet characteristically uses when speaking of her daughters' approaches to marriage. A young woman's proper endeavor, from her point of view, is to *get* a man.

7 Another suggestion that maternal efforts at daughters' marriages are a competitive activity.

8 As, of course, is she—invariably concerned with what, or whom, her daughters can "get."

9 Ill.

10 Austen had her own worries about long sleeves. On a visit to London, she writes to Cassandra, "I wear my gauze gown today, long sleeves & all; I shall see how they succeed, but as yet I have no reason to suppose long sleeves are allowable." Toward the end of the same letter: "Mrs Tilson had long sleeves too, & she assured me that they are worn in the evening by many. I was glad to hear this" (To Cassandra, 9 March 1814). Earlier in the century, long sleeves had not been acceptable evening wear.

11 Brief.

12 Fell through.

plain of. They had all been very ill-used since she last saw her sister. Two of her girls had been upon the point of marriage, and after all there was nothing in it.

"I do not blame Jane," she continued, "for Jane would have got[6] Mr. Bingley if she could. But, Lizzy! Oh, sister! it is very hard to think that she might have been Mr. Collins's wife by this time, had it not been for her own perverseness. He made her an offer in this very room, and she refused him. The consequence of it is, that Lady Lucas will have a daughter married before I have,[7] and that the Longbourn estate is just as much entailed as ever. The Lucases are very artful people indeed, sister. They are all for what they can get.[8] I am sorry to say it of them, but so it is. It makes me very nervous and poorly,[9] to be thwarted so in my own family, and to have neighbours who think of themselves before anybody else. However, your coming just at this time is the greatest of comforts, and I am very glad to hear what you tell us, of long sleeves."[10]

Mrs. Gardiner, to whom the chief of this news had been given before, in the course of Jane and Elizabeth's correspondence with her, made her sister a slight[11] answer, and in compassion to her nieces turned the conversation.

When alone with Elizabeth afterwards, she spoke more on the subject. "It seems likely to have been a desirable match for Jane," said she. "I am sorry it went off.[12] But these things happen so often! A young man, such as you describe Mr. Bingley, so easily falls in love with a pretty girl for a few weeks, and when accident separates them, so easily forgets her, that these sort of inconstancies are very frequent."

"An excellent consolation in its way," said Elizabeth, "but it will not do for *us*. We do not suffer by *accident*. It does not often happen that the interference of friends will persuade a young man of independent fortune to think no more of a girl, whom he was violently in love with only a few days before."

"But that expression of 'violently in love' is so hackneyed, so doubtful, so indefinite, that it gives me very little idea. It is as often applied to feelings which arise only from a half-hour's acquaintance, as to a real, strong attachment. Pray, how *violent was* Mr. Bingley's love?"

"I never saw a more promising inclination; he was growing quite inattentive to other people, and wholly engrossed by her. Every time they met, it was more decided and remarkable. At his own ball he offended two or three young ladies, by not asking them to dance; and I spoke to him twice myself, without receiving an answer. Could there be finer symptoms? Is not general incivility the very essence of love?"

"Oh, yes!—of that kind of love which I suppose him to have felt. Poor Jane! I am sorry for her, because, with her disposition, she may not get over it immediately. It had better have happened to *you*, Lizzy; you would have laughed yourself out of it sooner. But do you think she would be prevailed upon to go back with us? Change of scene might be of service—and perhaps a little relief from home, may be as useful as anything."

Elizabeth was exceedingly pleased with this proposal, and felt persuaded of her sister's ready acquiescence.

"I hope," added Mrs. Gardiner, "that no consideration with regard to this young man will influence her. We live in so different a part of town, all our connections[13] are so different, and, as you well know, we go out so little, that it is very improbable that they should meet at all, unless he really comes to see her."

"And *that* is quite impossible; for he is now in the custody of his friend, and Mr. Darcy would no more suffer[14] him to call on Jane in such a part of London! My dear aunt, how could you think of it? Mr. Darcy may perhaps have *heard* of such a place as Gracechurch Street,[15] but he would hardly think a month's ablution[16] enough to cleanse him from its impurities, were he once to enter it; and depend upon it, Mr. Bingley never stirs without him."

"So much the better. I hope they will not meet at all. But does not Jane correspond with the sister? *She* will not be able to help calling."

"She will drop the acquaintance entirely."

But in spite of the certainty in which Elizabeth affected to place this point, as well as the still more interesting[17] one of Bingley's being

13 Social alliances.

14 Allow.

15 The Gardiners' address, in the City of London, the commercial section, an unfashionable district.

16 The washing of the body as a religious rite.

17 Significant.

18 Concern.

19 Powers of entertainment.

20 Had had the means of.

21 Reputation.

withheld from seeing Jane, she felt a solicitude[18] on the subject which convinced her, on examination, that she did not consider it entirely hopeless. It was possible, and sometimes she thought it probable, that his affection might be re-animated, and the influence of his friends successfully combated by the more natural influence of Jane's attractions.

Miss Bennet accepted her aunt's invitation with pleasure; and the Bingleys were no otherwise in her thoughts at the same time, than as she hoped that, by Caroline's not living in the same house with her brother, she might occasionally spend a morning with her, without any danger of seeing him.

The Gardiners staid a week at Longbourn; and what with the Philipses, the Lucases, and the officers, there was not a day without its engagement. Mrs. Bennet had so carefully provided for the entertainment of her brother and sister, that they did not once sit down to a family dinner. When the engagement was for home, some of the officers always made part of it, of which officers Mr. Wickham was sure to be one; and on these occasions, Mrs. Gardiner, rendered suspicious by Elizabeth's warm commendation of him, narrowly observed them both. Without supposing them, from what she saw, to be very seriously in love, their preference of each other was plain enough to make her a little uneasy; and she resolved to speak to Elizabeth on the subject before she left Hertfordshire, and represent to her the imprudence of encouraging such an attachment.

To Mrs. Gardiner, Wickham had one means of affording pleasure, unconnected with his general powers.[19] About ten or a dozen years ago, before her marriage, she had spent a considerable time in that very part of Derbyshire, to which he belonged. They had, therefore, many acquaintance in common; and, though Wickham had been little there since the death of Darcy's father, five years before, it was yet in his power to give her fresher intelligence of her former friends, than she had been in the way[20] of procuring.

Mrs. Gardiner had seen Pemberley, and known the late Mr. Darcy by character[21] perfectly well. Here consequently was an inexhaustible subject of discourse. In comparing her recollection of Pemberley with the minute description which Wickham could give, and in bestowing her tribute of praise on the character of its late possessor, she was delighting both him and herself. On being made acquainted with the present Mr. Darcy's treatment of him, she tried to remember some of that gentleman's reputed disposition when quite a lad, which might agree with it, and was confident at last, that she recollected having heard Mr. Fitzwilliam Darcy formerly spoken of as a very proud, ill-natured boy.

Elaine Maylen, photograph of Stoneleigh Abbey. Stoneleigh Abbey in Warwickshire belonged for generations to the Leighs, members of Jane Austen's mother's family. Jane visited it only once, with her mother and her mother's cousin, the Reverend Thomas Leigh, in 1806. Her mother wrote an entertaining letter about the visit, emphasizing the quantity and quality of food, the number of windows (forty-five in front), and the number of rooms ("twenty-six bedchambers in the new part of the house and a great many, some very good ones, in the old").

3

1 Scrupulously.

2 Only one character in an Austen novel engages in such a marriage: Mrs. Price, in *Mansfield Park.* The possession of rich relatives who help her many children alleviates the difficulties of real poverty (and even Mrs. Price has two servant girls, unsatisfactory though they are), but the disorder and discomfort of her household suggest poverty's unpleasantness. It seems unquestionable that Austen would endorse Mrs. Gardiner's recommendation of financial prudence in matters of love.

3 Prudence is a virtue of high importance in eighteenth-century English fiction. The intricate plot of Henry Fielding's *Tom Jones* hinges on the hero's initial lack of the quality and on the arduous process through which he acquires the habits of prudence. Frances Burney's *Evelina,* with a female hero, articulates the different demands of prudence for a young woman. The characteristic may be defined as an "ability to recognize and follow the most suitable or sensible course of action" (*OED*). It thus implies capacities of discrimination or even wisdom, as well as the will to act. Often, prudence entails giving due weight to financial considerations. In acknowledging that she sees the imprudence of encouraging Wickham, Elizabeth in effect accepts the desirability of modifying her behavior.

MRS. GARDINER'S CAUTION TO ELIZABETH was punctually[1] and kindly given on the first favourable opportunity of speaking to her alone; after honestly telling her what she thought, she thus went on:

"You are too sensible a girl, Lizzy, to fall in love merely because you are warned against it; and, therefore, I am not afraid of speaking openly. Seriously, I would have you be on your guard. Do not involve yourself or endeavour to involve him in an affection which the want of fortune would make so very imprudent.[2] I have nothing to say against *him;* he is a most interesting young man; and if he had the fortune he ought to have, I should think you could not do better. But as it is—you must not let your fancy run away with you. You have sense, and we all expect you to use it. Your father would depend on *your* resolution and good conduct, I am sure. You must not disappoint your father."

"My dear aunt, this is being serious indeed."

"Yes, and I hope to engage you to be serious likewise."

"Well, then, you need not be under any alarm. I will take care of myself, and of Mr. Wickham too. He shall not be in love with me, if I can prevent it."

"Elizabeth, you are not serious now."

"I beg your pardon. I will try again. At present I am not in love with Mr. Wickham; no, I certainly am not. But he is, beyond all comparison, the most agreeable man I ever saw—and if he becomes really attached to me—I believe it will be better that he should not. I see the imprudence[3] of it. Oh! *that* abominable Mr. Darcy!—My father's opinion of me does me the greatest honor; and I should be miserable to forfeit it. My father, however, is partial to Mr. Wickham. In short, my dear aunt, I should be very sorry to be the means of making any of you unhappy; but since we see every day that where there is affection, young people are seldom withheld by immediate want of fortune, from entering into engagements with each other, how can I promise to be wiser than so many of my fellow creatures if I am tempted, or how am I even to know that it would be wisdom to resist?[4] All that I can promise you, therefore, is not to be in a hurry. I will not be in a hurry to believe myself his first object.[5] When I am in company with him, I will not be wishing.[6] In short, I will do my best."

"Perhaps it will be as well, if you discourage his coming here so very often. At least, you should not *remind* your Mother of inviting him."

"As I did the other day," said Elizabeth, with a conscious[7] smile; "very true, it will be wise in me to refrain from *that*. But do not imagine that he is always here so often. It is on your account that he has been so frequently invited this week. You know my mother's ideas as to the necessity of constant company for her friends. But really, and upon my honour, I will try to do what I think to be the wisest; and now, I hope you are satisfied."

Her aunt assured her that she was, and Elizabeth having thanked her for the kindness of her hints, they parted; a wonderful[8] instance of advice being given on such a point, without being resented.

Mr. Collins returned into Hertfordshire soon after it had been quitted by the Gardiners and Jane; but as he took up his abode with the Lucases, his arrival was no great inconvenience to Mrs. Bennet. His marriage was now fast approaching, and she was at length so far resigned as to think it inevitable, and even repeatedly to say in an ill-natured tone that she "*wished* they might be happy." Thursday was to be the wedding day, and on Wednesday Miss Lucas paid her farewell visit; and when she rose to take leave, Elizabeth, ashamed of her mother's ungracious and reluctant good wishes, and sincerely affected herself, accompanied her out of the room. As they went down stairs together, Charlotte said,

4 It is striking that Elizabeth finds imprudence in marriage easier to defend than prudence (as in Charlotte's case, where she redefines financial prudence as selfishness). In *Persuasion* (1818), Austen imagines the situation of a young woman persuaded by a motherly friend not to marry the man she loves, because of his uncertain financial prospects. Years later, the couple meet again and reunite. The heroine, however, does not consider herself wrong to have taken her mentor's advice at the time, although she declares that she would not herself offer such advice.

5 The chief object of his affections.

6 For Wickham's attention and perhaps his courtship.

7 The word used in this sense is usually defined as "self-conscious." C. S. Lewis points out, however, that its etymology does not allow for such a meaning. Rather, *conscious* implies knowledge of a secret—of something that other participants in the conversation do not know. In this context, it means that Elizabeth has in mind the history of her relationship with Wickham, more than her aunt can know. As Lewis goes on to say, "No doubt when one is *conscious,* when one has a secret, one tends to be, and to look, 'self-conscious'" (C. S. Lewis, *Studies in Words* [Cambridge: Cambridge University Press, 1960], 186).

8 Remarkable.

9 The adverb in this context calls attention to the fundamental irrationality of Mr. Collins's idolizing Lady Catherine and praising all that belongs to her.

"I shall depend on hearing from you very often, Eliza."

"*That* you certainly shall."

"And I have another favour to ask. Will you come and see me?"

"We shall often meet, I hope, in Hertfordshire."

"I am not likely to leave Kent for some time. Promise me, therefore, to come to Hunsford."

Elizabeth could not refuse, though she foresaw little pleasure in the visit.

"My father and Maria are coming to me in March," added Charlotte, "and I hope you will consent to be of the party. Indeed, Eliza, you will be as welcome to me as either of them."

The wedding took place; the bride and bridegroom set off for Kent from the church door, and every body had as much to say, or to hear, on the subject as usual. Elizabeth soon heard from her friend; and their correspondence was as regular and frequent as it had ever been; that it should be equally unreserved was impossible. Elizabeth could never address her without feeling that all the comfort of intimacy was over, and though determined not to slacken as a correspondent, it was for the sake of what had been, rather than what was. Charlotte's first letters were received with a good deal of eagerness; there could not but be curiosity to know how she would speak of her new home, how she would like Lady Catherine, and how happy she would dare pronounce herself to be; though, when the letters were read, Elizabeth felt that Charlotte expressed herself on every point exactly as she might have foreseen. She wrote cheerfully, seemed surrounded with comforts, and mentioned nothing which she could not praise. The house, furniture, neighbourhood, and roads, were all to her taste, and Lady Catherine's behaviour was most friendly and obliging. It was Mr. Collins's picture of Hunsford and Rosings rationally[9] softened; and Elizabeth perceived that she must wait for her own visit there, to know the rest.

Jane had already written a few lines to her sister to announce their safe arrival in London; and when she wrote again, Elizabeth hoped it would be in her power to say something of the Bingleys.

Her impatience for this second letter was as well rewarded as impatience generally is. Jane had been a week in town without either seeing or hearing from Caroline. She accounted for it, however, by supposing that her last letter to her friend from Longbourn had by some accident been lost.

"My aunt," she continued, "is going to-morrow into that part of the town, and I shall take the opportunity of calling in Grosvenor-street."

She wrote again when the visit was paid, and she had seen Miss Bingley. "I did not think Caroline in spirits," were her words, "but she was very glad to see me, and reproached me for giving her no notice of my coming to London. I was right, therefore; my last letter had never reached her. I enquired after their brother, of course.[10] He was well, but so much engaged with Mr. Darcy, that they scarcely ever saw him. I found that Miss Darcy was expected to dinner. I wish I could see her. My visit was not long, as Caroline and Mrs. Hurst were going out. I dare say I shall soon see them here."

Elizabeth shook her head over this letter. It convinced her, that accident only could discover[11] to Mr. Bingley her sister's being in town.

Four weeks passed away, and Jane saw nothing of him. She endeavoured to persuade herself that she did not regret it; but she could no longer be blind to Miss Bingley's inattention. After waiting at home every morning for a fortnight, and inventing every evening a fresh excuse for her, the visitor did at last appear; but the shortness of her stay, and yet more, the alteration of her manner, would allow Jane to deceive herself no longer. The letter which she wrote on this occasion to her sister, will prove what she felt.

> "My dearest Lizzy will, I am sure, be incapable of triumphing
> in her better judgment, at my expence, when I confess my-
> self to have been entirely deceived in Miss Bingley's regard
> for me. But, my dear sister, though the event[12] has proved
> you right, do not think me obstinate if I still assert, that,
> considering what her behaviour was, my confidence was as
> natural[13] as your suspicion. I do not at all comprehend her
> reason for wishing to be intimate with me; but if the same
> circumstances were to happen again, I am sure I should be

10 Politeness would demand that she make formal enquiries after the health of absent members of the household.

11 Reveal.

12 Outcome.

13 "Natural" is a striking word here. Jane is saying that the situation warranted either confidence or suspicion as a response. By observing that either would be "natural," she suggests—quite accurately—that the diverse interpretations by her and her sister emanate from their different natures.

deceived again. Caroline did not return my visit till yesterday; and not a note, not a line, did I receive in the mean time.
When she did come, it was very evident that she had no pleasure in it; she made a slight, formal, apology, for not calling
before, said not a word of wishing to see me again, and was in
every respect so altered a creature, that when she went away,
I was perfectly resolved to continue the acquaintance no
longer. I pity, though I cannot help blaming her. She was very
wrong in singling me out as she did; I can safely say, that every advance to intimacy began on her side. But I pity her, because she must feel that she has been acting wrong, and because I am very sure that anxiety for her brother is the cause
of it. I need not explain myself farther; and though *we* know
this anxiety to be quite needless, yet if she feels it, it will easily account for her behaviour to me; and so deservedly dear
as he is to his sister, whatever anxiety she must feel on his
behalf is natural and amiable. I cannot but wonder, however,
at her having any such fears now, because, if he had at all
cared about me, we must have met long, long ago. He knows
of my being in town, I am certain, from something she said
herself; and yet it should seem by her manner of talking, as
if she wanted to persuade herself that he is really partial to
Miss Darcy. I cannot understand it. If I were not afraid of
judging harshly, I should be almost tempted to say, that there
is a strong appearance of duplicity in all this. But I will endeavour to banish every painful thought, and think only of
what will make me happy, your affection, and the invariable
kindness of my dear uncle and aunt. Let me hear from you
very soon. Miss Bingley said something of his never returning to Netherfield again, of giving up the house, but not with
any certainty. We had better not mention it. I am extremely
glad that you have such pleasant accounts from our friends at
Hunsford. Pray go to see them, with Sir William and Maria. I
am sure you will be very comfortable there.

Yours, etc."

This letter gave Elizabeth some pain; but her spirits returned as she considered that Jane would no longer be duped, by the sister at least. All expectation from the brother was now absolutely over. She would not even wish for any renewal of his attentions. His character sunk on every review of it;[14] and as a punishment for him, as well as a possible advantage to Jane,[15] she seriously hoped he might really soon marry Mr. Darcy's sister, as, by Wickham's account, she would make him abundantly regret what he had thrown away.

Mrs. Gardiner about this time reminded Elizabeth of her promise concerning that gentleman, and required information; and Elizabeth had such to send as might rather give contentment to her aunt than to herself. His apparent partiality had subsided, his attentions were over, he was the admirer of some one else. Elizabeth was watchful enough to see it all, but she could see it and write of it without material[16] pain. Her heart had been but slightly touched, and her vanity was satisfied with believing that *she* would have been his only choice, had fortune permitted it. The sudden acquisition of ten thousand pounds was the most remarkable charm of the young lady, to whom he was now rendering himself agreeable; but Elizabeth, less clear sighted perhaps in his case than in Charlotte's, did not quarrel with him for his wish of independence.[17] Nothing, on the contrary, could be more natural; and while able to suppose that it cost him a few struggles to relinquish her, she was ready to allow it a wise and desirable measure for both, and could very sincerely wish him happy.

All this was acknowledged to Mrs. Gardiner; and after relating the circumstances, she thus went on:—"I am now convinced, my dear aunt, that I have never been much in love; for had I really experienced that pure and elevating passion, I should at present detest his very name, and wish him all manner of evil. But my feelings are not only cordial towards *him;* they are even impartial towards Miss King. I cannot find out that I hate her at all, or that I am in the least unwilling to think her a very good sort of girl. There can be no love in all this. My watchfulness has been effectual; and though I certainly should be a more interesting[18] object to all my acquaintance, were I distractedly in love with him, I cannot say that I regret my compar-

14 That is, every time she considered the situation she arrived at a more derogatory view of Bingley's character.

15 If Bingley married someone else, Jane, knowing him unattainable, might find it easier to get over her feeling for him.

16 Significant.

17 That is, financial independence, since his wife's fortune would automatically become his at the moment of marriage, unless other arrangements had been made by settlement. Charlotte, of course, also wished for "independence": marriage would remove her from dependence on her family, although she would necessarily remain dependent on her husband.

18 Elizabeth uses *interesting* here in its older sense: "That concerns, touches, affects, or is of importance." The *OED* cites as an example of this usage Hester Chapone, who writes of "a woman . . . thought meanly of in points the most interesting to her honour." Elizabeth knows that she would seem of more significance to her contemporaries if she were unhappily in love. She in effect echoes her father, who has earlier observed, "Next to being married, a girl likes to be crossed in love a little now and then. It is something to think of, and gives her a sort of distinction among her companions" (II, 1).

ative insignificance. Importance may sometimes be purchased too dearly. Kitty and Lydia take his defection much more to heart than I do. They are young in the ways of the world, and not yet open to the mortifying conviction that handsome young men must have something to live on, as well as the plain."

Charles Wild, "Carlton House, the Blue Velvet Room," 1816. Carlton House was the home of the prince regent, later King George IV, an admirer of Austen's novels; Austen visited the house in 1815.

4

WITH NO GREATER EVENTS THAN THESE in the Longbourn family, and otherwise diversified by little beyond the walks to Meryton, sometimes dirty[1] and sometimes cold, did January and February pass away.[2] March was to take Elizabeth to Hunsford. She had not at first thought very seriously of going thither; but Charlotte, she soon found, was depending on the plan and she gradually learned to consider it herself with greater pleasure as well as greater certainty. Absence had increased her desire of seeing Charlotte again, and weakened her disgust of[3] Mr. Collins. There was novelty in the scheme, and as, with such a mother and such uncompanionable sisters, home could not be faultless, a little change was not unwelcome for its own sake. The journey would moreover give her a peep at Jane; and, in short, as the time drew near, she would have been very sorry for any delay. Everything, however, went on smoothly, and was finally settled according to Charlotte's first sketch. She was to accompany Sir William and his second daughter. The improvement of spending a night in London was added in time, and the plan became perfect as plan could be.

The only pain was in leaving her father, who would certainly miss her, and who, when it came to the point, so little liked her going, that he told her to write to him, and almost promised to answer her letter.

The farewell between herself and Mr. Wickham was perfectly friendly; on his side even more. His present pursuit could not make him forget that Elizabeth had been the first to excite and to deserve

1 Muddy.

2 A sentence like this one calls attention to how uneventful external life in such a semi-rural setting as Longbourn can be. Aside from the arrival of the militia and of Wickham, virtually everything of significance that has happened in the novel so far has been psychological: Jane's developing feeling for Bingley and its frustration, Elizabeth's interest in Wickham and indignation at Darcy, Darcy's interest in her, Collins's successive proposals, their motivations, and their aftermath.

3 Distaste for.

4 Like her father. Ivor Morris, examining the similarities between Elizabeth and Mr. Bennet, argues that they share not only their delight in the absurd but a mutual capacity to distance themselves "from the immediacy of event and the threat of emotion's dominance." He declares this capacity "most often the distinguishing feature of a very able mind." Mr. Bennet's ability to distance himself is manifest; Elizabeth's, according to Morris, reveals itself in her tendency to rely on principle. The father and daughter are most obviously kindred spirits, however, in their witty mockery, which repeatedly reveals the power of their minds in action. See http://www.jasna.org/persuasions/on-line/vol25no1/morris.html.

5 Object of attention.

his attention, the first to listen and to pity, the first to be admired; and in his manner of bidding her adieu, wishing her every enjoyment, reminding her of what she was to expect in Lady Catherine de Bourgh, and trusting their opinion of her—their opinion of everybody—would always coincide, there was a solicitude, an interest which she felt must ever attach her to him with a most sincere regard; and she parted from him convinced, that whether married or single, he must always be her model of the amiable and pleasing.

Her fellow-travellers the next day, were not of a kind to make her think him less agreeable. Sir William Lucas, and his daughter Maria, a good humoured girl, but as empty-headed as himself, had nothing to say that could be worth hearing, and were listened to with about as much delight as the rattle of the chaise. Elizabeth loved absurdities,[4] but she had known Sir William's too long. He could tell her nothing new of the wonders of his presentation and knighthood; and his civilities were worn out like his information.

It was a journey of only twenty-four miles, and they began it so early as to be in Gracechurch-street by noon. As they drove to Mr. Gardiner's door, Jane was at a drawing-room window watching their arrival; when they entered the passage she was there to welcome them, and Elizabeth, looking earnestly in her face, was pleased to see it healthful and lovely as ever. On the stairs were a troop of little boys and girls, whose eagerness for their cousin's appearance would not allow them to wait in the drawing-room, and whose shyness, as they had not seen her for a twelvemonth, prevented their coming lower. All was joy and kindness. The day passed most pleasantly away; the morning in bustle and shopping, and the evening at one of the theatres.

Elizabeth then contrived to sit by her aunt. Their first object[5] was her sister; and she was more grieved than astonished to hear, in reply to her minute enquiries, that though Jane always struggled to support her spirits, there were periods of dejection. It was reasonable, however, to hope, that they would not continue long. Mrs. Gardiner gave her the particulars also of Miss Bingley's visit in Gracechurch-street, and repeated conversations occurring at different times between Jane and herself, which proved that the former had, from her heart, given up the acquaintance.

6 Teased, bantered with.

Mrs. Gardiner then rallied[6] her niece on Wickham's desertion, and complimented her on bearing it so well.

"But, my dear Elizabeth," she added, "what sort of girl is Miss King? I should be sorry to think our friend mercenary."

"Pray, my dear aunt, what is the difference in matrimonial affairs, between the mercenary and the prudent motive? Where does discretion end, and avarice begin? Last Christmas you were afraid of his marrying me, because it would be imprudent; and now, because he is trying to get a girl with only ten thousand pounds, you want to find out that he is mercenary."

"If you will only tell me what sort of girl Miss King is, I shall know what to think."

"She is a very good kind of girl, I believe. I know no harm of her."

"But he paid her not the smallest attention, till her grandfather's death made her mistress of this fortune."

"No—why should he? If it was not allowable for him to gain *my* affections, because I had no money, what occasion could there be for making love to a girl whom he did not care about, and who was equally poor?"

"But there seems indelicacy in directing his attentions towards her, so soon after this event."

"A man in distressed circumstances has not time for all those elegant decorums which other people may observe. If *she* does not object to it, why should *we?*"

"*Her* not objecting, does not justify *him*. It only shews her being deficient in something herself—sense or feeling."

"Well," cried Elizabeth, "have it as you choose. *He* shall be mercenary, and *she* shall be foolish."

"No, Lizzy, that is what I do *not* choose. I should be sorry, you know, to think ill of a young man who has lived so long in Derbyshire."

"Oh! if that is all, I have a very poor opinion of young men who live in Derbyshire; and their intimate friends who live in Hertford-

7 The Lake District in northwest England, still a popular tourist destination in the twenty-first century, had achieved popularity before the end of the eighteenth century. In the 1790s, "this was the most popular summer excursion in the kingdom," with trips to the Lakes encouraged by the fact that European travel, given the French Revolution, had become impossible (Esther Moir, *The Discovery of Britain: The English Tourists, 1540 to 1840* [London: Routledge & Kegan Paul, 1964], 139).

In 1778, Father Thomas West had published *A Guide to the Lakes,* celebrating the region's scenery and suggesting vantage points from which to achieve the best views. The book, along with William Gilpin's *Observations, Relative Chiefly to Picturesque Beauty*. . . stimulated a surge of travel to this landscape of lakes and mountains. In the early nineteenth century, before the publication of *Pride and Prejudice,* the poetry of Wordsworth and Coleridge, which included allusions to lakes such as Grasmere, Windermere, and Rydal Water, heightened general consciousness of the area's beauties. Wordsworth in 1810 published his own *Guide to the Lakes.*

8 Melancholy, gloom, irritability, or moroseness. "Spleen" was a term applied in the eighteenth century to diverse disorders that we might call neurotic. Alexander Pope, in *The Rape of the Lock,* imagines a cave of spleen, populated entirely by females, in which various kinds of dissatisfaction and mournfulness appear to emanate from sexual causes. Anne Finch, countess of Winchilsea, earlier in the eighteenth century wrote a long poem called *The Spleen,* in which she examined the disorder's many manifestations. Its opening lines suggest the range of emotions that could be categorized as spleen:

What art thou, Spleen, which everything dost ape?
    Thou Proteus to abused mankind,
    Who never yet thy real cause could find
Or fix thee to remain in one continued shape.
    Still varying thy perplexing form
    Now a Dead Sea thou'lt represent,
    A calm of stupid discontent,
Then, dashing on the rocks, with rage into a storm.
    Trembling sometimes thou dost appear

shire are not much better. I am sick of them all. Thank Heaven! I am going to-morrow where I shall find a man who has not one agreeable quality, who has neither manner nor sense to recommend him. Stupid men are the only ones worth knowing, after all."

"Take care, Lizzy; that speech savours strongly of disappointment."

Before they were separated by the conclusion of the play, she had the unexpected happiness of an invitation to accompany her uncle and aunt in a tour of pleasure which they proposed taking in the summer.

"We have not determined how far it shall carry us," said Mrs. Gardiner, "but perhaps to the Lakes."[7]

No scheme could have been more agreeable to Elizabeth, and her acceptance of the invitation was most ready and grateful. "Oh, my dear, dear aunt," she rapturously cried, "what delight! what felicity! You give me fresh life and vigour. Adieu to disappointment and spleen.[8] What are men to rocks and mountains? Oh! what hours of transport[9] we shall spend! And when we *do* return, it shall not be like other travellers, without being able to give one accurate idea of any thing. We *will* know where we have gone—we *will* recollect what we have seen. Lakes, mountains, and rivers, shall not be jumbled together in our imaginations; nor, when we attempt to describe any particular scene, will we begin quarreling about its relative situation. Let *our* first effusions be less insupportable than those of the generality of travellers."[10]

Dissolved into a panic fear;
  Or sleep intruding dost thy shadows spread
And crowd with boding dreams the melancholy
  head.

9 Rapture.

10 Tourism had exploded in the course of the eighteenth century, and nature had become an important attraction. The Grand Tour of Europe had long been a rite of passage for young men, but the idea of travel within England was a more recent development. Coaches had been greatly improved during the century, and roads as well; moreover, a network of turnpikes (the work of private developers, who maintained and profited from them) now crossed the country. As a result, domestic travel was far easier than it had been earlier.

Tourists eagerly visited country houses and literary shrines, but increasingly they recognized the aesthetic pleasures of nature. Edmund Burke published his important treatise *A Philosophic Inquiry into the Origins of Our Ideas of the Sublime and Beautiful* in 1756, arguing for the aesthetic power of the dark, obscure, and rugged. As a result, mountains, no longer perceived as "horrid," came to be seen as worthy objects of contemplation. William Gilpin, in a series of books about different parts of England, promoted the notion of the picturesque, which depended fundamentally on analogies between art and nature. Travelers were invited to see "pictures" in nature and instructed about how to look and what to look at.

Elizabeth's "rapturous" response to her aunt's suggestion that she accompany them is the kind of reaction that tourists were expected to have to the scenery of the Lake District and to other picturesque sites. Her claim that they would be able to describe accurately what they see, however, does not conform to Gilpin's understanding of the relation between sights seen and accounts of them. He writes: "Mountains, rocks, broken-ground, water, and wood, are the simple materials, which [Nature] employs in all her beautiful pictures: but the variety and harmony, with which she employs them are infinite. In description these words stand only for *general ideas,* on her charts each is *detailed* into a thousand varied forms. Words may give the great outlines of a country. . . . But their range extends no farther. They cannot mark the characteristic distinction of each scene—the touches of nature—her living tints—her endless varieties, both in form and colour.— In a word, all her elegant *peculiarities* are beyond their reach" (*Observations, on Several Parts of England, Particularly the Mountains and Lakes of Cumberland and Westmoreland, Relative Chiefly to Picturesque Beauty,* 3rd ed.).

5

1 Main road; the locution *high road* is the source for our *highway*.

2 Fencing.

3 Stakes in the ground, making a fence.

EVERY OBJECT IN THE NEXT DAY'S JOURNEY was new and interesting to Elizabeth; and her spirits were in a state for enjoyment; for she had seen her sister looking so well as to banish all fear for her health, and the prospect of her northern tour was a constant source of delight.

When they left the high road[1] for the lane to Hunsford, every eye was in search of the Parsonage, and every turning expected to bring it in view. The palings[2] of Rosings Park was their boundary on one side. Elizabeth smiled at the recollection of all that she had heard of its inhabitants.

At length the Parsonage was discernible. The garden sloping to the road, the house standing in it, the green pales[3] and the laurel hedge, every thing declared they were arriving. Mr. Collins and Charlotte appeared at the door, and the carriage stopped at the small gate, which led by a short gravel walk to the house, amidst the nods and smiles of the whole party. In a moment they were all out of the chaise, rejoicing at the sight of each other. Mrs. Collins welcomed her friend with the liveliest pleasure, and Elizabeth was more and more satisfied with coming, when she found herself so affectionately received. She saw instantly that her cousin's manners were not altered by his marriage; his formal civility was just what it had been, and he detained her some minutes at the gate to hear and satisfy his enquiries after all her family. They were then, with no other delay than his pointing out the neatness of the entrance, taken into the house; and as soon as they were in the parlour, he welcomed them a second time with ostentatious formality to his humble abode, and punctually[4] repeated all his wife's offers of refreshment.

Elizabeth was prepared to see him in his glory; and she could not help fancying that in displaying the good proportion of the room, its aspect[5] and its furniture, he addressed himself particularly to her, as if wishing to make her feel what she had lost in refusing him. But though everything seemed neat and comfortable, she was not able to gratify him by any sigh of repentance; and rather looked with wonder at her friend that she could have so cheerful an air, with such a companion. When Mr. Collins said any thing of which his wife might reasonably be ashamed, which certainly was not unseldom,[6] she involuntarily turned her eye on Charlotte. Once or twice she could discern a faint blush;[7] but in general Charlotte wisely did not hear. After sitting long enough to admire every article of furniture in the room, from the sideboard to the fender,[8] to give an account of their journey and of all that had happened in London, Mr. Collins invited them to take a stroll in the garden, which was large and well laid out, and to the cultivation of which he attended himself. To work in his garden was one of his most respectable pleasures;[9] and Elizabeth admired the command of countenance with which Charlotte talked of the healthfulness of the exercise, and owned[10] she encouraged it as much as possible. Here, leading the way through every walk and cross walk, and scarcely allowing them an interval to utter the praises he asked for, every view was pointed out with a minuteness which left beauty entirely behind. He could number the fields in every direction, and could tell how many trees there were in the most distant clump. But of all the views which his garden, or which the county, or the kingdom could boast, none were to be compared with the prospect of Rosings, afforded by an opening in the trees that bordered the park nearly opposite the front of his house. It was a handsome modern building, well situated on rising ground.

From his garden, Mr. Collins would have led them round his two meadows; but the ladies not having shoes to encounter the remains of a white frost, turned back; and while Sir William accompanied him, Charlotte took her sister and friend over the house, extremely well pleased, probably,[11] to have the opportunity of shewing it with-

4 In a manner attentive to details; scrupulously; punctiliously.

5 Exposure.

6 Paradoxically, *unseldom* frequently meant *seldom*. Mr. Collins often says things that might embarrass his wife.

7 An indispensable mode of unconscious communication.

8 Fire guard.

9 The comment may lead one to wonder what Mr. Collins's other pleasures might have been.

10 Acknowledged.

11 This "probably" issues from Elizabeth's perspective. Austen characteristically uses an omniscient narrator, who would know for sure whether Charlotte was pleased. But she also relies heavily on free indirect discourse, in which the tone and inflection of a specific character replace that of a dispassionate narrator. Thus Elizabeth's consciousness controls most of this paragraph.

12 Courteousness. The importance of Lady Catherine's courtesy, from Mr. Collins's point of view, seems to depend on its alliance with condescension: he values his patroness's utterances because they emerge from someone of high rank, who must always be conscious of his social inferiority.

13 In-laws were commonly referred to as though they were members of the immediate family.

14 These are terms of very moderate praise—but Mr. Collins promptly interprets them as justifying his own extravagant adulation of Lady Catherine.

15 Skill.

out her husband's help. It was rather small, but well built and convenient; and every thing was fitted up and arranged with a neatness and consistency of which Elizabeth gave Charlotte all the credit. When Mr. Collins could be forgotten, there was really a great air of comfort throughout, and by Charlotte's evident enjoyment of it, Elizabeth supposed he must be often forgotten.

She had already learnt that Lady Catherine was still in the country. It was spoken of again while they were at dinner, when Mr. Collins joining in, observed,

"Yes, Miss Elizabeth, you will have the honour of seeing Lady Catherine de Bourgh on the ensuing Sunday at church, and I need not say you will be delighted with her. She is all affability[12] and condescension, and I doubt not but you will be honoured with some portion of her notice when service is over. I have scarcely any hesitation in saying she will include you and my sister[13] Maria in every invitation with which she honours us during your stay here. Her behaviour to my dear Charlotte is charming. We dine at Rosings twice every week, and are never allowed to walk home. Her ladyship's carriage is regularly ordered for us. I *should* say, one of her ladyship's carriages, for she has several."

"Lady Catherine is a very respectable, sensible woman indeed,"[14] added Charlotte, "and a most attentive neighbour."

"Very true, my dear, that is exactly what I say. She is the sort of woman whom one cannot regard with too much deference."

The evening was spent chiefly in talking over Hertfordshire news, and telling again what had already been written; and when it closed, Elizabeth in the solitude of her chamber had to meditate upon Charlotte's degree of contentment, to understand her address[15] in guiding, and composure in bearing with her husband, and to acknowledge that it was all done very well. She had also to anticipate how her visit would pass, the quiet tenor of their usual employments, the vexatious interruptions of Mr. Collins, and the gaieties of their intercourse with Rosings. A lively imagination soon settled it all.

About the middle of the next day, as she was in her room getting ready for a walk, a sudden noise below seemed to speak the whole house in confusion; and after listening a moment, she heard some-body running upstairs in a violent hurry, and calling loudly after her. She opened the door, and met Maria in the landing place, who, breathless with agitation, cried out,

"Oh, my dear Eliza! pray make haste and come into the dining-room, for there is such a sight to be seen! I will not tell you what it is. Make haste, and come down this moment."

Elizabeth asked questions in vain; Maria would tell her nothing more, and down they ran into the dining-room, which fronted the lane, in quest of this wonder; it was two ladies stopping in a low phaeton at the garden gate.

"And is this all?" cried Elizabeth. "I expected at least that the pigs were got into the garden, and here is nothing but Lady Catherine and her daughter!"

"La!¹⁶ my dear," said Maria quite shocked at the mistake, "it is not Lady Catherine. The old lady is Mrs. Jenkinson, who lives with them. The other is Miss De Bourgh. Only look at her. She is quite a little creature. Who would have thought she could be so thin and small!"

"She is abominably rude to keep Charlotte out of doors in all this wind.¹⁷ Why does she not come in?"

"Oh! Charlotte says, she hardly ever does. It is the greatest of fa-vours when Miss De Bourgh comes in."

"I like her appearance," said Elizabeth, struck with other ideas. "She looks sickly and cross.—Yes, she will do for him very well. She will make him a very proper wife."

Mr. Collins and Charlotte were both standing at the gate in con-versation with the ladies; and Sir William, to Elizabeth's high diver-sion, was stationed in the door-way, in earnest contemplation of the greatness before him, and constantly bowing whenever Miss De Bourgh looked that way.

At length there was nothing more to be said; the ladies drove on, and the others returned into the house. Mr. Collins no sooner saw the two girls than he began to congratulate them on their good for-tune, which Charlotte explained by letting them know that the whole party was asked to dine at Rosings the next day.

16 An exclamation used to call attention to an em-phatic statement.

17 In *A Collection of Letters,* which Austen wrote at the age of sixteen, a young woman is made to stand by a coach talking with a noblewoman, "though the Wind was extremely high and very cold." Lady Greville agrees with her daughter that it is a horrible east wind, and comments that she can hardly stand having the window down. "But," she adds, "you are used to be blown about the wind Miss Maria & that is what has made your Complexion so ruddy & coarse. You young Ladies who cannot often ride in a Carriage never mind what weather you trudge in, or how the wind shews your legs. I would not have *my* Girls stand out of doors as you do in such a day as this. But some sort of people have no feelings either of cold or Delicacy." The epi-sode in which Miss De Bourgh keeps Charlotte stand-ing in the wind makes the same point more delicately: aristocrats often act as though they assume that lesser beings have no feelings.

6

1 Dressing for dinner.

MR. COLLINS'S TRIUMPH IN CONSEQUENCE of this invitation was complete. The power of displaying the grandeur of his patroness to his wondering visitors, and of letting them see her civility towards himself and his wife, was exactly what he had wished for; and that an opportunity of doing it should be given so soon, was such an instance of Lady Catherine's condescension, as he knew not how to admire enough.

"I confess," said he, "that I should not have been at all surprised by her ladyship's asking us on Sunday to drink tea and spend the evening at Rosings. I rather expected, from my knowledge of her affability, that it would happen. But who could have foreseen such an attention as this? Who could have imagined that we should receive an invitation to dine there (an invitation moreover including the whole party) so immediately after your arrival!"

"I am the less surprised at what has happened," replied Sir William, "from that knowledge of what the manners of the great really are, which my situation in life has allowed me to acquire. About the Court, such instances of elegant breeding are not uncommon."

Scarcely anything was talked of the whole day or next morning, but their visit to Rosings. Mr. Collins was carefully instructing them in what they were to expect, that the sight of such rooms, so many servants, and so splendid a dinner might not wholly overpower them.

When the ladies were separating for the toilette,[1] he said to Elizabeth,

"Do not make yourself uneasy, my dear cousin, about your apparel. Lady Catherine is far from requiring that elegance of dress in us which becomes herself and daughter. I would advise you merely to put on whatever of your clothes is superior to the rest, there is no occasion for any thing more.[2] Lady Catherine will not think the worse of you for being simply dressed. She likes to have the distinction of rank preserved."[3]

While they were dressing, he came two or three times to their different doors, to recommend their being quick, as Lady Catherine very much objected to be kept waiting for her dinner. — Such formidable accounts of her Ladyship, and her manner of living, quite frightened Maria Lucas, who had been little used to company,[4] and she looked forward to her introduction at Rosings, with as much apprehension, as her father had done to his presentation at St. James's.

As the weather was fine, they had a pleasant walk of about half a mile across the park. — Every park has its beauty and its prospects;[5] and Elizabeth saw much to be pleased with, though she could not be in such raptures as Mr. Collins expected the scene to inspire,[6] and was but slightly affected by his enumeration of the windows in front of the house, and his relation of what the glazing[7] altogether had originally cost Sir Lewis De Bourgh.[8]

When they ascended the steps to the hall, Maria's alarm was every moment increasing, and even Sir William did not look perfectly calm. — Elizabeth's courage did not fail her. She had heard nothing of Lady Catherine that spoke[9] her awful[10] from any extraordinary talents or miraculous virtue, and the mere stateliness of money or rank, she thought she could witness without trepidation.

From the entrance hall, of which Mr. Collins pointed out, with a rapturous air, the fine proportion and finished[11] ornaments, they followed the servants through an antichamber, to the room where Lady Catherine, her daughter, and Mrs. Jenkinson were sitting. Her ladyship, with great condescension,[12] arose to receive them; and as Mrs. Collins had settled it with her husband that the office of introduction should be hers, it was performed in a proper manner, without any of those apologies and thanks which he would have thought necessary.

2 It is a little difficult to imagine what more (than what is superior to the rest) could be managed.

3 As does Collins himself.

4 Social occasions.

5 Views.

6 The fact that Mr. Collins is inspired to rapture by the enumeration of windows and what they cost suggests his seriously distorted emotional responses. He pursues marriage apparently without erotic feeling but pursues patronage with real reverence, if not love, for riches and their possessors.

7 Installation of glass. Since there had been a tax on every window since the late seventeenth century, an abundance of windows signaled the presence of wealth.

8 In a short note in *Explicator,* Joan Klingel Ray argues that Rosings conveys the subtle message that the De Bourgh family was nouveau riche. The windows provide one piece of evidence. Since Sir Lewis paid for the original glazing, he must have overseen the construction of the house, which therefore had to be recent. See Joan Klingel Ray, "Pride and Prejudice: The Tale Told by Lady Catherine's House," *Explicator* 67: 1 (Fall 2008), 66–70.

9 Declared.

10 Declared her awe-inspiring.

11 Perfected, consummately executed.

12 Because of her high rank, Lady Catherine would not necessarily be expected to rise for inferior visitors.

In spite of having been at St. James's, Sir William was so completely awed by the grandeur surrounding him, that he had but just courage enough to make a very low bow, and take his seat without saying a word; and his daughter, frightened almost out of her senses, sat on the edge of her chair, not knowing which way to look. Elizabeth found herself quite equal to the scene, and could observe the three ladies before her composedly. Lady Catherine was a tall, large woman, with strongly-marked features, which might once have been handsome. Her air was not conciliating, nor was her manner of receiving them such as to make her visitors forget their inferior rank. She was not rendered formidable by silence; but whatever she said was spoken in so authoritative a tone, as marked her self-importance, and brought Mr. Wickham immediately to Elizabeth's mind; and

Fire screens; unknown artist, plate 108 from George Smith, *A Collection of Designs for Household Furniture and Interior Decoration in the Most Approved and Elegant Taste* (London: Published by J. Taylor, 1808). Mrs. Jenkinson would have used such highly decorated screens to shield Miss De Bourgh from the fire.

from the observation of the day altogether, she believed Lady Catherine to be exactly what he represented.

When, after examining the mother, in whose countenance and deportment she soon found some resemblance of Mr. Darcy, she turned her eyes on the daughter, she could almost have joined in Maria's astonishment, at her being so thin, and so small. There was neither in figure nor face, any likeness between the ladies. Miss De Bourgh was pale and sickly; her features, though not plain, were insignificant;[13] and she spoke very little, except in a low voice, to Mrs. Jenkinson, in whose appearance there was nothing remarkable, and who was entirely engaged in listening to what she said, and placing a screen in the proper direction before her eyes.[14]

After sitting a few minutes, they were all sent to one of the windows to admire the view,[15] Mr. Collins attending them to point out its beauties, and Lady Catherine kindly informing them that it was much better worth looking at in the summer.

The dinner was exceedingly handsome,[16] and there were all the servants and all the articles of plate[17] which Mr. Collins had promised; and, as he had likewise foretold, he took his seat at the bottom of the table,[18] by her ladyship's desire, and looked as if he felt that life could furnish nothing greater.—He carved, and ate, and praised with delighted alacrity; and every dish was commended, first by him, and then by Sir William, who was now enough recovered to echo whatever his son in law said, in a manner which Elizabeth wondered Lady Catherine could bear. But Lady Catherine seemed gratified by their excessive admiration, and gave most gracious smiles, especially when any dish on the table proved a novelty to them. The party did not supply much conversation. Elizabeth was ready to speak whenever there was an opening, but she was seated between Charlotte and Miss De Bourgh—the former of whom was engaged in listening to Lady Catherine,[19] and the latter said not a word to her all dinner time. Mrs. Jenkinson was chiefly employed in watching how little Miss De Bourgh ate, pressing her to try some other dish, and fearing she were indisposed. Maria thought speaking out of the question, and the gentlemen did nothing but eat and admire.

13 Small; devoid of meaning.

14 The screen would shield her from the light of the fire.

15 The narrative will draw many contrasts between Darcy's estate, Pemberley, and his aunt's, Rosings. One concerns this matter of "the view." At Rosings, there appears to be a single view that visitors are to contemplate; at Pemberley, the view keeps changing. Peter Knox-Shaw remarks, "Far from being self-empowered, the gaze of visitors to the Park is directed centripetally towards the presence of Lady Catherine who, in the interests of having 'the distinction of rank preserved,' frowns on conversation and is happiest when her guests dress down for dinner" (*Jane Austen and the Enlightenment* [Cambridge: Cambridge University Press, 2004], 93).

16 A curious adjective to apply to a dinner, suggesting that appearance is of primary importance. In the context, it emphasizes the narrator's failure to comment at all on the flavorfulness of the food.

17 Silver or gold dishes and accessories.

18 Heads of the household customarily sat at the head and foot of the table. Mr. Collins is therefore being assigned an important position.

19 Clearly a full-time occupation.

20 Family.

21 Susan J. Wolfson observes that Austen endows Lady Catherine with "qualities akin to what we admire in Elizabeth: fearless, forthright self-possession, indifference to norms of male admiration, and ability to manage, even without a husband" ("Re: Reading *Pride and Prejudice*," *A Companion to Jane Austen,* ed. Claudia L. Johnson and Clara Tuite [Chichester: Wiley-Blackwell, 2009], 118). The comment implies not that we are expected to find Lady Catherine attractive but that the novelist distributes admirable characteristics even among less than admirable characters.

22 The size and nature of a man's carriage indicated his wealth and social importance.

23 Lady Catherine's questions seem primarily designed to ascertain Elizabeth's precise social status—and whether any marriage of her siblings is likely to change it.

24 Excellent.

When the ladies returned to the drawing room, there was little to be done but to hear Lady Catherine talk, which she did without any intermission till coffee came in, delivering her opinion on every subject in so decisive a manner as proved that she was not used to have her judgment controverted. She enquired into Charlotte's domestic concerns familiarly and minutely, gave her a great deal of advice, as to the management of them all; told her how every thing ought to be regulated in so small a family as hers, and instructed her as to the care of her cows and her poultry. Elizabeth found that nothing was beneath this great Lady's attention, which could furnish her with an occasion of dictating to others. In the intervals of her discourse with Mrs. Collins, she addressed a variety of questions to Maria and Elizabeth, but especially to the latter, of whose connections[20] she knew the least, and who she observed to Mrs. Collins, was a very genteel, pretty kind of girl.[21] She asked her at different times, how many sisters she had, whether they were older or younger than herself, whether any of them were likely to be married, whether they were handsome, where they had been educated, what carriage her father kept,[22] and what had been her mother's maiden name?[23]—Elizabeth felt all the impertinence of her questions, but answered them very composedly.—Lady Catherine then observed,

"Your father's estate is entailed on Mr. Collins, I think. For your sake," turning to Charlotte, "I am glad of it; but otherwise I see no occasion for entailing estates from the female line.—It was not thought necessary in Sir Lewis de Bourgh's family.—Do you play and sing, Miss Bennet?"

"A little."

"Oh! Then—some time or other we shall be happy to hear you. Our instrument is a capital[24] one, probably superior to—You shall try it some day.—Do your sisters play and sing?"

"One of them does."

"Why did not you all learn?—You ought all to have learned. The Miss Webbs all play, and their father has not so good an income as yours.—Do you draw?"

"No, not at all."

"What, none of you?"

"Not one."

"That is very strange. But I suppose you had no opportunity. Your mother should have taken you to town every spring for the benefit of masters."[25]

"My mother would have had no objection, but my father hates London."

"Has your governess left you?"

"We never had any governess."

"No governess! How was that possible? Five daughters brought up at home without a governess!—I never heard of such a thing. Your mother must have been quite a slave to your education."

Elizabeth could hardly help smiling, as she assured her that had not been the case.

"Then, who taught you? who attended to you?—Without a governess you must have been neglected."

"Compared with some families, I believe we were; but such of us as wished to learn, never wanted[26] the means. We were always encouraged to read, and had all the masters that were necessary. Those who chose to be idle, certainly might."

"Aye, no doubt; but that is what a governess will prevent, and if I had known your mother, I should have advised her most strenuously to engage one. I always say that nothing is to be done in education without steady and regular instruction, and nobody but a governess can give it. It is wonderful[27] how many families I have been the means of supplying in that way. I am always glad to get a young person well placed out.[28] Four nieces of Mrs. Jenkinson are most delightfully situated through my means; and it was but the other day that I recommended another young person, who was merely accidentally mentioned to me, and the family are quite delighted with her. Mrs. Collins, did I tell you of Lady Metcalfe's calling yesterday to thank me? She finds Miss Pope a treasure. 'Lady Catherine,' said she, 'you have given me a treasure.' Are any of your younger sisters out,[29] Miss Bennet?"

"Yes, Ma'am, all."

25 Teachers (of drawing).

26 Lacked.

27 Astonishing.

28 Employed as a governess. In *Emma*, vulgar Mrs. Elton insists, against her protégée's will, on "placing" Jane Fairfax as governess with a wealthy family of her acquaintance.

29 In society. Entrance into society implied marriageability. Customarily, younger sisters did not come out until older ones were married, so Lady Catherine's surprise at the situation in the Bennet family is predictable. *Mansfield Park* contains a discussion between Mary Crawford and Edmund Bertram about the problem of how one decides whether a young woman is "out." Mary says, "Manners as well as appearance are, generally speaking, so totally different. Till now, I could not have supposed it possible to be mistaken as to a girl's being out or not. A girl not out, has always the same sort of dress; a close bonnet for instance, looks very demure, and never says a word. You may smile—but it is so I assure you—and except that it is sometimes carried a little too far, it is all very proper. Girls should be quiet and modest. The most objectionable part is, that the alteration of manners on being introduced into company is frequently too sudden. They sometimes pass in such very little time from reserve to quite the opposite—to confidence! *That* is the faulty part of the present system. One does not like to see a girl of eighteen or nineteen so immediately up to every thing—and perhaps when one has seen her hardly able to speak the year before" (I, 5).

30 Society.

31 Acknowledge.

32 Lady Catherine's questions and comments are indeed impertinent, but they serve the clear purpose of asserting her power. She insists on dominating the company—a company, of course, of her social inferiors. Her notion of the rights of aristocracy appears to include that of total control.

33 A card game for two, three, or four persons—in this instance, clearly for four. Players attempt to accumulate points by combinations of cards; the first person to gain twenty-one points wins.

34 Dull.

"All!—What, all five out at once?—Very odd!—And you only the second.—The younger ones out before the elder are married!—Your younger sisters must be very young?"

"Yes, my youngest is not sixteen. Perhaps she is full young to be much in company.[30] But really, Ma'am, I think it would be very hard upon younger sisters, that they should not have their share of society and amusement because the elder may not have the means or inclination to marry early.—The last born has as good a right to the pleasures of youth, as the first.—And to be kept back on *such* a motive!—I think it would not be very likely to promote sisterly affection or delicacy of mind."

"Upon my word," said her Ladyship, "you give your opinion very decidedly for so young a person.—Pray, what is your age?"

"With three younger sisters grown up," replied Elizabeth smiling, "your Ladyship can hardly expect me to own[31] it."

Lady Catherine seemed quite astonished at not receiving a direct answer; and Elizabeth suspected herself to be the first creature who had ever dared to trifle with so much dignified impertinence.[32]

"You cannot be more than twenty, I am sure,—therefore you need not conceal your age."

"I am not one and twenty."

When the gentlemen had joined them, and tea was over, the card tables were placed. Lady Catherine, Sir William, and Mr. and Mrs. Collins sat down to quadrille; and as Miss De Bourgh chose to play at cassino,[33] the two girls had the honour of assisting Mrs. Jenkinson to make up her party. Their table was superlatively stupid.[34] Scarcely a syllable was uttered that did not relate to the game, except when Mrs. Jenkinson expressed her fears of Miss De Bourgh's being too hot or too cold, or having too much or too little light. A great deal more passed at the other table. Lady Catherine was generally speaking—stating the mistakes of the three others, or relating some anecdote of herself. Mr. Collins was employed in agreeing to every thing her Ladyship said, thanking her for every fish he won, and apologising if he thought he won too many. Sir William did not say much. He was storing his memory with anecdotes and noble names.

When Lady Catherine and her daughter had played as long as they chose, the tables were broke up, the carriage was offered to Mrs. Collins, gratefully accepted, and immediately ordered. The party then gathered round the fire to hear Lady Catherine determine what weather they were to have on the morrow.[35] From these instructions they were summoned by the arrival of the coach, and with many speeches of thankfulness on Mr. Collins's side, and as many bows on Sir William's, they departed. As soon as they had driven from the door, Elizabeth was called on by her cousin, to give her opinion of all that she had seen at Rosings, which, for Charlotte's sake, she made more favourable than it really was. But her commendation, though costing her some trouble, could by no means satisfy Mr. Collins, and he was very soon obliged to take her Ladyship's praise into his own hands.

35 Lady Catherine, in other words, claims godlike capacity and prerogative.

Drawing room state chair; unknown artist, plate 58 from George Smith, *A Collection of Designs for Household Furniture and Interior Decoration in the Most Approved and Elegant Taste* (London: Published by J. Taylor, 1808). This uncomfortable-looking but elaborate chair might have inhabited Lady Catherine's drawing room.

1 A wonderfully ambiguous form of praise: like "That *is* a baby!"

2 A light, two-wheeled carriage drawn by a single horse.

3 Mr. Collins has earlier been described as "better fitted for a walker than a reader" (I, 15), so we may suspect that looking out the window occupies a large proportion of his time.

4 Faced the back.

5 Exposure.

6 Room.

SIR WILLIAM STAYED ONLY A WEEK at Hunsford; but his visit was long enough to convince him of his daughter's being most comfortably settled, and of her possessing such a husband and such a neighbour as were not often met with.[1] While Sir William was with them, Mr. Collins devoted his mornings to driving him out in his gig,[2] and shewing him the country; but when he went away, the whole family returned to their usual employments, and Elizabeth was thankful to find that they did not see more of her cousin by the alteration, for the chief of the time between breakfast and dinner was now passed by him either at work in the garden, or in reading and writing, and looking out of window in his own book room, which fronted the road.[3] The room in which the ladies sat was backwards.[4] Elizabeth had at first rather wondered that Charlotte should not prefer the dining parlour for common use; it was a better sized room, and had a pleasanter aspect;[5] but she soon saw that her friend had an excellent reason for what she did, for Mr. Collins would undoubtedly have been much less in his own apartment,[6] had they sat in one equally lively; and she gave Charlotte credit for the arrangement.

From the drawing room they could distinguish nothing in the lane, and were indebted to Mr. Collins for the knowledge of what carriages went along, and how often especially Miss De Bourgh drove by in her phaeton, which he never failed coming to inform them of, though it happened almost every day. She not unfrequently stopped at the Parsonage, and had a few minutes' conversation with Charlotte, but was scarcely ever prevailed on to get out.

Very few days passed in which Mr. Collins did not walk to Rosings, and not many in which his wife did not think it necessary to go likewise; and till Elizabeth recollected that there might be other family livings to be disposed of,[7] she could not understand the sacrifice of so many hours. Now and then they were honoured with a call from her Ladyship, and nothing escaped her observation that was passing in the room during these visits. She examined into their employments, looked at their work,[8] and advised them to do it differently; found fault with the arrangement of the furniture, or detected the housemaid in negligence; and if she accepted any refreshment, seemed to do it only for the sake of finding out that Mrs. Collins's joints[9] of meat were too large for her family.

Elizabeth soon perceived that though this great lady was not in the commission of the peace[10] of the county, she was a most active magistrate in her own parish, the minutest concerns of which were carried to her by Mr. Collins; and whenever any of the cottagers were disposed to be quarrelsome, discontented, or too poor, she sallied forth into the village to settle their differences, silence their complaints, and scold them into harmony and plenty.

The entertainment of dining at Rosings was repeated about twice a week; and, allowing for the loss of Sir William, and there being only one card table in the evening, every such entertainment was the counterpart of the first. Their other engagements were few; as the style of living in the neighbourhood in general, was beyond the Collinses' reach.[11] This however was no evil to Elizabeth, and upon the whole she spent her time comfortably enough; there were half hours of pleasant conversation with Charlotte, and the weather was so fine for the time of year, that she had often great enjoyment out of doors. Her favourite walk, and where she frequently went while the others were calling on Lady Catherine, was along the open grove which edged that side of the park, where there was a nice sheltered path, which no one seemed to value but herself, and where she felt beyond the reach of Lady Catherine's curiosity.

In this quiet way, the first fortnight of her visit soon passed away. Easter was approaching, and the week preceding it was to bring an addition to the family at Rosings, which in so small a circle must be

7 As a rich landowner, Lady Catherine would probably have the disposal of multiple livings. It was not uncommon for a clergyman to hold more than one clerical position at a time. He might preach at two churches and care for two parishes, if they were close together; or he might hire someone else (at a lower salary than the position's income) to perform the duties of a parish.

8 Needlework.

9 Roasts.

10 The authority to act as magistrate, or justice of the peace, and thus to adjudicate local disputes. Only men with estates worth more than £100 a year could hold such a commission, a fact that limited such officials to landowners and some clergymen. In order to be an active magistrate, a man had to pay a fee and take an oath. A woman—even an elevated one like Lady Catherine—could not officially serve at all.

11 Because their style of entertaining was too expensive for Mr. Collins's income.

12 Porters' lodges.

13 The other room.

14 Visit. Charlotte would not expect Darcy to visit immediately because she is of lower social rank than he and has no special connection with him.

15 Manner.

16 A minimal form of courtesy.

important. Elizabeth had heard soon after her arrival, that Mr. Darcy was expected there in the course of a few weeks, and though there were not many of her acquaintances whom she did not prefer, his coming would furnish one comparatively new to look at in their Rosings parties, and she might be amused in seeing how hopeless Miss Bingley's designs on him were, by his behaviour to his cousin, for whom he was evidently destined by Lady Catherine; who talked of his coming with the greatest satisfaction, spoke of him in terms of the highest admiration, and seemed almost angry to find that he had already been frequently seen by Miss Lucas and herself.

His arrival was soon known at the Parsonage; for Mr. Collins was walking the whole morning within view of the lodges[12] opening into Hunsford Lane, in order to have the earliest assurance of it; and after making his bow as the carriage turned into the Park, hurried home with the great intelligence. On the following morning he hastened to Rosings to pay his respects. There were two nephews of Lady Catherine to require them, for Mr. Darcy had brought with him a Colonel Fitzwilliam, the younger son of his uncle, Lord —— and to the great surprise of all the party, when Mr. Collins returned the gentlemen accompanied him. Charlotte had seen them from her husband's room, crossing the road, and immediately running into the other,[13] told the girls what an honour they might expect, adding,

"I may thank you, Eliza, for this piece of civility. Mr. Darcy would never have come so soon to wait upon[14] me."

Elizabeth had scarcely time to disclaim all right to the compliment, before their approach was announced by the door-bell, and shortly afterwards the three gentlemen entered the room. Colonel Fitzwilliam, who led the way, was about thirty, not handsome, but in person and address[15] most truly the gentleman. Mr. Darcy looked just as he had been used to look in Hertfordshire, paid his compliments, with his usual reserve, to Mrs. Collins; and whatever might be his feelings toward her friend, met her with every appearance of composure. Elizabeth merely curtseyed to him, without saying a word.[16]

Colonel Fitzwilliam entered into conversation directly with the readiness and ease of a well-bred man, and talked very pleasantly; but his cousin, after having addressed a slight observation on the house and garden to Mrs. Collins, sat for some time without speaking to any body. At length, however, his civility was so far awakened as to enquire of Elizabeth after the health of her family. She answered him in the usual way, and after a moment's pause, added,

"My eldest sister has been in town these three months. Have you never happened to see her there?"

She was perfectly sensible that he never had; but she wished to see whether he would betray any consciousness of what had passed between the Bingleys and Jane; and she thought he looked a little confused[17] as he answered that he had never been so fortunate as to meet Miss Bennet. The subject was pursued no farther, and the gentlemen soon afterwards went away.

17 As usual, Elizabeth is more than eager to interpret appearances.

8

1 To alleviate the boredom of a household consisting only of Lady Catherine, her daughter, and the daughter's companion.

2 That is, after dinner.

COLONEL FITZWILLIAM'S MANNERS WERE very much admired at the parsonage, and the ladies all felt that he must add considerably to the pleasures of their engagements at Rosings. It was some days, however, before they received any invitation thither, for while there were visitors in the house, they could not be necessary;[1] and it was not till Easter-day, almost a week after the gentlemen's arrival, that they were honoured by such an attention, and then they were merely asked on leaving church to come there in the evening.[2] For the last week they had seen very little of Lady Catherine or her daughter. Colonel Fitzwilliam had called at the parsonage more than once during the time, but Mr. Darcy they had only seen at church.

The invitation was accepted of course, and at a proper hour they joined the party in Lady Catherine's drawing room. Her ladyship received them civilly, but it was plain that their company was by no means so acceptable as when she could get nobody else; and she was, in fact, almost engrossed by her nephews, speaking to them, especially to Darcy, much more than to any other person in the room.

Colonel Fitzwilliam seemed really glad to see them; anything was a welcome relief to him at Rosings; and Mrs. Collins's pretty friend had moreover caught his fancy very much. He now seated himself by her, and talked so agreeably of Kent and Hertfordshire, of travelling and staying at home, of new books and music, that Elizabeth had never been half so well entertained in that room before; and they conversed with so much spirit and flow, as to draw the attention of

Lady Catherine herself, as well as of Mr. Darcy. *His* eyes had been soon and repeatedly turned towards them with a look of curiosity; and that her ladyship after a while shared the feeling, was more openly acknowledged, for she did not scruple to call out,

"What is that you are saying, Fitzwilliam? What is it you are talking of? What are you telling Miss Bennet? Let me hear what it is."

"We are speaking of music, Madam," said he, when no longer able to avoid a reply.

"Of music! Then pray speak aloud. It is of all subjects my delight. I must have my share in the conversation, if you are speaking of music. There are few people in England, I suppose, who have more true enjoyment of music than myself, or a better natural taste. If I had ever learnt, I should have been a great proficient. And so would Anne, if her health had allowed her to apply. I am confident that she would have performed delightfully.[3] How does Georgiana get on, Darcy?"

Mr. Darcy spoke with affectionate praise of his sister's proficiency.

"I am very glad to hear such a good account of her," said Lady Catherine; "and pray tell her from me, that she cannot expect to excel, if she does not practise a great deal."

"I assure you, Madam," he replied, "that she does not need such advice. She practises very constantly."

"So much the better. It cannot be done too much; and when I next write to her, I shall charge her not to neglect it on any account. I often tell young ladies, that no excellence in music is to be acquired, without constant practice. I have told Miss Bennet several times, that she will never play really well, unless she practises more; and though Mrs. Collins has no instrument, she is very welcome, as I have often told her, to come to Rosings every day, and play on the pianoforte in Mrs. Jenkinson's room. She would be in nobody's way, you know, in that part of the house."

Mr. Darcy looked a little ashamed of his aunt's ill breeding,[4] and made no answer.

When coffee was over, Colonel Fitzwilliam reminded Elizabeth of having promised to play to him; and she sat down directly to the

3 Lady Catherine is often confident about what would have happened if something else had only happened, or not happened. Her excessive faith in her imagination bears some affinity to her belief that she can argue the villagers into prosperity. Austen depicts her as an altogether dreadful person, arrogant, rude, and unaware of others' needs or feelings. One may fancy that Mrs. Bennet would be rather like her, if very rich. Despite her moral and psychological unattractiveness, though, her sheer force of personality makes her a figure of the powerful woman.

4 In suggesting that Elizabeth come in such a way that no member of the family would have to encounter her.

5 So much for her "true enjoyment of music."

6 Imposing grandeur.

instrument. He drew a chair near her. Lady Catherine listened to half a song, and then talked, as before, to her other nephew;[5] till the latter walked away from her, and moving with his usual deliberation towards the piano forte, stationed himself so as to command a full view of the fair performer's countenance. Elizabeth saw what he was doing, and at the first convenient pause, turned to him with an arch smile, and said,

"You mean to frighten me, Mr. Darcy, by coming in all this state[6] to hear me? I will not be alarmed though your sister *does* play so well. There is a stubbornness about me that never can bear to be fright-

John Smart, "Miss Harriet and Miss Elizabeth Binney," 1806. Watercolor on card. Although the instrument here is a harpsichord rather than a pianoforte, the image conveys the association between elegant young ladies and musical performance. John Smart (1741/2–1816) was a noted painter of miniatures.

ened at the will of others. My courage always rises at every attempt to intimidate me."

"I shall not say that you are mistaken," he replied, "because you could not really believe me to entertain any design of alarming you; and I have had the pleasure of your acquaintance long enough to know that you find great enjoyment in occasionally professing opinions which in fact are not your own."

Elizabeth laughed heartily at this picture of herself, and said to Colonel Fitzwilliam, "Your cousin will give you a very pretty notion of me, and teach you not to believe a word I say. I am particularly unlucky in meeting with a person so well able to expose my real character, in a part of the world, where I had hoped to pass myself off with some degree of credit. Indeed, Mr. Darcy, it is very ungenerous in you to mention all that you knew to my disadvantage in Hertfordshire—and, give me leave to say, very impolitic too—for it is provoking me to retaliate, and such things may come out, as will shock your relations to hear."

"I am not afraid of you," said he, smilingly.

"Pray let me hear what you have to accuse him of," cried Colonel Fitzwilliam. "I should like to know how he behaves among strangers."

"You shall hear then—but prepare yourself for something very dreadful. The first time of my ever seeing him in Hertfordshire, you must know, was at a ball—and at this ball, what do you think he did? He danced only four dances, though gentlemen were scarce; and, to my certain knowledge, more than one young lady was sitting down in want of a partner.[7] Mr. Darcy, you cannot deny the fact."

"I had not at that time the honour of knowing any lady in the assembly beyond my own party."

"True; and nobody can ever be introduced in a ball room. Well, Colonel Fitzwilliam, what do I play next? My fingers wait your orders."

"Perhaps," said Darcy, "I should have judged better, had I sought an introduction; but I am ill qualified to recommend myself to strangers."

7 Elizabeth deliberately reminds Darcy of his initial snub of her—she was, of course, one of the young ladies "sitting down in want of a partner"—and speaks of such a snub as a "very dreadful" failure of manners. Although her tone is joking, this is a remarkably bold move.

8 The world of society.

9 Austen herself practiced piano conscientiously from the age of twelve. She had a wide repertoire of both popular and serious music and copied out many scores in her own hand. Elizabeth, in contrast, has what Gillen D'Arcy Wood terms a "relaxed attitude toward piano practice," which, Wood continues, "contrasts appealingly both with Mary's sullen anxiety for 'display' and Georgiana's sequestration following the failed elopement with Wickham, for which she punishes herself with scales" ("Austen's Accomplishment: Music and the Modern Heroine," *A Companion to Jane Austen,* ed. Claudia L. Johnson and Clara Tuite [Chichester: Wiley-Blackwell, 2009], 367–368). Suggesting to Darcy the analogy between conversational and musical ease, Elizabeth indicates that she considers both manifestations valuable social skills and hints that Darcy, in his willingness to accept his own inadequacies, fails to fulfill social obligations.

10 However, they take manifest pleasure in performing for each other.

11 Although her proclamation that she herself would have been a fine musician if she had learned speaks only of her arrogance, Lady Catherine's claim (made twice) that her daughter would have played well conveys a certain pathos. Like Mrs. Bennet, although for different reasons, Lady Catherine feels desperate about her daughter, who is unable to fulfill any of her mother's fantasies.

"Shall we ask your cousin the reason of this?" said Elizabeth, still addressing Colonel Fitzwilliam. "Shall we ask him why a man of sense and education, and who has lived in the world,[8] is ill-qualified to recommend himself to strangers?"

"I can answer your question," said Fitzwilliam, "without applying to him. It is because he will not give himself the trouble."

"I certainly have not the talent which some people possess," said Darcy, "of conversing easily with those I have never seen before. I cannot catch their tone of conversation, or appear interested in their concerns, as I often see done."

"My fingers," said Elizabeth, "do not move over this instrument in the masterly manner which I see so many women's do. They have not the same force or rapidity, and do not produce the same expression. But then I have always supposed it to be my own fault—because I would not take the trouble of practising. It is not that I do not believe *my* fingers as capable as any other woman's of superior execution."[9]

Darcy smiled and said, "You are perfectly right. You have employed your time much better. No one admitted to the privilege of hearing you can think anything wanting. We neither of us perform to strangers."[10]

Here they were interrupted by Lady Catherine, who called out to know what they were talking of. Elizabeth immediately began playing again. Lady Catherine approached, and, after listening for a few minutes, said to Darcy,

"Miss Bennet would not play at all amiss if she practised more, and could have the advantage of a London master. She has a very good notion of fingering, though her taste is not equal to Anne's. Anne would have been a delightful performer, had her health allowed her to learn."[11]

Elizabeth looked at Darcy to see how cordially he assented to his cousin's praise; but neither at that moment nor at any other could she discern any symptom of love; and from the whole of his behaviour to Miss De Bourgh she derived this comfort for Miss Bingley, that he might have been just as likely to marry *her,* had she been his relation.

Lady Catherine continued her remarks on Elizabeth's performance, mixing with them many instructions on execution and taste. Elizabeth received them with all the forbearance of civility; and at the request of the gentlemen remained at the instrument till her Ladyship's carriage was ready to take them all home.

William Watts, "Godsmerham Park," 1785. Godsmerham Park, which belonged to the Knights, became Edward Austen Knight's principal residence. The great house, set among woods, belonged to the same general type as Darcy's estate, Pemberley. The engraver, Watts (1753–1851), specialized in "views."

9

1 From the servant who answered the door.

2 Conventional polite inquiries about the well-being of Rosings's inhabitants.

3 Emergency.

ELIZABETH WAS SITTING BY HERSELF the next morning, and writing to Jane, while Mrs. Collins and Maria were gone on business into the village, when she was startled by a ring at the door, the certain signal of a visitor. As she had heard no carriage, she thought it not unlikely to be Lady Catherine, and under that apprehension was putting away her half-finished letter that she might escape all impertinent questions, when the door opened, and to her very great surprise, Mr. Darcy, and Mr. Darcy only, entered the room.

He seemed astonished too on finding her alone, and apologised for his intrusion, by letting her know that he had understood[1] all the ladies were to be within.

They then sat down, and when her inquiries after Rosings[2] were made, seemed in danger of sinking into total silence. It was absolutely necessary, therefore, to think of something, and in this emergence[3] recollecting *when* she had seen him last in Hertfordshire, and feeling curious to know what he would say on the subject of their hasty departure, she observed,

"How very suddenly you all quitted Netherfield last November, Mr. Darcy! It must have been a most agreeable surprise to Mr. Bingley to see you all after him so soon; for, if I recollect right, he went but the day before. He and his sisters were well, I hope, when you left London?"

"Perfectly so—I thank you."

She found that she was to receive no other answer—and, after a short pause added,

"I think I have understood that Mr. Bingley has not much idea of ever returning to Netherfield again?"

"I have never heard him say so; but it is probable that he may spend very little of his time there in the future. He has many friends, and he is at a time of life when friends and engagements are continually increasing."

"If he means to be but little at Netherfield, it would be better for the neighbourhood that he should give up the place entirely, for then we might possibly get a settled family there. But perhaps Mr. Bingley did not take the house so much for the convenience of the neighbourhood as for his own, and we must expect him to keep or quit it on the same principle."

"I should not be surprised," said Darcy, "if he were to give it up as soon as any eligible purchase offers."[4]

Elizabeth made no answer. She was afraid of talking longer of his friend; and, having nothing else to say, was now determined to leave the trouble of finding a subject to him.

He took the hint, and soon began with, "This seems a very comfortable house. Lady Catherine, I believe, did a great deal to it when Mr. Collins first came to Hunsford."

"I believe she did—and I am sure she could not have bestowed her kindness on a more grateful object."

"Mr. Collins appears to be very fortunate in his choice of a wife."

"Yes, indeed; his friends may well rejoice in his having met with one of the very few sensible women who would have accepted him, or have made him happy if they had. My friend has an excellent understanding—though I am not certain that I consider her marrying Mr. Collins as the wisest thing she ever did.[5] She seems perfectly happy, however, and in a prudential light, it is certainly a very good match for her."

"It must be very agreeable for her to be settled within so easy a distance of her own family and friends."

"An easy distance, do you call it? It is nearly fifty miles."

"And what is fifty miles of good road? Little more than half a day's journey. Yes, I call it a *very* easy distance."

4 When he comes upon an estate that he likes enough to buy.

5 Elizabeth is remarkably frank with Darcy—perhaps because it is so important to her to distinguish her own point of view about marriage from Charlotte's.

6 For a family of moderate income, a fifty-mile distance would indeed be expensive. If one traveled post—that is, with hired horses changed at intervals, and with an attendant postilion to drive them—the cost would be roughly one shilling a mile, for a total of £2 10/—equivalent to about $250 today. Mr. Collins, having made three round trips between Rosings and Longbourn during his courtship, has invested a good deal in his endeavor to find a suitable wife.

7 He is implying that she seems more at ease in the larger world than does Charlotte, that she appears to have had more experience.

"I should never have considered the distance as one of the *advantages* of the match," cried Elizabeth. "I should never have said Mrs. Collins was settled *near* her family."

"It is a proof of your own attachment to Hertfordshire. Anything beyond the very neighbourhood of Longbourn, I suppose, would appear far."

As he spoke there was a sort of smile which Elizabeth fancied she understood; he must be supposing her to be thinking of Jane and Netherfield, and she blushed as she answered,

"I do not mean to say that a woman may not be settled too near her family. The far and the near must be relative, and depend on many varying circumstances. Where there is fortune to make the expence of travelling unimportant, distance becomes no evil.[6] But that is not the case *here*. Mr. and Mrs. Collins have a comfortable income, but not such a one as will allow of frequent journeys—and I am persuaded my friend would not call herself *near* her family under less than *half* the present distance."

Mr. Darcy drew his chair a little towards her, and said, "*You* cannot have a right to such very strong local attachment. *You* cannot have been always at Longbourn."[7]

Elizabeth looked surprised. The gentleman experienced some change of feeling; he drew back his chair, took a newspaper from the table, and glancing over it, said, in a colder voice,

"Are you pleased with Kent?"

A short dialogue on the subject of the country ensued, on either side calm and concise—and soon put an end to by the entrance of Charlotte and her sister, just returned from their walk. The tête-à-tête surprised them. Mr. Darcy related the mistake which had occasioned his intruding on Miss Bennet, and after sitting a few minutes longer without saying much to any body, went away.

"What can be the meaning of this?" said Charlotte, as soon as he was gone. "My dear Eliza he must be in love with you, or he would never have called us in this familiar way."

But when Elizabeth told of his silence, it did not seem very likely, even to Charlotte's wishes, to be the case; and after various conjectures, they could at last only suppose his visit to proceed from the difficulty of finding any thing to do, which was the more probable from the time of year. All field sports were over.[8] Within doors there was Lady Catherine, books, and a billiard table, but gentlemen cannot always be within doors; and in the nearness of the Parsonage, or the pleasantness of the walk to it, or of the people who lived in it, the two cousins found a temptation from this period of walking thither almost every day. They called at various times of the morning, sometimes separately, sometimes together, and now and then accompanied by their aunt.[9] It was plain to them all that Colonel Fitzwilliam came because he had pleasure in their society, a persuasion[10] which of course recommended him still more; and Elizabeth was reminded by her own satisfaction in being with him, as well as by his evident admiration of her, of her former favourite George Wickham; and though, in comparing them, she saw there was less captivating softness in Colonel Fitzwilliam's manners, she believed he might have the best informed mind.

But why Mr. Darcy came so often to the Parsonage, it was more difficult to understand. It could not be for society, as he frequently sat there ten minutes together without opening his lips; and when he did speak, it seemed the effect of necessity rather than of choice—a sacrifice to propriety, not a pleasure to himself. He seldom appeared really animated. Mrs. Collins knew not what to make of him. Colonel Fitzwilliam's occasionally laughing at his stupidity,[11] proved that he was generally different, which her own knowledge of him could not have told her; and as she would have liked to believe this change the effect of love, and the object of that love her friend Eliza, she set herself seriously to work to find it out.—She watched him whenever they were at Rosings, and whenever he came to Hunsford; but without much success. He certainly looked at her friend a great deal, but the expression of that look was disputable. It was an earnest, steadfast gaze, but she often doubted whether there were much admiration in it, and sometimes it seemed nothing but absence of mind.

She had once or twice suggested to Elizabeth the possibility of his being partial to her, but Elizabeth always laughed at the idea; and Mrs. Collins did not think it right to press the subject, from the danger of raising expectations which might only end in disappointment;

8 Since it is April, the season for hunting and shooting is past. Young men, therefore, have few obvious forms of entertainment in the country.

9 It seems rather surprising that Lady Catherine should walk, but evidently she does, since earlier in the chapter Elizabeth, not hearing a carriage, assumes that an unexpected visitor will prove to be Lady Catherine.

10 Conviction.

11 Dullness.

12 Again Charlotte indicates her conviction that marriage always turns on wealth and position. She also suggests clearly for the first time that she sees the preambles to courtship as a contest of power.

13 In other words, Charlotte's kind schemes for Elizabeth are marked by her customary "prudence": she considers her own interests as well as Elizabeth's.

for in her opinion it admitted not of a doubt, that all her friend's dislike would vanish, if she could suppose him to be in her power.[12]

In her kind schemes for Elizabeth, she sometimes planned her marrying Colonel Fitzwilliam. He was beyond comparison the most pleasant man; he certainly admired her, and his situation in life was most eligible; but, to counterbalance these advantages, Mr. Darcy had considerable patronage in the church, and his cousin could have none at all.[13]

IO

MORE THAN ONCE DID ELIZABETH, in her ramble within the Park, unexpectedly meet Mr. Darcy. — She felt all the perverseness of the mischance that should bring him where no one else was brought; and to prevent its ever happening again, took care to inform him at first,[1] that it was a favourite haunt of hers. — How it could occur a second time therefore was very odd! — Yet it did, and even a third. — It seemed like wilful ill-nature, or a voluntary penance,[2] for on these occasions it was not merely a few formal inquiries and an awkward pause and then away, but he actually thought it necessary to turn back and walk with her. He never said a great deal, nor did she give herself the trouble of talking or of listening much; but it struck her in the course of their third rencontre[3] that he was asking some odd unconnected questions — about her pleasure in being at Hunsford, her love of solitary walks, and her opinion of Mr. and Mrs. Collins's happiness; and that in speaking of Rosings and her not perfectly understanding the house, he seemed to expect that whenever she came into Kent again she would be staying *there* too. His words seemed to imply it. Could he have Colonel Fitzwilliam in his thoughts? She supposed, if he meant any thing, he must mean an allusion to what might arise in that quarter.[4] It distressed her a little, and she was quite glad to find herself at the gate in the pales opposite the Parsonage.

She was engaged one day as she walked, in re-perusing Jane's last letter, and dwelling on some passages which proved that Jane had not written in spirits,[5] when, instead of being again surprised by Mr. Darcy, she saw on looking up that Colonel Fitzwilliam was meeting

1 At his first appearance in her favorite haunt.

2 By this point even a first-time reader, noting the perverseness of Elizabeth's interpretations, must realize that her understanding of interpersonal situations is not necessarily trustworthy.

3 Accidental encounter.

4 This paragraph provides a striking instance of Elizabeth's blindness to Darcy's growing interest in her.

5 In a cheerful mood.

6 By the rules of primogeniture, an eldest son normally inherited all family land and most of the family wealth. Rich families provided also for younger sons and for daughters, but not nearly so lavishly. Younger sons, therefore, like Colonel Fitzwilliam, would have to support themselves at least partially by a profession. The acceptable professions for an earl's son would be the army, navy, law, or the church. The colonel, a member of the regular army (as opposed to the temporary militia), is presumably not "poor," except in relative terms.

7 Pointed, striking home.

her. Putting away the letter immediately and forcing a smile, she said,

"I did not know before that you ever walked this way."

"I have been making the tour of the Park," he replied, "as I generally do every year, and intended to close it with a call at the Parsonage. Are you going much farther?"

"No, I should have turned in a moment."

And accordingly she did turn, and they walked towards the Parsonage together.

"Do you certainly leave Kent on Saturday?" said she.

"Yes—if Darcy does not put it off again. But I am at his disposal. He arranges the business just as he pleases."

"And if not able to please himself in the arrangement, he has at least great pleasure in the power of choice. I do not know anybody who seems more to enjoy the power of doing what he likes than Mr. Darcy."

"He likes to have his own way very well," replied Colonel Fitzwilliam. "But so we all do. It is only that he has better means of having it than many others, because he is rich, and many others are poor. I speak feelingly. A younger son, you know, must be inured to self-denial and dependence."[6]

"In my opinion, the younger son of an Earl can know very little of either. Now, seriously, what have you ever known of self-denial and dependence? When have you been prevented by want of money from going wherever you chose, or procuring anything you had a fancy for?"

"These are home[7] questions—and perhaps I cannot say that I have experienced many hardships of that nature. But in matters of greater weight, I may suffer from the want of money. Younger sons cannot marry where they like."

"Unless where they like women of fortune, which I think they very often do."

"Our habits of expence make us too dependant, and there are not many in my rank of life who can afford to marry without some attention to money."

"Is this," thought Elizabeth, "meant for me?" and she coloured at the idea; but, recovering herself, said in a lively tone, "and pray, what is the usual price of an Earl's younger son? Unless the elder brother is very sickly, I suppose you would not ask above fifty thousand pounds."[8]

He answered her in the same style, and the subject dropped. To interrupt a silence which might make him fancy her affected with what had passed, she soon afterwards said,

"I imagine your cousin brought you down with him chiefly for the sake of having somebody at his disposal. I wonder he does not marry, to secure a lasting convenience of that kind. But, perhaps his sister does as well for the present, and, as she is under his sole care, he may do what he likes with her."

"No," said Colonel Fitzwilliam, "that is an advantage which he must divide with me. I am joined with him in the guardianship of Miss Darcy."

"Are you indeed? And pray what sort of guardians do you make? Does your charge give you much trouble? Young ladies of her age, are sometimes a little difficult to manage, and if she has the true Darcy spirit, she may like to have her own way."

As she spoke, she observed him looking at her earnestly; and the manner in which he immediately asked her why she supposed Miss Darcy likely to give them any uneasiness, convinced her that she had somehow or other got pretty near the truth. She directly[9] replied,

"You need not be frightened. I never heard any harm of her; and I dare say she is one of the most tractable creatures in the world. She is a very great favourite with some ladies of my acquaintance, Mrs. Hurst and Miss Bingley. I think I have heard you say that you know them."

"I know them a little. Their brother is a pleasant gentleman-like man—he is a great friend of Darcy's."

"Oh! yes," said Elizabeth drily—"Mr. Darcy is uncommonly kind to Mr. Bingley, and takes a prodigious deal of care of him."

"Care of him!—Yes, I really believe Darcy *does* take care of him in those points where he most wants care.[10] From something that

8 If the eldest son were very sickly, his younger brother might plausibly hope to become the heir—and a woman looking to make a good marriage might be inclined to accept him. In *Mansfield Park,* the younger son of a baronet, Edmund Bertram, has taken orders and plans a career in the church. When his elder brother, the heir to the estate, falls critically ill, the woman whom Edmund is courting becomes seriously interested in him because of the possibility that his brother's death would make him the heir.

9 Immediately.

10 "Darcy's concern for and tutelage of Bingley . . . suggest the hero's recognition that wealthy men of trade like Bingley are becoming vital resources in England's future—and these men must be taught to discipline their passions to ensure their maturation as stable men of the nation" (Michael Kramp, *Disciplining Love: Austen and the Modern Man* [Columbus: The Ohio State University Press, 2007], 80).

he told me in our journey hither, I have reason to think Bingley very much indebted to him. But I ought to beg his pardon, for I have no right to suppose that Bingley was the person meant. It was all conjecture."

"What is it you mean?"

"It is a circumstance which Darcy could not wish to be generally known, because if it were to get round to the lady's family, it would be an unpleasant thing."

"You may depend upon my not mentioning it."

"And remember that I have not much reason for supposing it to be Bingley. What he told me was merely this: that he congratulated himself on having lately saved a friend from the inconveniences of a most imprudent marriage, but without mentioning names or any other particulars, and I only suspected it to be Bingley from believing him the kind of young man to get into a scrape of that sort, and from knowing them to have been together the whole of last summer."

"Did Mr. Darcy give you his reasons for this interference?"

"I understood that there were some very strong objections against the lady."

"And what arts did he use to separate them?"

"He did not talk to me of his own arts," said Fitzwilliam, smiling. "He only told me, what I have now told you."

Elizabeth made no answer, and walked on, her heart swelling with indignation. After watching her a little, Fitzwilliam asked her why she was so thoughtful.

"I am thinking of what you have been telling me," said she. "Your cousin's conduct does not suit my feelings. Why was he to be the judge?"

"You are rather disposed to call his interference officious?"

"I do not see what right Mr. Darcy had to decide on the propriety of his friend's inclination, or why, upon his own judgment alone, he was to determine and direct in what manner his friend was to be happy. But," she continued, recollecting herself, "as we know none of the particulars, it is not fair to condemn him. It is not to be supposed that there was much affection in the case."

"That is not an unnatural surmise," said Fitzwilliam, "but it is lessening the honour of my cousin's triumph very sadly."

This was spoken jestingly; but it appeared to her so just a picture of Mr. Darcy,[11] that she would not trust herself with an answer; and, therefore, abruptly changing the conversation, talked on indifferent matters till they reached the parsonage. There, shut into her own room, as soon as their visitor left them, she could think without interruption of all that she had heard. It was not to be supposed that any other people could be meant than those with whom she was connected. There could not exist in the world *two* men, over whom Mr. Darcy could have such boundless influence. That he had been concerned in the measures taken to separate Bingley and Jane, she had never doubted; but she had always attributed to Miss Bingley the principal design and arrangement of them. If his own vanity, however, did not mislead him, *he* was the cause, his pride and caprice[12] were the cause of all that Jane had suffered, and still continued to suffer. He had ruined for a while every hope of happiness for the most affectionate, generous heart in the world; and no one could say how lasting an evil he might have inflicted.

"There were some very strong objections against the lady," were Colonel Fitzwilliam's words; and those strong objections probably were, her having one uncle who was a country attorney, and another who was in business in London. "To Jane herself," she exclaimed, "there could be no possibility of objection; all loveliness and goodness as she is! Her understanding excellent, her mind improved, and her manners captivating. Neither could any thing be urged against my father, who, though with some peculiarities, has abilities which Mr. Darcy himself need not disdain, and respectability which he will probably never reach."[13] When she thought of her mother indeed, her confidence gave way a little, but she would not allow that any objections *there* had material weight with Mr. Darcy, whose pride, she was convinced, would receive a deeper wound from the want of importance in his friend's connections, than from their want of sense; and she was quite decided at last, that he had been partly governed by this worst kind of pride,[14] and partly by the wish of retaining Mr. Bingley for his sister.

11 The justness of the picture must be its suggestion of Darcy's wish to "triumph."

12 In attributing Darcy's behavior to "pride and caprice," Elizabeth goes far beyond any evidence she has.

13 Elizabeth means that her father deserves and receives respect for his inherent qualities, which are more admirable than Darcy's, rather than for his rank or wealth.

14 Elizabeth apparently considers pride in social status to be the "worst kind of pride."

15 Elizabeth, it seems, is not to be understood only as a girl willing to stride three miles through mud. She is also a girl who bemoans her sister's misfortune with agitation and tears sufficient to bring on a headache— a process that indicates her devotion to Jane but also suggests her emotional vulnerability. Increasingly as the novel continues, Elizabeth, marked by her independence and forthrightness, nonetheless demonstrates some characteristics of the sentimental heroine, blushing and weeping and exclaiming. She is importantly rendered as possessing emotional depths of which she allows only glimpses.

The agitation and tears which the subject occasioned, brought on a headach;[15] and it grew so much worse towards the evening that, added to her unwillingness to see Mr. Darcy, it determined her not to attend her cousins to Rosings, where they were engaged to drink tea. Mrs. Collins, seeing that she was really unwell, did not press her to go, and as much as possible prevented her husband from pressing her, but Mr. Collins could not conceal his apprehension of Lady Catherine's being rather displeased by her staying at home.

II

WHEN THEY WERE GONE, ELIZABETH, as if intending to exasperate herself as much as possible against Mr. Darcy, chose for her employment the examination of all the letters which Jane had written to her since her being in Kent. They contained no actual complaint, nor was there any revival of past occurrences, or any communication of present suffering. But in all, and in almost every line of each, there was a want of that cheerfulness which had been used to characterize[1] her style, and which, proceeding from the serenity of a mind at ease with itself, and kindly disposed towards every one, had been scarcely ever clouded. Elizabeth noticed every sentence conveying the idea of uneasiness, with an attention which it had hardly received on the first perusal. Mr. Darcy's shameful boast of what misery he had been able to inflict, gave her a keener sense of her sister's sufferings. It was some consolation to think that his visit to Rosings was to end on the day after the next, and a still greater, that in less than a fortnight she should herself be with Jane again, and enabled to contribute to the recovery of her spirits, by all that affection could do.

She could not think of Darcy's leaving Kent, without remembering that his cousin was to go with him; but Colonel Fitzwilliam had made it clear that he had no intentions[2] at all, and agreeable as he was, she did not mean to be unhappy about him.

While settling this point, she was suddenly roused by the sound of the door bell, and her spirits were a little fluttered by the idea of its being Colonel Fitzwilliam himself, who had once before called late in the evening, and might now come to enquire particularly after her.

1 Mark.

2 Of marriage.

3 A blush, always an ambiguous sign, might indicate to Darcy Elizabeth's "consciousness"—that is, her secret love for him. Her silence could suggest the same thing.

4 Family position.

5 It's possible that Austen got the suggestion for Darcy's arrogant proposal from Frances Burney's *Cecilia, or Memoirs of an Heiress* (1784). Delvile, loved by Cecilia, simultaneously declares his love and the impossibility of a marriage that "with my own family would degrade me for ever!" As he explains, "From the hour that my ill-destined passion was fully known to myself, I weighed all the consequences of indulging it, and found, added to the extreme hazard of success, an impropriety even in the attempt. *My* honour in the honour of my family is bound" (III, vi, 9). He does not propose to his beloved at this point in the narrative, for the reason he has explained.

6 A man of such family pride, such social position, and such wealth.

7 Like Collins, it seems, Darcy couches his proposal as a series of statements about himself and his feelings. At least those feelings appear to include genuine attachment to Elizabeth, even though his way of expressing himself shows no concern for her emotions.

8 Darcy's proposal also resembles Collins's in the suitor's clear expectation of a positive response.

9 This blush, unlike the previous one, has clear meaning in relation to her words: it signifies anger.

But this idea was soon banished, and her spirits were very differently affected, when, to her utter amazement, she saw Mr. Darcy walk into the room. In an hurried manner he immediately began an enquiry after her health, imputing his visit to a wish of hearing that she were better. She answered him with cold civility. He sat down for a few moments, and then getting up walked about the room. Elizabeth was surprised, but said not a word. After a silence of several minutes, he came towards her in an agitated manner, and thus began,

"In vain I have struggled. It will not do. My feelings will not be repressed. You must allow me to tell you how ardently I admire and love you."

Elizabeth's astonishment was beyond expression. She stared, coloured, doubted, and was silent. This he considered sufficient encouragement;[3] and the avowal of all that he felt, and had long felt for her, immediately followed. He spoke well; but there were feelings besides those of the heart to be detailed; and he was not more eloquent on the subject of tenderness than of pride. His sense of her inferiority—of its being a degradation—of the family obstacles which judgment had always opposed to inclination, were dwelt on with a warmth which seemed due to the consequence[4] he was wounding, but was very unlikely to recommend his suit.[5]

In spite of her deeply-rooted dislike, she could not be insensible to the compliment of such a man's[6] affection, and though her intentions did not vary for an instant, she was at first sorry for the pain he was to receive; till, roused to resentment by his subsequent language, she lost all compassion in anger. She tried, however, to compose herself to answer him with patience, when he should have done. He concluded with representing to her the strength of that attachment which, in spite of all his endeavours, he had found impossible to conquer; and with expressing his hope that it would now be rewarded by her acceptance of his hand.[7] As he said this, she could easily see that he had no doubt of a favourable answer.[8] He *spoke* of apprehension and anxiety, but his countenance expressed real security. Such a circumstance could only exasperate farther, and when he ceased, the colour rose into her cheeks,[9] and she said,

"In such cases as this, it is, I believe, the established mode to express a sense of obligation for the sentiments avowed, however unequally they may be returned. It is natural that obligation should be felt, and if I could *feel* gratitude, I would now thank you. But I cannot—I have never desired your good opinion, and you have certainly bestowed it most unwillingly. I am sorry to have occasioned pain to any one. It has been most unconsciously done, however, and I hope will be of short duration. The feelings which, you tell me, have long prevented the acknowledgment of your regard, can have little difficulty in overcoming it after this explanation."[10]

Mr. Darcy, who was leaning against the mantel-piece with his eyes fixed on her face, seemed to catch her words with no less resentment than surprise. His complexion became pale with anger, and the disturbance of his mind was visible in every feature. He was struggling for the appearance of composure, and would not open his lips, till he believed himself to have attained it. The pause was to Elizabeth's feelings dreadful. At length, with a voice of forced calmness, he said,

"And this is all the reply which I am to have the honour of expecting! I might, perhaps, wish to be informed why, with so little *endeavour* at civility, I am thus rejected. But it is of small importance."

"I might as well enquire," replied she, "why with so evident a desire of offending and insulting me, you chose to tell me that you liked me against your will, against your reason, and even against your character?[11] Was not this some excuse for incivility, if I *was* uncivil? But I have other provocations. You know I have. Had not my feelings decided against you, had they been indifferent, or had they even been favourable, do you think that any consideration would tempt me to accept the man, who has been the means of ruining, perhaps for ever, the happiness of a most beloved sister?"

As she pronounced these words, Mr. Darcy changed colour;[12] but the emotion was short, and he listened without attempting to interrupt her while she continued,

"I have every reason in the world to think ill of you. No motive can excuse the unjust and ungenerous part you acted *there*. You dare not, you cannot deny that you have been the principal, if not the only

10 Elizabeth speaks with unusual formality and dignity in this speech—qualities appropriate to the situation's importance but also indicative of the self-control she is exercising.

11 In opposition to your sense of morality and propriety. *Character,* in the sense relevant here, means "the sum of the moral and mental qualities which distinguish an individual . . . viewed as a whole" *(OED).*

12 Another ambiguous sign.

13 Of course she cannot actually know whether Bingley is in fact in a state of acute misery.

14 Elizabeth still bases moral judgments on appearance, considering that his air, or manner, *proves* Darcy unmoved. Similarly, in the next sentence, she will interpret his smile as declaring his *affected* incredulity.

15 Darcy means that he has rescued his friend from the social degradation that he has risked suffering himself.

16 The metaphor suggests that character ordinarily remains folded up, thus obscure, until it is "unfolded" in narrative.

17 Darcy's remark, his "less tranquil tone," and his heightened color suggest that he suspects Elizabeth of having a romantic interest in Wickham.

18 Financial independence.

19 Deserving.

means of dividing them from each other, of exposing one to the censure of the world for caprice and instability, the other to its derision for disappointed hopes, and involving them both in misery of the acutest kind."[13]

She paused, and saw with no slight indignation that he was listening with an air which proved him wholly unmoved by any feeling of remorse.[14] He even looked at her with a smile of affected incredulity.

"Can you deny that you have done it?" she repeated.

With assumed tranquillity he then replied, "I have no wish of denying that I did every thing in my power to separate my friend from your sister, or that I rejoice in my success. Towards *him* I have been kinder than towards myself."[15]

Elizabeth disdained the appearance of noticing this civil reflection, but its meaning did not escape, nor was it likely to conciliate her.

"But it is not merely this affair," she continued, "on which my dislike is founded. Long before it had taken place my opinion of you was decided. Your character was unfolded[16] in the recital which I received many months ago from Mr. Wickham. On this subject, what can you have to say? In what imaginary act of friendship can you here defend yourself? or under what misrepresentation, can you here impose upon others?"

"You take an eager interest in that gentleman's concerns," said Darcy in a less tranquil tone, and with a heightened colour.[17]

"Who that knows what his misfortunes have been, can help feeling an interest in him?"

"His misfortunes!" repeated Darcy contemptuously; "yes, his misfortunes have been great indeed."

"And of your infliction," cried Elizabeth with energy. "You have reduced him to his present state of poverty, comparative poverty. You have withheld the advantages, which you must know to have been designed for him. You have deprived the best years of his life, of that independence[18] which was no less his due than his desert.[19] You have done all this! and yet you can treat the mention of his misfortunes with contempt and ridicule."

"And this," cried Darcy, as he walked with quick steps across the room, "is your opinion of me! This is the estimation in which you hold me! I thank you for explaining it so fully. My faults, according to this calculation, are heavy indeed! But perhaps," added he, stopping in his walk, and turning towards her, "these offenses might have been overlooked, had not your pride[20] been hurt by my honest confession of the scruples that had long prevented my forming any serious design.[21] These bitter accusations might have been suppressed, had I with greater policy[22] concealed my struggles, and flattered you into the belief of my being impelled by unqualified, unalloyed inclination; by reason, by reflection, by every thing. But disguise of every sort is my abhorrence. Nor am I ashamed of the feelings I related. They were natural and just. Could you expect me to rejoice in the inferiority of your connections? To congratulate myself on the hope of relations, whose condition in life is so decidedly beneath my own?"

Elizabeth felt herself growing more angry every moment; yet she tried to the utmost to speak with composure when she said,

"You are mistaken, Mr. Darcy, if you suppose that the mode of your declaration affected me in any other way, than as it spared the concern which I might have felt in refusing you, had you behaved in a more gentleman-like manner."[23]

She saw him start at this, but he said nothing, and she continued,

"You could not have made the offer of your hand in any possible way that would have tempted me to accept it."

Again his astonishment was obvious; and he looked at her with an expression of mingled incredulity and mortification. She went on.

"From the very beginning, from the first moment I may almost say, of my acquaintance with you, your manners impressing me with the fullest belief of your arrogance, your conceit, and your selfish disdain of the feelings of others, were such as to form the ground-work of disapprobation,[24] on which succeeding events have built so immoveable a dislike; and I had not known you a month before I felt that you were the last man in the world whom I could ever be prevailed on to marry."[25]

20 Darcy's accusation of pride comes as something of a surprise. Elizabeth has not accused him of pride in this scene, although she has taken pride for granted as his dominant characteristic. He sees her as suffering from the same fault.

21 To propose to Elizabeth.

22 Strategy.

23 In accusing Darcy, a man of elevated social stature, of not being gentleman-like, Elizabeth draws on the tradition that gentlemanliness inheres not in rank but in conduct. The point is made economically in Robert Bage's *Hermsprong, or Man As He Is Not* (1796), a novel that Austen had in her library, when the upstart clerk Fillygrove demands the "satisfaction of a gentleman" (a duel) from Hermsprong. His status as gentleman depends on the fact that his father has an income from land of £100 a year. Hermsprong responds, "I allow your title, sir, as far as your father's hundred a year can give it you. It does not seem to be due to you by your manners, or your morals" (Chapter 16).

24 Elizabeth acknowledges what the text has already made apparent: that she, like others in her circle, makes her primary judgments of character on the basis of manners.

25 Elizabeth's forthright rejection of Darcy issues not only from her "prejudice" against him but from her personal integrity. Charlotte has no doubt that all her friend's objections to this rich and powerful man would vanish if she thought him interested in her; Charlotte is altogether wrong. Unlike Charlotte, Elizabeth values men for who they are (or who she thinks they are), not for what they have. Her belief that Darcy has injured two persons she cares for damages him severely in her estimation, and his apparently pervasive lack of concern for others makes him, from her point of view, unmarriageable. She seems to acknowledge in this speech, though, that she has thought of the possibility of marrying him, even though she has definitively rejected it.

26 Leave.

27 *Support* here has its literal physical meaning: Elizabeth feels as though she can't stand up.

28 Another indication of her emotional nature.

29 In privacy Elizabeth returns to her conviction of Darcy's pride, which she has not mentioned to him.

30 Self-assurance, impudence.

"You have said quite enough, madam. I perfectly comprehend your feelings, and have now only to be ashamed of what my own have been. Forgive me for having taken up so much of your time, and accept my best wishes for your health and happiness."

And with these words he hastily left the room, and Elizabeth heard him the next moment open the front door and quit[26] the house.

The tumult of her mind was now painfully great. She knew not how to support herself,[27] and from actual weakness sat down and cried for half an hour.[28] Her astonishment, as she reflected on what had passed, was increased by every review of it. That she should receive an offer of marriage from Mr. Darcy! that he should have been in love with her for so many months! so much in love as to wish to marry her in spite of all the objections which had made him prevent his friend's marrying her sister, and which must appear at least with equal force in his own case, was almost incredible! it was gratifying to have inspired unconsciously so strong an affection. But his pride, his abominable pride,[29] his shameless avowal of what he had done with respect to Jane, his unpardonable assurance[30] in acknowledging, though he could not justify it, and the unfeeling manner in which he had mentioned Mr. Wickham, his cruelty towards whom he had not attempted to deny, soon overcame the pity which the consideration of his attachment had for a moment excited.

She continued in very agitated reflections till the sound of Lady Catherine's carriage made her feel how unequal she was to encounter Charlotte's observation, and hurried her away to her room.

12

ELIZABETH AWOKE THE NEXT MORNING to the same thoughts and meditations which had at length closed her eyes. She could not yet recover from the surprise of what had happened; it was impossible to think of any thing else, and totally indisposed for employment, she resolved soon after breakfast to indulge herself in air and exercise. She was proceeding directly to her favourite walk, when the recollection of Mr. Darcy's sometimes coming there stopped her, and instead of entering the park, she turned up the lane, which led farther from the turnpike road.[1] The park paling was still the boundary on one side, and she soon passed one of the gates into the ground.[2]

After walking two or three times along that part of the lane, she was tempted, by the pleasantness of the morning, to stop at the gates and look into the park. The five weeks which she had now passed in Kent had made a great difference in the country, and every day was adding to the verdure of the early trees. She was on the point of continuing her walk, when she caught a glimpse of a gentleman within the sort of grove which edged the park; he was moving that way; and fearful of its being Mr. Darcy, she was directly retreating. But the person who advanced, was now near enough to see her, and stepping forward with eagerness, pronounced her name. She had turned away; but on hearing herself called, though in a voice which proved it to be Mr. Darcy, she moved again towards the gate. He had by that time reached it also, and, holding out a letter, which she instinctively took, said, with a look of haughty composure,[3] "I have been walking in the

1 A public road maintained by tolls collected from travelers.

2 Of the park.

3 Elizabeth sees "haughty composure" in Darcy's look: she is committed to the view that pride is his most conspicuous characteristic.

Anonymous, "The Love Letter," 178[5]? Many novels of Austen's period testify
to the need for a female confidante in matters of the heart. Elizabeth has no
love letter to show, but she is eager to confide to Jane the substance of Darcy's
forthright epistle about the mistakes she has made.

grove some time in the hope of meeting you. Will you do me the honour of reading that letter?"[4]—And then, with a slight bow, turned again into the plantation,[5] and was soon out of sight.

With no expectation of pleasure, but with the strongest curiosity, Elizabeth opened the letter, and to her still increasing wonder, perceived an envelope containing two sheets of letter paper, written quite through,[6] in a very close[7] hand.—The envelope itself was likewise full.[8]—Pursuing her way along the lane, she then began it. It was dated from Rosings, at eight o'clock in the morning, and was as follows:—

"Be not alarmed, Madam, on receiving this letter, by the apprehension of its containing any repetition of those sentiments, or renewal of those offers, which were last night so disgusting[9] to you. I write without any intention of paining you, or humbling myself, by dwelling on wishes, which, for the happiness of both, cannot be too soon forgotten; and the effort which the formation, and the perusal of this letter must occasion, should have been spared, had not my character[10] required it to be written and read. You must, therefore, pardon the freedom with which I demand your attention; your feelings, I know, will bestow it unwillingly, but I demand it of your justice.

"Two offences of a very different nature, and by no means of equal magnitude, you last night laid to my charge. The first mentioned was, that, regardless of the sentiments of either, I had detached Mr. Bingley from your sister,—and the other, that I had, in defiance of various claims, in defiance of honour and humanity, ruined the immediate prosperity and blasted the prospects of Mr. Wickham.—Wilfully and wantonly to have thrown off the companion of my youth, the acknowledged favourite of my father, a young man who had scarcely any other dependence than on our patronage, and who had been brought up to expect its exertion, would be a depravity, to which the separation of two young persons, whose affection could be the growth of only a few weeks,

4 Because correspondence between a man and a woman was considered improper unless the couple were engaged, Darcy protects Elizabeth's reputation by giving her the letter in person instead of mailing it to her. His manners are neither "easy" nor "happy"; rather, they seem often formal, in his writing (of the letter Elizabeth is about to read) and in his direct interpersonal relations. But they are, except in the notable instance of his proposal, always correct.

5 Grove, wood of planted trees.

6 Covered with writing.

7 Tight, narrow.

8 In this period envelopes in the modern sense did not exist. A sheet of paper folded around the letter served the purposes of an envelope. Darcy's letter includes a full sheet of writing on the inside of the "envelope."

9 Distasteful.

10 Here suggesting both his nature—which compelled him to write—and his reputation, as far as Elizabeth is concerned.

11 The county, or that part of the world.

12 The observation suggests at least a smattering of contempt for Bingley's facility in falling in love.

13 A conventional phrase that seems rather ironic under the circumstances.

14 Special.

15 Sharing.

16 Temperament.

17 Like Elizabeth and Jane, coming to conclusions about Wickham on the basis of his appearance and manners, Darcy has concluded Jane's character from her "countenance and air." His mistaken deduction calls attention to the dubiety of visual evidence as a basis for psychological and moral insight. Of course, *Pride and Prejudice* may also lead one to reflect on how often such evidence is the only kind available.

could bear no comparison.—But from the severity of that blame which was last night so liberally bestowed, respecting each circumstance, I shall hope to be in the future secured, when the following account of my actions and their motives has been read.—If, in the explanation of them which is due to myself, I am under the necessity of relating feelings which may be offensive to yours, I can only say that I am sorry.—The necessity must be obeyed—and further apology would be absurd. I had not been long in Hertfordshire, before I saw, in common with others, that Bingley preferred your eldest sister to any other young woman in the country.[11]—But it was not till the evening of the dance at Netherfield that I had any apprehension of his feeling a serious attachment.—I had often seen him in love before.[12]—At that ball, while I had the honour of dancing with you,[13] I was first made acquainted, by Sir William Lucas's accidental information, that Bingley's attentions to your sister had given rise to a general expectation of their marriage. He spoke of it as a certain event, of which the time alone could be undecided. From that moment I observed my friend's behaviour attentively; and I could then perceive that his partiality for Miss Bennet was beyond what I had ever witnessed in him. Your sister I also watched.—Her look and manners were open, cheerful, and engaging as ever, but without any symptom of peculiar[14] regard, and I remained convinced from the evening's scrutiny, that though she received his attentions with pleasure, she did not invite them by any participation[15] of sentiment.—If *you* have not been mistaken here, *I* must have been in an error. Your superior knowledge of your sister must make the latter probable.—If it be so, if I have been misled by such error to inflict pain on her, your resentment has not been unreasonable. But I shall not scruple to assert, that the serenity of your sister's countenance and air was such, as might have given the most acute observer, a conviction that, however amiable her temper,[16] her heart was not likely to be easily touched.[17]—That I was desirous of believing her indifferent is certain,—but I will venture to say that my investigations and decisions are not usually influenced by my hopes or fears.—I did not believe her to be indifferent because I wished it;—I believed it on impartial conviction, as truly as I wished it in reason.—My objections to the marriage were not merely those, which I last night acknowledged to have required the utmost force of passion to put aside, in my own case; the want of connection[18] could not be so great an evil to my friend as to me.[19]—But there were other causes of repugnance;[20]—causes which, though still existing, and existing to an equal degree in both instances, I had myself endeavoured to forget, because they were not immediately before me.—These causes must be stated, though briefly.—The situation of your mother's family, though objectionable, was nothing in comparison to that total want of propriety[21] so frequently, so almost uniformly betrayed by herself, by your three younger sisters,[22] and occasionally even by your father.—Pardon me.—It pains me to offend you. But amidst your concern for the defects of your nearest relations, and your displeasure at this representation of them, let it give you consolation to consider that, to have conducted yourselves so as to avoid any share of the like censure, is praise no less generally bestowed on you and your eldest sister, than it is honourable to the sense and disposition of both.[23]—I will only say farther, that from what passed that evening, my opinion of all parties was confirmed, and every inducement heightened, which could have led me before, to preserve my friend from what I esteemed a most unhappy connection.—He left Netherfield for London, on the day following, as you, I am certain, remember, with the design of soon returning.—The part which I acted,[24] is now to be explained.—His sisters' uneasiness had been equally excited with my own; our coincidence[25] of feeling was soon discovered; and, alike sensible[26] that no time was to be lost in detaching their brother, we shortly resolved on joining him directly in London.—We accordingly went—and there I readily engaged in the office of pointing out to my friend, the cer-

18 Lack of good family connections.

19 Because Bingley does not belong to so great a family as Darcy does.

20 Distaste, aversion.

21 Good manners, decorousness, correctness. The attention to manners that has shaped so many judgments narrated in the novel now becomes a very serious matter: "want of propriety," Darcy says, matters more than poor social standing and provides the primary ground for his effort to dissuade Bingley from further courtship of Jane.

22 Darcy apparently considers Mary's propensity for self-display a failure of propriety comparable to the boisterousness of Lydia and Kitty.

23 Darcy's allusion to the general view of Elizabeth and Jane may remind us that community opinion, in Austen's world, affects everyone. Samuel Richardson's *Clarissa,* published in the mid-eighteenth century (1748), opens with a letter in which Clarissa's friend Anna tells her that she has become "the public talk" because of events that have taken place in her family (Letter 1). She knows how concerned Clarissa will be about this fact, and she asks for information that will help her influence public opinion. Throughout the eighteenth century, the importance of community manifests itself in fiction, drama, and letters. Despite Elizabeth Bennet's independent spirit, she is both influenced by the views of her community and concerned about them inasmuch as they bear on her.

24 Yet another of Darcy's performances.

25 Concurrence.

26 Conscious.

27 This is real condescension: a lowering of himself.

28 Artifice, deceit.

tain evils of such a choice.—I described, and enforced them earnestly.—But, however this remonstrance might have staggered or delayed his determination, I do not suppose that it would ultimately have prevented the marriage, had it not been seconded by the assurance which I hesitated not in giving, of your sister's indifference. He had before believed her to return his affection with sincere, if not with equal regard. —But Bingley has great natural modesty, with a stronger dependence on my judgment than on his own.—To convince him, therefore, that he had deceived himself, was no very difficult point. To persuade him against returning into Hertfordshire, when that conviction had been given, was scarcely the work of a moment.—I cannot blame myself for having done thus much. There is but one part of my conduct in the whole affair, on which I do not reflect with satisfaction; it is that I condescended[27] to adopt the measures of art[28] so far as to conceal from him your sister's being in town. I knew it myself, as it was known to Miss Bingley, but her brother is even yet ignorant of it.—That they might have met without ill consequence, is perhaps probable;—but his regard did not appear to me enough extinguished for him to see her without some danger.—Perhaps this concealment, this disguise, was beneath me.—It is done, however, and it was done for the best.—On this subject I have nothing more to say, no other apology to offer. If I have wounded your sister's feelings, it was unknowingly done; and though the motives which governed me may to you very naturally appear insufficient, I have not yet learnt to condemn them.—With respect to that other, more weighty accusation, of having injured Mr. Wickham, I can only refute it by laying before you the whole of his connection with my family. Of what he has *particularly* accused me I am ignorant; but of the truth of what I shall relate, I can summon more than one witness of undoubted veracity. Mr. Wickham is the son of a very respectable man, who had for many years the management of all the Pemberley estates; and whose good conduct in the discharge of his trust, naturally inclined my father to be of service to him, and on George Wickham, who was his god-son,[29] his kindness was therefore liberally bestowed. My father supported him at school, and afterwards at Cambridge;—most important assistance, as his own father, always poor from the extravagance of his wife, would have been unable to give him a gentleman's education.[30] My father was not only fond of this young man's society, whose manners were always engaging;[31] he had also the highest opinion of him, and hoping the church would be his profession, intended to provide for him in it. As for myself, it is many, many years since I first began to think of him in a very different manner. The vicious[32] propensities[33]—the want[34] of principle which he was careful to guard from the knowledge of his best friend, could not escape the observation of a young man of nearly the same age with himself, and who had opportunities of seeing him in unguarded moments, which Mr. Darcy could not have. Here again I shall give you pain—to what degree you only can tell. But whatever may be the sentiments which Mr. Wickham has created,[35] a suspicion of their nature shall not prevent me from unfolding[36] his real character. It adds even another motive. My excellent father died about five years ago; and his attachment to Mr. Wickham was to the last so steady, that in his will he particularly recommended it to me, to promote his advancement in the best manner that his profession might allow, and if he took orders,[37] desired that a valuable family living might be his as soon as it became vacant. There was also a legacy of one thousand pounds. His own father did not long survive mine, and within half a year from these events, Mr. Wickham wrote to inform me that, having finally resolved against taking orders, he hoped I should not think it unreasonable for him to expect some more immediate pecuniary advantage, in lieu of the preferment,[38] by which he could not be benefited. He had some intention, he added, of studying law, and I must be aware that the interest of one thousand pounds would be a very insufficient support

29 That is, the godson of Darcy's father.

30 At Cambridge or Oxford University. Members of the professional class customarily attended the university.

31 Wickham's manners have apparently been the cause of whatever success he has had—in his previous life as well as in Meryton.

32 Immoral.

33 Inherited from his extravagant mother? Austen often explains characters' weaknesses by parental inheritance or upbringing.

34 Lack.

35 Another hint that Darcy believes Elizabeth in love with Wickham.

36 Darcy's use of the verb *unfold* in relation to his revelations about Wickham—a verb that he repeats later in his account—not only echoes Elizabeth's use of the same verb about Wickham's revelations concerning him but prefigures Elizabeth's folding and unfolding of the envelope containing his letter in the next chapter, as she reads and rereads the letter. I owe the latter point to David Marshall, whose thorough and sensitive interpretation of this and the succeeding chapter appears in "Unfolding Characters: Attention and Autobiography in *Pride and Prejudice*," *Imagining Selves: Essays in Honor of Patricia Meyer Spacks,* ed. Rivka Swenson and Elise Lauterbach [Newark: University of Delaware Press, 2009], 209–234.

37 Became ordained as a clergyman.

38 Advancement in the church.

39 Because of his "vicious propensities"—presumably for gambling and womanizing.

40 London.

41 Clergyman who had been holding the church position earlier intended for Wickham.

42 Appointment to the living.

43 Financial circumstances.

44 Household.

therein. I rather wished, than believed him to be sincere; but at any rate, was perfectly ready to accede to his proposal. I knew that Mr. Wickham ought not to be a clergyman.[39] The business was therefore soon settled. He resigned all claim to assistance in the church, were it possible that he could ever be in a situation to receive it, and accepted in return three thousand pounds. All connection between us seemed now dissolved. I thought too ill of him to invite him to Pemberley, or admit his society in town.[40] In town I believe he chiefly lived, but his studying the law was a mere pretence, and being now free from all restraint, his life was a life of idleness and dissipation. For about three years I heard little of him; but on the decease of the incumbent of the living[41] which had been designed for him, he applied to me again by letter for the presentation.[42] His circumstances,[43] he assured me, and I had no difficulty in believing it, were exceedingly bad. He had found the law a most unprofitable study, and was now absolutely resolved on being ordained, if I would present him to the living in question—of which he trusted there could be little doubt, as he was well assured that I had no other person to provide for, and I could not have forgotten my revered father's intentions. You will hardly blame me for refusing to comply with this entreaty, or for resisting every repetition to it. His resentment was in proportion to the distress of his circumstances—and he was doubtless as violent in his abuse of me to others as in his reproaches to myself. After this period, every appearance of acquaintance was dropped. How he lived I know not. But last summer he was again most painfully obtruded on my notice. I must now mention a circumstance which I would wish to forget myself, and which no obligation less than the present should induce me to unfold to any human being. Having said thus much, I feel no doubt of your secrecy. My sister, who is more than ten years my junior, was left to the guardianship of my mother's nephew, Colonel Fitzwilliam, and myself. About a year ago, she was taken from school, and an establishment[44] formed for her in

London; and last summer she went with the lady who presided over it, to Ramsgate;[45] and thither also went Mr. Wickham, undoubtedly by design; for there proved to have been a prior acquaintance between him and Mrs. Younge,[46] in whose character we were most unhappily deceived; and by her connivance and aid, he so far recommended himself to Georgiana, whose affectionate heart retained a strong impression of his kindness to her as a child, that she was persuaded to believe herself in love, and to consent to an elopement. She was then but fifteen, which must be her excuse; and after stating her imprudence, I am happy to add, that I owed the knowledge of it to herself. I joined them unexpectedly a day or two before the intended elopement, and then Georgiana, unable to support the idea of grieving and offending a brother whom she almost looked up to as a father, acknowledged the whole to me. You may imagine what I felt and how I acted. Regard for my sister's credit[47] and feelings prevented any public exposure; but I wrote to Mr. Wickham, who left the place immediately, and Mrs. Younge was of course removed from her charge.[48] Mr. Wickham's chief object was unquestionably my sister's fortune, which is thirty thousand pounds;[49] but I cannot help supposing that the hope of revenging himself on me, was a strong inducement. His revenge would have been complete indeed. This, madam, is a faithful narrative of every event in which we have been concerned together; and if you do not absolutely reject it as false, you will, I hope, acquit me henceforth of cruelty towards Mr. Wickham. I know not in what manner, under what form of falsehood he had imposed on you; but his success is not perhaps to be wondered at, ignorant as you previously were of everything concerning either. Detection could not be in your power, and suspicion certainly not in your inclination. You may possibly wonder why all this was not told you last night. But I was not then master enough of myself to know what could or ought to be revealed. For the truth of everything here related, I can appeal more particularly to

45 A resort town on the southeastern coast of England, not far from London and very popular at the time.

46 The chaperone who presided over Miss Darcy's establishment.

47 Reputation. Any suggestion of sexual indiscretion would ruin a young woman's prospects for a good marriage.

48 Responsibility.

49 An extremely large fortune for a woman. An elopement, which would mean a marriage without the legal settlements that might protect a woman's money, would give Wickham complete possession of his bride's fortune and leave her penniless and totally dependent on him.

the testimony of Colonel Fitzwilliam, who from our near relationship and constant intimacy, and still more as one of the executors of my father's will, has been unavoidably acquainted with every particular of these transactions. If your abhorrence of *me* should make *my* assertions valueless, you cannot be prevented by the same cause from confiding in my cousin; and that there may be the possibility of consulting him, I shall endeavour to find some opportunity of putting this letter in your hands in the course of the morning. I will only add, God bless you.

"Fitzwilliam Darcy"

Harris Bigg-Wither, c. 1805. Bigg-Wither (1781–1833), the son of family friends, proposed marriage to Jane Austen in 1802. She accepted him but changed her mind overnight. He married someone else two years later and subsequently fathered ten children.

13

If Elizabeth, when Mr. Darcy gave her the letter, did not expect it to contain a renewal of his offers, she had formed no expectation at all of its contents. But such as they were, it may well be supposed how eagerly she went through them, and what a contrariety[1] of emotion they excited. Her feelings as she read were scarcely to be defined. With amazement did she first understand that he believed any apology to be in his power; and stedfastly was she persuaded that he could have no explanation to give, which a just sense of shame would not conceal.[2] With a strong prejudice against every thing he might say, she began his account of what had happened at Netherfield. She read, with an eagerness which hardly left her power of comprehension, and from impatience of knowing what the next sentence might bring, was incapable of attending to the sense of the one before her eyes. His belief of her sister's insensibility,[3] she instantly resolved to be false, and his account of the real, the worst objections to the match, made her too angry to have any wish of doing him justice. He expressed no regret for what he had done which satisfied her; his style was not penitent, but haughty.[4] It was all pride and insolence.

But when this subject was succeeded by his account of Mr. Wickham, when she read with somewhat clearer attention a relation[5] of events, which, if true, must overthrow every cherished[6] opinion of his[7] worth, and which bore so alarming an affinity to his own history of himself, her feelings were yet more acutely painful and more difficult of definition. Astonishment, apprehension, and even horror,

1 Inconsistency.

2 In other words, she thinks him shameless as well as arrogant. She is determined not to believe what he says, and she's already prepared the grounds for interpreting his self-defense as false.

3 Indifference, imperviousness.

4 Strikingly, despite Elizabeth's "strong prejudice," everything she says about Darcy's letter in her initial state of anger is quite true. He is indeed wrong about Jane's "insensibility," and "pride" certainly marks his tone, although "insolence" may be debatable. The truth Elizabeth perceives at this point is, however, not the whole truth.

5 Narrative.

6 "Cherished" both because of her lingering affection for Wickham and because she is generally fond of her own opinions.

7 Wickham's.

8 This sentence-by-sentence examination shapes the process of her rereading, which this chapter records in detail. David Marshall, in the essay cited in the previous chapter, examines the process closely. He also refers to the present chapter as "one of the most remarkable chapters in the novel" ("Unfolding Characters: Attention and Autobiography in *Pride and Prejudice*," *Imagining Selves: Essays in Honor of Patricia Meyer Spacks*, ed. Rivka Swenson and Elise Lauterbach [Newark: University of Delaware Press, 2009], 211).

9 In realizing that the events she has thought herself to understand are capable of a different "turn," Elizabeth for the first time fully acknowledges the power of interpretation, which the reader of *Pride and Prejudice* has probably pondered earlier. The community Elizabeth inhabits appears to be deeply engaged in a process of rapid but definitive interpretation, which converts itself instantly to conviction. Elizabeth herself exemplifies just such a process.

oppressed her. She wished to discredit it entirely, repeatedly exclaiming, "This must be false! This cannot be! This must be the grossest falsehood!"—and when she had gone through the whole letter, though scarcely knowing any thing of the last page or two, put it hastily away, protesting that she would not regard it, that she would never look in it again.

In this perturbed state of mind, with thoughts that could rest on nothing, she walked on; but it would not do; in half a minute the letter was unfolded again, and collecting herself as well as she could, she again began the mortifying perusal of all that related to Wickham, and commanded herself so far as to examine the meaning of every sentence.[8] The account of his connection with the Pemberley family, was exactly what he had related himself; and the kindness of the late Mr. Darcy, though she had not before known its extent, agreed equally well with his own words. So far each recital confirmed the other: but when she came to the will, the difference was great. What Wickham had said of the living was fresh in her memory, and as she recalled his very words, it was impossible not to feel that there was gross duplicity on one side or the other; and, for a few moments, she flattered herself that her wishes did not err. But when she read, and re-read with the closest attention, the particulars immediately following of Wickham's resigning all pretensions to the living, of his receiving in lieu, so considerable a sum as three thousand pounds, again was she forced to hesitate. She put down the letter, weighed every circumstance with what she meant to be impartiality—deliberated on the probability of each statement—but with little success. On both sides it was only assertion. Again she read on. But every line proved more clearly that the affair, which she had believed it impossible that any contrivance could so represent, as to render Mr. Darcy's conduct in it less than infamous, was capable of a turn which must make him entirely blameless throughout the whole.[9]

The extravagance and general profligacy which he scrupled not to lay to Mr. Wickham's charge, exceedingly shocked her; the more so, as she could bring no proof of its injustice. She had never heard of him before his entrance into the——shire Militia, in which he had engaged at the persuasion of the young man, who, on meeting him accidentally in town, had there renewed a slight acquaintance. Of his former way of life nothing had been known in Hertfordshire but what he told himself. As to his real character, had information been in her power, she had never felt a wish of enquiring. His countenance, voice, and manner, had established him at once in the possession of every virtue.[10] She tried to recollect some instance of goodness, some distinguished trait of integrity or benevolence, that might rescue him from the attacks of Mr. Darcy; or at least, by the predominance of virtue, atone for those casual[11] errors, under which she would endeavour to class, what Mr. Darcy had described as the idleness and vice of many years continuance. But no such recollection befriended her. She could see him instantly before her, in every charm of air and address;[12] but she could remember no more substantial good than the general approbation of the neighbourhood, and the regard which his social powers had gained him in the mess.[13] After pausing on this point a considerable while, she once more continued to read. But, alas! the story which followed of his designs on Miss Darcy, received some confirmation from what had passed between Colonel Fitzwilliam and herself only the morning before; and at last she was referred for the truth of every particular to Colonel Fitzwilliam himself—from whom she had previously received the information of his near concern in all his cousin's affairs, and whose character she had no reason to question. At one time she had almost resolved on applying to him, but the idea was checked by the awkwardness of the application, and at length wholly banished by the conviction that Mr. Darcy would never have hazarded such a proposal, if he had not been well assured of his cousin's corroboration.

She perfectly remembered everything that had passed in conversation between Wickham and herself, in their first evening at Mr. Philips's. Many of his expressions were still fresh in her memory. She was *now* struck with the impropriety of such communications to a stranger, and wondered it had escaped her before. She saw the indelicacy of putting himself forward as he had done, and the inconsistency of his professions[14] with his conduct. She remembered that he had boasted of having no fear of seeing Mr. Darcy—that Mr. Darcy might leave the country, but that *he* should stand his ground; yet he

10 Elizabeth here acknowledges for the first time that countenance, voice, and manner are not sufficient grounds for judging character. The situation of being forced to alter previously held views is unusual for her: she tends to state her opinions forthrightly and to believe in them absolutely. A case in point is her final articulated judgment of Wickham, when she has just parted with him: "she parted from him convinced, that whether married or single, he must always be her model of the amiable and pleasing" (II, 4). Now her conviction must give way, and the "must" that she employed so confidently turns out to be meaningless—like the "must" in her assertions earlier in this chapter: "This must be false . . . This must be the grossest falsehood!"

11 Accidental.

12 Manner in conversation.

13 A group of officers who eat together.

14 Claims.

15 Lowering others' opinion of Darcy.

16 Elizabeth now assesses evidence that she had simply ignored before. Acts of interpretation, this novel repeatedly suggests, depend partly on selectivity about what evidence will be admitted.

17 Aspirations.

18 Medium size.

19 Women in their premarital state face a difficult dilemma. Jane, it appears, has lost her man as a result of not showing her feelings; Elizabeth now suspects that she has encouraged an unworthy man by incautiously displaying hers.

20 Acknowledge.

21 Repellent, likely to push others away.

22 Lately.

23 Comparable moments of self-condemnation by a female protagonist occur in *Northanger Abbey, Sense and Sensibility,* and *Emma*. Catherine's self-assessment in *Northanger Abbey* is perhaps most extreme: "Most grievously was she humbled. Most bitterly did she cry. . . . She hated herself more than she could express" (II, 10). Such sentiments in every case mark the point of a figure's significant psychic change. Important essays discussing the humbling of central characters in Austen's fiction include Ruth Bernard Yeazell, "Sexuality, Shame, and Privacy in the English Novel," *Social Research* 68: 1 (2001), 119–144; and Mary Ann O'Farrell, "Austen's Blush," *Novel* (1994), 125–139.

An earlier example of this kind of wholesale self-reproach occurs in Charlotte Lennox's *The Female Quixote* (1752), a novel that delighted Austen and that the Austen family read aloud long after Jane Austen's first reading of it. The novelist reports to her sister that they gave up attempts at oral presentation of another work of fiction, because of its "indelicacy." "We changed it for the 'Female Quixotte [sic],' which now makes our evening amusement; to me a very high one, as I find the work quite equal to what I remembered it" (To Cassandra, 7–8 January 1807).

had avoided the Netherfield ball the very next week. She remembered also, that till the Netherfield family had quitted the country, he had told his story to no one but herself; but that after their removal it had been every where discussed; that he had then no reserves, no scruples in sinking Mr. Darcy's character,[15] though he had assured her that respect for the father, would always prevent his exposing the son.[16]

How differently did every thing now appear in which he was concerned! His attentions to Miss King were now the consequence of views[17] solely and hatefully mercenary; and the mediocrity[18] of her fortune proved no longer the moderation of his wishes, but his eagerness to grasp at any thing. His behaviour to herself could now have had no tolerable motive; he had either been deceived with regard to her fortune, or had been gratifying his vanity by encouraging the preference which she believed she had most incautiously shewn.[19] Every lingering struggle in his favour grew fainter and fainter; and in farther justification of Mr. Darcy, she could not but allow[20] that Mr. Bingley, when questioned by Jane, had long ago asserted his blamelessness in the affair; that proud and repulsive[21] were his manners, she had never, in the whole course of their acquaintance, an acquaintance which had latterly[22] brought them much together, and given her a sort of intimacy with his ways, seen any thing that betrayed him to be unprincipled or unjust—any thing that spoke him of irreligious or immoral habits. That among his own connections he was esteemed and valued—that even Wickham had allowed him merit as a brother, and that she had often heard him speak so affectionately of his sister as to prove him capable of *some* amiable feeling. That had his actions been what Wickham represented them, so gross a violation of every thing right could hardly have been concealed from the world; and that friendship between a person capable of it, and such an amiable man as Mr. Bingley, was incomprehensible.

She grew absolutely ashamed of herself.—Of neither Darcy nor Wickham could she think, without feeling that she had been blind, partial, prejudiced, absurd.

"How despicably I have acted!"[23] she cried.—"I, who have prided myself on my discernment!—I, who have valued myself on my abilities! who have often disdained the generous candour of my sister, and gratified my vanity, in useless or blameable distrust!—How humiliating is this discovery!—Yet, how just a humiliation!—Had I been in love, I could not have been more wretchedly blind![24] But vanity, not love, has been my folly.[25]—Pleased with the preference of one, and offended by the neglect of the other, on the very beginning of our acquaintance, I have courted prepossession[26] and ignorance, and driven reason away, where either were concerned. Till this moment, I never knew myself."[27]

From herself to Jane—from Jane to Bingley, her thoughts were in a line which soon brought to her recollection that Mr. Darcy's explanation *there,* had appeared very insufficient; and she read it again. Widely different was the effect of a second perusal.—How could she deny that credit to his assertions, in one instance, which she had been obliged to give in the other?—He declared himself to be totally unsuspicious of her sister's attachment;—and she could not help remembering what Charlotte's opinion had always been.—Neither could she deny the justice of his description of Jane.—She felt that Jane's feelings, though fervent, were little displayed, and that there was a constant complacency in her air and manner, not often united with great sensibility.

When she came to that part of the letter, in which her family were mentioned, in terms of such mortifying, yet merited reproach, her sense of shame was severe. The justice of the charge struck her too forcibly for denial, and the circumstances to which he particularly alluded, as having passed at the Netherfield ball, and as confirming all his first disapprobation, could not have made a stronger impression on his mind than on hers.

The compliment to herself and her sister, was not unfelt. It soothed, but it could not console her for the contempt which had thus been self-attracted by the rest of her family;—and as she considered that Jane's disappointment had in fact been the work of her nearest relations, and reflected how materially the credit of both

The heroine of *The Female Quixote,* Arabella, has been deluded by her reading of romances into believing that she herself participates in a romance plot—or, more accurately, many romance plots. A wise clergyman finally brings her to her senses. "My Heart yields to the Force of Truth," Arabella says. ". . . I begin to perceive that I have hitherto at least trifled away my Time, and fear that I have already made some Approaches to the Crime of encouraging Violence and Revenge" (IX, 11). Arabella is a precursor of Catherine in *Northanger Abbey,* whose reading of Gothic novels persuades her that she inhabits a Gothic plot.

24 Compare a speech by Lady Delacour in Maria Edgeworth's *Belinda* (1801): "if you would only open your eyes, which heroines make it a principle never to do—or else there would be an end of the novel—if you would only open your eyes, you would see that this man is in love with you; and whilst you are afraid of his contempt, he is a hundred times more afraid of yours" (I, 6).

25 After frequently accusing Darcy of pride, Elizabeth now accuses herself of vanity. The two forms of moral weakness often closely resemble each other in this novel, despite the fact that Mary Bennet early declares them quite different.

26 Prejudice.

27 In an important essay on the epistemology of *Pride and Prejudice,* emphasizing issues of gender, Susan C. Greenfield points out that when Elizabeth declares that previously she never knew herself, "her mind becomes its own uncertain object—uncertain because it can change without warning and uncertain because it can be unknown." Her own thoughts, Greenfield continues, can be "as deceptive and inaccessible as Wickham and Darcy" ("The Absent-Minded Heroine; or, Elizabeth Bennet Has a Thought," *Eighteenth-Century Studies* 39: 3 [2006], 344).

28 Object of interest.

must be hurt by such impropriety of conduct, she felt depressed beyond any thing she had ever known before.

After wandering along the lane for two hours, giving way to every variety of thought; re-considering events, determining probabilities, and reconciling herself as well as she could, to a change so sudden and so important, fatigue, and a recollection of her long absence, made her at length return home; and she entered the house with the wish of appearing cheerful as usual, and the resolution of repressing such reflections as must make her unfit for conversation.

She was immediately told that the two gentlemen from Rosings had each called during her absence; Mr. Darcy, only for a few minutes, to take leave, but that Colonel Fitzwilliam had been sitting with them at least an hour, hoping for her return, and almost resolving to walk after her till she could be found. — Elizabeth could but just *affect* concern in missing him; she really rejoiced at it. Colonel Fitzwilliam was no longer an object.[28] She could think only of her letter.

Austen's ivory cup-and-ball game. The game, which originated in the sixteenth century, was very popular in the eighteenth and nineteenth centuries. Its object is simply to get the ball into the cup, using only the hand and arm that hold the cup.

14

THE TWO GENTLEMEN LEFT ROSINGS the next morning; and Mr. Collins having been in waiting near the lodges, to make them his parting obeisance, was able to bring home the pleasing intelligence, of their appearing in very good health, and in as tolerable spirits as could be expected, after the melancholy scene so lately gone through at Rosings.[1] To Rosings he then hastened to console Lady Catherine, and her daughter; and on his return, brought back, with great satisfaction, a message from her Ladyship, importing[2] that she felt herself so dull[3] as to make her very desirous of having them all to dine with her.

Elizabeth could not see Lady Catherine without recollecting, that had she chosen it, she might by this time have been presented to her, as her future niece; nor could she think, without a smile, of what her ladyship's indignation would have been. "What would she have said? —how would she have behaved?" were questions with which she amused herself.

Their first subject was the diminution of the Rosings party.—"I assure you, I feel it exceedingly," said Lady Catherine; "I believe no one feels the loss of friends so much as I do. But I am particularly attached to these young men; and know them to be so much attached to me!—They were excessively[4] sorry to go! But so they always are. The dear colonel rallied his spirits tolerably till just at last; but Darcy seemed to feel it most acutely, more I think than last year. His attachment to Rosings, certainly increases."

1 The scene of their parting with Lady Catherine.

2 Communicating.

3 Depressed.

4 At this time *excessively* served as a mild intensifier, roughly equivalent to *very*.

5 To Darcy's presumed romantic interest in Lady Catherine's daughter.

6 Lady Catherine has just invited her to pay a longer visit to the Collinses. Elizabeth's polite expression of gratitude presumably contains some irony, since Lady Catherine has no right to offer such an invitation.

7 A barouche is a coach with two rows of interior seats, on which passengers sit facing one another. It has a roof for the passengers that can be raised, for sun and air, or let down, for protection, at will. Because its size and its elaborate construction made it expensive, the barouche was considered an appurtenance of the wealthy. During a visit to London, Austen writes to her sister about her comic discomfort at riding in a vehicle so inappropriate to her relative poverty: "[I] was ready to laugh all the time, at my being where I was.—I could not but feel that I had naturally small right to be parading about London in a Barouche" (To Cassandra, 24 May 1813). In *Emma,* the novelist generates considerable comedy from the social pretensions of Mrs. Elton, who insistently mentions the barouche-landau (a barouche of modified construction) owned by her sister.

The box that Lady Catherine alludes to is a closed luggage compartment outside and in front of the main body of the coach. The driver often sits on it; in this case, Lady Catherine suggests that a manservant could join him.

8 To travel post is to use one's own or a rented carriage and change horses at posting stations along the way, thus ensuring greater speed than could be achieved by tiring a single set of horses. Posting stations were customarily located at inns.

9 The two manservants, of course, could not protect her from the real danger at Ramsgate—Wickham.

Mr. Collins had a compliment, and an allusion to throw in here,[5] which were kindly smiled on by the mother and daughter.

Lady Catherine observed, after dinner, that Miss Bennet seemed out of spirits, and immediately accounting for it by herself, by supposing that she did not like to go home again so soon, she added,

"But if that is the case, you must write to your mother to beg that you may stay a little longer. Mrs. Collins will be very glad of your company, I am sure."

"I am much obliged to your ladyship for your kind invitation,"[6] replied Elizabeth, "but it is not in my power to accept it.—I must be in town next Saturday."

"Why, at that rate, you will have been here only six weeks. I expected you to stay two months. I told Mrs. Collins so before you came. There can be no occasion for your going so soon. Mrs. Bennet could certainly spare you for another fortnight."

"But my father cannot.—He wrote last week to hurry my return."

"Oh! your father of course may spare you, if your mother can. Daughters are never of so much consequence to a father. And if you will stay another *month* complete, it will be in my power to take one of you as far as London, for I am going there early in June, for a week; and as Dawson does not object to the barouche box,[7] there will be very good room for one of you—and indeed, if the weather should happen to be cool, I should not object to taking you both, as you are neither of you large."

"You are all kindness, Madam; but I believe we must abide by our original plan."

Lady Catherine seemed resigned.—"Mrs. Collins, you must send a servant with them. You know I always speak my mind, and I cannot bear the idea of two young women travelling post[8] by themselves. It is highly improper. You must contrive to send somebody. I have the greatest dislike in the world to that sort of thing.—Young women should always be properly guarded and attended, according to their situation in life. When my niece Georgiana went to Ramsgate last summer, I made a point of her having two men servants go with her.[9] —Miss Darcy, the daughter of Mr. Darcy, of Pemberley, and Lady Anne, could not have appeared with propriety in a different manner.

I am excessively attentive to all those things. You must send John with the young ladies, Mrs. Collins. I am glad it occurred to me to mention it; for it would really be discreditable to *you* to let them go alone."

"My uncle is to send a servant for us."

"Oh!—Your uncle!—He keeps a man-servant, does he?[10]—I am very glad you have somebody who thinks of these things. Where shall you change horses?—Oh! Bromley, of course.—If you mention my name at the Bell, you will be attended to."

Lady Catherine had many other questions to ask respecting their journey, and as she did not answer them all herself, attention was necessary, which Elizabeth believed to be lucky for her; or, with a mind so occupied, she might have forgotten where she was. Reflection must be reserved for solitary hours; whenever she was alone, she gave way to it as the greatest relief; and not a day went by without a solitary walk, in which she might indulge in all the delight of unpleasant recollections.[11]

Mr. Darcy's letter, she was in a fair way of soon knowing by heart. She studied every sentence: and her feelings towards its writer were at times widely different. When she remembered the style of his address,[12] she was still full of indignation; but when she considered how unjustly she had condemned and upbraided him, her anger was turned against herself; and his disappointed feelings became the object of compassion. His attachment excited gratitude, his general character respect; but she could not approve[13] him; nor could she for a moment repent her refusal, or feel the slightest inclination ever to see him again. In her own past behaviour, there was a constant source of vexation and regret;[14] and in the unhappy[15] defects of her family a subject of yet heavier chagrin. They were hopeless of remedy. Her father, contented with laughing at them, would never exert himself to restrain the wild giddiness of his youngest daughters; and her mother, with manners so far from right herself,[16] was entirely insensible of the evil. Elizabeth had frequently united with Jane in an endeavour to check the imprudence[17] of Catherine and Lydia; but while they were supported by their mother's indulgence, what chance could there be of improvement? Catherine, weak-spirited, irritable,

10 Since male servants demanded higher wages than women, having a manservant signals Mr. Gardiner's relative prosperity.

11 The "delight," that is, of considering the causes of these reflections in every possible aspect.

12 Proposal.

13 Commend. We may wonder why it is that Elizabeth still can't "approve" Darcy. Perhaps the haughtiness of his style continues to alienate her.

14 Because of her encouragement of Wickham and her willingness to be deceived by him.

15 Unfortunate.

16 Although Elizabeth has been forced to learn that manners do not provide an adequate basis for judgment, she knows that they nonetheless supply the grounds upon which most members of her society judge. Her mother's failures of manners—her deviations from proper behavior—will inevitably make others think badly of her.

17 By labeling their attitudes and behavior "imprudence," Elizabeth indicates a serious moral judgment.

18 The marriage would have been "desirable in every respect" because it offered the promise both of "advantage"—financial ease and social status—and "happiness," being based on true love.

19 Disclosure.

20 This time Lady Catherine considers herself to condescend (usually it's Mr. Collins who attributes condescension to her) in going so far as to wish the travelers a good journey.

and completely under Lydia's guidance, had been always affronted by their advice; and Lydia, self-willed and careless, would scarcely give them a hearing. They were ignorant, idle, and vain. While there was an officer in Meryton, they would flirt with him; and while Meryton was within a walk of Longbourn, they would be going there forever.

Anxiety on Jane's behalf, was another prevailing concern; and Mr. Darcy's explanation, by restoring Bingley to all her former good opinion, heightened the sense of what Jane had lost. His affection was proved to have been sincere, and his conduct cleared of all blame, unless any could attach to the implicitness of his confidence in his friend. How grievous then was the thought that, of a situation so desirable in every respect, so replete with advantage, so promising for happiness,[18] Jane had been deprived, by the folly and indecorum of her own family!

When to these recollections was added the developement[19] of Wickham's character, it may be easily believed that the happy spirits which had seldom been depressed before, were now so much affected as to make it almost impossible for her to appear tolerably cheerful.

Their engagements at Rosings were as frequent during the last week of her stay, as they had been at first. The very last evening was spent there; and her Ladyship again enquired minutely into the particulars of their journey, gave them directions as to the best method of packing, and was so urgent on the necessity of placing gowns in the only right way, that Maria thought herself obliged, on her return, to undo all the work of the morning, and pack her trunk afresh.

When they parted, Lady Catherine, with great condescension,[20] wished them a good journey, and invited them to come to Hunsford again next year; and Miss De Bourgh exerted herself so far as to curtsey and hold out her hand to both.

15

ON SATURDAY MORNING ELIZABETH and Mr. Collins met for breakfast a few minutes before the others appeared; and he took the opportunity of paying the parting civilities which he deemed indispensably necessary.

"I know not, Miss Elizabeth," said he, "whether Mrs. Collins has yet expressed her sense of your kindness in coming to us, but I am very certain you will not leave the house without receiving her thanks for it. The favour of your company has been much felt, I assure you. We know how little there is to tempt anyone to our humble abode. Our plain manner of living, our small rooms, and few domestics,[1] and the little we see of the world, must make Hunsford extremely dull to a young lady like yourself;[2] but I hope you will believe us grateful for the condescension, and that we have done every thing in our power to prevent your spending your time unpleasantly."

Elizabeth was eager with her thanks and assurances of happiness. She had spent six weeks with great enjoyment; and the pleasure of being with Charlotte, and the kind attentions she had received, must make *her* feel the obliged. Mr. Collins was gratified, and with a more smiling solemnity replied,

"It gives me the greatest pleasure to hear that you have passed your time not disagreeably. We have certainly done our best; and most fortunately having it in our power to introduce you to very superior society, and from our connection with Rosings, the frequent means of varying the humble home scene, I think we may flatter ourselves that your Hunsford visit cannot have been entirely irksome.

1 Servants.

2 It is curious that Mr. Collins now seems to consider Elizabeth someone socially above him. His earlier proposal, with its stress on her financial limitations, certainly suggested nothing of the sort. Perhaps, though, he thinks that Elizabeth, in rejecting him, appeared to consider herself too good for him, and he is taunting her with all that he in fact had to offer. In this reading, he would believe her someone who thinks herself socially above him but is actually not. I owe this suggestion to Deidre Lynch.

3 Charlotte is obviously doing a good job of filling her role as Mrs. Collins.

4 *Yet,* in this sentence, strikes an ominous note, suggesting that the distractions of Charlotte's life will eventually lose their charms. Most of this paragraph is couched in free indirect discourse, recording the operations of Elizabeth's consciousness. If the *yet* comes from Elizabeth, it reinforces other hints that Elizabeth has some investment in seeing Charlotte's marriage as inevitably unhappy. Her thoughts and comments on Charlotte's choice have been emphatic. The word may belong, however, to the narrator, in which case it would confirm Elizabeth's judgment that the marriage can't possibly be happy for Charlotte in the long run.

5 A smaller carriage than the barouche, capable of carrying three persons. It has presumably been brought from London by the manservant whom Mr. Gardiner had sent for the two young women.

Our situation with regard to Lady Catherine's family is indeed the sort of extraordinary advantage and blessing which few can boast. You see on what a footing we are. You see how continually we are engaged there. In truth I must acknowledge that, with all the disadvantages of this humble parsonage, I should not think any one abiding in it an object of compassion, while they are sharers of our intimacy at Rosings."

Words were insufficient for the elevation of his feelings; and he was obliged to walk about the room, while Elizabeth tried to unite civility and truth in a few short sentences.

"You may, in fact, carry a very favourable report of us into Hertfordshire, my dear cousin. I flatter myself at least that you will be able to do so. Lady Catherine's great attentions to Mrs. Collins you have been a daily witness of; and altogether I trust it does not appear that your friend has drawn an unfortunate—but on this point it will be as well to be silent. Only let me assure you, my dear Miss Elizabeth, that I can from my heart most cordially wish you equal felicity in marriage. My dear Charlotte and I have but one mind and one way of thinking. There is in every thing a most remarkable resemblance of character and ideas between us. We seem to have been designed for each other."3

Elizabeth could safely say that it was a great happiness where that was the case, and with equal sincerity could add that she firmly believed and rejoiced in his domestic comforts. She was not sorry, however, to have the recital of them interrupted by the lady from whom they sprang. Poor Charlotte!—it was melancholy to leave her to such society!—But she had chosen it with her eyes open; and though evidently regretting that her visitors were to go, she did not seem to ask for compassion. Her home and her housekeeping, her parish and her poultry, and all their dependent concerns, had not yet lost their charms.4

At length the chaise5 arrived, the trunks were fastened on, the parcels placed within, and it was pronounced to be ready. After an affectionate parting between the friends, Elizabeth was attended to the carriage by Mr. Collins, and as they walked down the garden, he was commissioning her with his best respects to all her family, not forgetting his thanks for the kindness he had received at Longbourn in the winter, and his compliments to Mr. and Mrs. Gardiner, though unknown. He then handed her in, Maria followed, and the door was on the point of being closed, when he suddenly reminded them, with some consternation, that they had hitherto forgotten to leave any message for the ladies of Rosings.

"But," he added, "you will of course wish to have your humble respects delivered to them, with your grateful thanks for their kindness to you while you have been here."

Elizabeth made no objection;—the door was then allowed to be shut, and the carriage drove off.

"Good gracious!" cried Maria, after a few minutes' silence, "it seems but a day or two since we first came!—and yet how many things have happened!"

"A great many indeed," said her companion, with a sigh.

"We have dined nine times at Rosings, besides drinking tea there twice!—How much I shall have to tell!"

Elizabeth added privately, "and how much I shall have to conceal."

Their journey was performed without much conversation, or any alarm; and within four hours of their leaving Hunsford they reached Mr. Gardiner's house, where they were to remain a few days.

Jane looked well, and Elizabeth had little opportunity of studying her spirits, amidst the various engagements which the kindness of her aunt had reserved for them. But Jane was to go home with her, and at Longbourn there would be leisure enough for observation.

It was not without an effort meanwhile, that she could wait even for Longbourn, before she told her sister of Mr. Darcy's proposals. To know that she had the power of revealing what would so exceedingly astonish Jane, and must, at the same time, so highly gratify whatever of her own vanity she had not yet been able to reason away,[6] was such a temptation to openness as nothing could have conquered, but the state of indecision in which she remained, as to the extent of what she should communicate; and her fear, if she once entered on the subject, of being hurried into repeating something of Bingley, which might only grieve her sister farther.

6 Now Elizabeth has a specific focus for the vanity of which she accused herself after her rereadings of Darcy's letter: she is vain about the fact of the proposal that she so fiercely rejected.

16

1 Where the Gardiners live.

2 They would have come from London in a rented carriage.

3 Across the street.

4 Preparing.

5 A cucumber was a particularly extravagant purchase at this time. It might have cost as much as the equivalent of $5 now.

6 Lunch was not a customary meal in this period, but travelers often sought refreshment in the middle of the day, after an early start.

7 Lydia's financial irresponsibility—she is an inveterate and careless consumer—reflects the same heedlessness that leads her to block out the words of others when she does not wish to hear them.

IT WAS THE SECOND WEEK IN MAY, in which the three young ladies set out together from Gracechurch-street,[1] for the town of — — in Hertfordshire; and, as they drew near the appointed inn where Mr. Bennet's carriage[2] was to meet them, they quickly perceived, in token of the coachman's punctuality, both Kitty and Lydia looking out of a dining room upstairs. These two girls had been above an hour in the place, happily employed in visiting an opposite[3] milliner, watching the sentinel on guard, and dressing[4] a sallad and cucumber.[5]

After welcoming their sisters, they triumphantly displayed a table set out with such cold meat as an inn larder usually affords, exclaiming, "Is not this nice? is not this an agreeable surprise?"[6]

"And we mean to treat you all," added Lydia, "but you must lend us the money, for we have just spent ours at the shop out there."[7] Then shewing her purchases: "Look here, I have bought this bonnet. I do not think it is very pretty; but I thought I might as well buy it as not. I shall pull it to pieces as soon as I get home, and see if I can make it up any better."

And when her sisters abused it as ugly, she added, with perfect unconcern, "Oh! but there were two or three much uglier in the shop; and when I have bought some prettier-coloured satin to trim it with fresh, I think it will be very tolerable. Besides, it will not much signify what one wears this summer, after the — —shire have left Meryton, and they are going in a fortnight."

"Are they indeed!" cried Elizabeth, with the greatest satisfaction.

"They are going to be encamped near Brighton;[8] and I do so want papa to take us all there for the summer! It would be such a delicious scheme; and I dare say would hardly cost any thing at all. Mamma would like to go too of all things! Only think what a miserable summer else we shall have!"

"Yes," thought Elizabeth, "*that* would be a delightful scheme, indeed, and completely do for us at once. Good Heaven! Brighton, and a whole campful of soldiers, to us, who have been overset[9] already by one poor regiment of militia, and the monthly balls of Meryton."

"Now I have got some news for you," said Lydia, as they sat down to table. "What do you think? It is excellent news, capital news, and about a certain person we all like."

Jane and Elizabeth looked at each other, and the waiter was told he need not stay. Lydia laughed, and said,

"Aye, that is just like your formality and discretion.[10] You thought the waiter must not hear, as if he cared! I dare say he often hears worse things said than I am going to say. But he is an ugly fellow![11] I am glad he is gone. I never saw such a long chin in my life. Well, but now for my news: it is about dear Wickham; too good for the waiter, is not it? There is no danger of Wickham's marrying Mary King. There's for you! She is gone down to her uncle at Liverpool;[12] gone to stay. Wickham is safe."[13]

"And Mary King is safe!" added Elizabeth; "safe from a connection[14] imprudent as to fortune."

"She is a great fool for going away, if she liked him."

"But I hope there is no strong attachment on either side," said Jane.

"I am sure there is not on *his*. I will answer for it he never cared three straws about her. Who *could* about such a nasty little freckled thing?"

Elizabeth was shocked to think that, however incapable of such coarseness of *expression* herself, the coarseness of the *sentiment* was little other than her own breast had formerly harboured and fancied liberal![15]

As soon as all had ate, and the elder ones paid, the carriage was ordered; and after some contrivance, the whole party, with all their

8 A resort town on the south coast that provided during the summer many entertainments besides those supplied by the militia.

9 Disordered.

10 Lydia, of course, considers both of these nouns negative terms.

11 Lydia's value system is apparent: she judges men solely on their physical attractions.

12 An industrial city in northwest England on the Mersey River; in Austen's time an important port.

13 The colloquial vigor of Lydia's speech suggests the force of her personality. Like Elizabeth herself, Lydia has a strong will.

14 Marriage.

15 Generous, free from prejudice. The word has an interesting history. Originally used to designate those arts and sciences considered "worthy of a free man," it came to mean "pertaining to or suitable to persons of superior social station," or, as Dr. Johnson put it in his *Dictionary*, "becoming [to] a gentleman" *(OED)*. In thinking herself liberal, Elizabeth not only declares herself free of prejudice but emphasizes her status as a gentlewoman.

16 Bags for needlework and its equipment.

17 Hat box. This instance of Lydia's notion of "fun" is striking because of its utter triviality.

18 Lydia makes quite clear what kind of happening alone interests her.

19 Since Lydia, like her mother, takes marriage as the marker of female success, early marriage signifies for her triumphant achievement as a woman.

20 One may suspect that Lydia could have made fun out of it.

21 Probably another officer.

22 Cross-dressing, which Lydia and Kitty make into a joke, was a serious issue in the 1790s, when anxiety pervaded England over women's alleged tendency to move toward a masculine mode of dress. Maria Edgeworth's *Belinda* delineates a female character who dresses like a man and is subsequently caught in a man trap that destroys the beauty of her leg. Male cross-dressing was apparently less frequent and less fraught, but it was nonetheless a potentially risky matter for joking. Jillian Heydt-Stevenson comments, "That certain members of the regiment and their wives enjoy cross-dressing as a form of recreation illustrates Wollstonecraft's link in the *Vindication* between idle women and a standing army—far from being purposeful, both are groups with nothing to do" (*Austen's Unbecoming Conjunctions: Subversive Laughter, Embodied History* [New York: Palgrave Macmillan, 2005], 85).

boxes, workbags,[16] and parcels, and the unwelcome addition of Kitty's and Lydia's purchases, were seated in it.

"How nicely we are all crammed in," cried Lydia. "I am glad I bought my bonnet, if it is only for the fun of having another bandbox![17] Well, now let us be quite comfortable and snug, and talk and laugh all the way home. And in the first place, let us hear what has happened to you all, since you went away. Have you seen any pleasant men? Have you had any flirting? I was in great hopes that one of you would have got a husband before you came back.[18] Jane will be quite an old maid soon, I declare. She is almost three and twenty! Lord, how ashamed I should be of not being married before three and twenty![19] My aunt Philips wants you so to get husbands, you can't think. She says Lizzy had better have taken Mr. Collins; but *I* do not think there would have been any fun in it.[20] Lord! how I should like to be married before any of you; and then I would chaperon you about to all the balls. Dear me! we had such a good piece of fun the other day at Colonel Forster's! Kitty and me were to spend the day there, and Mrs. Forster promised to have a little dance in the evening; (by the bye, Mrs. Forster and me are *such* friends!) and so she asked the two Harringtons to come, but Harriet was ill, and so Pen was forced to come by herself; and then, what do you think we did? We dressed up Chamberlayne[21] in woman's clothes on purpose to pass for a lady,—only think what fun![22] Not a soul knew of it, but Col. and Mrs. Forster, and Kitty and me, except my aunt, for we were forced to borrow one of her gowns; and you cannot imagine how well he looked! When Denny, and Wickham, and Pratt, and two or three more of the men came in, they did not know him in the least. Lord! how I laughed! and so did Mrs. Forster. I thought I should have died. And *that* made the men suspect something, and then they soon found out what was the matter."

With such kind of histories of their parties and good jokes, did Lydia, assisted by Kitty's hints and additions, endeavour to amuse her companions all the way to Longbourn. Elizabeth listened as little as she could, but there was no escaping the frequent mention of Wickham's name.

Their reception at home was most kind. Mrs. Bennet rejoiced to see Jane in undiminished beauty; and more than once during dinner did Mr. Bennet say voluntarily to Elizabeth,

"I am glad you are come back, Lizzy."

Their party in the dining-room was large, for almost all the Lucases came to meet Maria and hear the news: and various were the subjects that occupied them; Lady Lucas was enquiring of Maria across the table, after the welfare and poultry of her eldest daughter; Mrs. Bennet was doubly engaged, on one hand collecting an account of the present fashions from Jane, who sat some way below her, and, on the other, retailing them all to the younger Miss Lucases; and Lydia, in a voice rather louder than any other person's, was enumerating the various pleasures of the morning to any body who would hear her.

"Oh! Mary," said she, "I wish you had gone with us, for we had such fun! As we went along, Kitty and me drew up all the blinds, and pretended there was nobody in the coach; and I should have gone so all the way, if Kitty had not been sick; and when we got to the George, I do think we behaved very handsomely, for we treated the other three with the nicest cold luncheon in the world, and if you would have gone, we would have treated you too. And then when we came away it was such fun! I thought we never should have got into the coach.[23] I was ready to die of laughter. And then we were so merry all the way home! we talked and laughed so loud, that any body might have heard us ten miles off!"

To this, Mary very gravely replied, "Far be it from me, my dear sister, to depreciate such pleasures. They would doubtless be congenial with the generality of female minds. But I confess they would have no charms for *me*. I should infinitely prefer a book."

But of this answer Lydia heard not a word. She seldom listened to any body for more than half a minute, and never attended to Mary at all.

In the afternoon Lydia was urgent with the rest of the girls to walk to Meryton and to see how everybody went on;[24] but Elizabeth steadily opposed the scheme. It should not be said that the Miss

23 Because it was so crowded with their belongings.

24 Was getting along.

Bennets could not be at home half a day before they were in pursuit of the officers. There was another reason too for her opposition. She dreaded seeing Wickham again, and was resolved to avoid it as long as possible. The comfort to *her,* of the regiment's approaching removal, was indeed beyond expression. In a fortnight they were to go, and once gone, she hoped there could be nothing more to plague her on his account.

She had not been many hours at home, before she found that the Brighton scheme, of which Lydia had given them a hint at the inn, was under frequent discussion between her parents. Elizabeth saw directly that her father had not the smallest intention of yielding; but his answers were at the same time so vague and equivocal, that her mother, though often disheartened, had never yet despaired of succeeding at last.

G. F. Prosser, "Manydown Park," 1833. Manydown Park, in Hampshire, 2 1/2 miles from Steventon Rectory, where the Austens lived, belonged to the Bigg family and was the site of Harris Bigg-Wither's proposal to Jane Austen. The house was demolished in 1965.

17

ELIZABETH'S IMPATIENCE TO ACQUAINT JANE with what had happened could no longer be overcome; and at length resolving to suppress every particular in which her sister was concerned, and preparing her to be surprised, she related to her the next morning the chief of the scene between Mr. Darcy and herself.

Miss Bennet's astonishment was soon lessened by the strong sisterly partiality which made any admiration of Elizabeth appear perfectly natural; and all surprise was shortly lost in other feelings. She was sorry that Mr. Darcy should have delivered his sentiments in a manner so little suited to recommend them; but still more was she grieved for the unhappiness which her sister's refusal must have given him.

"His being so sure of succeeding, was wrong," said she; "and certainly ought not to have appeared;[1] but consider how much it must increase his disappointment."

"Indeed," replied Elizabeth, "I am heartily sorry for him; but he has other feelings which will probably soon drive away his regard for me. You do not blame me, however, for refusing him?"

"Blame you! Oh, no."

"But you blame me for having spoken so warmly of Wickham?"

"No—I do not know that you were wrong in saying what you did."

"But you *will* know it, when I tell you what happened the very next day."

1 In other words, if Darcy was sure of succeeding he should for the sake of civility have concealed that fact.

2 Gratifying.

3 Kind, variety.

4 Your abundant pouring out of feeling makes me more sparing of emotion—by analogy with the possible effect of someone's pouring out money, which might cause an onlooker to hold onto her own wealth.

5 The view that physiognomy conveys character is beginning to be challenged.

She then spoke of the letter, repeating the whole of its contents as far as they concerned George Wickham. What a stroke was this for poor Jane! who would willingly have gone through the world without believing that so much wickedness existed in the whole race of mankind, as was here collected in one individual. Nor was Darcy's vindication, though grateful[2] to her feelings, capable of consoling her for such discovery. Most earnestly did she labour to prove the probability of error, and seek to clear one, without involving the other.

"This will not do," said Elizabeth; "you never will be able to make both of them good for any thing. Take your choice, but you must be satisfied with only one. There is but such a quantity of merit between them; just enough to make one good sort[3] of man; and of late it has been shifting about pretty much. For my part, I am inclined to believe it all Darcy's, but you shall do as you chuse."

It was some time, however, before a smile could be extorted from Jane.

"I do not know when I have been more shocked," said she. "Wickham so very bad! It is almost past belief. And poor Mr. Darcy! dear Lizzy, only consider what he must have suffered. Such a disappointment! and with the knowledge of your ill opinion too! and having to relate such a thing of his sister! It is really too distressing. I am sure you must feel it so."

"Oh! no, my regret and compassion are all done away by seeing you so full of both. I know you will do him such ample justice, that I am growing every moment more unconcerned and indifferent. Your profusion makes me saving;[4] and if you lament over him much longer, my heart will be as light as a feather."

"Poor Wickham; there is such an expression of goodness in his countenance![5] such an openness and gentleness in his manner."

"There certainly was some great mismanagement in the education of those two young men. One has got all the goodness, and the other all the appearance of it."

"I never thought Mr. Darcy so deficient in the *appearance* of it as you used to do."

"And yet I meant to be uncommonly clever in taking so decided a dislike to him, without any reason. It is such a spur to one's genius, such an opening for wit to have a dislike of that kind. One may be continually abusive without saying any thing just; but one cannot always be laughing at a man without now and then stumbling on something witty."[6]

"Lizzy, when you first read that letter, I am sure you could not treat the matter as you do now."

"Indeed I could not. I was uncomfortable enough. I was very uncomfortable, I may say unhappy. And with no one to speak to, of what I felt, no Jane to comfort me and say that I had not been so very weak and vain[7] and nonsensical as I knew I had! Oh! how I wanted you!"

"How unfortunate that you should have used such very strong expressions in speaking of Wickham to Mr. Darcy, for now they *do* appear wholly undeserved."

"Certainly. But the misfortune of speaking with bitterness, is a most natural consequence of the prejudices[8] I had been encouraging. There is one point, on which I want your advice. I want to be told whether I ought, or ought not to make our acquaintance in general understand Wickham's character."

Miss Bennet paused a little, and then replied, "Surely there can be no occasion for exposing him so dreadfully. What is your own opinion?"

"That it ought not to be attempted. Mr. Darcy has not authorised me to make his communication public. On the contrary, every particular relative to his sister, was meant to be kept as much as possible to myself; and if I endeavour to undeceive people as to the rest of his conduct, who will believe me? The general prejudice against Mr. Darcy is so violent, that it would be the death of half the good people in Meryton, to attempt to place him in an amiable light.[9] I am not equal to it. Wickham will soon be gone; and therefore it will not signify[10] to any body here, what he really is. Sometime hence it will be all found out, and then we may laugh at their stupidity in not knowing it before. At present I will say nothing about it."

6 Compare John Gregory's comments on wit in women: "Wit is the most dangerous talent you can possess. It must be guarded with great discretion and good nature, otherwise it will create you many enemies. Wit is perfectly consistent with softness and delicacy; yet they are seldom found united. Wit is so flattering to vanity, that they who possess it become intoxicated, and lose all self-command" (John Gregory, *A Father's Legacy to his Daughters, The Young Lady's Pocket Library, or Parental Monitor* [Bristol: Thoemmes Press, 1995], 13).

7 Elizabeth continues to accuse herself of vanity.

8 Elizabeth also now blames herself for prejudice. A little later, she will speak of "general prejudice," which contributed to her own.

9 The collective opinion that has earlier justified and reinforced Elizabeth's negative view of Darcy now appears to her as prejudice, which misguides interpretation. As the original title of *Pride and Prejudice, First Impressions,* suggests, much of the novel turns on problems of interpretation and on the drama of changing interpretations.

10 Matter, have any importance.

11 Reputation.

12 By removing any possibility of his restoring his reputation. It is worth noticing how sharply the two sisters' rationales for not disclosing Wickham's past differ from each other. Elizabeth thinks about how difficult it would be to persuade the community and how she can laugh at her fellows once the truth is revealed; Jane worries about Wickham's moral and psychological welfare.

13 Memory of him.

14 Relatives.

15 Would necessarily be.

16 In *Sense and Sensibility*, Austen represents the effects of the opposite course. Marianne, disappointed in love, indulges her feelings to the utmost, threatening the tranquility of her sister, and eventually makes herself so ill that her life is threatened.

"You are quite right. To have his errors made public might ruin him for ever. He is now perhaps sorry for what he has done, and anxious to re-establish a character.[11] We must not make him desperate."[12]

The tumult of Elizabeth's mind was allayed by this conversation. She had got rid of two of the secrets which had weighed on her for a fortnight, and was certain of a willing listener in Jane, whenever she might wish to talk again of either. But there was still something lurking behind, of which prudence forbade the disclosure. She dared not relate the other half of Mr. Darcy's letter, nor explain to her sister how sincerely she had been valued by his friend. Here was knowledge in which no one could partake; and she was sensible that nothing less than a perfect understanding between the parties could justify her in throwing off this last incumbrance of mystery. "And then," said she, "if that very improbable event should ever take place, I shall merely be able to tell what Bingley may tell in a much more agreeable manner himself. The liberty of communication cannot be mine till it has lost all its value!"

She was now, on being settled at home, at leisure to observe the real state of her sister's spirits. Jane was not happy. She still cherished a very tender affection for Bingley. Having never even fancied herself in love before, her regard had all the warmth of first attachment, and from her age and disposition, greater steadiness than first attachments often boast; and so fervently did she value his remembrance,[13] and prefer him to every other man, that all her good sense, and all her attention to the feelings of her friends,[14] were requisite to check the indulgence of those regrets, which must have been[15] injurious to her own health and their tranquillity.[16]

"Well, Lizzy," said Mrs. Bennet one day, "what is your opinion now of this sad business of Jane's? For my part, I am determined never to speak of it again to anybody. I told my sister Philips so the other day. But I cannot find out that Jane saw any thing of him in London. Well, he is a very undeserving young man—and I do not suppose there is the least chance in the world of her ever getting him now. There is no talk of his coming to Netherfield again in the summer; and I have enquired of everybody too, who is likely to know."

"I do not believe he will ever live at Netherfield any more."

"Oh well! it is just as he chooses. Nobody wants him to come. Though I shall always say that he used my daughter extremely ill; and if I was her, I would not have put up with it. Well, my comfort is, I am sure Jane will die of a broken heart; and then he will be sorry for what he has done."

But as Elizabeth could not receive comfort from any such expectation, she made no answer.

"Well, Lizzy," continued her mother, soon afterwards, "and so the Collinses live very comfortable, do they? Well, well, I only hope it will last. And what sort of table do they keep? Charlotte is an excellent manager, I dare say. If she is half as sharp as her mother, she is saving[17] enough. There is nothing extravagant in *their* housekeeping, I dare say."

"No, nothing at all."

"A great deal of good management, depend upon it. Yes, yes. *They* will take care not to outrun their income. *They* will never be distressed for money. Well, much good may it do them! And so, I suppose, they often talk of having Longbourn when your father is dead. They look upon it as quite their own,[18] I dare say, whenever that happens."

"It was a subject which they could not mention before me."

"No. It would have been strange if they had. But I make no doubt, they often talk of it between themselves. Well, if they can be easy with an estate that is not lawfully their own,[19] so much the better. *I* should be ashamed of having one that was only entailed on me."[20]

17 Frugal.

18 Mrs. Bennet's formulation conveys her view that the Collinses have no right to the estate. Actually, they not only "look on it" as their own: it will in fact be their own.

19 As Mrs. Bennet cannot be made to understand, it is precisely by the agency of law that an entail operates.

20 John A. Dussinger comments about Mrs. Bennet, using her last two speeches here as an example, "Often she is a mouthpiece to spew out ideas prohibited in civil conversation but relevant to the circumstances, as is demonstrated emphatically in the scene upon Elizabeth's return from Hunsford." A little later, he adds, "Despite her muddled reasoning in an argument, Mrs. Bennet is at times disquietingly right about other characters, and her talk has the advantage of filling in many empty spaces in the dialogue and narrative" (*In the Pride of the Moment: Encounters in Jane Austen's World* [Columbus: The Ohio State University Press, 1990], 122). Dussinger argues that Austen's "artistic strength lies not so much in the larger design of the story as in its minute encounters, the ivory miniatures revelatory of the character's inner life" (16). He provides some compelling readings of those minute encounters.

18

1 Quickly.

2 Apathy; incapacity for feeling.

3 Immersing oneself in sea water was considered me-
dicinal. Brighton was, by the beginning of the nineteenth century, "quite clearly the most important seaside resort in England" (John K. Walton, *The English
Seaside Resort: A Social History, 1750–1914* [New York: St.
Martin's Press, 1983], 48). It had grown quickly, Walton
explains, as a result of "emulation and competition":
members of the aristocracy had begun to frequent it,
and those from lower classes quickly followed (216). By
1794, there were estimated to be 10,000 annual visitors, compared with a resident population of 5,700
(Sue Berry, *Georgian Brighton* [Chichester: Phillimore,
2005], 40). Books about the value of sea bathing were
frequently published in the final decades of the eighteenth century, many of them by Brighton doctors. In
1768, a Dr. Awsiter had published such a work, and the
next year he opened Brighton's first baths. A second
bath appeared in 1787 (Berry, *Georgian Brighton*, 25).

THE FIRST WEEK OF THEIR return was soon gone. The second began. It was the last of the regiment's stay in Meryton, and all the
young ladies in the neighbourhood were drooping apace.[1] The dejection was almost universal. The elder Miss Bennets alone were still
able to eat, drink, and sleep, and pursue the usual course of their employments. Very frequently were they reproached for this insensibility[2] by Kitty and Lydia, whose own misery was extreme, and who
could not comprehend such hard-heartedness in any of the family.

"Good Heaven! What is to become of us! What are we to do!"
would they often exclaim in the bitterness of woe. "How can you be
smiling so, Lizzy?"

Their affectionate mother shared all their grief; she remembered
what she had herself endured on a similar occasion, five and twenty
years ago.

"I am sure," said she, "I cried for two days together when Colonel Miller's regiment went away. I thought I should have broke my
heart."

"I am sure I shall break *mine,*" said Lydia.

"If one could but go to Brighton!" observed Mrs. Bennet.

"Oh, yes!—if one could but go to Brighton! But papa is so disagreeable."

"A little sea-bathing would set me up for ever."[3]

"And my aunt Phillips is sure it would do *me* a great deal of good,"
added Kitty.

Such were the kind of lamentations resounding perpetually through Longbourn House. Elizabeth tried to be diverted by them; but all sense of pleasure was lost in shame. She felt anew the justice of Mr. Darcy's objections; and never had she before been so much disposed to pardon his interference in the views[4] of his friend.

But the gloom of Lydia's prospect was shortly cleared away; for she received an invitation from Mrs. Forster, the wife of the Colonel of the regiment, to accompany her to Brighton. This invaluable friend was a very young woman, and very lately[5] married. A resemblance in good humour and good spirits had recommended her and Lydia to each other, and out of their *three* months' acquaintance they had been intimate *two*.

The rapture of Lydia on this occasion, her adoration of Mrs. Forster, the delight of Mrs. Bennet, and the mortification of Kitty, are scarcely to be described. Wholly inattentive to her sister's feelings, Lydia flew about the house in restless ecstacy, calling for every one's congratulations, and laughing and talking with more violence than ever; whilst the luckless Kitty continued in the parlour repining at her fate in terms as unreasonable as her accent was peevish.

"I cannot see why Mrs. Forster should not ask *me* as well as Lydia," said she, "though I am *not* her particular friend. I have just as much right to be asked as she has, and more too, for I am two years older."

In vain did Elizabeth attempt to make her reasonable,[6] and Jane to make her resigned. As for Elizabeth herself, this invitation was so far from exciting in her the same feelings as in her mother and Lydia, that she considered it as the death warrant of all possibility of common sense for the latter; and detestable as such a step must make her were it known, she could not help secretly advising her father not to let her go. She represented to him all the improprieties of Lydia's general behaviour, the little advantage she could derive from the friendship of such a woman as Mrs. Forster, and the probability of her being yet more imprudent[7] with such a companion at Brighton, where the temptations must be greater than at home. He heard her attentively, and then said,

4 Plans.

5 Recently.

6 Elizabeth's faith in rationality frequently proves ineffectual in her family.

7 Again, this serious moral term.

8 Rationality doesn't work even with Elizabeth's father, who counters it with his customary cynical self-removal.

9 Particular.

10 Self-assurance, audacity.

11 The notion of character as fixed was widespread in the eighteenth century. Novels focused on human development tended to conceive it as a process of accretion rather than change. Thus Tom Jones, forced to learn prudence, does not alter his fundamental nature of generosity and warmth; he only adds prudence to his other admirable characteristics. Austen often suggests a more flexible conception of human nature: her central characters frequently undergo essential change. Even in the eighteenth-century view, the young (and Lydia is not yet sixteen) were considered more malleable than their elders.

12 Lowest.

13 Physical appearance.

14 In *An Unfortunate Mother's Advice to her Absent Daughters,* a work first published in 1761 but republished into the nineteenth century, Sarah Pennington makes a strong case against the kind of life that Lydia and Kitty lead: "Diversions, properly regulated, are not only allowable, they are absolutely necessary to youth, and are never criminal but when taken to excess; that is, when they engross the whole thought, when they are made the chief business of life: they then give a distaste to every valuable employment, and, by a sort of infatuation, leave the mind in a state of restless impatience from the conclusion of one 'till the commencement of another. This is the unfortunate disposition of many; guard most carefully against it, for nothing can be attended with more pernicious consequences" (*An Unfortunate Mother's Advice to her Absent Daughters, The Young Lady's Pocket Library, or Parental Monitor* [Bristol: Thoemmes Press, 1995], 72). It is interesting that Elizabeth now sees in her younger sisters manifestations of vanity, the sin of which she has accused herself.

"Lydia will never be easy until she has exposed herself in some public place or other, and we can never expect her to do it with so little expense or inconvenience to her family as under the present circumstances."

"If you were aware," said Elizabeth, "of the very great disadvantage to us all, which must arise from the public notice of Lydia's unguarded and imprudent manner; nay, which has already arisen from it, I am sure you would judge differently in the affair."

"Already arisen?" repeated Mr. Bennet. "What, has she frightened away some of your lovers? Poor little Lizzy! But do not be cast down. Such squeamish youths as cannot bear to be connected with a little absurdity, are not worth a regret. Come, let me see the list of the pitiful fellows who have been kept aloof by Lydia's folly."[8]

"Indeed you are mistaken. I have no such injuries to resent. It is not of peculiar,[9] but of general evils, which I am now complaining. Our importance, our respectability in the world, must be affected by the wild volatility, the assurance[10] and disdain of all restraint which mark Lydia's character. Excuse me—for I must speak plainly. If you, my dear father, will not take the trouble of checking her exuberant spirits, and of teaching her that her present pursuits are not to be the business of her life, she will soon be beyond the reach of amendment. Her character will be fixed,[11] and she will, at sixteen, be the most determined flirt that ever made herself and her family ridiculous. A flirt too, in the worst and meanest[12] degree of flirtation: without any attraction beyond youth and a tolerable person;[13] and from the ignorance and emptiness of her mind, wholly unable to ward off any portion of that universal contempt which her rage for admiration will excite. In this danger Kitty is also comprehended. She will follow wherever Lydia leads. Vain, ignorant, idle, and absolutely uncontrolled![14] Oh! my dear father, can you suppose it possible that they will not be censured and despised wherever they are known, and that their sisters will not be often involved in the disgrace?"

Mr. Bennet saw that her whole heart was in the subject; and affectionately taking her hand, said in reply:

"Do not make yourself uneasy, my love. Wherever you and Jane are known, you must be respected and valued; and you will not appear to less advantage for having a couple of—or I may say, three very silly sisters. We shall have no peace at Longbourn if Lydia does not go to Brighton. Let her go then. Colonel Forster is a sensible man, and will keep her out of any real mischief; and she is luckily too poor to be an object of prey to any body. At Brighton she will be of less importance even as a common flirt than she has been here. The officers will find women better worth their notice. Let us hope, therefore, that her being there may teach her her own insignificance. At any rate, she cannot grow many degrees worse, without authorizing us to lock her up for the rest of her life."

With this answer Elizabeth was forced to be content; but her own opinion continued the same, and she left him disappointed and sorry. It was not in her nature, however, to increase her vexations by dwelling on them. She was confident of having performed her duty, and to fret over unavoidable evils, or augment them by anxiety, was no part of her disposition.

Had Lydia and her mother known the substance of her conference with her father, their indignation would hardly have found expression in their united volubility. In Lydia's imagination, a visit to Brighton comprised every possibility of earthly happiness. She saw with the creative eye of fancy, the streets of that gay bathing place covered with officers. She saw herself the object of attention, to tens and to scores of them at present unknown. She saw all the glories of the camp; its tents stretched forth in beauteous uniformity of lines, crowded with the young and the gay, and dazzling with scarlet; and to complete the view, she saw herself seated beneath a tent, tenderly flirting with at least six officers at once.[15]

Had she known her sister sought to tear her from such prospects and such realities as these, what would have been her sensations? They could have been understood only by her mother, who might have felt nearly the same. Lydia's going to Brighton was all that consoled her for her melancholy conviction of her husband's never intending to go there himself.

But they were entirely ignorant of what had passed; and their raptures continued with little intermission to the very day of Lydia's leaving home.

15 Because the militia would stay at Brighton only a short time, they inhabited tented encampments. Enlisted men would live in tents; officers might have better accommodations (Berry, *Georgian Brighton*, 71). Bharat Tandon comments on this passage, "At once elegant and ludicrous, Austen's comedy—like the mock-heroic of Pope and Swift, which it recalls here—maintains an inwardness and reciprocity with the object of its disapproval, 'the creative eye of fancy.' Lydia's vision of 'earthly happiness' manages to compact teenage daydream with the rhetoric of Biblical prophecy ('She saw [. . .] She saw [. . .] to tens and to scores of them [. . .] She saw all the glories of the camp [. . .] she saw')" (*Jane Austen and the Morality of Conversation* [London: Anthem Press, 2003], 86). Tandon's close attention to the working of Austen's text makes his study particularly valuable.

Susan Greenfield notes another aspect of Lydia's musing when she observes that it "speaks to the material basis of Lydia's near ruin"—and, it might be added, to the materiality of all that she imagines. Greenfield continues: "In a world where women are 'object[s],' Lydia truly believes that—like the master of a harem—she will sit 'beneath a tent,' and control 'scores' of 'unknown' men" ("The Absent-Minded Heroine; or, Elizabeth Bennet Has a Thought," *Eighteenth-Century Studies* 39: 3 [2006], 345).

16 "Learn[ing] to detect" suggests a willed change in interpretation. Such a change has taken place in Elizabeth, whose feelings toward Wickham have altered in accord with her new perceptions of his nature. She now notices the kind of evidence she has failed previously to see.

17 Cause distaste.

18 Now Elizabeth believes that Wickham detects in her the vanity she has seen in herself, and that he deliberately wishes to play on it.

Elizabeth was now to see Mr. Wickham for the last time. Having been frequently in company with him since her return, agitation was pretty well over; the agitations of former partiality entirely so. She had even learnt to detect,[16] in the very gentleness which had first delighted her, an affectation and a sameness to disgust[17] and weary. In his present behaviour to herself, moreover, she had a fresh source of displeasure, for the inclination he soon testified of renewing those attentions which had marked the early part of their acquaintance, could only serve, after what had since passed, to provoke her. She lost all concern for him in finding herself thus selected as the object of such idle and frivolous gallantry; and while she steadily repressed it, could not but feel the reproof contained in his believing, that however long, and for whatever cause, his attentions had been withdrawn, her vanity would be gratified and her preference secured at any time by their renewal.[18]

On the very last day of the regiment's remaining at Meryton, he dined with others of the officers at Longbourn; and so little was Elizabeth disposed to part from him in good humour, that on his making some enquiry as to the manner in which her time had passed at Hunsford, she mentioned Colonel Fitzwilliam's and Mr. Darcy's having both spent three weeks at Rosings, and asked him if he were acquainted with the former.

He looked surprised, displeased, alarmed; but with a moment's recollection and a returning smile, replied, that he had formerly seen him often; and after observing that he was a very gentlemanlike man, asked her how she had liked him. Her answer was warmly in his favour. With an air of indifference he soon afterwards added, "How long did you say he was at Rosings?"

"Nearly three weeks."

"And you saw him frequently?"

"Yes, almost every day."

"His manners are very different from his cousin's."

"Yes, very different. But I think Mr. Darcy improves upon acquaintance."

"Indeed!" cried Mr. Wickham with a look which did not escape her. "And pray may I ask?" but checking himself, he added in a gayer tone, "Is it in address[19] that he improves? Has he deigned to add aught[20] of civility to his ordinary style? for I dare not hope," he continued in a lower and more serious tone, "that he is improved in essentials."

"Oh, no!" said Elizabeth. "In essentials, I believe, he is very much what he ever was."

While she spoke, Wickham looked as if scarcely knowing whether to rejoice over her words, or to distrust their meaning.[21] There was a something in her countenance which made him listen with an apprehensive and anxious attention,[22] while she added,

"When I said that he improved on acquaintance, I did not mean that either his mind or manners were in a state of improvement, but that from knowing him better, his disposition was better understood."

Wickham's alarm now appeared in a heightened complexion and agitated look; for a few minutes he was silent; till, shaking off his embarrassment, he turned to her again, and said in the gentlest of accents,

"You, who so well know my feeling towards Mr. Darcy, will readily comprehend how sincerely I must rejoice that he is wise enough to assume even the *appearance* of what is right. His pride, in that direction, may be of service, if not to himself, to many others, for it must deter him from such foul misconduct as I have suffered by. I only fear that the sort of cautiousness, to which you, I imagine, have been alluding, is merely adopted on his visits to his aunt, of whose good opinion and judgment he stands much in awe. His fear of her, has always operated, I know, when they were together; and a good deal is to be imputed to his wish of forwarding the match with Miss De Bourgh, which I am certain he has very much at heart."[23]

Elizabeth could not repress a smile at this, but she answered only by a slight inclination of the head. She saw that he wanted to engage her on the old subject of his grievances, and she was in no humour to indulge him. The rest of the evening passed with the *appearance,* on his side, of usual cheerfulness, but with no farther attempt to distinguish[24] Elizabeth; and they parted at last with mutual civility, and possibly a mutual desire of never meeting again.

19 Manner of speaking.

20 Anything.

21 Elizabeth here deliberately plays with ambiguities. Her verbal exchanges with Darcy have frequently been marked by ambiguity, but it seems part of the author's rather than the characters' intention. Not so in this sequence.

22 Wickham, too, is a reader of countenances. He sees something that he can't quite interpret; his realization of that fact makes him seem cleverer than Elizabeth and Jane, who have believed that what they see testifies clearly to inner substance.

23 The reader who has been influenced by Elizabeth—as most readers are, in their first perusal of the novel—and enlightened by Darcy's letter will see the speciousness of Wickham's utterances in this sequence. His earlier statements about himself and Darcy were, of course, at least equally specious, but, like Elizabeth, we probably failed to notice. Susan C. Greenfield comments that "Elizabeth's gravest mistakes occur when she takes language too literally—when she assumes words are really true" ("The Absent-Minded Heroine," 343).

24 Single out.

When the party broke up, Lydia returned with Mrs. Forster to Meryton, from whence they were to set out early the next morning. The separation between her and her family was rather noisy than pathetic. Kitty was the only one who shed tears; but she did weep from vexation and envy. Mrs. Bennet was diffuse in her good wishes for the felicity of her daughter, and impressive in her injunctions that she would not miss the opportunity of enjoying herself as much as possible; advice, which there was every reason to believe would be attended to; and in the clamorous happiness of Lydia herself in bidding farewell, the more gentle adieus of her sisters were uttered without being heard.

David Dodd, portrait of George III, 1794. King George III, familiar to Americans as having imposed the taxes that led to the American War of Independence, ruled England throughout Austen's lifetime.

19

Had Elizabeth's opinion been all drawn from her own family, she could not have formed a very pleasing opinion of conjugal felicity or domestic comfort. Her father captivated by youth and beauty,[1] and that appearance of good humour, which youth and beauty generally give, had married a woman whose weak understanding[2] and illiberal[3] mind, had very early in their marriage put an end to all real affection for her. Respect, esteem, and confidence, had vanished for ever; and all his views[4] of domestic happiness were overthrown. But Mr. Bennet was not of a disposition to seek comfort for the disappointment which his own imprudence[5] had brought on, in any of those pleasures which too often console the unfortunate for their folly or their vice.[6] He was fond of the country and of books; and from these tastes had arisen his principal enjoyments. To his wife he was very little otherwise indebted, than as her ignorance and folly had contributed to his amusement. This is not the sort of happiness which a man would in general wish to owe to his wife; but where other powers of entertainment are wanting, the true philosopher will derive benefit from such as are given.

Elizabeth, however, had never been blind to the impropriety of her father's behaviour as a husband. She had always seen it with pain; but respecting his abilities, and grateful for his affectionate treatment of herself, she endeavoured to forget what she could not overlook, and to banish from her thoughts that continual breach of conjugal obligation and decorum which, in exposing his wife to the

1 In *Sense and Sensibility*, Austen reflects again about this kind of marriage. Her protagonist, Elinor, concludes about a minor character: "His temper might perhaps be a little soured by finding, like many others of his sex, that through some unaccountable bias in favour of beauty, he was the husband of a very silly woman,—but she knew that this kind of blunder was too common for any sensible man to be lastingly hurt by it" (I, 20).

As for Mr. Bennet, young and not yet worldly wise, he presumably once considered beauty and good humor sufficient qualifications for a wife. He could not remedy his mistake, once he realized it, by divorce, an expensive procedure that required an Act of Parliament, and was granted only on grounds of adultery. Trapped in his union with a foolish wife, he must have developed his delight in absurdity as a defense against misery.

2 Intellect.

3 Sordid.

4 Expectations.

5 His imprudence in marrying has nothing to do with money; it characterizes his failure to think about such matters as intellectual compatibility.

6 That is, such pleasures as gambling, drinking, and womanizing—common activities for gentlemen dissatisfied with their marriages.

7 As Mr. Bennet does by mocking his wife in terms comprehensible to at least her eldest daughters, if not to herself.

8 Social gatherings with others.

9 Spa, resort. Early in the eighteenth century, members of the upper classes had flocked to such inland spas as Bath, but seaside resorts became increasingly fashionable. Sea bathing was thought to have health benefits; a 1702 work called *History of Cold Bathing,* by Sir John Floyer and Edward Baynard, claimed that it could "cure cancer, rheumatism, ulcers, deafness, asthma, hernia, corns, leprosy, consumption, venereal diseases, tumours, a disordered mind and sundry other ailments." Sea bathing, it was alleged, also had aphrodisiac effects (Keith Parry, *Resorts of the Lancashire Coast* [North Pomfret, VT: David & Charles, 1983], 13).

Austen's last, unfinished novel, *Sanditon,* concerned a new resort and efforts to promote it. Mr. Parker, the principal promoter, "held it indeed as certain, that no person c^d be really well, no person . . . could be really in a state of secure & permanent Health without spending at least 6 weeks by the Sea every year. —The Sea air & Sea Bathing together were nearly infallible, one or the other of them being a match for every Disorder, of the Stomach, the Lungs or the Blood; They were anti-spasmodic, anti-pulmonary, anti-septic, anti-bilious & anti-rheumatic. Nobody could catch cold by the Sea, Nobody wanted Appetite by the Sea, Nobody wanted Spirits, Nobody wanted Strength" (Chapter 2).

Elizabeth's worry about Lydia at a watering place, however, does not concern her physical health. The psychological dangers of such a locale are suggested by a 1788 work, William Hutton's *Description of Blackpool in Lancashire, frequented for Sea Bathing.* Hutton writes, "Here is a full display of beauty and fashion. Here the eye faithful to its trust, conveys intelligence from the heart of one sex to that of the other; gentle tumults rise in the breast; intercourse opens in tender language; the softer passions are called into action. . . . Here may be seen folly flushed with money, shoe strings [often very elaborate at the time] and a phaeton and four [light carriage with four horses]. Keen envy sparkles

contempt of her own children,[7] was so highly reprehensible. But she had never felt so strongly as now, the disadvantages which must attend the children of so unsuitable a marriage, nor ever been so fully aware of the evils arising from so ill-judged a direction of talents; talents which rightly used, might at least have preserved the respectability of his daughters, even if incapable of enlarging the mind of his wife.

When Elizabeth had rejoiced over Wickham's departure, she found little other cause for satisfaction in the loss of the regiment. Their parties abroad[8] were less varied than before; and at home she had a mother and sister whose constant repinings at the dulness of every thing around them, threw a real gloom over their domestic circle; and, though Kitty might in time regain her natural degree of sense, since the disturbers of her brain were removed, her other sister, from whose disposition greater evil might be apprehended, was likely to be hardened in all her folly and assurance, by a situation of such double danger as a watering place[9] and a camp.[10] Upon the whole, therefore, she found, what has been sometimes been found before, that an event to which she had looked forward with impatient desire, did not in taking place, bring all the satisfaction she had promised herself. It was consequently necessary to name some other period for the commencement of actual felicity; to have some other point on which her wishes and hopes might be fixed, and by again enjoying the pleasure of anticipation, console herself for the present, and prepare for another disappointment. Her tour to the Lakes was now the object of her happiest thoughts; it was her best consolation for all the uncomfortable hours, which the discontentedness of her mother and Kitty made inevitable; and could she have included Jane in the scheme, every part of it would have been perfect.

"But it is fortunate," thought she, "that I have something to wish for. Were the whole arrangement complete, my disappointment would be certain. But here, by carrying with me one ceaseless source of regret in my sister's absence, I may reasonably hope to have all my expectations of pleasure realized. A scheme of which every part promises delight, can never be successful; and general disappoint-

"Return From Brighton, or A Journey to Town for the Winter Season," 1786. A caricature of a stage coach crammed with would-be fashionable people, returning from Brighton's dissipations to those of London. Lydia might not associate with such people, but in Brighton she would see them everywhere.

ment is only warded off by the defence of some little peculiar[11] vexation."

When Lydia went away, she promised to write very often and very minutely to her mother and Kitty; but her letters were always long expected, and always very short. Those to her mother, contained little else, than that they were just returned from the library, where such and such officers had attended them, and where she had seen such beautiful ornaments as made her quite wild;[12] that she had a new gown, or a new parasol, which she would have described more fully, but was obliged to leave off in a violent hurry, as Mrs. Forster called her, and they were going to the

in the eye at the display of a new bonnet" (quoted in Parry, *Resorts of the Lancashire Coast*, 15).

10 Military encampment, "dangerous" to young women because of the many young men it contained. Even Elizabeth never mentions or appears to consider the possible danger of invasion, the cause for the militia's stationing in Brighton. The fear of invasion was great in 1796–1798, 1801, and 1804–1805, and the coast "of Sussex was thought to be especially vulnerable for most of it is low lying. Brighton is located in a shallow bay that was especially tempting as the gently sloping beach that attracted bathers was also very suitable as a landing place for seaborn invasions" (Sue Berry, *Georgian Brighton* [Chichester: Phillimore, 2005], 63).

11 Special, distinctive.

12 Excited. Two circulating libraries had been founded in Brighton, in a conspicuous location on a popular promenade. Subscribers would stroll on the promenade to see and be seen; at the library "they would sign the visitors' book to record their subscription and announce their arrival to others who might call in to read, chat, listen to music, buy fripperies or gamble" (Berry, *Georgian Brighton*, 28–29). The owners of the libraries offered such special attractions as perfume for sale and dance music to listen to (36). Obviously, an appropriate environment for Lydia.

13 This formulation makes it clear that the Forsters lived in lodgings in town, while the camp of tents was elsewhere.

14 Wealthy families customarily spent winter in London, while Parliament was in session, and summer in the country.

15 It was only two weeks before it would begin.

16 Counted on.

17 According to Peter Knox-Shaw, Derbyshire is "a setting wilder in some respects than the Lakes in [William] Gilpin's view"—hence an appropriate environment for the emotional turmoil Elizabeth is about to undergo (*Jane Austen and the Enlightenment* [Cambridge: Cambridge University Press, 2004], 91).

18 Principal tourist attractions of northern Derbyshire. Matlock is a spa and resort in a river valley. Chatsworth, the splendid estate of the dukes of Devonshire; Dovedale, a beautiful river gorge; and the Peak, the rolling hills of the region, remain attractions even now.

19 Appointed task—like Mr. Collins's business of love-making.

20 Temperament.

camp;[13] — and from her correspondence with her sister, there was still less to be learnt—for her letters to Kitty, though rather longer, were much too full of lines under the words to be made public.

After the first fortnight or three weeks of her absence, health, good humour and cheerfulness began to re-appear at Longbourn. Every thing wore a happier aspect. The families who had been in town for the winter[14] came back again, and summer finery and summer engagements arose. Mrs. Bennet was restored to her usual querulous serenity, and by the middle of June Kitty was so much recovered as to be able to enter Meryton without tears; an event of such happy promise as to make Elizabeth hope, that by the following Christmas, she might be so tolerably reasonable as not to mention an officer above once a day, unless by some cruel and malicious arrangement at the War Office, another regiment should be quartered in Meryton.

The time fixed for the beginning of their Northern tour was now fast approaching; and a fortnight only was wanting of it,[15] when a letter arrived from Mrs. Gardiner, which at once delayed its commencement and curtailed its extent. Mr. Gardiner would be prevented by business from setting out till a fortnight later in July, and must be in London again within a month; and as that left too short a period for them to go so far, and see so much as they had proposed, or at least to see it with the leisure and comfort they had built on,[16] they were obliged to give up the Lakes, and substitute a more contracted tour; and, according to the present plan, were to go no farther northwards than Derbyshire.[17] In that county, there was enough to be seen, to occupy the chief of their three weeks; and to Mrs. Gardiner it had a peculiarly strong attraction. The town where she had formerly passed some years of her life, and where they were now to spend a few days, was probably as great an object of her curiosity as all the celebrated beauties of Matlock, Chatsworth, Dovedale, or the Peak.[18]

Elizabeth was excessively disappointed; she had set her heart on seeing the Lakes; and still thought there might have been time enough. But it was her business[19] to be satisfied—and certainly her temper[20] to be happy; and all was soon right again.

With the mention of Derbyshire, there were many ideas connected. It was impossible for her to see the word without thinking of Pemberley and its owner. "But surely," said she, "I may enter his county with impunity, and rob it of a few petrified spars[21] without his perceiving me."

The period of expectation was now doubled.[22] Four weeks were to pass away before her uncle and aunt's arrival. But they did pass away, and Mr. and Mrs. Gardiner, with their four children, did at length appear at Longbourn. The children, two girls of six and eight years old, and two younger boys, were to be left under the particular care of their cousin Jane, who was the general favourite, and whose steady sense and sweetness of temper exactly adapted her for attending to them in every way—teaching them, playing with them, and loving them.

The Gardiners staid only one night at Longbourn, and set off the next morning with Elizabeth in pursuit of novelty and amusement. One enjoyment was certain—that of suitableness as companions; a suitableness which comprehended health and temper to bear inconveniences—cheerfulness to enhance every pleasure—and affection and intelligence, which might supply it among themselves if there were disappointments abroad.[23]

It is not the object of this work to give a description of Derbyshire, nor of any of the remarkable places through which their route thither lay; Oxford, Blenheim, Warwick, Kenelworth, Birmingham,[24] &c. are sufficiently known. A small part of Derbyshire is all the present concern. To the little town of Lambton,[25] the scene of Mrs. Gardiner's former residence, and where she had lately learned some acquaintance still remained, they bent their steps, after having seen all the principal wonders of the country; and within five miles of Lambton, Elizabeth found from her aunt, that Pemberley was situated. It was not in their direct road, nor more than a mile or two out of it. In talking over their route the evening before, Mrs. Gardiner expressed an inclination to see the place again. Mr. Gardiner declared his willingness, and Elizabeth was applied to for her approbation.

21 Pieces of a luminous crystalline mineral called fluorspar, conspicuously present in Derbyshire caves and mines. Tourists might find pieces on the ground or in caves or buy them in stores.

22 Because of Mr. Gardiner's business commitments.

23 Outside themselves.

24 Oxford, the site of a major university; Blenheim, palace of the dukes of Marlborough; Warwick and Kenelworth, ancient castles; Birmingham, a large city in the process of becoming a great manufacturing center.

25 An imaginary town.

26 Acknowledge.

27 Derbyshire is particularly full of great country houses, many of which remain tourist attractions to this day. In the late eighteenth century, such houses were still in private hands. Visitors could nonetheless apply for admittance, sometimes only on specified days, and enjoy conducted tours of interiors, usually under the guidance of the housekeeper. Important houses in Derbyshire include Chatsworth; Haddon Hall, dating from the fourteenth and fifteenth century; and Hardwick Hall, especially noted for its tapestries.

28 Dullness.

"My love, should not you like to see a place of which you have heard so much?" said her aunt. "A place too, with which so many of your acquaintances are connected. Wickham passed all his youth there, you know."

Elizabeth was distressed. She felt that she had no business at Pemberley, and was obliged to assume a disinclination for seeing it. She must own[26] that she was tired of great houses; after going over so many, she really had no pleasure in fine carpets or satin curtains.[27]

Mrs. Gardiner abused her stupidity.[28] "If it were merely a fine house richly furnished," said she, "I should not care about it myself; but the grounds are delightful. They have some of the finest woods in the country."

Elizabeth said no more—but her mind could not acquiesce. The possibility of meeting Mr. Darcy, while viewing the place, instantly occurred. It would be dreadful! She blushed at the very idea; and thought it would be better to speak openly to her aunt, than to run such a risk. But against this, there were objections; and she finally resolved that it could be the last resource, if her private inquiries as to the absence of the family, were unfavourably answered.

Accordingly, when she retired at night, she asked the chambermaid whether Pemberley were not a very fine place, what was the name of its proprietor, and with no little alarm, whether the family were down for the summer. A most welcome negative followed the last question—and her alarms being now removed, she was at leisure to feel a great deal of curiosity to see the house herself; and when the subject was revived the next morning, and she was again applied to, could readily answer, and with a proper air of indifference, that she had not really any dislike to the scheme.

To Pemberley, therefore, they were to go.

VOLUME III

I

ELIZABETH, AS THEY DROVE ALONG, watched for the first appearance of Pemberley Woods with some perturbation; and when at length they turned in at the lodge,[1] her spirits were in a high flutter.

The park[2] was very large, and contained great variety of ground. They entered it in one of its lowest points, and drove for some time through a beautiful wood stretching over a wide extent.

Elizabeth's mind was too full for conversation, but she saw and admired every remarkable spot and point of view. They gradually ascended for half a mile, and then found themselves at the top of a considerable eminence, where the wood ceased, and the eye was instantly caught by Pemberley House, situated on the opposite side of a valley, into which the road with some abruptness wound. It was a large, handsome, stone building, standing well on rising ground, and backed by a ridge of high woody hills;—and in front, a stream of some natural importance was swelled into greater, but without any artificial appearance.[3] Its banks were neither formal, nor falsely adorned. Elizabeth was delighted. She had never seen a place for which nature had done more, or where natural beauty had been so little counteracted by an awkward taste.[4] They were all of them warm in their admiration; and at that moment she felt, that to be mistress of Pemberley might be something![5]

They descended the hill, crossed the bridge, and drove to the door; and, while examining the nearer aspect of the house, all her apprehensions of meeting its owner returned. She dreaded lest the chambermaid had been mistaken. On applying to see the place, they

1 Gatehouse or porter's lodge.

2 Grounds surrounding the house.

3 William Gilpin writes, "when it is apparent, that the view is contrived; the effect is lost" (*Observations, on Several Parts of England . . . Relative Chiefly to Picturesque Beauty*, 3rd ed., 2 vols. [London, 1808], II, 178). Views about landscape gardening had changed radically in the course of the eighteenth century. At the century's beginning, French ideas dominated English practice, mandating formality and symmetry. By 1800, "naturalness" held sway, and designers labored to produce effects that looked unplanned. The new principles of design had political as well as aesthetic import, suggesting British freedom as opposed to French restriction.

4 This is the first of many "scenes" or "vistas" that the travelers see at Pemberley. In all its scenes, the estate conforms to the standards of the "picturesque," which had become a powerful aesthetic criterion. "Landskip should contain variety enough to form a picture upon canvas," wrote William Shenstone in *Unconnected Thoughts on Gardening* (quoted in Malcolm Andrews, *The Search for the Picturesque: Landscape Aesthetics and Tourism in Britain, 1760–1800* [Stanford: Stanford University Press, 1989], 54). William Gilpin in 1768 defined the picturesque as "a term expressive of that peculiar kind of beauty, which is agreeable in a picture" (Andrews, p. 56). Like this first view of the big house backed by hills and fronted by a stream that has been augmented to heightened "importance," the vistas of Pemberley typically seem composed as though by a painter.

5 The political implications of *Pride and Prejudice* are debatable. The novel consistently emphasizes Darcy's wealth and social status, mainly (up to this point) in connection with his pride. Now, as Elizabeth receives an extensive view of Pemberley, she realizes fully for the first time exactly what wealth and status mean and is tempted by the possibility of acquiring riches and social position through marriage.

Such evidence leads some to conclude that Austen supports conservative values, the values of a stable aristocracy. Claudia L. Johnson, who does not herself accept this position, summarizes it well: "On the surface at least, *Pride and Prejudice* corroborates conservative myths which had argued that established forms cherished rather than prohibited true liberty, sustained rather than disrupted real happiness, and safeguarded rather than repressed individual merit. Its hero accordingly is a sober-minded exemplar of the great gentry, a dutiful son and affectionate brother. Its villain is an ungrateful upstart. . . . And its turning point is the heroine's contemplation of the household of a private gentleman. Prepared to find Pemberley a grandiose estate designed expressly to overbear subordinates with awe, Elizabeth finds instead an unpretentiously elegant manor, and rather than testimonials to the insolence of power, she hears tributes to a kind master, a beloved landlord" (*Women, Politics, and the Novel* [Chicago: University of Chicago Press, 1988], 74).

Johnson goes on, however, to argue that "the 'conservatism' of *Pride and Prejudice* is an imaginative experiment with conservative myths, and not a statement of faith in them as they had already stood in anti-Jacobin fiction. . . . [T]hroughout the course of the novel those myths become so transformed that they are made to accommodate what could otherwise be seen as subversive impulses and values, and in the process they themselves become the vehicles of incisive social criticism" (75). Darcy, to be sure, conforms to conservative requirements, but Elizabeth emphatically does not. Johnson sees Austen as eluding established doctrines by undercutting the period's moral certainties, providing evidence on opposite sides of many issues.

Johnson's subtly argued treatment places Austen in her immediate literary context and employs an avowedly feminist viewpoint. Equally well argued, though, and richly aware of Austen's literary and political circumstances, is an earlier work that reaches the opposite conclusion, Marilyn Butler's *Jane Austen and the War of Ideas* (Oxford: Oxford University Press, 1975). Butler refutes the claims of those who see the character of Elizabeth Bennet as radically opposed to the conservative position, as individualistic, independent, and intermittently iconoclastic. She emphasizes the process of Elizabeth's moral education, as rendered by the novel. Austen's "moral ideal is clear," Butler writes: "it is most nearly approached by Darcy and Elizabeth at the point when they have acknowledged the necessity of Jane and Bingley's humility and candour. In their ultimate state of enlightenment, Jane Austen's hero and heroine illustrate a view of human nature that derives from orthodox Christian pessimism, not from progressive optimism. The theme of the moral education of Elizabeth, which is paralleled by that of Darcy, does not sanction but rebukes the contemporary doctrine of faith in the individual" (212). As a whole, though, Butler maintains, *Pride and Prejudice* lacks the moral clarity characteristic of Austen's other works.

In the context of this chapter of *Pride and Prejudice*, Elizabeth's feeling about being mistress of Pemberley might be interpreted as an aesthetic rather than an economic response. Every described aspect of the house and grounds conforms precisely to the period's dominant aesthetic standards. To be mistress of such an estate would be "something" because of the beauty it embodies. Moreover, since Darcy's taste is presumably operative in the choices of landscape design, Elizabeth's perception of its lack of "awkwardness" and of the proprietor's willingness to allow nature rather than his own social pretensions to dictate arrangements is also a positive perception about Darcy's character. The idea of a country house itself would be attractive for more reasons than wealth and status. Mark Girouard points out that the period between 1800 and 1900 was "the golden age of the country house." As interest in nature became increasingly prevalent, people began to value country houses because in them they "could en-

A picturesque landscape, from William Gilpin (1724–1804), plate 2 from *Three Essays on Picturesque Beauty*, (London: Printed for R. Blamire, 1792). This landscape engraving, suggestive of the vistas that the travelers see at Pemberley, shows the kind of variety that William Gilpin valued in the picturesque: human beings in the landscape, land and water, cultivated and wild.

were admitted into the hall;[6] and Elizabeth, as they waited for the housekeeper, had leisure to wonder at her being where she was.

The housekeeper came; a respectable-looking elderly woman, much less fine,[7] and more civil, than she had any notion of finding her. They followed her into the dining-parlour. It was a large, well proportioned room, handsomely fitted up.[8] Elizabeth, after slightly surveying it, went to a window to enjoy its prospect.[9] The hill, crowned with wood, which they had descended, receiving increased abruptness from the distance, was a beautiful object. Every disposition[10] of the ground was good; and she looked on the whole scene, the river, the trees scattered on its banks, and the winding of the valley, as far as she could trace it, with delight.[11] As they passed into other rooms, these objects were taking different positions; but from every window there were beauties to be seen. The rooms were lofty and handsome, and their furniture suitable to the fortune of their proprietor; but Elizabeth saw, with admiration of his

joy the country without feeling imprisoned by it. . . . Solitude was made especially delicious by the knowledge that there was no problem about escaping from it"—both because roads had improved, making travel easier, and because it was always easy to fill a country house with company (*Life in the English Country House: A Social and Architectural History* [New Haven: Yale University Press, 1978], 218).

6 "Since snobbery is inbred in the English nation, the aristocracy have always exercised a lure for other members of society, and their wealth, taste and material possessions have aroused an interest which is by no means confined to the mid-twentieth century. Seeing round country houses has long been a popular English pastime . . . and a ring at the bell of some stately home, the purchase of a catalogue if one were on sale, a conducted tour by the housekeeper, were as familiar to the eighteenth-century tourist as they are to the visitors of today" (Esther Moir, *The Discovery of Britain: The English Tourists, 1540 to 1840* [London: Routledge & Kegan Paul, 1964], 58).

7 Finely attired, showy.

8 Equipped.

9 View.

10 Arrangement.

11 Delight is an appropriate response to a picturesque scene: "Even Gilpin acknowledged that the chief pleasure in Picturesque travel was not the 'scientifical' analysis of scenery (though that afforded great amusement) but the irrational response" (Andrews, *The Search for the Picturesque*, 44). The aspect of the picturesque most strongly emphasized in the accounts of views from the windows of Pemberley and of the scene outdoors is what Uvedale Price characterized as *intricacy*: "What most delights us in the intricacy of varied ground, of swelling knolls, and of vallies between them, retiring from the sight in different directions amidst trees or thickets, is, that according to Hogarth's expression, it leads the eye a kind of wanton chace; this is what he calls the *beauty* of intricacy" (*Essays on the Picturesque, as Compared with the Sublime and the Beautiful*

. . . , 3 vols. [London, 1810; first pub. 1794], I, 251–252). Price defines intricacy in landscape as *that disposition of objects . . . which, by a partial and uncertain concealment, excites and nourishes curiosity*" (I, 22).

12 Again, taste suggests character.

13 Elegance, one of Elizabeth's favorite terms of approval, connotes refinement and good taste. Elegant furnishings would be marked by their tasteful adornment and their refined grace of form.

14 Another hint that, despite Lady Catherine's social pretensions, Sir Lewis may have had a recent rather than an inherited fortune. It was not uncommon in the period for aristocrats to marry wealthy commoners. The contrast between Pemberley and Rosings is important. As Barbara Britton Wenner puts the point, "Elizabeth needs to see Rosings in order to appreciate Pemberley" (*Prospect and Refuge in the Landscape of Jane Austen* [Burlington, VT: Ashgate, 2006], 57). Wenner also offers an economical explanation for this chapter's emphasis on details of the estate: "Pemberley basically *is* Darcy. . . . [E]very feature of the estate represents Darcy's character" (57).

15 Collections of miniature portraits, popular in this period, were common.

16 Writing of eighteenth-century visitors to great houses, Ian Ousby explains, "The gardener showed them the grounds and the housekeeper took them through the rooms, an arrangement which had the merit of encouraging a little quiet gossip about their employer" (*The Englishman's England: Taste, Travel and the Rise of Tourism* [Cambridge: Cambridge University Press, 1990], 77).

17 Physical nature.

taste,[12] that it was neither gaudy nor uselessly fine; with less of splendor, and more real elegance,[13] than the furniture of Rosings.[14]

"And of this place," thought she, "I might have been mistress! With these rooms I might now have been familiarly acquainted! Instead of viewing them as a stranger, I might have rejoiced in them as my own, and welcomed to them as visitors my uncle and aunt. But no,"—recollecting herself,—"that could never be: my uncle and aunt would have been lost to me: I should not have been allowed to invite them."

This was a lucky recollection—it saved her from something like regret.

She longed to enquire of the housekeeper, whether her master were really absent, but had not courage for it. At length however, the question was asked by her uncle; and she turned away with alarm, while Mrs. Reynolds replied, that he was, adding, "but we expect him to-morrow, with a large party of friends." How rejoiced was Elizabeth that their own journey had not by any circumstance been delayed a day!

Her aunt now called her to look at a picture. She approached, and saw the likeness of Mr. Wickham suspended, amongst several other miniatures,[15] over the mantel-piece. Her aunt asked her, smilingly, how she liked it. The housekeeper came forward, and told them it was a picture of a young gentleman, the son of her late master's steward, who had been brought up by him at his own expence.—"He is now gone into the army," she added, "but I am afraid he has turned out very wild."[16]

Mrs. Gardiner looked at her niece with a smile, but Elizabeth could not return it.

"And that," said Mrs. Reynolds, pointing to another of the miniatures, "is my master—and very like him. It was drawn at the same time as the other—about eight years ago."

"I have heard much of your master's fine person,"[17] said Mrs. Gardiner, looking at the picture; "it is a handsome face. But, Lizzy, you can tell us whether it is like or not."

Mrs. Reynolds's respect for Elizabeth seemed to increase on this intimation of her knowing her master.

18 This is unquestionably a blush of "consciousness": Elizabeth knows Darcy in ways that she has not yet revealed even to her aunt.

19 She has not previously commented on Darcy's looks.

Unknown artist. Formerly attributed to John Wootton, 1682–1764, later to Jan Siberechts, 1627–ca. 1703, painting of Bifrons Park, Kent, c. 1695–1700. This was a house that Austen knew. Pemberley might resemble it. Siberechts was a Flemish artist who settled in England in the 1670s and made his name creating renditions of English country houses.

"Does that young lady know Mr. Darcy?"

Elizabeth coloured,[18] and said—"A little."

"And do not you think him a very handsome gentleman, Ma'am?"

"Yes, very handsome."[19]

"I am sure *I* know none so handsome; but in the gallery up stairs you will see a finer, larger picture of him than this. This room was my late master's favourite room, and these miniatures are just as they used to be then. He was very fond of them."

This accounted to Elizabeth for Mr. Wickham's being among them.

Mrs. Reynolds then directed their attention to one of Miss Darcy, drawn when she was only eight years old.

"And is Miss Darcy as handsome as her brother?" said Mrs. Gardiner.

20 Piano.

21 This is presumably Elizabeth's speculation: she would expect to see pride in Darcy's servant, although she also suggests a more benign interpretation.

"Oh! yes—the handsomest young lady that ever was seen; and so accomplished!—She plays and sings all day long. In the next room is a new instrument[20] just come down for her—a present from my master; she comes here to-morrow with him."

Mr. Gardiner, whose manners were easy and pleasant, encouraged her communicativeness by his questions and remarks; Mrs. Reynolds, either from pride[21] or attachment, had evidently great pleasure in talking of her master and his sister.

"Is your master much at Pemberley in the course of the year?"

"Not so much as I could wish, Sir; but I dare say he may spend half his time here; and Miss Darcy is always down for the summer months."

"Except," thought Elizabeth, "when she goes to Ramsgate."

"If your master would marry, you might see more of him."

"Yes, Sir; but I do not know when *that* will be. I do not know who is good enough for him."

Mr. and Mrs. Gardiner smiled. Elizabeth could not help saying, "It is very much to his credit, I am sure, that you should think so."

"I say no more than the truth, and what every body will say that knows him," replied the other. Elizabeth thought this was going pretty far; and she listened with increasing astonishment as the housekeeper added, "I have never had a cross word from him in my life, and I have known him ever since he was four years old."

This was praise, of all others most extraordinary, most opposite to her ideas. That he was not a good-tempered man, had been her firmest opinion. Her keenest attention was awakened; she longed to hear more, and was grateful to her uncle for saying,

"There are very few people of whom so much can be said. You are lucky in having such a master."

"Yes, Sir, I know I am. If I were to go through the world, I could not meet with a better. But I have always observed, that they who are good-natured when children, are good-natured when they grow up; and he was always the sweetest-tempered, most generous-hearted, boy in the world."

Elizabeth almost stared at her.—"Can this be Mr. Darcy!" thought she.

"His father was an excellent man," said Mrs. Gardiner.

"Yes, Ma'am, that he was indeed; and his son will be just like him— just as affable[22] to the poor."[23]

Elizabeth listened, wondered, doubted, and was impatient for more. Mrs. Reynolds could interest her on no other point. She related the subject of the pictures, the dimensions of the rooms, and the price of the furniture, in vain. Mr. Gardiner, highly amused by the kind of family prejudice,[24] to which he attributed her excessive commendation of her master, soon led again to the subject; and she dwelt with energy on his many merits, as they proceeded together up the great staircase.

"He is the best landlord, and the best master," said she, "that ever lived. Not like the wild young men now-a-days, who think of nothing but themselves. There is not one of his tenants or servants but will give him a good name.[25] Some people call him proud; but I am sure I never saw any thing of it. To my fancy, it is only because he does not rattle[26] away like other young men."

22 Benevolent.

23 A common complaint of eighteenth-century tourists was that the housekeepers who showed them around were illiterate and ill-informed: "Most tourists agreed that servants were both ignorant and insolent, and housekeepers proved so full of pretentious and wholly unreliable information that John Dodd could only conclude that it was a 'Laudable Custome of England that they should be unacquainted with what they were showing'" (Moir, *The Discovery of Britain*, 60). Mrs. Reynolds is obviously an exception: well-spoken and well-informed.

24 Elizabeth thinks it possible that the housekeeper is motivated by pride; Mr. Gardiner thinks it may be prejudice.

25 Sarah Pennington advises her daughters, in assessing men, "to lay no stress on outward appearances, which are too often fallacious, but to take the rule of judging from the simple, unpolished sentiments of those, whose dependent connections give them an undeniable certainty; who not only see, but hourly feel the good or bad effects of that disposition to which they are subjected. By this I mean, that if a man is equally respected, esteemed, and beloved by his tenants, by his dependents and domestics . . . from the proud steward to the submissive wretch, who, thankful for employment, humbly obeys the menial tribe; you may justly conclude he has that true good-nature, that real benevolence, which delights in communicating felicity, and enjoys the satisfaction it diffuses" (*An Unfortunate Mother's Advice to her Absent Daughters, The Young Lady's Pocket Library, or Parental Monitor* [Bristol: Thoemmes Press, 1995], 100–101).

26 Chatter, talk thoughtlessly.

Jane Austen's signature.

27 Since the "authority" was Wickham himself, the re-mark functions in the narrative as irony.

28 Recently.

29 "What really interested the tourists inside houses was not so much furniture as pictures" (Moir, *The Discovery of Britain*, 71). Ousby adds, "One simple fact . . . stands out. To most visitors the real proof that a country-house owner had taste as well as wealth and power was his collection of art" (*The Englishman's England*, 74).

30 This "striking resemblance" may remind us of the "faithful portrait" in I, 17. Elizabeth has suggested that she and Darcy share "an unsocial, taciturn disposition, unwilling to speak" unless they expect to say something to amaze the whole room; Darcy responds, "This is no very striking resemblance of your own character," but comments that Elizabeth undoubtedly thinks it a faithful portrait of him. The striking resemblance now is of Darcy with a smile, Darcy in good-humored guise.

31 Darcy has quite often been described as smiling at Elizabeth, but she has never appeared to notice the fact. Now, retrospectively, she does. Her capacity to realize Darcy's warmth toward her marks a significant change in her perceptions.

32 Tony Tanner sees Elizabeth's contemplation of the portrait as the definitive moment for her change of feeling toward its subject. He speaks of "the education of her vision" and suggests that the "physical penetration of the interior of Pemberley . . . is both an analogue and an aid for her perceptual penetration of the interior quality of its owner" (*Jane Austen* [Cambridge: Harvard University Press, 1986], 116). "Standing before the large and true image of the real Darcy," Tanner continues, "Elizabeth has in effect completed her journey. When she next meets the original, outside in the grounds, she is no longer in any doubt as to his true worth. . . . [T]he grounds, the house, the portrait all bespeak the real man—they represent a visible extension of his inner qualities, his true style" (120).

"In what an amiable light does this place him!" thought Elizabeth.

"This fine account of him," whispered her aunt, as they walked, "is not quite consistent with his behaviour to our poor friend."

"Perhaps we might be deceived."

"That is not very likely; our authority was too good."[27]

On reaching the spacious lobby above, they were shewn into a very pretty sitting-room, lately[28] fitted up with greater elegance and lightness than the apartments below; and were informed that it was but just done, to give pleasure to Miss Darcy, who had taken a liking to the room, when last at Pemberley.

"He is certainly a good brother," said Elizabeth, as she walked towards one of the windows.

Mrs. Reynolds anticipated Miss Darcy's delight, when she should enter the room. "And this is always the way with him," she added.—"Whatever can give his sister any pleasure, is sure to be done in a moment. There is nothing he would not do for her."

The picture-gallery, and two or three of the principal bed-rooms, were all that remained to be shewn. In the former were many good paintings; but Elizabeth knew nothing of the art; and from such as had been already visible below, she had willingly turned to look at some drawings of Miss Darcy's, in crayons, whose subjects were usually more interesting, and also more intelligible.

In the gallery there were many family portraits, but they could have little to fix the attention of a stranger.[29] Elizabeth walked in quest of the only face whose features would be known to her. At last it arrested her—and she beheld a striking resemblance[30] to Mr. Darcy, with such a smile over the face, as she remembered to have sometimes seen, when he looked at her.[31] She stood several minutes before the picture in earnest contemplation, and returned to it again before they quitted the gallery.[32] Mrs. Reynolds informed them that it had been taken in his father's life time.

There was certainly at this moment, in Elizabeth's mind, a more gentle sensation towards the original, than she had ever felt in the height of their acquaintance. The commendation bestowed on him by Mrs. Reynolds was of no trifling nature. What praise is more valuable than the praise of an intelligent servant? As a brother, a landlord,

Thomas Rowlandson (1756–1827), "A Gentleman's Art Gallery." As this print indicates, paintings crammed the picture galleries of great houses. Elizabeth's turning away from the gallery's fine art to Miss Darcy's drawings may have resulted partly from visual overload.

33 Elizabeth responds here to a realization of Darcy's immense social power, the power of a wealthy land-owner.

34 Contrary to the usual patterns of romance, Elizabeth's change of feeling toward Darcy takes place mainly in his absence, during the period when she does not see him at all. The shifts in her memory of past episodes in their relationship both register and help to determine the alteration of her feeling. Susan C. Greenfield examines in detail the importance of absence in the novel's narrative, claiming that *Pride and Prejudice* "aligns absence with productive thought" ("The Absent-Minded Heroine; or, Elizabeth Bennet Has a Thought," *Eighteenth-Century Studies* 39: 3 [2006], 338). When Elizabeth sees Darcy in the novel's first two volumes, she misunderstands him; when she thinks about him, she develops understanding: "As objects that women depend upon but never possess, men are ever absent and—at least in many novels—thus likely to occupy the female mind" (339).

35 This seems an instance of the blush as communication. He blushes and she blushes; the blushes express what they cannot say.

36 Moved abruptly or violently, in this instance from surprise.

37 The words *civil* and *civility* occur eleven times in this chapter, always with reference to Darcy (who is also characterized as "polite"). Here this language has no connotation of empty forms; it describes a profound change in Darcy's manners.

38 Formal expressions of courtesy.

a master, she considered how many people's happiness were in his guardianship!—How much of pleasure or pain it was in his power to bestow!—How much of good or evil must be done by him![33] Every idea that had been brought forward by the housekeeper was favourable to his character, and as she stood before the canvas, on which he was represented, and fixed his eyes upon herself, she thought of his regard with a deeper sentiment of gratitude than it had ever raised before; she remembered its warmth, and softened its impropriety of expression.[34]

When all of the house that was open to general inspection had been seen, they returned down stairs, and, taking leave of the housekeeper, were consigned over to the gardener, who met them at the hall door.

As they walked across the hall towards the river, Elizabeth turned back to look again; her uncle and aunt stopped also, and while the former was conjecturing as to the date of the building, the owner of it himself suddenly came forward from the road, which led behind it to the stables.

They were within twenty yards of each other, and so abrupt was his appearance, that it was impossible to avoid his sight. Their eyes instantly met, and the cheeks of both were overspread with the deepest blush.[35] He absolutely started,[36] and for a moment seemed immoveable from surprise; but shortly recovering himself, advanced towards the party, and spoke to Elizabeth, if not in terms of perfect composure, at least of perfect civility.[37]

She had instinctively turned away; but stopping on his approach, received his compliments[38] with an embarrassment impossible to be overcome. Had his first appearance, or his resemblance to the picture they had just been examining, been insufficient to assure the other two that they now saw Mr. Darcy, the gardener's expression of surprise, on beholding his master, must immediately have told it. They stood a little aloof while he was talking to their niece, who, astonished and confused, scarcely dared lift her eyes to his face, and knew not what answer she returned to his civil enquiries after her family. Amazed at the alteration of his manner since they last parted, every sentence that he uttered was increasing her embarrassment;

and every idea of the impropriety of her being found there, recurring to her mind, the few minutes in which they continued together, were some of the most uncomfortable of her life. Nor did he seem much more at ease; when he spoke, his accent[39] had none of its usual sedateness;[40] and he repeated his enquiries as to the time of her having left Longbourn, and of her stay in Derbyshire, so often, and in so hurried a way, as plainly spoke the distraction of his thoughts.

At length, every idea seemed to fail him; and, after standing a few moments without saying a word, he suddenly recollected himself, and took leave.

The others then joined her, and expressed admiration of his figure;[41] but Elizabeth heard not a word, and, wholly engrossed by her own feelings, followed them in silence. She was overpowered by shame and vexation. Her coming there was the most unfortunate, the most ill-judged thing in the world! How strange it must appear to him! In what a disgraceful light might it not strike so vain[42] a man! It might seem as if she had purposely thrown herself in his way again! Oh! why did she come? or, why did he thus come a day before he was expected? Had they been only ten minutes sooner, they should have been beyond the reach of his discrimination,[43] for it was plain that he was that moment arrived, that moment alighted from his horse or his carriage. She blushed again and again over the perverseness of the meeting. And his behaviour, so strikingly altered,—what could it mean? That he should even speak to her was amazing!—but to speak with such civility, to enquire after her family! Never in her life had she seen his manners so little dignified, never had he spoken with such gentleness as on this unexpected meeting. What a contrast did it offer to his last address in Rosings Park, when he put his letter into her hand! She knew not what to think, nor how to account for it.

They had now entered a beautiful walk by the side of the water, and every step was bringing forward a nobler fall of ground, or a finer reach of the woods to which they were approaching; but it was some time before Elizabeth was sensible of any of it; and, though she answered mechanically to the repeated appeals of her uncle and aunt, and seemed to direct her eyes to such objects as they pointed out, she distinguished no part of the scene. Her thoughts were all fixed

39 Tone.

40 Calmness.

41 Appearance.

42 Elizabeth's more frequent accusation has been that Darcy is proud. Now, seeing him as vain, she endows him with the same moral weakness that she has seen in herself.

43 Discernment.

44 That is, appearing more like her usual self. She distinctly does not want to appear like the self she currently is.

45 Woods on a steep slope.

46 A small stand of trees periodically cut for fuel or for other needs of the estate. The "roughness" of the planting suggests that the estate's planners may have responded to the aesthetic theories of Edmund Burke, whose *Philosophical Enquiry into the Origin of Our Ideas of the Sublime and Beautiful* (1757) had a long-lasting effect. Burke posited that the large, the terrifying, the dark, the obscure, and the confused might arouse a sense of the sublime, a more powerful emotion than the response to beauty. As a consequence, designers sometimes valued crudity over polish, as more likely to create an emotional reaction.

on that one spot of Pemberley House, whichever it might be, where Mr. Darcy then was. She longed to know what at that moment was passing in his mind; in what manner he thought of her, and whether, in defiance of every thing, she was still dear to him. Perhaps he had been civil, only because he felt himself at ease; yet there had been *that* in his voice, which was not like ease. Whether he had felt more of pain or of pleasure in seeing her, she could not tell, but he certainly had not seen her with composure.

At length, however, the remarks of her companions on her absence of mind aroused her, and she felt the necessity of appearing more like herself.[44]

They entered the woods, and bidding adieu to the river for a while, ascended some of the higher grounds; whence, in spots where the opening of the trees gave the eye power to wander, were many charming views of the valley, the opposite hills, with the long range of woods overspreading many, and occasionally part of the stream. Mr. Gardiner expressed a wish of going round the whole Park, but feared it might be beyond a walk. With a triumphant smile, they were told, that it was ten miles round. It settled the matter; and they pursued the accustomed circuit; which brought them again, after some time, in a descent among hanging woods,[45] to the edge of the water, in one of its narrowest parts. They crossed it by a simple bridge, in character with the general air of the scene; it was a spot less adorned than any they had yet visited; and the valley, here contracted into a glen, allowed room only for the stream, and a narrow walk amidst the rough coppice-wood[46] which bordered it. Elizabeth longed to explore its windings; but when they had crossed the bridge, and perceived their distance from the house, Mrs. Gardiner, who was not a great walker, could go no farther, and thought only of returning to the carriage as quickly as possible. Her niece was, therefore, obliged to submit, and they took their way towards the house on the opposite side of the river, in the nearest direction; but their progress was slow, for Mr. Gardiner, though seldom able to indulge the taste, was very fond of fishing, and was so much engaged in watching the occasional appearance of some trout in the water, and talking to the man about them, that he advanced but little. Whilst wandering on in this slow manner, they were again surprised, and Elizabeth's astonishment was quite equal to what it had been at first, by the sight of Mr. Darcy approaching them, and at no great distance. The walk here being here less sheltered than on the other side, allowed them to see him before they met. Elizabeth, however astonished, was at least more prepared for an interview than before, and resolved to appear and to speak with calmness, if he really intended to meet them. For a few moments, indeed, she felt that he would probably strike into some other path. The idea lasted while a turning in the walk concealed him from their view; the turning past, he was immediately before them. With a glance, she saw, that he had lost none of his recent civility; and, to imitate his politeness, she began, as they met, to admire the beauty of the place; but she had not got beyond the words "delightful," and "charming," when some unlucky recollections obtruded, and she fancied that praise of Pemberley from her, might be mischievously construed.[47] Her colour changed, and she said no more.

Mrs. Gardiner was standing a little behind; and on her pausing, he asked her if she would do him the honour of introducing him to her friends.[48] This was a stroke of civility for which she was quite unprepared; and she could hardly suppress a smile, at his being now seeking the acquaintance of some of those very people, against whom his pride had revolted, in his offer to herself. "What will be his surprise," thought she, "when he knows who they are! He takes them now for people of fashion."[49]

The introduction, however, was immediately made; and as she named their relationship to herself, she stole a sly look at him, to see how he bore it; and was not without the expectation of his decamping as fast as he could from such disgraceful companions. That he was *surprised* by the connexion[50] was evident; he sustained it however with fortitude, and so far from going away, turned back with them, and entered into conversation with Mr. Gardiner. Elizabeth could not but be pleased, could not but triumph. It was consoling, that he should know she had some relations for whom there was no need to

47 In other words, that she might be thought to have the feelings she had actually entertained, about how gratifying it might be to be mistress of Pemberley.

48 Because of Darcy's higher social status, it would not be proper for Elizabeth to introduce her aunt and uncle unless he requested the introduction.

49 Social standing.

50 Relationship.

51 A small town on the Wye River in Derbyshire.

blush. She listened most attentively to all that passed between them, and gloried in every expression, every sentence of her uncle, which marked his intelligence, his taste, or his good manners.

The conversation soon turned upon fishing, and she heard Mr. Darcy invite him, with the greatest civility, to fish there as often as he chose, while he continued in the neighbourhood, offering at the same time to supply him with fishing tackle, and pointing out those parts of the stream where there was usually most sport. Mrs. Gardiner, who was walking arm in arm with Elizabeth, gave her a look expressive of her wonder. Elizabeth said nothing, but it gratified her exceedingly; the compliment must be all for herself. Her astonishment, however, was extreme; and continually was she repeating, "Why is he so altered? From what can it proceed? It cannot be for *me,* it cannot be for *my* sake that his manners are thus softened. My reproofs at Hunsford could not work such a change as this. It is impossible that he should still love me."

After walking some time in this way, the two ladies in front, the two gentlemen behind, on resuming their places, after descending to the brink of the river for the better inspection of some curious waterplant, there chanced to be a little alteration. It originated in Mrs. Gardiner, who, fatigued by the exercise of the morning, found Elizabeth's arm inadequate to her support, and consequently preferred her husband's. Mr. Darcy took her place by her niece, and they walked on together. After a short silence, the lady first spoke. She wished him to know that she had been assured of his absence before she came to the place, and accordingly began by observing, that his arrival had been very unexpected—"for your housekeeper," she added, "informed us that you would certainly not be here till tomorrow; and indeed, before we left Bakewell,⁵¹ we understood that you were not immediately expected in the country." He acknowledged the truth of it all; and said that business with his steward had occasioned his coming forward a few hours before the rest of the party with whom he had been travelling. "They will join me early tomorrow," he continued, "and among them are some who will claim an acquaintance with you,—Mr. Bingley and his sisters."

Jane Austen was an accomplished seamstress. Examples of her needlework are on display in Chawton House, in Hampshire. Among them is the patchwork quilt (above) made by Jane, her sister, and their mother.

Elizabeth answered only by a slight bow. Her thoughts were instantly driven back to the time when Mr. Bingley's name had been last mentioned between them; and if she might judge by his complexion, *his* mind was not very differently engaged.[52]

"There is also one other person in the party," he continued after a pause, "who more particularly wishes to be known to you.—Will you allow me, or do I ask too much, to introduce my sister to your acquaintance during your stay at Lambton?"

The surprise of such an application was great indeed; it was too great for her to know in what manner she acceded to it. She immediately felt that whatever desire Miss Darcy might have of being acquainted with her, must be the work of her brother, and, without looking farther, it was satisfactory; it was gratifying to know that his resentment had not made him think really ill of her.

They now walked on in silence; each of them deep in thought. Elizabeth was not comfortable; that was impossible; but she was flattered and pleased. His wish of introducing his sister to her, was a compliment of the highest kind. They soon outstripped the others, and when they had reached the carriage, Mr. and Mrs. Gardiner were half a quarter of a mile behind.

He then asked her to walk into the house—but she declared herself not tired, and they stood together on the lawn. At such a time, much might have been said, and silence was very awkward. She wanted to talk, but there seemed an embargo on every subject. At last she recollected that she had been travelling, and they talked of Matlock and Dove Dale[53] with great perseverance. Yet time and her aunt moved slowly[54]—and her patience and her ideas were nearly worn out before the tete-a-tete was over. On Mr. and Mrs. Gardiner's coming up, they were all pressed to go into the house and take some refreshment; but this was declined, and they parted on each side with the utmost politeness. Mr. Darcy handed the ladies into the carriage, and when it drove off, Elizabeth saw him walking slowly towards the house.

The observations of her uncle and aunt now began; and each of them pronounced him to be infinitely superior to any thing they had

52 Another instance of the blush as communication.

53 Both are famous scenic locales in the Peak District of Derbyshire. Although Austen does not tell us of the beauty spots Elizabeth and her aunt and uncle have visited, they have presumably enjoyed the rugged scenery of the mountainous region. Gilpin sounds a little uncertain about just how "picturesque" this part of the world is: he seems to find it a bit too rugged. Commenting on Chatsworth, the great house that some have thought a model for Pemberley, he remarks that it wouldn't seem striking "except in the wilds of Derbyshire" (*Observations, on Several Parts of England . . . Relative Chiefly to Picturesque Beauty,* 3rd ed., 2 vols. [London, 1808], II, 216). He writes of the vale of Matlock, however, that it is "a romantic, and most delightful scene, in which the ideas of sublimity and beauty are blended in a high degree" (II, 217–218).

54 Michael Wood provides a brilliant exegesis of the phrase "time and her aunt" and of its functions in this passage. He writes that "it offers us a glimpse of Austen's ironic philosophy, or if you prefer, her irony about philosophy. It brings together, as if to mirror life's confluences in a trick of grammar, two very different orders of contingency. There is the world of aunts, and everything they represent of family and society, kindness and curiosity. It's a world of aunts and not of uncles because it's a world of women. And there is the world of time, which is also the world of chance meetings (one day earlier and the visitors would have missed Darcy, one day later, knowing he was supposed to be there, they would not have visited), and the world of aging and healing. Time is the enemy of marriage for women in Austen, which is why its supposed healing powers are so often treated with skepticism. Aunts and time, together or separately, determine much of life—determine all of life, Austen's irony cryptically suggests—that we do not manage to take into our own hands" ("Time and Her Aunt," *A Companion to Jane Austen,* ed. Claudia L. Johnson and Clara Tuite [Chichester: Wiley-Blackwell, 2009], 198–199). Wood's full essay is well worth reading: it demonstrates the subtlety with which Austen generates her effects.

Engraving by J. Bluck (1791–1819) after Thomas Barber (1768–1843), "Dove Dale No.4," from T. C. Hofland, *Six Views in Derbyshire* (Nottingham: Published by T. Barber and T. Hofland, 1805). A view of Dove Dale, one of the scenic spots that Elizabeth and her relatives have visited, a subject of conversation between Elizabeth and Darcy at Pemberley.

Engraving by J. Bluck (1791–1819) after T. C. Hofland (1777–1843), Matlock No.6," from *Six Views in Derbyshire* (Nottingham: Published by T. Barber and T. Hofland, 1805). Matlock, another scenic site, praised by William Gilpin as "romantic." Darcy and Elizabeth discuss this, too.

expected. "He is perfectly well behaved, polite, and unassuming," said her uncle.

"There *is* something a little stately in him to be sure," replied her aunt, "but it is confined to his air, and is not unbecoming. I can now say with the housekeeper, that though some people may call him proud, *I* have seen nothing of it."

"I was never more surprised than by his behaviour to us. It was more than civil; it was really attentive; and there was no necessity for such attention. His acquaintance with Elizabeth was very trifling."

"To be sure, Lizzy," said her aunt, "he is not so handsome as Wickham; or, rather, he has not Wickham's countenance,[55] for his features are perfectly good. But how came you to tell us that he was so disagreeable?"

Elizabeth excused herself as well as she could; said that she had liked him better when they had met in Kent than before, and that she had never seen him so pleasant as this morning.

"But perhaps he may be a little whimsical in his civilities," replied her uncle. "Your great men[56] often are; and therefore I shall not take him at his word about fishing, as he might change his mind another day, and warn me off his grounds."

Elizabeth felt that they had entirely mistaken his character,[57] but said nothing.

"From what we have seen of him," continued Mrs. Gardiner, "I really should not have thought that he could have behaved in so cruel a way by any body, as he has done by poor Wickham. He has not an ill-natured look. On the contrary, there is something pleasing about his mouth when he speaks. And there is something of dignity in his countenance, that would not give one an unfavourable idea of his heart. But to be sure, the good lady who shewed us the house, did give him a most flaming character![58] I could hardly help laughing aloud sometimes. But he is a liberal[59] master, I suppose, and *that* in the eye of a servant comprehends every virtue."

Elizabeth here felt herself called on to say something in vindication of his behaviour to Wickham; and therefore gave them to understand, in as guarded a manner as she could, that by what she had heard from his relations in Kent, his actions were capable of a very

55 Appearance (as a whole): in other words, he doesn't give as good a physical impression of himself as Wickham does.

56 Men of high social position.

57 It is something new for Elizabeth to be defending Darcy, even internally.

58 Extravagantly positive characterization.

59 Generous.

different construction;[60] and that his character was by no means so faulty, nor Wickham's so amiable, as they had been considered in Hertfordshire. In confirmation of this, she related the particulars of all the pecuniary transactions in which they had been connected, without actually naming her authority, but stating it to be such as such as might be relied on.

Mrs. Gardiner was surprised and concerned; but as they were now approaching the scene of her former pleasures, every idea gave way to the charm of recollection; and she was too much engaged in pointing out to her husband all the interesting spots in its environs, to think of anything else. Fatigued as she had been by the morning's walk, they had no sooner dined than she set off again in quest of her former acquaintance, and the evening was spent in the satisfactions of a intercourse renewed after many years discontinuance.

The occurrences of the day were too full of interest to leave Elizabeth much attention for any of these new friends; and she could do nothing but think, and think with wonder, of Mr. Darcy's civility, and above all, of his wishing her to be acquainted with his sister.

2

ELIZABETH HAD SETTLED IT[1] that Mr. Darcy would bring his sister to visit her, the very day after her reaching Pemberley; and was consequently resolved not to be out of sight of the inn the whole of that morning. But her conclusion was false; for on the very morning after their own arrival at Lambton, these visitors came. They had been walking about the place with some of their new friends, and were just returned to the inn to dress themselves for dining with the same family, when the sound of a carriage drew them to a window, and they saw a gentleman and a lady in a curricle,[2] driving up the street. Elizabeth immediately recognising the livery,[3] guessed what it meant, and imparted no small degree of surprise to her relations, by acquainting them with the honour which she expected. Her uncle and aunt were all amazement; and the embarrassment[4] of her manner as she spoke, joined to the circumstance itself, and many of the circumstances of the preceding day, opened to them a new idea on the business. Nothing had ever suggested it before, but they felt that there was no other way of accounting for such attentions from such a quarter, than by supposing a partiality for their niece. While these newly-born notions were passing in their heads, the perturbation of Elizabeth's feelings was every moment increasing. She was quite amazed at her own discomposure; but amongst other causes of disquiet, she dreaded lest the partiality of the brother should have said too much in her favour; and more than commonly anxious to please,[5] she naturally suspected that every power of pleasing would fail her.

1 Decided.

2 A light, two-wheeled carriage drawn by two horses. A curricle was a fashionable equipage, often elegantly fitted up, with matched (therefore expensive) horses drawing it—much superior to, for example, Mr. Collins's gig. John Thorpe, in *Northanger Abbey,* boasts of *his* gig—an inferior conveyance, with only one horse— that it is "curricle hung": in other words, from his self-aggrandizing point of view, almost equivalent to a curricle.

3 The costume worn by servants; its color and design, often adapted from their employers' coat of arms, identifies the family for whom they work.

4 Embarrassment was a rather new element in novels; Frances Burney's first novel, *Evelina* (1778), was probably the first work to explore it. Novelists' desire to pay attention to such a feeling indicated their growing concern with rendering realistic social interactions and psychological nuance.

5 Women were thought "naturally" to have a particular desire to please. As the marchioness de Lambert put the point, "women are designed to please" (*Advice of a Mother to Her Daughter, The Young Lady's Pocket Library, or Parental Monitor* [Bristol: Thoemmes, 1995], 144). They were nonetheless frequently advised to cultivate their capacity for pleasing others. The marchioness explains, "Politeness is a desire of pleasing: nature gives it, education and the world improve it. . . . True

politeness is modest; and as it aims to please, it knows that the way to carry its point, is to shew that we do not prefer ourselves to others, but give them the first rank in our esteem" (180).

Even the most pious moralists considered pleasing a primary desideratum for women. The clergyman James Fordyce frequently makes it a criterion for female action. Thus he has no objection to dancing as an activity for young women, since it displays "that easy graceful carriage, to which Nature has annexed very pleasing perceptions in the beholders" (*Sermons to Young Women,* 3rd American ed., from 12th London ed. [Philadelphia, 1809], 119).

Thomas Rowlandson, "Boy Bringing Round a Citizen's Curricle," 1787. The light and speedy curricle, a vehicle frequently chosen by fashionable young men, was usually drawn by two horses. The grim and prosperous couple—far from fashionable—looking at this one-horse version will provide considerable weight for the single horse to pull. Rowlandson (1757–1827) was a famous printmaker and caricaturist.

She retreated from the window, fearful of being seen; and as she walked up and down the room, endeavouring to compose herself, saw such looks of enquiring surprise in her uncle and aunt, as made every thing worse.

Miss Darcy and her brother appeared, and this formidable introduction took place. With astonishment did Elizabeth see, that her new acquaintance was at least as much embarrassed as herself. Since her being at Lambton, she had heard that Miss Darcy was exceedingly proud; but the observation of a very few minutes convinced her, that she was only exceedingly shy. She found it difficult to obtain even a word from her beyond a monosyllable.

Miss Darcy was tall, and on a larger scale than Elizabeth; and, though little more than sixteen, her figure was formed, and her appearance womanly and graceful. She was less handsome than her brother, but there was sense[6] and good humour in her face, and her manners were perfectly unassuming and gentle. Elizabeth, who had expected to find in her as acute and unembarrassed an observer as ever Mr. Darcy had been, was much relieved by discerning such different feelings.

They had not long been together, before Mr. Darcy told her that Bingley was also coming to wait on[7] her; and she had barely time to express her satisfaction, and prepare for such a visitor, when Bingley's quick step was heard on the stairs, and in a moment he entered the room. All Elizabeth's anger against him had been long done away;[8] but had she still felt any, it could hardly have stood its ground against the unaffected cordiality with which he expressed himself, on seeing her again. He enquired in a friendly, though general way, after her family, and looked and spoke with the same good-humoured ease that he had ever done.

To Mr. and Mrs. Gardiner he was scarcely a less interesting personage than to herself. They had long wished to see him. The whole party before them, indeed, excited a lively attention. The suspicions which had just arisen of Mr. Darcy and their niece, directed their observation towards each with an earnest though guarded enquiry; and they soon drew from those enquiries the full conviction that one of them at least knew what it was to love. Of the lady's sensations they remained a little in doubt; but that the gentleman was overflowing with admiration was evident enough.[9]

Elizabeth, on her side, had much to do. She wanted to ascertain the feelings of each of her visitors, she wanted to compose her own, and to make herself agreeable to all; and in the latter object, where she feared most to fail, she was most sure of success, for those to whom she endeavoured to give pleasure were prepossessed in her favour. Bingley was ready, Georgiana was eager, and Darcy determined, to be pleased.

In seeing Bingley, her thoughts naturally flew to her sister; and, oh! how ardently did she long to know, whether any of his were directed in a like manner. Sometimes she could fancy, that he talked less than on former occasions, and once or twice pleased herself with the notion that as he looked at her, he was trying to trace a resem-

6 Sensibleness, good sense, with overtones of capacity for feeling.

7 Call on.

8 Dismissed.

9 To the Gardiners, but not to Elizabeth.

10 A phrase that suggests the degree to which Elizabeth's feelings shape her understanding.

11 Elizabeth is still busy interpreting—but aware now of the possibility of mistake.

12 Desire to please.

13 A curious—although not inaccurate—adjective for the scene of Darcy's rejected proposal.

14 And desire to please is emphatically not "natural" for Darcy.

15 Social status.

blance. But, though this might be imaginary, she could not be deceived as to his behaviour to Miss Darcy, who had been set up as a rival to Jane. No look appeared on either side that spoke particular regard. Nothing occurred between them that could justify the hopes of his sister. On this point she was soon satisfied; and two or three little circumstances occurred ere they parted, which, in her anxious interpretation,[10] denoted a recollection of Jane, not untinctured by tenderness, and a wish of saying more that might lead to the mention of her, had he dared. He observed to her, at a moment when the others were talking together, and in a tone which had something of real regret, that it "was a very long time since he had had the pleasure of seeing her;" and, before she could reply, he added, "It is above eight months. We have not met since the 26th of November, when we were all dancing together at Netherfield."

Elizabeth was pleased to find his memory so exact; and he afterwards took occasion to ask her, when unattended to by any of the rest, whether *all* her sisters were at Longbourn. There was not much in the question, nor in the preceding remark, but there was a look and a manner which gave them meaning.[11]

It was not often that she could turn her eyes on Mr. Darcy himself; but, whenever she did catch a glimpse, she saw an expression of general complaisance,[12] and in all that he said, she heard an accent so removed from hauteur or disdain of his companions, as convinced her that the improvement of manners which she had yesterday witnessed, however temporary its existence might prove, had at least outlived one day. When she saw him thus seeking the acquaintance, and courting the good opinion of people, with whom any intercourse a few months ago would have been a disgrace; when she saw him thus civil, not only to herself, but to the very relations whom he had openly disdained, and recollected their last lively[13] scene in Hunsford Parsonage, the difference, the change was so great, and struck so forcibly on her mind, that she could hardly restrain her astonishment from being visible. Never, even in the company of his dear friends at Netherfield, or his dignified relations at Rosings, had she seen him so desirous to please,[14] so free from self-consequence, or unbending reserve as now, when no importance[15] could result from the success of his endeavours, and when even the acquaintance of those to whom his attentions were addressed, would draw down the ridicule and censure of the ladies both of Netherfield and Rosings.

Their visitors stayed with them above half an hour, and when they arose to depart, Mr. Darcy called on his sister to join him in expressing their wish of seeing Mr. and Mrs. Gardiner, and Miss Bennet, to dinner at Pemberley, before they left the country.[16] Miss Darcy, though with a diffidence which marked her little in the habit of giving invitations, readily obeyed. Mrs. Gardiner looked at her niece, desirous of knowing how *she,* whom the invitation most concerned, felt disposed as to its acceptance, but Elizabeth had turned away her head. Presuming, however, that this studied avoidance spoke rather a momentary embarrassment, than any dislike of the proposal, and seeing in her husband, who was fond of society, a perfect willingness to accept it, she ventured to engage for[17] her attendance, and the day after the next was fixed on.

Bingley expressed great pleasure in the certainty of seeing Elizabeth again, having still a great deal to say to her, and many enquiries to make after all their Hertfordshire friends. Elizabeth, construing all this into a wish of hearing her speak of her sister, was pleased; and on this account, as well as some others, found herself, when their visitors left them, capable of considering the last half hour with some satisfaction, though while it was passing, the enjoyment of it had been little. Eager to be alone, and fearful of enquiries or hints from her uncle and aunt, she staid with them only long enough to hear their favourable opinion of Bingley, and then hurried away to dress.

But she had no reason to fear Mr. and Mrs. Gardiner's curiosity; it was not their wish to force her communication. It was evident that she was much better acquainted with Mr. Darcy than they had before any idea of; it was evident that he was very much in love with her. They saw much to interest, but nothing to justify enquiry.

Of Mr. Darcy it was now a matter of anxiety to think well; and, as far as their acquaintance reached, there was no fault to find. They could not be untouched by his politeness; and had they drawn his character from their own feelings, and his servant's report, without any reference to any other account, the circle in Hertfordshire to

16 Locality.

17 Promise.

18 Information.

19 Because, presumably, they had no social equals in the town.

20 Paid.

21 Now she has to interpret herself, as well as others.

22 Here is Dr. Gregory's account of how a woman falls in love: gratitude is a key element. "Some agreeable qualities recommend a gentleman to your common good liking and friendship. In the course of his acquaintance, he contracts an attachment to you. When you perceive it, it excites your gratitude: this gratitude rises into a preference, and this preference perhaps at last advances to some degree of attachment, especially if it meets with crosses and difficulties; for these, and a state of suspense, are very great incitements to attachment, and are the food of love in both sexes. If attachment was not excited in your sex in this manner, there is not one of a million of you that could ever marry with any degree of love" (John Gregory, *A Father's Legacy to his Daughters, The Young Lady's Pocket Library, or Parental Monitor* [Bristol: Thoemmes Press, 1995], 33).

23 Elizabeth's self-assessment emphasizes her faults, which are undeniably present. As Austen wrote to her niece, with reference to a Mr. Wildman who apparently disliked one of the novelist's works, "He & I should not in the least agree of course, in our ideas of Novels & Heroines;—pictures of perfection as you know make me sick & wicked" (To Fanny Knight, 23–25 March 1817).

which he was known, would not have recognised it for Mr. Darcy. There was now an interest, however, in believing the housekeeper; and they soon became sensible that the authority of a servant who had known him since he was four years old, and whose own manners indicated respectability, was not to be hastily rejected. Neither had any thing occurred in the intelligence[18] of their Lambton friends, that could materially lessen its weight. They had nothing to accuse him of but pride; pride he probably had, and if not, it would certainly be imputed by the inhabitants of a small market-town, where the family did not visit.[19] It was acknowledged, however, that he was a liberal man, and did much good among the poor.

With respect to Wickham, the travellers soon found that he was not held there in much estimation; for though the chief of his concerns, with the son of his patron, were imperfectly understood, it was yet a well known fact that, on his quitting Derbyshire, he had left many debts behind him, which Mr. Darcy afterwards discharged.[20]

As for Elizabeth, her thoughts were at Pemberley this evening more than the last; and the evening, though as it passed it seemed long, was not long enough to determine her feelings towards *one* in that mansion; and she lay awake two whole hours, endeavouring to make them out.[21] She certainly did not hate him. No; hatred had vanished long ago, and she had almost as long been ashamed of ever feeling a dislike against him, that could be so called. The respect created by the conviction of his valuable qualities, though at first unwillingly admitted, had for some time ceased to be repugnant to her feelings; and it was now heightened into somewhat of a friendlier nature, by the testimony so highly in his favour, and bringing forward his disposition in so amiable a light, which yesterday had produced. But above all, above respect and esteem, there was a motive within her of good will which could not be overlooked. It was gratitude.[22]—Gratitude, not merely for having once loved her, but for loving her still well enough, to forgive all the petulance and acrimony of her manner in rejecting him, and all the unjust accusations accompanying her rejection.[23] He who, she had been persuaded, would avoid her as his greatest enemy, seemed, on this accidental meeting, most eager to preserve the acquaintance, and without any indelicate display of regard, or any peculiarity[24] of manner, where their two selves only were concerned, was soliciting the good opinion of her friends,[25] and bent on making her known to his sister. Such a change in a man of so much pride, excited not only astonishment but gratitude—for to love, ardent love, it must be attributed; and as such its impression on her was of a sort to be encouraged, as by no means unpleasing, though it could not be exactly defined. She respected, she esteemed, she was grateful to him, she felt a real interest in his welfare; and she only wanted to know how far she wished that welfare to depend upon herself, and how far it would be for the happiness of both that she should employ the power, which her fancy told her she still possessed, of bringing on her the renewal of his addresses.

It had been settled in the evening between the aunt and the niece, that such a striking civility as Miss Darcy's, in coming to see them on the very day of her arrival at Pemberley, for she had reached it only to a late breakfast, ought to be imitated, though it could not be equalled, by some exertion of politeness on their side; and, consequently, that it would be highly expedient[26] to wait on her at Pemberley the following morning. They were, therefore, to go.—Elizabeth was pleased, though, when she asked herself the reason, she had very little to say in reply.

Mr. Gardiner left them soon after breakfast. The fishing scheme had been renewed the day before, and a positive engagement made of his meeting some of the gentlemen at Pemberley by noon.[27]

24 Special attentiveness to her.

25 Here meaning relatives.

26 Proper, suitable.

27 Michael Kramp sees in Darcy's kindness to Mr. Gardiner evidence of England's changing social arrangements. He writes that *Pride and Prejudice* "dramatizes how England and its ancestral leaders are beginning to recognize the social potential of new classes of men, represented by Bingley and Gardiner, who have either wealth or a sense of duty—but not both. Indeed, Darcy's close relationship with Bingley suggests that the gap between new and old money is shrinking, and the hero's kindness and collaboration with Gardiner demonstrate an astonishing degree of cooperation between the aristocracy and the tradesmen of London" (*Disciplining Love: Austen and the Modern Man* [Columbus: The Ohio State University Press, 2007], 76).

3

1 Drawing room, or salon.

2 Exposure.

3 The fact that they are "scattered" rather than symmetrically arranged makes them conform to the standards of the picturesque.

4 Acknowledged.

CONVINCED AS ELIZABETH NOW was that Miss Bingley's dislike of her had originated in jealousy, she could not help feeling how very unwelcome her appearance at Pemberley must be to her, and was curious to know with how much civility on that lady's side, the acquaintance would now be renewed.

On reaching the house, they were shewn through the hall into the saloon,[1] whose northern aspect[2] rendered it delightful for summer. Its windows opening to the ground, admitted a most refreshing view of the high woody hills behind the house, and of the beautiful oaks and Spanish chesnuts which were scattered over the intermediate lawn.[3]

In this room they were received by Miss Darcy, who was sitting there with Mrs. Hurst and Miss Bingley, and the lady with whom she lived in London. Georgiana's reception of them was very civil; but attended with all that embarrassment which, though proceeding from shyness and the fear of doing wrong, would easily give to those who felt themselves inferior, the belief of her being proud and reserved. Mrs. Gardiner and her niece, however, did her justice, and pitied her.

By Mrs. Hurst and Miss Bingley, they were noticed[4] only by a curtsey; and on their being seated, a pause, awkward as such pauses must always be, succeeded for a few moments. It was first broken by Mrs. Annesley, a genteel, agreeable-looking woman, whose endeavour to introduce some kind of discourse, proved her to be more truly well bred than either of the others; and between her and Mrs. Gardiner, with occasional help from Elizabeth, the conversation was carried on. Miss Darcy looked as if she wished for courage enough to join in it; and sometimes did venture a short sentence, when there was least danger of its being heard.

Elizabeth soon saw that she was herself closely watched by Miss Bingley, and that she could not speak a word, especially to Miss Darcy, without calling her attention. This observation would not have prevented her from trying to talk to the latter, had they not been seated at an inconvenient distance; but she was not sorry to be spared the necessity of saying much. Her own thoughts were employing her. She expected every moment that some of the gentlemen would enter the room. She wished, she feared that the master of the house might be amongst them; and whether she wished or feared it most, she could scarcely determine. After sitting in this manner a quarter of an hour, without hearing Miss Bingley's voice, Elizabeth was roused by receiving from her a cold enquiry after the health of her family.[5] She answered with equal indifference and brevity, and the other said no more.

The next variation which their visit afforded was produced by the entrance of servants with cold meat, cake, and a variety of all the finest fruits in season;[6] but this did not take place till after many a significant look and smile from Mrs. Annesley to Miss Darcy had been given, to remind her of her post.[7] There was now employment for the whole party; for though they could not all talk, they could all eat; and the beautiful pyramids of grapes, nectarines, and peaches,[8] soon collected them round the table.

While thus engaged, Elizabeth had a fair opportunity of deciding whether she most feared or wished for the appearance of Mr. Darcy, by the feelings which prevailed on his entering the room; and then, though but a moment before she had believed her wishes to predominate, she began to regret that he came.

He had been some time with Mr. Gardiner, who, with two or three other gentlemen from the house, was engaged by the river,[9] and had left him only on learning that the ladies of the family intended a visit to Georgiana that morning. No sooner did he appear, than Elizabeth wisely resolved to be perfectly easy and unembarrassed;—a resolu-

5 Such an inquiry would be a conventional opening gambit—part of what is implied by someone's offering "compliments." Waiting fifteen minutes to make it, however, is seriously rude.

6 During such a "morning visit" as this, refreshments would not necessarily be served at all. The abundance of food offered at Pemberley indicates the generous hospitality that Darcy wishes to provide for his guests. Since luncheon was not yet an established meal, such a repast might be served whenever guests appeared. "As the meal had no name," Maggie Lane writes, "it is not surprising that it had no fixed hour" (*Jane Austen and Food* [London: The Hambledon Press, 1995], 35).

7 As hostess. Miss Darcy is the youngest woman present, but her position as sister of the estate's owner makes her responsible for the entertainment, as is Miss Bingley in her brother's home at Netherfield. Indeed, technically she oversees the running of the household, since no other woman inhabits Darcy's estate.

8 All of which would have been grown in hothouses on the estate, a fact indicative of Darcy's wealth.

9 In other words, he was fishing.

10 Encouraged.

11 Blushing—perhaps because he still suspects that Elizabeth retains a romantic preference for Wickham.

12 An emotion.

13 Family.

tion the more necessary to be made, but perhaps not the more easily kept, because she saw that the suspicions of the whole party were awakened against them, and that there was scarcely an eye which did not watch his behaviour when he first came into the room. In no countenance was attentive curiosity so strongly marked as in Miss Bingley's, in spite of the smiles which overspread her face whenever she spoke to one of its objects; for jealousy had not yet made her desperate, and her attentions to Mr. Darcy were by no means over. Miss Darcy, on her brother's entrance, exerted herself much more to talk; and Elizabeth saw that he was anxious for his sister and herself to get acquainted, and forwarded,[10] as much as possible, every attempt at conversation on either side. Miss Bingley saw all this likewise; and, in the imprudence of anger, took the first opportunity of saying, with sneering civility,

"Pray, Miss Eliza, are not the — —shire Militia removed from Meryton? They must be a great loss to *your* family."

In Darcy's presence she dared not mention Wickham's name; but Elizabeth instantly comprehended that he was uppermost in her thoughts; and the various recollections connected with him gave her a moment's distress; but, exerting herself vigorously to repel the ill-natured attack, she presently answered the question in a tolerably disengaged tone. While she spoke, an involuntary glance shewed her Darcy with an heightened complexion,[11] earnestly looking at her, and his sister overcome with confusion, and unable to lift up her eyes. Had Miss Bingley known what pain she was then giving her beloved friend, she undoubtedly would have refrained from the hint; but she had merely intended to discompose Elizabeth, by bringing forward the idea of a man to whom she believed her partial, to make her betray a sensibility[12] which might injure her in Darcy's opinion, and perhaps to remind the latter of all the follies and absurdities, by which some part of her family were connected with that corps. Not a syllable had ever reached her of Miss Darcy's meditated elopement. To no creature had it been revealed, where secrecy was possible, except to Elizabeth; and from all Bingley's connections[13] her brother was particularly anxious to conceal it, from that very wish which Elizabeth had long ago attributed to him, of their becoming hereafter her own.[14] He had certainly formed such a plan, and without meaning that it should affect his endeavour to separate him from Miss Bennet, it is probable that it might add something to his lively concern for the welfare of his friend.

Elizabeth's collected[15] behaviour, however, soon quieted his emotion; and as Miss Bingley, vexed and disappointed, dared not approach nearer to Wickham, Georgiana also recovered in time, though not enough to be able to speak any more. Her brother, whose eye she feared to meet, scarcely recollected her interest in the affair, and the very circumstance which had been designed to turn his thoughts from Elizabeth, seemed to have fixed them on her more, and more cheerfully.

Their visit did not continue long after the question and answer above-mentioned; and while Mr. Darcy was attending them to their carriage, Miss Bingley was venting her feelings in criticisms on Elizabeth's person, behaviour, and dress. But Georgiana would not join her. Her brother's recommendation was enough to ensure her favour: his judgment could not err, and he had spoken in such terms of Elizabeth, as to leave Georgiana without the power of finding her otherwise than lovely and amiable. When Darcy returned to the saloon, Miss Bingley could not help repeating to him some part of what she had been saying to his sister.

"How very ill[16] Miss Eliza Bennet looks this morning, Mr. Darcy," she cried; "I never in my life saw any one so much altered as she is since the winter. She is grown so brown[17] and coarse! Louisa and I were agreeing that we should not have known her again."

However little Mr. Darcy might have liked such an address, he contented himself with coolly replying, that he perceived no other alteration than her being rather tanned,—no miraculous consequence of travelling in the summer.

"For my own part," she rejoined, "I must confess that I never could see any beauty in her. Her face is too thin; her complexion has no brilliancy;[18] and her features are not at all handsome. Her nose wants character; there is nothing marked in its lines. Her teeth are tolerable, but not out of the common way;[19] and as for her eyes, which have sometimes been called so fine, I could never see anything extraordi-

14 Through a marriage between Bingley and Georgiana.

15 Composed.

16 Imperfect, not up to ordinary standards.

17 Tanned—at a time when white skin was fashionable.

18 Luster.

19 Nothing special, not unusual.

20 Excessive self-confidence; conceit. Miss Bingley implies that such conceit might be justified if its possessor were fashionable.

nary in them. They have a sharp, shrewish look, which I do not like at all; and in her air altogether there is a self-sufficiency[20] without fashion, which is intolerable."

Persuaded as Miss Bingley was that Darcy admired Elizabeth, this was not the best method of recommending herself; but angry people are not always wise; and in seeing him at last look somewhat nettled, she had all the success she expected. He was resolutely silent however; and, from a determination of making him speak, she continued,

"I remember, when we first knew her in Hertfordshire, how amazed we all were to find that she was a reputed beauty; and I particularly recollect your saying one night, after they had been dining at Netherfield, '*She* a beauty!—I should as soon call her mother a wit.' But afterwards she seemed to improve on you, and I believe you thought her rather pretty at one time."

"Yes," replied Darcy, who could contain himself no longer, "but *that* was only when I first knew her, for it is many months since I have considered her as one of the handsomest women of my acquaintance."

He then went away, and Miss Bingley was left to all the satisfaction of having forced him to say what gave no one any pain but herself.

Mrs. Gardiner and Elizabeth talked of all that had occurred, during their visit, as they returned, except what had particularly interested them both. The looks and behaviour of every body they had seen were discussed, except of the person who had mostly engaged their attention. They talked of his sister, his friends, his house, his fruit, of every thing but himself; yet Elizabeth was longing to know what Mrs. Gardiner thought of him, and Mrs. Gardiner would have been highly gratified by her niece's beginning the subject.

4

Elizabeth had been a good deal disappointed in not finding a letter from Jane, on their first arrival at Lambton; and this disappointment had been renewed on each of the mornings that had now been spent there; but on the third, her repining was over, and her sister justified by the receipt of two letters from her at once, on one of which was marked that it had been missent elsewhere.[1] Elizabeth was not surprised at it, as Jane had written the direction[2] remarkably ill.

They had just been preparing to walk as the letters came in; and her uncle and aunt, leaving her to enjoy them in quiet, set off by themselves. The one missent must first be attended to; it had been written five days ago. The beginning contained an account of all their little parties and engagements, with such news as the country afforded;[3] but the latter half, which was dated a day later, and written in evident agitation, gave more important intelligence. It was to this effect:

> "Since writing the above, dearest Lizzy, something has occurred of a most unexpected and serious nature; but I am afraid of alarming you—be assured that we are all well. What I have to say relates to poor Lydia.[4] An express[5] came at twelve last night, just as we were all gone to bed, from Colonel Forster, to inform us that she was gone off to Scotland[6] with one of his officers; to own[7] the truth, with Wickham!— Imagine our surprise. To Kitty, however, it does not seem so

1 Postal service in Great Britain had greatly improved in the course of the eighteenth century, with the range of service widening and speed increasing. By the middle of the century, "[l]etters were sent every night to the principal South and Midland towns of England" (J. C. Hemmeon, *The History of the British Post Office* [Cambridge: Harvard University Press, 1912], 38). Earlier, post boys on horseback had delivered mail between one town and another, but in 1784 mail coaches were introduced. As the report of a parliamentary committee observed, "They have lessened the chance of robbery [and] diminished the need for special messengers and expresses" (41).

2 Address.

3 Exactly the kind of communication in Austen's typical letters to her sister.

4 No one but Jane would use the adjective *poor* for Lydia under these circumstances.

5 A message carried by a special messenger.

6 A plan to go to Scotland implied an intention of marriage. Lord Hardwicke's Marriage Act (1753) specified that both men and women under the age of twenty-one must have parental consent to marry. The law did not apply to Scotland, where boys could marry at fourteen and girls at twelve, with or without parental consent.

7 Acknowledge.

8 From a financial point of view.

9 Let us rejoice, in other words, that Wickham planned to marry Lydia, rather than simply to live with her.

10 Jane is trying to pretend to herself that Wickham's wickedness, their knowledge of which was acquired from Darcy, is mere rumor.

11 Just inside the Scottish border, frequently the site for marriages of English elopers. The Gretna Green marriage was a convention of eighteenth-century fiction, particularly in instances when a man wished to marry a woman for her money and thus had a special incentive to avoid parental knowledge.

wholly unexpected. I am very, very sorry. So imprudent[8] a match on both sides!—But I am willing to hope the best, and that his character has been misunderstood. Thoughtless and indiscreet I can easily believe him, but this step (and let us rejoice over it)[9] marks nothing bad at heart. His choice is disinterested at least, for he must know my father can give her nothing. Our poor mother is sadly grieved. My father bears it better. How thankful am I, that we never let them know what has been said against him;[10] we must forget it ourselves. They were off Saturday night about twelve, as is conjectured, but were not missed till yesterday morning at eight. The express was sent off directly. My dear Lizzy, they must have passed within ten miles of us. Colonel Forster gives us reason to expect him here soon. Lydia left a few lines for his wife, informing her of their intention. I must conclude, for I cannot be long from my poor mother. I am afraid you will not be able to make it out, but I hardly know what I have written."

Without allowing herself time for consideration, and scarcely knowing what she felt, Elizabeth on finishing this letter instantly seized the other, and opening it with the utmost impatience, read as follows: it had been written a day later than the conclusion of the first.

"By this time, my dearest sister, you have received my hurried letter; I wish this may be more intelligible, but though not confined for time, my head is so bewildered that I cannot answer for being coherent. Dearest Lizzy, I hardly know what I would write, but I have bad news for you, and it cannot be delayed. Imprudent as a marriage between Mr. Wickham and our poor Lydia would be, we are now anxious to be assured it has taken place, for there is but too much reason to fear they are not gone to Scotland. Colonel Forster came yesterday, having left Brighton the day before, not many hours after the express. Though Lydia's short letter to Mrs. F. gave them to understand that they were going to Gretna Green,[11] something was dropped by Denny expressing his belief that W. never intended to go there, or to marry Lydia at all, which was repeated to Colonel F. who instantly taking the alarm, set off from B. intending to trace their route. He did trace them easily to Clapham,[12] but no further; for on entering that place, they removed into a hackney-coach[13] and dismissed the chaise that brought them from Epsom.[14] All that is known after this is, that they were seen to continue the London road. I know not what to think. After making every possible enquiry on that side London, Colonel F. came on into Hertfordshire, anxiously renewing them at all the turnpikes,[15] and at the inns in Barnet and Hatfield,[16] but without any success, no such people had been seen to pass through. With the kindest concern he came on to Longbourn, and broke his apprehensions to us in a manner most creditable to his heart. I am sincerely grieved for him and Mrs. F. but no one can throw any blame on them. Our distress, my dear Lizzy, is very great. My father and mother believe the worst, but I cannot think so ill of him. Many circumstances might make it more eligible[17] for them to be married privately in town[18] than to pursue their first plan; and even if *he* could form such a design against a young woman of Lydia's connections, which is not likely, can I suppose her so lost to every thing?[19]—Impossible. I grieve to find, however, that Colonel F. is not disposed to depend upon their marriage; he shook his head when I expressed my hopes, and said he feared W. was not a man to be trusted. My poor mother is really ill and keeps her room. Could she exert herself it would be better but this is not to be expected; and as to my father, I never in my life saw him so affected. Poor Kitty has anger for having concealed their attachment; but as it was a matter of confidence, one cannot wonder. I am truly glad, dearest Lizzy, that you have been spared something of these distressing scenes; but now as the first shock is over, shall I own that I long for your return? I am not so selfish, however, as to press for it, if inconvenient. Adieu! I take up my pen again to do, what I

12 In south London.

13 A hired coach, equivalent to a modern taxi, for transportation around town. The couple had taken a hired chaise for the relatively long journey from Brighton; their transfer to a hackney coach suggests that they planned to remain in London.

14 A town a few miles south of London.

15 Stops where travelers would have to pay a toll.

16 Where the couple might have paused to eat or to change horses.

17 Desirable.

18 Young people wishing to marry without parental consent might do so in London by making use of banns, public notices of a proposed marriage on three successive Sundays in church. If no one appeared to reveal legal impediments to the marriage, it could take place. Couples from outside London could reasonably assume that their parents would not hear of the banns, and London parishes were likely far too large for a clergyman to ascertain the ages and residency of all who presented themselves for marriage.

19 Every moral imperative.

20 Emergency.

21 It would be considered impolite to ask such a personal question.

22 That is, unable to stand up.

23 In registering her feelings so dramatically on her body, Elizabeth resembles the heroines of sensibility who had abounded throughout the eighteenth century. Unlike Mrs. Bennet, whose ailments, although intended to register her delicate feelings, appear to

GENERAL POSTMAN.

Pub. by R. Ackermann, London.

"The General Postman," from Rudolph Ackermann, *World in Miniature*, 1827. Mail service in the early nineteenth century was typically frequent and efficient.

have just told you I would not, but circumstances are such, that I cannot help earnestly begging you all to come here, as soon as possible. I know my dear uncle and aunt so well, that I am not afraid of requesting it, though I have still something more to ask of the former. My father is going to London with Colonel Forster instantly, to try to discover her. What he means to do, I am sure I know not; but his excessive distress will not allow him to pursue any measure in the best and safest way, and Colonel Forster is obliged to be at Brighton again to-morrow evening. In such an exigence[20] my uncle's advice and assistance would be every thing in the world; he will immediately comprehend what I must feel, and I rely upon his goodness."

"Oh! where, where is my uncle?" cried Elizabeth, darting from her seat as she finished the letter, in eagerness to follow him, without losing a moment of the time so precious; but as she reached the door, it was opened by a servant, and Mr. Darcy appeared. Her pale face and impetuous manner made him start, and before he could recover himself enough to speak, she, in whose mind every idea was superseded by Lydia's situation, hastily exclaimed, "I beg your pardon, but I must leave you. I must find Mr. Gardiner this moment, on business that cannot be delayed; I have not an instant to lose."

"Good God! what is the matter?" cried he, with more feeling than politeness;[21] then recollecting himself, "I will not detain you a minute; but let me, or let the servant, go after Mr. and Mrs. Gardiner. You are not well enough;—you cannot go yourself."

Elizabeth hesitated, but her knees trembled under her, and she felt how little would be gained by her attempting to pursue them. Calling back the servant, therefore, she commissioned him, though in so breathless an accent as made her almost unintelligible, to fetch his master and mistress home, instantly.

On his quitting the room she sat down, unable to support herself,[22] and looking so miserably ill,[23] that it was impossible for Darcy to leave her, or to refrain from saying, in a tone of gentleness and

GRETNA GREEN, or the RED-HOT MARRIAGE.
Oh! M.r Blacksmith ease our Pains, and Tye us fast in Wedlocks Chains.

Anonymous, "Gretna Green, or The Red-Hot marriage," c. 1795. Although marriages did not customarily take place in blacksmiths' shops, couples seeking to be married at Gretna Green were often in haste, caring less about environment than about efficiency. Note that the prospective groom here is, like Wickham, a soldier—perhaps a member of the militia.

be imaginary, such heroines genuinely express strong emotion by blushing, weeping, fainting, or—like Elizabeth here—proving unable to support themselves. In Frances Burney's *Evelina* (1778), the title character goes through a similar sequence when she encounters a poverty-stricken man who appears about to commit suicide. Like Elizabeth, although with far less experience, Evelina proves capable of acting effectively when necessary, but her conventional symptoms of female weakness demonstrate her proper femininity. In many of the earlier novels, such expressions of a woman's bodily weakness serve as catalysts for a man's realization of love.

24 No family connections of importance.

25 Two of Austen's other major novels, *Sense and Sensibility* and *Mansfield Park,* also contain stories of sexual impropriety. In *Sense and Sensibility,* Colonel Brandon tells the story of a woman he loved, whose seduction (by another) eventuates in a life of prostitution and the birth of an illegitimate daughter, also later a victim of seduction. *Mansfield Park* contains a character who, although married, elopes with another man and for a time lives with him. None of Austen's fiction, however, centers on the seduced woman—who had been a staple of eighteenth-century novels, most notably Samuel Richardson's *Clarissa.* In virtually all the eighteenth-century examples, the seduced maiden is punished (or rewarded) by death; Austen resorts to this denouement only in *Sense and Sensibility.* Unlike most of her predecessors, Austen explores the possibility that female as well as male desire contributes to the "fall" of young women. She invariably uses her vignettes of sexual misbehavior to expose potential dangers for the heroine—dangers often more subtle than those of seduction.

Lydia's misbehavior could not possibly tempt Elizabeth as a model. But Lydia, exemplifying irresponsible lust, and Charlotte, exemplifying financial prudence of a perhaps excessively responsible nature, suggest polarized possible bases for marital choice. A woman could, and can, be influenced by many forces in deciding whom she wishes to marry. Austen makes the reader aware of possibilities that Elizabeth herself would never consider.

26 Influenced.

commiseration, "Let me call your maid. Is there nothing you could take, to give you present relief?—A glass of wine;—shall I get you one?—You are very ill."

"No, I thank you," she replied, endeavouring to recover herself. "There is nothing the matter with me. I am quite well; I am only distressed by some dreadful news which I have just received from Longbourn."

She burst into tears as she alluded to it, and for a few minutes could not speak another word. Darcy, in wretched suspense, could only say something indistinctly of his concern, and observe her in compassionate silence. At length, she spoke again. "I have just had a letter from Jane, with such dreadful news. It cannot be concealed from any one. My younger sister has left all her friends—has eloped;—has thrown herself into the power of—of Mr. Wickham. They are gone off together from Brighton. *You* know him too well to doubt the rest. She has no money, no connections,[24] nothing that can tempt him to—she is lost for ever."[25]

Darcy was fixed in astonishment. "When I consider," she added, in a yet more agitated voice, "that *I* might have prevented it!—*I,* who knew what he was. Had I but explained some part of it only—some part of what I learnt, to my own family! Had his character been known, this could not have happened. But it is all, all too late now."

"I am grieved indeed," cried Darcy; "grieved—shocked. But is it certain, absolutely certain?"

"Oh, yes!—They left Brighton together on Sunday night, and were traced almost to London, but not beyond; they are certainly not gone to Scotland."

"And what has been done, what has been attempted, to recover her?"

"My father is gone to London, and Jane has written to beg my uncle's immediate assistance, and we shall be off, I hope, in half an hour. But nothing can be done; I know very well that nothing can be done. How is such a man to be worked on?[26] How are they even to be discovered? I have not the smallest hope. It is every way horrible!"

Darcy shook his head in silent acquiescence.

"When *my* eyes were opened to his real character.—Oh! had I known what I ought, what I dared, to do! But I knew not—I was afraid of doing too much. Wretched, wretched, mistake!"

Darcy made no answer. He seemed scarcely to hear her, and was walking up and down the room in earnest meditation, his brow contracted, his air gloomy. Elizabeth soon observed, and instantly understood it.[27] Her power was sinking;[28] every thing *must* sink under such a proof of family weakness, such an assurance of the deepest disgrace. She could neither wonder nor condemn, but the belief of his self-conquest brought nothing consolatory to her bosom, afforded no palliation of her distress. It was, on the contrary, exactly calculated to make her understand her own wishes; and never had she so honestly felt that she could have loved him, as now, when all love must be vain.

But self, though it would intrude, could not engross her. Lydia—the humiliation, the misery, she was bringing on them all,[29] soon swallowed up every private care; and covering her face with her handkerchief, Elizabeth was soon lost to every thing else; and, after a pause of several minutes, was only recalled to a sense of her situation by the voice of her companion, who, in a manner which, though it spoke compassion, spoke likewise restraint, said, "I am afraid you have been long desiring my absence, nor have I any thing to plead in excuse of my stay, but real, though unavailing, concern. Would to Heaven that any thing could be either said or done on my part, that might offer consolation to such distress. But I will not torment you with vain wishes, which may seem purposely to ask for your thanks. This unfortunate affair will, I fear, prevent my sister's having the pleasure of seeing you at Pemberley today."

"Oh, yes. Be so kind as to apologize for us to Miss Darcy. Say that urgent business calls us home immediately. Conceal the unhappy truth as long as it is possible.—I know it cannot be long."

He readily assured her of his secrecy—again expressed his sorrow for her distress, wished it a happier conclusion than there was at present reason to hope, and leaving his compliments for her relations, with only one serious, parting, look, went away.

27 Elizabeth's characteristic confidence that she has "instantly understood" Darcy underlines her tendency to believe firmly in the rightness of her own opinions.

28 This is the first time that Elizabeth's language has suggested a perception that her relationship with Darcy is one in which she has power.

29 The disgrace of a family member would damage the reputation of the entire family.

30 Austen's concern for psychological realism leads her to comment more than once in her fiction on the likelihood that gratitude may eventuate in love. In *Northanger Abbey*, the male rather than the female protagonist is thus motivated. "I must confess," the narrator explains, "that his affection originated in nothing better than gratitude, or, in other words, that a persuasion of her partiality for him had been the only cause of giving her a serious thought. It is a new circumstance in romance, I acknowledge, and dreadfully derogatory of an heroine's dignity; but if it be as new in common life, the credit of a wild imagination will at least be all my own" (II, 15).

31 That is, the love at first sight celebrated in countless works of romantic fiction.

As he quitted the room, Elizabeth felt how improbable it was that they should ever see each other again on such terms of cordiality as had marked their several meetings in Derbyshire; and as she threw a retrospective glance over the whole of their acquaintance, so full of contradictions and varieties, sighed at the perverseness of those feelings which would now have promoted its continuance, and would formerly have rejoiced in its termination.

If gratitude and esteem are good foundations of affection,[30] Elizabeth's change of sentiment will be neither improbable nor faulty. But if otherwise, if the regard springing from such sources is unreasonable or unnatural, in comparison of what is so often described as arising on a first interview with its object, and even before two words have been exchanged,[31] nothing can be said in her defence, except that she had given somewhat of a trial to the latter method, in her partiality for Wickham, and that its ill success might perhaps authorise her to seek the other less interesting mode of attachment. Be that as it may, she saw him go with regret; and in this early example of what Lydia's infamy must produce, found additional anguish as she reflected on that wretched business. Never, since reading Jane's second letter, had she entertained a hope of Wickham's meaning to marry her. No one but Jane, she thought, could flatter herself with such an expectation. Surprise was the least of her feelings on this developement. While the contents of the first letter remained on her mind, she was all surprise—all astonishment that Wickham should marry a girl, whom it was impossible he could marry for money; and how Lydia could ever have attached him, had appeared incomprehensible. But now it was all too natural. For such an attachment as this, she might have sufficient charms; and though she did not suppose Lydia to be deliberately engaging in an elopement, without the intention of marriage, she had no difficulty in believing that neither her virtue nor her understanding would preserve her from falling an easy prey.

She had never perceived, while the regiment was in Hertfordshire, that Lydia had any partiality for him, but she was convinced that Lydia had wanted only encouragement to attach herself to any body.

Sometimes one officer, sometimes another had been her favourite, as their attentions raised them in her opinion. Her affections had continually been fluctuating, but never without an object. The mischief of neglect and mistaken indulgence towards such a girl.—Oh! how acutely did she now feel it.

She was wild to be at home—to hear, to see, to be upon the spot, to share with Jane in the cares that must now fall wholly upon her, in a family so deranged;[32] a father absent, a mother incapable of exertion, and requiring constant attendance; and though almost persuaded that nothing could be done for Lydia, her uncle's interference seemed of the utmost importance, and till he entered the room, the misery of her impatience was severe. Mr. and Mrs. Gardiner had hurried back in alarm, supposing, by the servant's account, that their niece was taken suddenly ill;—but satisfying them instantly on that head, she eagerly communicated the cause of their summons, reading the two letters aloud, and dwelling on the postscript of the last with trembling energy.[33]—Though Lydia had never been a favourite with them, Mr. and Mrs. Gardiner could not but be deeply afflicted. Not Lydia only, but all were concerned in it; and after the first exclamations of surprise and horror, Mr. Gardiner promised every assistance in his power.—Elizabeth, though expecting no less, thanked him with tears of gratitude; and all three being actuated by one spirit, every thing relating to their journey was speedily settled. They were to be off as soon as possible. "But what is to be done about Pemberley?" cried Mrs. Gardiner. "John told us Mr. Darcy was here when you sent for us;—was it so?"

"Yes; and I told him we should not be able to keep our engagement. *That* is all settled."

"That is all settled;" repeated the other, as she ran into her room to prepare. "And are they upon such terms as for her to disclose the real truth! Oh, that I knew how it was!"

But wishes were vain; or at best could only serve to amuse her in the hurry and confusion of the following hour. Had Elizabeth been at leisure to be idle, she would have remained certain that all employment was impossible to one so wretched as herself; but she had

32 Disordered.

33 Several phrases in this paragraph—for example, "wild to be at home," "misery of her impatience," "trembling energy," "tears of gratitude"—call attention to the intensity of Elizabeth's emotional capacity, an important aspect of her character. Although she cultivates a witty façade and wants to be seen as a rational being—although she *is* emphatically a rational being—Austen represents her also as a woman of strong feeling. Indeed, her outrage at Charlotte's marital choice, in contrast with Jane's mild acceptance, indicates the same thing. The love for Darcy that she is beginning to recognize will turn into a passionate commitment.

her share of business as well as her aunt, and amongst the rest there were notes to be written to all their friends at Lambton, with false excuses for their sudden departure. An hour, however, saw the whole completed; and Mr. Gardiner meanwhile having settled his account at the inn, nothing remained to be done but to go; and Elizabeth, after all the misery of the morning, found herself, in a shorter space of time than she could have supposed, seated in the carriage, and on the road to Longbourn.

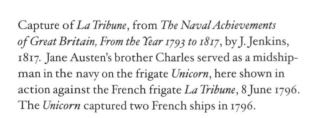

Capture of *La Tribune*, from *The Naval Achievements of Great Britain, From the Year 1793 to 1817*, by J. Jenkins, 1817. Jane Austen's brother Charles served as a midshipman in the navy on the frigate *Unicorn*, here shown in action against the French frigate *La Tribune*, 8 June 1796. The *Unicorn* captured two French ships in 1796.

5

"I HAVE BEEN THINKING IT OVER AGAIN, ELIZABETH," said her uncle, as they drove from the town; "and really, upon serious consideration, I am much more inclined than I was to judge as your eldest sister does of the matter. It appears to me so very unlikely, that any young man should form such a design against a girl who is by no means unprotected or friendless, and who was actually staying in his colonel's family,[1] that I am strongly inclined to hope the best. Could he expect that her friends would not step forward?[2] Could he expect to be noticed[3] again by the regiment, after such an affront to Colonel Forster? His temptation is not adequate to the risk!"

"Do you really think so?" cried Elizabeth, brightening up for a moment.

"Upon my word," said Mrs. Gardiner, "I begin to be of your uncle's opinion. It is really too great a violation of decency, honour, and interest,[4] for him to be guilty of. I cannot think so very ill of Wickham. Can you yourself, Lizzy, so wholly give him up, as to believe him capable of it?"

"Not, perhaps, of neglecting his own interest. But of every other neglect I can believe him capable. If, indeed, it should be so! But I dare not hope it. Why should they not go on to Scotland, if that had been the case?"

"In the first place," replied Mr. Gardiner, "there is no absolute proof that they are not gone to Scotland."

1 That is, the family of his commanding officer.

2 To fight a duel in defense of Lydia's honor. Duels were not so common as they had been in the early eighteenth century, but they persisted well into the nineteenth century, although they had long been banned by law. Traditionally, a woman's male family members should defend her honor. Colonel Brandon, in *Sense and Sensibility*, reports fighting a duel with the seducer of Eliza, illegitimate daughter of the woman he had once loved. His duel, however, was mainly symbolic. "We met by appointment," Brandon says, "he to defend, I to punish his conduct. We returned unwounded, and the meeting, therefore, never got abroad" (II, 9). *Sir Charles Grandison,* the novel by Samuel Richardson that Austen declared her favorite, heavily criticizes the practice of dueling as unchristian and immoral.

3 Acknowledged.

4 Self-interest.

5 An elopement without marriage.

6 Going on.

"Oh! but their removing from the chaise into a hackney coach is such a presumption! And, besides, no traces of them were to be found on the Barnet road."

"Well, then—supposing them to be in London. They may be there, though for the purpose of concealment, for no more exceptionable purpose. It is not likely that money should be very abundant on either side; and it might strike them that they could be more economically, though less expeditiously, married in London, than in Scotland."

"But why all this secrecy? Why any fear of detection? Why must their marriage be private? Oh! no, no, this is not likely. His most particular friend, you see by Jane's account, was persuaded of his never intending to marry her. Wickham will never marry a woman without some money. He cannot afford it. And what claims has Lydia, what attractions has she beyond youth, health, and good humour, that could make him for her sake, forego every chance of benefiting himself by marrying well? As to what restraint the apprehension of disgrace in the corps might throw on a dishonourable elopement[5] with her, I am not able to judge; for I know nothing of the effects that such a step might produce. But as to your other objection, I am afraid it will hardly hold good. Lydia has no brothers to step forward; and he might imagine, from my father's behaviour, from his indolence and the little attention he has ever seemed to give to what was going forward[6] in his family, that *he* would do as little, and think as little about it, as any father could do, in such a matter."

"But can you think that Lydia is so lost to every thing but love of him, as to consent to live with him on any other terms than marriage?"

"It does seem, and it is most shocking indeed," replied Elizabeth, with tears in her eyes, "that a sister's sense of decency and virtue in such a point should admit of doubt. But, really, I know not what to say. Perhaps I am not doing her justice. But she is very young; she has never been taught to think on serious subjects; and for the last half year, nay, for a twelvemonth, she has been given up to nothing but amusement and vanity. She has been allowed to dispose of her time in the most idle and frivolous manner, and to adopt any opinions that

came in her way. Since the — —shire were first quartered in Meryton, nothing but love, flirtation, and officers, have been in her head.
She has been doing every thing in her power by thinking and talking
on the subject, to give greater—what shall I call it? susceptibility to
her feelings; which are naturally lively enough. And we all know that
Wickham has every charm of person and address[7] that can captivate
a woman."

"But you see that Jane," said her aunt, "does not think so ill of
Wickham, as to believe him capable of the attempt."

"Of whom does Jane ever think ill? And who is there, whatever
might be their former conduct, that she would think capable of such
an attempt, till it were proved against them? But Jane knows, as well
as I do, what Wickham really is. We both know that he has been
profligate in every sense of the word.[8] That he has neither integrity
nor honour. That he is as false and deceitful, as he is insinuating."

"And do you really know all this?" cried Mrs. Gardiner, whose curiosity as to the mode of her intelligence was all alive.

"I do indeed," replied Elizabeth, colouring.[9] "I told you the other
day, of his infamous behaviour to Mr. Darcy; and you yourself, when
last at Longbourn, heard in what manner he spoke of the man, who
had behaved with such forbearance and liberality towards him. And
there are other circumstances which I am not at liberty—which it is
not worth while to relate; but his lies about the whole Pemberley
family are endless. From what he said of Miss Darcy, I was thoroughly
prepared to see a proud, reserved, disagreeable girl. Yet he knew to
the contrary himself. He must know that she was as amiable and un-
pretending[10] as we have found her."

"But does Lydia know nothing of this? Can she be ignorant of
what you and Jane seem so well to understand?"

"Oh, yes!—that, that is the worst of all. Till I was in Kent, and saw
so much both of Mr. Darcy and his relation, Colonel Fitzwilliam, I
was ignorant of the truth myself. And when I returned home, the
— —shire was to leave Meryton in a week or fortnight's time. As that
was the case, neither Jane, to whom I related the whole, nor I,
thought it necessary to make our knowledge public; for of what use
could it apparently[11] be to any one, that the good opinion which all

7 Elizabeth has learned to consider Wickham's
"charms" superficial.

8 The word's meanings include "debauched or licen-
tious," "recklessly extravagant," and "lacking in moderation."

9 The narrator rarely interprets Elizabeth's blushes;
the reader is challenged to do so. This particular blush
is probably what Austen would call a "conscious" one:
her aunt's question has brought to mind the many aspects of her connection with Darcy that she has not
revealed.

10 Unpretentious.

11 Seemingly.

12 Important.

13 A small enclosure where horses are turned out to graze.

the neighbourhood had of him, should then be overthrown? And even when it was settled that Lydia should go with Mrs. Forster, the necessity of opening her eyes to his character never occurred to me. That *she* could be in any danger from the deception never entered my head. That such a consequence as *this* should ensue, you may easily believe was far enough from my thoughts."

"When they all removed to Brighton, therefore, you had no reason, I suppose, to believe them fond of each other?"

"Not the slightest. I can remember no symptom of affection on either side; and had any thing of the kind been perceptible, you must be aware that ours is not a family, on which it could be thrown away. When first he entered the corps, she was ready enough to admire him; but so we all were. Every girl in, or near Meryton, was out of her senses about him for the first two months; but he never distinguished *her* by any particular attention, and, consequently, after a moderate period of extravagant and wild admiration, her fancy for him gave way, and others of the regiment, who treated her with more distinction, again became her favourites."

It may be easily believed, that however little of novelty could be added to their fears, hopes, and conjectures, on this interesting[12] subject, by its repeated discussion, no other could detain them from it long, during the whole of the journey. From Elizabeth's thoughts it was never absent. Fixed there by the keenest of all anguish, self-reproach, she could find no interval of ease or forgetfulness.

They travelled as expeditiously as possible; and sleeping one night on the road, reached Longbourn by dinner-time the next day. It was a comfort to Elizabeth to consider that Jane could not have been wearied by long expectations.

The little Gardiners, attracted by the sight of a chaise, were standing on the steps of the house, as they entered the paddock;[13] and, when the carriage drove up to the door, the joyful surprise that lighted up their faces, and displayed itself over their whole bodies, in a variety of capers and frisks, was the first pleasing earnest[14] of their welcome.[15]

Elizabeth jumped out; and, after giving each of them a hasty kiss, hurried into the vestibule, where Jane, who came running down stairs from her mother's apartment,[16] immediately met her.

Elizabeth, as she affectionately embraced her, whilst tears filled the eyes of both, lost not a moment in asking whether any thing had been heard of the fugitives.

"Not yet," replied Jane. "But now that my dear uncle is come, I hope every thing will be well."

"Is my father in town?"

"Yes, he went on Tuesday as I wrote you word."

"And have you heard from him often?"

"We have heard only once. He wrote me a few lines on Wednesday, to say that he had arrived in safety, and to give me his directions,[17] which I particularly begged him to do. He merely added that he should not write again, till he had something of importance to mention."

"And my mother—How is she? How are you all?"

"My mother is tolerably well, I trust; though her spirits are greatly shaken. She is up stairs, and will have great satisfaction in seeing you all. She does not yet leave her dressing-room. Mary and Kitty, thank Heaven! are quite well."

"But you—How are you?" cried Elizabeth. "You look pale. How much you must have gone through!"

Her sister, however, assured her, of her being perfectly well; and their conversation, which had been passing while Mr. and Mrs. Gardiner were engaged with their children, was now put an end to, by the approach of the whole party. Jane ran to her uncle and aunt, and welcomed and thanked them both, with alternate smiles and tears.

When they were all in the drawing room, the questions which Elizabeth had already asked, were of course repeated by the others, and they soon found that Jane had no intelligence to give. The sanguine hope of good, however, which the benevolence of her heart suggested, had not yet deserted her; she still expected that it would

14 Pledge.

15 Austen's novels frequently treat children generically rather than individually. Even when a single child inhabits a scene, as in *Persuasion* an unruly nephew clings to Anne Elliot's back, the child is assigned little personality. More characteristic is the kind of episode sketched here, of unspecified capers and frisks, or comments like this one, from *Sense and Sensibility:* "On every formal visit a child ought to be of the party, by way of provision for discourse. In the present case it took up ten minutes to determine whether the boy were most like his father or mother, and in what particular he resembled either, for of course every body differed, and every body was astonished at the opinion of the others" (I, 6). A striking exception to Austen's general practice, though, is Fanny Price in *Mansfield Park,* whom we first encounter as a sympathetically portrayed child.

16 A suite of rooms assigned to a particular person.

17 Address.

18 This is the sharpest explicit judgment of Mrs. Bennet in *Pride and Prejudice*.

19 Mrs. Bennet realistically imagines the family's utter poverty, given the loss of her husband's property and income.

20 Mrs. Bennet's self-dramatizing imagination now has more than usual to work on. Her projection of dire events is partly calculated (presumably unconsciously) to keep her at the center of the unfolding drama.

21 Dreadful.

all end well, and that every morning would bring some letter, either from Lydia or her father, to explain their proceedings, and perhaps announce the marriage.

Mrs. Bennet, to whose apartment they all repaired, after a few minutes conversation together, received them exactly as might be expected; with tears and lamentations of regret, invectives against the villainous conduct of Wickham, and complaints of her own sufferings and ill usage; blaming every body but the person to whose ill judging indulgence the errors of her daughter must be principally owing.[18]

"If I had been able," said she, "to carry my point in going to Brighton, with all my family, *this* would not have happened; but poor dear Lydia had nobody to take care of her. Why did the Forsters ever let her go out of their sight? I am sure there was some great neglect or other on their side, for she is not the kind of girl to do such a thing, if she had been well looked after. I always thought they were very unfit to have the charge of her; but I was overruled, as I always am. Poor dear child! And now here's Mr. Bennet gone away, and I know he will fight Wickham, wherever he meets him, and then he will be killed, and what is to become of us all?[19] The Collinses will turn us out, before he is cold in his grave; and if you are not kind to us, brother, I do not know what we shall do."[20]

They all exclaimed against such terrific[21] ideas; and Mr. Gardiner, after general assurances of his affection for her and all her family, told her that he meant to be in London the very next day, and would assist Mr. Bennet in every endeavour for recovering Lydia.

"Do not give way to useless alarm," added he; "though it is right to be prepared for the worst, there is no occasion to look on it as certain. It is not quite a week since they left Brighton. In a few days more, we may gain some news of them, and till we know that they are not married, and have no design of marrying, do not let us give the matter over as lost. As soon as I get to town, I shall go to my brother, and make him come home with me to Gracechurch Street, and then we may consult together as to what is to be done."

"Oh! my dear brother," replied Mrs. Bennet, "that is exactly what I could most wish for. And now do, when you get to town, find them out, wherever they may be; and if they are not married already, *make* them marry. And as for wedding clothes,[22] do not let them wait for that, but tell Lydia she shall have as much money as she chuses, to buy them, after they are married. And, above all things, keep Mr. Bennet from fighting. Tell him what a dreadful state I am in,—that I am frightened out of my wits; and have such tremblings, such flutterings, all over me, such spasms in my side, and pains in my head, and such beatings at heart, that I can get no rest by night nor by day. And tell my dear Lydia, not to give any directions about her clothes, till she has seen me, for she does not know which are the best warehouses.[23] Oh, brother, how kind you are! I know you will contrive it all."

But Mr. Gardiner, though he assured her again of his earnest endeavours in the cause, could not avoid recommending moderation to her, as well in her hopes as her fears; and after talking with her in this manner till dinner was on the table, they left her to vent all her feelings on the housekeeper, who attended, in the absence of her daughters.

Though her brother and sister were persuaded that there was no real occasion for such a seclusion from the family, they did not attempt to oppose it, for they knew that she had not prudence enough to hold her tongue before the servants, while they waited at table, and judged it better that *one* only of the household, and the one whom they could most trust, should comprehend all her fears and solicitude on the subject.[24]

In the dining-room they were soon joined by Mary and Kitty, who had been too busily engaged in their separate apartments, to make their appearance before. One came from her books, and the other from her toilette. The faces of both, however, were tolerably calm; and no change was visible in either, except that the loss of her favourite sister, or the anger which she had herself incurred in this business, had given something more of fretfulness than usual, to the accents of Kitty. As for Mary, she was mistress enough of herself to

22 Trousseau.

23 Shops. "Warehouse" was considered a more dignified term. Mrs. Bennet sees in the subject of Lydia's wardrobe another opportunity for being important herself.

24 The insistence in eighteenth- and nineteenth-century servants' manuals that servants must keep their employers' secrets suggests by implication how likely they were to spread them. In the Bennet household, there are approximately as many servants as there are family members: it is easy to be overheard, even if one is not, like Mrs. Bennet, always indiscreet. What servants hear, they may well pass on. Eliza Haywood, in 1743, warns against "discover[ing] the Affairs of the Family where you live. The smallest and most trivial Action *there* should never escape your Lips, because you cannot be a Judge what are really such, and what are the contrary. Things that may seem to you Matters of perfect Indifference, may happen to prove of great Importance to those concerned in them" (Eliza Haywood, *A Present for a Servant-Maid. Or, The Sure Means of Gaining Love and Esteem* [New York: Garland, 1985], 13). An early-nineteenth-century manual has special warnings for the hall porter, whose "best qualities are patience and good temper, to which may be added, secrecy in regard to the affairs, connections, and intercourse of the family. A close tongue, and an inflexible countenance, are, therefore, indispensable, and he should practice the maxim of hearing and seeing all, but saying nothing" (Samuel Adams and Sarah Adams, *The Complete Servant* (1825), ed. Ann Haley [Lewes: Southover Press, 1989], 150). Elizabeth and Jane hope that the housekeeper will keep to herself the knowledge of their mother's responses to domestic crisis.

25 Such observations appear not only in many conduct books but also in virtually all novels that deal with sexual impropriety. Under the circumstances, though, Mary's reliance on these standard observations registers her lack of emotional involvement with her sister's situation or with the potential damage to the entire family. Her books protect her from real life and real feeling. Even Kitty, in comparison, shows some slight emotional response, self-centered though it is.

26 Mentally overwhelmed.

27 Lydia's continuing to live with Wickham without marrying him, and the consequent disgrace of the entire family.

28 Acknowledge.

whisper to Elizabeth with a countenance of grave reflection, soon after they were seated at table,

"This is a most unfortunate affair; and will probably be much talked of. But we must stem the tide of malice, and pour into the wounded bosoms of each other, the balm of sisterly consolation."

Then, perceiving in Elizabeth no inclination of replying, she added, "Unhappy as the event must be for Lydia, we may draw from it this useful lesson; that loss of virtue in a female is irretrievable—that one false step involves her in endless ruin—that her reputation is no less brittle than it is beautiful,—and that she cannot be too much guarded in her behaviour towards the undeserving of the other sex."[25]

Elizabeth lifted up her eyes in amazement, but was too much oppressed[26] to make any reply. Mary, however, continued to console herself with such kind of moral extractions from the evil before them.

In the afternoon, the two elder Miss Bennets were able to be for half an hour by themselves; and Elizabeth instantly availed herself of the opportunity of making many enquiries, which Jane was equally eager to satisfy. After joining in general lamentations over the dreadful sequel of this event,[27] which Elizabeth considered as all but certain, and Miss Bennet could not assert to be wholly impossible, the former continued the subject, by saying, "But tell me all and every thing about it, which I have not already heard. Give me farther particulars. What did Colonel Forster say? Had they no apprehension of any thing before the elopement took place? They must have seen them together for ever."

"Colonel Forster did own[28] that he had often suspected some partiality, especially on Lydia's side, but nothing to give him any alarm. I am so grieved for him. His behaviour was attentive and kind to the utmost. He *was* coming to us, in order to assure us of his concern, before he had any idea of their not being gone to Scotland: when that apprehension first got abroad, it hastened his journey."

"And was Denny convinced that Wickham would not marry? Did he know of their intending to go off? Had Colonel Forster seen Denny himself?"

"Yes; but, when questioned by *him,* Denny denied knowing any thing of their plan, and would not give his real opinion about it. He did not repeat his persuasion of their not marrying—and from *that,* I am inclined to hope, he might have been misunderstood before."

"And till Colonel Forster came himself, not one of you entertained a doubt, I suppose, of their being really married?"

"How was it possible that such an idea should enter our brains! I felt a little uneasy—a little fearful of my sister's happiness with him in marriage, because I knew that his conduct had not been always quite right. My father and mother knew nothing of that, they only felt how imprudent a match it must be.[29] Kitty then owned, with a very natural triumph on knowing more than the rest of us, that in Lydia's last letter, she had prepared her for such a step. She had known, it seems, of their being in love with each other, many weeks."

"But not before they went to Brighton?"

"No, I believe not."

"And did Colonel Forster appear to think ill of Wickham himself? Does he know his real character?"

"I must confess that he did not speak so well of Wickham as he formerly did. He believed him to be imprudent and extravagant. And since this sad affair has taken place, it is said, that he left Meryton greatly in debt; but I hope this may be false."

"Oh, Jane, had we been less secret, had we told what we knew of him, this could not have happened!"

"Perhaps it would have been better," replied her sister. "But to expose the former faults of any person, without knowing what their present feelings were, seemed unjustifiable. We acted with the best intentions."

"Could Colonel Forster repeat the particulars of Lydia's note to his wife?"

"He brought it with him for us to see."

Jane then took it from her pocket-book,[30] and gave it to Elizabeth. These were the contents:

29 Again, from a financial point of view.

30 A book carried in the pocket for notes and papers.

31 Laughter figures prominently in *Pride and Prejudice,* with different meanings for different characters. Mr. Bennet expresses his philosophical stance through his laughter, a fact made explicit later in the novel. Elizabeth uses laughter as a defense against strong feeling. Lydia, whether laughing in the carriage with Kitty or reporting her laughter in a letter, laughs mindlessly and conveys her lack of reflectiveness by her laughter. See Patricia Meyer Spacks, "Austen's Laughter," *Women's Studies: An Interdisciplinary Journal,* 15 (1988), 71–85.

32 Decorated with needlework.

33 Lydia sounds anything but serious, but Elizabeth means that she seriously expects to be married.

"My dear Harriet,

"You will laugh when you know where I am gone, and I cannot help laughing myself at your surprise to-morrow morning, as soon as I am missed.[31] I am going to Gretna Green, and if you cannot guess with who, I shall think you a simpleton, for there is but one man in the world I love, and he is an angel. I should never be happy without him, so think it no harm to be off. You need not send them word at Longbourn of my going, if you do not like it, for it will make the surprise the greater, when I write to them, and sign my name Lydia Wickham. What a good joke it will be! I can hardly write for laughing. Pray make my excuses to Pratt, for not keeping my engagement, and dancing with him to night. Tell him I hope he will excuse me when he knows all, and tell him I will dance with him at the next ball we meet, with great pleasure. I shall send for my clothes when I get to Longbourn; but I wish you would tell Sally to mend a great slit in my worked[32] muslin gown, before they are packed up. Good bye. Give my love to Colonel Forster, I hope you will drink to our good journey.

"Your affectionate friend,
"Lydia Bennet."

"Oh! thoughtless, thoughtless Lydia!" cried Elizabeth when she had finished it. "What a letter is this, to be written at such a moment! But at least it shews, that *she* was serious on the subject of their journey.[33] Whatever he might afterwards persuade her to, it was not on her side a *scheme* of infamy. My poor father! how he must have felt it!"

"I never saw any one so shocked. He could not speak a word for full ten minutes. My mother was taken ill immediately, and the whole house in such confusion!"

"Oh! Jane," cried Elizabeth, "was there a servant belonging to it, who did not know the whole story before the end of the day?"

"I do not know.—I hope there was.—But to be guarded at such a time, is very difficult. My mother was in hysterics, and though I endeavoured to give her every assistance in my power, I am afraid I did not do so much as I might have done! but the horror of what might possibly happen, almost took from me my faculties."

"Your attendance upon her, has been too much for you. You do not look well. Oh! that I had been with you, you have had every care and anxiety upon yourself alone."

"Mary and Kitty have been very kind, and would have shared in every fatigue, I am sure; but I did not think it right for either of them. Kitty is slight and delicate and Mary studies so much, that her hours of repose should not be broken in on. My aunt Phillips came to Longbourn on Tuesday, after my father went away; and was so good as to stay till Thursday with me. She was of great use and comfort to us all, and Lady Lucas has been very kind; she walked here on Wednesday morning to condole with us, and offered her services, or any of her daughters, if they could be of use to us."

"She had better have stayed at home," cried Elizabeth; "perhaps she *meant* well, but, under such a misfortune as this, one cannot see too little of one's neighbours. Assistance is impossible; condolence, insufferable. Let them triumph over us at a distance, and be satisfied."

She then proceeded to inquire into the measures which her father had intended to pursue, while in town, for the recovery of his daughter.

"He meant I believe," replied Jane, "to go to Epsom, the place where they last changed horses, see the postilions[34] and try if any thing could be made out from them. His principal object must be, to discover the number of the hackney coach which took them from Clapham. It had come with a fare from London; and as he thought the circumstance of a gentleman and lady's removing from one carriage into another, might be remarked, he meant to make enquiries at Clapham. If he could any how discover at what house the coachman had before set down his fare, he determined to make enquiries there, and hoped it might not be impossible to find out the stand and number of the coach. I do not know of any other designs that he had formed: but he was in such a hurry to be gone, and his spirits so greatly discomposed, that I had difficulty in finding out even so much as this."

34 Men, hired from the places where one changed horses when traveling post, who rode on one of the horses in order to guide them.

6

1 Mail.

2 Lawless behavior.

3 Flirtations. Rumor now has it that Wickham has seduced, or attempted to seduce, every tradesman's daughter.

THE WHOLE PARTY WERE IN hopes of a letter from Mr. Bennet the next morning, but the post[1] came in without bringing a single line from him. His family knew him to be on all common occasions, a most negligent and dilatory correspondent; but at such a time, they had hoped for exertion. They were forced to conclude, that he had no pleasing intelligence to send, but even of *that* they would have been glad to be certain. Mr. Gardiner had waited only for the letters before he set off.

When he was gone, they were certain at least of receiving constant information of what was going on, and their uncle promised, at parting, to prevail on Mr. Bennet to return to Longbourn, as soon as he could, to the great consolation of his sister, who considered it as the only security for her husband's not being killed in a duel.

Mrs. Gardiner and the children were to remain in Hertfordshire a few days longer, as the former thought her presence might be serviceable to her nieces. She shared in their attendance on Mrs. Bennet, and was a great comfort to them, in their hours of freedom. Their other aunt also visited them frequently, and always, as she said, with the design of cheering and heartening them up, though as she never came without reporting some fresh instance of Wickham's extravagance or irregularity,[2] she seldom went away without leaving them more dispirited than she found them.

All Meryton seemed striving to blacken the man, who, but three months before, had been almost an angel of light. He was declared to be in debt to every tradesman in the place, and his intrigues,[3] all honoured with the title of seduction, had been extended into every tradesman's family. Every body declared that he was the wickedest young man in the world; and every body began to find out, that they had always distrusted the appearance of his goodness.[4] Elizabeth, though she did not credit[5] above half of what was said, believed enough to make her former assurance of her sister's ruin[6] still more certain; and even Jane, who believed still less of it, became almost hopeless, more especially as the time was now come, when if they had gone to Scotland, which she had never before entirely despaired of, they must in all probability have gained some news of them.

Mr. Gardiner left Longbourn on Sunday; on Tuesday, his wife received a letter from him; it told them that, on his arrival, he had immediately found out his brother, and persuaded him to come to Gracechurch Street. That Mr. Bennet had been to Epsom[7] and Clapham,[8] before his arrival, but without gaining any satisfactory information; and that he was now determined to enquire at all the principal hotels in town, as Mr. Bennet thought it possible they might have gone to one of them, on their first coming to London, before they procured lodgings. Mr. Gardiner himself did not expect any success from this measure, but as his brother was eager in it, he meant to assist him in pursuing it. He added, that Mr. Bennet seemed wholly disinclined at present, to leave London, and promised to write again very soon. There was also a postscript to this effect.

"I have written to Colonel Forster to desire him to find out, if possible, from some of the young man's intimates in the regiment, whether Wickham has any relations or connections, who would be likely to know in what part of town he has now concealed himself. If there were any one, that one could apply to with a probability of gaining such a clue as that, it might be of essential consequence. At present we have nothing to guide us. Colonel Forster will, I dare say, do every thing in his power to satisfy us on this head. But, on second thoughts, perhaps Lizzy could tell us what relations he has now living, better than any other person."

Elizabeth was at no loss to understand from whence this deference to her authority proceeded;[9] but it was not in her power to give

4 Community opinion, in other words, is not only undependable but fickle.

5 Believe.

6 That is, her seduction without the hope of marriage.

7 A town in Surrey, southwest of London; in Austen's time, the location of a spa. Epsom salts derive their name from the fact that they were originally made by boiling down mineral water from Epsom.

8 South of London; now a part of Greater London. In the late eighteenth and nineteenth centuries, it was a locale for residents of wealthy London merchants, who built splendid houses there.

9 Since the Gardiners suspect that Elizabeth and Darcy love each other, they may also suspect that Darcy has shared with his beloved intimate details about Wickham. Elizabeth has told them explicitly that she has sources of information about Wickham's character and history.

10 We would say "looked over her shoulder."

any information of so satisfactory a nature, as the compliment deserved.

She had never heard of his having had any relations, except a father and mother, both of whom had been dead many years. It was possible, however, that some of his companions in the——shire might be able to give more information; and, though she was not very sanguine in expecting it, the application was a something to look forward to.

Every day at Longbourn was now a day of anxiety; but the most anxious part of each was when the post was expected. The arrival of letters was the first grand object of every morning's impatience. Through letters, whatever of good or bad was to be told, would be communicated, and every succeeding day was expected to bring some news of importance.

But before they heard again from Mr. Gardiner, a letter arrived for their father, from a different quarter, from Mr. Collins; which, as Jane had received directions to open all that came for him in his absence, she accordingly read; and Elizabeth, who knew what curiosities his letters always were, looked over her,[10] and read it likewise. It was as follows:

"My dear Sir,

"I feel myself called upon, by our relationship, and my situation in life, to condole with you on the grievous affliction you are now suffering under, of which we were yesterday informed by a letter from Hertfordshire. Be assured, my dear Sir, that Mrs. Collins and myself sincerely sympathise with you, and all your respectable family, in your present distress which must be of the bitterest kind, because proceeding from a cause which no time can remove. No arguments shall be wanting on my part, that can alleviate so severe a misfortune; or that may comfort you, under a circumstance that must be of all others most afflicting to a parent's mind. The death of your daughter would have been a blessing in comparison of this. And it is the more to be lamented, because there is reason to suppose, as my dear Charlotte informs me, that this licentiousness of behaviour in your daughter, has proceeded from a faulty degree of indulgence, though, at the same time, for the consolation of yourself and Mrs. Bennet, I am inclined to think that her own disposition must be naturally bad, or she could not be guilty of such an enormity, at so early an age. Howsoever that may be, you are grievously to be pitied, in which opinion I am not only joined by Mrs. Collins, but likewise by Lady Catherine and her daughter, to whom I have related the affair. They agree with me in apprehending that this false step in one daughter will be injurious to the fortunes of all the others, for who, as Lady Catherine herself condescendingly[11] says, will connect themselves with such a family. And this consideration leads me moreover to reflect with augmented satisfaction on a certain event of last November, for had it been otherwise, I must have been involved in all your sorrow and disgrace.[12] Let me then advise you then, my dear Sir, to console yourself as much as possible, to throw off your unworthy child from your affection for ever, and leave her to reap the fruits of her own heinous offense.

"I am, dear Sir, &c.&c."

Mr. Gardiner did not write again, till he had received an answer from Colonel Forster; and then he had nothing of a pleasant nature to send. It was not known that Wickham had a single relation, with whom he kept up any connection, and it was certain that he had no near one living. His former acquaintances had been numerous; but since he had been in the militia, it did not appear that he was on terms of particular friendship with any of them. There was no one therefore who could be pointed out, as likely to give any news of him. And in the wretched state of his own finances, there was a very powerful motive for secrecy, in addition to his fear of discovery by Lydia's relations, for it had just transpired that he had left gaming[13] debts behind him, to a very considerable amount. Colonel Forster believed

11 A strange instance of Lady Catherine's "condescension." Does Mr. Collins consider it "condescending" for her even to mention such a subject?

12 Mr. Collins's notion of "comfort" seems peculiar.

13 Gambling.

14 That is, to tradesmen.

15 Usually meaning gambling debts, which, unlike debts to merchants, were not legally enforceable. A man who failed to pay debts of honor, however, would be ostracized by his fellows.

16 In much eighteenth-century fiction, a gamester is the very type of the dishonorable man. *Cecilia* contains a particularly vivid instance in Mr. Harrell, one of the heroine's guardians, who lives a life of conspicuous extravagance, who apparently tries to sell Cecilia herself to a dissipated nobleman in order to pay a gambling debt, and who finally commits suicide when his losses overwhelm him.

17 A letter from Darcy to Elizabeth would have signaled their engagement, since only if engaged could a man and woman properly correspond. In *Emma,* Jane Fairfax and Frank Churchill take part in a secret correspondence—but only because they are secretly engaged.

that more than a thousand pounds would be necessary to clear his expences at Brighton. He owed a good deal in the town,[14] but his debts of honour[15] were still more formidable. Mr. Gardiner did not attempt to conceal these particulars from the Longbourn family, Jane heard them with horror. "A gamester!"[16] she cried. "This is wholly unexpected. I had not an idea of it."

Mr. Gardiner added in his letter, that they might expect to see their father at home on the following day, which was Saturday. Rendered spiritless by the ill success of all their endeavours, he had yielded to his brother-in-law's intreaty that he would return to his family, and leave it to him to do, whatever occasion might suggest to be advisable for continuing their pursuit. When Mrs. Bennet was told of this, she did not express so much satisfaction as her children expected, considering what her anxiety for his life had been before.

"What, is he coming home, and without poor Lydia!" she cried. "Sure he will not leave London before he has found them. Who is to fight Wickham, and make him marry her, if he comes away?"

As Mrs. Gardiner began to wish to be at home, it was settled that she and her children should go to London, at the same time that Mr. Bennet came from it. The coach, therefore, took them the first stage of their journey, and brought its master back to Longbourn.

Mrs. Gardiner went away in all the perplexity about Elizabeth and her Derbyshire friend, that had attended her from that part of the world. His name had never been voluntarily mentioned before them by her niece; and the kind of half-expectation which Mrs. Gardiner had formed, of their being followed by a letter from him,[17] had ended in nothing. Elizabeth had received none since her return, that could come from Pemberley.

The present unhappy state of the family, rendered any other excuse for the lowness of her spirits unnecessary; nothing, therefore, could be fairly conjectured from *that,* though Elizabeth, who was by this time tolerably well acquainted with her own feelings, was perfectly aware, that, had she known nothing of Darcy, she could have borne the dread of Lydia's infamy somewhat better. It would have spared her, she thought, one sleepless night out of two.

Thomas Rowlandson (1756–1827), "The Gaming Table." The facial expressions of
the gambling men in this satiric print suggest the intensity of their involvement.
The military officer, unlike Wickham, is only an onlooker, but the eagerness of his
face and posture hints that he may soon become an active participant.

18 Outcome.

19 Display.

20 A garment worn when a man is having his hair powdered, usually an old dressing gown, since the procedure inevitably soils whatever a person is wearing.

21 East of Brighton on the Sussex coast. In Austen's time it was only a village, not yet significant as a resort, although several of King George III's children had visited it in the summer of 1780. It began to develop as a resort around 1841 (John K. Walton, *The English Seaside Resort: A Social History, 1750–1914* [New York: St. Martin's Press, 1983], 80). Kitty would not have found it an exciting destination.

When Mr. Bennet arrived, he had all the appearance of his usual philosophic composure. He said as little as he had ever been in the habit of saying; made no mention of the business that had taken him away, and it was some time before his daughters had courage to speak of it.

It was not till the afternoon, when he joined them at tea, that Elizabeth ventured to introduce the subject; and then, on her briefly expressing her sorrow for what he must have endured, he replied, "Say nothing of that. Who should suffer but myself? It has been my own doing, and I ought to feel it."

"You must not be too severe upon yourself," replied Elizabeth.

"You may well warn me against such an evil. Human nature is so prone to fall into it! No, Lizzy, let me once in my life feel how much I have been to blame. I am not afraid of being overpowered by the impression. It will pass away soon enough."

"Do you suppose them to be in London?"

"Yes; where else can they be so well concealed?"

"And Lydia used to want to go to London," added Kitty.

"She is happy, then," said her father drily; "and her residence there will probably be of some duration."

Then, after a short silence, he continued, "Lizzy, I bear you no ill-will for being justified in your advice to me last May, which, considering the event,[18] shews some greatness of mind."

They were interrupted by Miss Bennet, who came to fetch her mother's tea.

"This is a parade,"[19] he cried, "which does one good; it gives such an elegance to misfortune! Another day I will do the same; I will sit in my library, in my night cap and powdering gown,[20] and give as much trouble as I can,—or, perhaps, I may defer it, till Kitty runs away."

"I am not going to run away, Papa," said Kitty fretfully; "if *I* should ever go to Brighton, I would behave better than Lydia."

"*You* go to Brighton.—I would not trust you so near it as East Bourne,[21] for fifty pounds! No, Kitty, I have at last learnt to be cautious, and you will feel the effects of it. No officer is ever to enter into my house again, nor even to pass through the village. Balls will be absolutely prohibited, unless you stand up[22] with one of your sisters. And you are never to stir out of doors, till you can prove, that you have spent ten minutes of every day in a rational manner."

Kitty, who took all these threats in a serious light, began to cry.

"Well, well," said he, "do not make yourself unhappy. If you are a good girl for the next ten years, I will take you to a review[23] at the end of them."

22 To dance.

23 Public military ceremony, a formal inspection of the troops by senior officers.

7

1 They are "girls," although Jane is twenty-three years old, until they are married.

TWO DAYS AFTER MR. BENNET'S RETURN, as Jane and Elizabeth were walking together in the shrubbery behind the house, they saw the housekeeper coming towards them, and, concluding that she came to call them to their mother, went forward to meet her; but, instead of the expected summons, when they approached her, she said to Miss Bennet, "I beg your pardon, madam, for interrupting you, but I was in hopes you might have got some good news from town, so I took the liberty of coming to ask."

"What do you mean, Hill? We have heard nothing from town."

"Dear madam," cried Mrs. Hill, in great astonishment, "don't you know there is an express come for master from Mr. Gardiner? He has been here this half hour, and master has had a letter."

Away ran the girls,[1] too eager to get in to have time for speech. They ran through the vestibule into the breakfast room; from thence to the library;—their father was in neither; and they were on the point of seeking him upstairs with their mother, when they were met by the butler, who said,

"If you are looking for my master, ma'am, he is walking towards the little copse."

Upon this information, they instantly passed through the hall once more, and ran across the lawn after their father, who was deliberately pursuing his way towards a small wood on one side of the paddock.

Jane, who was not so light, nor so much in the habit of running as Elizabeth,[2] soon lagged behind, while her sister, panting for breath, came up with him, and eagerly cried out,

"Oh, Papa, what news? what news? have you heard from my uncle?"

"Yes, I have had a letter from him by express."

"Well, and what news does it bring? good or bad?"

"What is there of good to be expected?" said he, taking the letter from his pocket; "but perhaps you would like to read it."

Elizabeth impatiently caught it from his hand. Jane now came up.

"Read it aloud," said their father, "for I hardly know myself what it is about."

> "Gracechurch-street,
> Monday,
> August 2.

"My Dear Brother,

"At last I am able to send you some tidings of my niece, and such as, upon the whole, I hope will give you satisfaction. Soon after you left me on Saturday, I was fortunate enough to find out in what part of London they were. The particulars, I reserve till we meet. It is enough to know they are discovered, I have seen them both—"

"Then it is, as I always hoped," cried Jane; "they are married!"

Elizabeth read on; "I have seen them both. They are not married, nor can I find there was any intention of being so; but if you are willing to perform the engagements[3] which I have ventured to make on your side, I hope it will not be long before they are. All that is required of you is, to assure to your daughter, by settlement,[4] her equal share of the five thousand pounds, secured among your children after the decease of yourself and my sister; and, moreover, to enter into an engagement of allowing her, during your life, one hundred pounds per annum. These are conditions which, considering

2 The information that Elizabeth is in the habit of running makes it retrospectively clear that her unconventional journey to Netherfield to see Jane was not anomalous.

3 Commitments.

4 A legally binding agreement, customarily entered into before marriage, governing the distribution of money for a couple. Ordinarily, such an agreement would assign money from the groom's family for the wife's personal spending, for children who survived their father, and for the wife in widowhood. Money from the bride's family would go to the groom as a dowry. In this case, however, no money from the groom's family is forthcoming.

5 To make part of the marriage settlement providing for Lydia if she is widowed.

6 Presumably his attorney.

7 In other words, that she should stay with them until she is married.

every thing, I had no hesitation in complying with, as far as I thought myself privileged, for you. I shall send this by express, that no time may be lost in bringing me your answer. You will easily comprehend, from these particulars, that Mr. Wickham's circumstances are not so hopeless as they are generally believed to be. The world has been deceived in that respect; and I am happy to say, there will be some little money, even when all his debts are discharged, to settle on my niece,[5] in addition to her own fortune. If, as I conclude will be the case, you send me full powers to act in your name, throughout the whole of this business, I will immediately give directions to Haggerston[6] for preparing a proper settlement. There will not be the smallest occasion for your coming to town again; therefore stay quietly at Longbourn, and depend on my diligence and care. Send back your answer as soon as you can, and be careful to write explicitly. We have judged it best, that my niece should be married from this house,[7] of which I hope you will approve. She comes to us to-day. I shall write again as soon as any thing more is determined on. Yours, &c.

"Edw. Gardiner."

"Is it possible!" cried Elizabeth, when she had finished. "Can it be possible that he will marry her?"

"Wickham is not so undeserving, then, as we thought him," said her sister. "My dear father, I congratulate you."

"And have you answered the letter?" cried Elizabeth.

"No; but it must be done soon."

Most earnestly did she then intreat him to lose no more time before he wrote.

"Oh! my dear father," she cried, "come back, and write immediately. Consider how important every moment is, in such a case."

"Let me write for you," said Jane, "if you dislike the trouble yourself."

"I dislike it very much," he replied; "but it must be done."

And so saying, he turned back with them, and walked towards the house.

"And may I ask?" said Elizabeth, "but the terms, I suppose, must be complied with."

"Complied with! I am only ashamed of his asking so little."

"And they *must* marry! Yet he is *such* a man!"

"Yes, yes, they must marry. There is nothing else to be done.[8] But there are two things that I want very much to know:—one is, how much money your uncle has laid down, to bring it about; and the other, how am I ever to pay him."

"Money! My uncle!" cried Jane, "what do you mean, Sir?"

"I mean, that no man in his senses, would marry Lydia on so slight a temptation as one hundred a-year during my life, and fifty[9] after I am gone."

"That is very true," said Elizabeth; "though it had not occurred to me before. His debts to be discharged, and something still to remain! Oh! it must be my uncle's doings! Generous, good man, I am afraid he has distressed himself. A small sum could not do all this."

"No," said her father, "Wickham's a fool, if he takes her with a farthing[10] less than ten thousand pounds. I should be sorry to think so ill of him, in the very beginning of our relationship."

"Ten thousand pounds! Heaven forbid! How is half such a sum to be repaid?"

Mr. Bennet made no answer, and each of them, deep in thought, continued silent till they reached the house. Their father then went to the library to write, and the girls walked into the breakfast-room.

"And they are really to be married!" cried Elizabeth, as soon as they were by themselves. "How strange this is! And for *this* we are to be thankful. That they should marry, small as is their chance of happiness, and wretched as is his character, we are forced to rejoice. Oh, Lydia!"

"I comfort myself with thinking," replied Jane, "that he certainly would not marry Lydia, if he had not a real regard for her.[11] Though our kind uncle has done something towards clearing him, I cannot believe that ten thousand pounds, or anything like it, has been ad-

8 Marriage, and only marriage, would effectively erase the disgrace incurred by Lydia's sexual misconduct.

9 The amount of interest to be expected from the thousand pounds that Lydia will inherit. Mr. Bennet, too, considers money the motive for marriage, although he himself has married for other reasons; it doesn't occur to him as even a remote possibility that someone might want to marry Lydia because of her personal attractions.

10 A coin of tiny value, worth a quarter of a penny.

11 Only Jane could comfort herself thus: Wickham is clearly motivated by financial considerations.

12 Support, favor.

13 She should be miserable from a sense of how badly she has behaved and how generous her aunt and uncle are in taking her in despite her disgrace.

14 In other words, she is determined to believe this: she doesn't believe it at present.

15 Please myself with the hope.

16 It is difficult to imagine Wickham and Lydia living in a rational manner. Jane's expectation that they will do so indicates not only her characteristic optimism and insistence on thinking well of everyone but also her commitment, which she shares with Elizabeth, to the idea that reason should govern behavior.

17 State of excitement.

vanced. He has children of his own, and may have more. How could he spare half ten thousand pounds?"

"If we are ever able to learn what Wickham's debts have been," said Elizabeth, "and how much is settled on his side on our sister, we shall exactly know what Mr. Gardiner has done for them, because Wickham has not sixpence of his own. The kindness of my uncle and aunt can never be requited. Their taking her home, and affording her their personal protection and countenance,[12] is such a sacrifice to her advantage, as years of gratitude cannot enough acknowledge. By this time she is actually with them! If such goodness does not make her miserable now, she will never deserve to be happy![13] What a meeting for her, when she first sees my aunt!"

"We must endeavour to forget all that has passed on either side," said Jane: "I hope and trust they will yet be happy. His consenting to marry her is a proof, I will believe,[14] that he is come to a right way of thinking. Their mutual affection will steady them; and I flatter myself[15] they will settle so quietly, and live in so rational a manner,[16] as may in time make their past imprudence forgotten."

"Their conduct has been such," replied Elizabeth, "as neither you, nor I, nor any body can ever forget. It is useless to talk of it."

It now occurred to the girls that their mother was in all likelihood perfectly ignorant of what had happened. They went to the library, therefore, and asked their father, whether he would not wish them to make it known to her. He was writing and, without raising his head, coolly replied,

"Just as you please."

"May we take my uncle's letter to read to her?"

"Take whatever you like, and get away."

Elizabeth took the letter from his writing table, and they went up stairs together. Mary and Kitty were both with Mrs. Bennet: one communication would, therefore, do for all. After a slight preparation for good news, the letter was read aloud. Mrs. Bennet could hardly contain herself. As soon as Jane had read Mr. Gardiner's hope of Lydia's being soon married, her joy burst forth, and every following sentence added to its exuberance. She was now in an irritation[17] as violent from delight, as she had ever been fidgetty from alarm and vexation. To know that her daughter would be married was enough. She was disturbed by no fear for her felicity, nor humbled by any remembrance of her misconduct.

"My dear, dear Lydia!" she cried: "This is delightful[18] indeed!—She will be married!—I shall see her again!—She will be married at sixteen!—My good, kind brother!—I knew how it would be—I knew he would manage every thing. How I long to see her! and to see dear Wickham too! But the clothes, the wedding clothes! I will write to my sister Gardiner about them directly. Lizzy, my dear, run down to your father, and ask him how much he will give her. Stay, stay, I will go myself. Ring the bell, Kitty, for Hill. I will put on my things in a moment. My dear, dear Lydia!—How merry we shall be together when we meet!"

Her eldest daughter endeavoured to give some relief to the violence of these transports, by leading her thoughts to the obligations which Mr. Gardiner's behaviour laid them all under.

"For we must attribute this happy conclusion," she added, "in a great measure, to his kindness. We are persuaded that he has pledged himself to assist Mr. Wickham with money."

"Well," cried her mother, "it is all very right; who should do it but her own uncle? If he had not had a family of his own,[19] I and my children must have had all his money you know; and it is the first time we have ever had any thing from him, except a few presents. Well! I am so happy. In a short time, I shall have a daughter married. Mrs. Wickham! How well it sounds. And she was only sixteen last June. My dear Jane, I am in such a flutter, that I am sure I can't write; so I will dictate, and you write for me. We will settle with your father about the money afterwards; but the things should be ordered immediately."

She was then proceeding to all the particulars of calico, muslin, and cambric, and would shortly have dictated some very plentiful orders, had not Jane, though with some difficulty, persuaded her to wait, till her father was at leisure to be consulted. One day's delay, she observed, would be of small importance; and her mother was too happy, to be quite so obstinate as usual. Other schemes too came into her head.

18 A weirdly inappropriate adjective that emphasizes once more Mrs. Bennet's total commitment to her daughters' marriages as the denouement resolving every difficulty and declaring her own success in the world.

19 A very large "if."

20 Jane expects that Lydia and Wickham would live in a rational manner; Elizabeth realizes that rational happiness cannot be expected for them—and she does not value the notion of *irrational* happiness.

"I will go to Meryton," said she, "as soon as I am dressed, and tell the good, good news to my sister Phillips. And as I come back, I can call on Lady Lucas and Mrs. Long. Kitty, run down and order the carriage. An airing would do me a great deal of good, I am sure. Girls, can I do anything for you in Meryton? Oh! here comes Hill. My dear Hill, have you heard the good news? Miss Lydia is going to be married; and you shall all have a bowl of punch, to make merry at her wedding."

Mrs. Hill began instantly to express her joy. Elizabeth received her congratulations amongst the rest, and then, sick of this folly, took refuge in her own room, that she might think with freedom.

Poor Lydia's situation must, at best, be bad enough; but that it was no worse, she had need to be thankful. She felt it so; and though, in looking forward, neither rational happiness[20] nor worldly prosperity, could be justly expected for her sister; in looking back to what they had feared, only two hours ago, she felt all the advantages of what they had gained.

8

MR. BENNET HAD VERY OFTEN WISHED, before this period of his life, that, instead of spending his whole income, he had laid by an annual sum, for the better provision of his children, and of his wife, if she survived him. He now wished it more than ever. Had he done his duty in that respect, Lydia need not have been indebted to her uncle, for whatever of honour or credit[1] could now be purchased for her. The satisfaction of prevailing on one of the most worthless young men in Great Britain[2] to be her husband, might then have rested in its proper place.

He was seriously concerned, that a cause of so little advantage to any one, should be forwarded at the sole expence of his brother-in-law, and he was determined, if possible, to find out the extent of his assistance, and to discharge the obligation as soon as he could.

When first Mr. Bennet had married, economy was held[3] to be perfectly useless; for, of course, they were to have a son. The son was to join in cutting off the entail,[4] as soon as he should be of age, and the widow and younger children would by that means be provided for. Five daughters successively entered the world, but yet the son was to come; and Mrs. Bennet, for many years after Lydia's birth, had been certain that he would. This event had at last been despaired of, but it was then too late to be saving.[5] Mrs. Bennet had no turn[6] for economy, and her husband's love of independence[7] had alone prevented their exceeding their income.

Five thousand pounds was settled by marriage articles on Mrs. Bennet and the children. But in what proportions it should be di-

1 Reputation. The idea of *purchasing* honor or reputation is of course ironic.

2 The phrase emphatically summarizes the new evaluation of Wickham.

3 Considered.

4 Since the entail was intended to ensure male inheritance, a son, the prospective heir, could join with his father in breaking it off and making new arrangements for the transmission of the estate.

5 Frugal.

6 Aptitude, capacity.

7 Austen usually uses *independence* and its cognates with financial reference, and she does so here. But this usage is unusual in implying the more familiar sense of the word as well: "freedom from subjection, or from the influence of others; individual liberty of thought or action" *(OED)*. Because Mr. Bennet loves his individual liberty, it is crucial for him to preserve the financial resources that make it possible.

8 Commitments.

9 The preceding paragraph and this one exemplify once more Austen's skill at manipulating and modulating the techniques of free indirect discourse. The sentences immediately before this appear to be a third-person summary of Mr. Bennet's letter, but they strongly suggest his voice: put into the first person, they might well be sentences from the letter. One can't be sure about the sentence opening this paragraph: would Mr. Bennet acknowledge in a letter to his brother-in-law his wish to have as little trouble as possible? Perhaps; perhaps not. The next sentence, however, refers to his transports of rage: we're now securely in the consciousness of the narrator. The movement between Mr. Bennet's mind and the narrator's suggests that Elizabeth's father, who claims to get his pleasure from laughing at people, may have depths of feeling that he does not customarily reveal.

10 Appropriate or tolerable resignation.

11 Become a prostitute—a common fate, especially in literary renditions, of young women who "lost their virtue."

12 If a girl's parents were able and willing to help her, seclusion would be a relatively benign alternative to prostitution. Since known deviation from chastity in an unmarried woman made her permanently unmarriageable and permanently disgraced, she could no longer function in polite society but must be kept out of sight. A married woman's deviation from sexual propriety was considered equally reprehensible. Thus after committing adultery, Maria in *Mansfield Park* is sent off to live with an aunt in permanent banishment.

13 Having her married.

14 The "good-natured wishes" of spiteful ladies are of course ironic: they wish that Lydia may come out well, while firmly expecting the opposite.

vided amongst the latter, depended on the will of the parents. This was one point, with regard to Lydia, at least, which was now to be settled, and Mr. Bennet could have no hesitation in acceding to the proposal before him. In terms of grateful acknowledgment for the kindness of his brother, though expressed most concisely, he then delivered on paper his perfect approbation of all that was done, and his willingness to fulfil the engagements[8] that had been made for him. He had never before supposed that, could Wickham be prevailed on to marry his daughter, it would be done with so little inconvenience to himself, as by the present arrangement. He would scarcely be ten pounds a-year the loser, by the hundred that was to be paid them; for, what with her board and pocket allowance, and the continual presents in money, which passed to her, through her mother's hands, Lydia's expences had been very little within that sum.

That it would be done with such trifling exertion on his side, too, was another very welcome surprise; for his chief wish at present, was to have as little trouble in the business as possible.[9] When the first transports of rage which had produced his activity in seeking her were over, he naturally returned to all his former indolence. His letter was soon dispatched; for though dilatory in undertaking business, he was quick in its execution. He begged to know farther particulars of what he was indebted to his brother; but was too angry with Lydia, to send any message to her.

The good news quickly spread through the house; and with proportionate speed through the neighbourhood. It was borne in the latter with decent philosophy.[10] To be sure it would have been more for the advantage of conversation, had Miss Lydia Bennet come upon the town;[11] or, as the happiest alternative, been secluded from the world, in some distant farmhouse.[12] But there was much to be talked of, in marrying her;[13] and the good-natured wishes for her well-doing, which had proceeded before, from all the spiteful old ladies in Meryton, lost but a little of their spirit in this change of circumstances, because with such an husband, her misery was considered certain.[14]

It was a fortnight since Mrs. Bennet had been down stairs, but on this happy day she again took her seat at the head of her table, and in spirits oppressively high.[15] No sentiment of shame gave a damp to her triumph. The marriage of a daughter, which had been the first object of her wishes, since Jane was sixteen, was now on the point of accomplishment, and her thoughts and her words ran wholly on those attendants[16] of elegant nuptials, fine muslins, new carriages, and servants.[17] She was busily searching through the neighbourhood for a proper situation[18] for her daughter, and, without knowing or considering what their income might be, rejected many as deficient in size and importance.

"Haye-Park might do," said she, "if the Gouldings would quit it, or the great house at Stoke, if the drawing-room were larger; but Ashworth is too far off! I could not bear to have her ten miles from me; and as for Purvis Lodge, the attics are dreadful."

Her husband allowed her to talk on without interruption, while the servants remained. But when they had withdrawn, he said to her, "Mrs. Bennet, before you take any, or all of these houses, for your son and daughter, let us come to a right understanding. Into *one* house in this neighbourhood, they shall never have admittance. I will not encourage the impudence[19] of either, by receiving them at Longbourn."

A long dispute followed this declaration; but Mr. Bennet was firm: it soon led to another; and Mrs. Bennet found, with amazement and horror, that her husband would not advance a guinea[20] to buy clothes for his daughter. He protested that she should receive from him no mark of affection whatever, on the occasion. Mrs. Bennet could hardly comprehend it. That his anger could be carried to such a point of inconceivable resentment, as to refuse his daughter a privilege, without which her marriage would scarcely seem valid, exceeded all she could believe possible. She was more alive to the disgrace, which the want of new clothes must reflect on her daughter's nuptials, than to any sense of shame at her eloping and living with Wickham, a fortnight before they took place.

Elizabeth was now most heartily sorry that she had, from the distress of the moment, been led to make Mr. Darcy acquainted with their fears for her sister; for since her marriage would so shortly give the proper termination to the elopement, they might hope to con-

15 Oppressive to the listeners, or some of them: certainly Mrs. Bennet feels no oppression.

16 Such material appurtenances seem to Mrs. Bennet inevitably attendant on a marriage.

17 Concomitants of an upper-class marriage—all of which required wealth.

18 Place to live.

19 Shamelessness.

20 At this time a gold coin with a value of twenty-one shillings, or one shilling more than a pound.

21 Lydia's "frailty" is moral: "moral weakness . . . liability to err or yield to temptation" (OED). The noun nonetheless has ironic overtones when applied to the girl who will be described in the next chapter as "untamed, unabashed, wild, noisy, and fearless."

22 Elizabeth strives always to be rational. Rationality tells her that Darcy cannot be expected to wish an alliance with her family; her emotions yet continue to assert her desire to have him do just that.

23 Perhaps she repented her earlier misjudgment of Darcy, or her cavalier refusal of his proposal.

24 Zealous for the preservation of.

25 News.

26 Magnanimous.

27 The community had disapproved of him from the outset on the basis of his manners.

28 The notion that members of a married couple with contrasting personalities can modify each other recurs in Austen's novels. Thus, in *Persuasion,* Anne Elliot reflects about Charles Musgrove, who had married her sister after being rejected by Anne: "Anne could believe, with Lady Russell, that a more equal match might have greatly improved him; and that a woman of real understanding might have given more consequence to his character, and more usefulness, rationality, and elegance to his habits and pursuits" (I, 6). And in *Emma,* Knightley contemplates Frank's forthcoming marriage to Jane Fairfax: "as he is, beyond a doubt, really attached to Miss Fairfax, and will soon, it may be hoped, have the advantage of being constantly with her, I am very ready to believe his character will improve, and acquire from her's the steadiness and delicacy of principle that it wants" (III, 15).

ceal its unfavourable beginning, from all those who were not immediately on the spot.

She had no fear of its spreading farther, through his means. There were few people on whose secrecy she would have more confidently depended; but at the same time, there was no one, whose knowledge of a sister's frailty[21] would have mortified her so much. Not, however, from any fear of disadvantage from it, individually to herself; for at any rate, there seemed a gulf impossible between them. Had Lydia's marriage been concluded on the most honourable terms, it was not to be supposed that Mr. Darcy would connect himself with a family, where to every other objection would now be added, an alliance and relationship of the nearest kind with the man whom he so justly scorned.

From such a connection she could not wonder that he should shrink. The wish of procuring her regard, which she had assured herself of his feeling in Derbyshire, could not in rational expectation[22] survive such a blow as this. She was humbled, she was grieved; she repented, though she hardly knew of what.[23] She became jealous[24] of his esteem, when she could no longer hope to be benefited by it. She wanted to hear of him, when there seemed the least chance of gaining intelligence.[25] She was convinced that she could have been happy with him; when it was no longer likely they should meet.

What a triumph for him, as she often thought, could he know that the proposals which she had proudly spurned only four months ago, would now have been gladly and gratefully received! He was as generous,[26] she doubted not, as the most generous of his sex. But while he was mortal, there must be a triumph.

She began now to comprehend that he was exactly the man, who, in disposition and talents, would most suit her. His understanding and temper, though unlike her own, would have answered all her wishes. It was an union that must have been to the advantage of both; by her ease and liveliness, his mind might have been softened, his manners improved,[27] and from his judgment, information, and knowledge of the world, she must have received benefit of greater importance.[28]

But no such happy marriage could now teach the admiring multitude what connubial felicity really was.[29] An union of a different tendency, and precluding the possibility of the other, was soon to be formed in their family.

How Wickham and Lydia were to be supported in tolerable independence,[30] she could not imagine. But how little of permanent happiness could belong to a couple who were only brought together because their passions were stronger than their virtue, she could easily conjecture.

Mr. Gardiner soon wrote again to his brother.[31] To Mr. Bennet's acknowledgments he briefly replied, with assurances of his eagerness to promote the welfare of any of his family; and concluded with intreaties that the subject might never be mentioned to him again. The principal purport of his letter was to inform them, that Mr. Wickham had resolved on quitting the Militia.

"It was greatly my wish that he should do so," he added, "as soon as his marriage was fixed on. And I think you will agree with me, in considering a removal from that corps as highly advisable, both on his account and my niece's.[32] It is Mr. Wickham's intention to go into the regulars;[33] and, among his former friends, there are still some who are able and willing to assist him in the army.[34] He has the promise of an ensigncy[35] in General — —'s regiment, now quartered in the North. It is an advantage to have it so far from this part of the kingdom. He promises fairly,[36] and I hope among different people, where they may each have a character[37] to preserve, they will both be more prudent. I have written to Colonel Forster, to inform him of our present arrangements, and to request that he will satisfy the various creditors of Mr. Wickham in and near Brighton, with assurances of speedy payment, for which I have pledged myself. And will you give

29 It is difficult to tell whether this observation is Elizabeth's irony at her own expense or the narrator's ironic comment on her imaginings.

30 How they would manage financially.

31 Brother-in-law. In-laws were commonly referred to as though they were natural relatives.

32 Both because the members of the regiment would know about Wickham's misdeeds and because of the general association of the militia with frivolity.

33 The regular units of the army, which, unlike the militia, might engage in fighting abroad.

34 He would need assistance to purchase a commission.

35 The lowest officer rank.

36 Makes fair promises (of reformation).

37 Reputation. If Wickham returned to his militia regiment, his companions would know of his gambling, his unpaid debts, and his elopement.

38 Reported.

39 Social importance.

40 Another indication, like Mrs. Bennet's references to Jane's failure to "get" Bingley, of her tendency to reduce everything to physical terms. She wishes to "shew" her daughter as she might show a new carriage or a new dress.

yourself the trouble of carrying similar assurances to his creditors in Meryton, of whom I shall subjoin a list, according to his information? He has given in[38] all his debts; I hope at least he has not deceived us. Haggerston has our directions, and all will be completed in a week. They will then join his regiment, unless they are first invited to Longbourn; and I understand from Mrs. Gardiner, that my niece is very desirous of seeing you all, before she leaves the South. She is well, and begs to be dutifully remembered to you and her mother.—Yours, &c.

"E. Gardiner."

Mr. Bennet and his daughters saw all the advantages of Wickham's removal from the— —shire, as clearly as Mr. Gardiner could do. But Mrs. Bennet was not so well pleased with it. Lydia's being settled in the North, just when she had expected most pleasure and pride in her company, for she had by no means given up her plan of their residing in Hertfordshire, was a severe disappointment; and, besides, it was such a pity that Lydia should be taken from a regiment where she was acquainted with every body, and had so many favourites.

"She is so fond of Mrs. Forster," said she, "it will be quite shocking to send her away! And there are several of the young men, too, that she likes very much. The officers may not be so pleasant in General — —'s regiment."

His daughter's request, for such it might be considered, of being admitted into her family again, before she set off for the North, received at first an absolute negative. But Jane and Elizabeth, who agreed in wishing, for the sake of their sister's feelings and consequencem,[39] that she should be noticed on her marriage by her parents, urged him so earnestly, yet so rationally and so mildly, to receive her and her husband at Longbourn, as soon as they were married, that he was prevailed on to think as they thought, and act as they wished. And their mother had the satisfaction of knowing, that she should be able to shew her married daughter,[40] in the neighbourhood, before she was banished to the North. When Mr. Bennet wrote again to his brother, therefore, he sent his permission for them to come; and it was settled, that as soon as the ceremony was over, they should proceed to Longbourn. Elizabeth was surprised, however, that Wickham should consent to such a scheme, and had she consulted only her own inclination, any meeting with him would have been the last object of her wishes.

Letter of 1801 from Jane Austen, living in Bath, to her sister, Cassandra, who was staying with the family of her late fiancé, Thomas Fowle. Fowle, serving as a chaplain, died of yellow fever in the West Indies in 1797. Cassandra was always Jane's most frequent correspondent.

9

1 They feel the shame that Lydia never experiences.

2 Lydia and Wickham.

3 Lydia, of course, is incapable of even feeling herself a culprit.

4 Self-assurance, lack of embarrassment.

THEIR SISTER'S WEDDING DAY ARRIVED; and Jane and Elizabeth felt for her probably more than she felt for herself.[1] The carriage was sent to meet them[2] at — —, and they were to return in it, by dinnertime. Their arrival was dreaded by the elder Miss Bennets; and Jane more especially, who gave Lydia the feelings which would have attended herself, had *she* been the culprit,[3] was wretched in the thought of what her sister must endure.

They came. The family were assembled in the breakfast room, to receive them. Smiles decked the face of Mrs. Bennet, as the carriage drove up to the door; her husband looked impenetrably grave; her daughters, alarmed, anxious, uneasy.

Lydia's voice was heard in the vestibule; the door was thrown open, and she ran into the room. Her mother stepped forwards, embraced her, and welcomed her with rapture; gave her hand with an affectionate smile to Wickham, who followed his lady, and wished them both joy, with an alacrity which shewed no doubt of their happiness.

Their reception from Mr. Bennet, to whom they then turned, was not quite so cordial. His countenance rather gained in austerity; and he scarcely opened his lips. The easy assurance[4] of the young couple, indeed, was enough to provoke him. Elizabeth was disgusted, and even Miss Bennet was shocked. Lydia was Lydia still; untamed, unabashed, wild, noisy, and fearless. She turned from sister to sister, demanding their congratulations, and when at length they all sat down, looked eagerly round the room, took notice of some little alteration in it, and observed, with a laugh, that it was a great while since she had been there.

Wickham was not at all more distressed than herself, but his manners were always so pleasing,[5] that had his character and his marriage been exactly what they ought, his smiles and his easy address,[6] while he claimed their relationship, would have delighted them all. Elizabeth had not before believed him quite equal to such assurance; but she sat down, resolving within herself, to draw no limits in future to the impudence[7] of an impudent man. *She* blushed, and Jane blushed; but the cheeks of the two who caused their confusion, suffered no variation of colour.[8]

There was no want of discourse.[9] The bride and her mother could neither of them talk fast enough; and Wickham, who happened to sit near Elizabeth, began enquiring after his acquaintance in that neighbourhood, with a good humoured ease, which she felt very unable to equal in her replies. They seemed each of them to have the happiest memories in the world.[10] Nothing of the past was recollected with pain; and Lydia led voluntarily to subjects, which her sisters would not have alluded to for the world.

"Only think of its being three months," she cried, "since I went away; it seems but a fortnight I declare; and yet there have been things enough happened in the time. Good gracious! when I went away, I am sure I had no more idea of being married till I came back again! though I thought it would be very good fun[11] if I was."

Her father lifted up his eyes. Jane was distressed. Elizabeth looked expressively at Lydia; but she, who never heard nor saw any thing of which she chose to be insensible,[12] gaily continued, "Oh! mamma, do the people hereabouts know I am married today? I was afraid they might not; and we overtook William Goulding in his curricle, so I was determined he should know it, and so I let down the side glass next to him, and took off my glove, and let my hand just rest upon the window frame, so that he might see the ring, and then I bowed and smiled like any thing."[13]

Elizabeth could bear it no longer. She got up, and ran out of the room; and returned no more, till she heard them passing through the hall to the dining parlour. She then joined them soon enough to see

5 These pleasing manners accounted for the universal approval that Wickham earlier encountered. The novel underlines the inadequacy of manners as a standard of moral judgment—even as it suggests manners' importance by, for instance, Elizabeth's suffering over her mother's social misconduct.

6 Manner of speaking.

7 Shameless effrontery; unabashed presumption. Lydia and Wickham are equally impudent. Far from acting like a culprit, Lydia, like her mother, feels triumphant.

8 *Pride and Prejudice* contains a good deal of blushing. As moral commentators of the period frequently observed, there are many reasons for a girl to blush. If she blushes at an off-color remark, for instance, the blush may damage her social standing because it indicates that she understands the reference: she is not "innocent." Most often in Austen's work, young women blush from embarrassment. Here, they appear to blush on behalf of their unembarrassed sister, feeling for her what she does not feel for herself.

9 Lack of conversation.

10 In company with Lydia, Wickham reveals for the first time how completely he shares her moral unawareness and essential frivolity. The two of them seem ideally suited to each other—but not because, as in Elizabeth's imaginings of herself with Darcy, one compensates for the weaknesses of the other.

11 "Fun" appears to be Lydia's main standard of judgment.

12 Unconscious.

13 Lydia—in every other way so unlike her—resembles Charlotte in her "culturally determined desperation to compete for and win a husband," which drives both women "to self-destructive choices" (Jillian Heydt-Stevenson, *Austen's Unbecoming Conjunctions: Subversive Laughter, Embodied History* [New York: Palgrave Macmillan, 2005], 99).

14 Ostentation.

15 By the rules of precedence, the heads of the household, Mr. and Mrs. Bennet, would enter the dining room first, followed by their unmarried daughters in the order of their birth. A married woman took precedence over a single one, so now Lydia, the youngest, and thus previously the last in line, comes immediately after her parents. Her concern about precedence, however, is unattractive. One of the Miss Musgroves, in *Persuasion,* complains to Anne about similar behavior in Anne's sister, Mary, who is the daughter of a baronet and thus high in the order of precedence: "I wish any body could give Mary a hint that it would be a great deal better if she were not so very tenacious; especially, if she would not be always putting herself forward to take place of mamma. Nobody doubts her right to have precedence of mamma, but it would be more becoming in her not to be always insisting on it. It is not that mamma cares about it the least in the world, but I know it is taken notice of by many persons" (I, 6).

16 A town on the northeast coast of England, on the Tyne River, famous from the thirteenth century for its shipping of coal—not a very glamorous site for Lydia.

Lydia, with anxious parade,[14] walk up to her mother's right hand, and hear her say to her eldest sister, "Ah! Jane, I take your place now, and you must go lower, because I am a married woman."[15]

It was not to be supposed that time would give Lydia that embarrassment, from which she had been so wholly free at first. Her ease and good spirits increased. She longed to see Mrs. Phillips, the Lucasses, and all their other neighbours, and to hear herself called "Mrs. Wickham," by each of them; and in the mean time, she went after dinner to shew her ring, and boast of being married, to Mrs. Hill and the two housemaids.

"Well, mamma," said she, when they were all returned to the breakfast room, "and what do you think of my husband? Is not he a charming man? I am sure my sisters must all envy me. I only hope they may have half my good luck. They must all go to Brighton. That is the place to get husbands. What a pity it is, mamma, we did not all go."

"Very true; and if I had my will, we should. But my dear Lydia, I don't at all like your going such a way off. Must it be so?"

"Oh, lord! yes;—there is nothing in that. I shall like it of all things. You and papa, and my sisters, must come down and see us. We shall be at Newcastle[16] all the winter, and I dare say there will be some balls, and I will take care to get good partners for them all."

"I should like it beyond any thing!" said her mother.

"And then when you go away! you may leave one or two of my sisters behind you; and I dare say I shall get husbands for them before the winter is over."

"I thank you for my share of the favour," said Elizabeth; "but I do not particularly like your way of getting husbands."

Their visitors were not to remain above ten days with them. Mr. Wickham had received his commission before he left London, and he was to join his regiment at the end of a fortnight.

No one but Mrs. Bennet, regretted that their stay would be so short; and she made the most of the time by visiting about with her daughter, and having very frequent parties at home. These parties were acceptable to all; to avoid a family circle was even more desirable to such as did think, than such as did not.

Wickham's affection for Lydia was just what Elizabeth had expected to find it; not equal to Lydia's for him. She had scarcely needed her present observation to be satisfied, from the reason of things,[17] that their elopement had been brought on by the strength of her love, rather than by his; and she would have wondered why, without violently caring for her, he chose to elope with her at all, had she not felt certain that his flight was rendered necessary by distress of circumstances;[18] and if that were the case, he was not the young man to resist an opportunity of having a companion.

Lydia was exceedingly fond of him. He was her dear Wickham on every occasion; no one was to be put in competition with him. He did every thing best in the world; and she was sure he would kill more birds on the first of September,[19] than any body else in the country.[20]

One morning, soon after their arrival, as she was sitting with her two elder sisters, she said to Elizabeth:

"Lizzy, I never gave *you* an account of my wedding, I believe. You were not by, when I told mamma, and the others, all about it. Are not you curious to hear how it was managed?"

"No really," replied Elizabeth; "I think there cannot be too little said on the subject."

"La! You are so strange! But I must tell you how it went off. We were married, you know, at St. Clement's, because Wickham's lodgings were in that parish. And it was settled that we should all be there by eleven o'clock. My uncle and aunt and I were to go together; and the others were to meet us at the church. Well, Monday morning came, and I was in such a fuss! I was so afraid you know that something would happen to put it off, and then I should have gone quite distracted. And there was my aunt, all the time I was dressing, preaching and talking away just as if she was reading a sermon. However, I did not hear above one word in ten, for I was thinking, you may suppose, of my dear Wickham. I longed to know whether he would be married in his blue coat.

"Well, and so we breakfasted at ten as usual; I thought it would never be over; for, by the bye, you are to understand, that my uncle and aunt were horrid unpleasant all the time I was with them. If you'll believe me, I did not once put my foot out of doors, though I

17 We would probably say "the nature of things." Elizabeth's phrasing, although commonplace, suggests her fundamental commitment to rationality. Although she, like everyone, deviates from reason frequently, she wishes to be, and to have others be, reasonable.

18 Financial distress.

19 The beginning of the season for hunting partridges. In Austen's juvenile work *Sir William Mountague,* the eponymous character proposes to a "young, accomplished & lovely" woman, who accepts him and, when pressed to name a day for their marriage, fixes on the first of September. Sir William, who "could not support the idea of losing such a Day, even for such a Cause," begs her to delay the wedding for a short time. Enraged, she returns to London. "Sir William was sorry to lose her, but as he knew that he should have been much more greived [sic] by the Loss of the 1st of September, his Sorrow was not without a mixture of Happiness."

20 Region.

21 Plan for activity.

22 Only three theaters in London were allowed to offer spoken drama, by the current Licensing Act. The
Little Theater in the Haymarket was open from June
to September, when the other two theaters were closed
and when London was relatively sparsely populated,
since many prosperous people went to the country for
the summer.

23 By law, marriages had to be performed between 8
A.M. and noon.

24 To give her away.

was there a fortnight. Not one party, or scheme,[21] or any thing. To be
sure London was rather thin, but however, the Little Theatre[22] was
open. Well, and so just as the carriage came to the door, my uncle was
called away upon business to that horrid man Mr. Stone. And then,
you know, when once they get together, there is no end of it. Well, I
was so frightened I did not know what to do, for my uncle was to
give me away; and if we were beyond the hour,[23] we could not be married all day. But, luckily, he came back again in ten minutes time,
and then we all set out. However, I recollected afterwards that if he
had been prevented going, the wedding need not be put off, for Mr.
Darcy might have done as well."[24]

"Mr. Darcy!" repeated Elizabeth, in utter amazement.

"Oh, yes!—he was to come there with Wickham, you know. But
gracious me! I quite forgot! I ought not to have said a word about it.
I promised them so faithfully! What will Wickham say? It was to be
such a secret!"

"If it was to be secret," said Jane, "say not another word on the
subject. You may depend upon my seeking no further."

"Oh! certainly," said Elizabeth, though burning with curiosity; "we
will ask you no questions."

"Thank you," said Lydia, "for if you did, I should certainly tell you
all, and then Wickham would be angry."

On such encouragement to ask, Elizabeth was forced to put it out
of her power, by running away.

But to live in ignorance on such a point was impossible; or at least
it was impossible not to try for information. Mr. Darcy had been at
her sister's wedding. It was exactly a scene, and exactly among people, where he had apparently least to do, and least temptation to go.
Conjectures as to the meaning of it, rapid and wild, hurried into her
brain; but she was satisfied with none. Those that best pleased her, as
placing his conduct in the noblest light, seemed most improbable.
She could not bear such suspense; and hastily seizing a sheet of paper, wrote a short letter to her aunt, to request an explanation of
what Lydia had dropt, if it were compatible with the secrecy which
had been intended.

"You may readily comprehend," she added, "what my curiosity must be to know how a person unconnected with any of us, and (comparatively speaking) a stranger to our family, should have been amongst you at such a time. Pray write instantly, and let me understand it—unless it is, for very cogent reasons, to remain in the secrecy which Lydia seems to think necessary; and then I must endeavour to be satisfied with ignorance."

"Not that I *shall,* though," she added to herself, as she finished the letter; "and my dear aunt, if you do not tell me in an honourable manner, I shall certainly be reduced to tricks and stratagems to find it out."

Jane's delicate sense of honour would not allow her to speak to Elizabeth privately of what Lydia had let fall; Elizabeth was glad of it;—till it appeared whether her inquiries would receive any satisfaction, she had rather be without a confidante.

Illustration from *Little Journeys to the Homes of Famous Women*, 1897 (later coloration). This nineteenth-century engraving of Jane Austen seems to be based on the famous drawing by her sister, Cassandra.

10

ELIZABETH HAD THE SATISFACTION of receiving an answer to her letter, as soon as she possibly could. She was no sooner in possession of it, than hurrying into the little copse, where she was least likely to be interrupted, she sat down on one of the benches and prepared to be happy;[1] for the length of the letter convinced her, that it did not contain a denial.

"Grace-church street, Sept. 6.

"My dear niece,

"I have just received your letter, and shall devote this whole morning to answering it, as I foresee that a *little* writing will not comprise what I have to tell you. I must confess myself surprised by your application;[2] I did not expect it from *you*. Don't think me angry, however, for I only mean to let you know, that I had not imagined such enquiries to be necessary on *your* side. If you do not choose to understand me,[3] forgive my impertinence. Your uncle is as much surprised as I am—and nothing but the belief of your being a party concerned, would have allowed him to act as he has done. But if you are really innocent and ignorant, I must be more explicit. On the very day of my coming home from Longbourn, your uncle had a most unexpected visitor. Mr. Darcy called, and was shut up with him several hours. It was all over before I arrived; so my curiosity was not so dreadfully racked as *yours* seems to have been. He came to tell Mr.

---

[1] This formulation suggests that she expected to learn that Darcy has behaved nobly, even though she earlier told herself how unlikely such behavior would be. Or would she perhaps be "happy" at any news of Darcy?

[2] Request.

[3] Mrs. Gardiner's considering Elizabeth's possible claim not to understand a matter of choice reveals her conviction of the closeness between Darcy and her niece.

Gardiner that he had found out where your sister and Mr. Wickham were, and that he had seen and talked with them both; Wickham repeatedly, Lydia once. From what I can collect,[4] he left Derbyshire only one day after ourselves, and came to town with the resolution of hunting for them. The motive professed, was his conviction of its being owing to himself that Wickham's worthlessness had not been so well known, as to make it impossible for any young woman of character, to love or confide in him.[5] He generously imputed the whole to his mistaken pride, and confessed that he had before thought it beneath him, to lay his private actions open to the world. His character was to speak for itself. He called it, therefore, his duty to step forward, and endeavour to remedy an evil, which had been brought on by himself. If he *had another* motive, I am sure it would never disgrace him. He had been some days in town, before he was able to discover them; but he had something to direct his search, which was more than *we* had; and the consciousness of this, was another reason for his resolving to follow us. There is a lady, it seems, a Mrs. Younge, who was some time ago governess to Miss Darcy, and was dismissed from her charge on some cause of disapprobation, though he did not say what. She then took[6] a large house in Edward-street, and has since maintained herself by letting lodgings. This Mrs. Younge was, he knew, intimately acquainted with Wickham; and he went to her for intelligence of him, as soon as he got to town. But it was two or three days before he could get from her what he wanted. She would not betray her trust, I suppose, without bribery and corruption, for she really did know where her friend was to be found. Wickham indeed had gone to her, on their first arrival in London, and had she been able to receive them into her house, they would have taken up their abode with her. At length, however, our kind friend procured the wished-for direction.[7] They were in — — street. He saw Wickham, and afterwards insisted on seeing Lydia. His first object with her, he acknowledged, had been to persuade her to quit her pres-

4 Gather.

5 Darcy blames himself, in other words, for not having made it publicly known how reprehensibly Wickham had behaved in the matter of the church living. He would not under any circumstances have revealed Wickham's attempted seduction of his sister, which would have damaged Miss Darcy's reputation.

6 Rented.

7 Address.

8 Family, relatives.

9 This is ungentlemanly behavior. To accuse a woman of initiating a sexual liaison violates social norms and expectations about female nature.

10 Because he would be disgraced in the regiment for his failure to pay his gambling debts.

11 That is, his financial situation.

12 Region.

13 Invulnerable.

14 Either because a father's closer relationship might be expected to make him more reluctant to allow a nonrelative to intervene or because Darcy considered Mr. Gardiner a more judicious person.

ent disgraceful situation, and return to her friends[8] as soon as they could be prevailed on to receive her, offering his assistance, as far as it would go. But he found Lydia absolutely resolved on remaining where she was. She cared for none of her friends; she wanted no help of his; she would not hear of leaving Wickham. She was sure they should be married some time or other, and it did not much signify when. Since such were her feelings, it only remained, he thought, to secure and expedite a marriage, which, in his very first conversation with Wickham, he easily learnt had never been *his* design. He confessed himself obliged to leave the regiment, on account of some debts of honour, which were very pressing; and scrupled not to lay all the ill-consequences of Lydia's flight, on her own folly alone.[9] He meant to resign his commission immediately;[10] and as to his future situation, he could conjecture very little about it. He must go somewhere, but he did not know where, and he knew he should have nothing to live on. Mr. Darcy asked him why he had not married your sister at once. Though Mr. Bennet was not imagined to be very rich, he would have been able to do something for him, and his situation[11] must have been benefited by marriage. But he found, in reply to this question, that Wickham still cherished the hope of more effectually making his fortune by marriage in some other country.[12] Under such circumstances, however, he was not likely to be proof[13] against the temptation of immediate relief. They met several times, for there was much to be discussed. Wickham of course wanted more than he could get; but at length was reduced to be reasonable. Every thing being settled between *them,* Mr. Darcy's next step was to make your uncle acquainted with it, and he first called in Gracechurch-street the evening before I came home. But Mr. Gardiner could not be seen, and Mr. Darcy found, on farther enquiry, that your father was still with him, but would quit town the next morning. He did not judge your father to be a person whom he could so properly consult as your uncle,[14] and therefore readily postponed seeing him, till after the departure of the former. He did not leave his name, and till the next day, it was only known that a gentleman had called on business. On Saturday he came again. Your father was gone, your uncle at home, and, as I said before, they had a great deal of talk together. They met again on Sunday, and then *I* saw him too. It was not all settled before Monday: as soon as it was, the express was sent off to Longbourn. But our visitor was very obstinate. I fancy, Lizzy, that obstinacy is the real defect of his character after all. He has been accused of many faults at different times; but *this* is the true one. Nothing was to be done that he did not do himself; though I am sure (and I do not speak it to be thanked, therefore say nothing about it,) your uncle would most readily have settled the whole. They battled it together for a long time, which was more than either the gentleman or lady concerned in it deserved. But at last your uncle was forced to yield, and instead of being allowed to be of use to his niece, was forced to put up with only having the probable credit of it, which went sorely against the grain; and I really believe your letter this morning gave him great pleasure, because it required an explanation that would rob him of his borrowed feathers,[15] and give the praise where it was due. But, Lizzy, this must go no farther than yourself, or Jane at most. You know pretty well, I suppose, what has been done for the young people. His debts are to be paid, amounting, I believe, to considerably more than a thousand pounds, another thousand in addition to her own settled upon *her,* and his commission purchased. The reason why all this was to be done by him alone, was such as I have given above. It was owing to him, to his reserve, and want of proper consideration, that Wickham's character had been so misunderstood, and consequently that he had been received and noticed[16] as he was. Perhaps there was some truth in *this;* though I doubt whether *his* reserve, or *anybody's* reserve, can be answerable for the event.[17] But in spite of all this fine talking, my dear Lizzy, you may rest perfectly assured, that your uncle would never have yielded, if we had

15 In Aesop's fable "The Jackdaw and His Borrowed Feathers," a jackdaw (a small black bird of the crow genus) envies the beautiful feathers of peacocks. He picks up fallen feathers and inserts them among his own, then patronizes the other jackdaws as ugly. When he tries to associate with the peacocks, however, they recognize his fraud and peck away not only the borrowed feathers but the jackdaw's original feathers as well, leaving him bald, to be mocked by others of his species.

16 Entertained and treated politely and attentively.

17 Mrs. Gardiner is partly joking here about Lydia's conspicuous lack of reserve.

18 Narration.

19 The meanings of *prudent* include "discreet, cautious, far-sighted" *(OED).* Mrs. Gardiner is joking that discretion in Darcy's case would imply willingness to subject himself to less cautious influence.

not given him credit for *another interest* in the affair. When all this was resolved on, he returned again to his friends, who were still staying at Pemberley; but it was agreed that he should be in London once more when the wedding took place, and all money matters were then to receive the last finish. I believe I have now told you every thing. It is a relation[18] which you tell me is to give you great surprise; I hope at least it will not afford you any displeasure. Lydia came to us; and Wickham had constant admission to the house. *He* was exactly what he had been, when I knew him in Hertfordshire; but I would not tell you how little I was satisfied with *her* behaviour while she staid with us, if I had not perceived, by Jane's letter last Wednesday, that her conduct on coming home was exactly of a piece with it, and therefore what I now tell you, can give you no fresh pain. I talked to her repeatedly in the most serious manner, representing to her all the wickedness of what she had done, and all the unhappiness she had brought on her family. If she heard me, it was by good luck, for I am sure she did not listen. I was sometimes quite provoked, but then I recollected my dear Elizabeth and Jane, and for their sakes had patience with her. Mr. Darcy was punctual in his return, and as Lydia informed you, attended the wedding. He dined with us the next day, and was to leave town again on Wednesday or Thursday. Will you be very angry with me, my dear Lizzy, if I take this opportunity of saying (what I was never bold enough to say before) how much I like him. His behaviour to us has, in every respect, been as pleasing as when we were in Derbyshire. His understanding and opinions all please me; he wants nothing but a little more liveliness, and *that,* if he marry *prudently,*[19] his wife may teach him. I thought him very sly;—he hardly ever mentioned your name. But slyness seems the fashion. Pray forgive me, if I have been very presuming, or at least do not punish me so far as to exclude me from P. I shall never be quite happy till I have been all round the park. A low phaeton, with a nice little pair of ponies, would be the very thing. But I must write

no more. The children have been wanting me this half hour.
Yours, very sincerely,

"M. Gardiner."

The contents of this letter threw Elizabeth into a flutter of spirits, in which it was difficult to determine whether pleasure or pain bore the greatest share. The vague and unsettled suspicions which uncertainty had produced of what Mr. Darcy might have been doing to

Two young ladies in calico gowns, from Humphry Repton, *Gallery of Fashion,* vol. I, August 1794. A low phaeton, with a nice little pair of ponies, carrying two women: exactly what Mrs. Gardiner imagined for a visit to Pemberley.

20 Respect.

21 Among all the references to vanity and pride, Elizabeth has earlier accused herself of vanity. Now she considers it vain to believe that Darcy could possibly still cherish tender feelings for her. Her self-doubt as she learns about Darcy's generosity signals the crumbling of some of her defensive devices, like turning a potential insult into a matter for laughter.

22 In most contexts, this would seem an automatic phrase, merely intensifying the degree of pride attributed. In a novel so centrally concerned with the operations of pride, it has more specific meaning. Elizabeth has mentally accused Darcy of various sorts of pride: in his family, his social status, his character. She means here that every kind of pride he might imaginably possess would be violated.

23 Her restoration to her family and to society.

24 Reputation. Once Lydia was married, the disgrace of having lived with a man outside of marriage would be obviated.

25 Pride has been mainly a reprehensible characteristic throughout the novel. This is the first time that a character is described as being proud of someone else.

forward her sister's match, which she had feared to encourage as an exertion of goodness too great to be probable, and at the same time dreaded to be just, from the pain of obligation, were proved beyond their greatest extent to be true! He had followed them purposely to town, he had taken on himself all the trouble and mortification attendant on such a research; in which supplication had been necessary to a woman whom he must abominate and despise, and where he was reduced to meet, frequently meet, reason with, persuade, and finally bribe, the man whom he always most wished to avoid, and whose very name it was punishment to him to pronounce. He had done all this for a girl whom he could neither regard[20] nor esteem. Her heart did whisper, that he had done it for her. But it was a hope shortly checked by other considerations, and she soon felt that even her vanity[21] was insufficient, when required to depend on his affection for her, for a woman who had already refused him, as able to overcome a sentiment so natural as abhorrence against relationship with Wickham. Brother in law of Wickham! Every kind of pride[22] must revolt from the connection. He had to be sure done much. She was ashamed to think how much. But he had given a reason for his interference, which asked no extraordinary stretch of belief. It was reasonable that he should feel he had been wrong; he had liberality, and he had the means of exercising it; and though she would not place herself as his principal inducement, she could, perhaps, believe that remaining partiality for her might assist his endeavours in a cause where her peace of mind must be materially concerned. It was painful, exceedingly painful, to know that they were under obligations to a person who could never receive a return. They owed the restoration of Lydia,[23] her character,[24] every thing to him. Oh! how heartily did she grieve over every ungracious sensation she had ever encouraged, every saucy speech she had ever directed towards him. For herself she was humbled; but she was proud of him.[25] Proud that in a cause of compassion and honour, he had been able to get the better of himself. She read over her aunt's commendation of him again and again. It was hardly enough; but it pleased her. She was even sensible of some pleasure, though mixed with regret, on finding how steadfastly both she and her uncle had been persuaded that affection and confidence subsisted between Mr. Darcy and herself.

She was roused from her seat, and her reflections, by some one's approach; and before she could strike into another path, she was overtaken by Wickham.

"I am afraid I interrupt your solitary ramble, my dear sister?" said he, as he joined her.

"You certainly do," she replied with a smile; "but it does not follow that the interruption must be unwelcome."

"I should be sorry indeed, if it were. *We* were always good friends; and now we are better."

"True. Are the others coming out?"

"I do not know. Mrs. Bennet and Lydia are going in the carriage to Meryton. And so, my dear sister, I find from our uncle and aunt, that you have actually seen Pemberley."

She replied in the affirmative.

"I almost envy you the pleasure, and yet I believe it would be too much for me, or else I could take it in my way to Newcastle. And you saw the old housekeeper, I suppose? Poor Reynolds, she was always very fond of me. But of course she did not mention my name to you."

"Yes, she did."

"And what did she say?"

"That you were gone into the army, and she was afraid had—not turned out well. At such a distance as *that,* you know, things are strangely misrepresented."

"Certainly," he replied, biting his lips. Elizabeth hoped she had silenced him; but he soon afterwards said,

"I was surprised to see Darcy in town last month. We passed each other several times. I wonder what he can be doing there."

"Perhaps preparing for his marriage with Miss de Bourgh," said Elizabeth. "It must be something particular, to take him there at this time of year."

"Undoubtedly. Did you see him while you were at Lambton? I thought I understood from the Gardiners that you had."

"Yes; he introduced us to his sister."

Jane Austen's portable writing desk, made of mahogany, with an inlaid leather top. Austen's father bought it for her in December 1794, presumably as a birthday or Christmas gift.

"And do you like her?"

"Very much."

"I have heard, indeed, that she is uncommonly improved within this year or two. When I last saw her, she was not very promising. I am very glad you liked her. I hope she will turn out well."

"I dare say she will; she has got over the most trying age."

"Did you go by the village of Kympton?"

"I do not recollect that we did."

"I mention it, because it is the living which I ought to have had. A most delightful place! Excellent Parsonage House! It would have suited me in every respect."

"How should you have liked making sermons?"

"Exceedingly well. I should have considered it as part of my duty, and the exertion would soon have been nothing. One ought not to repine;—but, to be sure, it would have been such a thing for me! The quiet, the retirement of such a life, would have answered all my ideas of happiness! But it was not to be. Did you ever hear Darcy mention the circumstance, when you were in Kent?"

"I *have* heard from authority, which I thought *as good,* that it was left you conditionally only, and at the will of the present patron."

"You have. Yes, there was something in *that;* I told you so from the first, you may remember."

"I *did* hear, too, that there was a time, when sermon-making was not so palatable to you, as it seems to be at present; that you actually declared your resolution of never taking orders, and that the business had been compromised accordingly."

"You did! and it was not wholly without foundation. You may remember what I told you on that point, when first we talked of it."

They were now almost at the door of the house, for she had walked fast to get rid of him; and unwilling, for her sister's sake, to provoke him, she only said in reply, with a good-humoured smile,

"Come, Mr. Wickham, we are brother and sister, you know. Do not let us quarrel about the past. In future, I hope we shall be always of one mind."

She held out her hand; he kissed it with affectionate gallantry, though he hardly knew how to look, and they entered the house.

II

Mr. Wickham was so perfectly satisfied with this conversation, that he never again distressed himself, or provoked his dear sister Elizabeth, by introducing the subject of it; and she was pleased to find that she had said enough to keep him quiet.

The day of his and Lydia's departure soon came, and Mrs. Bennet was forced to submit to a separation, which, as her husband by no means entered into her scheme of their all going to Newcastle, was likely to continue at least a twelvemonth.

"Oh! my dear Lydia," she cried, "when shall we meet again?"

"Oh, lord! I don't know. Not these two or three years, perhaps."

"Write to me very often, my dear."

"As often as I can. But you know married women have never much time for writing. My sisters may write to *me*. They will have nothing else to do."[1]

Mr. Wickham's adieus were much more affectionate than his wife's. He smiled, looked handsome, and said many pretty things.

"He is as fine a fellow," said Mr. Bennet, as soon as they were out of the house, "as ever I saw. He simpers, and smirks, and makes love to us all. I am prodigiously proud[2] of him. I defy even Sir William Lucas himself, to produce a more valuable son-in-law."[3]

The loss of her daughter made Mrs. Bennet very dull[4] for several days.

"I often think," said she, "that there is nothing so bad as parting with one's friends. One seems so forlorn without them."

1 The sense of importance that Lydia has acquired by marriage emphasizes the social significance of the married state for women. It may also enable the reader to feel faint retrospective pity for the girl who previously could achieve little status within her family.

2 Another instance of being proud of someone else—this time ironically.

3 Since Sir William's son-in-law is Mr. Collins, Mr. Bennet is suggesting that Wickham provides a better target for his mockery than even the obsequious clergyman. It may be remembered, however, that earlier Mr. Bennet, like his daughters, had been taken in by Wickham. When Mrs. Gardiner warns Elizabeth against the imprudence of falling in love with Wickham, Elizabeth unironically observes, "My father, however, is partial to Mr. Wickham" (II, 3).

4 Gloomy.

5 Bingley's housekeeper.

6 This change of color is presumably caused by self-consciousness.

"This is the consequence you see, Madam, of marrying a daughter," said Elizabeth. "It must make you better satisfied that your other four are single."

"It is no such thing. Lydia does not leave me because she is married; but only because her husband's regiment happens to be so far off. If that had been nearer, she would not have gone so soon."

But the spiritless condition which this event threw her into, was shortly relieved, and her mind opened again to the agitation of hope, by an article of news, which then began to be in circulation. The housekeeper at Netherfield had received orders to prepare for the arrival of her master, who was coming down in a day or two, to shoot there for several weeks. Mrs. Bennet was quite in the fidgets. She looked at Jane, and smiled, and shook her head by turns.

"Well, well, and so Mr. Bingley is coming down, sister," (for Mrs. Phillips first brought her the news.) "Well, so much the better. Not that I care about it, though. He is nothing to us, you know, and I am sure *I* never want to see him again. But, however, he is very welcome to come to Netherfield, if he likes it. And who knows what *may* happen? But that is nothing to us. You know, sister, we agreed long ago never to mention a word about it. And so, is it quite certain he is coming?"

"You may depend on it," replied the other, "for Mrs. Nicholls[5] was in Meryton last night; I saw her passing by, and went out myself on purpose to know the truth of it; and she told me that it was certain true. He comes down on Thursday at the latest, very likely on Wednesday. She was going to the butcher's, she told me, on purpose to order in some meat on Wednesday, and she has got three couple of ducks, just fit to be killed."

Miss Bennet had not been able to hear of his coming, without changing colour.[6] It was many months since she had mentioned his name to Elizabeth; but now, as soon as they were alone together, she said,

"I saw you look at me today, Lizzy, when my aunt told us of the present report; and I know I appeared distressed. But don't imagine it was from any silly cause. I was only confused for the moment, because I felt that I *should* be looked at. I do assure you, that the news does not affect me either with pleasure or pain. I am glad of one thing, that he comes alone; because we shall see the less of him. Not that I am afraid of *myself*, but I dread other people's remarks."

Elizabeth did not know what to make of it. Had she not seen him in Derbyshire, she might have supposed him capable of coming there, with no other view than what was acknowledged; but she still thought him partial to Jane, and she wavered as to the greater probability of his coming there *with* his friend's permission, or being bold enough to come without it.

"Yet it is hard," she sometimes thought, "that this poor man cannot come to a house, which he has legally hired, without raising all this speculation! I *will* leave him to himself."

In spite of what her sister declared, and really believed to be her feelings, in the expectation of his arrival, Elizabeth could easily perceive that her spirits were affected by it. They were more disturbed, more unequal,[7] than she had often seen them.

The subject which had been so warmly canvassed[8] between their parents, about a twelvemonth ago, was now brought forward again.

"As soon as ever Mr. Bingley comes, my dear," said Mrs. Bennet, "you will wait on him of course."

"No, no. You forced me into visiting him last year, and promised if I went to see him, he should marry one of my daughters. But it ended in nothing, and I will not be sent on a fool's errand again."

His wife represented to him how absolutely necessary such an attention would be from all the neighbouring gentlemen, on his returning to Netherfield.

"'Tis an etiquette I despise," said he. "If he wants our society, let him seek it. He knows where we live. I will not spend *my* hours in running after my neighbours every time they go away, and come back again."

"Well, all I know is, that it will be abominably rude if you do not wait on him. But, however, that shan't prevent my asking him to dine here, I am determined. We must have Mrs. Long and the Gouldings soon. That will make thirteen with ourselves, so there will be just room at table for him."

7 Variable.

8 Discussed.

9　The formulation suggests that she enjoys her anxiety and fretfulness—which, of course, direct the attention of others toward her.

Probably Jane Austen, by an unknown artist, c. 1810–1815. This silhouette appeared in the second volume of the first edition of *Mansfield Park,* inscribed "L'aimable Jane."

Consoled by this resolution, she was the better able to bear her husband's incivility; though it was very mortifying to know that her neighbours might all see Mr. Bingley in consequence of it, before *they* did. As the day of his arrival drew near,

"I begin to be sorry that he comes at all," said Jane to her sister. "It would be nothing; I could see him with perfect indifference, but I can hardly bear to hear it thus perpetually talked of. My mother means well; but she does not know, no one can know how much I suffer from what she says. Happy shall I be, when his stay at Netherfield is over!"

"I wish I could say any thing to comfort you," replied Elizabeth; "but it is wholly out of my power. You must feel it; and the usual satisfaction of preaching patience to a sufferer is denied me, because you have always so much."

Mr. Bingley arrived. Mrs. Bennet, through the assistance of servants, contrived to have the earliest tidings of it, that the period of anxiety and fretfulness on her side, might be as long as it could.[9] She counted the days that must intervene before their invitation could be sent; hopeless of seeing him before. But on the third morning after his arrival in Hertfordshire, she saw him from her dressing-room window, enter the paddock, and ride towards the house.

Her daughters were eagerly called to partake of her joy. Jane resolutely kept her place at the table; but Elizabeth, to satisfy her mother, went to the window—she looked,—she saw Mr. Darcy with him, and sat down again by her sister.

"There is a gentleman with him, mamma," said Kitty; "who can it be?"

"Some acquaintance or other, my dear, I suppose; I am sure I do not know."

"La!" replied Kitty, "it looks just like that man that used to be with him before. Mr. what's his name. That tall, proud man."

"Good gracious! Mr. Darcy!—and so it does I vow. Well, any friend of Mr. Bingley's will always be welcome here to be sure; but else I must say that I hate the very sight of him."

Jane looked at Elizabeth with surprise and concern. She knew but little of their meeting in Derbyshire, and therefore felt for the awkwardness which must attend her sister, in seeing him almost for the first time after receiving his explanatory letter. Both sisters were uncomfortable enough. Each felt for the other, and of course for themselves; and their mother talked on, of her dislike of Mr. Darcy, and her resolution to be civil to him only as Mr. Bingley's friend, without being heard by either of them. But Elizabeth had sources of uneasiness which could not be suspected by Jane, to whom she had never yet had courage to shew Mrs. Gardiner's letter, or to relate her own change of sentiment towards him. To Jane, he could be only a man whose proposals she had refused, and whose merit she had undervalued; but to her own more extensive information, he was the person, to whom the whole family were indebted for the first of benefits, and whom she regarded herself with an interest, if not quite so tender, at least as reasonable and just,[10] as what Jane felt for Bingley. Her astonishment at his coming—at his coming to Netherfield, to Longbourn, and voluntarily seeking her again, was almost equal to what she had known on first witnessing his altered behaviour in Derbyshire.

The colour which had been driven from her face, returned for half a minute with an additional glow, and a smile of delight added lustre to her eyes, as she thought for that space of time, that his affection and wishes must still be unshaken. But she would not be secure.[11]

"Let me first see how he behaves," said she; "it will then be early enough for expectation."

She sat intently at work,[12] striving to be composed, and without daring to lift up her eyes, till anxious curiosity carried them to the face of her sister, as the servant was approaching the door. Jane looked a little paler than usual, but more sedate than Elizabeth had expected. On the gentlemen's appearing, her colour increased; yet she received them with tolerable ease, and with a propriety of behaviour equally free from any symptom of resentment, or any unnecessary complaisance.

Elizabeth said as little to either as civility would allow, and sat down again to her work, with an eagerness which it did not often command.[13] She had ventured only one glance at Darcy. He looked serious as usual; and she thought, more as he had been used to look in Hertfordshire, than as she had seen him at Pemberley. But, per-

10 Elizabeth's assessment of her feeling for Darcy as "reasonable and just" provides another indication of how insistently she seeks to govern herself by rationality.

11 She dares not allow herself to feel sure.

12 Needlework.

13 This is the first clear indication that Elizabeth does not take pleasure in a young woman's conventional pursuits. Her walking to Netherfield to see her sister was taken by the Bingley sisters as evidence that she is not ladylike; the later information that she is more in the habit of running than is Jane also hints her preference for vigorous activity. Yet she is often represented as at her needlework, whether she likes it or not. On the present occasion, of course, that work provides an occupation that may serve to conceal her embarrassment at Darcy's advent.

14 Because she knows that he has in fact seen her uncle and aunt more recently than she has.

15 Relatives.

haps he could not in her mother's presence be what he was before her uncle and aunt. It was a painful, but not an improbable, conjecture.

Bingley, she had likewise seen for an instant, and in that short period saw him looking both pleased and embarrassed. He was received by Mrs. Bennet with a degree of civility, which made her two daughters ashamed, especially when contrasted with the cold and ceremonious politeness of her curtsey and address to his friend.

Elizabeth particularly, who knew that her mother owed to the latter the preservation of her favourite daughter from irremediable infamy, was hurt and distressed to a most painful degree by a distinction so ill applied.

Darcy, after enquiring of her how Mr. and Mrs. Gardiner did, a question which she could not answer without confusion,[14] said scarcely any thing. He was not seated by her; perhaps that was the reason of his silence; but it had not been so in Derbyshire. There he had talked to her friends,[15] when he could not to herself. But now several minutes elapsed without bringing the sound of his voice; and when occasionally, unable to resist the impulse of curiosity, she raised her eyes to his face, she as often found him looking at Jane, as at herself, and frequently on no object but the ground. More thoughtfulness, and less anxiety to please than when they last met, were plainly expressed. She was disappointed, and angry with herself for being so.

"Could I expect it to be otherwise!" said she. "Yet why did he come?"

She was in no humour for conversation with any one but himself; and to him she had hardly courage to speak.

She enquired after his sister, but could do no more.

"It is a long time, Mr. Bingley, since you went away," said Mrs. Bennet.

He readily agreed to it.

"I began to be afraid you would never come back again. People *did* say you meant to quit the place entirely at Michaelmas; but, however, I hope it is not true. A great many changes have happened in the neighbourhood, since you went away. Miss Lucas is married and settled. And one of my own daughters. I suppose you have heard of it; indeed, you must have seen it in the papers. It was in the Times and the Courier, I know; though it was not put in as it ought to be. It was only said, 'Lately, George Wickham, Esq. to Miss Lydia Bennet,' without there being a syllable said of her father, or the place where she lived, or any thing. It was my brother Gardiner's drawing up too, and I wonder how he came to make such an awkward business of it. Did you see it?"

Bingley replied that he did, and made his congratulations. Elizabeth dared not lift up her eyes. How Mr. Darcy looked, therefore, she could not tell.

"It is a delightful thing, to be sure, to have a daughter well married,"[16] continued her mother; "but at the same time, Mr. Bingley, it is very hard to have her taken such a way from me. They are gone down to Newcastle, a place quite northward, it seems, and there they are to stay, I do not know how long. His regiment is there; for I suppose you have heard of his leaving the — —shire, and of his being gone into the regulars. Thank Heaven! he has *some* friends, though perhaps not so many as he deserves."

Elizabeth, who knew this to be levelled at Mr. Darcy, was in such misery of shame, that she could hardly keep her seat. It drew from her, however, the exertion of speaking, which nothing else had so effectually done before; and she asked Bingley, whether he meant to make any stay in the country at present. A few weeks, he believed.

"When you have killed all your own birds, Mr. Bingley,"[17] said her mother, "I beg you will come here, and shoot as many as you please, on Mr. Bennet's manor. I am sure he will be vastly happy to oblige you, and will save all the best of the covies[18] for you."

Elizabeth's misery increased, at such unnecessary, such officious attention! Were the same fair prospect to arise at present, as had flattered them a year ago, every thing, she was persuaded, would be hastening to the same vexatious conclusion. At that instant, she felt that years of happiness could not make Jane or herself amends, for moments of such painful confusion.

"The first wish of my heart," said she to herself, "is never more to be in company with either of them. Their society can afford no plea-

16 Only Mrs. Bennet could call Lydia "well married."

17 Mrs. Bennet clearly does not know much about hunting. A gentleman would want to make sure that birds would remain for future years' hunting; he would take care *not* to kill all his own birds.

18 Broods of partridge.

19 Convinced.

For the last eight years of her life, Austen and her mother inhabited Chawton Cottage, which was part of her brother's estate.

sure, that will atone for such wretchedness as this! Let me never see either one or the other again!"

Yet the misery, for which years of happiness were to offer no compensation, received soon afterwards material relief, from observing how much the beauty of her sister re-kindled the admiration of her former lover. When first he came in, he had spoken to her but little; but every five minutes seemed to be giving her more of his attention. He found her as handsome as she had been last year; as good natured, and as unaffected, though not quite so chatty. Jane was anxious that no difference should be perceived in her at all, and was really persuaded[19] that she talked as much as ever. But her mind was so busily engaged, that she did not always know when she was silent.

When the gentlemen rose to go away, Mrs. Bennet was mindful of her intended civility, and they were invited and engaged to dine at Longbourn in a few days time.

"You are quite a visit in my debt, Mr. Bingley," she added, "for when you went to town last winter, you promised to take a family dinner with us, as soon as you returned. I have not forgot, you see; and I assure you, I was very much disappointed that you did not come back and keep your engagement."

Bingley looked a little silly at this reflection, and said something of his concern, at having been prevented by business. They then went away.

Mrs. Bennet had been strongly inclined to ask them to stay and dine there, that day; but, though she always kept a very good table, she did not think any thing less than two courses, could be good enough for a man on whom she had such anxious designs, or satisfy the appetite and pride of one who had ten thousand a-year.

12

As soon as they were gone, Elizabeth walked out to recover her spirits; or in other words, to dwell without interruption on those subjects that must deaden them more.[1] Mr. Darcy's behaviour astonished and vexed her.

"Why, if he came only to be silent, grave, and indifferent," said she, "did he come at all?"

She could settle it in no way that gave her pleasure.

"He could be still amiable, still pleasing, to my uncle and aunt, when he was in town; and why not to me? If he fears me, why come hither? If he no longer cares for me, why silent?[2] Teazing, teazing,[3] man! I will think no more about him."

Her resolution was for a short time involuntarily kept by the approach of her sister, who joined her with a cheerful look, which shewed her better satisfied with their visitors, than Elizabeth.

"Now," said she, "that this first meeting is over, I feel perfectly easy. I know my own strength, and I shall never be embarrassed again by his coming. I am glad he dines here on Tuesday. It will then be publicly seen that, on both sides, we meet only as common and indifferent acquaintance."

"Yes, very indifferent indeed," said Elizabeth, laughingly. "Oh, Jane, take care."

"My dear Lizzy, you cannot think me so weak, as to be in danger now?"

"I think you are in very great danger of making him as much in love with you as ever."

1 She tells herself that she's going out in order to feel better, but what she really wants is a chance to brood over the problem that obsesses her.

2 This series of questions, none of which Elizabeth can answer satisfactorily, calls attention to the fact that, as Bruce Stovel puts it, "Elizabeth is no longer someone who knows exactly what to think" ("Asking Versus Telling," *The Talk in Jane Austen,* ed. Bruce Stovel and Lynn Weinlos Gregg [Edmonton: University of Alberta Press, 2002], 38). Earlier in the novel, her customary certainty has characteristically contrasted with Jane's efforts to find alternate interpretations.

3 Irritating, vexatious.

4 General.

5 At dinner parties in this period, there were ordinarily no assigned seats, except for the host and hostess. Guests filed into the dining room, and each in turn chose a place to sit. Ladies would enter first, followed by the men in order of precedence.

They did not see the gentlemen again till Tuesday; and Mrs. Bennet, in the meanwhile, was giving way to all the happy schemes, which the good humour, and common[4] politeness of Bingley, in half an hour's visit, had revived.

On Tuesday there was a large party assembled at Longbourn; and the two, who were most anxiously expected, to the credit of their punctuality as sportsmen, were in very good time. When they repaired to the dining-room, Elizabeth eagerly watched to see whether Bingley would take the place, which, in all their former parties, had belonged to him, by her sister. Her prudent mother, occupied by the same ideas, forbore to invite him to sit by herself. On entering the room, he seemed to hesitate; but Jane happened to look round, and happened to smile: it was decided. He placed himself by her.[5]

Elizabeth, with a triumphant sensation, looked towards his friend. He bore it with noble indifference, and she would have imagined that Bingley had received his sanction to be happy, had she not seen his eyes likewise turned towards Mr. Darcy, with an expression of half-laughing alarm.

His behaviour to her sister was such, during dinner time, as shewed an admiration of her, which, though more guarded than formerly, persuaded Elizabeth, that if left wholly to himself, Jane's happiness, and his own, would be speedily secured. Though she dared not depend upon the consequence, she yet received pleasure from observing his behaviour. It gave her all the animation that her spirits could boast; for she was in no cheerful humour. Mr. Darcy was almost as far from her, as the table could divide them. He was on one side of her mother. She knew how little such a situation would give pleasure to either, or make either appear to advantage. She was not near enough to hear any of their discourse, but she could see how seldom they spoke to each other, and how formal and cold was their manner, whenever they did. Her mother's ungraciousness, made the sense of what they owed him more painful to Elizabeth's mind; and she would, at times, have given any thing to be privileged to tell him, that his kindness was neither unknown nor unfelt by the whole of the family.

She was in hopes that the evening would afford some opportunity of bringing them together; that the whole of the visit would not pass away without enabling them to enter into something more of conversation, than the mere ceremonious salutation attending his entrance. Anxious and uneasy, the period which passed in the drawing-room, before the gentlemen came, was wearisome and dull to a degree, that almost made her uncivil.[6] She looked forward to their entrance, as the point on which all her chance of pleasure for the evening must depend.

"If he does not come to me, *then*," said she,[7] "I shall give him up for ever."

The gentlemen came; and she thought he looked as if he would have answered her hopes; but, alas! the ladies had crowded round the table, where Miss Bennet was making tea, and Elizabeth pouring out the coffee, in so close a confederacy, that there was not a single vacancy near her, which would admit of[8] a chair. And on the gentlemen's approaching, one of the girls moved closer to her than ever, and said, in a whisper,

"The men shan't come and part us, I am determined. We want none of them; do we?"

Darcy had walked away to another part of the room. She followed him with her eyes, envied every one to whom he spoke, had scarcely patience enough to help anybody to coffee; and then was enraged against herself for being so silly!

"A man who has once been refused! How could I ever be foolish enough to expect a renewal of his love? Is there one among the sex,[9] who would not protest against such a weakness as a second proposal to the same woman? There is no indignity so abhorrent to their feelings!"[10]

She was a little revived, however, by his bringing back his coffee cup himself; and she seized the opportunity of saying,

"Is your sister at Pemberley still?"

"Yes, she will remain there till Christmas."

"And quite alone? Have all her friends left her?"

6 Almost, but not quite. The obligation to social decorum was felt as commanding by all the well-bred.

7 To herself.

8 Allow [room for].

9 The male sex.

10 Elizabeth's categorical allegations about the male sex constitute an effort to regain her sense of rational control.

11 A resort town in north Yorkshire, northeast England, on the North Sea. For centuries it was the site of the Scarborough Fair, a six-week trading festival beginning in late summer. This fair survived into the eighteenth century, by which time the town's main attraction had become its spa, which made it England's first seaside resort. Visitors could also take pleasure in the ruins of a medieval castle.

12 Well prepared.

13 Despite England's conflicts with France, French cooking remained the standard for elegant cuisine. (Remember Mr. Hurst's apparent contempt for Elizabeth when he discovered that she preferred a simple dish to a [French] ragout; I, 8.) Mrs. Bennet is striving for elegance by serving game (venison and partridges), and she appears satisfied with what she has achieved.

14 Therefore not, from Mrs. Bennet's point of view, dangerous rivals for her own girls, as she has earlier thought them to be.

15 If Jane marries someone as wealthy as Bingley, Mrs. Bennet thinks, she will thus improve the lot of the entire family. The match will provide Jane with money that she might transmit on occasion to her siblings and will arguably increase the Bennet family's social status, thus improving the other daughters' marital prospects.

"Mrs. Annesley is with her. The others have been gone on to Scarborough,[11] these three weeks."

She could think of nothing more to say; but if he wished to converse with her, he might have better success. He stood by her, however, for some minutes, in silence; and, at last, on the young lady's whispering to Elizabeth again, he walked away.

When the tea-things were removed, and the card tables placed, the ladies all rose, and Elizabeth was then hoping to be soon joined by him, when all her views were overthrown, by seeing him fall a victim to her mother's rapacity for whist players, and in a few moments after seated with the rest of the party. She now lost every expectation of pleasure. They were confined for the evening at different tables, and she had nothing to hope, but that his eyes were so often turned towards her side of the room, as to make him play as unsuccessfully as herself.

Mrs. Bennet had designed to keep the two Netherfield gentlemen to supper; but their carriage was unluckily ordered before any of the others, and she had no opportunity of detaining them.

"Well girls," said she, as soon as they were left to themselves, "What say you to the day? I think every thing has passed off uncommonly well, I assure you. The dinner was as well dressed[12] as any I ever saw. The venison was roasted to a turn—and everybody said, they never saw so fat a haunch. The soup was fifty times better than what we had at the Lucases' last week; and even Mr. Darcy acknowledged, that the partridges were remarkably well done; and I suppose he has two or three French cooks[13] at least. And, my dear Jane, I never saw you look in greater beauty. Mrs. Long said so too, for I asked her whether you did not. And what do you think she said besides? 'Ah! Mrs. Bennet, we shall have her at Netherfield at last.' She did indeed. I do think Mrs. Long is as good a creature as ever lived—and her nieces are very pretty behaved girls, and not at all handsome:[14] I like them prodigiously."

Mrs. Bennet, in short, was in very great spirits; she had seen enough of Bingley's behaviour to Jane, to be convinced that she would get him at last; and her expectations of advantage to her family,[15] when in a happy humour, were so far beyond reason, that she was quite disappointed at not seeing him there again the next day, to make his proposals.

"It has been a very agreeable day," said Miss Bennet to Elizabeth. "The party seemed so well selected, so suitable one with the other. I hope we may often meet again."

Elizabeth smiled.

"Lizzy, you must not do so. You must not suspect me. It mortifies me. I assure you that I have now learnt to enjoy his conversation as an agreeable and sensible young man, without having a wish beyond it. I am perfectly satisfied from what his manners now are, that he never had any design of engaging my affection. It is only that he is blessed with greater sweetness of address, and a stronger desire of generally pleasing than any other man."

"You are very cruel," said her sister, "you will not let me smile, and are provoking me to it every moment."

"How hard it is in some cases to be believed!"

"And how impossible in others!"

"But why should you wish to persuade me that I feel more than I acknowledge?"

"That is a question which I hardly know how to answer. We all love to instruct, though we can teach only what is not worth knowing. Forgive me; and if you persist in indifference, do not make *me* your confidante."

Cassandra Austen, portrait of Jane Austen, c. 1810. This portrait, the only reasonably certain depiction of Austen from her lifetime, did not altogether please her relatives, who did not unanimously agree that it provided a genuine likeness. The late nineteenth-century engraving of Austen probably derives from this watercolor (see p. 361).

13

1 So early.

2 More advanced, ahead of.

A FEW DAYS AFTER THIS VISIT, Mr. Bingley called again, and alone. His friend had left him that morning for London, but was to return home in ten days time. He sat with them above an hour, and was in remarkably good spirits. Mrs. Bennet invited him to dine with them; but, with many expressions of concern, he confessed himself engaged elsewhere.

"Next time you call," said she, "I hope we shall be more lucky."

He should be particularly happy at any time, &c. &c.; and if she would give him leave, would take an early opportunity of waiting on them.

"Can you come to-morrow?"

Yes, he had no engagement at all for to-morrow; and her invitation was accepted with alacrity.

He came, and in such very good time,[1] that the ladies were none of them dressed. In ran Mrs. Bennet to her daughter's room, in her dressing gown, and with her hair half finished, crying out,

"My dear Jane, make haste and hurry down. He is come—Mr. Bingley is come.—He is, indeed. Make haste, make haste. Here, Sarah, come to Miss Bennet this moment, and help her on with her gown. Never mind Miss Lizzy's hair."

"We will be down as soon as we can," said Jane; "but I dare say Kitty is forwarder[2] than either of us, for she went up stairs half an hour ago."

"Oh! hang Kitty! what has she to do with it? Come be quick, be quick! Where is your sash, my dear?"

But when her mother was gone, Jane would not be prevailed on to go down without one of her sisters.

The same anxiety to get them by themselves, was visible again in the evening. After tea, Mr. Bennet retired to the library, as was his custom, and Mary went up stairs to her instrument. Two obstacles of the five being thus removed, Mrs. Bennet sat looking and winking at Elizabeth and Catherine for a considerable time, without making any impression on them. Elizabeth would not observe her; and when at last Kitty did, she very innocently said, "What is the matter mamma? What do you keep winking at me for? What am I to do?"

"Nothing child, nothing. I did not wink at you." She then sat still five minutes longer; but unable to waste such a precious occasion, she suddenly got up, and saying to Kitty, "Come here, my love, I want to speak to you," took her out of the room. Jane instantly gave a look at Elizabeth, which spoke her distress at such premeditation, and her intreaty that *she* would not give into it. In a few minutes, Mrs. Bennet half opened the door and called out,

"Lizzy, my dear, I want to speak with you."

Elizabeth was forced to go.

"We may as well leave them by themselves you know;" said her mother as soon as she was in the hall. "Kitty and I are going up stairs to sit in my dressing room."

Elizabeth made no attempt to reason with her mother, but remained quietly in the hall, till she and Kitty were out of sight, then returned into the drawing room.

Mrs. Bennet's schemes for this day were ineffectual. Bingley was every thing that was charming, except the professed lover of her daughter. His ease and cheerfulness rendered him a most agreeable addition to their evening party; and he bore with the ill-judged officiousness of the mother, and heard all her silly remarks with a forbearance and command of countenance, particularly grateful[3] to the daughter.

He scarcely needed an invitation to stay supper; and before he went away, an engagement was formed, chiefly through his own and Mrs. Bennet's means, for his coming next morning to shoot with her husband.

3 Pleasing, gratifying.

Thomas Medland (1744–1823) after Edward Bell (1794–1847), "Richard Badham Thornhill, Esq," frontispiece to *The Shooting Directory* by R. B. Thornhill (London: Printed for Longman, Hurst, Rees, and Orme, 1804). The engraving shows a gentleman perhaps just returned from shooting, with gun and dogs.

After this day, Jane said no more of her indifference. Not a word passed between the sisters concerning Bingley; but Elizabeth went to bed in the happy belief that all must speedily be concluded, unless Mr. Darcy returned within the stated time. Seriously, however, she felt tolerably persuaded that all this must have taken place with that gentleman's concurrence.

Bingley was punctual to his appointment; and he and Mr. Bennet spent the morning together, as had been agreed on. The latter was much more agreeable than his companion expected. There was nothing of presumption or folly in Bingley, that could provoke his ridicule, or disgust him into silence; and he was more communicative, and less eccentric than the other had ever seen him. Bingley of course returned with him to dinner; and in the evening Mrs. Bennet's invention was again at work to get every body away from him and her daughter. Elizabeth, who had a letter to write, went into the breakfast room for that purpose soon after tea; for as the others were all going to sit down to cards, she could not be wanted to counteract her mother's schemes.

But on returning to the drawing room, when her letter was finished, she saw, to her infinite surprise, there was reason to fear that her mother had been too ingenious for her. On opening the door, she perceived her sister and Bingley standing together over the hearth, as if engaged in earnest conversation; and had this led to no suspicion, the faces of both as they hastily turned round, and moved away from each other, would have told it all. Their situation was awkward enough; but *hers* she thought was still worse. Not a syllable was uttered by either; and Elizabeth was on the point of going away again, when Bingley, who as well as the others had sat down, suddenly rose, and whispering a few words to her sister, ran out of the room.

Jane could have no reserves from Elizabeth, where confidence would give pleasure; and instantly embracing her, acknowledged, with the liveliest emotion, that she was the happiest creature in the world.[4]

"'Tis too much!" she added, "by far too much. I do not deserve it. Oh! why is not every body as happy?"

4 Jane does not ordinarily resort to clichés, but in this situation nothing more eloquent comes to her mind.

5 Jane's happiness at the prospect of marrying Bingley derives partly from the satisfaction it will give her family. Her genuine selflessness expresses itself even at this moment when self-concern might be expected to dominate.

6 A good marriage, in Elizabeth's view and in that of eighteenth-century moralists, must be founded on reason. As she has thought a bit earlier, the marriage between Jane and Bingley is "the happiest, wisest, most reasonable end" of their relationship.

Elizabeth's congratulations were given with a sincerity, a warmth, a delight, which words could but poorly express. Every sentence of kindness was a fresh source of happiness to Jane. But she would not allow herself to stay with her sister, or say half that remained to be said, for the present.

"I must go instantly to my mother;" she cried. "I would not on any account trifle with her affectionate solicitude; or allow her to hear it from any one but myself. He is gone to my father already. Oh! Lizzy, to know that what I have to relate will give such pleasure to all my dear family! how shall I bear so much happiness!"[5]

She then hastened away to her mother, who had purposely broken up the card party, and was sitting up stairs with Kitty.

Elizabeth, who was left by herself, now smiled at the rapidity and ease with which an affair was finally settled, that had given them so many previous months of suspense and vexation.

"And this," said she, "is the end of all his friend's anxious circumspection! of all his sister's falsehood and contrivance! the happiest, wisest, most reasonable end!"

In a few minutes she was joined by Bingley, whose conference with her father had been short and to the purpose.

"Where is your sister?" said he hastily, as he opened the door.

"With my mother up stairs. She will be down in a moment I dare say."

He then shut the door, and coming up to her, claimed the good wishes and affection of a sister. Elizabeth honestly and heartily expressed her delight in the prospect of their relationship. They shook hands with great cordiality; and then till her sister came down, she had to listen to all he had to say, of his own happiness, and of Jane's perfections; and in spite of his being a lover, Elizabeth really believed all his expectations of felicity, to be rationally founded,[6] because they had for basis the excellent understanding, and super-excellent disposition of Jane, and a general similarity of feeling and taste between her and himself.

It was an evening of no common delight to them all; the satisfaction of Miss Bennet's mind gave a glow of such sweet animation to her face, as made her look handsomer than ever. Kitty simpered and smiled, and hoped her turn was coming soon. Mrs. Bennet could not give her consent, or speak her approbation in terms warm enough to satisfy her feelings, though she talked to Bingley of nothing else, for half an hour; and when Mr. Bennet joined them at supper, his voice and manner plainly shewed how really happy he was.

Not a word, however, passed his lips in allusion to it, till their visitor took his leave for the night; but as soon as he was gone, he turned to his daughter and said,

"Jane, I congratulate you. You will be a very happy woman."

Jane went to him instantly, kissed him, and thanked him for his goodness.

"You are a good girl;" he replied, "and I have great pleasure in thinking you will be so happily settled. I have not a doubt of your doing very well together. Your tempers[7] are by no means unlike. You are each of you so complying, that nothing will ever be resolved on; so easy,[8] that every servant will cheat you; and so generous, that you will always exceed your income."

"I hope not so. Imprudence or thoughtlessness in money matters, would be unpardonable in *me*."[9]

"Exceed their income! My dear Mr. Bennet," cried his wife, "what are you talking of? Why, he has four or five thousand a-year, and very likely more." Then addressing her daughter, "Oh! my dear, dear Jane, I am so happy! I am sure I shan't get a wink of sleep all night. I knew how it would be. I always said it must be so, at last. I was sure you could not be so beautiful for nothing![10] I remember, as soon as ever I saw him, when he first came into Hertfordshire last year, I thought how likely it was that you should come together. Oh! he is the handsomest young man that ever was seen!"[11]

Wickham, Lydia, were all forgotten. Jane was beyond competition her favourite child. At that moment, she cared for no other. Her youngest sisters soon began to make interest[12] with her for objects of happiness which she might in future be able to dispense.

Mary petitioned for the use of the library at Netherfield; and Kitty begged very hard for a few balls there every winter.

Bingley, from this time, was of course a daily visitor at Longbourn; coming frequently before breakfast, and always remaining till after

7 Temperaments, dispositions.

8 Easy-going.

9 Because she is not bringing money to the marriage. She feels responsible for using prudently whatever part she is allotted of Bingley's wealth.

10 Mrs. Bennet believes that for the business of getting girls married, no other asset compares in value with beauty. Throughout the novel, she never mentions other qualities of her daughters that might attract men. In this respect she resembles many contemporary novelists, who frequently offered stock descriptions of their heroines that amounted to codes for "attractive to men." Not until *Jane Eyre* (1847) was a novelistic heroine explicitly described as plain. As the marchioness de Lambert wrote early in the eighteenth century, "Beauty inspires a pleasing sentiment which prepossesses people in its favour" (Ann-Thérèse, Marchioness de Lambert, *Advice of a Mother to her Daughter, The Young Lady's Pocket Library, or Parental Monitor* [Bristol: Thoemmes Press, 1995], 144).

11 Even in a man, it seems, good looks supply an emblem of eligibility from Mrs. Bennet's point of view.

12 Make special pleas.

supper; unless when some barbarous neighbour, who could not be enough detested, had given him an invitation to dinner, which he thought himself obliged to accept.

Elizabeth had now but little time for conversation with her sister; for while he was present, Jane had no attention to bestow on any one else; but she found herself considerably useful to both of them in those hours of separation that must sometimes occur. In the absence of Jane, he always attached himself to Elizabeth, for the pleasure of talking of her; and when Bingley was gone, Jane constantly sought the same means of relief.

"He has made me so happy," said she, one evening, "by telling me, that he was totally ignorant of my being in town last spring! I had not believed it possible."

"I suspected as much," replied Elizabeth. "But how did he account for it?"

"It must have been his sister's doing. They were certainly no friends to his acquaintance with me, which I cannot wonder at, since he might have chosen so much more advantageously in many respects. But when they see, as I trust they will, that their brother is happy with me, they will learn to be contented, and we shall be on good terms again; though we can never be what we once were to each other."

"That is the most unforgiving speech," said Elizabeth, "that I ever heard you utter. Good girl! It would vex me, indeed, to see you again the dupe of Miss Bingley's pretended regard."

"Would you believe it, Lizzy, that when he went to town last November, he really loved me, and nothing but a persuasion of *my* being indifferent, would have prevented his coming down again!"

"He made a little mistake to be sure; but it is to the credit of his modesty."

This naturally introduced a panegyric from Jane on his diffidence, and the little value he put on his own good qualities.

Elizabeth was pleased to find, that he had not betrayed the interference of his friend; for, though Jane had the most generous and forgiving heart in the world, she knew it was a circumstance which must prejudice her against him.

"I am certainly the most fortunate creature that ever existed!" cried Jane. "Oh! Lizzy, why am I thus singled from my family, and blessed above them all! If I could but see *you* as happy! If there *were* but such another man for you!"

"If you were to give me forty such men, I never could be so happy as you. Till I have your disposition, your goodness, I never can have your happiness. No, no, let me shift for myself; and, perhaps, if I have very good luck, I may meet with another Mr. Collins in time."

The situation of affairs in the Longbourn family could not be long a secret. Mrs. Bennet was privileged to whisper it to Mrs. Phillips, and *she* ventured, without any permission, to do the same by all her neighbours in Meryton.

The Bennets were speedily pronounced to be the luckiest family in the world, though only a few weeks before, when Lydia had first run away, they had been generally proved to be marked out for misfortune.

J. Cordrey (c. 1765–1825), "The London to Dartford Stage-Coach," 1813. Jane and Cassandra would often have taken this coach on their way to their brother's house in mid-Kent.

14

1 Not literally on the grass: up the driveway that passed through the lawn.

2 Carriage and horses.

3 Correspond to.

4 Hired, like the horses used by Elizabeth and Jane for returning to Longbourn. The fact that the horses were hired indicated that the visitor came from some distance, since callers would use their own horses for visits in the neighborhood.

5 If present when visitors came, Bingley and Jane would be expected to remain in the room to help entertain them.

6 Expecting.

7 Lady Catherine, as the superior in rank, should have asked to be introduced to Elizabeth's mother.

ONE MORNING, ABOUT A WEEK after Bingley's engagement with Jane had been formed, as he and the females of the family were sitting together in the dining room, their attention was suddenly drawn to the window, by the sound of a carriage; and they perceived a chaise and four driving up the lawn.[1] It was too early in the morning for visitors, and besides, the equipage[2] did not answer to[3] that of any of their neighbours. The horses were post;[4] and neither the carriage, nor the livery of the servant who preceded it, were familiar to them. As it was certain, however, that somebody was coming, Bingley instantly prevailed on Miss Bennet to avoid the confinement of such an intrusion,[5] and walk away with him into the shrubbery. They both set off, and the conjectures of the remaining three continued, though with little satisfaction, till the door was thrown open, and their visitor entered. It was Lady Catherine de Bourgh.

They were of course all intending[6] to be surprised; but their astonishment was beyond their expectation; and on the part of Mrs. Bennet and Kitty, though she was perfectly unknown to them, even inferior to what Elizabeth felt.

She entered the room with an air more than usually ungracious, made no other reply to Elizabeth's salutation, than a slight inclination of the head, and sat down without saying a word. Elizabeth had mentioned her name to her mother on her ladyship's entrance, though no request of introduction had been made.[7]

Mrs. Bennet all amazement, though flattered by having a guest of such high importance, received her with the utmost politeness.

After sitting for a moment in silence, she said very stiffly to Elizabeth,

"I hope you are well, Miss Bennet. That lady I suppose is your mother."

Elizabeth replied very concisely that she was.

"And *that* I suppose is one of your sisters."

"Yes, madam," said Mrs. Bennet, delighted to speak to a Lady Catherine.[8] "She is my youngest girl but one. My youngest of all, is lately married, and my eldest is somewhere about the grounds, walking with a young man, who I believe will soon become a part of the family."

"You have a very small park here," returned Lady Catherine after a short silence.

"It is nothing in comparison of Rosings, my lady, I dare say; but I assure you it is much larger than Sir William Lucas's."

"This must be a most inconvenient sitting room for the evening, in summer; the windows are full west."

Mrs. Bennet assured her that they never sat there after dinner, and then added,

"May I take the liberty of asking your ladyship whether you left Mr. and Mrs. Collins well."

"Yes, very well. I saw them the night before last."

Elizabeth now expected that she would produce a letter for her from Charlotte, as it seemed the only probable motive for her calling. But no letter appeared, and she was completely puzzled.

Mrs. Bennet, with great civility, begged her ladyship to take some refreshment; but Lady Catherine very resolutely, and not very politely, declined eating any thing; and then rising up, said to Elizabeth,

"Miss Bennet, there seemed to be a prettyish kind of a little wilderness[9] on one side of your lawn. I should be glad to take a turn in it, if you will favour me with your company."

"Go, my dear," cried her mother, "and shew her ladyship about the different walks. I think she will be pleased with the hermitage."[10]

Elizabeth obeyed, and running into her own room for her parasol, attended her noble guest down stairs. As they passed through the

8 Having been more or less introduced, Mrs. Bennet is now free to speak to her high-ranking guest.

9 A group of trees in an elaborate arrangement. This is presumably the "copse" to which Elizabeth often retreats. Calling it a wilderness is in accord with the contemporary taste for "natural" landscaping.

10 The construction of mock hermitages on landscaped grounds was a fashionable enterprise in the eighteenth century, when interest in the solitary and the medieval rose high. Men were sometimes hired to act the part of their hermit residents, but more often the building itself, frequently constructed as an imitation ruin, was the attraction.

Such hermitages belonged to the larger category of "follies," buildings without a practical purpose erected for aesthetic reasons. Towers, pyramids, and temples were other favored forms, often also presented as ruins, in accord with the principles of the picturesque. The enthusiasm for follies lasted through the seventeenth and much of the eighteenth century. It was waning by the century's end.

11 One may wonder who has celebrated it.

12 Importance.

13 Yet another reason for blushing.

hall, Lady Catherine opened the doors into the dining-parlour and drawing room, and pronouncing them, after a short survey, to be decent looking rooms, walked on.

Her carriage remained at the door, and Elizabeth saw that her waiting-woman was in it. They proceeded in silence along the gravel walk that led to the copse; Elizabeth was determined to make no effort for conversation with a woman, who was now more than usually insolent and disagreeable.

"How could I ever think her like her nephew?" said she, as she looked in her face.

As soon as they entered the copse, Lady Catherine began in the following manner:—

"You can be at no loss, Miss Bennet, to understand the reason of my journey hither. Your own heart, your own conscience, must tell you why I come."

Elizabeth looked with unaffected astonishment.

"Indeed, you are mistaken, Madam. I have not been at all able to account for the honour of seeing you here."

"Miss Bennet," replied her ladyship, in an angry tone, "you ought to know, that I am not to be trifled with. But however insincere *you* may choose to be, you shall not find *me* so. My character has ever been celebrated[11] for its sincerity and frankness, and in a cause of such moment[12] as this, I shall certainly not depart from it. A report of a most alarming nature reached me two days ago. I was told, that not only your sister was on the point of being most advantageously married, but that *you,* that Miss Elizabeth Bennet, would, in all likelihood, be soon afterwards united to my nephew, my own nephew, Mr. Darcy. Though I *know* it must be a scandalous falsehood; though I would not injure him so much as to suppose the truth of it possible, I instantly resolved on setting off for this place, that I might make my sentiments known to you."

"If you believed it impossible to be true," said Elizabeth, colouring with astonishment and disdain,[13] "I wonder you took the trouble of coming so far. What could your ladyship propose by it?"

"At once to insist upon having such a report universally contradicted."

"Your coming to Longbourn, to see me and my family," said Elizabeth coolly, "will be rather a confirmation of it; if, indeed, such a report is in existence."

"If! do you then pretend to be ignorant of it? Has it not been industriously circulated by yourselves? Do you not know that such a report is spread abroad?"

"I never heard that it was."

"And can you likewise declare, that there is no *foundation* for it?"

"I do not pretend to possess equal frankness with your ladyship. *You* may ask questions, which *I* shall not choose to answer."

"This is not to be borne. Miss Bennet, I insist on being satisfied. Has he, has my nephew, made you an offer of marriage?"

"Your ladyship has declared it to be impossible."

"It ought to be so; it must be so, while he retains the use of his reason. But *your* arts and allurements may, in a moment of infatuation, have made him forget what he owes to himself and to all his family. You may have drawn him in."[14]

"If I have, I shall be the last person to confess it."

"Miss Bennet, do you know who I am? I have not been accustomed to such language as this. I am almost the nearest relation he has in the world, and am entitled to know all his dearest concerns."

"But you are not entitled to know *mine;* nor will such behaviour as this, ever induce me to be explicit."

"Let me be rightly understood. This match, to which you have the presumption to aspire, can never take place. No, never. Mr. Darcy is engaged to *my daughter.* Now what have you to say?"

"Only this; that if he is so, you can have no reason to suppose he will make an offer to me."

Lady Catherine hesitated for a moment, and then replied,

"The engagement between them is of a peculiar kind. From their infancy, they have been intended for each other. It was the favourite wish of *his* mother, as well as of her's. While in their cradles, we planned the union: and now, at the moment when the wishes of both sisters[15] would be accomplished, in their marriage, to be prevented by a young woman of inferior birth, of no importance in the world, and wholly unallied to the family? Do you pay no regard to the wishes

14 Women were frequently accused of drawing men in. Austen offers several representations of women attempting to do just that, Miss Bingley conspicuous among them. Mary Crawford, in *Mansfield Park,* also exemplifies the skill—as Elizabeth emphatically does not.

15 Marriages of first cousins, especially in the upper ranks of society, were not uncommon in this period. Moreover, in the recent past, marriages based on arrangements made at the time of the participants' birth still took place, although they were becoming outmoded by the end of the eighteenth century.

Title page illustration from *Pride and Prejudice,* 1833, published by Richard Bentley, London. This illustration shows the confrontation between Elizabeth and Lady Catherine.

of his friends? To his tacit engagement with Miss De Bourgh? Are you lost to every feeling of propriety and delicacy? Have you not heard me say, that from his earliest hours he was destined for his cousin?"

"Yes, and I had heard it before. But what is that to me? If there is no other objection to my marrying your nephew, I shall certainly not be kept from it, by knowing that his mother and aunt wished him to marry Miss De Bourgh. You both did as much as you could, in planning the marriage. Its completion depended on others. If Mr. Darcy is neither by honour nor inclination confined to his cousin, why is not he to make another choice? And if I am that choice, why may not I accept him?"

"Because honour, decorum, prudence, nay, interest,[16] forbid it. Yes, Miss Bennet, interest; for do not expect to be noticed[17] by his family or friends, if you wilfully act against the inclinations of all. You will be censured, slighted, and despised, by every one connected with him.[18] Your alliance will be a disgrace; your name will never even be mentioned by any of us."

"These are heavy misfortunes," replied Elizabeth. "But the wife of Mr. Darcy must have such extraordinary sources of happiness necessarily attached to her situation, that she could, upon the whole, have no cause to repine."

"Obstinate, headstrong girl! I am ashamed of you! Is this your gratitude for my attentions to you last spring? Is nothing due to me on that score?

"Let us sit down. You are to understand, Miss Bennet, that I came here with the determined resolution of carrying my purpose; nor will I be dissuaded from it. I have not been used to submit to any person's whims. I have not been in the habit of brooking disappointment."

"*That* will make your ladyship's situation at present more pitiable; but it will have no effect on *me*."

"I will not be interrupted. Hear me in silence. My daughter and my nephew are formed for each other. They are descended on the maternal side, from the same noble line; and, on the father's, from respectable, honourable, and ancient, though untitled families. Their

16 Self-interest.

17 Given social recognition.

18 Lady Catherine appears to share Mrs. Bennet's belief that a woman marries for her own advantage and that of her family. The information she imparts, that Darcy's relatives will ignore her, she assumes, will cancel the main reason Elizabeth might want the marriage.

19 This is a bold assertion on Elizabeth's part. It is technically true to say that she and Darcy belong to the same social sphere, if the status of "gentleman" is broadly defined. Mr. Bennet is indeed a gentleman: he does not have to work for a living. But the social gap between him and Darcy, who has an income of £10,000 pounds a year and never needs to worry about whether the horses for the carriage are needed for the farm, remains large. Elizabeth is quite aware of this fact, but her defiance of Lady Catherine leads her to rely on the technicality.

20 Social status.

fortune on both sides is splendid. They are destined for each other by the voice of every member of their respective houses; and what is to divide them? The upstart pretensions of a young woman without family, connections, or fortune. Is this to be endured! But it must not, shall not be. If you were sensible of your own good, you would not wish to quit the sphere, in which you have been brought up."

"In marrying your nephew, I should not consider myself as quitting that sphere. He is a gentleman; I am a gentleman's daughter; so far we are equal."[19]

"True. You *are* a gentleman's daughter. But who was your mother? Who are your uncles and aunts? Do not imagine me ignorant of their condition."[20]

"Whatever my connections may be," said Elizabeth, "if your nephew does not object to them, they can be nothing to *you*."

Anna Lefroy, "Steventon Rectory," c. 1814. Jane Austen was born at Steventon Rectory and lived there until she was twenty-five, when her father retired from his role as active clergyman and the family moved to Bath. An early version of *Pride and Prejudice* was completed there. Beyond its title ("First Impressions"), little is known about this preliminary text. Anna Lefroy was Austen's niece.

"Tell me once for all, are you engaged to him?"

Though Elizabeth would not, for the mere purpose of obliging Lady Catherine, have answered this question; she could not but say, after a moment's deliberation,

"I am not."[21]

Lady Catherine seemed pleased.

"And will you promise me, never to enter into such an engagement?"

"I will make no promise of the kind."

"Miss Bennet, I am shocked and astonished. I expected to find a more reasonable young woman. But do not deceive yourself into a belief that I will ever recede. I shall not go away, till you have given me the assurance I require."

"And I certainly *never* shall give it. I am not to be intimidated into anything so wholly unreasonable. Your ladyship wants Mr. Darcy to marry your daughter; but would my giving you the wished-for promise, make *their* marriage at all more probable? Supposing him to be attached to me, would my refusing to accept his hand, make him wish to bestow it on his cousin? Allow me to say, Lady Catherine, that the arguments with which you have supported this extraordinary application,[22] have been as frivolous as the application was ill-judged. You have widely[23] mistaken my character, if you think I can be worked on by such persuasions as these. How far your nephew might approve of your interference in *his* affairs, I cannot tell; but you have certainly no right to concern yourself in mine. I must beg, therefore, to be importuned no farther on the subject."

"Not so hasty, if you please. I have by no means done. To all the objections I have already urged, I have still another to add. I am no stranger to the particulars of your youngest sister's infamous elopement. I know it all; that the young man's marrying her was a patched-up business, at the expence of your father and uncles. And is *such* a girl to be my nephew's sister? Is *her* husband, is the son of his late father's steward, to be his brother? Heaven and earth!—of what are you thinking? Are the shades of Pemberley to be thus polluted?"

"You can *now* have nothing farther to say," she resentfully an-

21 Perhaps she does not wish it known—by the Collinses, for example, or ultimately by Darcy—that she by silence allowed the possibility that she was in fact engaged.

22 Appeal.

23 Greatly.

24 Reputation.

25 By using this word, Lady Catherine indicates again her assumption that Elizabeth would marry Darcy for the sake of worldly advantage.

26 Test.

27 It would be customary politeness to send compliments to the titular hostess if unable to say goodbye to her in person.

swered. "You have insulted me in every possible method. I must beg to return to the house."

And she rose as she spoke. Lady Catherine rose also, and they turned back. Her ladyship was highly incensed.

"You have no regard, then, for the honour and credit[24] of my nephew! Unfeeling, selfish girl! Do you not consider that a connection with you, must disgrace him in the eyes of everybody?"

"Lady Catherine, I have nothing further to say. You know my sentiments."

"You are then resolved to have him?"

"I have said no such thing. I am only resolved to act in that manner, which will, in my own opinion, constitute my happiness, without reference to *you,* or to any person so wholly unconnected with me."

"It is well. You refuse, then, to oblige me. You refuse to obey the claims of duty, honour, and gratitude. You are determined to ruin him in the opinion of all his friends, and make him the contempt of the world."

"Neither duty, nor honour, nor gratitude," replied Elizabeth, "have any possible claim on me, in the present instance. No principle of either, would be violated by my marriage with Mr. Darcy. And with regard to the resentment of his family, or the indignation of the world, if the former *were* excited by his marrying me, it would not give me one moment's concern—and the world in general would have too much sense to join in the scorn."

"And this is your real opinion! This is your final resolve! Very well. I shall now know how to act. Do not imagine, Miss Bennet, that your ambition[25] will ever be gratified. I came to try[26] you. I hoped to find you reasonable; but depend upon it I will carry my point."

In this manner Lady Catherine talked on, till they were at the door of the carriage, when turning hastily round, she added,

"I take no leave of you, Miss Bennet. I send no compliments[27] to your mother. You deserve no such attention. I am most seriously displeased."

Elizabeth made no answer; and without attempting to persuade her ladyship to return into the house, walked quietly into it herself.

She heard the carriage drive away as she proceeded up stairs. Her mother impatiently met her at the door of the dressing room, to ask why Lady Catherine would not come in again and rest herself.

"She did not choose it," said her daughter, "she would go."

"She is a very fine-looking woman! and her calling here was prodigiously civil! for she only came, I suppose, to tell us the Collinses were well. She is on her road somewhere, I dare say, and so passing through Meryton, thought she might as well call on you. I suppose she had nothing particular to say to you, Lizzy?"

Elizabeth was forced to give into a little falsehood here; for to acknowledge the substance of their conversation was impossible.[28]

28 The scene between Elizabeth and Lady Catherine owes something to an episode in Samuel Richardson's *Pamela*. Shortly after the improbable marriage between the servant girl Pamela and her rich master, Mr. B, his sister, Lady Davers, appears unexpectedly at their home. Mr. B is at a neighbor's, where Pamela is supposed to join him. Lady Davers prevents her from leaving, refuses to believe that she is married, emphasizing her lowliness in comparison to Mr. B's high status, and calls her a whore. Pamela shows her a loving letter from Mr. B that refers to her as his wife, thus enraging Lady Davers even more: "[Y]ou shew'd it me, to upbraid me with his stooping to such painted Dirt, to the Disgrace of a Family, ancient and untainted beyond most in the Kingdom; and now I will give thee One hundred Guineas for one bold Word, that I may fell thee at my Foot ('Tuesday, 11 in the Morning')." When Lady Davers calls her "beggarly Brat," Pamela defends her parents as "honest and industrious," only subject to misfortune. She infuriates Lady Davers to the utmost by saying, "I scorn your Words, and am as much marry'd as your Ladyship!"

The stakes are different for Elizabeth and Pamela: Pamela is defending her marriage as well as herself. The two episodes, however, engage the same issues. By verbal triumph over an aristocratic opponent, a young woman of lower social status in a society operating largely on the basis of class distinctions can demonstrate her appropriateness as a mate for Prince Charming. Both Pamela and Elizabeth refuse to be cowed. Both employ moral, mental, and verbal resources in frustrating the aristocratic claim to automatic dominance. Elizabeth can claim, as Pamela cannot, that she is the daughter of a gentleman and would not marry outside her class if she married Darcy, but Darcy's enormous wealth and his aristocratic mother ("Lady Anne") give him status quite different from hers.

Unlike Elizabeth, Pamela mingles her defiance with proclamations of deference. Published in 1740, *Pamela* belongs to a different era from *Pride and Prejudice*. Elizabeth makes it far clearer that her right to marry Darcy if she chooses (and if he chooses) derives from her distinctive character, not from her financial or social position.

15

1 By suggesting that Lady Catherine's behavior was not rational, Elizabeth of course levels a serious criticism at her.

2 Pondering.

THE DISCOMPOSURE OF SPIRITS, which this extraordinary visit threw Elizabeth into, could not be easily overcome; nor could she for many hours, learn to think of it less than incessantly. Lady Catherine it appeared, had actually taken the trouble of this journey from Rosings, for the sole purpose of breaking off her supposed engagement with Mr. Darcy. It was a rational scheme, to be sure![1] but from what the report of their engagement could originate, Elizabeth was at a loss to imagine; till she recollected that *his* being the intimate friend of Bingley, and *her* being the sister of Jane, was enough, at a time when the expectation of one wedding, made every body eager for another, to supply the idea. She had not herself forgotten to feel that the marriage of her sister must bring them more frequently together. And her neighbours at Lucas lodge, therefore, (for through their communication with the Collinses, the report she concluded had reached Lady Catherine) had only set *that* down, as almost certain and immediate, which *she* had looked forward to as possible, at some future time.

In revolving[2] Lady Catherine's expressions, however, she could not help feeling some uneasiness as to the possible consequence of her persisting in this interference. From what she had said of her resolution to prevent their marriage, it occurred to Elizabeth that she must meditate an application to her nephew; and how *he* might take a similar representation of the evils attached to a connection with her, she dared not pronounce. She knew not the exact degree of his affection for his aunt, or his dependence on her judgment, but it was natural to suppose that he thought much higher of her ladyship than *she* could do; and it was certain, that in enumerating the miseries of a marriage with *one,* whose immediate connections were so unequal to his own, his aunt would address him on his weakest side. With his notions of dignity, he would probably feel that the arguments, which to Elizabeth had appeared weak and ridiculous, contained much good sense and solid reasoning.

If he had been wavering before as to what he should do, which had often seemed likely, the advice and intreaty of so near a relation might settle every doubt, and determine him at once to be as happy, as dignity unblemished could make him.[3] In that case he would return no more. Lady Catherine might see him in her way through town; and his engagement to Bingley of coming again to Netherfield must give way.

"If, therefore, an excuse for not keeping his promise, should come to his friend within a few days," she added, "I shall know how to understand it. I shall then give over[4] every expectation, every wish of his constancy. If he is satisfied with only regretting me, when he might have obtained my affections and hand, I shall soon cease to regret him at all."

The surprise of the rest of the family, on hearing who their visitor had been, was very great; but they obligingly satisfied it, with the same kind of supposition, which had appeased Mrs. Bennet's curiosity; and Elizabeth was spared from much teazing on the subject.

The next morning, as she was going down stairs, she was met by her father, who came out of his library with a letter in his hand.

"Lizzy," said he, "I was going to look for you; come into my room."

She followed him thither; and her curiosity to know what he had to tell her, was heightened by the supposition of its being in some manner connected with the letter he held. It suddenly struck her that it might be from Lady Catherine; and she anticipated with dismay all the consequent explanations.

3 This reflection of Elizabeth's makes it clear that even if she's in love, she does not relinquish her habit of making quick, certain judgments about people. If Darcy does not pursue her, she has decided, his choice must have been made on the basis of his sense of dignity—which she feels inclined to mock.

4 Give up.

5 Embarrassment? Excitement? Modesty?

6 *Conviction,* not *guess.* Elizabeth tends to be sure of her conclusions, regardless of their basis.

7 Self-conscious, aware of something secret.

8 Notified.

9 Which would of course seem important to an aspiring clergyman.

10 Mr. Collins shares the view held by Mrs. Bennet and Lady Catherine: that a woman marries for personal and family financial and social advantage.

She followed her father to the fire place, and they both sat down. He then said,

"I have received a letter this morning that has astonished me exceedingly. As it principally concerns yourself, you ought to know its contents. I did not know before, that I had *two* daughters on the brink of matrimony. Let me congratulate you, on a very important conquest."

The colour now rushed into Elizabeth's cheeks[5] in the instantaneous conviction[6] of its being a letter from the nephew, instead of the aunt; and she was undetermined whether most to be pleased that he explained himself at all, or offended that his letter was not rather addressed to herself; when her father continued,

"You look conscious.[7] Young ladies have great penetration in such matters as these; but I think I may defy even *your* sagacity, to discover the name of your admirer. This letter is from Mr. Collins."

"From Mr. Collins! and what can *he* have to say?"

"Something very much to the purpose of course. He begins with congratulations on the approaching nuptials of my eldest daughter, of which it seems he has been told by some of the good-natured, gossiping Lucases. I shall not sport with your impatience, by reading what he says on that point. What relates to yourself, is as follows. 'Having thus offered you the sincere congratulations of Mrs. Collins and myself on this happy event, let me now add a short hint on the subject of another; of which we have been advertised[8] by the same authority. Your daughter Elizabeth, it is presumed, will not long bear the name of Bennet, after her elder sister has resigned it, and the chosen partner of her fate, may be reasonably looked up to, as one of the most illustrious personages in this land.'

"Can you possibly guess, Lizzy, who is meant by this?' 'This young gentleman is blessed in a peculiar way, with every thing the heart of mortal can most desire,—splendid property, noble kindred, and extensive patronage.[9] Yet in spite of all these temptations, let me warn my cousin Elizabeth, and yourself, of what evils you may incur, by a precipitate closure with this gentleman's proposals, which, of course, you will be inclined to take immediate advantage of.'[10]

"Have you any idea, Lizzy, who this gentleman is? But now it comes out."

"My motive for cautioning you is as follows. We have reason to imagine that his aunt, Lady Catherine de Bourgh, does not look on the match with a friendly eye."

"*Mr. Darcy,* you see, is the man! Now, Lizzy, I think I *have* surprised you. Could he, or the Lucases, have pitched on any man, within the circle of our acquaintance, whose name would have given the lie more effectually to what they related? Mr. Darcy, who never looks at any woman but to see a blemish, and who probably never looked at *you* in his life! It is admirable!"

Elizabeth tried to join in her father's pleasantry, but could only force one most reluctant smile. Never had his wit been directed in a manner so little agreeable to her.

"Are you not diverted?"

"Oh! yes. Pray read on."

"After mentioning the likelihood of this marriage to her ladyship last night, she immediately, with her usual condescension,[11] expressed what she felt on the occasion; when it become apparent, that on the score of some family objections on the part of my cousin, she would never give her consent to what she termed so disgraceful a match. I thought it my duty to give the speediest intelligence[12] of this to my cousin, that she and her noble admirer may be aware of what they are about, and not run hastily into a marriage which has not been properly sanctioned." "Mr. Collins moreover adds, 'I am truly rejoiced that my cousin Lydia's sad business has been so well hushed up, and am only concerned that their living together before the marriage took place, should be so generally known. I must not, however, neglect the duties of my station, or refrain from declaring my amazement, at hearing that you received the young couple into your house as soon as they were married. It was an encouragement of vice; and had I been the rector of Longbourn, I should very strenuously have opposed it. You ought certainly to forgive them as a christian, but never to admit them in your sight, or allow their names to be mentioned in your hearing.' *That* is his notion of christian forgiveness!

11 This is probably Mr. Collins's most inappropriate use of his favorite form of praise for Lady Catherine.

12 News.

G. Engleheart, "Thomas Lefroy," 1799. Thomas Lefroy (1776–1869) was Austen's partner in a youthful flirtation. He eventually became Lord Chief Justice of Ireland, long after having married someone else.

13 A baby: Charlotte is pregnant.

14 Affectedly prim.

15 This explicit statement of Mr. Bennet's mode of existence provides new focus for the theme of laughter. His laughter, he now says, is not only defensive, like Elizabeth's, but also aggressive. It fosters a sense of superiority—his form of "pride"—and provides the entertainment that gets him through his days. He likes the idea of sharing this vision of the world with his favorite daughter; he seems to assume, mistakenly, that her laughter means what his does.

16 This despite the fact that he has earlier said that his son-in-law, Wickham, was more "valuable" than Sir William's son-in-law, Collins.

17 The contrast between her position and her father's now becomes striking. Her laughter serves as protection against his inquiry, against the world's perception of her new emotional vulnerability.

The rest of his letter is only about his dear Charlotte's situation, and his expectation of a young olive-branch.[13] But, Lizzy, you look as if you did not enjoy it. You are not going to be *Missish,*[14] I hope, and pretend to be affronted at an idle report. For what do we live, but to make sport for our neighbours, and laugh at them in our turn?"[15]

"Oh!" cried Elizabeth, "I am excessively diverted. But it is so strange!"

"Yes—*that* is what makes it amusing. Had they fixed on any other man it would have been nothing; but *his* perfect indifference, and *your* pointed dislike, make it so delightfully absurd! Much as I abominate writing, I would not give up Mr. Collins's correspondence for any consideration. Nay, when I read a letter of his, I cannot help giving him the preference even over Wickham, much as I value the impudence and hypocrisy of my son-in-law.[16] And pray, Lizzy, what said Lady Catherine about this report? Did she call to refuse her consent?"

To this question his daughter replied only with a laugh; and as it had been asked without the least suspicion, she was not distressed by his repeating it. Elizabeth had never been more at a loss to make her feelings appear what they were not. It was necessary to laugh, when she would rather have cried.[17] Her father had most cruelly mortified her, by what he said of Mr. Darcy's indifference, and she could do nothing but wonder at such a want of penetration, or fear that perhaps, instead of his seeing too *little,* she might have fancied too *much.*

16

Instead of receiving any such letter of excuse from his friend, as Elizabeth half expected Mr. Bingley to do, he was able to bring Darcy with him to Longbourn before many days had passed after Lady Catherine's visit. The gentlemen arrived early; and, before Mrs. Bennet had time to tell him of their having seen his aunt, of which her daughter sat in momentary dread,[1] Bingley, who wanted to be alone with Jane, proposed their all walking out. It was agreed to. Mrs. Bennet was not in the habit of walking; Mary could never spare time, but the remaining five set off together. Bingley and Jane, however, soon allowed the others to outstrip them. They lagged behind, while Elizabeth, Kitty, and Darcy, were to entertain each other. Very little was said by either; Kitty was too much afraid of him to talk; Elizabeth was secretly forming a desperate resolution; and perhaps he might be doing the same.[2]

They walked towards the Lucases, because Kitty wished to call upon Maria; and as Elizabeth saw no occasion for making it a general concern, when Kitty left them, she went boldly on with him alone. Now was the moment for her resolution to be executed, and, while her courage was high, she immediately said,

"Mr. Darcy, I am a very selfish creature; and, for the sake of giving relief to my own feelings, care not how much I may be wounding your's. I can no longer help thanking you for your unexampled kindness to my poor sister. Ever since I have known it, I have been most anxious to acknowledge to you how gratefully I feel it. Were it known

1 That is, dreading her mother's announcement at every moment.

2 Only occasionally does Austen's narrator pretend not to know what's going on in a character's mind. The "perhaps" in this sentence is a deliberate tease of the reader.

3 Carefully unspecified emotion.

4 It may come as a surprise to the reader as well as to Elizabeth to have Darcy professing respect for other members of the Bennet family.

5 Ashley Tauchert comments on the relation between Darcy's two proposals and Elizabeth's responses to them: "It is easy to assume that the heroine has undergone a great change in character to allow for this reversal, but her stance in both scenes is identical with regard to her claim for autonomy. The specific difference illuminated by reversal between the parallel scenes is in her perception of Darcy, now a collaborator in her narrative of possible freedom" (*Romancing Jane Austen: Narrative, Realism, and the Possibility of a Happy Ending* [New York: Palgrave Macmillan, 2005], 80).

6 Again, the narrator professes not to know something about a character that she has created.

7 Fervently.

8 Austen here slyly alludes to the earlier conversation between Elizabeth and her aunt in which Elizabeth claims that Bingley has been "violently in love" with Jane, and Mrs. Gardiner challenges the phrase, saying that the expression "is so hackneyed, so doubtful, so indefinite, that it gives me very little idea. It is as often applied to feelings which arise from an half-hour's acquaintance, as to a real, strong attachment" (II, 2). In the case of Darcy, however, we can believe in "a real, strong attachment." As usual, though, Austen refuses to tell her readers what exactly was said in a proposal scene. The most notorious example of her technique occurs in *Emma*. Knightley proposes (his words are actually given), and it remains for Emma to reply: "What did she say?—Just what she ought, of course. A lady always does" (III, 13).

9 The historian Linda Colley claims that *Pride and Prejudice* "is a deliberate essay in fantasy," since a man with an inherited estate and an annual income of £10,000 would be unlikely to invite the daughter of a small country gentleman and niece of a Cheapside attorney to dance, much less seek her hand in marriage: "Indeed, real-life Darcys would scarcely have wasted

to the rest of my family, I should not have merely my own gratitude to express."

"I am sorry, exceedingly sorry," replied Darcy, in a tone of surprise and emotion,[3] "that you have ever been informed of what may, in a mistaken light, have given you uneasiness. I did not think Mrs. Gardiner was so little to be trusted."

"You must not blame my aunt. Lydia's thoughtlessness first betrayed to me that you had been concerned in the matter; and, of course, I could not rest till I knew the particulars. Let me thank you again and again, in the name of all my family, for that generous compassion which induced you to take so much trouble, and bear so many mortifications, for the sake of discovering them."

"If you *will* thank me," he replied, "let it be for yourself alone. That the wish of giving happiness to you, might add force to the other inducements which led me on, I shall not attempt to deny. But your *family* owe me nothing. Much as I respect them,[4] I believe I thought only of *you*."

Elizabeth was too much embarrassed to say a word. After a short pause, her companion added, "You are too generous to trifle with me. If your feelings are still what they were last April, tell me so at once. *My* affections and wishes are unchanged, but one word from you will silence me on this subject for ever."

Elizabeth, feeling all the more than common awkwardness and anxiety of his situation, now forced herself to speak; and immediately, though not very fluently, gave him to understand that her sentiments had undergone so material a change, since the period to which he alluded, as to make her receive with gratitude and pleasure, his present assurances.[5] The happiness which this reply produced, was such as he had probably[6] never felt before; and he expressed himself on the occasion as sensibly[7] and as warmly as a man violently in love can be supposed to do.[8] Had Elizabeth been able to encounter his eye, she might have seen how well the expression of heartfelt delight, diffused over his face, became him; but, though she could not look, she could listen, and he told her of feelings, which, in proving of what importance she was to him, made his affection every moment more valuable.[9]

They walked on, without knowing in what direction. There was too much to be thought, and felt, and said, for attention to any other objects. She soon learnt that they were indebted for their present good understanding to the efforts of his aunt, who *did* call on him in her return through London, and there relate her journey to Longbourn, its motive, and the substance of her conversation with Elizabeth; dwelling emphatically on every expression of the latter, which, in her ladyship's apprehension, peculiarly denoted her perverseness and assurance,[10] in the belief that such a relation[11] must assist her endeavours to obtain that promise from her nephew, which *she* had refused to give. But, unluckily for her ladyship, its effect had been exactly contrariwise.

"It taught me to hope," said he, "as I had scarcely ever allowed myself to hope before. I knew enough of your disposition to be certain, that, had you been absolutely, irrevocably decided against me, you would have acknowledged it to Lady Catherine, frankly and openly."

Elizabeth coloured and laughed as she replied, "Yes, you know enough of my *frankness* to believe me capable of *that*. After abusing you so abominably to your face, I could have no scruple in abusing you to all your relations."

"What did you say of me, that I did not deserve? For, though your accusations were ill-founded, formed on mistaken premises, my behaviour to you at the time, had merited the severest reproof. It was unpardonable. I cannot think of it without abhorrence."

"We will not quarrel for the greater share of blame annexed to that evening," said Elizabeth. "The conduct of neither, if strictly examined, will be irreproachable; but since then, we have both, I hope, improved in civility."

"I cannot be so easily reconciled to myself. The recollection of what I then said, of my conduct, my manners, my expressions during the whole of it, is now, and has been many months, inexpressibly painful to me. Your reproof, so well applied, I shall never forget: 'had you behaved in a more gentlemanlike manner.' Those were your words. You know not, you can scarcely conceive, how they have tortured me;—though it was some time, I confess, before I was reasonable enough to allow their justice."

their precious bachelor youth on rural Hertfordshire. London, with its indulgences, its political life and its marriage market offering more eligible future wives even than Miss Bingley, would have been the automatic draw." John Wiltshire, who quotes this passage, also disputes it, citing a contemporary comment by Annabella Milbanke, the future Lady Byron, declaring *Pride and Prejudice* the most *probable* fiction she has ever read. Wiltshire goes on to acknowledge, however, that "Colley's insistence points to the great gulf that does exist between the two main figures" (*Recreating Jane Austen* [Cambridge: Cambridge University Press, 2001], 159).

The novel's fantasy element is apparent in its adherence to the patterns of romance and fairy tale. Yet its psychological realism enables the reader readily to suspend disbelief.

10 Self-assurance, impudence.

11 Narration.

12 Expression.

13 All of Austen's novels seem designed for rereading: second and subsequent readings typically reveal aspects of plot and characterization necessarily invisible the first time through. *Pride and Prejudice* contains a central episode of rereading (Elizabeth's repeated readings of Darcy's letter), and at the present juncture it appears to direct the reader to read that letter herself yet again. Certainly one wants to know—and is unlikely to remember—just what expressions Darcy is talking about.

"I was certainly very far from expecting them to make so strong an impression. I had not the smallest idea of their being ever felt in such a way."

"I can easily believe it. You thought me then devoid of every proper feeling, I am sure you did. The turn[12] of your countenance I shall never forget, as you said that I could not have addressed you in any possible way, that would induce you to accept me."

"Oh! do not repeat what I then said. These recollections will not do at all. I assure you, that I have long been most heartily ashamed of it."

Darcy mentioned his letter. "Did it," said he, "did it *soon* make you think better of me? Did you, on reading it, give any credit to its contents?"

She explained what its effect on her had been, and how gradually all her former prejudices had been removed.

"I knew," said he, "that what I wrote must give you pain, but it was necessary. I hope you have destroyed the letter. There was one part especially, the opening of it, which I should dread your having the power of reading again. I can remember some expressions which might justly make you hate me."[13]

"The letter shall certainly be burnt, if you believe it essential to the preservation of my regard; but, though we have both reason to think my opinions not entirely unalterable, they are not, I hope, quite so easily changed as that implies."

"When I wrote that letter," replied Darcy, "I believed myself perfectly calm and cool, but I am since convinced that it was written in a dreadful bitterness of spirit."

"The letter, perhaps, began in bitterness, but it did not end so. The adieu is charity itself. But think no more of the letter. The feelings of the person who wrote, and the person who received it, are now so widely different from what they were then, that every unpleasant circumstance attending it, ought to be forgotten. You must learn some of my philosophy. Think only of the past as its remembrance gives you pleasure."

"I cannot give you credit for any philosophy of the kind. *Your* retrospections must be so totally void of reproach, that the contentment arising from them, is not of philosophy, but what is much better, of innocence. But with *me,* it is not so. Painful recollections will intrude, which cannot, which ought not to be repelled. I have been a selfish being all my life, in practice, though not in principle. As a child I was taught what was *right,* but I was not taught to correct my temper. I was given good principles, but left to follow them in pride and conceit. Unfortunately an only son, (for many years an only *child*) I was spoilt by my parents, who though good themselves, (my father particularly, all that was benevolent and amiable), allowed, encouraged, almost taught me to be selfish and overbearing, to care for none beyond my own family circle, to think meanly[14] of all the rest of the world, to *wish* at least to think meanly of their sense and worth compared with my own.[15] Such I was, from eight to eight and twenty; and such I might still have been but for you, dearest, loveliest Elizabeth! What do I not owe you! You taught me a lesson, hard indeed at first, but most advantageous. By you, I was properly humbled. I came to you without a doubt of my reception. You shewed me how insufficient were all my pretensions to please a woman worthy of being pleased."

"Had you then persuaded yourself that I should?"

"Indeed I had. What will you think of my vanity? I believed you to be wishing, expecting my addresses."[16]

"My manners must have been in fault, but not intentionally I assure you. I never meant to deceive you, but my spirits might often lead me wrong.[17] How you must have hated me after *that* evening?"

"Hate you! I was angry perhaps at first, but my anger soon began to take a proper direction."[18]

"I am almost afraid of asking what you thought of me; when we met at Pemberley. You blamed me for coming?"

"No indeed; I felt nothing but surprise."

"Your surprise could not be greater than *mine* in being noticed[19] by you. My conscience told me that I deserved no extraordinary politeness, and I confess that I did not expect to receive *more* than my due."

"My object *then*," replied Darcy, "was to shew you, by every civility in my power, that I was not so mean[20] as to resent the past; and I

14 Disdainfully.

15 Lovelace, Clarissa's seducer in Samuel Richardson's 1748 novel, offers a similar account of his own development. Many other eighteenth-century novelists drew in comparable ways on the notion of parental responsibility for the flaws of adult children.

16 Proposal.

17 She is suggesting that her sheer exuberance might have misled Darcy.

18 Turning, presumably, toward Wickham and toward himself.

19 Paid attention to.

20 Small-minded.

21 Elizabeth at the time, it will be remembered, ana-
lyzed his behavior "rationally" and "instantly understood it." She attributed his thoughtfulness and gloom
to the sinking of her power as Darcy realized that he
could not connect himself with such a family as hers.
She was wrong, as she had often been wrong, because
her feelings (in this instance her anxiety over whether
he could still care for her) interfered with her judgment.

22 Protested.

hoped to obtain your forgiveness, to lessen your ill opinion, by letting you see that your reproofs had been attended to. How soon any
other wishes introduced themselves I can hardly tell, but I believe in
about half an hour after I had seen you."

He then told her of Georgiana's delight in her acquaintance, and
of her disappointment at its sudden interruption; which naturally
leading to the cause of that interruption, she soon learnt that his
resolution of following her from Derbyshire in quest of her sister,
had been formed before he quitted the inn, and that his gravity and
thoughtfulness there, had arisen from no other struggles than what
such a purpose must comprehend.[21]

She expressed her gratitude again, but it was too painful a subject
to each, to be dwelt on farther.

After walking several miles in a leisurely manner, and too busy
to know any thing about it, they found at last, on examining their
watches, that it was time to be at home.

"What could become of Mr. Bingley and Jane!" was a wonder
which introduced the discussion of *their* affairs. Darcy was delighted
with their engagement; his friend had given him the earliest information of it.

"I must ask whether you were surprised?" said Elizabeth.

"Not at all. When I went away, I felt that it would soon happen."

"That is to say, you had given your permission. I guessed as much."
And though he exclaimed at[22] the term, she found that it had been
pretty much the case.

"On the evening before my going to London," said he, "I made a
confession to him, which I believe I ought to have made long ago. I
told him of all that had occurred to make my former interference in
his affairs, absurd and impertinent. His surprise was great. He had
never had the slightest suspicion. I told him, moreover, that I believed myself mistaken in supposing, as I had done, that your sister
was indifferent to him; and as I could easily perceive that his attachment to her was unabated, I felt no doubt of their happiness together."

Elizabeth could not help smiling at his easy manner of directing
his friend.

"Did you speak from your own observation," said she, "when you told him that my sister loved him, or merely from my information last spring?"

"From the former. I had narrowly[23] observed her during the two visits which I had lately made here; and I was convinced of her affection."

"And your assurance of it, I suppose, carried immediate conviction to him."

"It did. Bingley is most unaffectedly modest. His diffidence had prevented his depending on his own judgment in so anxious a case, but his reliance on mine, made every thing easy. I was obliged to confess one thing, which for a time, and not unjustly, offended him. I could not allow myself to conceal that your sister had been in town three months last winter, that I had known it, and purposely kept it from him. He was angry. But his anger, I am persuaded, lasted no longer than he remained in any doubt of your sister's sentiments. He has heartily forgiven me now."

Elizabeth longed to observe that Mr. Bingley had been a most delightful friend; so easily guided that his worth was invaluable; but she checked herself.[24] She remembered that he had yet to learn to be laught at,[25] and it was rather too early to begin. In anticipating the happiness of Bingley, which of course was to be inferior only to his own, he continued the conversation till they reached the house. In the hall they parted.

23 Closely, rigorously.

24 In an earlier argument with Darcy (I, 10), Elizabeth had supported the position that ready persuadability by a friend marked an agreeable disposition that merited praise rather than mockery. In that instance too, Bingley supplied the available example of the trait.

25 Elizabeth retains the impulse to laugh, although in her present situation she hardly needs laughter as a defensive tactic. She also considers the effect as well as the provocation of her laughter.

Sir Henry Raeburn, "Sir Walter Scott," 1822. Sir Walter, Austen's contemporary, the most popular novelist of their time, admired Austen's work and reviewed it favorably. Sir Henry Raeburn (1756–1823), a Scotsman knighted in 1822, was probably the most famous portraitist of his day.

1 An unusual formulation for Jane, who is generally less certain of her views than is her sister.

"MY DEAR LIZZY, where can you have been walking to?" was a question which Elizabeth received from Jane as soon as she entered the room, and from all the others when they sat down to table. She had only to say in reply, that they had wandered about, till she was beyond her own knowledge. She coloured as she spoke; but neither that, nor any thing else, awakened a suspicion of the truth.

The evening passed quietly, unmarked by anything extraordinary. The acknowledged lovers talked and laughed, the unacknowledged were silent. Darcy was not of a disposition in which happiness overflows in mirth; and Elizabeth, agitated and confused, rather *knew* that she was happy, than *felt* herself to be so; for, besides the immediate embarrassment, there were other evils before her. She anticipated what would be felt in the family when her situation became known; she was aware that no one liked him but Jane; and even feared that with the others it was a *dislike* which not all his fortune and consequence might do away.

At night she opened her heart to Jane. Though suspicion was very far from Miss Bennet's general habits, she was absolutely incredulous here.

"You are joking, Lizzy. This cannot be!—engaged to Mr. Darcy! No, no, you shall not deceive me. I know it to be impossible."1

"This is a wretched beginning indeed! My sole dependence was on you; and I am sure nobody else will believe me, if you do not. Yet, indeed, I am in earnest. I speak nothing but the truth. He still loves me, and we are engaged."

Jane looked at her doubtingly. "Oh, Lizzy! it cannot be. I know how much you dislike him."

"You know nothing of the matter. *That* is all to be forgot. Perhaps I did not always love him so well as I do now. But in such cases as these, a good memory is unpardonable. This is the last time I shall ever remember it myself."

Miss Bennet still looked all amazement. Elizabeth again, and more seriously assured her of its truth.

"Good Heaven! can it be really so! Yet now I must believe you," cried Jane. "My dear, dear Lizzy, I would—I do congratulate you—but are you certain? forgive the question—are you quite certain that you can be happy with him?"

"There can be no doubt of that. It is settled between us already, that we are to be the happiest couple in the world. But are you pleased, Jane? Shall you like to have such a brother?"

"Very, very much. Nothing could give either Bingley or myself more delight. But we considered it, we talked of it as impossible. And do you really love him quite well enough? Oh, Lizzy! do any thing rather than marry without affection. Are you quite sure that you feel what you ought to do?"

"Oh, yes! You will only think I feel *more* than I ought to do, when I tell you all."

"What do you mean?"

"Why, I must confess that I love him better than I do Bingley. I am afraid you will be angry."

"My dearest sister, now *be* serious. I want to talk very seriously. Let me know every thing that I am to know, without delay. Will you tell me how long you have loved him?"

"It has been coming on so gradually, that I hardly know when it began. But I believe I must date it from my first seeing his beautiful grounds at Pemberley."[2]

Another intreaty that she would be serious, however, produced the desired effect; and she soon satisfied Jane by her solemn assur-

2 This "joke" has particular resonance because in fact Elizabeth's feelings did undergo a considerable change at Pemberley. She does not, like Charlotte, make her marital choice purely from the desire for an establishment, yet she felt at Pemberley that to be mistress of such an estate "would be something." To ignore Darcy's wealth and status would hardly be possible; Elizabeth has a realistic sense of the advantage that will accrue to her in the marriage.

3 Regard.

4 The same accusation that Mrs. Gardiner implicitly made.

ances of attachment. When convinced on that article, Miss Bennet had nothing further to wish.

"Now I am quite happy," said she, "for you will be as happy as myself. I always had a value[3] for him. Were it for nothing but his love of you, I must always have esteemed him; but now, as Bingley's friend and your husband, there can be only Bingley and yourself more dear to me. But Lizzy, you have been very sly,[4] very reserved with me. How little did you tell me of what passed at Pemberley and Lambton! I owe all that I know of it, to another, not to you."

Elizabeth told her the motives of her secrecy. She had been unwilling to mention Bingley; and the unsettled state of her own feelings had made her equally avoid the name of his friend. But now she would no longer conceal from her, his share in Lydia's marriage. All was acknowledged, and half the night spent in conversation.

"Good gracious!" cried Mrs. Bennet, as she stood at a window the next morning, "if that disagreeable Mr. Darcy is not coming here again with our dear Bingley! What can he mean by being so tiresome as to be always coming here? I had no notion but he would go a shooting, or something or other, and not disturb us with his company. What shall we do with him? Lizzy, you must walk out with him again, that he may not be in Bingley's way."

Elizabeth could hardly help laughing at so convenient a proposal; yet was really vexed that her mother should be always giving him such an epithet.

As soon as they entered, Bingley looked at her so expressively, and shook hands with such warmth, as left no doubt of his good information; and he soon afterwards said aloud, "Mrs. Bennet, have you no more lanes hereabouts in which Lizzy may lose her way again today?"

"I advise Mr. Darcy, and Lizzy, and Kitty," said Mrs. Bennet, "to walk to Oakham Mount this morning. It is a nice long walk, and Mr. Darcy has never seen the view."

"It may do very well for the others," replied Mr. Bingley; "but I am sure it will be too much for Kitty. Won't it, Kitty?"

Kitty owned that she had rather stay at home. Darcy professed a great curiosity to see the view from the Mount, and Elizabeth silently consented. As she went up stairs to get ready, Mrs. Bennet followed her, saying:

"I am quite sorry, Lizzy, that you should be forced to have that disagreeable man all to yourself. But I hope you will not mind it: it is all for Jane's sake, you know; and there is no occasion for talking to him, except just now and then. So, do not put yourself to inconvenience."

During their walk, it was resolved that Mr. Bennet's consent should be asked in the course of the evening. Elizabeth reserved to herself the application for her mother's. She could not determine how her mother would take it; sometimes doubting whether all his wealth and grandeur would be enough to overcome her abhorrence of the man. But whether she were violently set against the match, or violently delighted with it, it was certain that her manner would be equally ill adapted to do credit to her sense; and she could no more bear that Mr. Darcy should hear the first raptures of her joy, than the first vehemence of her disapprobation.

In the evening, soon after Mr. Bennet withdrew to the library, she saw Mr. Darcy rise also and follow him, and her agitation on seeing it was extreme. She did not fear her father's opposition, but he was going to be made unhappy; and that it should be through her means, that *she,* his favourite child, should be distressing him by her choice, should be filling him with fears and regrets in disposing of her, was a wretched reflection, and she sat in misery till Mr. Darcy appeared again, when, looking at him, she was a little relieved by his smile. In a few minutes he approached the table where she was sitting with Kitty; and, while pretending to admire her work[5] said in a whisper, "Go to your father, he wants you in the library." She was gone directly.

5 Needlework.

6 Elizabeth thus reminds the reader that her frequent invocations of reason stem partly from what she recognizes as irrational tendencies in herself.

7 A crucial distinction. Elizabeth now believes that Darcy's is "proper" pride, appropriate to his character and his status. Charlotte, it may be remembered, thought this much earlier.

8 Unlike Lady Catherine, Darcy "condescends" because, by character rather than by rank—by virtue of the "kind of man" he is—he is recognized, even by Mr. Bennet, as superior.

9 In this rare moment of perfect seriousness, Mr. Bennet hints the pain of his own marital lot.

Her father was walking about the room, looking grave and anxious. "Lizzy," said he, "what are you doing? Are you out of your senses, to be accepting this man? Have not you always hated him?"

How earnestly did she then wish that her former opinions had been more reasonable,[6] her expressions more moderate! It would have spared her from explanations and professions which it was exceedingly awkward to give; but they were now necessary, and she assured him, with some confusion, of her attachment to Mr. Darcy.

"Or, in other words, you are determined to have him. He is rich, to be sure, and you may have more fine clothes and fine carriages than Jane. But will they make you happy?"

"Have you any other objection," said Elizabeth, "than your belief of my indifference?"

"None at all. We all know him to be a proud, unpleasant sort of man; but this would be nothing if you really liked him."

"I do, I do like him," she replied, with tears in her eyes, "I love him. Indeed he has no improper pride.[7] He is perfectly amiable. You do not know what he really is; then pray do not pain me by speaking of him in such terms."

"Lizzy," said her father, "I have given him my consent. He is the kind of man, indeed, to whom I should never dare refuse any thing, which he condescended to ask.[8] I now give it to *you,* if you are resolved on having him. But let me advise you to think better of it. I know your disposition, Lizzy. I know that you could be neither happy nor respectable, unless you truly esteemed your husband; unless you looked up to him as a superior. Your lively talents would place you in the greatest danger in an unequal marriage. You could scarcely escape discredit and misery. My child, let me not have the grief of seeing *you* unable to respect your partner in life.[9] You know not what you are about."

Elizabeth, still more affected, was earnest and solemn in her reply; and at length, by repeated assurances that Mr. Darcy was really the object of her choice, by explaining the gradual change which her estimation of him had undergone, relating her absolute certainty that his affection was not the work of a day, but had stood the test of many months' suspense, and enumerating with energy all his good qualities, she did conquer her father's incredulity, and reconcile him to the match.

"Well, my dear," said he, when she ceased speaking, "I have no more to say. If this be the case, he deserves you. I could not have parted with you, my Lizzy, to any one less worthy."

To complete the favourable impression, she then told him what Mr. Darcy had voluntarily done for Lydia. He heard her with astonishment.

"This is an evening of wonders, indeed! And so, Darcy did every thing; made up the match, gave the money, paid the fellow's debts, and got him his commission! So much the better. It will save me a world of trouble and economy. Had it been your uncle's doing, I must and *would* have paid him; but these violent young lovers carry every thing their own way. I shall offer to pay him to-morrow; he will rant and storm about his love for you, and there will be an end of the matter."

He then recollected her embarrassment a few days before, on his reading Mr. Collins's letter; and after laughing at her some time,[10] allowed her at last to go—saying, as she quitted the room, "If any young men come for Mary or Kitty, send them in, for I am quite at leisure."

Elizabeth's mind was now relieved from a very heavy weight; and, after half an hour's quiet reflection in her own room, she was able to join the others with tolerable composure. Every thing was too recent for gaiety, but the evening passed tranquilly away; there was no longer anything material[11] to be dreaded, and the comfort of ease and familiarity would come in time.

When her mother went up to her dressing-room at night, she followed her, and made the important communication. Its effect was most extraordinary; for on first hearing it, Mrs. Bennet sat quite still, and unable to utter a syllable. Nor was it under many, many minutes that she could comprehend what she heard; though not in general backward to credit what was for the advantage of her family, or that came in the shape of a lover to any of them. She began at length to recover, to fidget about in her chair, get up, sit down again, wonder, and bless herself.

10 Thus Mr. Bennet restores his equilibrium.

11 Significant.

Frontispiece of *Pride and Prejudice*, 1833, published by Richard Bentley, London. The illustration shows Elizabeth and her father discussing her desire to marry Darcy.

"Good gracious! Lord bless me! only think! dear me! Mr. Darcy! Who would have thought it! And is it really true? Oh! my sweetest Lizzy! how rich and how great you will be! What pin money,[12] what jewels, what carriages you will have! Jane's is nothing to it—nothing at all. I am so pleased—so happy. Such a charming man!—so handsome! so tall![13]—Oh, my dear Lizzy! pray apologise for my having disliked him so much before. I hope he will overlook it. Dear, dear Lizzy. A house in town![14] Every thing that is charming! Three daughters married! Ten thousand a year! Oh, Lord! What will become of me. I shall go distracted."

This was enough to prove that her approbation need not be doubted: and Elizabeth, rejoicing that such an effusion was heard only by herself, soon went away. But before she had been three minutes in her own room, her mother followed her.

"My dearest child," she cried, "I can think of nothing else! Ten thousand a year, and very likely more! 'Tis as good as a Lord! And a special licence.[15] You must and shall be married by a special licence. But my dearest love, tell me what dish Mr. Darcy is particularly fond of, that I may have it to-morrow."

This was a sad omen of what her mother's behaviour to the gentleman himself might be; and Elizabeth found, that though in the certain possession of his warmest affection, and secure of her relations' consent, there was still something to be wished for. But the morrow passed off much better than she expected; for Mrs. Bennet luckily stood in such awe of her intended son-in-law, that she ventured not to speak to him, unless it was in her power to offer him any attention, or mark her deference for his opinion.

Elizabeth had the satisfaction of seeing her father taking pains to get acquainted with him; and Mr. Bennet soon assured her that he was rising every hour in his esteem.

"I admire all my three sons-in-law highly," said he. "Wickham, perhaps, is my favourite; but I think I shall like *your* husband quite as well as Jane's."[16]

12 Allowance for clothes and personal expenses, often specified in marriage settlements.

13 Mrs. Bennet has quickly reverted to her usual standards of judgment.

14 London.

15 A marriage license granted by the archbishop of Canterbury, which allowed a couple to ignore such customary regulations as those specifying the times and places legal for marriage. It permitted, for example, marriage at home rather than in a church. Since only the wealthy could procure such licenses, they carried social prestige.

16 Twenty-first-century readers of Austen apparently see Darcy as very attractive indeed. Ashley Tauchert reports on a BBC poll to find the fictional figure that women thought most compelling: "Mr Darcy emerged triumphant . . . in a recent BBC vote to find the most fancied fictional figure of woman's desire—leaving James Bond with all his bedroom skills and gadgets in second place" (*Romancing Jane Austen: Narrative, Realism, and the Possibility of a Happy Ending* [New York: Palgrave Macmillan, 2005], 75).

18

1 In mentioning beauty and manners first, Elizabeth invokes the most common standards for communal judgment.

2 It is indeed a reasonable theory, especially considering the great emphasis placed on manners throughout the text. Elizabeth is suggesting that her manners genuinely express her personality, and that Darcy responded to their authenticity—in contrast to the formulaic "civility" of several other characters.

ELIZABETH'S SPIRITS SOON RISING to playfulness again, she wanted Mr. Darcy to account for his having ever fallen in love with her. "How could you begin?" said she. "I can comprehend your going on charmingly, when you had once made a beginning; but what could set you off in the first place?"

"I cannot fix on the hour, or the spot, or the look, or the words, which laid the foundation. It is too long ago. I was in the middle before I knew that I *had* begun."

"My beauty you had early withstood, and as for my manners[1]—my behaviour to *you* was at least always bordering on the uncivil, and I never spoke to you without rather wishing to give you pain than not. Now be sincere; did you admire me for my impertinence?"

"For the liveliness of your mind, I did."

"You may as well call it impertinence at once. It was very little less. The fact is, that you were sick of civility, of deference, of officious attention. You were disgusted with the women who were always speaking, and looking, and thinking for *your* approbation alone. I roused, and interested you, because I was so unlike *them*. Had you not been really amiable, you would have hated me for it; but in spite of the pains you took to disguise yourself, your feelings were always noble and just; and in your heart, you thoroughly despised the persons who so assiduously courted you. There—I have saved you the trouble of accounting for it; and really, all things considered, I begin to think it perfectly reasonable.[2] To be sure, you knew no actual good of me—but nobody thinks of *that* when they fall in love."

"Was there no good in your affectionate behaviour to Jane, while she was ill at Netherfield?"

"Dearest Jane! who could have done less for her? But make a virtue of it by all means. My good qualities are under your protection, and you are to exaggerate them as much as possible; and, in return, it belongs to me to find occasions for teazing and quarrelling with you as often as may be; and I shall begin directly by asking you what made you so unwilling to come to the point at last. What made you so shy of me, when you first called, and afterwards dined here? Why, especially, when you called, did you look as if you did not care about me?"

"Because you were grave and silent, and gave me no encouragement."

"But I was embarrassed."

"And so was I."

"You might have talked to me more when you came to dinner."

"A man who had felt less, might."[3]

"How unlucky that you should have a reasonable answer to give, and that I should be so reasonable as to admit it! But I wonder how long you *would* have gone on, if you had been left to yourself. I wonder when you *would* have spoken, if I had not asked you! My resolution of thanking you for your kindness to Lydia had certainly great effect. *Too much,* I am afraid; for what becomes of the moral, if our comfort springs from a breach of promise, for I ought not to have mentioned the subject? This will never do."[4]

"You need not distress yourself. The moral will be perfectly fair. Lady Catherine's unjustifiable endeavours to separate us, were the means of removing all my doubts. I am not indebted for my present happiness to your eager desire of expressing your gratitude. I was not in a humour to wait for any opening of your's. My aunt's intelligence[5] had given me hope, and I was determined at once to know every thing."

"Lady Catherine has been of infinite use, which ought to make her happy, for she loves to be of use. But tell me, what did you come down to Netherfield for? Was it merely to ride to Longbourn and be embarrassed? or had you intended any more serious consequence?"

3 Darcy, too, is one who has, and often conceals, deep feelings. This is not the first time that the novel has hinted at his social awkwardness and shyness.

4 Austen makes a similar joke about the moral of *Northanger Abbey.* After suggesting that General Tilney's injustice toward Catherine probably encouraged the match between her and Henry, the narrator comments, "I leave it to be settled by whomsoever it may concern, whether the tendency of this work be altogether to recommend parental tyranny, or reward filial disobedience" (II, 16).

5 Information.

6 In his emphasis on judgment, Darcy, like Elizabeth, tries to employ rationality in conducting his affair of the heart.

7 Like Elizabeth, Darcy has and cultivates a strong sense of moral responsibility.

8 Elizabeth employs the same cliché that Jane had used, but with full awareness that her sentiment is hackneyed.

9 The most delightful and purely joyous of Elizabeth's laughs. In claiming to be happier even than Jane, Elizabeth contradicts her earlier statement to her sister: "If you were to give me forty such men, I never could be so happy as you. Till I have your disposition, your goodness, I never can have your happiness" (III, 13).

"My real purpose was to see *you,* and to judge, if I could, whether I might ever hope to make you love me.[6] My avowed one, or what I avowed to myself, was to see whether your sister were still partial to Bingley, and if she were, to make the confession to him which I have since made."

"Shall you ever have courage to announce to Lady Catherine what is to befall her?"

"I am more likely to want time than courage, Elizabeth. But it ought to be done,[7] and if you will give me a sheet of paper, it shall be done directly."

"And if I had not a letter to write myself, I might sit by you and admire the evenness of your writing, as another young lady once did. But I have an aunt, too, who must not be longer neglected."

From an unwillingness to confess how much her intimacy with Mr. Darcy had been over-rated, Elizabeth had never yet answered Mrs. Gardiner's long letter; but now, having *that* to communicate which she knew would be most welcome, she was almost ashamed to find, that her uncle and aunt had already lost three days of happiness, and immediately wrote as follows:

"I would have thanked you before, my dear aunt, as I ought to have done, for your long, kind, satisfactory, detail of particulars; but to say the truth, I was too cross to write. You supposed more than really existed. But *now* suppose as much as you chuse; give a loose to your fancy, indulge your imagination in every possible flight which the subject will afford, and unless you believe me actually married, you cannot greatly err. You must write again very soon, and praise him a great deal more than you did in your last. I thank you, again and again, for not going to the Lakes. How could I be so silly as to wish it! Your idea of the ponies is delightful. We will go round the Park every day. I am the happiest creature in the world.[8] Perhaps other people have said so before, but not one with such justice. I am happier even than Jane; she only smiles, I laugh.[9] Mr. Darcy sends you all the love in the world, that he can spare from me. You are all to come to Pemberley at Christmas. Yours, &c."

Mr. Darcy's letter to Lady Catherine was in a different style; and
still different from either was what Mr. Bennet sent to Mr. Collins,
in reply to his last.

> "Dear Sir,
>
> "I must trouble you once more for congratulations. Eliza-
> beth will soon be the wife of Mr. Darcy. Console Lady Cath-
> erine as well as you can. But, if I were you, I would stand by
> the nephew. He has more to give.
>
> "Your's sincerely, &c."

Miss Bingley's congratulations to her brother, on his approaching marriage, were all that was affectionate and insincere. She wrote
even to Jane on the occasion, to express her delight, and repeat all
her former professions of regard. Jane was not deceived, but she was
affected; and though feeling no reliance on her, could not help writing her a much kinder answer than she knew was deserved.

The joy which Miss Darcy expressed on receiving similar information, was as sincere as her brother's in sending it. Four sides of paper
were insufficient to contain all her delight, and all her earnest desire
of being loved by her sister.

Before any answer could arrive from Mr. Collins, or any congratulations to Elizabeth, from his wife, the Longbourn family heard that
the Collinses were come themselves to Lucas Lodge. The reason of
this sudden removal was soon evident. Lady Catherine had been rendered so exceedingly angry by the contents of her nephew's letter,
that Charlotte, really rejoicing in the match, was anxious to get away
till the storm was blown over. At such a moment, the arrival of her
friend was a sincere pleasure to Elizabeth, though in the course of
their meetings she must sometimes think the pleasure dearly bought,
when she saw Mr. Darcy exposed to all the parading[10] and obsequious civility of her husband. He bore it, however, with admirable
calmness. He could even listen to Sir William Lucas, when he complimented him on carrying away the brightest jewel of the country,
and expressed his hopes of their all meeting frequently at St. James's,

10 Ostentatious show.

11 In an investigation of the moral pattern of *Pride and Prejudice,* Alison Searle maintains, "Humility, self-knowledge and love are crucial to the progress of both Elizabeth and Darcy in coming to a true knowledge and appreciation of each other that facilitates a complementary mutuality in 'all the comfort and elegance of their family party at Pemberley'" ("The Moral Imagination: Biblical Imperatives, Narrative and Hermeneutics in *Pride and Prejudice," Renascence* 59: 1 [2006], 26). She demonstrates how Austen draws on biblical doctrine and how her narrative technique enforces her moral perspective.

with very decent composure. If he did shrug his shoulders, it was not till Sir William was out of sight.

Mrs. Phillips's vulgarity was another, and perhaps a greater tax on his forbearance; and though Mrs. Phillips, as well as her sister, stood in too much awe of him to speak with the familiarity which Bingley's good humour encouraged, yet, whenever she *did* speak, she must be vulgar. Nor was her respect for him, though it made her more quiet, at all likely to make her more elegant. Elizabeth did all she could, to shield him from the frequent notice of either, and was ever anxious to keep him to herself, and to those of her family with whom he might converse without mortification; and though the uncomfortable feelings arising from all this took from the season of courtship much of its pleasure, it added to the hope of the future; and she looked forward with delight to the time when they should be removed from society so little pleasing to either, to all the comfort and elegance of their family party at Pemberley.[11]

19

HAPPY FOR ALL HER MATERNAL feelings was the day on which Mrs. Bennet got rid of[1] her two most deserving daughters. With what delighted pride she afterwards visited Mrs. Bingley and talked of Mrs. Darcy[2] may be guessed. I wish I could say, for the sake of her family, that the accomplishment of her earnest desire in the establishment[3] of so many of her children, produced so happy an effect as to make her a sensible, amiable, well-informed woman for the rest of her life; though perhaps it was lucky for her husband, who might not have relished domestic felicity in so unusual a form, that she still was occasionally nervous and invariably silly.[4]

Mr. Bennet missed his second daughter exceedingly; his affection for her drew him oftener from home than any thing else could do. He delighted in going to Pemberley, especially when he was least expected.

Mr. Bingley and Jane remained at Netherfield only a twelvemonth. So near a vicinity to her mother and Meryton relations was not desirable even to *his* easy temper, or *her* affectionate heart. The darling wish of his sisters was then gratified; he bought an estate in a neighbouring county to Derbyshire, and Jane and Elizabeth, in addition to every other source of happiness, were within thirty miles of each other.

Kitty, to her very material advantage, spent the chief of her time with her two elder sisters. In society so superior to what she had generally known, her improvement was great. She was not of so ungov-

1 A curious locution that emphasizes Mrs. Bennet's confusion of people and commodities.

2 In 1813 Austen reports going to an exhibition and seeing "a small portrait of Mrs Bingley, excessively like her. I went in hopes of seeing one of her Sister, but there was no Mrs Darcy. . . . Mrs Bingley's [portrait] is exactly herself, size, shaped face, features & sweetness; there never was a greater likeness. She is dressed in a white gown, with green ornaments, which convinces me of what I had always supposed, that green was a favourite color with her. I dare say Mrs Darcy will be in Yellow." Later in the letter, on the evening of the same day, she adds that they have gone to two further exhibitions, "and I am disappointed, for there was nothing like Mrs D. at either.—I can only imagine that M^r D prizes any Picture of her too much to like it should be exposed to the public eye.—I can imagine he w^d have that sort of feeling—that mixture of Love, Pride & Delicacy" (To Cassandra, 24 May 1813).

3 Marriage.

4 The comment suggests that Mr. Bennet gets much of his pleasure from overtly or covertly mocking his wife.

William Blake, "Portrait of Mrs. Q" (1820). Austen in a letter to Cassandra reports seeing a painting of Mrs. Bingley in a white gown with green ornaments. This engraving is actually a depiction of Harriet Quentin, a mistress to George IV when he was prince regent, based on a portrait by François Huet-Villier. It may, however, resemble the painting that Austen saw.

ernable a temper[5] as Lydia; and, removed from the influence of Lydia's example, she became, by proper attention and management, less irritable, less ignorant, and less insipid.[6] From the further disadvantage of Lydia's society she was of course carefully kept, and though Mrs. Wickham frequently invited her to come and stay with her, with the promise of balls and young men, her father would never consent to her going.

Mary was the only daughter who remained at home; and she was necessarily drawn from the pursuit of accomplishments by Mrs. Bennet's being quite unable to sit alone. Mary was obliged to mix more with the world, but she could still moralize over every morning visit; and as she was no longer mortified by comparisons between her sisters' beauty and her own, it was suspected by her father that she submitted to the change without much reluctance.[7]

As for Wickham and Lydia, their characters suffered no revolution[8] from the marriage of her sisters. He bore with philosophy the conviction that Elizabeth must now become acquainted with whatever of his ingratitude and falsehood had before been unknown to her; and in spite of every thing, was not wholly without hope that Darcy might yet be prevailed on to make his fortune. The congratulatory letter which Elizabeth received from Lydia on her marriage, explained to her that, by his wife at least, if not by himself, such a hope was cherished. The letter was to this effect:

"My Dear Lizzy,

"I wish you joy. If you love Mr. Darcy half as well as I do my dear Wickham, you must be very happy. It is a great comfort to have you so rich, and when you have nothing else to do, I hope you will think of us. I am sure Wickham would like a place at court[9] very much, and I do not think we shall have quite money enough to live upon without some help. Any place would do, of about three or four hundred a year; but, however, do not speak to Mr. Darcy about it, if you had rather not.

"Your's, &c."

5 Temperament.

6 Uninteresting, foolish.

7 Steven D. Scott makes a valiant effort to defend Mary, insisting that she occupies "a privileged space in the novel." Scott continues: "She is a reader (of books and people), an observer, a surprisingly compassionate person who detects potential in the most unlikely places, refusing to condemn Mr. Collins outright, for instance, and staying at home with her mother at the novel's end. She is a young woman who is 'plain' in a world that values only beauty; a young woman who pursues 'accomplishments,' not for the goal of catching a husband, as most of the young women in this novel do, from the opening sentence onward, but for the activity itself and for the personal satisfaction it offers. . . . In her approaches and her attitudes, Mary reminds me more and more of Jane Austen herself" ("Making Room in the Middle," *The Talk in Jane Austen,* ed. Bruce Stovel and Lynn Weinlos Gregg [Edmonton: University of Alberta Press, 2002], 227). I find myself unpersuaded: Mary strikes me as a poor reader, as someone who pursues accomplishments in the hope of impressing others, and as eager for a husband, even if it's Collins. The narrator's tone continually criticizes her, despite the moments of compassion for her. And the text announces explicitly that "vanity" motivates her attention to accomplishments (I, 6).

8 Underwent no great change.

9 In a regiment attached to the court, where he would be better paid and have more social prestige.

10 Perhaps the Peace of Amiens, in 1802, which temporarily ended the hostilities between England and France during the French Revolutionary Wars. If so, the novel is set during the late 1790s, around the time of its original composition. It is possible, though, that Austen is anticipating a final treaty between the French and the English and that the novel therefore is set later. Such a treaty, of course, did not occur until 1815, after the publication of *Pride and Prejudice*.

11 Living place.

12 The novel early established Lydia's tendency to extravagance, as well as Wickham's propensity to incur gambling debts.

13 Visit.

14 Those visits emphasize the social realignment that the marriage of Darcy and Elizabeth suggests. Ashley Tauchert comments, "The common resolution offered to Austen's heroines, providential marriage, works explicitly to align individual and social destiny. Elizabeth and Darcy's union at one and the same time signals the positive reform of the female character, of the male suitor, and of the social world in which they figure" (*Romancing Jane Austen: Narrative, Realism, and the Possibility of a Happy Ending* [New York: Palgrave Macmillan, 2005], 79).

15 Aware.

16 The distance between the novel's famous first sentence and this final one calls attention to the kind of success that the marriage of Elizabeth and Darcy most significantly represents. It is, of course, a fairy-tale marriage: Prince Charming with a castle and immense wealth whisks away the beautiful maiden. More importantly, it is a marriage of true feeling. The first sentence of *Pride and Prejudice* suggests the view of marriage as a business transaction, held by Mrs. Bennet and Charlotte, among others: single man plus fortune equals, in the eyes of the community, need for a wife. The last sentence speaks of feeling: of love reaching outward, of "warmest gratitude." It occurs at the end of an account suggesting how Darcy and Elizabeth build a community around themselves, a community based

As it happened that Elizabeth had *much* rather not; she endeavoured in her answer to put an end to every intreaty and expectation of the kind. Such relief, however, as it was in her power to afford, by the practice of what might be called economy in her own private expences, she frequently sent them. It had always been evident to her that such an income as theirs, under the direction of two persons so extravagant in their wants, and heedless of the future, must be very insufficient to their support; and whenever they changed their quarters, either Jane or herself were sure of being applied to, for some little assistance towards discharging their bills. Their manner of living, even when the restoration of peace[10] dismissed them to a home, was unsettled in the extreme. They were always moving from place to place in quest of a cheap situation,[11] and always spending more than they ought.[12] His affection for her soon sunk into indifference; her's lasted a little longer; and in spite of her youth and her manners, she retained all the claims to reputation which her marriage had given her.

Though Darcy could never receive *him* at Pemberley, yet, for Elizabeth's sake, he assisted him farther in his profession. Lydia was occasionally a visitor there, when her husband was gone to enjoy himself in London or Bath; and with the Bingleys they both of them frequently staid so long, that even Bingley's good humour was overcome, and he proceeded so far as to *talk* of giving them a hint to be gone.

Miss Bingley was very deeply mortified by Darcy's marriage; but as she thought it advisable to retain the right of visiting at Pemberley, she dropt all her resentment; was fonder than ever of Georgiana, almost as attentive to Darcy as heretofore, and paid off every arrear of civility to Elizabeth.

Pemberley was now Georgiana's home; and the attachment of the sisters was exactly what Darcy had hoped to see. They were able to love each other, even as well as they intended. Georgiana had the highest opinion in the world of Elizabeth; though at first she often listened with an astonishment bordering on alarm, at her lively, sportive, manner of talking to her brother. He, who had always inspired in herself a respect which almost overcame her affection, she now saw the object of open pleasantry. Her mind received knowledge which had never before fallen in her way. By Elizabeth's instructions she began to comprehend that a woman may take liberties with her husband, which a brother will not always allow in a sister more than ten years younger than himself.

Lady Catherine was extremely indignant on the marriage of her nephew; and as she gave way to all the genuine frankness of her character, in her reply to the letter which announced its arrangement, she sent him language so very abusive, especially of Elizabeth, that for some time all intercourse was at an end. But at length, by Elizabeth's persuasion, he was prevailed on to overlook the offence, and seek a reconciliation; and, after a little farther resistance on the part of his aunt, her resentment gave way, either to her affection for him, or her curiosity to see how his wife conducted herself; and she condescended to wait on[13] them at Pemberley, in spite of that pollution which its woods had received, not merely from the presence of such a mistress, but the visits of her uncle and aunt from the city.[14]

With the Gardiners, they were always on the most intimate terms. Darcy, as well as Elizabeth, really loved them; and they were both ever sensible[15] of the warmest gratitude towards the persons who, by bringing her into Derbyshire, had been the means of uniting them.[16]

not on convention but on affective ties. Elizabeth has escaped not only her mother's commercialism but her father's cynicism.

The detailed account of an idyllic marriage differentiates *Pride and Prejudice* from Austen's other novels. To be sure, all end in marriage. Typically, though, the text hints at qualifications of the happiness to be anticipated. Even Anne Elliot's long-awaited marriage to Captain Wentworth, in *Persuasion,* will include the "quick alarms" to which a sailor's wife must be subject. *Northanger Abbey* suggests that Henry Tilney's attitude toward Catherine will change after a year of marriage; *Sense and Sensibility* has Marianne persuaded into marriage with a man she has previously scorned and Elinor married to a depressive lover of uncertain future; *Mansfield Park* hints that happiness will come to Fanny Price only at the cost of excluding a great deal; *Emma* marries its heroine to a much older man who has acted more as mentor than as lover. *Pride and Prejudice* also has its exclusions: Wickham cannot come to Pemberley; Charlotte and her husband are not mentioned. But, excluding the vice of Wickham and the folly of Collins, Pemberley yet includes a great deal—even ferocious Lady Catherine, even silly Mrs. Bennet. Darcy and Elizabeth, both of whom have undergone experiences of dramatic moral growth, clearly aspire to exemplify the generosity of spirit that they have learned.

FURTHER READING

ILLUSTRATION CREDITS

ACKNOWLEDGMENTS

Further Reading

This list of critical and biographical works about Austen (in some instances, about *Pride and Prejudice* alone) includes only books, not any of the numerous articles and book chapters that illuminate the novelist and her work. The notes of the present volume, however, include full publication information about many shorter pieces.

Baker, William. *Critical Companion to Jane Austen: A Literary Reference to Her Life and Work.* New York: Facts on File, 2008.

Birtwhistle, Sue, and Susie Conklin. *The Making of "Pride and Prejudice."* London: Penguin, 1995.

Butler, Marilyn. *Jane Austen and the War of Ideas.* Oxford: Oxford University Press, 1975.

Duckworth, Alistair. *The Improvement of the Estate: A Study of Jane Austen's Novels.* Baltimore: Johns Hopkins University Press, 1971.

Dussinger, John A. *In the Pride of the Moment: Encounters in Jane Austen's World.* Columbus: The Ohio State University Press, 1990.

Fergus, Jan. *Jane Austen and the Didactic Novel: "Northanger Abbey," "Sense and Sensibility," and "Pride and Prejudice."* Totowa, NJ: Barnes and Noble, 1983.

Galperin, William. *The Historical Austen.* Philadelphia: University of Pennsylvania Press, 2003.

Grey, David A., Walton Litz, and Brian Southam, eds. *The Jane Austen Handbook: With a Dictionary of Jane Austen's Life and Works.* London: Athlone Press, 1986.

Harman, Claire. *Jane's Fame: How Jane Austen Conquered the World.* New York: Canongate, 2009.

Heydt-Stevenson, Jillian. *Austen's Unbecoming Conjunctions: Subversive Laughter, Embodied History.* New York: Palgrave Macmillan, 2005.

Johnson, Claudia L. *Women, Politics, and the Novel.* Chicago: University of Chicago Press, 1988.

Johnson, Claudia L., and Clara Tuite, eds. *A Companion to Jane Austen.* Chichester: Wiley-Blackwell, 2009.

Kaplan, Deborah. *Jane Austen among Women.* Baltimore: Johns Hopkins University Press, 1992.

Kirkham, Margaret. *Jane Austen: Feminism and Fiction.* Totowa, NJ: Barnes and Noble, 1983.

Knox-Shaw, Peter. *Jane Austen and the Enlightenment.* Cambridge: Cambridge University Press, 2004.

Kramp, Michael. *Disciplining Love: Austen and the Modern Man.* Columbus: The Ohio State University Press, 2007.

Lane, Maggie. *Jane Austen and Food.* London: Hambledon Press, 1995.

Lynch, Deidre Shauna, ed. *Janeites: Austen's Disciples and Devotees.* Princeton: Princeton University Press, 2000.

Morgan, Susan. *In the Meantime: Character and Perception in Jane Austen's Fiction.* Chicago: University of Chicago Press, 1980.

Morris, Ivor. *Mr. Collins Considered: Approaches to Jane Austen.* London: Routledge and Kegan Paul, 1987.

Mudrick, Marvin. *Jane Austen: Irony as Defense and Discovery.* Berkeley: University of California Press, 1980.

Neill, Edward. *The Politics of Jane Austen.* New York: St. Martin's Press, 1999.

Nicolson, Nigel. *The World of Jane Austen.* London: Weidenfeld and Nicolson, 1991.

Southam, Brian, ed. *Jane Austen: The Critical Heritage,* 2 vols. New York: Routledge and Kegan Paul, 1987.

Stovel, Bruce, and Lynn Winlos Gregg, eds. *The Talk in Jane Austen.* Edmonton: University of Alberta Press, 2002.

Tandon, Bharat. *Jane Austen and the Morality of Conversation.* London: Anthem Press, 2003.

Tanner, Tony. *Jane Austen.* Cambridge, MA: Harvard University Press, 1986.

Tauchert, Ashley. *Romancing Jane Austen: Narrative, Realism, and the Possibility of a Happy Ending.* New York: Palgrave Macmillan, 2005.

Tave, Stuart. *Some Words of Jane Austen.* Chicago: University of Chicago Press, 1973.

Thompson, James. *Between Self and World: The Novels of Jane Austen.* University Park: Pennsylvania State University Press, 1988.

Tomalin, Claire. *Jane Austen: A Life.* New York: Knopf, 1998.

Troost, Linda, and Sayre Greenfield, eds. *Jane Austen in Hollywood.* Lexington: University of Kentucky Press, 1998.

Waldron, Mary. *Jane Austen and the Fiction of Her Time.* Cambridge: Cambridge University Press, 1999.

Wiltshire, John. *Recreating Jane Austen.* Cambridge: Cambridge University Press, 2001.

Illustration Credits

Watercolor of Jane Austen by her sister, Cassandra, painted about 1802. Private Collection. *Frontispiece*

Cover of the 1813 first edition of *Pride and Prejudice.* Courtesy Houghton Library, Harvard University. *3*

Title page of the first edition of *Pride and Prejudice.* Courtesy Houghton Library, Harvard University. *3*

Amy Lowell's bookplate in the Houghton Library first edition of *Pride and Prejudice.* Courtesy Houghton Library, Harvard University. *3*

Poster of the 1940 movie *Pride and Prejudice.* PRIDE AND PREJUDICE © Turner Entertainment Co. A Warner Bros. Entertainment Company. All rights reserved. *33*

Day bonnets, fashion plate from Rudolph Ackermann, *Repository of Arts,* 1817. Picture Collection, New York Public Library, Astor, Lenox, and Tilden Foundations. *35*

Full dress, June 1814, from Ackermann's *Repository of Arts, Literature, Commerce, Manufacture, Fashions and Politics.* Private Collection / The Bridgeman Art Library International. *41*

Full dress, *Le Beau Monde*, 1806. © V&A Images, Victoria and Albert Museum. *41*

Edward Francisco Burney, "Frances d'Arblay," c. 1784–1785. © National Portrait Gallery, London. *44*

Portrait of Maria Edgeworth, from E. A. Duyckinck, Portrait Gallery of Eminent Women, 1813. Harvard College Library, Widener H 1158.72.7. *44*

Edward Francis Burney, "An Elegant Establishment for Young Ladies," c. 1805. © V&A Images, Victoria and Albert Museum. *50*

Silhouette of Cassandra Austen, c. 1809 by John Meiers (nineteenth century). Private Collection / The Bridgeman Art Library. *55*

Engraving of a uniform worn by the Oxfordshire Militia. Courtesy of Jane Austen Memorial Trust. *63*

Anonymous, "The Charms of a Red Coat," 1787. Courtesy of The Lewis Walpole Library, Yale University. *64*

Designs for a library reading chair from Ackermann's *Repository of Arts, Literature, Commerce, Manufacture, Fashions and Politics*, 1810. Private Collection / The Bridgeman Art Library International. *72*

Library table; unknown artist, plate 89 from George Smith, *A Collection of Designs for Household Furniture and Interior Decoration in the Most Approved and Elegant Taste* (London: Published by J. Taylor, 1808). Yale Center for British Art, Paul Mellon Collection. *73*

Print from Progress of Female Virtue, engraved by Antoine Cardon (1772–1813), from original drawings by Maria Cecilia Louisa Cosway (1759–1838) (London: Pub. April 10, 1800, at R. Ackermann's, *Repository of Arts*). Yale Center for British Art, Paul Mellon Collection. *74*

Hugh Thomson, Illustrations for *Pride and Prejudice,* 1894. Mrs. Bennet with Lydia and Mary. Courtesy Houghton Library, Harvard University. *78*

Promenade dress, fashion plate from Ackermann's *Repository of Arts* (colored engraving). Private Collection / The Stapleton Collection / The Bridgeman Art Library International. *78*

James Barry, "Samuel Johnson," 1778–1780. © National Portrait Gallery, London. *84*

Plate 27 from William Gilpin, *Observations, Relative Chiefly to Picturesque Beauty, Made in the Year 1772, on Several Parts of England; Particularly the Mountains, and Lakes of Cumberland, and Westmoreland* (London: Printed for R. Blamire, 1786). Yale Center for British Art, Paul Mellon Collection. *88*

Plate 28 from William Gilpin, *Observations, Relative Chiefly to Picturesque Beauty, Made in the Year 1772, on Several Parts of England; Particularly the Mountains, and Lakes of Cumberland, and Westmoreland* (London: Printed for R. Blamire, 1786). Yale Center for British Art, Paul Mellon Collection. *88*

Edward Austen Knight (1768–1852) at the time of his Grand Tour (oil on canvas), English School (nineteenth century). Jane Austen House, Chawton, Hampshire, UK / The Bridgeman Art Library International.   *92*

"Military Flogging," *Illustrated London News,* 1846. Hulton Archive, Getty Images.   *96*

Anonymous, "The Circulating Library," 1804. Courtesy of The Lewis Walpole Library, Yale University.   *105*

Hugh Thomson, Illustrations for *Pride and Prejudice*, 1894. Mr. Collins reacts to the sight of a novel. Courtesy Houghton Library, Harvard University.   *108*

Title page of James Fordyce, *Sermons to Young Women*, 1767. Courtesy Beinecke Rare Book and Manuscript Library, Yale University.   *108*

Sir Thomas Banks, chimneypiece in Daylesford House, Gloucestershire, built 1789–1793. English Heritage National Monuments Record.   *115*

"The Cloakroom, Clifton Assembly Rooms" (oil on canvas), Rolinda Sharples (1794–1838). © Bristol City Museum and Art Gallery, UK / The Bridgeman Art Library International.   *130*

Hugh Thomson, Illustrations for *Pride and Prejudice*, 1894. Sir William Lucas compliments Darcy on his dancing. Courtesy Houghton Library, Harvard University.   *133*

Bound sheet music from Austen's own collection. Courtesy of Jane Austen Memorial Trust.   *141*

"The Concert, 25th September 1805" (pen and ink on paper), by John Harden (1772–1847). Abbot Hall Art Gallery, Kendal, Cumbria, UK. © Lakeland Arts Trust.   *141*

"View of a Drawing Room," 1780, Anonymous. Private Collection / The Bridgeman Art Library International.   *144*

"The Great House and Park at Chawton," c. 1780 (gouache on paper), Adam Callander (fl.1780–1811). Chawton House, Hampshire, UK / The Bridgeman Art Library International.   *178*

Elaine Maylen, photograph of Stoneleigh Abbey. Courtesy of Stoneleigh Abbey Ltd., stoneleighabbey.org.   *183*

Charles Wild, "Carlton House, the Blue Velvet Room," 1816. The Royal Collection © 2010, Her Majesty Queen Elizabeth II RL 22184.   *190*

Fire screens; unknown artist, plate 108 from George Smith, *A Collection of Designs for Household Furniture and Interior Decoration in the Most Approved and Elegant Tast*e (London: Published by J. Taylor, 1808). Yale Center for British Art, Paul Mellon Collection. *202*

Drawing room state chair; unknown artist, plate 58 from George Smith, *A Collection of Designs for Household Furniture and Interior Decoration in the Most Approved and Elegant Taste* (London: Published by J. Taylor, 1808). Yale Center for British Art, Paul Mellon Collection. *207*

John Smart, "Miss Harriet and Miss Elizabeth Binney," 1806. © V&A Images, Victoria and Albert Museum. *214*

"Godmersham Park," Kent, the Seat of Thomas Knight Esq., pub. in 1785 (engraving) (b/w photo), William Watts (1752–1851). Private Collection / The Bridgeman Art Library International. *217*

Anonymous, "The Love Letter," 178[5]? Courtesy of The Lewis Walpole Library, Yale University. *236*

Harris Bigg-Wither, c. 1805. Courtesy www.Bigg-Wither.com. *244*

Austen's ivory cup-and-ball game. Courtesy of Jane Austen Memorial Trust. *250*

G. F. Prosser, "Manydown Park," 1833. Collection Centre Canadien d'Architecture / Canadian Centre for Architecture, Montréal. *262*

Portrait of George III (1738–1820), 1794 (oil on canvas), David Dodd (1760-1790). Private Collection / The Bridgeman Art Library International. *274*

"Return From Brighton, or A Journey to Town for the Winter Season," 1786. Courtesy of The Lewis Walpole Library, Yale University. *277*

"A Picturesque Landscape," from William Gilpin (1724–1804), plate 2 from *Three Essays on Picturesque Beauty* (London: Printed for R. Blamirc, 1792). Yale Center for British Art, Paul Mellon Collection. *285*

Unknown artist. Formerly attributed to John Wootton, 1682–1764, later to Jan Siberechts, 1627–ca. 1703, painting of Bifrons Park, Kent, c. 1695–1700. Yale Center for British Art, Paul Mellon Collection B1977.14.83. *287*

Jane Austen's signature. Courtesy of Jane Austen Memorial Trust. *289*

Thomas Rowlandson (1756–1827), "A Gentleman's Art Gallery." Yale Center for British Art, Paul Mellon Collection B1981.25.2682. *291*

Detail of a patchwork quilt made by Mrs Austen, late eighteenth century. Jane Austen House, Chawton, Hampshire, UK / The Bridgeman Art Library International. *296*

Engraving by J. Bluck (1791–1819) after T. C. Hofland (1777–1843), "Matlock No. 6," from *Six Views in Derbyshire* (Nottingham: Published by T. Barber and T. Hofland, 1805). Yale Center for British Art, Paul Mellon Collection. *298*

Engraving by J. Bluck (1791–1819) after Thomas Barber (1768–1843), "Dove Dale No. 4." from T. C. Hofland, *Six Views in Derbyshire* (Nottingham: Published by T. Barber and T. Hofland, 1805). Yale Center for British Art, Paul Mellon Collection. *298*

Thomas Rowlandson, "Boy Bringing Round a Citizen's Curricle." Courtesy of The Lewis Walpole Library, Yale University. *302*

"The General Postman," from Ackermann's *World in Miniature*, pub. 1827 by Frederic Shoberl (1755–1853) (after) London Library, St. James's Square, London, UK. The Bridgeman Art Library International. *316*

Anonymous, "Gretna Green, or, The red-hot marriage," c. 1795. Courtesy of The Lewis Walpole Library, Yale University. *317*

Capture of *La Tribune*, from *The Naval Achievements of Great Britain, From the Year 1793 to 1817*, by J. Jenkins, 1817. The Unicorn Preservation Society, HM Frigate Unicorn, Dundee, Scotland. www.frigateunicorn.org. *322*

Thomas Rowlandson (1756–1827), "The Gaming Table." Yale Center for British Art, Paul Mellon Collection B1975.4.912. *339*

1801 letter from Jane Austen, living in Bath, to her sister, Cassandra. Courtesy of Jane Austen Memorial Trust. *355*

Jane Austen (1775–1817) illustration from *Little Journeys to the Homes of Famous Women*, published 1897. Engraving with later coloration, English School (nineteenth century) / Private Collection / Ken Welsh / The Bridgeman Art Library International. *361*

Two young ladies in calico gowns, taking an airing in a phaeton, from *Gallery of Fashionism,* Repton, Humphry (1752–1818). Victoria and Albert Museum, London, UK / The Bridgeman Art Library International. *367*

Jane Austen's portable writing-desk. © The British Library Board. All rights reserved. *370*

Probably Jane Austen, by an unknown artist, c. 1810–1815. © National Portrait Gallery, London. *374*

Chawton Cottage. Courtesy of Jane Austen Memorial Trust. *378*

Acknowledgments

Like much of my previous work, this volume is indebted to generations of students, both graduate and undergraduate, at Wellesley College, Yale University, and the University of Virginia. I have taught *Pride and Prejudice* in many different contexts and have invariably learned from my students and from the processes of shared critical investigation.

More specifically and immediately, I am grateful to the late Aubrey Williams, whose acuity and high critical standards influenced this book as they have affected all my writing for the past thirty years, and whose presence enriched my life; to Liliane Greene and Shirley Quinn, for conversations about Austen that stimulated and enlightened me; to Deidre Lynch, who gave my manuscript a thoughtful reading and rescued me from some embarrassing mistakes; to Myra Jehlen, who read and commented on many of the notes, as well as the Introduction, with her usual acumen; and to Jude Spacks, whose penetrating reading of the Introduction significantly improved it. My editor at Harvard University Press, John Kulka, went far beyond the call of duty, locating illustrative material and supporting this project in more ways than I could possibly have anticipated.